The Eighth Continent
Tales of the Foreign Service

THE EIGHTH CONTINENT

Tales of the Foreign Service

PHILIP GOULD

AN AUTHORS GUILD BACKINPRINT.COM EDITION

AN AUTHORS GUILD BACKINPRINT.COM EDITION

Published by iUniverse.com, Inc.

For information address:
iUniverse.com, Inc.
620 North 48th Street, Suite 201
Lincoln, NE 68504-3467
www.iuniverse.com

Originally published by Algonquin Books of Chapel Hill

This is a work of fiction. While, as in all fiction, the literary perceptions and
insights are based on experience, all names, characters, places, and incidents are
either products of the author's imagination or are used fictiously. No reference
to any real person is intended or should be inferred.

ISBN: 0-595-09451-1

Printed in the United States of America

For Molly, Michael, Constance, and Philip
and in memory of Michael Tyszkiewicz

Acknowledgments

The author would like to thank his agent, Nat Sobel, and his editors, Louis D. Rubin, Jr., and Marjorie Hudson, for their patience and guidance.

A
EUROPEAN
EPISODE

1

At twenty-five, three years behind the century, believing in nothing, Stefan, Count Z——, toyed with ending his life. Instead, he wrote a short novel about a young man who plays Russian roulette, pulls the trigger, and lives. Then the young man (called Adam, a popular Polish name) says to himself, "Now I am living but really I am dead since I chose death. What shall I do with myself? I am a puppet, therefore I must act like one." Adam begins to exist mechanically, concentrating only on the petty routines of the day. But by involving himself in the minute-by-minute process of existence he is unable to ignore the harsh surface beauty of the world, and that has an unexpected effect. He cannot bear to leave it.

Stefan showed Caroline a published copy, dated 1928. The Poles use the Latin alphabet, so she was able to read his name, though nothing else. The story, called in Stefan's verbal translation "Second Chance," had never been rendered into any other language. Captivated and unsatisfied, Caroline coaxed a more detailed outline from Stefan and the *un*motivated, and fatal, *good* act of his hero near the end of the story seemed to her original and moving. Stefan shrugged away the praise.

"My Adam is only the reverse of Gide's 'Lafcadio,'" he said.

"But who else ever thought of anything like that? It's a great idea! You should translate the book into English, Stefan, really. Or French, or something."

Stefan waved that away too. "Too old-fashioned for today's tastes. The work of a very young man under the influence of Lermontov's 'Hero of Our Time' and Turgenev's 'Desperate Character.'"

"I don't know the second story—you've left me no choice; I'll have to read it—but Pechorin is cruel," Caroline protested. "Your character doesn't believe in hurting anyone."

The maladies of Stefan's family seemed to be tuberculosis or a propensity to suicide. A rather bizarre early example: Great-grandfather S——, whose policies became unpopular, set sail on a private lake in a caravel of his own design, and blew himself from a cannon.

Stefan began telling Caroline these stories many years afterward as they sat at Café-Konditoreis, named after kings, prince-regents, Electors, founders. Newspapers, clipped at the fold to thin wooden poles, hung on wooden racks. The time now was early October, 1956. Everyone was watching Eastern Europe. That year, Khrushchev had exposed some of Stalin's crimes and, even worse from the point of view of the Kremlin old guard, had apologized to Tito, and blew the lid off Pandora's box. The Polish Titoist Gomułka was released from prison, readmitted to the party. Rioting Poles were killed in Poznan but their momentum was unstopped. Ferment frothed in Hungary. Stefan seemed to feel a certain urgency to tell Caroline about his life. Caroline caught the same need to hurry and wondered if there would be time enough to get everything down.

She had arrived in Munich from Belgrade in late September,

having published a series of think-pieces on the political situations in Morocco, Cyprus, and Yugoslavia. Munich, crowded with East European refugees and with its powerful radio broadcasting and receiving stations, had become a leading information center on the edge of even more significant events. Caroline, twenty-seven, had been a professional journalist since her graduation from Smith in '51, first in Boston—she was a New Englander—then in New York and Paris. For the past year she had free-lanced. Though she had sold articles so far to the *Paris Herald Tribune, Atlantic, The Boston Globe,* and several smaller publications and had a loose arrangement with a news-feature syndicate, her volume of sales was not large. She would not have been able to support herself and afford extensive travel without the aid of savings and parental loans. Munich was relatively inexpensive. She had a room in a clean *pension* and ate in cafés and *gasthauses.* A Pole she had interviewed about the present situation in his country—Stefan's chief at the U.S.-run East European refugee broadcasting service where both were employed—had referred her to Stefan. Stefan, a widower who lived alone, had a story he wanted to tell. He was fluent in nine languages but did not believe he would be able to write his autobiography well enough himself in English, French, or German, the primary languages of publication in the West. And no one wanted it in his native Polish.

His colleagues and compatriots showed Caroline photographs of him in old books and newspapers in their files. One asked, "Have you read Turgenev, Tolstoy? Of course. They will give you some idea of the lives these people led—and twenty years longer than their Russian tsarist cousins. But he was different too. Immensely rich like the others, but different. Everything happened to him. Everything that happened to us happened to him too. Most of us were in prisons, in the camps, and we have all lost our homes, our country. But before that? Never did I see pairs of footmen in knee britches holding lighted candles standing on each step of the grand staircase in one, just one of my grandmother's palaces. Never, I assure you, did I have my own estate of 25,000 acres. Nor a celebrated actress for a wife . . ."

A deputy said, "I am a socialist. I cannot possibly approve of people like him, no, even now when he has of course nothing of that left . . ."

The chief came to Stefan's defense. "I beg your pardon, Bronisław, but if possessing wealth is some kind of transgression, may I point out that he not only lost his, he redeemed it. He saved the lives of many people, many Jews . . ."

Before it vanished off the map in 1795, the centuries-old Commonwealth of Poland-Lithuania had reached not only great size and power but a high civilization. Weakened by flaws in its unique system of the less government the better, not the least among them the oriental self-indulgence, irresponsibility, even treason of too many of its landed magnates—Stefan's ancestors—the once "noble republic" had been carved into thirds. Until the First World War every inhabitant, from poor peasants to members of its titled families, had been subject to the kaiser, the emperor, or the tsar. Stefan, descended from a fifteenth-century Lithuanian boyar from Kiev, had been born a citizen of Russia.

In 1910, in Stefan's seventh year, his mother had been a patient in a Swiss TB sanatorium, her condition deteriorating. To distract himself, his father climbed mountains; too distracted, he lost his footing and fell to his death. Against all medical advice, the Countess Z—— insisted on accompanying her husband's body back to Poland and died en route aboard the train. In Vienna, Stefan and his siblings were met by their maternal grandmother with whom they would live from then on.

Stefan showed Caroline a photograph, one of many collected

from relatives who had lived in France, England, Italy for generations (he, himself, had left Poland one day with absolutely no possessions except the clothes on his back and had never returned)—a handsome grande dame wrapped in furs, seated imperiously in a horse-drawn landau, a fur toque like a diadem set upon her head.

"She was really quite unique, even in my country," Stefan said. "At times when she was a child her parents made her sleep under the piano while they played duets—Liszt, you know, and other stormy pieces. In order to develop her ability to sleep under any circumstances. One has duties and responsibilities and must be ready for every occasion, every emergency. Well, you see, under the same slightly mad Polish-Victorian system she trained us all, her children and grandchildren."

He smiled a little as he told Caroline this, with an expression that seemed to her intelligent, modest, even apologetic, kindly, but was there something else, something expectant and feverish in his eyes, extraordinarily blue? Was he slightly mad himself? Fey he certainly was. He leaned forward to light her cigarette, unfailingly courteous, lit his own, ordered coffee (their waiter was standing beside them now) in his rich, resonant voice. It was always a pleasure to listen to him speaking her own language with the cultivated diction of the trained classical actor he never was. Charmed, you listened and heard Joseph Schildkraut, Paul Lukas, Anton Walbrook—the slight central European accents she would never in the wide world want them to get rid of.

He fit Caroline's admittedly romantic notion of what an aristocrat ought to look like. He might, of course, have been a misshapen dwarf (like one prince he had told her about), might easily have appeared vain, stupid, foppish, depraved, cruel. He was, in fact, tall, athletic, once a tennis champion. His hair, dark brown and thick, was neatly brushed. She thought he had a noble face in the sense of having striking features that were not decadent and weak in their evenness but that reflected the qualities of excellence in the man himself, forged in the experiences and trials of a remarkable life.

He sometimes held cigarettes in the Russian manner in the tips of his thumb, fore and middle fingers, turned up.

In the fading late afternoon sunlight they sat at the Hofgarten-Café Annast which had stood on the Odeonsplatz since 1810. Stefan remembered it from the 1920s. At right angles, the Feldherrnhalle, an ersatz copy of the Loggia dei Lanzi in Florence, where Hitler's putsch of 1923 had been aborted in a bloody gun battle. The Theatinerkirche across the way had stood on its site since the seventeenth century. Both church and café were golden yellow with high arched doorways. From the three green domes of the basilica, as from the other great baroque and gothic towers of the old city soaring in tiers behind it, one might see on a clear day like this the snow peaks of the Alps forty miles to the south.

At other tables stout, dowdy women under beige felt hats with wide brims and bulbous crowns ate whipped cream alongside slim and stylish girls sipping Campari and soda. Wearing a raincoat, silk foulard tied at the throat, and carrying a rolled umbrella, Caroline joined the ranks of the latter, though her choice was coffee and she was the only American.

She looked at the Feldherrnhalle and visualized Hitler's thwarted putsch, which had not stopped him, and saw too reruns in her mind of old newsreels, TV documentaries, the massed Nazi troops in the Odeonsplatz, the blood-red banners, delirious crowds. . . . Stefan's narrative now had reached the opening days of World War I when aristocratic Poles, with estates and town houses and family members in three monarchies, suddenly found themselves on opposite sides of hostile frontiers.

"My grandmother was pro-French, pro–Triple Entente, which included Great Britain and Russia. Her husband sided with Austria-Hungary and they separated over this. Divided allegiances like these created a state of utter political, physical, and moral confusion and chaos. Poles were killed fighting each other as in your Civil War."

He paused after this perhaps preliminary, perhaps final, summing up of an enormous problem, and Caroline, whose mind was half elsewhere, broke in, "Stefan, may I jump ahead for a minute? There's a question I don't want to forget to ask. Sitting here in the Odeonsplatz made me think of Hitler rallies and that reminds me of something your boss told me. How you'd saved the lives of so many Jews. Can you tell me something about that?"

Stefan frowned. "He exaggerates my role. Don't think of me as any kind of Wallenberg. It was simply my job for a while to work with refugees. After the two invasions of Poland I was appointed a refugee relief coordinator by the Polish government-in-exile because of where I was—in still independent and neutral Lithuania, a crossroads of one of the early escape routes. We tried to secure identity papers—real and false—and transportation—for a variety of people. Some of them were relatives of mine. Some happened to be Jews. In Helena's theatrical world in Vienna and Warsaw and Budapest we knew a number of Jews. We simply did what we could as they came along . . . and I was not always successful."

He said that with such a sad and bitter look and with a tone, and gesture of his cigarette, of finality, that Caroline, for the moment, suspended this line of questioning.

"Nineteen-fifteen," she said gently. "You were twelve."

From a Red Cross station set up on the grounds of a family estate near Wilno (as the Poles spell Vilna, the Lithuanians call Vilnius) he had watched the retreat of the Russian army from its defeat in East Prussia. He had been old enough to distribute food parcels and to write letters for illiterate *muzhiks*. At seventeen, against his grandmother's wishes, he had run off to join the Polish legions of Marshal Piłsudski in that forgotten 1920 war against the Bolsheviks.

"We fought against Marshal Budyonny's cavalry in southeastern Poland and defeated them. Did you know that? Bolshevik armies under Budyonny, Tukhachevsky, Stalin himself, had reached the gates of Warsaw. Piłsudski's legions drove them back, whipped them so soundly Lenin sued for peace . . .

"Is that enough for today?" Stefan asked. "Or shall we have dinner somewhere and continue a while? I . . . will have to leave later but that gives us more than two hours."

"Fine with me as long as we go Dutch," Caroline said and saw that he understood the expression.

2

Clouds gathered and darkened ominously. A wind came up, scattered leaves and flung pasteboard drink coasters to the pavement. The temperature dropped ten degrees in seconds. A few drops of rain fell.

"Do you know Boettner's?"

"Not yet."

"It's not far but we'd best hurry."

Caroline's ear heard his accent but also the ease with which he used English contractions. From the cut of it his suit looked French, not like the expensive English tweed he is wearing in one of the old photographs he had shown her, but tailored from a sturdy, rather sober broadcloth she thought he had probably brought with him from France when he came to Munich in '52. Something else she had noticed was that he was too clean-shaven, his shirt too crisp, for him to have met her directly from work. He must have stopped off at his apartment to spruce up. She found this touching and smiled at him as they stood to leave the café and she snapped open her

11

umbrella. He did not know why she was smiling at him and for a moment a puzzled look wrinkled his eyebrows, but he said nothing.

Traffic was heavy. Mercedes-Benz taxis peeled away from a stand on the Odeonsplatz. Trams turning into and out of Briennerstrasse were filled with office workers and shoppers. At the intersection, clumps of orderly pedestrians under umbrellas waited dutifully for traffic lights to change. Caroline saw two prevailing uniforms on both men and women: chocolate brown belted raincoats and mustard brown shoes, or some version of the Bavarian national costume—feathered huntsmen's hats, wool and felt jackets with matching trousers or skirts in grey or forest green. Virtually every male carried a leather briefcase with straps. No office worker, butcher, or plumber would be without one.

They crossed and moved with the crowds along the narrow, elegant Theatinerstrasse. The sky was violent and lights were on in fashionable shops. Rain began to fall heavily. Stefan held a copy of the *Süddeutsche Zeitung* over his head.

Boettner's had a small luxury food shop off the street entrance. Beyond it was a cozy, clubby dining room, walls covered thickly with paintings, etchings, lithographs, photographs. Seated at the end of a banquette across a small table for two with an empty chair facing him was a young American vice-consul of thirty-one named Charles McKay. From his vantage point he could survey many of his fellow diners without appearing to stare. One of them happened to be a well-known German film actor, well enough known in American films too, in intimate converse with an intimidatingly glamorous woman, her perfect, tuck-pointed face as glazed as a china doll's. A slim green bottle of Riesling *auslese* stayed chilled in a silver bucket beside McKay's table, and a golden glass of it sat before him on the white linen cloth just to the right of a plate of crayfish in a dill-perfumed cream sauce. He could hear the rain outside and see it slanting past the show window of the gourmet shop. He was about as temporarily content as he ever was in those extremely interesting though rather lonely months of his first year at his first post, as attuned and receptive as he would ever be, when the tallish girl in the raincoat and silk scarf entered the shop. She furled her umbrella, smoothed her straight, dark-blond hair with one hand, stepped forward and stood at the entrance to the dining room, elevated slightly in small blue leather pumps, and waited for the advancing maître d'. Behind and above her was a distinguished-looking older man, old enough to be her father, a Pole. McKay recognized him from his neighborhood café, the Maximilian, though he didn't know his name.

A miserable, rainy autumn evening; but a lovely girl appearing in the midst of it and it may hold more promise than any evening in spring. Fall isn't so restless, so diffused. Fall is a gathering-in.

With Stefan across from her, Caroline asked above her menu, above reading glasses pushed down to the end of her nose, "What are krebse?"

"Krebse . . . like little lobsters. You call them crayfish. Crawfish?"

"I think I'll have some of those to start and then a venison chop. I've learned the name for that. But first a scotch on the rocks."

Stefan ordered one too, linked his fingers waiting for it.

"Now you must tell me your story," he said.

"Pouf. I have no story worth telling. Standard prosperous American parents. My father's an architect. He's sweet but my shameful secret is I don't really like the looks of most of his buildings. You know where I went to school, whom I've worked for, where I've been so far. What else can I tell you? At twenty-four I was engaged to a very handsome ex-BMOC—and I see by your puzzled expression for once *I* must translate—Big Man On Campus, a

university leader, very popular—who turned out to be . . . let's say
I discovered what I had carefully avoided noticing earlier (we partied and petted and partied and petted and I didn't have to notice,
Caroline thought but did not say), that we were intellectually—and
ideologically—incompatible. I broke it off. You can't imagine—or
perhaps you can—how worried my family and friends were about
me. As it was, they thought that at twenty-four I had already
reached the outer limits of marriageability. You can't blame them.
I thought so myself. It was what we were conditioned to think. To
get married between twenty-one and twenty-three was the goal of
every girl in my class, every girl I knew, except those few oddballs
who said they wanted a career—in medicine or what-have-you.
Then I fell for a guy who began to show signs of being seriously
unstable and that scared me too much to go on with it. So I went
to Paris and fell for a newspaper correspondent who left me for another girl because he thought I was too career-oriented to make him
a good wife. Twice burned and hedging my bets, I suppose that's
the way I must have appeared."

She decided not to mention the married Frenchman she had
been mixed up with for a while.

"Now at twenty-seven? Over the hill! A hopeless case!"

"My dear, that's ridiculous. You're an exceptionally lovely
young woman. Only an idiot would find you other than eminently
nubile."

"Thank you, kind sir. Oh, I'm poking fun at myself and at the
system, but the system is real. I've heard enough American men on
the subject. No matter what she looks like if she's my age and still
single there must be something the matter with her. . . . Now look
what I've picked up at that bookstore near the university." She un-
snapped her handbag and pulled out a copy of Gide's *Les Caves du
Vatican*. Stefan arched his eyebrows at the sight of it and seemed—
amused? Pleased with her?

"I couldn't find 'Lafcadio's Adventures' in English, or that Turgenev story in any language, but I can read this pretty well. I read it in college but I'd forgotten half of it. What I noticed particularly is that one of those 'uncles' of Lafcadio's courtesan mother is a Polish prince in the diplomatic service of Russia."

"Bielkowski . . ." Stefan murmured.

"And, you know, I'd completely forgotten that *before* Lafcadio pushes that man off the train for no reason—that's what sticks in your mind—he'd rescued a child he didn't know from a burning building. But your Adam commits a crime *first* and *then* does something heroic on the spur of the moment—"

"But you see, right there, it's Gide who's original."

"And perverse."

"Isn't perversity more true to life?"

"Does it have to be? Wasn't Gide simply reacting against hypocrisy, sanctimonious virtue? Well, maybe he was one of the first to do it way back then. But by now it's been done and done. What's so original anymore about cynicism? All it is is the easiest, safest, most conventional point of view. Seriously, I know you don't have time now but if things in Poland ever settle down I really wish you'd reconsider and turn your novel into English. Even part of it. A good friend of mine works for a publisher in New York. I'm sure she could get it read."

It was to this friend in New York Caroline had written, "I think I'm falling for the guy. He's older than my father but that doesn't seem to make any difference, and what has going with guys 'the right age' ever gotten me?" The friend had written back, "OK, he sounds wonderful (and looks incredibly handsome in that photograph!) and I don't mean to be a wet blanket, but don't forget, when you're thirty-five, still young, he'll be over sixty. When you're his age *now,* he'll be almost *eighty.* . . ." Caroline had long since worked out this equation for herself and wasn't troubled by it.

"So where were we?" she asked. "World War I is over. Poland is independent for the first time since the eighteenth century . . ."

McKay was only one course ahead of them. If he nursed his wine, and chewed his veal cutlet properly as his mother had once persistently admonished him to do and he often didn't, had dessert, coffee, a cognac, he could stay as long as this girl and her companion stayed. She faced him a little to the right across the small room, and what interested and excited him, beyond her physical appeal, was the fact that as she listened to whatever the older man was telling her, she took notes. And occasionally asked him questions—though McKay could hear only an occasional word—in American English. She was *interviewing* him. Theirs was a *business* dinner. Then, when they divided the bill and the Pole left alone, Charlie was elated . . .

Stefan had sighed and had fallen silent. It had been a long day. His narrative had become more complex. He had had to explain less familiar history—the breakdown of parliamentary democracy in Poland—thirty-one political parties, fourteen coalition governments in the first eight years of the republic—Piłsudski's coup d'etat of 1926. He had had to spell Polish names. It was eight-thirty.

"I don't want to make you late for your appointment," Caroline said.

Stefan signaled for the check and divided it with her, pulled the table away from the banquette.

"If I have time again next week . . ." he said. "These days . . . who can tell? There is so much more to translate, more than we can possibly handle. I may be asked to postpone my days off. . . . But here is something to read. I've finished translating my notes." He took folded paper from the inside of his jacket and she put it in her handbag.

"Oh, I understand. We'll do it when we can do it, but thanks for this. . . . Stefan, I meant to tell you before. You're much too

modest about your ability to write in English. You really don't need
me at all."

"Far from it. Far from it."

"Don't let me keep you. I need to make a phone call myself."

"Then, good night."

Who's he meeting at nine o'clock at night? she asked herself
as he went out. Well, it wasn't any of her business. They'd had another professional interview, not a date. She was on her own. Munich was safe and she went everywhere in it by herself at all hours
so there was no reason for him to escort her anywhere. He owed
her nothing.

But after hesitating half a minute—she did not really have a
phone call to make—she left the restaurant and began walking
quickly up the street to the right, in the direction she had seen him
turn. It was damp and chill but the rain had stopped. She crossed
the intersection but did not see him up ahead and assumed he had
made a turn. Left drew her because it was more familiar, down a
short block across from the Max-Joseph Platz, and then she saw him
standing at the far corner of the square in the shadow of scaffolding
around the bombed-out opera house, talking to a woman.

Caroline ducked quickly into the entrance to a boutique, a
woman's accessory shop, closed and locked but illuminated by night
lights. Handbags were displayed in the window, sachets, costume
jewelry, decorated boxes. Burning with shame, she stayed there until she saw Stefan and the woman walk up Maximilianstrasse and
get into a cab in front of the *Vier Jahreszeiten* hotel and then she
recrossed the street and hurried, half-running for two spurts, along
the facade of the Residenz, the royal palace, towards Odeonsplatz
and the cab stand there. A streetwalker! He left me and picked up
a streetwalker! She wanted to go someplace and hide and so she hid
in the back seat of a Mercedes taxi and then hid in her room at the
pension with the lights off, wondering whom it was she was ashamed
of, and decided it was only herself.

3

A few days after she'd appeared at Boettner's out of the rain, Charlie McKay saw her crossing the Englischer Garten by herself, not such a coincidence. He knew the Pole worked at Radio Free Europe on the other side of the park.

It was a Sunday and the weather was pleasant again. McKay was walking along a *fussweg*, a wide gravel path across the park leading to the Chinesischer Turm, a replica of a Chinese pagoda around which was laid out an outdoor beer garden where he'd planned to have brunch. Along an intersecting allée up ahead, a horse-drawn phaeton flickered through the trees and cut off the view for a few moments and then the girl reappeared, walking towards him. If she was the correspondent he thought she was she'd be used to talking to strangers—and curious. He began speaking—in English—when she was still a dozen feet away—"Hi, how are things going? Weren't you one of the reporters the political officer at the consulate gave a briefing to last week?"

She took a few more steps and stopped, chin raised slightly, a puzzled, but not unfriendly, half-smiling expression on her face.

"No-o," she said, drawling the word a bit, and smiled fully. "But maybe I should ask him to."

"Oh, well, sorry," McKay said. "You looked familiar."

"No need to apologize. I *do* get political briefings from time to time as a matter of fact and I *am* a reporter. I guess it must show."

"No, wait a minute, now I know where it was," McKay said, putting on a show of remembering, with a forefinger stabbing the air. "You were in Boettner's interviewing a Polish fellow. Older man . . . I'm Charlie McKay. The information officer at the consulate. I used to be with the UP."

"Caroline Draper," she said, shaking hands quickly.

"'v you been over to the RFE newsroom? Anything big going on? Join me in a cup of coffee?"

"I'm . . ." she started to say, then glanced at her wristwatch. "OK, I guess it's early enough." She turned and began walking along beside him. "What's going on? Which dateline d'you want to hear about first—Moscow, Warsaw, or Budapest . . . ?"

He'd had his brunch. Both were on second cups of coffee.

"The United Press, where?" Caroline asked.

"Pittsburgh, then New York."

"You a Pennsylvanian?"

"Illinois. Clarksville, on the east bank of the Mississippi about equidistant from the Iowa side and Missouri. The heartland. Population ten thousand."

"White frame houses with elm trees."

"Sycamores. How different is your street?"

"Well, you worry about tornadoes and we worry about hurricanes."

"New England or Long Island?"

"Little town on the Connecticut coast called Eastbrook about halfway between New Haven and New London."

"That's pretty country. We flew in there during the war."

"So when did you get to New York?"

"Forty-nine."

"I was there from fifty-two to fifty-four on the *Wall Street Journal.*"

"We probably covered some of the same stories," McKay said, thinking, no, I would have remembered. "Where'd you go after that?"

"To Paris to work on the *Trib.* We happy few."

"You bet your life. I think you've been pretty lucky all along. Classy jobs like that while I was breathing bad air on East Forty-Second Street. Working inside at UP was a little like working out at Stillman's gym. The only place lower was the International News Service. Ever read a story called 'That Tree,' by Katherine Anne Porter?"

"About Mexico?"

"Exactly. I know a couple of lines by heart. 'If there was one brand of bum on earth he despised it was a newspaper bum. Or anyhow the drunken illiterates the United Press and Associated Press seemed to think were good enough for Mexico and South America.'"

Caroline had a brief fit of giggling.

"Reading that didn't exactly disillusion me," McKay said. "After the first few weeks at UP I'd seen I was going to want to move on to something more respectable eventually. But that paragraph was a little disconcerting anyway. It made me restless."

"Working for UP was good training, though, wasn't it?"

"Oh, absolutely. And mostly a good—and talented—bunch of people. It was the organization itself that seemed so fly-by-night. It didn't own anything. That's what I heard anyway. Every office, every piece of equipment, every wire was leased. The place breathed insecurity. It wasn't homelike. Sometimes I felt like a shill in a Big Store con game. I always felt expendable. Seeing some of those nice

guys on every shift around the clock was educational too. Pale, over-
worked, and underpaid, any spirit they might have had leached out
of them, the older guys with families to support and better news
jobs tough to find. Could this be me in a few years? Maybe I ought
to look around while I was still single."

"Which you did."

"Which I did. It got to be a grind and what I was looking for
was glamor. I wanted to travel. The UP kept putting me off. Either
I was too young and needed more stateside seasoning, or there were
no overseas openings. They liked to hire people overseas so they
could pay them starvation wages below Guild scale. Then I heard
the government was recruiting people to work in Germany."

"And you'd rather write propaganda than news? . . . I'm sorry.
I made that sound a little bit nasty and provocative."

"Well, I don't have to write any lies. And at UP it seemed to
me I was churning out—or editing—an awful lot of trivia. I covered
less than catastrophic fires, ship launchings. I interviewed minor
politicians, deposed Latin American dictators, second-rate Hollywood actresses. All about equally unimportant. At the very least,
pretty ephemeral stuff. Nature of the beast, but still . . ."

"So now you get more satisfaction from what you're doing?"

"I enjoy the work enough. I don't feel Western civilization
would collapse if I wasn't here."

"I'm beginning to think you may be a cynic, Mr. McKay."

"Not really. I'd rather think of myself as an idealist with open
eyes. I realize how self-serving that may sound."

"Disarming is the word. After all, idealists have to have ideals,
don't they? . . . Listen, I've enjoyed this conversation and thanks
for the coffee but I do have to get to work."

"I'm heading back the way you were going originally. Where
are you staying?"

"The Pension Saint Rupert on Georgenstrasse."

"I live on Kaulbachstrasse, not too far from there."

They began retracing their steps through the Englischer Garten.

"You haven't been back to New York recently?" McKay asked.

"Not for two years."

"So neither of us knows what Third Avenue looks like without the El. I just can't picture it. Just as I can't imagine the street without the Irish pubs. I hung out at Costello's."

"I've been there but P.J. Clark's was my *querencia* when we were up that way."

"I lived just around the corner from both of them so to speak. You obviously lived further downtown."

"I shared an apartment on Christopher Street in the Village."

"There *are* things I miss here, no getting around it," McKay said. "New York food, New York bars, New York entertainment. Mabel Mercer at the Byline Room. Mae Barnes at Bon Soir."

"Café Nicholson."

"Luchow's."

"Café Brittany. The Little Club."

"The Blue Angel."

"You're making me homesick!" Caroline said.

"I had some good times, can't deny that," McKay said. "I shared an apartment with another UP guy named Sam Adams I'd met at Northwestern. He was older and went to New York a year earlier than I did. So he knew all the girls by the time I got there. Saved me a helluva lot of time. Stubby guy with a snub nose and thinning hair who sunburned easily—and a living example of something being greater than the sum of its parts. I'm still not sure what his secret was, the source of his appeal for women, but he sure had it."

"Speaking of which, do you know Stefan?"

"I know him to see him."

"He's really a fabulous guy. Or has had a fabulous life. Some of each I guess. What he's telling me should make a fascinating profile or full-length book."

At Leopoldstrasse near the Siegestor, they parted, Caroline walking left, McKay, returning her wave, turning right.

Talking to Caroline for the first time had stirred up a fresh batch of old emotions and the recollection of old emotions in McKay's ever responsive breast. As he continued on down the block to the Maximilian Café on the next corner and seated himself at a table by himself he found himself seeing Caroline on one side of his brain and viewing a projection of New York scenes on the other. There was some clear, though indirect, connection between the two that called for a sorting out, a clarification, if possible. The direction of his life seemed to be in question.

All those lovely, promising New York girls—ad agency assistants, *Time* researchers, secretaries, the more exotic Nina who danced, Belinda the flutist, Annabelle the guide at the UN—all gone a-glimmering for one reason or another, their decision or his. And no real luck in Munich thus far. Hilary, the virtually catatonic remittance girl from England. Bruni, certifiably crazy, or at least she drove *him* to the brink of that state with her suicide threats and anyway had gone back to her German lover in spite of his alleged cruelties. Now suddenly here was Caroline, who existed on a far superior plane of being, and how scintillating and more than that to have her around for a while, but that was it, what can come of this? McKay asked himself. She was a wanderer, in Munich temporarily, and he was stuck there for at least another year. Not to mention the fact that she was obviously enthralled and possibly enamored of her middle-aged Polish count. To confirm this, in the middle of that same week McKay ran into her at the Maximilian and all she could talk about, besides the great events of the day, was Stefan Stefan Stefan and the story of his life. She needed a confidant and McKay was handy, now her one other acquaintance in town.

Within days, however, the nature of their relationship had to be set aside, at least temporarily, as a matter of quite secondary importance.

4

The weekend of October 19, 1956, the balloon went up. Munich was charged with some of the atmosphere of Vienna, Berlin, and the capitals of the Triple Entente after August, 1914; of Munich itself in September of '39. Cafés were filled with newspaper readers and radio listeners. In the newsroom at Stefan's broadcasting headquarters people lined up to peer at chattering teletype machines. Khrushchev, Molotov, Mikoyan, Kaganovich had flown to Warsaw in a towering collective rage to try to prevent the election of Gomułka as first secretary, to demand that Polish-born Soviet Marshal Rokossovsky and other Stalinists be kept on the Polish politburo. Gomułka and his majority refused. Khrushchev warned that Rokossovsky's troops were ready to attack and that a Soviet division in East Germany was on the march towards Warsaw. The Polish leaders said if the Russians tried a putsch it would mean war and the Poles were ready for it. Khrushchev shouted, "We will crush you!" But the talks continued until 2:00 A.M. Saturday morning. Shortly afterwards Khrushchev and company flew back to Moscow.

Polish troops fired at Soviet contingents trying to cross from East Germany and the Soviet force had halted. On Sunday Gomułka was elected party secretary and Rokossovsky was kicked off the politburo. Soviet troops were reported drawing away from Warsaw. Polish defiance of the Kremlin leaders had an immediate galvanizing effect in Hungary. Thousands of Hungarian university students demanded an end to Stalinist rule and the departure of Soviet troops. Already on Monday Hungarian police were firing on demonstrators marching against the Gerő regime.

Stefan was to work fifteen straight days without a day off—ten- and twelve-hour days and longer—and Caroline was able to see him only in passing—in the corridors at Radio Free Europe when she visited the center RFE had set up for correspondents. Those days Munich was the place to be for foreign reporters. Vienna was a little closer to the action, but still well outside it, and did not have the radio monitoring facilities available in Munich. And it was through broadcasts from numerous central and regional radio stations across Poland and Hungary and the other countries of Eastern Europe that the most accurate, in-depth stories could be pieced together. The few Western correspondents in Warsaw and Budapest had to operate in a much narrower range of rumor, confusion, and official statements.

As for Charlie McKay, he had less to do than at any other time during his tour of duty. Who among his contacts in the local media wanted to hear that the United States was sitting on its hands? Doing nothing, making vague, timid statements, seemingly paralyzed by the events in Eastern Europe over which it had less control than the Russians but might have exercised some moral influence. The door was open. The Russians seemed equally bewildered by what was going on, caught in a bind of paralysis themselves.

So he busied himself by taking two-hour lunches and long walks to RFE to read the news and saw Caroline every day there or at the Café Maximilian.

She'd had to suspend work on Stefan's personal story, but she'd typed up some of her notes and Charlie could decipher her handwriting. In her manila envelope he also found a snapshot of a much younger Stefan looking like an English lord in his nineteen-thirties tweeds standing with a pair of enormous shaggy French sheepdogs, briards, before the massive white-columned portico of a neoclassical *dwor* that dated from Napoleonic times. McKay found the location Caroline had circled on her up-to-date map—startlingly deep inside the Soviet Union. That must have had its effect, living on the edge, as the clock ticked through the twenties and thirties, as Hitler came to power across Poland's western frontier, as Stalin consolidated his power in the even nearer East.

Earlier photos in Stockholm and Riga. One career always open to a member of the aristocracy was the diplomatic service, especially for a young man with a law degree from Cracow University. Still directionless after writing his novel, after his spiritual recovery, he had gone on to spend a year each in the Swedish and Latvian capitals, had learned both languages. Then he was asked to resign.

In her semieliptical note-taking style, still in longhand, Caroline had written: "Stefan, maverick among his generally reactionary relatives, and without foreign ministry approval, had published article in literary-current affairs journal (see attached clipping and translation) condemning anti-Semitism of Catholic ultra conservatives. Gave them St. Paul's 'sounding brass' or 'tinkling cymbal' with a twist of the pen—in English. Cymbal, spelled same in Polish, also means dunce, booby, fool."

"Who are these people?" McKay asked. A snapshot of a couple in citified nineteen-thirties clothes, standing in the garden of the manor house. Charlie turned the photo over. Someone had written Karl/Hilda Friedland, 1938.

"Friends from Vienna who left after the Anschluss, that's all I know. He doesn't seem to want to talk about them."

More pictures, faded photos clipped from newspapers and society magazines, Stefan dancing the Charleston, schussing on the slopes at Zakopane, with his bride Helena, Poland's most popular musical comedy star. This last was front page news in 1930 Warsaw.

"Family boycott," Caroline said. "With one exception—the grandmother, who had the brains and prestige to be different too, and who admired Helena. They were two of a kind."

In her day the grandmother had presided over a glittering salon. Carrying on that tradition, Stefan opened his country house to an almost constant procession of actors, writers, painters, composers, this in the brilliant, stylish cultural milieu of the era.

"'While it lasted, an amazing and delightful life,'" Caroline quoted from her hand-written notes. "Not so delightful when Helena began an affair with an actor-director who had convinced her to do Shakespeare. But Stefan didn't divorce her and after a year, as he'd predicted, she broke with the director, professionally and otherwise, went back to lighter roles. And Stefan took her back. *I* don't have to forgive her," Caroline said, "but apparently Stefan did. She was an actress. She lived for the theater, for the moment. But he knew that when he married her. And what his role was going to be—besides writing some of her material—to take care of her for the rest of her life. He did. Now I think it's time somebody took care of him."

Sinking heart. How long, McKay silently asked, would it take her to realize Stefan was too old for her? Fifty-three to twenty-seven, twenty-six years apart, three times too many.

By 1939 everyone believed war would break out, but Stefan and Helena imagined there would be long-lasting fronts as in 1914–1918. On Stefan's estate the rye fields splashed with cornflowers rolled to a far horizon. Reapers and sickles flashed under a brilliant summer sun. A sheaf of grain, the first cutting of the new harvest, was displayed in the entrance hall of the manor house. Raspberries had never grown in such profusion, had never tasted so sweet. The great pillars of the house gleamed white in the moonlight. Fires of St. John flickered across the darkened gardens cut by paths of silver.

Helena planned to return to Warsaw in late August to prepare as usual for the autumn theatrical season but at Stefan's insistence delayed her departure to recover completely from a throat infection. Thus they were both on the estate when German armies invaded Poland on September first. September seventeenth, Soviet armies invaded from the east.

Stefan had written a short memoir of some of the events that followed. It was this he had translated into English for Caroline. An account of his arrest by the Soviet NKVD, his two years in the Lubyanka and Butyrki prisons in Moscow: Dickensian, Gogolesque scenes in communal cells, harrowing black comedy, hundreds of nights when he could tell his interrogators nothing that could possibly be of any real use to them . . .

"Wasn't it enough to be a bloodsucking landlord, an enemy of the people?" Stefan wrote. "Why these charges of 'subversive activities' in Lithuania? The modern tyrant's need to wrap his crime in legalisms? Some of that, but more than that, as I was to learn . . ."

There were pages ahead of Charlie. He laid them down for a while.

"What's this about 'subversive activities'?" he asked.

"Helping people escape the Nazis," Caroline said. "The *Germans,* enemies of the Soviet Union by this time, but never mind that. Anybody who can get a passport or a visa forged must be subversive. But, as he says, more than that. Someone who knew him in Kaunas must have turned him in. There were too many accurate details in the charges to be a coincidence. He suspected a Latvian diplomat he'd known since the twenties."

"You know, when I think back to my grade school and high school days," Charlie said, "I'll bet there were at least one or two people who would have turned me in later on if they'd had the chance."

They are packed into sealed freight cars. For twenty-four hours the train does not move at all. Later, it is stalled for many hours during a German bombing attack. The journey lasts three weeks, a forced march three days through lifeless, eroded woods. A man steps out of line to piss and is shot dead on the spot.

From a distance the camp looks like an amusement park with its towers and gaily colored banners. Close up, the banners are emblazoned with slogans. "WE GREET STALIN, BUILDER OF SOCIALISM. HE WHO DOES NOT WORK DOES NOT EAT . . ."

Half-starved, they fell logs twelve hours a day under a brutal Arctic sun. Giant mosquitoes torture them in clouds. Rats run over their bodies as they try to sleep. Men die routinely of exhaustion, illness, and despair. Dressed in quilted cotton uniforms, felt caps with ear flaps, and boots fashioned from old automobile tires, they resemble ludicrous medieval knights as they march out the gates to Brahms' Hungarian Dance Number II played by a gypsy on a prison-made fiddle and an eyeless Russian strumming a guitar. Stefan's legs swell, his heart pains him, he believes his health is ruined, that he cannot survive this.

One accomplishment may have prolonged his life. He is one of the few prisoners who can swim. As a child he had learned in the lakes and rivers on family estates, off the beach at Deauville, had swum on the Riviera, off Capri (still swam in Lake Starnberg on warm weather weekends). Now, in 1942, swimmers are needed to

help break up logjams in the river Dvina. The luckier few who can
do this job are given extra rations, and the work itself is a little less
killing than wielding an axe.

Less than a month later, two months after leaving the Butyrki
prison in Moscow, he is free, saved by an accident of history. As
German armies advanced towards Moscow, Stalin gave in to Allied
pressure and agreed to sign a pact with the Polish government-in-
exile. An amnesty was declared for all Poles confined in the Soviet
Union. Polish military units would be formed on Soviet soil of former prisoners of war, political prisoners and deportees, to fight the
German invader.

5

Throughout the week of October 21, 1956, the Poles stood firm and appeared to have won their peaceful revolution. Gomułka met a street crowd waving Polish and Hungarian flags, thanked them for their devotion, but told them to go home. Most of them did.

In Hungary the rebels fought on, against Soviet units now. The estimated death toll was four to five thousand. Reports said Soviet troops were quelling the revolt but some rioting continued in the capital.

GERŐ OUT. NAGY TAKES OVER.
SOVIET TANKS FIRE ON UNARMED CROWD.

Nagy pleaded with the rebels to stop fighting and by Saturday, the twenty-sixth, announced that peace talks were under way with the Russians. By Sunday he said the Russians would leave Budapest. But fighting went on. The rebels were reported to hold key Hungarian cities.

Still reeling from these events, Caroline and McKay were stunned and took it personally when they heard the totally unexpected and unwelcome news that Israel had invaded Egypt and that Britain and France were moving to take over the Suez Canal.

"Has there ever been a week like this one?" Caroline said when they ran into each other outside the RFE newsroom. "Oh, those goddamned Israelis! I thought I admired them, but to pull a stunt like this when everybody's back is turned! And the French and Brits are just despicable! Grabbing the limelight, and what does that tell the Russians? That the West doesn't give a damn about Eastern Europe. I'm going to Vienna. I don't know if it's possible to get into Hungary but at least I'll be closer. Stefan's taking leave to go with me. We'll take the train tomorrow morning. He's known Vienna for forty years. He has friends there. He'll be a big help."

All McKay could do was hide his true feelings, but it wasn't necessary to hide any obvious, appropriate, and expected expressions of anger, frustration, and concern. As he listened to Caroline, people hurried along the corridors toward the street entrance. It didn't matter who they were or where they were actually going, they conjured up a picture of Western correspondents moving eastward, drawn closer towards Vienna and beyond, sensing greater danger for the rebels in a distracted world, the threat of disaster, some impending doom.

"Take care of yourself," was the only feeble comment Charlie could come up with just before Caroline, weighted with plans and responsibilities, charged away.

Enormously restless, McKay walked back to his office and spent most of the afternoon—Wednesday afternoon, October 31—staring out the window at the Hofgarten next to the royal palace, that expanse raw and windy on this late day in autumn, its umbrellas and café tables only a memory of summer. At four o'clock he filled out a leave slip for Thursday and Friday and took it to his boss, hoping he wouldn't turn it down for giving him such short notice. But he signed it readily enough, asking only, "What are *you* up to?"

"To tell you the truth I don't know yet."

"Well, stay loose," he advised.

McKay's apartment with its silences was a twenty-minute walk from the consulate along Kaulbachstrasse and that was one thing that always gave him a certain amount of pleasure, walking down this old, very European street of baroque houses and apartment buildings. On rainy evenings it seemed to him—movie trained as he was—agreeably sinister. A hanging restaurant sign creaked under a single entrance light, and were the headlights from the black Mercedes, cruising slowly, then gaining speed, aimed at anyone along the walls? But it was only another taxi.

His car was parked out front. When he saw it he made up his mind, climbed the stairs to his flat two at a time, made himself a quick supper of eggs and bread, packed a bag, and by seven o'clock was outside the city on the autobahn to Salzburg where he spent the night. Early Thursday morning he drove on to Vienna.

The last of the bright, winey fall had gone. The autumn was on the edge of winter now, overcast and chill, full of waiting snow.

At the Munich Hauptbahnhof, Caroline and Stefan bought *Die Welt*, the *Neue Züricher Nachrichten*, the London *Telegraph*, *Figaro*, the Paris *Herald Tribune* and an illustrated Italian magazine with photographs of Hungarian university students and even younger boys—some looked to be no more than fourteen—throwing Molotov cocktails at Soviet tanks. The news was the same, told and analyzed a dozen different ways. Nagy had called on the Soviet Union to discuss an immediate withdrawal of Soviet troops from Hungary. Fighting continued in Hungarian provinces. And in the Sinai desert. The Polish and Hungarian cardinals had been freed. Gomułka and

the Polish reformers were consolidating their gains. All almost unbelievable. Because Caroline could not go much beyond the headlines in the German language papers, she finished first. Stefan read
on, wearing shell-rimmed glasses, and looked ministerial. Caroline
smoked and looked out the window. The Munich suburbs, industrial
outskirts, and satellite towns were behind them. Grey-green farmers' fields were empty of activity, the harvest long over. Villages,
small stations rushing backward, gone. She knew it by the changed
sound even with her eyes closed. After the train had stopped briefly
at Rosenheim and had started up again, she got an issue of *Encounter* from her handbag, opened it to a bookmark, and began
reading an essay by Isaiah Berlin on the birth of the Russian intel-
ligentsia. Knees crossed, the heel of one navy blue leather pump
dangled off that silk-stockinged foot. Then she slipped off both
shoes and curled her legs beneath her skirt on the blue plush seat.
She read until the train began slowing as it approached the Austrian
border just west of Salzburg.

Caroline and Stefan returned from the buffet car. The woman
who had been in their compartment had left at Salzburg with her
luggage. The one German gentleman who had boarded at Munich
was still in place. In the other seat beside the corridor bulkhead they
found a plump little man, bald on the top of his head, drably suited,
who struck Caroline at a glance as being embarrassed to be where
he was. He sat with his hands clasped between his knees. She smiled
at him as she stepped beyond his knees and he smiled faintly in
return. Stefan nodded cordially. The train was already in motion.
Stefan, speaking German, proffered the German language papers
across the aisle and the new traveler accepted them with thanks, in
German. The train sped on towards Linz. "Mountains," Caroline
said, looking out the window to the south. There was snow on some
of the peaks.

The plump balding man read little beyond the front pages of the newspapers and one inside page in each. He started to hand them back to Stefan but Stefan shook his head politely and the new passenger placed the folded newspapers on the empty seat beside him. Stefan studied him for a few moments and then began speaking to him in the unique, rapidly cascading sounds of Hungarian, to which the new passenger responded eagerly with an agglutinative, dactylar flow of his own, his face brightened not so much with pleasure as with relief, a release of emotion. The apparently napping German across the way opened his eyes for a moment, closed them again. Caroline's attention was entirely wakeful. Abruptly, the newcomer looked at Caroline, who had said "mountains," and said, "Please excuse me. I also speak English."

"Oh, thank you for your courtesy," Caroline said. "But, please. Speak Hungarian. This is the time to speak Hungarian if you can. I wish I could. But my friend can translate later. I need to excuse myself anyway."

When she had returned from the W.C. at the end of the car, Caroline stood in the corridor looking out the window at the hilly Austrian landscape. Stefan came out of the compartment with the Hungarian, who smiled briefly at Caroline and walked up toward the buffet car. The train picked up speed. Stefan stayed in the corridor beside Caroline, holding on to the brass window rail.

"His name is Kovács. László," Stefan said. "A common name, perhaps his real one. He's been living in Salzburg. He is a violinist and plays in a café. His wife is in Győr, on the way to Budapest. He is going to Vienna to meet a friend. They'll try to drive to Győr to bring his wife out."

"Was she just visiting someone?"

"No. He's been in Austria a year without her."

"Why did he leave her in the first place?"

"He claims the AVO, the secret police, were after him for

something. I doubt if he was important, but whatever he did or said, or didn't do, wouldn't have to be important in the Western sense. But they might leave his wife alone. She could pretend to repudiate him. If he stayed, they would both be in trouble. The plan was, she would try to join him later. Even if they were estranged he might still try to help her at a time like this. I think he is a decent man, repetitious, a little dull, but under present circumstances I would be the last to deny him courage."

The letters of a suburban town fell slowly backward at the end of a station platform.

"Vienna," Stefan said. "We're very close."

6

Heavy six-story buildings, grey and brown, pressed close together under an overcast sky, pedestrians in overcoats, raincoats, hats, hurrying, each man or woman alone it seemed, isolated islands. A gloomy city, Caroline thought, and too big, of course, for what it was and had been now since the fall of the Habsburgs.

The RFE bureau occupied a small suite of rooms on the second floor of a mixed residential-commercial building on the Köstlergasse. MacKenzie, who ran it, was an Englishman married to a Viennese woman, a resident of the city since the end of the war. Stefan had said MacKenzie had published a collection of doggerel written in Viennese street dialect he had translated into English cockney. Short, sandy-haired, unkempt, he had watery blue eyes behind black-rimmed glasses, bad teeth. There was a piece of sticking plaster on his chin where he had cut himself shaving. He was not rude but not cordial, perhaps simply too busy, rushed. A Hungarian, a Romanian, and a Yugoslav occupied the other offices. The Hungarian was a woman. There were no introductions. The Hungarian woman spent the entire time on the telephone.

Late Thursday afternoon, November first. Nagy had declared Hungary neutral, no longer a member of the Warsaw Pact, and had appealed to the United Nations for support.

"My God," Caroline said. "What are the Russians doing?"

"Ringing Budapest with tanks," MacKenzie said.

"Can he get away with it? Khrushchev backed down in Warsaw."

MacKenzie declined comment but said Caroline could use the telephone.

She phoned three auto-rental agencies. Nothing was available and nothing was likely to be for days. She phoned the AP and UP bureaus. The UP staffers were all out. The Austrian woman who answered said she had no idea with whom Caroline might hitch a ride. Neither did the AP man, who had a dead voice and was curt and unhelpful.

"Where do correspondents hang out?" Caroline asked.

"Café Hawelka. Bristol Hotel bar. But if you want my opinion you'd be wasting your time in those places. I'll drive you to the border in the morning. Much easier to get a ride onward from there if there is one. Hell's own mess down there now, I'm told. Utter chaos at night."

"Well, thank you very much," Caroline said. "If I don't find anything sooner I'll certainly take you up on that offer. What time should I be ready to go, and where?"

Stefan telephoned a Polish couple who invited him to dinner, Caroline too when they heard about her, but she said, "No, I'd be in the way. You'd have to speak English. I'll pick up some goulash somewhere. I'm too nervous to eat very much. Besides, I'd really like to get in a nap. I don't have your energy, Stefan. I suddenly feel zonked."

"Then let us meet, say at nine, at the hotel. There is a Hungarian cabaret we would do well to visit. People there will know everything there is to know."

The narrow streets of the inner city were mostly empty. Shops were shuttered. Two taxis went past, one other car. A man crossed an intersection up ahead.

"Here," Stefan called, and Caroline realized she had walked past the entrance without noticing it. Stefan held aside one of the leather curtains hung around the entrance to keep out the chill night air, and they went inside. The room was dark and smoky and there was the sound of zithers and violins. The sound of Hungarian came from every corner. Stefan spoke it to a headwaiter up front.

"There are no tables at the moment. We must sit at the bar," Stefan said.

Halfway there, Caroline saw László Kovács. The violinist was the fifth at a round table but seemed to be alone, an outsider. The others were talking and gesturing to each other. Kovács sat slightly turned away from them, taking no part in the conversation. Caroline supposed the headwaiter had simply asked strangers to make room for him.

Caroline felt sorry for Kovács, but she had barely met him and wasn't inclined to approach him now. She had no power to do anything for him. Stefan too did not seem to be in any hurry to speak to the man. He had seated himself firmly at the bar, had ordered glasses of wine, wasn't even looking in Kovács' direction.

"Stefan, did you notice . . ."

"Yes. Poor fellow. I wonder if he located his friend."

"It doesn't look that way. Maybe he's supposed to meet him here."

But Kovács saw *them*. They saw his face in the mirror behind the bar. He was standing behind them.

"I beg your pardon," he said in English. "For intruding. I recognized you from the train. It seemed a coincidence. . . . I . . ."
   "A pleasure, my dear fellow," Stefan said. "Please join us. Are
you here to meet your friend?"
   "I have left a message . . ." Kovács said forlornly. "He had not
arrived. I waited four hours, five . . . then I came here. It is a place
he knows. . . . I have the car . . ."
   "You have a car? You've rented a car?" Caroline said.
   "Someone I know—a Hungarian—was able to hold one for me
at the auto agency where he works. They are very much in demand.
It is quite small—a Fiat."
   "Where are you staying, Mr. Kovács?" Caroline asked.
   "A small hotel. The Radetsky. Near the Ostbahnhof."
   "What time were you planning to leave?"
   "Planning to leave? I don't know. It was not certain. It would
depend on the arrangements my friend had made. . . ." He looked
back at the crowded room for a moment.
   "Do have something with us, Mr. Kovács," Stefan said. "Wine?
A whiskey?"
   Kovács held up the palm of a small soft hand. "Nothing, thank
you."
   "Are you sure?" Caroline asked, matching Stefan's cordial
tone.
   "No, you are very kind. I must go. I should not have stayed
here as long as I have."
   "We're at the Savoy if we can do anything," Caroline said.
   When Kovács had left, Stefan spoke to the barman in Hungar-
ian and leaning forward listened to the response. Caroline heard the
Magyar sounds and watched the gestures. A violin sobbed in the
background.
   "No change," Stefan said. "Everyone is waiting. Would you like
another glass of wine?"

"No, really. That was absolutely enough. Why don't we go on back."

Outside, Stefan hailed a cruising taxi.

A night porter inside the dimmed lobby of the Savoy unlocked the outside doors. Stefan said, "My dear, it's been a habit of mine to walk a while by myself before turning in. It pleases me to imagine the exercise helps me to sleep a little better. I hope you won't mind."

Caroline remembered the streetwalker he had picked up in Munich and her face felt on fire. But she kept her voice under control.

"No, of course not. Everybody needs a quiet time alone at least once a day."

With the ease of someone who has been doing it for years, Stefan leaned over—he didn't have far to lean; she was a fairly tall girl in heels—and tilting her chin with one hand, kissed her lightly on the lips.

"Goodnight, Caroline."

"Goodnight, Stefan. Thank you for everything."

Striding off down the dark street, he left her, quite astonished and happy and uncertain, with the night porter still waiting for her to enter.

In careful German, Caroline left a call for seven and said that in the morning she would be checking her suitcase for several days.

7

She had fallen asleep in her slip with the light on and when the light woke her she thought it was the middle of the day and she had missed the biggest story of her life. But it was only two in the morning. Switched into darkness she fell off again into oceanic deeps. When she woke the second time to no ringing phone her first thought was THEY DIDN'T WAKE US!

No. It was only ten to seven.

What then? Nerves. You're not psychic. Just get moving.

She got out of bed immediately and when she came out of the bathroom began dressing quickly, peeled off her slip and climbed into longjohns, wool slacks, and socks and sheepskin-lined boots. The ringing phone interrupted her. "Thank you. I'm up. Danke." Both hands free again, she pulled a long-sleeved cotton jersey over her head and combed her hair in a hurry.

Phone Kovács now? No, let Stefan or the desk clerk do it from the lobby. Viennese German was different. This was no time not to be understood by this clerk or the one at the Radetsky. Comb still in one hand she rapped on the connecting door and called Stefan's name. Once again after ten seconds. Still no answer. He'd gone down already.

She'd unpacked very little. Now she transferred a sweater and a half dozen changes of underpants from her suitcase to her commodious shoulder bag, packed her raincoat inside the suitcase, and strapped her umbrella to the side of it. Loaded down with this luggage and her sheepskin-lined coat she went out to the elevator, waited for it to come up, rode down.

In a small room off the lobby, tables were set for breakfast and a few of the other hotel guests were already seated at them, but not Stefan. He wasn't in the lobby either. The concierge on duty indicated her breakfast table with an outstretched hand.

"The gentleman in room three-seventeen . . ." Caroline began in German.

"He has not yet come downstairs, Madame."

Caroline stepped over to the house phone and dialed three-seventeen. She listened to seven long rings, eight . . . ten. A chill passed through her and her mouth dried.

"Could he have taken a walk?" she asked the concierge. *He took a walk last night* her own voice told her, but what did that have to do with it?

"No, Madame," the concierge said in English. "I have been here since six hours and have not seen him."

"He may be ill!" Caroline said. "Can someone let me in to see?"

The concierge summoned a bellman from his post, handed him the second key from box 317, and Caroline walked with him to the elevator. The arrow above the doors was arcing slowly toward the numbers of higher floors.

"Please, can we walk up?" Caroline asked.

She climbed up behind the bellman, her heart racing. She didn't know what to expect. Whatever it would be she feared it so much she had to fight off terror.

Stefan's room was empty, the bed made, unslept in. But his small suitcase was still open on the luggage rack. The bellman quickly opened the bathroom door, switched on the light, then turned and shook his head.

Caroline descended, half running, to the lobby.

"The night porter . . ." she said.

"He is off duty, Madame."

"Can you telephone him?"

"Alas, he has no phone."

"Can you get a message to him?"

"It would take a great deal of time. He lives many kilometers from here."

"Oh, it wouldn't do any good anyway!" Caroline said, distraught. "My friend took a walk last night just before I came in. Obviously he never came back! Can you make a call for me? To the Radetsky Hotel? Please ask for a László Kovács."

The concierge went to the open doorway to the telephone operator's room and gave instructions. Caroline and the concierge stood waiting, the reception desk and a silent telephone between them. Then it rang. The concierge spoke into it in Viennese German Caroline could barely understand. Still keeping the connection open, the concierge said, "There is no László Kovács registered at the Radetsky Hotel."

"But he was there as late as last evening!"

The concierge spoke to his counterpart again, listened, replaced the receiver.

"There has been no one by that name in the hotel for at least the past ten days."

"A small Hungarian . . ." Caroline said.

"There are so many small Hungarians," the concierge said sadly.

"Where can I use the outside phone?"

The cabin was across the lobby. Caroline gave the operator MacKenzie's office number. No one answered. It was still too early.

MacKenzie had said to meet him at eight-thirty. She gave the operator MacKenzie's home number. A woman answered. If she spoke English she refused to speak it now, spoke in irritated German too rapidly for Caroline to follow.

"*Bitte?*"

"*Im büro!*" Mrs. MacKenzie said testily, no doubt for the second time, and hung up.

He won't have arrived yet, Caroline told herself. Conscious of hunger but unable to eat, she crossed the lobby and went out to the street. The air was cold. She looked down the narrow street in the direction Stefan had walked but the sight gave her no clue, no inspiration. Had he been mugged? She didn't believe it. This was Vienna, not Naples or New York. Had he gotten sick, had a heart attack, fallen? Was he lying somewhere dead, dying, unattended? Why was it she didn't believe those always very real possibilities either, not with any premonition, any visceral force?

Now it was eight o'clock. She went back to the phone booth and an unfamiliar male voice answered MacKenzie's office number. He spoke German but with some other kind of accent. She identified herself in English and in good English the man at the other end called himself Corneliu.

"I expect him at any moment. There was a letter addressed to you in our mailbox when I came in."

"A letter?"

"Yes. I have it."

For two blocks she couldn't find a cab to save her life. Then one pulled up at the corner beside her while she was looking up and down the cross street frantically waving at what were all private cars speeding past her on the roadway.

Caroline held the unopened envelope in her hands. Her hunger now was making her queasy, light-headed, and was a source of con-

cern she could not ignore any longer. She had a journey ahead of
her. She had to take practical precautions, toughen her vital mechanism, and keep her wits about her. It was eight-twenty-five but
MacKenzie still hadn't arrived.

"Is there someplace nearby I can get some breakfast?"

"Directly across the street, a coffee house," Corneliu said.

"I didn't notice it. I wasn't paying attention."

"I will tell Mr. MacKenzie where you are. There is enough
time. He will not be able to leave until he goes through the
mail."

At the café there was an empty table beside a working tile
stove. A waiter brought a basket of rolls from a sideboard, a pot of
coffee, before she had completely settled herself. There was milk
and jam on the table already. In a matter of seconds the waiter returned with a small crock of sweet butter. She ate a little and then
when she was certain her queasiness had passed, she opened the
letter. It was written on Radetsky Hotel stationery. Even before she
began comprehending the words she first saw as simply horizontal
rows of marks across the page it occurred to her she had never before seen Stefan's handwriting, and the sight of this hitherto unknown aspect of his personality struck her with an independent
anguish of its own.

Caroline, my dear, Kovács' friend never arrived and there
is no more time to wait. Kovács—and that, it seems, is not his
real name—is too fearful and, I suspect, too ineffectual, to go
by himself. I am going to escort him or, if necessary, go alone.
I know the country.

I think now you should stay in Vienna and write your stories from there, especially since you do not have to cover day
to day events as the wire service reporters and other fast media

people do. I am sure there will be many stories here. Mac-Kenzie can help you.

My dear, you must go on. You have everything ahead of you. But I am one of the shadows in limbo. I have no future. I carry a stateless passport that hardly has any meaning for anyone. One might say I exist on Confederate money, Weimar marks or tsarist bonds. Oh, I have every intention of surviving for a while—though at this point it is not possible to know exactly where.

Whether he was interrupted at this point and was unable to continue writing or whether he could think of no way to conclude his message was not clear, but perhaps the answer was the former because there was more space on the page—and no signature.

Frozen into an unnatural stillness, incapable for the moment of the will to move in any direction, Caroline saw without seeing what was before her eyes—the decorative blond and painted wood of the café, the crystal chandeliers, the painting of Franz-Joseph, an old turtle in his bemedaled tunic and mutton chops, with his sad, brooding look of disillusionment.

MacKenzie found her there.

"I say, if you're ready we can be off."

8

As MacKenzie charged down the street, hunched over the wheel of his battered and dusty Opel, Caroline told him what Stefan had done and only in the telling did she remember Stefan's fascination—perhaps obsession—with his original concept of the gratuitous good act he had conceived thirty years before.

"Who does he think he is, the bloody Scarlet Pimpernel!" MacKenzie said.

"Don't ask me why he's done such a crazy thing," she said. "I think I know but it's too complicated to explain."

"Oh, he's quite mad," MacKenzie said. "Most Poles are, but Stefan most of all. Well, there goes his bloody job if he's interested, which obviously he isn't."

And his life? But she didn't say it.

"How long would it take to drive to Győr?"

"Fifty minutes to the border. Then however long it takes to get through the border formalities. Informalities these days, I should say. Assuming no delay, another thirty minutes? Then still another sixty kilometers or so. Highway is adequate but there could easily be obstructions—road blocks, checkpoints. Best to count on another hour and a half, even longer. You have no idea exactly when he left? No, I don't suppose so. Might have been 4:00 or 5:00 A.M. If he got to the border at 6:00, could easily be there by now."

For a while until they had left the city they rode in silence. On the highway, MacKenzie relaxed a bit at the wheel.

"Resourceful fellow I should imagine," he said. "Had to be. Been through all manner of muck in his day. Doesn't look Hungarian, though. Oh, I don't know. Perhaps he could pass. In parts of Spain, if you can suspend disbelief, Spaniards who've never seen a foreigner take *me* for Spanish—from some part of the country where they've never been."

"He doesn't look particularly like what I think of as Polish either," Caroline said. Talking was physically painful for her but she needed to talk in spite of it.

"No, there's that. Palm himself off as almost anybody I suppose so long as he isn't picked up. Then they'll find out soon enough. Hungarians won't mind a bit. Might even look on him as a kind of hero. Russians or Hungarian AVOs, another story."

"How well do you know him?"

"Never as well as one assumes, I suppose. Seen a fair amount of him over the past three or four years. Travels a lot, you know, on his time off. Has friends all over. Some friends do a bit of contract work for me. I think he's restless in Munich. No great love for the Germans, can't blame him for that."

Caroline looked straight ahead at the highway they were consuming.

"I've been helping him with his autobiography," she said. "Did he ever say anything about people named Friedland?"

"*He* didn't. The Polish friends I just mentioned told me a little."

"Jews he helped escape?"

"From Vienna, yes. But they didn't make it all the way."

"To the West."

"No. . . . He was the editor of a theater and film review. She was a prominent gynecologist," MacKenzie added after a bit. "From an old distinguished line. I looked them up in prewar Who's Whos. Archetypical Viennese intellectuals, evidently very close to Helena and Stefan. After the Anschluss, Stefan and Helena offered them asylum in Poland. When the Germans invaded the following year, they fled to Vilna where Stefan and Helena hid them when the bloody Russians marched in. Russkie's stayed two-and-a-half months that first time, then pulled out and turned the city over to the Lithuanians. Still no place for Jews to stay very long. Stefan got them British visas from the legation in Kaunas and whatever else was necessary—Latvian and Swedish transit visas I should imagine—so they could cross to Riga and board a Swedish ship. No evidence they ever did. They never reached Sweden. I don't know the details, if anyone does, but I think Stefan believes they must have been betrayed. Why don't you ask Stefan's friends when you get back to Vienna? I have their address."

But the tragic, terrible fates of other people so long ago seemed to Caroline less significant to her now than questions about Stefan himself, and Stefan's Helena.

"What happened to Helena after Stefan was arrested?"

"Kept on performing. Toured Russia with a troupe she'd organized, hoping to get some word of him. While she was living in the Moskva Hotel, Stefan was in the Lubyanka prison only a few blocks away but she had no idea how close she was. Worked her way to Tashkent and met up with him after his release."

"When did she die? Where?"

"Nineteen-forty-four would it be? Or forty-five? No, forty-four. In India."

"*India?* Well, why should anything surprise me."

"Simple enough explanation. When Stalin let them go, a quarter of a million Poles in Soviet camps and Siberian exile poured into Persia, under British military control. An enormous problem, what to do with them, especially civilians, and Stefan was an experienced refugee administrator. So that was the job he took on. Many of the women and children, old people, were packed off to British East Africa and British India. Eventually Helena too. She had TB, you know. Carried it around for years, and it got worse after two years of performing for Polish army units in Iraq and Palestine. Coughing fits on stage until even she admitted it was time to quit. But Tehran, where Stefan was working, was no city for a TB patient. He sent her to a sanatorium in Poona, near Bombay. And got himself transferred to India on temporary duty to check into Polish refugee welfare.

"But Helena wasn't happy in Poona and her doctors weren't encouraging. Someone told her how beautiful it was in Shillong, a mile high in the Khasi hills of Assam. Been there yourself?"

"No, never," Caroline said.

"Pretty place. Lots of Scots out that way and the meadows remind them of the highlands of home. Close to the Burma front but far enough away from it. Even in wartime, fresh vegetables and milk and sometimes fish from mountain streams. Stefan took leave and rented a little house. He knew now Helena couldn't last much longer, and in her own house, with him to take care of her, she could paint, something she'd done for years in her spare time.

"He got a letter from a relative who'd survived the war inside Poland. Through some channel or other this elderly woman heard Stefan's manor house near Vilna had caught fire—deliberately set or accidentally no one seemed to know—and had burned to the ground. Then the business about the dogs. Helena had a pair of terriers. Next door a neighbor kept a mastiff. One day the beast leapt the fence and killed the little dogs. Stefan said he knew then the mastiff was a symbol of death. The same day a chandelier crashed to the floor. Three omens, if you believe that sort of thing. I don't say I don't. In any case Helena died not long afterward.

"Nineteen-forty-four, Stefan only forty or so, a fine figure of a man. That voice. Five minutes with him and you'd know he was exceptional. With a great deal of experience as a wartime administrator used to dealing with people at the top, generals, diplomats. He had diplomatic status himself.

"The British put him to work in Calcutta. Glad to have him. Liaison, supply, personnel, something along those lines, possibly all three. It was a natural arrangement. All Polish forces were under British command by this time. And the Polish government-in-exile was fast fading away. Worked there a while, then drifted to the Lebanon to work with the last lot of refugees."

They were both silent a while. Then MacKenzie said, "Extraordinary life when you come to think of it. What he's up to now must seem a bit of a lark. No, then again I suppose not."

9

Nickelsdorf, the Austrian town at the Hungarian border, was a muddy, dung-spattered farmers' village with geese honking their right of way in the unpaved streets. Now it was crowded with Austrian gendarmerie, farmers risking Austrian neutrality by carrying bushel baskets of food and medicine to the border, Hungarian students and other civilians who had crossed into Austria for one purpose and another, and Red Cross convoys with food and medical supplies from many countries. None so far were from the United States.

McKay had been there since 7:00 A.M. By half past nine the number of correspondents and photographers had thinned out to a scattering, some of whom had gone into Hungary and come out again. It appeared that most of those who were going in had gone already.

Charlie spotted Caroline even before she had climbed out of the passenger seat of the beat-up Opel, Nickelsdorf was that small a place. For a moment or two he was embarrassed to be there, pos-

sibly to appear as though he was following her as an unwanted in-
truder. But then he saw it was not Stefan behind the wheel and that
Caroline was collecting her gear and walking away alone. He got out
of his car, stood beside it, and waited for her to discover him.

"Charlie!" she said, but there was no joy in her surprise. She
left her big shoulder bag against a stone wall and hurried up. "Charlie, Stefan's disappeared!" she said, distraught. "Into Hungary!
How long have you been here?"

"Couple of hours. But I haven't seen him. Why . . . ?"

"I'll explain later. It's so mixed up but I've got to try to find
him. . . . How did you get here? Do you know anybody who's driving in?"

"I drove my own car from Munich. I think everybody who's
going in has gone."

"Why are you here?"

McKay shrugged. "To see what there is to see. On my own.
I'm not on official duty. . . . Where do you expect to find him? It's
a small country as countries go, but big enough when you get there."

"I don't know. But I can't sit here and wonder about it." Her
eyes had gotten wet. "I *do* know where to find him—somewhere
between here and Györ, about a third of the way to Budapest. He
was going there to try to help someone. . . . Do you remember the
theme of his novel? He found a chance to act it out for himself."

Very suddenly McKay found himself inside a very large moment in his life. He calculated the hazards for a member of the
American diplomatic service, driving a car with consular corps
plates, unofficially entering a Communist country during a revolution, a revolution that might still fail though hope (blowing hot and
cold) was irresistibly, irrationally high when it was high. Imprisoned—or shot—as a provocateur, a spy? Had he been alone he
knew he would not cross the frontier. Alone he would not follow
Stefan, who was much better equipped to take care of himself. But

Caroline gave him no choice but to play the great fool on her behalf.
He could hardly toss her the keys to his car and stay behind. Who
could live the rest of his life with that even if she went in and out
without a scratch?

"I'm your lift," he said. "Let's go."

"Charlie, I can't ask you to."

"You haven't. Look, all bets are off, all rules are suspended
for the duration." He was a little short of breath.

As McKay began driving slowly toward the Austrian checkpoint, a man called to him in American English, "You got room?"
He was about thirty-five, stocky with curly hair starting high off his
forehead and turning grey. Pinned to his parka were a small American flag and a square of pasteboard with *Philadelphia Inquirer* written on it. McKay invited him to climb into the back seat and he
introduced himself as Allen Goodman. McKay planned quickly to
call himself a free-lance, but Goodman didn't ask. For a few minutes
Charlie found it reassuring to have another man along. Safety in
numbers. But reassurance began to thin out soon enough.

The Iron Curtain, Churchill's grim and memorable image, was
more than symbol or metaphor. It was real barbed wire and bullets,
prison watchtowers, border police with stony faces, and behind all
that, steel tanks and troop carriers, prison trains and Arctic camps,
and even when you couldn't see it, could see only silent, empty,
wintry fields stretching north and south, it was there, ominous and
waiting. Revolutionaries had broken a narrow opening in it but their
fight was still a desperate one. The iron was still in place, still im-
placable, and the opening could close behind you as unexpectedly
and quickly as it had appeared. For McKay, as the car his own foot
was powering moved slowly to the east, the concept and the reality
of what he was approaching, about to cross, to enter, and the possible implications for him, for Caroline too in spite of her "inde-

pendent" status, should anything go wrong, was more than a little sobering. Safety slipped away behind them. He did not feel trapped, he still had freedom of action, but at the same time the forward motion of the car seemed inexorable. There was no way he could have turned back.

Caroline, leaking hope, felt simply numb and fated.

McKay picked up a second hitchhiker in a belted leather coat, hip boots, a battered fedora, carrying a satchel of medical supplies, a doctor from Mosonmagyaróvár, a town ten kilometers or so across the frontier. He spoke good English. The very presence of this calm and competent-looking older man now riding behind him sent a large infusion of new and irrational confidence into McKay's spirit. *Daddy's here. Everything is going to be all right.* McKay laughed briefly as if at some private joke, one low-decibel bark, and Caroline looked at him for a moment. Goodman gave the doctor a cigar and they both lit up. Caroline rolled down the nearest window a little. It was cold and there was scattered snow in the three-kilometer strip between the Austrian and Hungarian frontier posts. It might have been a county line in an American plains state were it not for the Austrian guards in neat, grey-green uniforms with capes, the Hungarian guards and soldiers in red-trimmed olive drab, rifles strapped to their backs, some cradling Soviet tommy guns. They showed no interest in anybody's passport. How easy it is! McKay thought, euphoric now. There were few cars, many trucks, bicycles, people on foot. The walkers and cyclists waved and saluted. In the village of Hegyeshalom students passed out handbills and newly published newspapers, single sheets or four-page productions. The doctor translated headlines. They called for unity of all democratic forces, willing Marxists included, a neutral socialist state on the Scandinavian pattern. Caroline snapped a number of shots with the Leica hanging from the strap around her neck.

The countryside was like a poor corner of Austria. In the doctor's town the solid Germanic buildings needed paint and repair. Workers wearing assorted caps, pants, and suit jackets that seldom matched stood along the walls of buildings, smoking and gesturing.

The doctor invited them into his house for coffee.

"We haven't time," Caroline said.

"Five minutes," Goodman said. "He's already helped us to part of a story. There's more. When was the last time you were inside a Hungarian home?"

They filed into an old-fashioned parlor. A chiming clock, a radio, a small piano, all many years old; on the walls a crucifix, a portrait of the Virgin, a tacked up oriental rug. The room was warm near a brown porcelain stove. The doctor set out tiny glasses of *barackpálinka,* apricot brandy, on a lace-covered table, pointed to the tiny Hungarian and American flags tied to the cut-glass chandelier. Everyone toasted both flags, but McKay and Caroline, at least, did so half-reluctantly. Then the doctor's wife, dressed for the outdoors and carrying string bags filled with wrapped parcels from the market, entered the house talking, anxious-faced. The doctor translated. Soviet tanks were reported moving in to surround the town. The road to Budapest was believed to be already cut off.

"You had better go back to Austria immediately," the doctor said.

"Do you want to go with us?" Goodman asked the doctor.

The doctor spoke to his wife.

"*Nem!*" she said, and shook her head.

"Thank you, no," the doctor said.

"Is there any other way to get to Győr?" Caroline asked.

"To try to go there now would be very unwise," the doctor said. He walked with them out to the car.

"In a war you travel with the *friendly* side," Goodman said to Caroline. "You think the Russians are going to let anybody 'cover' this thing once they start shooting? Hand out interviews? If you're *lucky* you'd be interned until it's all over. Unraped."

"Why did we come here, then?" Caroline said.

"I don't know about you. I hoped for the best. I got a Hungarian grandmother back home. We're too late, baby. That's the answer. Just like that, we're too late."

McKay drove back, quickly, out of the town, towards Austria. There was a roadblock up ahead, all Hungarians manning it. All spoke German. Soviet tanks had closed the frontier. The Hungarians advised them to return to the first crossroads and drive twenty kilometers to the southwest where there was a small country border crossing.

They didn't see any tanks along the way but there was an awful moment coming up to the barrier, the line of soldiers. The soldiers were all Hungarian but for some reason the non-com in charge hesitated and looked carefully at their passports, McKay's black and gold diplomatic passport especially. Then the non-com stepped aside, shouted, and the barrier went up.

McKay had a map but it didn't show this corner of Burgenland in enough detail. One wrong turn led them quite a distance out of the way towards Graz until at a crossroads hamlet "*Nach Wien?*" got a farmer's finger pointed in the right direction. A second error led them up to impassable road construction and they lost another half hour retracing the way. "Oh God!" Caroline said, exasperated and tearful. It was five-thirty and dark before they got back to Nickelsdorf. A fellow from Reuters said no Soviet tanks were in sight but the Hungarians weren't letting anyone through.

Goodman got a ride back to Vienna. McKay and Caroline stayed. Charlie didn't try to make conversation. There wasn't anything to say. Caroline didn't talk to him or to anyone else. She sat at a table in the dining room of the *gasthaus* sipping coffee and harsh Austrian brandy and smoking cigarettes. McKay asked the waitress if the inn had two rooms they could have for the night and she went to ask the owner. He came back with her and demanded twice what

McKay and Caroline were paying in Vienna, paid in advance. Caroline checked in soon after that, refusing dinner. Just before she began climbing the stairs she took McKay's hand for a moment and said hoarsely, "Charlie, thank you for your help."

In the morning there were a lot of German, French, Swiss, and Scandinavian correspondents and photographers in the dining room. The Reuters man was at the bar drinking coffee.

"What's the latest?" Caroline tried to ask, her voice inadequate to the task. She coughed it into some kind of better shape. ". . . latest."

"Tanks out there now, just over the line. You can see them. Large-scale Soviet troop movements crossing Poland."

Caroline started walking toward the door but McKay caught her by the arm and stopped her.

"Eat something first," he told her. "You haven't eaten anything except a chocolate bar in twenty-four hours. It won't do you any good to pass out."

When they'd had breakfast they went outside to the street of frozen mud and walked up the seventy-five yards to the Austrian frontier post. The barriers were down. No vehicles were attempting to go through in either direction but people on foot were held up too. A French correspondent said, "They are waiting for instructions."

It wasn't possible to see anything from there. They leaned against the side of the customs and immigration shed and McKay wondered if there was any point in waiting at all. After a while an Austrian army jeep drove up from the village and the barrier went up before the jeep reached it so the vehicle had only to slow down momentarily before it went on. An officer drove and another sat beside him. Twenty minutes later the jeep returned and the officers went inside the shed. A border guard came out and raised the barrier. A dozen correspondents crossed over on foot and Caroline and

Charlie followed. Everyone spread out. The others were men who could walk faster but McKay held back to Caroline's pace and they were soon trudging along together up the side of the two-lane highway, crossing the treeless no-man's land under a wide, overcast sky. It took them thirty minutes to reach a point about three hundred yards from the Hungarian line where they could begin to make out the tanks, three, possibly four of them. A trickle of refugees had already begun to walk around the tanks across the barren fields, all of them middle-aged or older, one man carrying a child on his back. At two hundred yards they saw there were three Soviet tanks behind the border, guns pointing away across the fields. They came up to the other correspondents who had stopped in several clusters a hundred yards from the Hungarian line. Some had field glasses. When the Frenchman had finished looking through his and saw that Caroline was trying to see better by making a visor out of the edge of one gloved hand, he handed over his glasses without being asked and she focused on one tank after the other. Then McKay looked. The tanks seemed very close but Charlie couldn't make out any faces inside their turrets.

"*Merci bien,*" Caroline said, and McKay returned the binoculars.

One of the other correspondents said, "I'm ashamed to call myself an American down here. Not one goddamned truckload of anything, not one word of support for any new government and now it's too late. All along we promised support and they believed us. When they revolt, we do nothing. The Russians wait, day after day, practically beg us to make a move. Now they know we don't give a damn and they can do any fucking thing they please. What was to stop us from lending fifty planes to the Swiss to fly in nonmilitary supplies? What was to stop us from sending in UN observers? The Hungarians asked for them and for five days this border has been wide open. Would that have started a war, for Christ's sweet sake?"

10

McKay's car was still Caroline's only transportation, back to Vienna now on that dark, purposeless Saturday, where they waited, each alone in their separate hotels, until their separate silences became unbearable. Then they wandered the streets, briefly together, mostly by themselves, and slept fitfully into that terrible Sunday of massacre inside Hungary, and the beginning of mass flight to the West, the crushing of hopes.

For Caroline, not yet the end of hope when she heard of that phenomenal exodus of people into Austria and Yugoslavia, a siphoning off of talent—and problems—Soviet troop commanders and the new-old Hungarian bosses either could not or did not want to prevent. She saw it with her own eyes as she moved from refugee camp to refugee camp looking for the one survivor about whom she really cared. McKay extended his leave by a week to go with her. In Vienna, MacKenzie was one of the best sources of possible information through his multinational contacts and their chain of relatives, friends, and informants reaching in and listening-in to four surrounding countries. But at the end of that week no one had found any trace of Stefan Z——. McKay had no choice but to return to his job. But Caroline had no more business in Munich. Sunday afternoon, November the eleventh, McKay drove her to Vienna's Südbahnhof, where she could catch the direct express to Venice. Moments before she boarded it she gave him a sisterly kiss.

"Keep in touch," Charlie said.

"I will."

But by mid-December he had virtually given up hope of hearing from her again. And about the possible or probable or actual fate of Stefan there was only conjecture. He was not a public figure and so of no particular interest to the news media, and no Western government would be likely to intervene on his behalf. From MacKenzie and from some of Stefan's former colleagues in the Polish service at RFE, McKay heard alleged facts that might just as easily be traceable to rumor and back further still to speculation and vapor. There were reports he had been arrested and shot, that he had escaped into Yugoslavia, that he had managed to return to Poland, the last the least probable because it would have involved crossing both the width of quiescent but hard-line Czechoslovakia, and the Tatra mountains. He might, of course, be in hiding somewhere. By the turn of the new year the only fact, call it ninety percent incontrovertible, was that he had not turned up or chosen to reveal himself anywhere in the West.

"He's become a kind of legend," MacKenzie said when McKay called on him in Vienna two months later. "Let him stay one. I think that's how he would have wanted it. A mystery or an unmarked grave. He had surprisingly little vanity, really. We ought to allow him that much."

In mid-January, McKay, exalted by the sight of it, received a postcard from Rome providing a one-line weather report—and the return address of Caroline's *pensione*. McKay sent her a postcard of his own. It was the start of a correspondence. They were both lonely. McKay had not met or re-met anyone whose company he cared to share longer than the length of a bottle of *Hopfenperle*. Caroline had reached a stage in life where from time to time she might allow herself to be amused by Italian men but would never take any of them seriously. The messages on their postcards and in their letters weren't long. They discussed books they'd read (McKay thought *Lolita* a comic masterpiece; as a woman, Caroline had mixed feelings), movies (Caroline agreed *Beat the Devil*—which McKay had just seen for the third time—was inspired mania). McKay described a short trip he had taken to Alsace. He studiously avoided mentioning Munich but Caroline could tell him about Siena and Florence and about hearing Callas sing *Tosca* at La Scala in Milan. In mid-February she wrote: "Do you ski? Even if you don't, I'm told Cortina is the place to be. Can you get away for a few days?"

Glamor is in the eye of the beholder but clearly, for everyone, some places have it and some don't and, for McKay, high on a short list of the most glamorous places on earth was the little town of Cortina d'Ampezzo in the Dolomites of the Italian Alps.

He stopped his car on the edge of town, got out to look at it, and shivered with awe and a sense of infinite possibilities. The setting was spectacular, magnificent. Giant massifs broken by deep gorges towered ten thousand feet above the valley. Exposed limestone walls breaking out of the snow here and there into jagged ridges emphasized the sheer dramatic heights. In the gorgeous sunset they took on color—gold, pink, and vermillion deepening to violet and indigo. Wisps of snow swirled around the summits. The air was cold and exhilarating. His eye fell to the lower slopes and the floor of the valley and the steep roofs and steeples of the town where lights were going on.

They met in the lobby of the Hotel de la Poste (the French name perhaps in honor of the Frenchman who had first explored the surrounding mountains) and the kiss they exchanged was neither sisterly nor brotherly. It was all right to be glad to see each other, to be happy. Their room was on the third floor overlooking the square. The bellboy switched on a lamp and showed them in. A four-poster walnut bed, an armoire, a blanket chest painted grey-blue and decorated with green leaves and scarlet flowers. The bellboy opened the inside and outside shutters and they saw strings of ascending lights up the mountainside, and below in the square a bus pulling in from somewhere and discharging passengers. The driver climbed to the roof and began handing down suitcases and bundles.

Wide-eyed, Caroline sank into snowy billows of eiderdown. Arched as a longbow, wheeling, she drew the perfect angle, and drew him skyrocketing to discovery.

They went down to the crowded, lively bar, a town magnet. *I have arrived,* McKay, still dazzled, told himself. Beautiful women everywhere under the warm golden lights of the room, lovely girls, fascinating older women, distinguished-looking men, and beside him a girl as strikingly delectable as any girl there, who turned heads herself, who was his. One of the older men reminded them of Stefan, still missing, presumed dead, but with Stefan who could be sure? Caroline mourned him, but now, McKay thought, only as he did.

From their window they watched the orange torches of the night skiers zigzag slowly down the mountain, rise again, up, up, in a measured line, to repeat the descending pattern of lights until the torchlights went out like fireworks falling in the sea.

They made love again, and again in the morning beneath the mountains of the huge eiderdown comforter almost higher than their heads as the room got gradually warmer and the frost melted on the windows to reveal the blurred edge of the mountain, a cold sun, and the sky. Caroline lay silent, smiling, her eyes open, arms at her sides. A branch of some tree outside cracked under the weight of ice.

"When did you know how I felt about you?" Charlie asked. "In what postcard or letter did I give myself away?"

He had flattered himself that in all the time Caroline had been in thrall to Stefan he had successfully hidden his true feelings from her, but she shattered that illusion with a slow, back-and-forth, you-are-so-innocent shaking of her head.

"Charlie, Charlie, you can't hide anything. You gave yourself away the day we first crossed paths in the Englischer Garten." She touched his face with one hand. "What I appreciated most . . ." She didn't complete the sentence.

"Was me not making a pest of myself?" he said.

"I was going to say—not trying to be masterful."

"Now I think that's exactly what I want to be."

"Yes, be. Please be. I'll be a good girl."

They lunched on pasta with wild mushrooms. The hotel dining room had splendid views of heroic scenery through tall windows. They strolled along the main street of the town looking in shop windows. They sat at a table in the window of a café, sipping cappuccino. Then the cable car took them to the stupendous heights for the terrorizing thrill of the descent.

THE
NEW
PEOPLE

1

I rode beside Mr. Brown, the Anglo-Indian driver, in the front seat of the consulate's black Ford station wagon. At this moment, if our timing was well coordinated, the Greers, coming from Dacca by car, would be approaching West Bengal from the East Pakistani side.

In the year I had been stationed in Calcutta I had never been over this way before. I had had no professional need to make the trip, and recreational areas were north and south, not east. Meeting someone like Elliott Greer here now was highly unusual, possibly unprecedented.

"Some kind of difficulty with Chambers, the Dacca CG," Houston "Hud" Perry, the consul general, had said. "I'm not overly surprised. Chambers is a decent fellow but a stuffed shirt. Blinkered." By way of illustration he placed the heels of both thumbs against his eye sockets and stiffened his fingers in a forward direction. "Washington tells me the Greers are an exceptionally bright young couple. Who probably wanted out from under. God knows they're needed here."

Perry had been without a political officer for two months. Washington had not managed to recruit a replacement for the former incumbent until the latter was due to leave, and the new man, studying the Bengali language at the Foreign Service Institute in Virginia, would not reach the post for another half a year. Then Greer, who was qualified in Bengali—as well as Chinese—suddenly became available, and Perry had snapped him up.

It began to rain again, heavily, noisily, straight down. The Greers evidently couldn't even wait for the best season, the autumn, to travel in. It was June now. The monsoon had just begun and would go on for four months and when it wasn't raining it was hot and steamy. The rain pounded and splashed around us, ahead of us, reducing visibility. Mr. Brown slowed down. But a truck came at us, passed us—a lorry, I should say. At least the road ahead wasn't flooded, or so flooded as to be impassable. About ten minutes or five miles later the rain stopped. The forests on both sides of the road were luxuriant with tall, broad-leaved trees, ferns, elephant creepers, and elephant vines, moist and tangled, intensely green. Hanuman monkeys chattered, quarreled, screamed. There were cobras around here—a big one had whipped itself across the road ahead of us a while back—but no tigers. If there were any tigers left they were in the tall grasses and mangrove swamps of the Sundarbans farther south towards the Bay of Bengal. We drove past marshes here too, in what was called the Moribund Delta, shallow lakes and stagnant streams cut off from the Ganges and choked with water hyacinth, though beautiful now with violet flowers. Dense thickets of bamboo came up. Palms, pipal, banyan, rosewood, sal. Flame of the forest trees. We had four of them, and a mango tree, in our front garden on Moira Street where the Greers would be living too, one floor above us.

A direct transfer in midtour seemed such a severe breach of the rules, a violation of the system, I couldn't help wondering what had brought it on. The Greers might well have wanted to get out from under, as Hud Perry had said, but I had never heard of that being reason enough for leaving a post unless you were resigning. Subordinates don't successfully challenge and complain about a supervisor unless—and this is pure theory; I've never heard of it actually happening—unless the supervisor has lost his mind or has physically attacked the subordinate, or threatened him with violence. Something pretty drastic. The "decent" Chambers hardly seemed to fit into either scenario. The answer then could only be, it seemed to me, that Chambers had asked for Greer's transfer. On what grounds? Not incompetence, or Greer would not have the reputation of being "exceptionally bright" nor would Hud Perry have accepted him. Insubordination seemed equally unlikely. That was never tolerated. I could only imagine some kind of irreconcilable clash over policy or operating methods that neither side could live with and that both would have nerve enough to risk bringing out into the open. Their reputations were at stake. Greer apparently hadn't been damaged by the affair. Had Chambers? I would probably never know. I had looked him up in the stud book. A grade 1 already and nearing retirement age. Unlike Perry, who was only fifty-five, Chambers had probably given up any ambition to become an ambassador—even before Greer had arrived in Dacca.

I wondered how much Hud knew. I imagined some kind of face-saving formula had been worked out. But as well as I had gotten to know Hud I would not question him about it. The answer was privileged information and no official concern of mine, therefore I had no need to know it. And though my curiosity would not be satisfied—unless Greer himself volunteered the answer—that was fine by me. I did not work for the State Department. I told Indians about the United States. Greer's reporting would flow in the opposite direction. Though, to keep myself informed, I would read the cables he would draft, and he might observe some of my projects from time

to time, we would be independent of each other. I happened to outrank him by one grade—I'd reached a plateau I could expect to
remain on for years—but in the hierarchy of the post we would probably occupy about the same position above the salt. I had looked
Greer up too. He was thirty-two, younger than I was by seven years.
After an initial tour in Washington he had been an ambassador's
aide in Cairo, then had studied Chinese in Taipei and had worked
there and in Singapore. In Washington again he had studied Bengali
and then had been sent to Dacca. A native of Philadelphia. B.A.
from the University of Pennsylvania. Wife's maiden name Angelica
something or other. No year of birth or educational attainments
listed for wives. A standard short biography, nothing extraordinary
about it, nothing that revealed very much except that he had been
promoted at an average successful rate and was good at difficult
languages. Fluency in Chinese, if he really had it, was a real accomplishment. As for me, I knew some German and French, that was
all. I had picked up a little kitchen Bengali (as I had acquired a
smattering of Hebrew and Arabic) but had not been given any formal training in it. Fluency in Bengali was desirable in Calcutta but
not an absolute requirement. Hud Perry didn't speak it either, nor
for that matter had his former political officer. English was still very
much the link language of India. Three of the six major Calcutta
newspapers were published in it. Most servants, shopkeepers, and
even rickshaw wallahs, hawkers, and beggars spoke and understood
enough of it to get along.

Round a last curve and we were there. A striped wooden barrier, men in khaki uniforms, one a Sikh. Across a space of about a
dozen yards, a second barrier and East Pakistanis in uniforms with
slightly different markings. But no counterpart American station
wagon as yet.

Mr. Brown checked his wristwatch. "Five minutes ahead of
schedule."

Dark clouds gathered overhead. I hoped any flooding on the much more watery east side of Bengal wouldn't delay the arrival unduly. I had carelessly gone off without anything to read and there was nothing here except the jungle, not a tea shop or a fruit stall. And no preoccupying sign of tension to help pass the time as I had once seen at the frontier in Jerusalem. There was tension here all right but it was not overt. Not long before I had seen my Muslim bearer good-naturedly tweak the beard of a Sikh taxi driver come to pick me up and the Sikh laughing, but the two groups had massacred each other less than a generation earlier, and overnight, given the pretext, would again, no one doubted.

So Mr. Brown and I waited in the car.

Greer was apparently undamaged by whatever had happened in Dacca. That seemed to add up to self-confident, stubborn—and adroit. "Exceptionally bright." In short, formidable. Interesting. I found myself looking forward to welcoming him to West Bengal. And right on the dot at three o'clock, auspiciously, another black Ford came out of the forest on the other side and stopped at the barrier.

2

My immediate impression was that the Greers were one of the most attractive-looking couples, most attractive-looking *families,* I had ever seen. Elliott Greer, thick dark hair casually but neatly combed, not too long but not too short either, tanned face and arms, refined features, a nonsmiling look that was mature, then a smile that was boyish, as we approached each other.

Angelica, dark as Elliott, was a slender beauty and my soul flipped a bit appreciatively at the first sight of her.

The children, a boy and a girl of eight and seven respectively— facts in the administrative telegram Hud Perry had showed me of considerable interest to Caroline and me since our two were seven and six—were clearly Greers, with their coloring, but with individual faces, not simply carbon copies of their parents.

Mr. Brown now had the two suitcases Angelica had been carrying and half the children's packages and was toting them quickly back to our car. Elliott set his two suitcases on the ground as we met in the center of the strip.

"Beautiful timing," I called and then, "Charlie McKay, El-liott," I said, extending my hand.

He shook it firmly but corrected me.

"Tony."

Elliott Anthony, of course.

"Tony it is," I said and then shook hands with her.

"Hello, Anthony," I said to the boy. "And Amanda. Amanda, my daughter, Meredith, can't wait to meet you. She's seven too and you'll be living in the same apartment building."

"I know," Amanda said. "She can call me Mandy."

"Richard is only six," I said to Anthony apologetically, "but there's another boy your age in the building and more in school."

"That's OK," Anthony said.

I took one of Elliott's—Tony's—suitcases and tried to take the other but he said quickly, "I've got it."

"Well, welcome. I hate to pour you right back into an identical car, but we should be at Moira Street in about an hour and fifteen minutes if the rain doesn't hold us up. Have you ever been over here before—by air?"

"Never," Angelica said. "I know people joke about Dacca people going to Calcutta for R and R, Dacca being so much worse, or duller, but so far we've only been up to Kathmandu." Her voice was throaty, easy, practiced, gathering in the listener.

At the frontier, Tony Greer, with evident fluency, exchanged remarks in Bengali with a West Bengal immigration inspector who smiled broadly, flattered and impressed, and returned Greer's diplomatic passports with a flourish and a salute. Winning ways from the very first, I thought, impressed too.

Soon settled in the car, we moved along at Mr. Brown's steady fifty miles per hour.

"Did you have an easy trip?" I asked, and it occurred to me as I asked, that once the Greers had left their car on the other side they had not once looked back nor had I seen them saying any last words to their Dacca consulate driver.

"Uneventful and boring," Angelica said.

"All your servants are in place, ready to start in," I said. "All but one worked for your predecessors—who were satisfied with them as far as we know."

"What if we wanted to make changes?" Angelica asked.

"That's strictly up to you. The labor market being what it is, if a servant has a good position he wants to hang on to it. But there's a British woman, wife of a fellow at the High Commission, who runs a kind of nonprofit employment agency to keep busy. If you have any problems you might talk to her. The Kirklands had no need of a children's ayah, that's one gap you'll need to fill. However, Caroline—or should I say Rita, the Khasi woman who works for us— has a possibility for you waiting in the wings, a cousin of hers. I haven't seen her but Rita's a gem. In any case, your cook's prepared to fix dinner for you this evening and your bearer to serve it. We thought you'd rather unwind at home your first evening."

"You seem to have thought of everything," Angelica said, looking at me directly with her very wide-open eyes. What she had said was not in any way said sarcastically or critically, but it was not a compliment easy to respond to, a bit intimidating in its way.

"As Jeeves used to say, 'I endeavor to give satisfaction.' "

Perhaps that wasn't easy to respond to, either, though Angelica smiled.

I wondered if, when they were together, Tony Greer let Angelica do most of the talking, and I wanted to hear him say something. Looking at him directly I said, "I admire your Bengali—and envy it."

"Admire it, but don't envy it," Greer said in a voice of medium resonance that matched his medium age and medium size but there was controlled strength in it too.

"Oh? Explain."

"How many miles to the city?" Tony asked, his eyes looking away from mine, pointedly changing the subject, perhaps because of the presence of Mr. Brown. I didn't pursue the question.

"Fifty kilometers," Mr. Brown said, "a bit over thirty miles."

"Here. You might be looking at these," I said, and handed Tony two square white envelopes pulled from the door pocket of the car. One was a dinner invitation from Hud and Clarissa for the following evening, Sunday. The Greers would be the only guests. The other card invited the Greers to a reception the following Saturday evening, also at the congen's residence, at which they would be the guests of honor, a gathering to introduce them to official contacts and the American staff.

"I'm to tell you," I said, "you won't need to make any official courtesy calls on either Hud or Clarissa except at dinner tomorrow evening. The Perrys really try to reduce protocol to the absolute minimum. Result, I think you'll find—a refreshingly relaxed atmosphere. So, aside from dinner, Sunday is your own."

Tony handed Angelica each invitation as he finished looking at it. Neither commented. I waited for Tony to ask me questions. He didn't. After a while I glanced in the rearview mirror. Both appeared to be dozing. At least their eyes were closed. The children had climbed into the back end of the station wagon and had stretched out alongside the luggage.

The forest ended in paddy fields, then closed in again. Then the flat alluvial landscape was given over mostly to rice cultivation with only patches of forest interspersed between the paddy fields. Intermittently it rained. People worked in the fields and more and more people walked along the sides of the road, country people, men in loincloths, naked children, barefoot old women in saris but no cholis, their dried-up breasts swinging loose.

The road from the border joined the trunk road from the north

just above Dum Dum airport, so the Greers would get the same full
dose of the city all at once as would any travelers. Of course they
were already used to a large measure of South Asian urban conges-
tion. Still, Dacca was religiously, linguistically, and politically ho-
mogeneous, or mostly so, and Calcutta was far from that and
considerably more populous. Were there seven million or eight? Or
more? No one was really sure.

Abruptly we drove into bazaars and jostling crowds, into mad,
anarchic traffic—fiercely competing autos, lorries, rickshaws, bullock carts, two-wheeled carts under enormous loads of every com-
modity under the sun pulled by bare-chested peons; wandering
cows, and swarms and hordes of people in the many varieties of
cotton dress and undress of the East, standing, squatting, streaming, overflowing the ramshackle balconied buildings, the shanties,
the endless rows of tin-awninged, signboard-plastered shops below,
jamming the broken pavements, the filthy gutters, the littered roadways: plunged into color-splashed squalid cacophonous chaos, into
one of the great, vital, awful cities of the world.

Into the maw of this urban jungle, this metropolitan nightmare
gripped by elemental forces, we crossed streets near the university
down which brighter colors flashed—blood-red flags and arm
bands—where the cheap film music blaring at full volume over
scratchy loudspeakers clashed against the strident exhortations of
militant rabble-rousers, where the shouting in the streets was no
longer simply the transmission of information through the din, an
argument with a shopkeeper, a domestic quarrel, bawdy humor, but
the venting of rage, calls to violence. The level of tension was high
but seemed to have stabilized temporarily, was recent but not new,
compounded of and divided by communal hatreds: Hindu-Muslim,
Muslim-Sikh; right and left Communist struggles against the Congress government; rivalries and violent feuding among a bewildering
spectrum of leftist parties and political groups, between employed

and unemployed workers and factory owners, and so many other grievances of the exploited and forgotten, rising out of devastating poverty, disease, appalling misery, horrors, degradation, death. Out of the daily, weekly, monthly permutations of this raw material, Tony Greer would fashion the analyses he would, over Hud Perry's signature, and possible emendations and comments, cable to Washington.

Tony's eyes were open now and so were Angelica's and their children knelt behind them looking out the windows too. We turned into Chittaranjan Avenue, still densely crowded but wider, more Westernized, leading to the center of the city, the financial district, the hotels, government offices, the port. The buildings were taller, more substantial, some of them imposing. Near the beginning of the *maidan*, that vast park between Chowringhee Road and the river, some were grand indeed—the eighteenth-century East India Company Writers Building, the scandalous nineteenth-century extravagance of Lord Wellesley's Government House, now the governor's mansion, the Raj Bhavan. Here the swelling crowds were gayer, better dressed, streaming to the several motion picture theaters, to the better shops, crowding around sidewalk vendors and pitchmen. Mr. Brown entered Chowringhee Road, boulevard-wide and thick with taxis, private cars, and overloaded buses.

"My shop," I said, and pointed as we passed it to the U.S. Information Service building with its large exhibits (Space exploration; Oceanography) in show windows on either side of the main entrance. "And that's what it used to be—Whiteways & Laidlaw— biggest department store east of Suez. Appropriately enough. Two hundred years ago Calcutta 'Europe Shops' were probably the world's first department stores. Even back then you could buy a piano, a lady's hat, or a barrel of pickles, all under one roof.

"Firpo's restaurant," I said as I continued to recite at intervals. "Faded European elegance. Food is good enough if you stick to certain dishes. . . . Grand Hotel. . . . Park Street. . . . And now we're almost there."

Mr. Brown swung left onto Theatre Road, lined with crumbling colonial houses, weather-faded pink and ochre, dun-colored, some flush with the pavement, some set behind walled gardens. The great crowds were abruptly behind us. Only a few pedestrians were in sight. Right again and left into Moira Street. The *durwan* saluted as Mr. Brown drove through the gate of the compound and up the driveway beside the garden. Caroline and the kids, who had been sitting on our open verandah, stood when they saw us. Our building had six two-bedroom flats, six verandahs. On the second floor verandah to the right of ours, servants stood waiting and watching too. Abdul, who would be the Greer's bearer, wearing a black lambswool cap, one like Mohammad Ali Jinnah had worn, disappeared abruptly. He reappeared downstairs, standing in the driveway beside the main entrance when Mr. Brown drove up to it. Behind him stood the Greer's cook, sweeper, and ayah-to-be on one side of the staircase, Caroline, Meredith, and Richard on the other side.

I was attracted to Angelica Greer, no question of that, but looking at Caroline then I found her as pretty as always and was proud of her. Tony Greer shook hands with her, and embraced her with his engaging smile. I think she may have blushed a shade or two. I experienced a foolish, unwarranted twinge of jealousy. He let go her hand and turned to me.

"It's a quarter to five now," he said with sudden compelling congeniality and forcefulness. "Come up for a drink about six. We've been somnambulistic for the past couple of hours but we wake up when the sun goes down. Bring your kids."

It was as much as he had said since he had crossed the frontier.

Alone in our large, square living room with two electric-powered punkahs whirring below the high ceiling, sipping the cold *nimbu panis*—limeades—Osman, our bearer, had brought us, the children off somewhere with Rita, not yet able to play with their new friends upstairs, I said, "She's cute as a bug. I haven't quite figured him out yet. Complex, I suspect. Well? More interesting for that."

"They're certainly decorative, the two of them," Caroline said.

"Well, what d'you think?" I asked, gesturing to include all the rooms of the Greer's new home and their locally made furniture.

"Everything is lovely," Angelica said. "Nicer than what we had."

We went out to their verandah. Abdul brought us the drinks we had ordered, served on *our* silver tray he had borrowed from Osman. The Greers hadn't had time to unpack their first shipment of effects which had arrived by air freight a few days earlier. A ship was bringing the rest.

"I'd prefer a ground floor flat like yours—more convenient for guests," Tony said. "But this is fine. Fine. How long have your next door neighbors been here?"

"Two years. They're on home-leave and round-tripping."

"Maybe they wouldn't mind switching. What does he do?"

"Gerry? He's the consular officer."

"Who doesn't have to entertain more than once a year."

"You could give it a try, but I think they're entrenched down there."

Tony grinned. "I'm being facetious. Better view from up here anyway. Do you have your own car?"

"That's my Rover back there, yes."

"Are you two going out this evening?"

"For a change, no."

"After dinner, take me for a spin. I want to see what it's like down by the river. I won't sleep unless I know what the city looks like at night. Leave the girls and the kids here to get acquainted away from us. We can talk."

Here he was giving orders already, but what he had suggested suited me well enough. I wanted to talk.

I drove across the *maidan* on Queens Way, Kidderpur and St. George's Gate roads to the Strand Road along the river. Small and medium-sized freighters were lit up at anchor and dinghies moved along the bank. Far up behind them rose the fantastically overburdened Howrah Bridge and beyond the city end of it the modern towers of the financial district where crores of rupees were made in jute and tea, coal, iron, steel. . . . From this vantage point at night Calcutta seemed huge and grand, the old imperial capital. The Raj Bhavan was lit up in its acres of gardens; the skyline of the Esplanade and Chowringhee stood out along the edges of the great greensward of the *maidan*; behind us, farther down river, Fort William, cricket fields, the white dome of the Victoria Memorial, the spires of the Anglican cathedral, the white grandstand of the race course, finest in the East.

"Why did you tell me not to envy your ability to speak Bengali?" I asked.

"Why? Letting myself be talked into taking that much time to learn it was a costly mistake. Not only because it's useless anywhere outside of Dacca and Calcutta. But because Washington doesn't give a shit what happens in either place."

"Maybe we haven't been telling them clearly enough or forcefully enough why we're important," I said. "Here's your chance."

He laughed briefly, as though I might have said something naive and foolish, but then he struck me playfully on the arm with a fist. "Maybe you have a point," he said. "If nothing else, I've got to do something in a hurry. I've got only three, three-and-a-half months to come up with an 'exceptional' performance so Perry will have something sexy to put in my annual evaluation. Chambers and I didn't exactly see eye to eye." He grinned. "Have to get my Three this year if I expect to make One before I'm forty. Change of subject—I get the impression you and Caroline and the Perrys are pretty close."

"Well, he's a great guy and she's a lovely lady. I think of him as being one of the last of the old school gentlemen. We get along. I'm happy here. I think you will be too."

"Anyone I should watch out for?"

"In your position? No. Not everyone is always scintillating or always agreeable or even always very intelligent, but they're relatively harmless. Well, let's get on back."

So he was ambitious. I had hardly expected less and couldn't fault him for that.

In our air-conditioned bedroom Caroline said, "She's decided she doesn't want Rita's cousin as an ayah. Because they're related. 'Too chummy.' She thinks they'd be tea-klatching all day long instead of tending to business. She's wrong and I said so but she'd made up her mind. I think she's being foolish but what can I do? Except of course, guess who's going to have to baby-sit tomorrow evening—Rita. Unless they drag their children along to the Perrys—who would not be pleased. Next weekend too. I'm annoyed. If she's this fussy it may take her a couple of weeks or more to find a woman who satisfies her, and she will *have* to find one."

"How did things go otherwise?"

Caroline shrugged. "All right, I guess. . . . Not to worry. I'll get along. We'll get along."

3

That Sunday, Caroline and I and the children attended the late morning service at the old St. Andrew's Scottish Presbyterian Church downtown. St. Paul's, the Anglican cathedral, was much closer but too high-church for Caroline. When we drove back into the compound at half past twelve, Angelica Greer saw us as she stood leaning over the railing of her verandah, waved, and called down, "Come on up for brunch!" When I drove around to the back parking area out of sight Caroline said, "I guess we have no choice. But the kids expect to go swimming."

"Rita can take them. And she can take Anthony and Mandy too. Why don't we suggest it. Later on we can all go over to show the Greers the club, which I was going to do anyway."

So upstairs we went and the first thing Angelica announced was: "I found an ayah."

"What?" Caroline said.

"She just showed up this morning while we were unpacking our air freight—through some servants' grapevine, I suppose. She had two good letters of recommendation—from some Dutch woman who's just left the country, and that British woman you told us about. Just to make sure, I asked Abdul's opinion and he said, 'All right, memsahib.' They always *know*, don't they? They did in Dacca. Her name is Rose, a Christian from Madras, a Harijan probably. Not young anymore but she looks healthy and has a recent doctor's certificate too. Of course I *had* to have someone and soon. So I've been lucky, haven't I?"

Mostly redeemed in Caroline's eyes—Caroline was looking surprised and relieved—Angelica said, "What would you like—Abdul, could you come in here, please" (and Abdul materialized in his white uniform and black cap and white shoes) "—Bloody Marys? Gin and tonic? Your pleasure. Tony'll be out in just a minute. He's back there wrestling with one last crate. We're having eggs Benedict, how does that sound?"

The Greers had already unpacked a good deal and their living room was already stamped with their particular flair and good taste. The decorative emphasis, not surprisingly, was more Chinese and Malayan than subcontinental Indian, with dashes of Javanese and Balinese from vacation trips to Indonesia. There were several paintings by the same two, probably young, Asian artists unknown to me. I was sure the Greers would appreciate the opportunity to consider the work of many talented Indian painters on sale in Calcutta galleries and exhibitions at reasonable prices. A hi-fi had been set up and a Prokofiev violin concerto was playing. The bookcases were filled. Other books were stacked on top and on the floor. At that particular period of my life I was engrossed in Henry James and here were what appeared to be his complete works, including paperback duplicates of some novels and story collections in hardcover. I experienced the pleasure, you might even call it excitement, of discovering someone who shares a passion of yours, out of so many other people, the majority, the multitude, who don't know about it, or care.

"Which one of you is the James afficionado?" I asked Angelica.

"Tony, mostly."

"Who's the fan of Lewis Mumford?" I called through the open doorway to the master bedroom after spotting *The City in History* on a bottom shelf. At that moment, Tony emerged from the bedroom, brushing curls of excelsior from his hands.

"Great book," he said.

"You know, don't you, you've come to one of the most architecturally interesting cities anywhere," I said. "And you're living right in the middle of one of the oldest and most interesting neighborhoods."

"Lunch ready, memsahib," Abdul announced, and we trooped into the dining room.

As suggested, the Greer children had gone off swimming with ours, chaperoned by Rita and Rose, so there were just the four of us. Abdul served our eggs Benedict, constructed of local muffins and "English" eggs, that is to say chicken eggs, to distinguish them from ordinary duck eggs which were to be avoided, slices of tinned ham imported from a Singapore purveyor, a loan from the McKay godown until the Greers received their first order, and—

"I didn't know Ali could make hollandaise," I said.

"Now he can," Angelica said off-handedly. "I taught him this morning."

Abdul also served the white wine we'd included as a welcoming gift.

"You two have really been very sweet," Angelica said, raising her glass. "A toast to the McKays."

"Hear, hear," Tony said, raising his, and we all clinked glasses.

For conversation, Caroline and Angelica could draw on a fund of common gossip based on mutual foreign service acquaintances, mostly foreign service wives I should say, and a mutual wealth of amusing/appalling servant stories from both sides of the Bengali frontier and from the Far East to the Mideast and North Africa. Both Greers responded knowledgeably to everything that interested us. They'd read even the more obscure earlier works of the under-appreciated author we liked, knew who'd played the character roles in that old movie, remembered the specialties in our favorite Paris restaurants, took the words right out of our mouths, positive and negative, on a half dozen other subjects. They knew wickedly hilarious anecdotes about political figures we detested to the same degree, scandals new to us involving Hollywood stars, café society, and members of the international set. You can't help being impressed with people like that. We were predisposed to like them. We'd hoped they'd be interesting. There weren't that many Americans and it was certainly stimulating to have a pair of sparkling, unpredictable newcomers.

"You've aroused my curiosity," Tony said. "Architecturally—besides the invention of the bungalow—and the department store—what makes Calcutta so interesting as a city?"

We were sitting on the verandah under the spinning punkah fans, looking at the monsoon rain falling steadily through the *gul mohur*—flame of the forest—trees and sluicing the narrow street over the wall of the compound. The fat, bare-chested owner of the *pan* shop, seated cross-legged in his chest-high cubbyhole recessed into the wall of the building across the way, had closed half of his wooden shutters to protect his betal palm leaves, lime paste, nuts, herbs, spices, anise, tobacco, hashish, and other chewables.

"You've just stolen half my answer," I said. "Well, for another example, it has the earliest known garden suburbs. From the late eighteenth century. Spanish colonizers in hot countries built terrace houses with courtyards which more or less had to be in the central city. The British here thought free-standing houses with porches to catch the breeze from all sides would be cooler and healthier. And they could be put up outside of town too. The East India Company suburbanites commuted by riverboat. But these were big houses on big plots. The small Bengal-O peasant huts were further out, in exurbia—weekend retreats."

"You really like it here, don't you?" Tony asked.

"I don't know if anyone can decently *like* a place with so much misery in it, but, yes, I've grown attached to it. My chief local, and good friend, Chitu Chatterjee, describes himself as an 'incorrigible Calcuttan' who wouldn't live anywhere else. And he could. He's got the brains and the wherewithal to emigrate. He's one of a couple of million middle-class Bengalis foreign reporters never mention. Palaces and slums are more colorful to write about. I admire people like Chitu. They hold the place together. They're not to blame for the tripling of the population since the British left. There's a rich culture here that comes out of Chitu's middle class and the old aristocracy. Truly great music, first-rate world-class films. Painting, poetry, a literature, intellectual ferment. A livelier press than in any American city. The kind of press we used to have in New York and Chicago but no more. For all its poverty it's still one of the most prosperous cities in Asia, the main port for a huge hinterland. If the State Department would stop and look at it, the Calcutta consular district has a bigger population than most countries of the world—something like a hundred-and-forty-five million people in four states, two territories, two semi-independent Himalayan kingdoms, assorted tribal areas, and the Northeast Frontier Agency. It borders on two hostile countries. One of them—China—invaded not very long ago and might again. I can't believe it's a place that doesn't matter."

Tony listened. Even if he had read and heard all this before maybe he hadn't heard it put together exactly the way I had done it. It struck me then and later that Tony Greer was a young man who didn't waste words, he weighed and measured them and dealt them out carefully. He seemed to listen more than talk—he was a rare, first-class listener. He did not try to be particularly clever or witty but he listened so well and asked such appropriate, to-the-point questions and his sentences parsed and made such good sense that I thought he'd be able to command the attention of almost anyone. Oh, I was impressed! I thought, too, he would make a clever politician who would have an appeal for a more educated, thinking electorate, and later he admitted, in answer to my question, that he might consider going into politics.

That afternoon Caroline and I drove the Greers around our neighborhood "south of Park Street" as it was known, Park Street being a social dividing line, and in between rain showers I parked and we walked along Wood, Camac, Loudon, and other quiet streets between Park and Lower Circular Road, including Harrington, where the consulate and British High Commission were situated and where the Perrys lived, and looked at the flat-roofed nineteenth-century houses, with their high first floors, Palladian-pillared and shuttered with green blinds and gleaming with *chunaur,* a white stucco worn down in some cases to a patina like pink marble. About three o'clock I drove through a gate into the courtyard of the Lancer's Club.

It had seen grander days. There was a rather imposing entrance under a portico—wide marble steps flanked by potted ferns in polished brass tubs—but the green carpet in the lobby was worn and faded. Half the ground floor opposite the bar and restaurant was taken up by a rather bleak barnlike hall with a wood floor which could serve as a theater, banquet room, or badminton court. As we all climbed out of the Rover we could hear, distinctly, a bouncing, loose-stringed piano, the brushing of a Western snare drum, and a somewhat straggly chorus of voices singing a number from an English review. As we passed the open doors to the auditorium we

could see, up on the stage, men and women, all white and most
likely all British (though the club membership was more than half
Indian), in shorts and other sports attire, rehearsing their amateur
musical.

"Straight out of Waugh in the thirties," Angelica murmured.
"I love it."

The club bar and restaurant had a pleasant enough atmosphere,
perhaps best described as "continental-colonial." The food wasn't
bad, on the average better than most Calcutta hotel-restaurant fare,
though that, it must be admitted, wasn't saying much. We strolled
past it and went outside and sat at a table on the terrace.

"Rita will look for us here," I said, and ordered *nimbu pani*
from a turbaned bearer in white, sashed pajamas and bare feet. We
watched the ayahs squatting on the lawn to supervise the games of
small children and gossip among themselves, watched the tennis
games on the clay courts beyond.

"We belong for the swimming, tennis, and the good collection
of British mysteries in the library," I said. "It's no good for entertaining contacts, mine at any rate. It was whites only until Independence. The journalists and academics I know remember that and
don't like coming here even now. They look down on the less-than-
top-drawer English, and rather despise the middle-level, Westernized Indian businessmen—climbers—who do belong. You can
never really be sure of it, but they don't seem to mind that I'm a
member. So we simply do all our entertaining at home, once in a
great while in a restaurant. My representational allowance usually
runs out about three months into the new fiscal year and I'm out-
of-pocket enough as it is. What else. Bengal Club—stuffy anachronism. Full of desiccated Colonel Blimps who fall asleep at their
tables. If you're looking for a place to entertain I think the Calcutta
Club would be your best bet. It at least had titled Indian members.
They founded the place during the British raj and contacts seem to

feel comfortable there—from what little I've been able to observe. Quite a bit fancier than this place—and more expensive—a little too formal and pukka sahib for my taste. Swimming and tennis too. Do you golf?"

"No."

"Neither do we. Then the Tollygunge Club—Tolly to its friends—wouldn't do you much good either. That about covers it unless you happen to be into squash, cricket, soccer, or horse racing. If you're interested in the pool and the courts here, let me know and I'll put you up."

"Do it," Tony said. "You've sold me."

"Oh, fun," Angelica said. "Some nights when we don't have anything better to do we can sit in the bar, get sloshed on gin slings and sneer at all the nouveau Indians and seedy colonials. But we'd best be nice to them until they let us in, hadn't we?"

4

The Perrys had an excellent turnout that following Saturday evening, virtually all the right people. The chief minister's office, the Raj Bhavan, Fort William, and the leading newspapers were represented at high levels. There were other politicians and journalists. The inspector of police was there, more state and municipal officials, top civil servants. Pretty Bengali women, some in gorgeous saris, brightened the room. The hot, moist climate kept their skin looking youthful even into old age. A few old-fashioned wives spoke little or no English, sipped orange juice, and kept each other company in a corner of the large living room, but there were enough Western educated women, traveled, well-informed, to make a stimulating contribution to the evening. All had come less out of curiosity about the new American political officer, though there had to be some of that, than because they liked the Perrys and because the consul general's house was one of the most charming and comfortable official residences in the U.S. foreign service network. Inside, one might have been in Savannah, New York, or London. The food, Indian and eclectic American—Clarissa Perry made some of it with her own hands—was invariably imaginative and first rate. There was no shortage of alcohol.

In this sophisticated gathering, the Greers conveyed just the right mix of modesty and self-assurance. Tony's Bengali was a great hit. Angelica's beauty and charm were equally appreciated, in some cases even more so. Off to one side as the reception began to wind down—some of the guests were leaving—Hud Perry, his voice lowered, said to me, "Well, I think they were a huge success, don't you?"

"Certainly seems that way."

"Thank you, Charlie. And Caroline, for getting them off and running last week."

"We didn't do a thing," I said. "We just sort of watched them do it themselves. They're self-starters."

"No, quite the contrary. Tony is impressed by your knowledge of the area and very appreciative of the briefings and help you provided. I am too. . . . . I think we've got the makings of an outstanding team here now."

Hud was shorter than I was but projected a lean, aristocratic impression. A prominent aquiline nose contributed to this effect. He kept himself in trim. He still played singles with me and beat me about forty percent of the time, but more often we teamed up for doubles.

Clarissa Perry, a small, stylish, radiant woman with extraordinarily brilliant eyes and a husky voice, whose photograph one might expect to see in the copies of *Vogue* she kept around, was turned away from Hud, being gracious to the wife of the British deputy high commissioner and Lady Banerji, whose husband was an industrialist. Seeing Clarissa reminded me to ask Hud, "When do you expect your son?"

"Any day. Actually, more like two weeks, even a bit longer. He's following a rather leisurely course across Europe."

I had never met Thad Perry but there were photographs of him on display in the Perrys' living room and study. He was twenty, an only child, and I had gathered from certain looks and remarks that Hud and Clarissa were concerned about him. He had dropped out of college, then had drifted from job to job, none of them with much career potential. Now he was en route to Calcutta to stay an indefinite length of time.

Chatting with Hud had been a brief breather. There were still guests to help entertain, guests taking yet another drink from a bearer's tray, and I went back to work. Tony Greer was in a deep conversation, in Bengali, with the elected chief minister's chief secretary, that is to say the top Indian Administrative Service professional in the state government, who really ran that office. Angelica was hanging on every word coming from under the hawk nose and waxed mustache of the adjutant general, the number two man at Fort William (the commanding general of the military district happened to be in Delhi that evening), a spit and polish Sandhurst/ Dehra Dun graduate from Rajasthan. A senior aide to the governor joined Tony and the chief secretary and regarded Tony avidly, as avidly as General Singh seemed to be looking at Angelica.

No question about it, the Greers were launched, and after such a debut, from then on for a while all they had to do was walk into a room and not say anything to be appreciated.

Now as the weeks passed I had my own responsibilities and priorities to focus on. As public affairs officer I directed a staff of six Americans and more than a hundred local employees who kept me hopping. I was only half conscious of the activities of Tony and Angelica Greer. Tony, I knew, was out constantly all over town, calling on officials and editors for their political insights, making new contacts day and evening, being seen, Mr. Brown and other drivers reported to me, emerging from meetings with garlands of marigolds draped around his neck, a mark of esteem. He had his

work cut out for him. The Communist party of India had split into
two factions, left and right, the majority right wing aligned with the
Soviet Union, the left with China. In July and August massive and
frequent processions of strikers and university students paraded past
my offices on Chowringhee Road, shaking raised fists and shouting
slogans. Drawn outside once by a break in the rhythmic yelling,
sounds of a melee, I saw stone throwing broken up by police. In the
university area on the way to our smaller cultural center there, a
tram car was burning. Traffic was tied up for blocks and hours. In
the newspapers were photographs of police, protected by wicker
shields, making *lathi* charges and cracking heads. Elections were
scheduled in the fall and the Congress party was expected to win
again. Army troops inside Fort William were said to be on the alert.
Routinely I read copies of outgoing cables from the consulate.
Tony's reports to Washington were crisp and authoritative, syn-
theses of the best-informed official and unofficial assessments of
what was going on. Clearly, though, in the volatile situation prevailing, no one from the chief minister, commanding general, or divided communist leadership on down could predict the future with
any degree of assurance.

Unlike us, the Greers didn't seem to go in for large cocktail or
dinner parties but had a few people over at a time or took them to
restaurants and Park Street nightclubs. Evidently they had more
private funds at their disposal than we did. Apart from consulate
wives' meetings once a month, Caroline didn't see too much of Angelica during the day. Angelica had her own agenda. By this time
she seemed to know almost as many Indian and British women and
ladies of other nationalities as Caroline and apparently shopped
with them or lunched with them often—in their homes or in Park
Street or hotel restaurants. So our paths crossed only occasionally
to the extent that we would see the Greers at some function where
our professional interests converged, but then we might not have

the time or opportunity even to wave. However, at one national day reception at the Great Eastern Hotel—I believe it was the Burmese, but they were all alike—the Greers did wave and waved us over.

"This thing is useless and the food is inedible," Tony said. "Let's go to Chinatown and get something decent to eat."

The place he named wasn't one we knew but we were happy to leave with them. Chinese food was the best in the city but there were few restaurants to choose from and one had become "Tibetan" after the Chinese invasion of '62. The former owners had left— spies, some said.

Tony had bought a Triumph Vitesse from a departing Britisher. He drove us, squeezed into the tiny back seat, to a malodorous, still gas-lit cul-de-sac off Bentinck Street. Glimpsed through swinging doors, old Chinese men gambled with cards and counters. The restaurant was minute—three plain deal tables in two small rooms— with bare walls. We were the only customers. A woman came out of the dim back room and seemed to recognize Tony, who spoke to her in Chinese. In a few minutes an old man came out with cold bottles of beer and then the woman brought empty bowls and a large tureen of steaming Shanghai noodle soup thick with pasta strands, chicken, mushrooms, and other bits of things, a meal in itself. It was delicious. It, and the place itself, told us, as maybe it was meant to tell us, that already Tony Greer knew parts of the city better than I did.

There was a third figure in the place, a younger Chinese man in the back room. Leaving his soup half finished and not excusing himself, Tony got up suddenly and walked back. I could see him standing and talking to the young Chinese. The rest of us helped ourselves to more soup.

"There's not much left around here anymore, I guess," I said, to have something to say. "One temple, a couple of restaurants. I'm surprised this place still exists. Leave it to you to find it."

"I like it because it's a kind of secret inside a secret, like a Chinese box," Angelica said.

Angelica ate heartily and didn't seem perturbed that Tony had abandoned us. He reappeared just then but his expression was inward-looking. He sat down but said, "You about ready to go? I have to stop off at the residence."

We didn't talk driving back to the Great Eastern. I picked up my car there and we said goodnight. We said it, and Angelica. I'm not sure Tony did. When we were alone, Caroline said, "There are times when Tony verges on being rude."

"Oh, I'd call it preoccupied," I said. "He's a workaholic. After all, he wanted us to come along and I'm glad he introduced us to that place. I'll take you back there sometime, just the two of us."

A week later Tony was all cordiality as he invited us to a non-work party, "strictly to relax, absolutely casual. We just thought of it five minutes ago. Something everybody needs once in a while."

There were ten other people, no one we knew well but all but three—a Swedish sea captain in port for a week or so, and an Indian couple—were people we had run across before, two British couples, an Indian business executive and his wife, and an Anglo-Indian girl, a vocalist from The Blue Fox on Park Street the captain was escorting. That was where the Greers had met him one late evening. The Brits—the men were in business too—were rather silly people who liked to wear native headdress and other funny hats at parties but might be said to have been halfway amusing at the beginning of an evening, before they began on the copious variety of alcohol they would consume before they left. Caroline and I had always suspected one couple in particular were capable of going in for odd fun and games. The Indian I didn't know, introduced as A. K. Ghosh, was extraordinarily ugly with a pockmarked, misshapen face. I knew the other, dapper and foppish, a masquerade Englishman.

Their wives were chic, jeweled, expensively saried. If Caroline and I, the only other Americans besides the Greers, were flattered to be included, singled out, we would have been happier with more interesting people, of whom there were many in the city, in many creative walks of life. Still, a couple of drinks put us at our ease, the food was out of the ordinary—once again Angelica displayed her flair for cooking or teaching her cook new tricks—good music played in the background, and we hadn't had far to go—just upstairs. One of the Indian ladies who had zeroed in on me had been to Europe recently and it was enjoyable enough exchanging reminiscences with her for a while.

Tony went into his kitchen for something and I followed.

"A. K. Ghosh is new to me," I said. "What does he do?"

"Import-export business. He was a close associate of Netaji."

"Ah," I said. "I've never met one before."

Netaji, a title, a sobriquet, meant something like "revered leader" and as far as I knew the only Netaji was the charismatic and now legendary Bengali revolutionary Subhas Chandra Bose, reported killed in a plane crash on Formosa in 1945. Bose had been high up in the Congress party, a mayor of Calcutta, and parted with Gandhi over the philosophy of nonviolence. Anything to get the British out, he'd made a daring escape from house detention, gone to Hitler's Germany in disguise, made propaganda broadcasts over Radio Berlin, hoping to persuade Indian army prisoners of the Nazis, captured in North Africa, to join a new Indian National Army. He didn't have much success. On a German submarine and then a Japanese sub he'd gone to Tokyo, managed to convince some Indian army prisoners of the Japanese in Malaya and Burma—a tiny percentage of the two million Indian troops who fought bravely and well on the side of the Allies—to desert to the INA on the side of the Japanese—to "free" India. INA units in combat proved more hindrance than help and many deserted a second time. In 1945 one whole INA division surrendered en masse. Bose's death helped to transform him into even more of a legend, a folk hero. Many of his followers claimed to believe he had survived the plane crash to end his life as a sadhu, a holy man, at some undisclosed place. Various dates in connection with his life were ritually celebrated every year with certain chauvinistic newspapers devoting page after page to his exploits, real and inflated.

This remembered, it seemed to me I had nothing much to say to Ghosh and nothing to ask him. I wasn't going to bait him.

Fourteen people drifting around the living room, dining room, verandah, shifting allegiances, drinking quite a bit. Angelica took me by the hand out to the verandah, where we leaned over the railings to look at the shadowy garden below. Her lightly encased left breast brushed against my bare upper arm in passing.

"You and I have not had a real chance to talk since we arrived in Calcutta," Angelica said, looking up at me. Her parted lips glistened, her eyes radiated light and interest. There was alcohol on her breath but the scent was not unpleasant. There were a few light freckles on her pretty nose, endearing imperfections. She was arousing me and she knew it and wanted to. At the same time I have always found statements like the one she had just made rather intimidating, a countervailing effect in this instance. Yet I didn't think it was a miscalculation on her part. It seemed unlikely this particular party would get so wild she would expect to be able to get the two of us into bed before dawn. But she was sending me a message for the future to join her in a very grown-up game of post office, of that I was certain. But in case I wasn't absolutely certain, she let the fingers of one hand fall casually along the front of my leg for a moment, the leg turned toward the railing. I stepped back half a foot to turn toward the living room to look for Caroline but didn't see her. I offered Angelica a cigarette. She shook her head but I lit one.

"Well, what would you like to talk about?" I said.

"Just not about your work! Or Tony's. Tell me about the things you really like to do."

I decided, rather quickly, no, I wasn't going to do that. In what little spare time I had I was slowly writing an impressionistic travel book about India, but that was private information I wasn't sharing with anyone except Caroline. And, something warned me, maybe especially not with Angelica Greer.

"Read, listen to classical music, go to Shillong and Darjeeling and Kathmandu as often as possible."

A perfectly true and good enough answer but I think she sensed I was withholding something, including myself, and the interest in her expression turned into something ever so slightly hostile.

"You need another drink," she said. "And so do I."

She began walking back into the living room. I followed a few steps behind her but she stayed ahead of me—and away from me— attaching herself most immediately to the sea captain and the Anglo-Indian singer.

I found Caroline in the hall with A. K. Ghosh. She looked at me over his shoulder, asking to be rescued.

It was late enough. "I think we'd better be thinking about leaving," I said, and Caroline said, "Yes."

I found Tony to thank him and hear his "Sure," simply a quick break in the conversation he was having with one of the Brits, called to Angelica, "Thanks. It was fun," and saw her turn her head halfway for no more than three seconds to smile at us automatically, and then we could make our escape.

It wasn't until we were back in our apartment, and Osman, who had been baby-sitting, had left, that Caroline said, "Tony made a pass at me."

"While Angelica . . ." I said. "Join the club."

"Were you tempted?" I asked as I took off my shirt and hung my pants in the bedroom closet.

"I was angry," Caroline said, sounding that way.

"I believe you. But that doesn't answer my question."

"He was very flattering, very charming, and I enjoyed that before I realized what he was getting at. Tony is smooth, not crude, very subtle. He's undeniably physically attractive—as you seem to find Angelica . . ."

A slight but unmistakable current of apprehension ran through me. I thought I had no intention of ever getting involved with Angelica Greer, but objectively—or subjectively—I could see it happening easily enough, and I didn't resent her. Maybe I was flattered too. But Caroline resented Tony for putting her in the position of being tempted by him. And I resented him for his arrogance, his disregard for me (Caroline may have felt the same way about Angelica) but even more importantly because it suggested, it put the thought into my head, that Caroline, at thirty-five still a damn good-looking woman, might be ready for an adventure with someone as yet unknown who might only have to be nicer than Tony Greer. I didn't brood long about this. Perhaps I hadn't earned the right and it was Tony who was to blame for my unjustified fear of Caroline's theoretical betrayal, not Caroline herself. I watched her undress, saw her pause a moment, looking past me.

"Penny for your thoughts," I said.

"I was just thinking about Stefan. That captain reminded me."

"The captain?"

"The Swedish sea captain."

"But he didn't look remotely like Stefan."

"Not that. Being Swedish. Don't you remember? Stefan lived in Sweden one year as a third secretary in the Polish embassy."

"I thought that was in Latvia."

"Latvia one year too."

"Oh, and then got sacked for publishing an article condemning anti-Semitism."

Caroline was sitting up in bed in a very pretty, simple, white cotton nightgown, looking alluring, particularly exciting. We made love that night, made a point of it.

From then on the Greers were polite enough, especially in front of others, but seemed a little cool, a little distant. "I think we may have been dropped," I said.

"Or set aside," Caroline said.

Everyone in my office except Chitu Chatterjee had called me "Mr. McKay" since the day I arrived and I'd let them continue. I was truly less interested in deference than in not making things awkward for them—or me. Chitu was different. He'd called me Charlie from the first minute with the natural ease of an equal; indeed, in the Calcutta context, "equal" flattered me more than Chitu. Chitu knew who was already important and who was likely to become so. He knew the important people intimately, had known them since his school days, and they obviously respected him. He knew their quirks and weaknesses and rivalries and who should not be invited to the same gathering. He knew what was going on and how things worked. He was invaluable. When I'd arrived at the post he was one grade below the top level. An ignorant American predecessor of mine, convinced no local employee anywhere could be fully trusted, especially in the Third World, had refused to promote him—indeed, wanted to demote him. I was convinced incoming Americans, knowing less than nothing, *had* to trust their locals so long as those locals continued to prove themselves competent and trustworthy. Chitu got his promotion and I got a friend.

A week or so after the Greers' little gathering, Chitu came into my office and suggested we take a stroll down Chowringhee. Once outside he got straight to the point.

"Charlie, Tony Greer has been seen in several places hobnobbing with one A. K. Ghosh. I don't believe Ghosh can be described as a legitimate contact for an American political officer and he has a dubious reputation. He has never been known as a clever or successful businessman. His family was until recently in a state of genteel poverty. A few rents to collect, gold jewelry to sell. He doesn't appear to work at anything yet just in this past year or so is able to take costly trips to Japan, Hong Kong, Europe. And to spend a great deal of time and money in The Blue Fox and elsewhere on expensive tarts and other entertainment. Tony, being fairly new here, may not be aware of all these things."

"Drugs?" I said.

Chitu shrugged.

"Something profitable."

"Was Ghosh really high up in the INA?"

"I don't know. He might have been. In any case he trades on it."

In Calcutta it was impolitic to say anything openly against Subhas Chandra Bose. Chitu may have been brought up to revere him too, I didn't know. It was a subject I didn't need to discuss with him and preferred not to since I could not share any such admiration. But Chitu was highly intelligent and had never exhibited the slightest signs of fanaticism. The British were long gone. I somehow didn't think Chitu needed, as the masses did, as some politicians and newspaper publishers did, a hero to worship as a distraction from present difficulties or to exploit for their own purposes. "He trades on it" was more than most would say and all I really needed to know.

"Thank you, Chitu. I'm sure Tony will appreciate the information."

I wasn't sure of this at all but that same afternoon I passed it along anyway as Tony and I stood outside the back entrance to the Moira Street apartments. I'd arrived home first and waited on our verandah until I saw his car turn into the driveway.

"Something I thought you ought to know," I said.

His manner was cool and impatient.

"Can this wait?" He looked at his wristwatch. "I have less than half an hour to shower and shave before we go out for the evening."

"Sure, it can wait, but both of us seem to be endlessly busy these days and since what I have to tell you concerns you not me I'd just as soon be rid of it." And I went on quickly to repeat what Chitu had told me.

"Well, that's very very interesting," Tony said flatly, clearly not accepting Chitu's assessment. "Are you always sure Mr. Chatterjee knows what he's talking about?"

"Flawless record so far," I said confidently and cheerfully with a rising inflection. "But don't let me keep you. Of course you're the best judge of who your contacts are. I'm only a conduit here and I hereby retire from that role."

Tony smiled slightly and his eyes held mine just a shade longer than was friendly. Then he turned and climbed the stairs two at a time.

Angelica accompanied Tony on official trips to other states in the district, Bihar, Orissa, and Assam, leaving the children with their servants. Well, we had done that too, though not as often.

There were five more children in the building besides ours, and others scattered in apartments within walking or rickshaw distance, and Mandy did not become as steadfast a friend of Meredith as my little girl had probably hoped she would, and except in a pinch Anthony considered Richard too young to play with. Meredith seemed to be in and out of favor with Mandy every other week or so and one evening just before bedtime, during one of the latter periods, she said to me, "They make fun of us because we go to church and say our prayers at night. Anthony says there isn't any God at all."

Caroline looked at me for a moment, then asked Meredith, "Did you say there is?"

"Yes."

I was disturbed. It was the first time I'd had to deal with this kind of situation and though I should have been prepared, I wasn't, I had been too complacent. I motioned to Meredith and she came and sat beside me in my chair. I put my arm around her.

"There are people like us and there are people like them," I said. "There are people who believe and people who don't and all your life you're going to run into both kinds. We think we're right, they think they are, but it doesn't do any good to fight about it. It's much better not to as a matter of fact. Live and let live, have you ever heard that expression?"

"No."

"Well, it means just what it says and I think it's a good short way to put what I've just been saying. So don't worry about any of this. Just try to talk about something else if the subject comes up again."

Unburdened of this Solomonic homily I kissed her goodnight and said, "Off you go. Scoot. Sweet dreams."

It was Caroline's turn to read them a story. When she came back into the living room she said, "Well . . . ," without any question mark or exclamation point but with an ellipsis implied. For the moment I was willing to leave it at that, but Caroline said, "It's one thing not to practice anything—how many good friends—including the Perrys—do we have who don't—and after all you're a renegade Catholic. And another to turn your children into militant proselytizing atheists."

"Well, we don't know that. The Greer kids may simply have overheard their parents talking."

"I don't believe that for a minute. All I know is this sort of thing hasn't happened before. And those friends I just mentioned have children too."

"Hedging their bets?" I said.

"Whether they are or not, it's a question of manners. Of respect."

Caroline bit one corner of her lower lip for a moment. "I wasn't going to tell you this," she said. "I know how you dislike show-offs, and it didn't seem important at the time, it still may not be important, and we still have to live with the Greers, like it or not, but it seems Anthony and Mandy like to parade around in the nude and claim their parents do it all the time."

"Is that a fact," I said, after a moment of reflection, sudden images. "I guess I'm a bit stuffy but that does startle me a little. On the other hand, because we don't doesn't mean it isn't their privilege. My main concern is what effect, if any, has this had on Meredith and Richard."

"Well, you know Meredith is going through a perfectly normal phase of excessive modesty. She said she clamped her eyes shut until they put their clothes on. I think Richard was probably pretty indifferent about the whole thing. I also think it may have been a case of streaking from bathroom to bedroom, all over as soon as the ayah caught them at it."

"Rose."

"Yes. Rita was down here at the time. No harm done. Just an interesting bit of information we might not have known about otherwise."

I said, "I'm beginning to see—or am I too suspicious?—why Angelica didn't want to have Rita's cousin as an ayah. Rita—and we—might get to know too much."

"I'm not exactly surprised," Caroline said. "I've seen a touch of this myself. Not *Tony*, but the day of the last wives' meeting, Angelica phoned to say she'd drive me over and then phoned again to say she was running late, why didn't I come up to keep her company while she dressed. Called from the bedroom to say come on in, make myself at home. Which I did and then out she waltzed from the bathroom buck naked, no robe and not putting one on while she started to take her time looking for the right underwear. I was embarrassed. I don't care for that sort of thing. There was a girl at school used to run around in the buff from the shower room to her room clear at the end of the hall. I wasn't the only one who objected. This babe was the only one who didn't. All the rest of us signed a petition—or maybe it was an ultimatum—suggesting she at least put on underpants like everybody else. . . . So I told Angelica I'd wait in the living room until she got ready."

Osman broke up this conversation by coming in to ask if he could fix us a nightcap before he left for the evening. But I couldn't get out of my head the image Caroline had conjured up of Angelica Greer, one flight up and across the hall, walking naked across the room.

5

Sir Joynarain Coomar Dass Bahadur, O.B.E., K.C.I.E., the Maharajah of Chittipore, invited us to his annual monsoon concert, featuring the great sarodist Bahar Siddiq Khan. The Maharajah's tiny, once princely state was in north Bengal. Now his former subjects elected him to the state legislature and he lived much of the year in his Calcutta palace. On this occasion Clarissa Perry was genuinely not feeling well and that was Hud Perry's excuse not to have to sit on a rug to listen to music he really didn't care for. The Greers would represent them.

The Chittipore town house was set behind high walls and a gate guarded by a pair of small Gurkha *durwans* in their khaki shorts and shirts and black pillbox caps, sheathed *kukris* in their wide leather belts. During the Second World War out here, Chinese soldiers were said to fear the Japanese while Japanese troops were said to be terrified of Nepalese Gurkhas, whose ferocity and bravery in battle were legendary. Even mortally wounded by rifle or machine-gun fire, Gurkha warriors were reputed to be still capable of charging forward long enough to lop off one last head.

Roughly forty percent of the maharajah's former subjects were of Gurkha origin and traditionally served in the British-Indian army. The maharajah, traditionally, held a king's commission in that army. When the war broke out he'd gone on active duty, nominally at least, at the head of his troops, and had served with distinction in the reconquest of Burma from the Japanese.

I parked between a Bentley and a Jaguar. The Bentley's uniformed driver read a newspaper under a light in his front seat. The street was very quiet, empty of pedestrians. A mist was settling. Shards of broken glass, embedded along the top of the maharajah's wall, glinted in the light from street lamps.

The concert was already under way. Caroline and I could hear the music from a distance. A bearer wearing a red sash around his waist and a cockade in his turban ushered us across a vast entrance hall dominated by the mounted heads of a bull elephant and four tigers. He led us down a wide paneled corridor to a long drawing room filled with sixty or seventy people, all seated on cushions on the Persian carpets or on the carpets themselves. The three musicians sat cross-legged on a small dais at the far end of the room. Their feet were bare and they wore white, Muslim-style pajamas, loose, long-sleeved collarless shirts, and tan vests: the sarodist, Bahar Khan; Chowdhury, the tabla drummer; and a younger man behind them, Khan sahib's eldest son, who played the tamboura, the twanging drone.

The evening raga was still in its slow, sinuous early stages, weaving a moonlit path through some exquisitely tinted Mogul miniature, some mythical sixteenth-century rain forest, only the sarod and the drone playing, while the drummer sat waiting, resting the tips of his long fingers on the rims of his drums, one drum smaller than the other. We found a place to sit on the carpet where I could lean against a wall. Caroline had no trouble folding herself tailor fashion, she was still slender and limber. But I could never get myself quite comfortable enough, though I had learned to appreciate the sound of this classic medieval music.

The strange, sharp, resonant notes of the sarod turned a corner suddenly into a faster, more rhythmic variation of the thematic melody and just as suddenly the drums began—lightly, insinuatingly, excitingly, like the first rapid raindrops on roofs and leaves in the monsoon. The sad, serious, haunting melody and the drumbeats got into my blood. The raga gained momentum, speed, complexity, intensity. The sarodist sent out showers of dazzling notes and the drummer, as much a virtuoso, echoed him, tried to surpass him. They dueled with electric, inspired emotion and went beyond themselves. Many times the music seemed about to end but climax succeeded climax and the raga went on. Abruptly, after almost thirty minutes, it ended. Applause burst throughout the room.

Some in the audience remained seated but I was one of the first to stand. Turbaned bearers passed amongst us with silver trays of whiskey soda, orange juice, and *nimbu pani*.

"Delighted to have you," said our host, who passed himself along from hand to hand. The maharajah was a tiny man with silver hair and a small black mustache, a round protruding belly under skin-tight leggings below a navy blue Nehru tunic, a neat little doll one might see on a shelf in a small girl's collection from around the world. He wore an intricately wound pink silk turban jauntily on one side of his little white head and carried a short, ivory-headed malacca stick.

A father, a grandfather even, the maharajah was also well known as the elder statesman of a small homosexual elite that included Narendra, the governor's aide; a Scottish tea planter and several other Brits who had stayed on, become Indian citizens, and worked in various official capacities in tribal and frontier areas; and assorted Tibetan and Nepali pets and valets de chambre. Frequent travelers, they could be seen periodically lunching at the same table upstairs at Firpos, at the races and at The Blue Fox on Park Street. They were very active socially, rather exotic and picturesque, amusing.

Handsome Tony Greer—this may have been their first meeting—had caught the maharajah's admiring eye.

"Dear boy, come along. You must meet . . ." I heard him say, and taking Angelica's hand added, "And you, of course, my dear."

"Hi, Mr. McKay. I'd like you to meet Nalini Roy."

It was Thad Perry and the Indian girl Hud had told us about.

"How do you do," she said and I shook her hand.

". . . pleasure to . . . Caroline? Come and meet . . ."

The girl had a sweet, plain face and was rather thin, a little stoop-shouldered. An orphan, she had been adopted by an English couple who had had her keep her original name. They had sent her to a convent school where she had become a Catholic and now taught.

Thad was a frail version of his father—who, no less than Clarissa, seemed relieved he had found a nice girl so soon after his arrival, but I wondered how long it could last. He had nothing to do in Calcutta. How long could he stay?

Caroline and I moved off. We knew many of the other guests to one degree or another. General Singh was there as well as his commanding officer, General Captain, the second word not a rank but a Parsi family name. There were film actors and actresses and one director with an international reputation; a well-known alcoholic painter who was not on the wagon and would have to be carted home in one; a highly eccentric poet in this city of eccentrics, people who lived on illusions and the memory of Tagore; a Bhutanese prince wearing a short, striped robe of many colors—and knee socks and suede shoes like an English schoolboy. But from a distance, striding, he looked rather like a fifteenth-century Florentine noble-man. There were also merchant princes and one knighted captain of industry. The law, academia, and the fourth estate were well rep-resented.

Tony Greer was off in a corner with Narendra, the governor's aide, working as always, finding out whatever he could find out.

Seeing him—and seeing myself—in this palatial drawing room alongside the knight, the princes, the maharajah, and the film stars, I reflected one more time on the hazards and delusions of foreign service life. From hints Tony and Angelica had thrown out I gath-ered they had both escaped from some kind of lower middle class life in Philadelphia. Back home in America the McKays as well as the Greers and most if not all of our colleagues and fellow country-men—who did not have inherited money—would immediately melt into the mass of the merely moderately successful, standing in line to ride commuter buses, making mortgage payments, deciding if we could afford that week on Cape Cod or the Outer Banks this sum-mer or whether it would be more prudent to skip a year in favor of the college education fund. But overseas, especially in the Third World, we moved in the highest circles and lived like nabobs in the finest neighborhoods, waited on by servants, and were driven through the streets above the common herd. Over here it was easy to imagine—as some all too often did—that one's true importance was at last being recognized. I thought Tony Greer was probably too hard-headed a realist to fool himself. But if one stayed overseas very many years at a time, the temptations were great to believe that *this* was the real life, not the life you had left behind.

The British, still relatively numerous in Calcutta, most of them in business, could be considered a separate breed and were recog-nizable instantly a block away. There were far fewer other "Euro-peans"—which included Americans (and even Japanese)—and I thought I recognized them all, even the Russians who kept mostly to themselves. There were few tourists in those days, aside from official visitors, specialists we'd invite to meet counterparts and lecture to invited audiences. So I wondered who the tall European was I didn't recognize from across the room. In his late fifties, possibly older. His white hair was not snowy but coin dull, vainly long and carefully combed straight back in a European style, a prewar style. He wore a white suit, adding to the impression of fussy vanity. His rather craggy, sun-stained face was arrogant, there was no other word for it. He was standing with the maharajah and one of the maharajah's upcountry British cronies.

A long sliding note of a sarod string summoned us back to our places. Bearers had brought in a few upholstered chairs for the maharani, a thin old woman who chain-smoked cigarettes, and several other elderly ladies. I was not so favored and envied them as I once again tried to find a comfortable position on the floor against the wall. Caroline reached over and squeezed my hand sympathetically.

During the second intermission General Singh's squat, ugly wife left the room and did not return. The general stayed, and did not leave the side of Angelica Greer. Tony and Narendra were still thick as thieves across the room. Caroline and I, aware of our social responsibilities, also joined separate groups, but for a moment we looked at each other over the shoulders of others and Caroline raised her eyebrows.

I found myself stuck with Vivekananda Majumdar, the poet. He wore a long brocaded scarf draped over one shoulder like academic colors and had flowing white hair. In a relentless, unstoppable voice he began explaining the significance of the raga we had just heard. I didn't understand a word of it. But since he spoke either with eyes closed or raised heavenward I could let my gaze wander toward two extraordinarily lovely film starlets, one in a simple blue sari with gold trim, the other wearing a golden salwar kamiz.

Majumdar had gone back to Vedic days. He was going into the history of Indian music.

"One must begin with Bhava, Vibhava, Anubhava, Satvabhava, the stages of emotion one might say. The insistence, of course, is on the lyrical impulse rather than the dramatic. . . ." He chuckled, amused at what he was about to say. "Though Hindustani music and the Carnatic are both branches of the same tree, Bhairavi, for example, means something quite different in the north as does the Tala Roopak . . ."

I'm not at all sure I'm quoting him exactly but that was more or less the flavor of his monologue.

"Tell me, Mr. McKay. Do you sense the essential or should I say quintessential difference between the morning and evening raga? Of course—"

A burst of exuberant Bengali deflected him. Chitu Chatterjee had appeared to rescue me, to draw me aside to safety as though he had an urgent message to impart.

"Bless you, Chitu," I murmured.

"Majumdar was a good poet once," Chitu said, "but now he is merely tiresome."

After a third raga the concert ended and most guests prepared to leave.

"Tony is giving me a lift," I heard Narendra tell the maharajah.

They walked ahead of us as Caroline and I left the house. Angelica wasn't with them. Tony and Narendra drove off in the Greer's Vitesse. Caroline and I sat in the front seat of our car but I didn't start the engine. Other guests came out. Angelica was with General Singh. They walked through the gate to where the general's staff car waited, evidently after the driver had taken the general's wife back to Fort William.

"Tony was flirting with Narendra," Caroline said.

I couldn't believe it.

"Of course he was friendly, that's his job," I said. "Everyone knows Narendra is gay. He's also very well informed about the situation in Bengal."

"It wasn't just being friendly," Caroline said. "I saw their eyes, the way they smiled at each other. Narendra was flirting and Tony was flirting back. I don't know how else to describe it. If Tony was putting on an act, teasing Narendra to coax something out of him, what kind of behavior is that? . . . Then Angelica goes off with the general. Do we say anything? I'm not talking about gossip. I mean to Hud."

"How can we? What have we seen? Something that may be entirely innocent. We're not tale bearers."

Caroline sighed.

"Oh, no, of course you're right. But I doubt if we were the only people who noticed."

"We have no control over that. . . . It doesn't *look* good, that I'll admit. At the very least it looks indiscreet."

The Greers' indiscretion angered me suddenly because it might be Hud and Clarissa Perry who would have to be embarrassed by it. Possibly worse than embarrassed.

I drove down a couple of blocks before Caroline said, "Remember I told you about Angelica displaying herself in the raw and how I said I'd wait in the living room if she didn't mind? When I walked out she called out, 'What are you afraid of, Caroline?' and laughed as though it was all a joke. A joke in poor taste but at the time I didn't attach any more importance to it than that. Now I hear her in my head and I wonder. Implied invitations to swap partners. What I just told you. And now tonight. I really don't want Meredith and Richard playing with Amanda and Anthony, but of course if we forbid them to nothing will throw them together faster. I'm not satisfied with the quality of the American school and neither are you, and this is a problem we're going to have to face anywhere—with the possible exception of Western Europe—for a long time to come. Like another ten years. I still think you'd make a good teacher."

I sighed. "No, because I've never wanted to teach and therefore

I'd be no good at it. Look, stop and think. Things like we think we saw tonight could happen anywhere—including the nicest college towns in America."

"I'm sure you're right. But there'd be more room to avoid them than in this inbred, claustrophobic foreign service life."

"Come on. You'd be no happier as a faculty wife than as a foreign service wife."

"At Georgetown? Columbia? Oh, I'd do just fine in Washington or New York, thank you very much."

"We've had some good posts," I said. "Munich. Tel Aviv. Tunis. This one. We've seen places we might never have seen otherwise, met fascinating people, good people. We were good there ourselves."

"I don't deny that," Caroline said. "I'm not going to rewrite history. But when circumstances change then it's time to move on.

"Why do I have to say any of this?" Caroline continued. "You have your own reservations and quarrels. The system getting to be an anachronism. What are you really accomplishing out here? You're the one who asked the question, Charlie. A shoe salesman can tell you how many pairs he's sold, a consular officer how many visas he's issued. A journalist can at least show you his clippings. A diplomat or a propagandist can be honest and say he doesn't know—or try to deceive you with razzle dazzle rationalizations."

"You're oversimplifying."

"Not by much."

So far these weren't arguments exactly. They were friendly discussions. Neither were we joking, and neither could I deny some of Caroline's reasoning. But it wasn't that easy. My options were limited. I'd be forty in a few months. I'd built up almost fifteen years of retirement credit that at this point could only be converted into a lump sum of cash that wouldn't last long. And I still wanted to travel. Staying in the foreign service was the only way we could afford to do it.

But we said no more about any of this that evening.

The following day, a Saturday, I had a morning tennis date with Hud Perry. The sky was overcast, the air warm, moist, and heavy, and walking from Moira Street I carried with me the weight of malaise.

Hud played well that day, without a wasted motion, conserving his energy by simply conceding some net shots when he was in his back court and some cross-court returns that would have involved too much dashing back and forth, building his strategy on beautiful serves and precision net and corner placements of his own I couldn't reach in time. With that control and my semidistracted state he won handily.

After we had showered we had a cold drink at the club bar.

"I met Nalini last evening," I said. "She seems like a solid sort of girl and quite sweet."

"Well, she may make a man of him," Hud said. He took a swallow of his drink. "He's taken up Sanskrit and she's helping him with that, teaching him Bengali too. Something may come of it. He paints, you know. I've been wondering if one of your exhibit artists—Amalendu's the best, isn't he?—would have time to give him some advanced lessons. I'd pay of course."

"I should think he'd be interested."

"I wouldn't want you to put any pressure on him. He may have a full enough schedule."

"It won't hurt to ask. I think he'll give me an honest answer."

"The Greers have sort of adopted Thad, which is nice for him. More their age. Tony was there last night, I suppose?"

"Oh, yes," I said, on top of a little *frisson* of dismay.

"He's extraordinarily innovative, you know. One of the keenest minds I've run across. Gets right to the heart of a situation. Brilliant ideas."

Hud had delivered this praise with intensity, speaking more

rapidly than usual and a tone louder. He seemed excited about something but he cut himself off then, finished his drink with a long swallow, and said he had to get back to the residence.

There was an outgoing cable by Tony in the Tuesday file and I read it with particular interest. In spite of my misgivings about him I couldn't deny its excellence. I was struck by the clarity of the language—in refreshing contrast to the turgid oatmeal and obfuscation that passed for so much diplomatic reporting, some of that clarity conceivably the result of Hud Perry's editing. But it also struck me that the content, as well-informed as it was, probably no more than matched similar reporting from equally smart, ambitious young political officers across the map. And if, as Tony Greer maintained, the Calcutta consular district ranked low in importance in Washington, he would be up against stiff competition that fall for far fewer promotions than there were aspirants to fill them.

I couldn't get the parting scenes of that evening at the maharajah's out of my mind but as days passed I began to see them in a different light. I believed Caroline had seen what she thought she had seen, but I couldn't bring myself to believe it was either an invitation to a homosexual assignation or a calculated pretended one. It seemed to me what Caroline probably saw was a spontaneous facial expression projecting Tony Greer's understanding of Narendra's predilection—or predicament—a liberal heterosexual's joshing to match the gay's: just kidding around, one half of a mutual slap on the back. I'd have to have a lot more to go on before I could conclude otherwise, let alone say anything to anyone, least of all Tony himself. Strictly speaking it wasn't any of my business. The uneasiness I still felt was simply vestigial prejudice I needed to rid myself of. Why then did Tony and Narendra go off alone? For one thing the concert intermissions had been relatively short; they might not have had time to finish their discussion and went to finish it elsewhere. Perhaps Narendra had taken Tony to a restaurant or bar unknown to foreigners, where Tony might meet leftist spokesmen who would avoid American "imperialists" otherwise. In either case Angelica, a beautiful Western girl in Western dress, would be a distraction, an inhibiting factor. Angelica and General Singh? That was another kettle of fish—or can of worms. But until something else happened, if it was going to, we seemed to have no other choice but to let the matter rest.

6

The monsoon ended. The autumn and the autumn social season, the season of festivals, began in the pleasant, sunny days, in the cool of the evenings. In spite of the usual booby traps and obstructions—dung, puddles, garbage, loose paving stones; crowds and cows and antediluvian traffic—rickshaws, horse carriages, handcarts and bullock carts, ancient autos, buses, trams—we were drawn away from verandahs to markets and commercial arteries and their quickening animation, their endless variety of life. Where Chitpur Road curved into an intersection near the Nakhoda Mosque, rising and overlapping tiers of awnings, tropical facades, shutters, wrought-iron balconies, cupolas, casement windows, tin signs, billboards, followed the perspective to the near vanishing point at the foot of a deceptively narrower continuation of the road off to the right, and then through a skein of power lines, tram wires, and the overhanging brackets of street lamps, rose domes and minarets, a reminder that the Muslims of Calcutta had been around, under the Mogul emperor Aurangzeb, before there was a city, before the Ar-

menians—who may have been the first non-Asian settlers—before
the British set foot in Bengal in the 1650s.

On Free School Street, Sikh cab-drivers, looking for fares,
squeezed the rubber bulbs of their brass hand horns, honking for
attention. Rickshaw wallahs rapped small hand bells against their
wooden pull poles and called "Sahib! Sahib! Memsahib! Memsahib!" Hindu and Muslim shopkeepers from every part of the subcontinent, for the moment harmoniously coexisting, lolled in their
doorways or sat inside, tailor fashion, on sheet-covered platforms.
Bathers, one an old woman naked to the waist, squatted by curb-
stones, soaping and laving themselves. Other street people scrubbed
brass eating pans. Eight barefoot peons in loincloths marched down
the middle of the roadway, shouting for a clear passage, carrying an
upended conference table on their heads. Curbstone barbers did a
brisk business. Scribes at little tables wrote letters for the illiterate.
Hawkers sold Japanese fountain pens, cheap toys, cut pieces of papaya, and clay cups of sweet lime juice. Flies settled on the papaya
slices, were fanned away, returned. Cholera? The risk was fairly
high. A stagecoach rattled past drawn by a bony horse, a family
inside, children spilling out the windows, roof piled high with tin
chests and cooking ware. At the entrance to the vast covered maze
of the New Market (Thackeray, Calcutta-born, hadn't quite lived to
see it open) we were immediately besieged by a battalion of basket
boys. The only way to defeat them as a group was to select one to
carry our purchases, however light they might turn out to be. I
pointed to the most persistent, the loudest, cockiest, at which ri-
poste the others dispersed, scattering elsewhere to concentrate their
attack. Number 10, the winner, a bright little Muslim teenager, kept
suggesting various commodities: "Silk sari . . . brass . . . Kashmir
carpet . . ." Caroline shook her head. I pretended not to hear him.

Our cook bought our meat, fowl, fish; one brief visit to the
overpowering animal and bird market under this same roof, but

mercifully around the other side of the building, would convince any American newcomers who thought they might do without kitchen help to leave local custom well enough alone. And since the cook bought the meat he might as well buy all the groceries. That was how things were done. Caroline bought flowers, material, gifts, artifacts.

Her favorite Muslim curio shop was shuttered, locked.

"That's odd," Caroline said. "Why would he be closed today?"

The Muslim basket boy had disappeared in the crowd, without anything, we hadn't bought anything, without his baksheesh, and that was odder still.

Other Muslim shops were closed. We heard loud talk. Walking alongside us in the same direction, an educated-looking Bengali gentleman in a starched and billowing dhoti, gold studs holding his kurta buttoned, had paused too, head cocked to one side.

"Do you know what's going on?" I asked.

"I cannot quite make it out," he said.

He reversed direction to walk back forty yards or so to the intersection of a corridor where he joined a knot of people. We waited until he returned. His expression was pained. He threw the end of a long scarf over an opposite shoulder.

"There are rumors," he said cautiously, "that human heads were found in baskets of fish from East Pakistan."

Caroline stared at him.

"Here in the *New Market*?" I asked.

The gentleman shrugged. "I think not. No one I spoke to had seen anything. Or had spoken to anyone who had seen anything. There are only these rumors, you see. Whatever the truth it is a bad business."

I thanked him and Caroline and I hurried out to the street entrance. Bright sunshine, no sign of tension, nothing out of the ordinary.

We took a taxi to Harrington Street. The cab was a battered

rattletrap with ravaged upholstery driven by a grandfatherly Sikh, a big old man with muscular arms in short sleeves, a fine grey beard, bushy grey hair coming loose under his unkempt baby-blue turban, a dagger at his side hanging from a leather strap across his solid pot belly and barrel chest. I looked at the back of his head and thought about that dagger. Similar atrocities had been authenticated at other times and places. Yet I was inclined to believe this new report was false, and maliciously false.

"Are there any Hindus *left* over there?" Caroline asked in a low voice.

"Oh, I suppose so," I said. "But even if nothing really happened to them, someone wants us to think so."

Hud put it another way: "Of course it doesn't matter a whit if it's true or not. I'll get on to Tony right away."

From the roof of our apartment building on Moira Street you could see the smoke of fires curling straight up in the windless air about three miles to the north. Unlike those unspeakable three days of the Great Calcutta Killing of 1946 when thousands were slaughtered—mostly in the open, when mutilated corpses lined the gutters—unlike that public carnage, the pattern now was arson, so we had heard, though what else might be going on, might have gone on in the past twenty-four hours inside shops and living quarters and stairwells and in the narrow, hidden alleys of the Muslim quarter, might not be known for days and might never be accurately reported. Police and army units were out in force but did not even attempt to station patrols in every street or to investigate every overcrowded, wretched building. Armed men swept the area in moving vehicles and saw only what they could see driving past. All that Sunday, firemen with mostly antiquated equipment managed to confine the extent of the burning, to keep the flames from spreading into other neighborhoods.

Osman, our bearer, and the other Muslim servants in the building did not go home for five straight nights but slept in the normally unused servants' rooms above the garages. Like so many servants, their families lived in villages and in the city they lived alone.

Monday morning a handful of American newsmen flew in from Delhi. With Mr. Brown driving an office station wagon I escorted them into the besieged area. Caroline, notebook in hand, came along. She'd put in overseas calls to the *Boston Globe* and a news-feature syndicate she'd reported for across Europe and in North Africa and the Mideast not quite a decade earlier, and they'd said, go ahead, send us something. I had encouraged her. She had the time now with the kids in school and servants to take care of them afterwards, and here was a story.

Neither police nor army patrols tried to stop us but there were detours we had to follow, presumably to avoid fire engines and other impassable obstructions. We came to a deserted square. Mr. Brown parked and everyone got out. The two wire service photographers with us moved out to the middle of the open space and began snapping pictures. Broken glass was everywhere. The cheap and broken dregs from looted shops littered the roadways. Gutted and half-ruined shops and buildings still smouldered. An automobile, charred almost to the melting point, sat across an empty tram line. Shuttered or eyeless open windows looked down at us from the floors of residential buildings on the far side of the square, buildings that might have been deserted were it not for the white flags flying from the roofs. Had there been fighting as well as one-sided attacks? But of what use were flags of surrender and pleas for amnesty in this murderous religious war where the only rules were to kill or to hide?

From a side street emerged a dozen barefoot men in the meager, knicker-length soiled dhotis of the poor below bare chests or cotton undershirts, men in their twenties, thirties, some older. When they saw us several of them shook their fists above their heads but they were all smiling or laughing. They came closer.

"Americans?" one called in English. "Don't worry, Americans," he crowed. "We have taken good care of them!"

The photographers didn't try to take their picture. We got back in the car and Mr. Brown backed the station wagon up on the curb and turned in the direction we had come. When we were moving, one photographer took some shots of the little mob of men through the back window. I was oppressed and haunted by the hidden horrors we had left behind, by the laughter, the smiles. By the memory of photographs. The outskirts of towns in Indiana and the American South in the 1930s. The grinning faces underneath the trees.

"There were bodies in that car," the AP photographer said.

The newspapers, one of which had reported the rumor of the heads in the baskets of fish, thus spreading it further, showed greater responsibility by publishing, on inside pages, brief, euphemistic reports of "disturbances and instances of arson in minority communities," blamed on "goondas"—hoodlums—to quote one cautious journal, and the Governor's injunction to remain calm, avoid incidents, and to cooperate with the police in maintaining law and order. No casualty figures were given. Tony Greer's cable to Washington gave two: an official estimate that five hundred persons had died and an unofficial claim, based on a wide variety of highly authoritative sources, backed by an unimpeachable official source—whose identity had to be protected—that the actual death toll was in excess of sixteen hundred.

I read this, as I read all outgoing and incoming cables, in Hud Perry's outer office. When I got up from the couch to carry the classified file back to the communications unit, Varina, Hud's American secretary, came out of his office and said, "Charlie, Mr. Perry has something else for you to read." In the inner sanctum Hud was on one foot and half-sitting on the front edge of his desk. He held out a thin folder to me. The outside was labeled SECRET. LIMDIS. EYES ONLY. NO FOREIGN DISSEMINATION.

"As closely involved as you've been, I thought you ought to see this too, Charlie," Hud said.

It was a second cable drafted by Tony Greer. In it, Tony, noting his Chinese language capability and the Chinese contacts he had cultivated over the past several months—he described them as disaffected former agents of the Maoist regime—maintained he had firm evidence the communal killings had been deliberately fomented by the Chinese government to create upheaval and raise the level of tension well past the danger point. Motive: an attempt—successful—to bring on the existing emergency President's Rule, thus postponing the scheduled elections. This would prevent the pro-Soviet Communist party from, as predicted, greatly increasing its strength in the legislature at the expense of the weaker pro-Chinese party. The broader implications seemed self-evident. The cable raised the question, though cautiously did not attempt to answer it one way or the other: Had the bitter Chinese-Soviet, Mao-Khrushchev ideological quarrel taken the direction of great power rivalry over eastern India, perceived by both sides as being in their sphere of influence and strategically vital to their expansionist ambitions?

Hud was silent a moment, thinking, and when, looking over my head, he spoke, it was more to himself than to me.

"It all ties in," he said.

"May I ask, ties in to what?"

My question brought him down a little closer to earth. He beamed at me.

"Charlie, I don't mean to be mysterious. You will definitely be one of the first to know if it works but I'm thinking of something not completely formulated yet. Bear with me. It might be bad luck to talk about it prematurely. Indulge an old man in his superstitions."

"I don't see any old men," I said.
"Well, you're very kind."

I couldn't pass on this new classified information to Caroline for her journalistic needs but she had most of the same Indian sources Tony did, enough of them to be able to write solid follow-up action and think pieces for the *Globe* and the news syndicate. In due course, tear sheets came in the mail. Her signed pieces hadn't been cut very much. She was a pro who still knew how to write tightly, stick to essentials and vivid detail, and keep up reader interest. Seeing herself in print again gave her obvious satisfaction she probably needed. The restlessness was still there but now she had an outlet for some of it. And now she could sit back and take the long view for a publication like *The Atlantic,* which had published her in the fifties too. This was an exotic, colorful place after all, seldom visited by American journalists. There were innumerable feature pieces waiting to be written. I was surprised she hadn't gotten the bug again sooner than this in spite of her determination to be a good mother and a good foreign service wife. The ages of the children had a lot to do with it when they were younger, the felt need to be with them, play with them often, to supervise even the ayah's supervision of their activities. At any rate now she'd taken up her old trade again and I'd come home some days to hear the typewriter clacking in the dining room where she did her work.

7

There was a letter in my interoffice mailbox clipped under a covering note from Hud.

"This lady would seem to be in your field, Charlie. I'll put her up at the residence and give a reception for her but could you meet her flight and do whatever else you can to make her comfortable? I'll need your guest list for the reception—say, about ten names to start with. We can always add or cut later. Could I have that by COB today? The lead time is a little shorter than I'd prefer."

The letter, addressed to Hud, was from Henry Belknap, the country officer in Washington, telling us Jenny Trevilians, Mrs. Marshall Trevilians, was en route to Sikkim as a guest of the royal family and would be spending two days in Calcutta. The Secretary, a close personal friend, was anxious that every courtesy be extended to her.

Jenny Trevilians had published her memoirs a year or so earlier, thus she was in "my field," that is to say, information and cultural affairs. I hadn't read her book but I vaguely remembered a review in the *New York Times*.

I groaned audibly but there didn't happen to be anyone around

128

to hear me. I read the biographic sheet Belknap had enclosed. The lady had led an adventurous, interesting life to be sure—but the more interesting and adventurous a life the more difficult and demanding she might easily turn out to be. I'd had enough experience dealing with similar VIPs to be apprehensive. Born to a great deal of money and now in her mid-sixties. Breeder of racehorses, mountain climber (Himalayas, Andes), explorer (she'd crossed great stretches of the Sahara and was the first woman to set foot in one of the sacred, Islamic cities of Africa). She'd been a pioneer woman pilot and during the Second World War had been the only woman to fly C-54s over The Hump to China. The very proper biography didn't mention any lovers besides her late husband but I supposed she might have had a string of them, such high-powered types so often did.

Her flight was due in from Rangoon. I'd brought Caroline along to the airport for protection. We waited in the scruffy arrival-departure lounge at Dum Dum, I, at least, wishing profoundly I were somewhere else. Caroline looked cool and pretty and intelligent as she invariably did and I particularly appreciated having her around at a time like this. However I might appear to others alone, if I was clever enough to have snagged a girl like this for a wife I must be someone to reckon with. And how churlish it would be to be rude to someone so attractive. Caroline's presence might generate better behavior. Or so I reasoned, but you could never be sure. Some VIPs seemed to enjoy starting out outrageous so that when they later turned on the charm you'd want to clasp them about their ankles in whimpering gratitude. Others would leave you guessing for a while and then would start hacking away gradually, a hair or a knuckle at a time. Totally unreasonable or impossible requests and exasperation over the failure to fulfill them. Insults insinuated, threats veiled, and so forth.

The arrival of the flight was announced. There were few Europeans among the small number of passengers disembarking and only one of them could possibly be the woman we were expecting. Tall, thin, freckled, self-assured, wind-blown, and neither particularly stylish nor flamboyant. Comfortable shoes and cotton traveling clothes. A not-too-large canvas carry-on bag was strapped over one shoulder. Spotting us, she pulled horn-rimmed spectacles from her bag, put them on and barked loudly, "You from the consulate? I'm Jenny Trevilians. How nice of you to meet me. Where do we pick up the bags? I don't have much."

Surprisingly, she didn't—one medium-sized suitcase already on the counter in Customs. An inspector chalked it without asking her to open it.

"This is it?" I asked.

"Well, I don't blame you for expecting me to have more. Rich old ladies usually do. But I've learned to travel light. The trick is in knowing how to pack. Men can't pack a suitcase worth a damn. Can't fold maps, can't pack a suitcase." She smiled. "They can do a lot of other nice things, though. Tell me about yourselves."

What could we do but comply, taking turns telling her how long we'd been in Calcutta, where else in the world we'd served, our native states, not for longer than thirty seconds, though—by which time I had already decided I liked her.

"Mrs. Trevilians," Caroline was inspired to ask as we began walking out to the car, "when—"

"Jenny," Mrs. Trevilians interrupted. "Call me Jenny. I not only give you my permission, I insist on it. Getting old doesn't make you any stuffier if you haven't been that way all along. I have a younger sister who's been an old woman since the age of eleven."

Caroline laughed. "Jenny, during the war did you get down here very often from the Chabua air base?"

"My dear, I was the toast of the town. Only female for miles around, aside from the whores. I exaggerate of course and I'm bragging shamelessly—there were some lovely English and Indian girls about—but we did have some marvelous times in '44 and '45—those two relatively good years between the famine and the communal massacre. Life on the high wire, as I've written."

That was the title of her book.

"Actually I was only up at Chabua about six months. Then they transferred me to headquarters at Barrackpore just outside of town."

"Then I was wondering if you'd ever run into a Polish count, Stefan Z____?"

"Tall? Good-looking as all get out?" She stopped and clasped one of Caroline's hands. "Oh my God, of course! You knew Stefan! Whatever became of him?"

"He went into Hungary during the revolution in '56 to try to bring out someone who was a total stranger. He might have succeeded in helping that person in some way—we never found out—but Stefan himself never came back."

We'd reached the consulate car by then and getting the luggage arranged and ourselves seated interrupted Caroline for a few minutes but then she continued her narrative and summed up the story succinctly. Jenny Trevilians hung on every word.

"A man to the very end then," she said. "Before the Bolshies arrested him he'd rescued *hundreds* of Jews from the Nazis, you know, or did you know? He never said a word about this himself. I heard about it later from a cousin of his in Paris."

I didn't correct her but I thought "hundreds" might be overstated, that twenty-five to fifty would be more likely, and fine enough for any man. He had had so little time.

"No, we hadn't heard about hundreds," Caroline said. "That was the one thing he didn't want to tell me much about because two people he was very close to he'd failed to get out. Apparently they were betrayed by someone he trusted."

Trevilians shook her head sadly. "May he rest in peace. . . . Tell me, will Chitty be at this shindig the CG is having? The maharajah of Chittipore?"

"He's invited and he usually shows up," I said. "I gather you're old friends, in which case I'm sure he'll be there."

"Queer as Dick's hatband you know but a gutsy little man all the same."

"Did he know Stefan too?" I asked.

"Oh, those titled people always know each other," Jenny said. "Chitty'd been to Cambridge, knocked about Europe in the thirties. They'd met in some castle or other."

Over the past year and a half of our tour I'd asked other older Calcuttans, Indians, if they'd ever met Stefan when he'd been out here during the war years and they hadn't. I suppose that's why I'd never asked the maharajah, that and the fact our relationship had been infrequent and somewhat formal. And it occurred to me that people like Jenny Trevilians and the maharajah—and Stefan too— had traveled a great deal around the globe and yet lived in a small world. Like old-family Southerners and foreign service people, everybody knew everybody else and no matter where you went you seemed bound to run into somebody you knew or somebody who knew the people you knew.

Trevilians looked keenly through the car windows on both sides. "Place hasn't changed much," she said.

"Were you at the wedding last year?" I asked.

"That's the thing," she said hoarsely. "Missed it! Laid low by the grippe at the last minute. Tremendous disappointment. All that pageantry. How often do you get to see any of it these days? Hope and the Chogyal insisted I come out this year. I knew his father you see, the old king."

Then we'd arrived at the residence.

Hud and Clarissa's reception for Jenny Trevilians was intended to be more entertaining than official. The emphasis was to be on wit and good conversation, handsome and charming men and pretty and charming women. Eccentricity was acceptable if it was amusing and neither boring nor disruptive. Majumdar, the poet, and the alcoholic artist, for example, were not included.

As a guest at the residence and, I suspect, a lady who devoted little time to primping, Jenny Trevilians was already downstairs when we arrived, with Nigel Cumberland, one of the last British editors of *The Statesman,* at our heels, florid and wheezing, spilling cigarette ash on his jacket. He was accompanied by one of his brightest Indian subs.

"Lettie's hosting a vernissage but she'll be along shortly," he told Hud and Clarissa. "Jenny! Good God, how have you managed to reverse the aging process?"

With Jenny to inspire him and his young colleague—and me— as an audience, it didn't take Nigel long to get on to the old days, the war years and earlier. He'd been with the paper since the midthirties.

". . . It all seems so childishly simple when one looks back on it now," I heard him going on, "but I'm gratified to recall *The Statesman* recognized early on the great issue of the time—the true meaning of Nazism, that it had to be eradicated, when such ideas weren't any more popular with the burra sahibs out here than they were in Britain. We were a Liberal paper and Chamberlain and the Tories were in power. We gave them no quarter even though we caught hell for it . . ."

The maharajah arrived and he and Jenny greeted each other with glad cries and embraced effusively. Caroline and I were standing alongside. Released to do so, Jenny took one of Caroline's hands and one of mine and said, "Chitty, these nice young people knew Stefan! Lost in Hungary during the revolution of fifty-six I've only just heard. God, how easily we lose touch!"

"Ah, what a great pity," the maharajah said. "Mr. McKay, you must tell me the details when there is more time. . . . It's been so long since I've thought of him. But I think Stefan spent his life having to take risks. You've taken them too, Jenny."

"And *you*," Jenny said. "Don't be modest."

"I understand you'd met Stefan even before the war," Caroline said to the maharajah.

The maharajah thought back. "He and his wife were in so many places that year. I suppose every year, she being a performer always on tour. Not that I personally saw them everywhere, but there was more than one occasion. What stands out is a week-long shoot in Bohemia. He and his wife were only there out of politeness. They didn't really care much for that sort of hunting. He was an interesting chap, more serious than most, something of a scholar. He quite surprised me with his knowledge of Indian history and philosophy."

"Did you see her perform?" Caroline asked.

"No, but there were recordings. Someone had a gramophone."

Gesturing with his right hand, and in a low baritone, the maharajah tried to reproduce the first few notes of a nostalgic ballad. "Da dee da dee dee da dee . . ." he crooned, and faded out.

At that point Jenny took one of "Chitty's" hands, palms together, patted the large emerald ring the maharajah was wearing, said, "Come tell me all about . . ." and drew him to a sitting position beside her on a loveseat. Caroline and I left them to reminisce uninterrupted, and we separated. We'd probably moved around together a little too long as it was.

Not long after that, Tony—without Angelica, who was officially expected to be there too—showed up with that white-haired Arctic-eyed European we'd noticed at the maharajah's sarod concert—and A. K. Ghosh.

I was angered at the sight of him. It was one thing for Tony to thumb his nose at me in spite of what I'd told him, but to flaunt Ghosh in Hud and Clarissa's home where he didn't belong . . .

The sentence came to me whole: *Hud is slipping.* Hadn't he checked his guest list, questioned Tony? He hadn't needed to ask me about my recommendations because he was well acquainted with all of them. But I was reasonably sure Hud either didn't know Ghosh or would disapprove of him if he did know him. Had Tony just given him some song and dance about Ghosh and the other man too, who was not a contact at all but clearly some third-country outsider, that Hud had accepted because in Hud's eyes Tony Greer hung the moon? It appeared that way.

There wasn't any kind of commotion. Caroline and I—separately—simply avoided Tony, which we were supposed to do anyway at a gathering like this. Our job wasn't to chitchat with American colleagues. And, by extension, avoided Tony's pals too, which we could do with a clear conscience since they were anything but official contacts. So we simply looked away, and I continued to swap anecdotes about W. C. Fields with a well-known character actor in Bengali films while Caroline listened to a leading man and his wife, friends of ours. And, as I say, there was no commotion, simply that when the character actor moved somewhere else and I looked around to see who else might need attention, that turned out to be Jenny Trevilians. She was sitting by herself on the loveseat. The maharajah was nowhere in sight. I supposed he might be in the bathroom but when I asked "Jenny, can I get you anything?" she shook her head and patted the seat beside her. I sat down.

"Chitty left," she said. "Royal prerogative. You seem to have an odd situation of some sort going on at this post. Chitty took one look at what the cat dragged in—one of the people your political officer had in tow, a rather repulsive-looking Indian fellow—where is he?" She craned her neck and peered around the room. "Well, I don't happen to see him at the moment—and said—Chitty said—he would not stay in the same room with the man and could not understand why he was here in the first place. The fellow was a Jif, I gather, but after all these years there must be more to it than that.

I'm lunching with Chitty tomorrow before my flight to Baghdogra. Perhaps I'll find out then. He also seemed upset with some wintry-looking European who came in at the same time."

"Jif" stood for Japanese-inspired fifth column—in other words, the defunct Indian National Army. That plus Ghosh's unsavory reputation would account for the maharajah's extreme displeasure. But an expression of post solidarity seemed called for—I had Hud's reputation in mind rather than Tony's—and I said, "I'm as baffled as you are. You can never be entirely sure about the chemistry at these affairs. Sometimes even with the best information and the best intentions you guess wrong. Tony Greer is a very experienced and astute political officer. His work isn't in my bailiwick but he must have some reason to consider—the man's name is Ghosh by the way—consider Ghosh important. I'm sure he wouldn't deliberately set out to antagonize the maharajah. But I'm sorry you had to be exposed to anything unpleasant and to have your reunion dampened."

"Of the two of you I think you're the better diplomat," Jenny Trevilians said with what seemed a genuinely cordial smile.

I soon put her with the leading man and hoped for Hud's sake I'd appeased her enough so that she wouldn't grumble to the Secretary when she got home, and apart from saying goodbye and bon voyage when the party broke up and how much I'd enjoyed meeting her, that was the last time we talked.

Alone and walking home I told Caroline what had happened. "She hit the nail on the head: 'An odd situation of some sort seems to be going on at this post,'" I mimicked.

"Don't we know," Caroline said. "I liked *her,* though. She's a sketch."

We took a few more strides without saying anything. The night air was misty and cool. Then Caroline said, "Ever get that strange feeling—how did I get here? How in God's name do I find myself on Harrington Street in the city of Calcutta of all places, halfway around the world from Eastbrook, Connecticut, or Manhattan or Clarksville, Illinois? It must have something to do with a critical fusion of the familiar and the alien. The sidewalk under your feet feels exactly like a sidewalk anywhere and then you look towards the curb and there's a brown man with bare feet wearing a loincloth and a t-shirt and a cloth around his head, standing between the shafts of his rickshaw."

"It doesn't have to be that exotic," I said. "It happened to me once in Munich, riding on a streetcar at dusk."

There it was again, echo and resonance. Caroline heard it too. I knew all the recollections of Stefan she'd heard over the past two days must have been thrilling and sad for her. They were for me. Caroline had been in thrall to him and in some residual way probably still was, a fact that did not leave me disturbed with jealousy. I admired him too much for that. He had set a standard of behavior most men don't even aspire to, let alone have the capacity to achieve. Simply knowing it had existed was a source of hope, of strength.

Caroline took my hand as we walked the rest of the way in silence.

8

Ninety-nine percent of my life was spent at street level or only a few steps above it. I hadn't been a climber of church steeples, the pinnacles of minarets were barred to the infidel, and the businessmen whose offices were perched on the upper floors of high rises in the financial district were not my contacts to call on. But a new luxury apartment building was opened that fall and Caroline and I were invited to a cocktail party in its fifteenth floor penthouse by a Calcutta newspaper magnate. We arrived at dusk. The sky was pink and fading. Over the *maidan* and the river the sun was setting under great, mountainous banks of clouds. From the open terrace I could see for the first time almost the entire sprawl of the long, narrow city, the rows of ships berthed far down in the Kidderpore docks at Garden Reach, the smoke rising from factory chimneys and a million cow dung stoves. The great height hid the death and the misery, the bodies jammed together in tenements and *bustees,* nine hundred to the square block, but in the opposite direction, every roof below us, trees, parks, gardens, "tanks"—those square, tree-lined pools placed benignly throughout the city, where people bathed and washed their clothing, gossiped, got away from overcrowding for a while, where children played in the late afternoons—presented a green, shimmering pattern of tropical beauty. Let three-quarters of the population voluntarily go back to where they had originally come, I thought, then spend a fortune renovating and rebuilding, and Calcutta, that urban catastrophe, might become one of the world's handsome cities.

My new cultural affairs officer and his wife had recently arrived and were guests that evening. They too had become members of the Lancers Club and from inside the apartment I heard Lettie Cumberland, Nigel's wife of many years, telling her Lancers Club story. Lettie came from an old, distinguished Bengali family. "Lettie," I supposed, was a nickname or some anglicized diminutive of an Indian name, but though I was curious about it I had never been quite curious enough to remember to ask anyone who might know the answer. Lettie was a patroness of the arts, well-informed and witty, and I was very fond of her.

"Well, this was in the late twenties," I heard her say in her penetrating voice. "Douglas Fairbanks, senior, visited Calcutta. You're all too young to have seen him in person or even on the screen but you've probably seen photographs. He always had that very dark California tan. Well, someone invited him to have a swim at the Lancers Club but not every member knew he was there. Suddenly this British woman dashed out into the lobby and was heard to scream, 'There's a *black* Indian in the swimming pool! There's a *black* Indian in the swimming pool!' You can imagine the to-do in those days until they were able to straighten her out."

Lettie saw me and came out on the terrace. We both looked far down at the *maidan* in the near distance.

"Oh, I've seen it from on high before but not so recently," Lettie said. "Different perspectives give one—well, exactly that—different perspectives, don't you agree? You know it wasn't just a park at first, a pleasure ground. It was a buffer zone the British created after the first Fort William was sacked by a local nawab. After the British built the present fort on the river they razed all the buildings up to Chowringhee—a good cannon fire width—and then the rich Europeans and Indians had an esplanade to promenade on in the cool of the evenings. Just imagine the parade of elephants and camels, palanquins and carriages! From palanquins and palkee bearers to rickshaws and rickshaw wallahs in two hundred years. We haven't progressed very far, have we? . . . There were so few of them in proportion to the men, the British women in those days had a reputation for being dashing—something like Angelica I imagine."

I turned my head to look back into the apartment but then I remembered the Greers weren't there. This wasn't their crowd. And I wondered what Lettie might be getting at.

"When they went out for carriage rides the men lolled back while the women held the reins. And speaking of reins, have you been to the races this year?"

"Not so far."

We both looked at the white grandstand of the racecourse at the southern end of the Esplanade, reduced to dollhouse size by the elevation and distance.

"Hud and Clarissa don't go, either. Well, Nigel and I go and the young Greers seem to go quite often," Lettie said. "It seems to be a regular thing with them. They arrive together, watch one race together or perhaps none at all, and then without any evidence of having quarrelled, Angelica goes off with General Singh. The general is in mufti but still of course everyone recognizes him anyway. Well, I'm broad-minded, darling. It seems inevitable someone I know is going to have an affair sooner or later, but the idea of Tony *delivering* his wife to Singh, pimping in broad daylight, is a bit much, don't you think? They've blotted their copybooks as far as we're concerned. What disturbs me as much as anything is that Tony doesn't seem to care what 'we' think, the 'natives,' don't you know. Is his position with Hud so unassailable they can do exactly what they please with immunity, not care a fig for public opinion?"

"Lettie, I simply don't know. But I appreciate your candidness."

I had suddenly, it seemed to me, been handed a major problem that weighed me down and set my pulse racing.

"We like you chaps, you know," Lettie said. "By and large. I mean you and Caroline and Hud and Clarissa and many, if not all, of your colleagues and predecessors we've gotten to know. We've learned to expect better of you."

"I'm flattered and honored to hear you say it," I said. "And struck a bit dumb otherwise . . ."

It was only afterwards I recalled that Lettie hadn't said anything about Tony and Narendra. Maybe there was nothing to say about that. But Lettie had said quite enough as it was. But could I repeat it to Hud? In doubt, I didn't. I wonder to this day if things might have worked out differently if I had.

Clarissa Perry's sister and her husband arrived in Calcutta and Clarissa set off with them on a six-week trek to see the wonders of India and Nepal. With luck they might also get permission to visit Sikkim and Bhutan.

At the festival of Durga Puja I hired a dinghy to show the new CAO and his wife the climactic ceremony from the middle of the river. We were rowed out by a squatting Charon folded in a cloak. Freighters sat at anchor lit up in the night. The multitudes, a million?—thousands will not do—descended by truck and on foot bearing their more-than-life-size clay statues of Durga, the Earth Mother, some lit by candles, to float them in the sacred Ganga where they broke apart, disintegrated, sank, and disappeared.

For the second year in a row Narendra invited us to his family mansion to celebrate Diwali—Kali Puja. Others invited us to observe the same festival of light elsewhere in the city. Having been once to Narendra's, Caroline and I would have preferred a new location but the new CAO was included in all invitations and there was no question, for him and his wife Narendra's palace would be too unforgettable to miss.

The crumbling mansion where Narendra lived as one member of a large joint family was situated in a very old section of the city in the midst of ramshackle tenements. A narrow alley packed with one-room shops, some nothing more than poles, canvas, and corrugated iron roofs set up in spaces between buildings, crowded close upon the arched entrance to the courtyard. Three musicians—a flutist, a drummer, and a man fingering a harmonium—were stationed just inside the arch, squatting on the stones and playing a slow, repetitious melody. People from the neighborhood, poorly or simply dressed, filed in and out, the one day of the year—servants, repairmen, and peons with something to deliver, the exceptions—when they were permitted inside. The central courtyard was large, ringed by open balconies on each of three stories above, and open to the sky. Kites and crows wheeled above but were kept out by a wire net sagging from roof to roof. The crows protested angrily in the dusk.

In a small gallery off the courtyard stood a monstrous clay statue of Kali. She was black and eight feet high, with bloody hands and eyes and swollen tongue. Her waist was entwined with cobras and a girdle of severed limbs and she wore a necklace of skulls. In one of her several hands she clutched a strangler's noose. Death and life, darkness and light, violence and love, opposing natures in one. But I oversimplify. No two people agreed on the exact nature of this goddess or any other in the Hindu pantheon. Explanations ran like quicksilver out of my mind's reach; I hadn't the patience to sort them out. Did she bring pestilence in her wake or did one pray to her for deliverance from it? Possibly both. It was a fact that Calcutta was named for her, that "thugs" had murdered in her honor—probably a perversion—that human sacrifice was offered to propitiate her well into the nineteenth century. (There were rumors it still went on in remote places even now. In Calcutta, only goats were slaughtered.)

Worshipers walked up the two steps into the gallery, recited their prayers, and backed out, bowing respectfully. Three men entered the courtyard carrying enormous drums slung by straps around their necks. They began beating suddenly with bare hands and sticks and the sound exploded inside our heads. We clapped hands over our ears as we hurried to the stone staircase leading to the flight above. Beyond a terrace and in a long, Victorian drawing room, glass doors closed behind us; the terrible sound was diminished.

Narendra saw us and came up, sandals clapping. He had been giggling about something moments before and in an unsuccessful attempt to restore a dignified host's expression to his face in time to greet us, simpered, let another giggle escape, then a burst of laughter. Under those circumstances one tends to feel left out, laughed at, though I hadn't known Narendra to be malicious.

Like many upper-class Bengalis he looked Roman in his toga-like dhoti and kurta and with his classic features. In profile his might have been the face on one of the marble busts in his drawing room.

Over his shoulder I saw Tony Greer. Thad Perry was with him. His father, I knew, was having dinner with a High Court justice and the rector of the university. I didn't see Angelica and I didn't see Nalini Roy. But there were many people and then there was a power failure. There were always power failures. No one seemed to notice. Below the second-story verandah, oil lamps flickered around the courtyard where the frenzied drummers danced. Through tall windows fireworks over opposite rooftops lit the drawing room, went out. Interior electric lights went on again but slowly dimmed almost beyond usefulness. Like the house itself the drawing room was crumbling. Nothing appeared to have been refurbished or reupholstered, polished or even dusted in a hundred years. A collection of clocks was set about under glass bells or on mahogany etageres. None of them worked. Time had stopped here long ago. The mirrors were so tarnished they barely reflected all the old and middle-aged family members in dhotis and saris and Western dress, resurrected ghosts among their European guests, and the light was too dim in any case. In here was a faded dead world of manners, and the jungle sounded just outside. An elderly lady kept asking me about Australia where I had never been. I tried to tell her this but under the drumming perhaps she couldn't hear me. An elderly gentleman with red and white markings on his forehead, and a handlebar mustache which obscured speech already slurred and peculiarly intonated, asked me about people I had never met. A second old gentleman said he had written a poem dedicated to Norma Shearer, "star of the silver screen," and wondered if my office might like to publish it. I fobbed him off with some vague stalling tactic or other.

"Come and take a look at the inner courtyard," I said to the CAO and his wife and, with Caroline, the four of us crossed the length of the drawing room to a pair of tall, opened, shuttered doors. We stepped out onto a marble terrace and leaned over a marble balustrade. Oil lamps on tall wrought-iron stands were ranged along two sides of a reflecting pool one story below. On the balcony and beside the pool huge blue and green parrots screeched and stared. Some were more than two feet tall. They stood in wire cages with domed covers or perched outside on stands, like weather vanes. Mynahs and other rare birds preened in smaller cages, painted all the colors of the semiprecious stones set in floral and geometric designs in *pietra dura* tables. Peacocks and pelicans strutted free and left their droppings on the marble patio. Parvenu crows flew in off the street through a tear in the roof netting and hung around insolently on the heads of marble nymphs, on the capitals of Ionic columns, on the lips of Grecian urns.

We went back inside the drawing room.

Candles had been lit. Outside the windows, rockets flashed and burst, crackled suspensefully and exploded into sprays of multi-colored lights. I saw Thad with a Tibetan boy and the white-haired European I had seen at the maharajah's sarod concert and at Hud's. The maharajah was missing, an absence that struck me. This was an annual event. I would have expected to see him here. Perhaps he was ill. Or perhaps they were spatting. From the expression on his candlelit face, the way his eyes focused, I was sure Thad was on something—bhang or some variant. He was quite slender and in tight jeans looked even more so. Narendra came up behind him and put the palm of one hand on Thad's bottom. Thad started a little, like a nervous colt. I searched for Tony and found him half in and half out of some conversation. I thought he might be on bhang too.

"Is Nalini Roy here?" I asked him.

"How should I know?" He smiled. "Didn't make it, I suppose you'd say."

"If you have any influence on Thad Perry you ought to get him out of here."

"Why, whatever for, McKay? He's a grown boy who's enjoying himself. What right have I to interfere? Or you? His father knows where he is and what he is. You might want to check that out."

He turned and walked off. I wanted to fling one of those clocks at the back of his handsome head and frightened myself at the violence of my thoughts. *Thad didn't have to be led, pushed into the company of Narendra and his pals. He didn't have to be set up! That might have made a difference. Might.* But did I really have enough evidence to accuse Tony of complicity in the seduction of Thad Perry? It seemed to me my own friendship with Houston Perry might also be at stake.

"Have you seen enough?" I asked the CAO and his wife. "Why don't we have dinner somewhere."

We took a cab to the Amber restaurant, which specialized in tandoori chicken, but there were too many people waiting for tables. We took another cab to Nizams. The streets were mobbed with celebrating people. Nizams was jammed too but it was a bigger place and we decided to wait. It was a messy, glaringly lit modern Moorish rabbit warren of tile cubicles augmented by tables outside in a back alley where you could watch and smell the charcoal grilling. After a twenty-minute wait we got a table back there. We ate delicious lamb kabobs wrapped in chapatis washed down with Indian beer and for a while I felt free of other people's troubles. But when we went home the children were still up, playing a game with Rita on the living room floor, and I questioned, as Caroline questioned, if we were doing right by them, dragging them along into this foreign service life. We refused to send them off to boarding school somewhere in the mountains or even in Europe and certainly not to England. The British did that routinely and it was a terrible idea. Turning boys into little Thads or exposing them to the danger of it.

In December, Clarissa Perry returned from her long trip. And the promotion lists were published. Among a short list of grade 4's elevated to grade 3, the fifth name down was Elliott Anthony Greer.

9

The day he'd arrived in Calcutta, Tony Greer had coveted the consular officer's ground floor apartment on Moira Street and in the next breath I had talked him out of it. Now I knew why he had given in so easily. He had even grander notions.

Next door to the consul general's residence, on the opposite side of the residence from the consulate, was a quite elegant two-flat apartment house, each unit more spacious than the Moira Street flats, with third bedrooms—or studies. The upper apartment was occupied by the economic affairs officer, the lower by Martin, the administrative officer. Like the consular officer, Martin did not need to entertain officially more than once or twice a year. Martin was, however, next to Hud, the senior ranking man at the post, a veteran Hud's age with a solid reputation for competence. He looked the part—a little stout, a little bald—reassuring, like a family physician, an old lady's attorney, unflappable. Behind this facade was irreverence for the stuffier forms of bureaucracy and great skill at poker. These attributes allowed him to keep his cool when Hud awarded

Martin's apartment to Tony and moved Martin and his wife (their children were all grown and on their own) to Moira Street.

"The bastard!" Caroline commented to the Martins when we had them down for a welcoming drink. "Of course I'm selfishly delighted to have you here instead, but the nerve! The gall!"

"Gall runs in Tony's veins," I said. "Ice water and gall. I am rather surprised at Hud, though."

Martin was a master of indirection and his wife the soul of discretion. They did not need to agree with us verbally. In their half smiles there was great cold clarity. Martin did remark, however, "Onward and upward. Climbing those stairs will be just the exercise we need. Let us be delighted with you, Caroline."

At the end of January we heard from Martin that Clarissa Perry had flown back to the States for medical tests. After the weekly country team meeting in Hud's office I asked after her and Hud said, "Just a precaution. She hasn't been up to par lately. Something she might have picked up on that trip." He seemed anxious to end the discussion and I didn't press him further. Caroline and I had seen Clarissa only in passing once during the month, at some reception or other. She hadn't scheduled a wives' meeting in January. She had been gone three days before we heard about it. Then Hud came to a screening of a new film on the history of American art. I had asked him to make a few introductory remarks. His behavior was subdued, distracted. He was a little distant and formal with us, and left early. Later, he turned down a dinner invitation.

Thad was gone too, traveling in Nepal. That was something else Martin had told us rather than Hud.

The pleasant winter weather receded. The days and nights grew quickly warmer and by late February the hot season had begun. Hud said it was too hot for tennis, though I continued to play with others.

In reply to questions about Clarissa, Hud gave us a series of brief replies. "Too soon to tell. . . . They're thinking about scheduling exploratory surgery. . . . Oh, that biopsy was negative. But she'll stay with her sister a while longer. For the next six months the weather here wouldn't do her any good. She may have had too many years of tropical heat and tropical bugs . . ." At that point we stopped asking.

Our life went on. We saw Hud and the Greers routinely off and on in various places as we would see any colleagues or consulate neighbors, saw the Greers, that is to say glimpsed them, but avoided their company as much as possible. We may have had to speak to them at some point but I can't remember doing so.

But once after I had picked up some interesting political information almost accidentally and had sent it by memo addressed to Hud slash Tony, Hud asked me to come over and initial the telegram in which my information was incorporated. Hud said Tony had it in his office and so I had no other choice but to walk down the hall and go in.

I'd had occasion to glimpse Tony in action a few times before as he dealt with others. Now he was dealing with me and the effect was considerably sharper. Tony knew how to use silence, and a show of not noticing your presence, as a calculated weapon. I once called him a good listener and he was—when it suited him. This was the dark side of silence. I haven't found the tactic to be uncommon and it crosses social lines. The ignorant and uneducated use it too—with less finesse and more out of a sense of inferiority and resentment than contempt—but with the same end in view—dominance, control. I had worked for such people at both ends of the social scale and might, if I was not careful or lucky, have to do it again. Freedom, for me, was freedom from the likes of them. The only power I really coveted was to have the financial resources to insist on that freedom.

"Tony," I said. "If you could let me see that telegram so I can initial it, I'll be on my way."

He didn't look up. He continued typing a rather long sentence but then stopped abruptly, turned to me with that foolproof handsome grin of his—there seemed to be no way, from any angle, it could look ugly, sinister, foolish, or in any other way unattractive, a physical gift he shared with certain Hollywood actors—Ronald Colman and Douglas Fairbanks, Jr., come to mind—and handing me the multicopied telegram with its green top sheet, got to his feet and said, "I've got to dash. Just leave it with Varina." And off he did dash, and disappear, in his white duck trousers and open-neck short-sleeved bush shirt, the hot season outfit I was wearing too that was favored by the Calcutta man of affairs, Indian as well as foreign, who wore Western dress, except for a certain category of Indian businessmen who continued to wear coats and ties even on the most unbearable days. And I was so glad to see him go I almost didn't mind not being thanked for my contribution to his telegram. That was the reverse effect of the tactic of silence—the relief when it was over. We thank our tormentor for leaving us in peace.

Now the southern breeze blew in from the Bay of Bengal, raising humidity in its path, and in the early mornings a thick mist lay along the ground. Planes were delayed at Dum Dum and trains could proceed only with fog signals. In the late afternoons and early evenings of oppressively hot days in April and May, nor'westers, high winds with little rain, brought some cool relief and sometimes destruction in their wake, flimsy country dwellings flattened, small boats sunk. On Chowringhee Road so many nonpaying passengers hung to the outsides of double-decker buses the vehicles listed like capsizing ships. On the sidewalk at the entrance to Firpo's restaurant the stark naked holy man and the spider man who begged on all fours plied their vocations. Another body was found in a trunk at Howrah Station and *The Statesman* published a photograph of its face, above the notice: "Anyone having any information concerning the identity of this person is asked to communicate with . . ." At the city dump, a vision of hell, under a sun that raised the Fahrenheit temperature to as high as 120 in midday, the last scavengers sifted through the truckloads of refuse, already assiduously picked over en route, for anything—rags, bones, hair, glass, metal, plastic, that might fetch a few *naya paise* to keep them alive another day.

It was Varina who phoned me one May afternoon.

"Charlie, it's about Mr. Perry. He got a letter from the country officer in Washington half an hour ago—it came in the classified pouch and I brought it in to him. Then he came out of his office looking terrible. He said he was going to the residence. I asked him if he wanted me to call his doctor but he said, 'No. Forget doctors.' I said 'Mr. Greer isn't back yet, is there anyone else I should get in touch with?' and he said, 'Yes, Charlie McKay. Please ask him to come over.' I'm really terribly concerned, Charlie. I've never seen him like this. He's always been so cheerful, optimistic. And with Mrs. Perry away. . . . He misses her, I know that, and sometimes lately I've thought he might be feeling sad but a minute later he'd kid me about something, the way he does, full of the old bounce."

"I'm on my way," I said.

"After you see him, let me know if I can do anything."

Mr. Brown drove me over. The Perrys' bearer, Ahmed, opened the door. The air conditioning hit me full blast. The blinds were drawn in the living room. I didn't see Hud at first. He was sitting in a high-backed wing chair facing away from me.

"Hud?"

He didn't reply.

"Houston?"

For a moment I was frightened but when I walked over to him he turned his head slightly in my direction and said, "Come in, Charlie. It's a little early but would you like a drink? I'm having one."

He was having a strong one. An outsize Old-Fashioned glass

in his right hand was full and darkly tinted. A thick business-size white envelope lay on the end table.

"Sahib?" Ahmed asked.

"I'll have a *nimbu pani,* Ahmed," I said.

"Nothing stronger than that, Charlie?" Hud said. "I think you may need it."

"Then please let me have a light bourbon and ice."

Fortified with it I sat across from Hud in a matching wing chair. Varina hadn't exaggerated his state. Hud's arms and hands were tanned from tennis but he mostly kept himself out of the sun. Twice he'd had suspected skin cancer spots removed from his nose. He wore slacks on the courts and always a brimmed canvas hat and on the street during the day wore an old-fashioned panama. Normally then his face was only a healthy pink. Some of that color seemed to be returning, perhaps from the effect of alcohol, but across his forehead, under his eyes, and around his mouth his skin was still ashen. Fifty-six wasn't old, but Hud dated from another era. He'd been in the foreign service class of 1930, the year some newly commissioned young diplomats had to pay their own way to their first posts.

"The State Department was broke," he had told me once. "There were only funds to send people to the American republics. The rest of us were on our own, take it or leave it. I had to borrow the money from my father to buy a second-class ticket on a ship to Genoa where I'd been told there was a job for me as a diplomatic clerk. But it was worth it. Clarissa and I have had a good life."

Now he looked at me and it was clear he thought that good life was over.

"They've zapped me, Charlie," he said. "They've knocked the pins right out from under me. And I'm persuaded it's young Mr. Greer—in whom I'd placed so much confidence and trust—and who has powerful friends at court—who's sold me down the river."

He paused to take another sip of his drink and I waited, still unenlightened but already raging.

"There are two plans involved," he said. "The results of plan number two are in that envelope and I might tell you about that first but I think I will begin in chronological order with plan number one. Mr. Greer broached it last fall just a couple of months after he arrived here and I fell for it hook, line, and sinker. In a nutshell, he would propose to formally recognize the strategic importance and great size of the Calcutta consular district by raising the rank of the chief of mission from consul general to minister. Mind you, with my second tour of duty coming to an end here this year, even if such a plan were to be approved in record time, it would not be me who would become the first minister to eastern India. No, I could rightfully and honestly claim objective personal disinterestedness. And then Mr. Greer convinced me that I, not he, should take full credit for this brilliant proposal. Though I would never be the first minister here, I did hope for an ambassadorship somewhere to round out my career, and successful implementation of plan number one, it seemed to young Mr. Greer, and I agreed, would enhance that possibility. Using Mr. Greer's carefully reasoned arguments, some of which Mr. Greer said he'd heard from you, Charlie, and which I felt could certainly be justified, I dispatched the proposal to Washington in the form of a letter to Henry Belknap, the country officer. Months went by and I heard nothing other than an acknowledgment of receipt but didn't expect to. Such matters are dealt with very slowly and cautiously. But I was confident. The proposal made as much sense as anything else. Today I got my answer."

He reached to the side, picked up the envelope there with shaky fingers, and handed it across to me.

"Just ignore that 'EYES ONLY,'" Hud said. "The entire post will find out what's in it all too soon."

As I began to read I heard Hud say, "Mr. Greer, you know, though not a believer, went to a Jesuit high school. He was captain of the debating team. He was taught to be able to take either side of any question and argue convincingly for or against it. I'm sure it must have been splendid training for a man with his bent and career ambitions."

What Belknap, the country officer, had to say was an announcement of an established fact: to take effect before the start of the new fiscal year in October and to be implemented in phases over a three-year period, the American and local staffs of the Calcutta consular district would be reduced in size to approximately twenty-five percent of current totals. My office would be equally affected. Ultimately, over one hundred local employees would be pensioned off or let go with severance pay. The argument behind this drastic reduction in force was that the alleged "strategic importance" of the consular district was more apparent than real. It was clear from the fact the Chinese had *withdrawn,* after invading in 1962 to "adjust" their border claims, that the Maoist regime had no intention of taking on the endless, unprofitable, and ultimately impossible task—not to mention the opprobrium of world opinion—of attempting to conquer, hold, and administer a territory with a mostly racially alien population. Moreover, all geopolitical calculations rendered the threat of a Russian takeover equally remote. The Department acknowledged that Communists might be able to take power in Bengal through the electoral process and, though such an outcome would be inimical to U.S. interests, it should be borne in mind that a communist government already existed in the state of Kerala but nonetheless U.S. relations with the national Indian government were excellent. The alleged Chinese plot to upset the political timetable in Bengal by fomenting a communal riot, even if true, may have been the work of maverick or overzealous Chinese agents. No additional evidence had been put forth to indicate the Chinese would attempt any more serious adventures. Streamlining the Calcutta operation would be in the interests of economy. The reduction in force would serve to conform to more realistic priorities and goals.

"Hud," I said, "I've got no use for Tony Greer, for reasons I'll be glad to share with you, but why do you believe he engineered this? You must have some proof?"

"Proof? No, I have no proof at hand, though I'm convinced it exists in Belknap's file of correspondence. One, Tony is too smart, too shrewd, to have miscalculated as badly as I did in my innocence and dotage. His modesty—in letting *me* take credit for *his* proposal—I've come to question seriously ever since he got his promotion. No, there is nothing really very modest about young Mr. Greer. Over the past month—little things and not so little things here and there. Hanging up the phone a few seconds too soon to be truly courteous. Arguing with me in private—and at country team meetings, as you may have noticed, the private arguments tinged with mockery. Being late for appointments and not apologizing. Showing up *two hours* late at that reception—for the private American foreign policy group? A clear embarrassment for me, he being the political officer, and I'd promised them a briefing. Of course after he did arrive he charmed the socks off them and made me look even more of a fool. Just in the past week an attitude verging on open contempt, as if he *knew* I was through, that I simply don't count anymore. I'm sure he's the real author of plan number two and he had to send it in secretly, over my head, because he knew I'd never pass it along and cut my own throat. I've been betrayed and now I'm being destroyed." And then he added, without any attempt at introducing a transition, "Clarissa has left me, Charlie. I made a fool of myself over Angelica too. Clarissa got wind of it and I didn't deny it. I don't deserve any sympathy over that, do I? But it's killing me."

How can I describe my surprise that wasn't surprise?

"She'll take you back," I said. "She's a wonderful woman."

"Yes, she's that, but she won't. What I did was unnecessary and unforgivable."

"What Angelica did was what was unforgivable. I'm not asking,

I'm only hazarding a guess, a conviction, that this was the first and only time you ever strayed."

"But don't you see, a woman who puts up with a weak philanderer can always forgive him one more time. What I destroyed overnight was something we'd spent thirty years building up. Clarissa's pride simply won't take that. And everything wasn't perfect between us. It never is, is it? We'd begun to blame each other for what Thad has become. When a child dies it's the same thing, I'm told. You might think the tragedy would bring you closer but often it doesn't. Just the opposite. Once that starts . . ."

"Hud, why did Chambers have Greer transferred out of Dacca?"

"I don't know. We may never know. I do know it was Belknap who engineered some face-saving formula. If you're thinking of getting poor old Chambers to testify against Greer in some fashion you can forget it. I'm sure the face-saving formula would preclude it."

"How well do you know Chambers?"

Hud shook his head. "Never close friends—nor enemies either. We served in Washington at the same time for a while but that was a number of years ago. I'd see him at meetings, in the cafeteria, forget him a second later."

"What's his wife like?"

"Never laid eyes on her."

"You must have wondered, as I have, how Tony was able to spring himself loose from Dacca, from Chambers, reputation untarnished."

"Of course."

"And what did you guess? Would simple incompatibility have been enough?"

"A rare enough thing, I suppose, but anything is possible if you have powerful friends interested in advancing your career and not interested in the other fellow's. That was my assumption and I was so glad at first to have Tony I didn't waste time speculating further. Water under the bridge."

"Then. What about now?"

"Still a good enough reason. What difference does it make?"

"What about the threat of blackmail? What if Tony found out something compromising about Chambers?"

"Tony may be lucky, but don't you think that would have been a little too convenient to be believable?"

"Not if it was Tony who provoked Chambers into the compromising situation."

I told him what Lettie Cumberland had told me.

"I've heard that rumor, yes. This town reeks of gossip."

"This may anger you but I have to say it. But you hesitate to hold Tony accountable because he can turn around and accuse you of unfairly seducing your subordinate's wife." And as he stared at me I told him what Caroline had seen at the maharajah's party, what I had seen at Narendra's, things, it was obvious, he hadn't heard about before.

"Tony may have had an affair with Narendra himself," I said. "Maybe he seduced Chambers too and then accused Chambers of an 'attempted' seduction—rejected, of course—and reported him to Belknap. Angelica made a pass at Caroline—and me, and Tony tried to seduce Caroline. I think they're both capable of anything."

Ahmed had made himself scarce and had left the bourbon bottle and an ice bucket on the coffee table and while I was talking Hud had poured himself still another drink he didn't need and was working on it diligently.

"Do you believe his Chinese plot theory now?" I asked.

"I don't know what to believe. But I do know there's no way to prove it wasn't so."

I was literally, physically nauseated, and the bourbon wasn't helping.

"Hud, take leave. Now. Emergency leave if you have to. Get out of here. Fly to the States and try to see Clarissa. Talk to someone on the grievance board. Someone who knows the ins and outs and can take an objective look at any case you might have and your chances of getting satisfaction." Even as I was saying it I knew it wouldn't work.

"Thank you, Charlie. I know you're trying to be as helpful as you can. Why I let Varina call you. I value your friendship. Maybe I *will* take some leave—at least go as far as Hong Kong for a week or so, to get my bearings. Now I'm half-drunk and had better try to sleep it off. Will you excuse me, Charlie? Give my love to Caroline."

It was three-thirty in the afternoon. In the state of mind I was in if I went back to the office I'd get nothing worthwhile accomplished. I told Mr. Brown to drive back without me, that I'd walk home from the residence and phone my secretary from there.

I didn't need convincing but as I walked to Moira Street I thought Hud's theory about Tony wouldn't hold up five minutes before any grievance board or court of law. And who else could he appeal to? I'd always believed he and the ambassador in Delhi had a high regard for each other, but the ambassador, a political appointee, was a self-made millionaire business executive in private life who took one ceremonial trip to Calcutta a year and had his own agenda for the entire country which might be summed up in one word—modernize. It seemed unlikely he'd fight a streamlining of the Calcutta consulate operation. Maybe we *were* overstaffed. Maybe it *was* a good idea to cut us down to size. It was what had been done to Hud that left me enraged and frustrated. But what could he do about it, or I? It was common knowledge that Angelica was misbehaving but that—per se—couldn't be held against Tony and in any case could easily be dismissed as unprovable—and unfounded—rumor. The same held for any innuendos concerning

Tony and Narendra. The Tony-Narendra-Thad Perry equation?
Hud, and Clarissa too, acknowledged their son was a homosexual.
Could that be blamed on Tony? It would never get off the ground.

Caroline was home and I told her everything.

"God, this does it!" she said. "I've had it with this kind of life!
We've got to get out of here."

"We'll be getting out in exactly thirty-seven days."

"Out of the post on home leave at the end of just another tour
is not what I'm talking about. The odds are they'll ask you to round-
trip but even if they don't where does that get us—to someplace like
Bombay where everything will just repeat itself?"

"I couldn't teach in a university without the necessary degrees,
you know that. Five years of study, minimum. At my age?"

"Other people have done it. Your pension fund could pay for
some of it and I can work."

"Caroline, be practical."

"All right, all right, in Washington there're all kinds of things
you're qualified to do, even if you don't go back into news. Congressional staff work."

"Burnoutsville for the under thirty-five crowd. And the pay is
too low."

"Congressional Research Service."

"Where you have to have a doctorate in something, so that
takes us back where we started from."

"Foundations, think tanks, PR firms, consulting . . ."

I didn't bother to reply and for the moment she had run out of
ideas. Anyway, the phone was ringing.

Caroline answered it. She listened a moment, then thrust the
phone at me with a look of horror as though it might be some loath-
some live thing she couldn't get unstuck from her fingers.

"Hud's *dead*!" she said, her voice rising piercingly, this abom-
inable revelation something she believed but could not accept.

Martin was on the other end.

Hud's dead, he repeated. Killed in a smashup with a Sikh taxi on Eden Gardens Road. In his own car. Driving his own car. Head-on collision. Gas tanks exploded. Terrible thing. Terrible, terrible thing.

I was hit with such grief and rage as I'd never felt before in my life. And then with guilt for having given Hud what I had thought might be ammunition against Tony—how Tony had led Thad into Narendra's spiderweb—but was really too much knowledge Hud didn't need to know.

"Does Tony know this yet?" I heard myself shouting into the phone.

"He's been informed."

"I've got to talk to you!" I said.

Everything Martin had told me I'd repeated aloud to Caroline as I was hearing it, and in tears she had flung herself on the living room couch. I went down to the Rover and drove to the consulate. Martin was in his office, just sitting there. He'd done all he could do, informed Delhi, Washington, who would inform Clarissa and Thad. What was left of the body was in the morgue, awaiting further disposition.

"He was drunk," I said. "He told me he was going to sleep it off but he changed his mind."

I told Martin everything. He knew the rumors about Angelica and General Singh and said he'd also heard hints about Tony and Narendra.

"Like it or not, and I don't," he said, "I'm acting CG now and God knows when they'll get a replacement out here. And the first thing is I am simply going to refuse to work at the same post with him. . . . Set that aside for a moment. This is going to be front page news in the Calcutta papers, of course, and I'm designated spokesman. Reporters are due an hour from now. I held them off until I could talk to you. Varina said you were the last person to see Hud.

"I'm not going to cover up," Martin went on. "I'm going to say the consul general had heard some deeply disturbing personal news, had been drinking, and tragically went for a drive. We'll make a generous settlement on the Sikh cabbie's family. All these details, of course, will blow up the story that much more. But Hud was very popular with the press. Maybe they'll avoid sensationalizing things."

"Will it be such a bad thing if they do?" I said. "Hud's beyond hurting and Clarissa and Thad will probably never read it or hear what people here say about it. I think the publicity will only help our case against Tony and Angelica."

"There's only one way to take a bull by the horns," Martin said, "and that's to do it before I lose my nerve." He picked up the phone. "Varina, please get me Mr. Belknap at his home number."

In Washington it was only 5:00 A.M. but when the call went through Martin didn't apologize.

"Henry, I won't mince words. It's come to light that there's a perception of Tony—and Angelica—among some of our oldest— and most loyal—contacts . . . detrimental . . . to U.S. interests. Hud knew about it. Others know. You might say it's public knowledge. If you need me to spell it out I'll put all this in writing but I think I can sum it up for you now: sexual indiscretion on a rather startling scale—involving our most important political contacts. Coming on top of Hud's death and the peculiar circumstances of that . . ."

Martin's face reddened perceptibly as he listened. His posture stiffened, challenged.

"It occurred to us, Henry," he said, measuring out his words, "that as country officer—and knowing Tony *so much better*—than the rest of us—you might possibly have some ideas how we might cope with what I consider—an untenable—situation. We know how the ambassador feels. He expects personnel problems to be handled at the appropriate level below him . . ."

". . . Yes, but I think what we're talking about here is damage *control,* Henry, not letting the situation get any *worse* than it is already. I'm thinking in terms of *immediate* action. I don't have the authority myself but I'm not prepared to overlook things or let them slide. With Hud's death, things have gone too far. If you'd rather I bring the DCM in on this I'll be guided by that decision and fly up to Delhi this evening. . . . Henry, I've got every reporter in town waiting in the outer office. If you could get back to me within the next hour . . ."

He listened again, still unsmiling, but his expression grew calmer. There weren't any reporters in the outer office. They weren't due for another forty-five minutes. The deputy chief of mission in Delhi, of far less humble origins than the ambassador, far more autocratic and ferociously ambitious, could be, would be, far more choleric over this than the ambassador himself, who had really struck me as quite a patient, kindly man on the two occasions I'd been in his presence.

". . . Well, thank you, Henry. I can appreciate how painful this must be for you but I really believe that's the wisest course. . . ." Martin put down the receiver.

"Fuck him," he said. "I'm too old to worry about making enemies." He picked up the phone again.

"Varina?" Then his voice abruptly became more gentle. "Now Varina, you have to try to pull yourself together. . . . I'll tell you what. Why don't you get Cindy to sit in for you and you take the rest of the day off. Tomorrow I'm going to need you more than ever and I'll need you on your feet, everybody's strong right arm. But before you go, please get on to the Pan Am office right away and book four seats on the New York flight day after tomorrow." He sighed. "The Greer family will be going back to Washington. They'll need that connecting flight too . . ."

Martin arranged a memorial service that was held late the following morning in the Anglican cathedral. With the conspicuous exception of the Greers, the entire American contingent and the entire local staffs were there except for skeleton crews left behind to answer phones in otherwise empty offices. A remarkable number of prominent Calcuttans and representatives of the consular corps filled the pews behind us. Afterwards, Caroline and Martin's wife went back to Moira Street and Martin and I drove to the Lancer's Club.

"What was his reaction? Did he put up a squawk?" I asked. This was the first time since he'd put in that second call to Belknap that I'd been alone with Martin.

"Total silence," Martin said. "Picked the tickets off my desk, turned on his heels and walked out."

Martin began on his second drink as we waited for lunch to be served.

"There's not going to be any immediate assignment for him," Martin said. "They'll stick him in Belknap's office to cool his heels, an albatross around Belknap's neck, a raven on his shoulder. Belknap may not be quite the prick Tony is but if you shake hands with him, count your fingers afterward. How long do you suppose it'll be before he cuts his losses to protect his own position?"

Tony Greer knew from Varina that Martin and I were lunching at the club. Tony and Angelica were evidently on the verandah when Martin and I left the dining room but the verandah was behind us and we didn't see them. Tony caught up with me in the courtyard after Martin had driven out.

"I have something to say to you," Greer said. Angelica watched us from the portico, Messalina, Lady MacBeth, the angel of death.

"I have nothing to say to you," I said.

"I'm going to call you as a sworn witness," Tony said. "I have a very good friend in Washington who earns six figures in his law practice. He's renowned for getting people like you indicted and destroyed. It's going to be so easy for him he may feel he can assign the case to a junior partner. But you're finished, McKay, washed up! You've been a washout all your life but now you don't have a prayer!"

Greer had acquired power in his career and knew how to use it as I never had. I had some of it, statutorily, and had to exercise it in the performance of my job, but I disliked administration and was never comfortable with it. Tony relished it and drew on his full reserves of it now as he leveled this threat with the sound of righteous anger and complete conviction. And he frightened me. Hit suddenly, unexpectedly, with such a threat, even the most innocent, at least for a few moments, search wildly for a breach in their defenses, full of doubt, weak and shaking from imagined vulnerability and fear of the power of authority. And I was not completely innocent. I had dealt, with Hud, with Martin, in rumor, gossip, conjecture. Hud had been ruined and now was dead and I believed enough of the web of suspicion Tony and Angelica had woven round themselves in full view of a number of people, and Martin believed it and Belknap had accepted it, and having once done that and made his decision would not back down. But the law is complex and full of hidden traps. I felt no true guilt and the panic passed but I continued to feel a residue of fear and would until Tony Greer was utterly defeated.

I started to walk away from him but he got in front of me.

"One other thing," he said. "I screwed Caroline. In *your* bed."

"Still the liar! You made a pass that missed!"

I knew suddenly that he had been bluffing a minute before or he would not have groped for some parting shot of malice to poison the atmosphere. "But you don't talk about my wife that way under any circumstances!"

I grabbed his shoulders and slammed him against a solid gate

post. Angelica screamed something. A British club member entering on foot at that moment said, "I say!" and put a restraining hand
on my shoulder.

"Piss off!" I told him, and he backed away.

"Still the fool!" Tony spat at me. "That was months ago!"

I've never hated anyone so much as at that moment, not because I believed it was true but because for a moment he had made
me wonder if it was.

"You'll never be up to it," I said, and with thumb and forefinger
twisted his pretty nose to the right until he let out a raucous little
shriek of pain.

Less than twenty-four hours later the Greers were gone. Then
Caroline and I had five weeks to wait before we flew back to Washington ourselves. We waited for something more than that, some
conclusion to this story, realizing we might be kept in suspense for
months. The fact was, as Martin learned, Tony walked State Department corridors for only three weeks, unassigned, before he resigned. But he'll land on his feet. People like him always do. Hadn't
he said he might consider going into politics? Whatever he does, in
or out of government, it behooves the rest of us to keep our eyes
open and watch our step.

As I remember all this and write it down I'm getting ready to
return to Calcutta—alone. One more two-year tour will complete
ten straight years overseas and then I'll be due for a three-year
Washington assignment. And then I'll have time to work out what
I'm going to do with the rest of my life. Caroline has landed a job
as a Washington correspondent for a newspaper chain. Meredith
and Richard are enrolled at the excellent Friends School in the District. We've taken out a mortgage on a house in the American University area. With two incomes coming in we'll be able to afford it.

It's not the best solution but it seems to me the only one immediately possible. I'm not due for Washington yet and no exceptions are granted except for medical reasons, which don't apply. All of us have passed the State Department physical exams: fully qualified for overseas duty. During the few weeks we've all had in Washington for my routine consultations, when we weren't making the expected, required home leave visits to Caroline's parents in Connecticut and mine in Illinois, I have looked for but have not found any nongovernment job that interests me remotely. I know Caroline thinks I haven't looked hard enough. So be it. I don't want to leave my family, but put it another way: I don't want them to leave me. I simply need to go back, if for no other reason than that we need the money. I have to continue getting paid. And I want to go back. I want to be able to finish that travel book about India. That's what I really want to do.

THE
EIGHTH
CONTINENT

1

Porters at the entrance to the pier had swooped down to carry off luggage, leaving me to wonder if I'd ever see it again—were any of them wearing official badges?—and now the line of passengers, if it could be called a line at all, was scarcely moving and the heat was not to be borne.

The pier had been jammed with people all along and chaos reigned. Crowds pressed forward from the rear entrance to dock-side, some clots of people were close to being out of control, and the threat of some weaker person falling and being trampled was distinctly real. The woman with the two small children immediately ahead of me looked ready to faint from exhaustion or the humidity.

It was at that moment the white-haired older man and the young man with him hurried up alongside the line to the left, el-bowing aside steerage passengers, porters, anyone in their path, and did not stop until they'd reached the fence beside the entrance gate.

"Did you *see* that? I don't believe it!" the woman ahead gasped in some Commonwealth accent.

I was simply speechless with rage. What made his behavior somewhat worse was that I recognized the older man.

The line surged forward briefly. The woman, her children, and I almost toppled over. The gate had been opened. The white-haired man and his companion had timed their move, their assault, to coincide with the opening of the gate and had successfully managed to push in brutally ahead of everyone else. I couldn't actually see this outrage at its moment of execution but the clear evidence of it was plain enough when I caught sight of the pair at the top of the gangplank, stepping on board. Raging and suffering through the same procedure, helping the woman ahead of me by carrying one of the children, we squeezed past the gate and left the worst of the crowd behind. By the time we had made it to the deck the line-crashers had disappeared.

"Thank you, you've been so kind—I don't know what I'd have done without your help," the woman said. "I'm Penny Graves."

I acknowledged her name and gratitude with mine, "Charlie McKay," and a nod, and headed for one of the Lascar stewards standing below hanging placards and a range of cabin numbers that included my own.

The S.S. *Nairobi* sailed at seven in the evening and it was a good five hours before the Bombay heat was finally behind us. Stripped to my underwear, I lay sweating on my bunk reading *The Road to Oxiana,* sipping occasionally from the third bottle of beer the steward had brought me. I had eaten a very early dinner at the Taj Mahal Hotel in order to avoid the steamy dining saloon aboard ship where the punkah fans the first evening out would be no more effective than the fan in my cabin, stirring the sluggish September air, air that never, the year round, held a breath of coolness in it.

The air finally fresh enough at almost midnight, I dressed in shorts, tied the laces on tennis shoes over sockless feet and made my way through empty corridors and up one flight to an open deck. I had not had to steady myself by holding on to any corridor railing. The Indian Ocean was smooth as a millpond. The ship seemed to cleave through the water almost without creating a furrow, leaving scarcely a wake behind. A full moon was out, stars were profuse. I could see far out to a faint horizon across what seemed a refreshing immensity of space. There was little wind, but the ship's motion created the breeze I showered in for ten minutes or so before turning in. I slept well, dreamlessly.

From designated hardship posts like Calcutta, foreign service officers and staff personnel were required to take Rest and Rehabilitation leave once every two-year tour, the transportation, less the first hundred dollars, paid for by the government, all other expenses to be borne by the officer for himself and his family. If one had a family. I had one, a wife and two children, but they were in Washington. My wife had resumed a suspended profession to become a newspaper correspondent on Capitol Hill, and had recently signed a contract to appear once weekly as a TV panelist. Thus she was absolutely unable to accompany me on my latest assignment as a government public affairs officer. This was only one rather extreme example of the rebellion of American diplomatic wives that had begun in—well, no studies I was aware of had been done on the subject, but it seemed to have gotten under way sometime around the mid-1960s. Bolder and more discontented wives had begun vocally and in writing to resent a number of things, but their grievances might be boiled down to one concept: They were fed up with providing the diplomatic service with two professionals for the price of one. Wives not only had to cohost their husband's representational gatherings, sometimes several times weekly—doing most of the planning, ordering, and supervising of servants themselves—but had to accompany their spouses to work parties given by others.

They were bossed by the senior officer's wife. They were officially rated along with their husbands. And for all of which they were paid not one extra nickel. Thus some, like Caroline McKay, were saying the hell with it. So for a year now I had lived alone, not quite halfway around the world from my wife of ten years and my children, aged eight and seven. It had not been a good idea. We had both been wrong, Caroline and I, and both of us admitted it, me saying I should have resigned from the foreign service to take any kind of job in Washington until I could line up something that suited me, Caroline regretting she and the kids hadn't come back to the post with me for one last two-year tour before a Washington assignment. Of course our individual regrets canceled each other out and in any case came too late. We were too committed at both ends and stuck with our decision—for another long year.

R and R to the States was not authorized. I could pay for it myself but Caroline and I both agreed, reluctantly, that we could not afford it, not with substantial mortgage payments to make on our house in Washington, and with Meredith and Richard in an expensive private school. A rendezvous in Europe would be prohibitively expensive, too.

We had all taken R and R in Hong Kong two years earlier. This time I planned to go to Penang, where I'd never been. But at a reception at the Raj Bhavan I mentioned this trip to the Maharajah of Chittipore, who convinced me I'd regret it.

"Overrated," he said. "Not enough different from Calcutta. You'd be disappointed, Mr. McKay. Take my word for it. Go to Seychelles! No comparison. The ideal place for a holiday. The Garden of Eden! And a sea voyage in the bargain."

I'd considered the Seychelles too. Departed colleagues had raved about the place. So had others recommended Penang, which also sounded livelier, and being alone. . . . I was puzzled why the maharajah was down on the place but I supposed he had his reasons.

And so I changed my mind and booked passage to those granite islands in a coral sea, nine hundred and some miles east of the Kenya coast of Africa, four hundred miles north of Madagascar.

Going there had to mean taking almost a month off, adding two weeks of annual leave to the prescribed fortnight of R and R. The only way to get there was by ship—from Bombay or Karachi. The ship, the same ship, after depositing a passenger at the end of a five-day voyage from Bombay, for example, proceeded on to Mombassa, Zanzibar, Dar Es Salaam, and Durban, from whence it returned, calling at the same ports, twelve days later en route back to the subcontinent.

There were not so many first class passengers that I could not have a table in the dining room to myself. Waking early, extraordinarily hungry, not having eaten in almost fifteen hours, I was one of the first in to breakfast. Feeling rested, clean, cool, comfortable, my hunger soon enough appeased, I poured myself another cup of coffee and looked at the sunshine through a range of windows—blocked partially for a moment by the figures of the line-crashers of the evening before—that unholy pair—who were seated by a steward at a table directly in my line of vision not fifteen feet away.

Old anger rose quickly in my chest and just as quickly gave way to intense interest.

The maharajah's friend. No, I couldn't say that fairly. I had seen him with the maharajah only once, two years before at the latter's sarod concert. At Hud Perry's party for Jenny Trevilians later on, the maharajah had been upset with the man for being with A. K. Ghosh. Tony Greer had brought both of them. Tony Greer's friend then, or A. K. Ghosh's, and both were scum. I held Greer responsible for Hud's ruin and death, and Ghosh was believed reliably to be a trafficker in drugs. Fine friends. I could hear his European accent. Not German I didn't think, nor Dutch, clearly neither French nor Spanish nor Italian, not Slavic. Something else.

The younger man was considerably younger, by twenty-five

years at least, possibly thirty. French was the first nationality that occurred to me, but who knows?—Spanish, Catalan, Corsican, Italian, Lebanese, or any combination of ethnic stock from around the entire rim of the Mediterranean. Trim, tanned, muscular arms in a red-and-white-striped short-sleeved sailor's jersey, a shirt that suggested a boutique rather than a ship chandler's. Dark hair trimmed and brushed neatly into a pompadour. An unlikely pair—or all too likely, though if I'd seen them separately I would not have singled them out as homosexual.

I glanced briefly at my coffee cup before raising it off its saucer again, glanced back and for a few moments met the eyes of the older man.

A killer's eyes, utterly ruthless, utterly merciless. And powerfully, physically chilling. The flesh crawled across my neck. I looked away, rejecting the challenge to outstare the bastard and at the same time, I told myself, in order to mask my conviction. And a conviction it was, though I myself had been known to say it was not really possible, without prior knowledge, to read such a thing in a person's face. Yet there is a power in intuition and there needn't be anything supernatural about it. We flip the switch on wireless radios the size of cigarette packages and have long since ceased to marvel when we hear voices reaching our ears from miles, even thousands of miles away. Why couldn't it be possible for the complex human brain to transmit messages, reveal thoughts, over shorter distances?

In any case, what court was there, what authority, on this ship or anywhere else to rob me of my conviction, of entertaining it and speculating on it if I wished? After all, there was more than the look of the man and more than intuition to go on. There were the dates of recent history. Recent enough. What had this man of about sixty been doing a quarter century earlier? With that accent, where? If he had not killed anyone personally, even as a soldier, whose death had he ordered? Supervised? And why was he now aboard a ship whose eventual destination was South Africa?

But if thoughts could be read, I suddenly became aware, then *mine* too were open to possible transmission and scrutiny. And mind-reading aside, anyone who stares, hangs around, is open to suspicion. Although it had been long before, and in crowds, we'd been present at three of the same gatherings. If I recognized him I had better assume he recognized me. I drained my coffee and left, quickly, without a backward glance.

The ship ploughed on across a glassy sea. The S.S. *Nairobi* was neither a large vessel nor a cruise ship and so had few distractions—dining room, lounge, bar, a minute library, and that was about it. No swimming pool. Bingo in the evening, which I had every intention of avoiding religiously. Plenty of fresh air, of course, and more than enough deck chairs to lounge in. Decks to walk on. The captain's cocktail reception that evening. An invitation in a square white envelope was on my bunkside table when I returned from breakfast.

I spent the day in my cabin, on deck, and at lunch finishing Robert Byron's travel odyssey to the ruins of Persia. I had other books of the same nature by Pritchett, Durrell, and Leigh Fermor—the British had a near monopoly on the genre, which I thought needed a friendly challenge in the form of greater American input, my own for example; in my spare time I had almost completed a full-length impressionistic account of my travels to odd corners of India. The remembered satisfaction from this continuing effort fused to the pleasure of present reading put me into a mood of rare contentment, to be savored while it lasted. Every so often, though, I found myself lowering my book to glance at my fellow passengers.

I lunched late and whoever he was and his boyfriend were not at their table. The other diners seemed to be white Commonwealth types mostly, plus one turbaned Sikh in white duck trousers and a white bush shirt, his wife sari-draped, and a stocky, jovial-looking Seychelleois of obviously mixed ancestry, including Chinese, his attractive wife who looked perhaps Egyptian, and their two pretty little girls. Mrs. Graves, the woman I had helped board the ship, chatted with them from an adjoining table, her boy and girl having already made friends with the Seychelleois children. One look at these kids and I missed my own, acutely. Another long year before I'd see them again, see how they'd changed. They were nice kids—I had Caroline more than myself to thank for that—but independent-minded, their own selves. Meredith was going to be pretty like her mother. Already she was a great reader. Richard was full of curiosity about the world around him.

The other Commonwealth types seemed all elderly or well into middle age, with the exception of a rather striking-looking girl in her twenties who sat with a severe-looking older couple.

In midafternoon, I saw the white-haired man and his companion strolling about fifty feet ahead in the same direction. I paused at the rail, pretending to look for dolphins or whales, and waited until the pair had almost reached the barrier at the stern end of the ship, where they would be forced to reverse direction. Just before they turned, I walked forward again briskly as though that was the pace I had been maintaining all along. The turn made, the gap closed quickly. The white-haired man looked at his companion, not straight ahead, not directly at me, and after allowing myself one long searching look, I averted my eyes too, and then we were passing each other. I was conscious of being a couple of inches shorter than the older man, the same height as his young friend.

And I could scarcely believe my ears. I heard the older man say clearly and viciously, in accented English, "Stupid Americans!"

My face flamed. I could feel the heat. I spun around and watched my enemy striding arrogantly, unconcernedly, contemptuously away from me, not looking back.

"Oh, yes," said the purser, consulting his manifest. "I think you mean Mr. Peterson and Mr. Pontalba."

"I thought I'd recognized him!" I said. "Thank you for your trouble." I left the purser's office quickly then, berating myself for my timid, half-hearted measures. *You'd make a rotten investigator. First name! Citizenship! Destination! Why the hell didn't you have nerve enough to ask? Guilt, that's why. Unsure of yourself. The man may be obnoxious but for all you really know not guilty of any crime at all.*

I did not dress (necktie, jacket) for the captain's cocktail party with any expectation of enjoying myself. Routine, perfunctory, British India Steam Navigation Company public relations of course, no more. Nothing wrong with that, but nothing very exciting either. Of my fellow passengers I'd seen so far, only Peterson and Pontalba engaged my interest—possibly that good-looking girl (if she's actually that up close), though clearly way too young, not to mention chaperoned. Still, you never knew. Someone might prove to be interesting, someone I hadn't yet seen. Curiosity sustained me as I put a part in my hair in front of the cabin mirror, propelled me down and around corridors to the lounge.

I was neither early nor the last to arrive.

A quick glance around. Peterson and Pontalba not there. Tall young girl—young woman—and the older pair talking to the captain, the Sikhs, a third couple. Two other uniformed officers stationed widely apart from the captain and each other, the focal points of other groups. Same people I'd seen in the dining room and on deck. I took a scotch and water from a steward's tray and moved toward the group containing Penny Graves. Widowed, divorced, simply traveling alone for whatever reason, she was not my type, but pleasant enough and no doubt easier to talk to than some of the others would be.

"Managed to find someone to watch the kids?" I asked.

"Oh, the Mintos, the family from the Seychelles, have their own ayah with them who's keeping an eye on all four children while they play. A perfect godsend. Mr. McKay, I'd like you to meet . . ."

Brewster? Baxter? Bixby? Dixon? Hastings? Two too many names there, since there were only three other couples besides Mrs. Graves and the chief engineer, whose name was Da Souza, and maybe I had misheard all of them, but no matter, they were interchangeable and quite forgettable, wherever they were from—Britain, Rhodesia, South Africa, Australia—I'd definitely heard Australia mentioned. In my work, I had attended so many affairs of this kind in so many countries that I believed I was an expert at sizing up people quickly. You make a few pleasantries, listen a bit, sometimes more than a bit if it's awkward getting away, and nine times out of ten that's all it takes to determine that only one person in fifty—a generous estimate—is anyone you'd care to meet a second time. If no shared interests or experiences or ideas are revealed within the first few minutes—if indeed the very opposite is evident—move on. Life is too short to dally here. Better to be alone if that's the only other choice.

"Everyone seems to be here except our friends the gate-crashers," I said, to make conversation with Penny Graves.

"No, one other, the poor man," Penny Graves said. "Ill in his cabin and not just seasick apparently. The purser thinks he may be going home to die."

"Not a pleasant thought," I said, then slipped to one side, murmuring ". . . freshen this up" and first looked around again for Peterson. Not a sign of him and the party half over at least. I felt certain Peterson and Pontalba had been invited—but had chosen to snub or boycott the affair. *So he despises all of us.* I was not surprised. But I could easily imagine him striding into the lounge followed by armed men, a riding crop in one hand and death in his eyes.

I moved toward the other side of the room.

The girl had detached herself from the older pair, who were still conversing with the captain, and had moved into the group around the third officer, a sunburned redhead, balding. But before I had reached this cluster of people the girl had turned away, rather indecisively, looking footloose, bored—and really quite pretty. Conscious that though she might well snub me, too, I was also aware I had absolutely no competition.

I smiled, not too eagerly I hoped.

"Hello. I'm Charlie McKay."

Her response was immediately gratifying, rather surprisingly so in fact—the bright, rapt expression, the hand extended to shake mine.

"Nicola Montaldo. You may call me Nicky."

Very little accent. Really only her phrasing said not American—probably not Canadian either.

Before I could call her Nicky or say anything at all she said, "Tell me about yourself. You're American, I saw that at once. I like Americans. Some people don't, but I do."

"Well, you see you already know all about me so why don't you tell me about yourself instead."

"No, that's not fair. I asked first. I'm twenty-three. How old are you? Let me guess. Thirty . . . thirty. . . . No, you tell me."

"Forty," I said, resisting the temptation to lower the truth by a couple of years.

She clapped her hands once.

"I was *very* close. What do you do?"

"Work at the American consulate in Calcutta. Taking a vacation in the Seychelles. Where—"

"Where is your wife? You must have a wife somewhere. You like girls, I can tell."

"I do and I do, you're absolutely right. She's in Washington. You see, she has a very good job there she didn't want to leave."

"Do you miss her?"

"I try not to think about it."

"Do you like *me?*"

I was really quite startled.

"Well, of course." What else was I to say?

"Then meet me on the upper deck at eleven tonight. Promise?"

Her eyes shifted suddenly from looking directly into mine to looking over my right shoulder.

"Beth."

I turned to see the severe-looking older couple.

"Mr. McKay," the girl said, "may I present Mr. and Mrs. Hugo DeWitt."

I said, "Good evening," and raised my right hand, but seeing no hands lifted to shake mine—only cold nods—slowly lowered it.

"We are leaving now," said Mrs. DeWitt.

"Oh, very well," the girl said, and walked away with them out of the lounge. Soon afterward, I left too.

Beth?

In my cabin, I put film in my Nikon but inside one jacket pocket the camera made too noticeable a bulge and pulled the lightweight seersucker out of alignment. And I wasn't going to reveal it slung around my neck with a strap. No. No need to be precipitous. Wait. Telephoto lens from a safe distance in daylight. I returned the camera to its case.

Peterson and the young man and the girl of several names and the DeWitts were at their tables when I came in to dinner and behind my book I studiously avoided looking at any of them. I did not know if I myself was the object of any sort of attention. The food, I had discovered at lunch, this confirmed now at dinner, was going to be English "continental" and relentlessly dull—pallid clear soup, some unidentifiable meat in gravy, squash—what the English called vegetable marrow—certainly nothing to savor and linger over. I might have had some wine but decided to save that until later in the evening. Pudding was brought. I ate half of it and left.

At ten I went to the bar with my book. Two Commonwealth couples sitting together at a table were the only customers. Half bottles of Bordeaux were available and one was uncorked at my table. I sipped slowly, read, and let the time go by. Should I keep the rendezvous with the strange, possibly batty girl with the two names? I hadn't promised to. We'd been interrupted before I could answer her question. I wasn't sure what I would have said had there been time. But no harm in simply flirting with her a little, was there? At ten to eleven I went out on deck, climbed the forward stairs, saw no one. Higher still, two figures moved about behind the lighted glass panels of the helmsman's bridge.

And waited until half past eleven. Stood up! Unless the DeWitts were responsible for her failure to appear. Feeling rather foolish, regretful, and also rather relieved to tell the truth, I went back to my cabin. Who would believe I'd been faithful to Caroline for one year already, but that too was the truth, and virtue, or more accurately, simply no guilt, would still have to be its own reward.

2

I was on the upper deck at 8:00 A.M., having breakfasted even earlier than the previous morning, and quickly, before Peterson and company had put in an appearance. There were a few lounge chairs on the upper level and in one of them I left two books and my camera case.

Telephoto zoom lens snapped onto my camera, I explored the upper deck around its horseshoe loop, scanning the ocean for signs of porpoises or whales, and what of the lower deck could be seen from my vantage point, either with the naked eye or through the viewfinder of the Nikon. All these preparations took only a few minutes. I returned camera and lens to their carrying case and put the case beside my chair, relatively out of sight. I descended the stairs and began striding quickly in the manner of a man taking a constitutional. I passed two couples, a single woman, a ship's officer, smiled and nodded at them all. I crossed through the lounge to the identical starboard deck, climbed the forward stairs on that side, walked around to my commandeered chair and found everything as I had left it.

There was only one good possibility, doubled. From the heads of the port and starboard staircases on the upper deck I could see only a few yards along the roofed promenade decks below. Standing halfway down the stairs extended the range but not to the full length of the decks. Risky or not, I'd have to descend to the level of my quarry, almost all the way down, to get a shot at him at all from any distance.

Could Penny Graves or Nicky/Beth help? As a decoy model? As photographer?

The first decision was made for me seconds later.

I was two steps above the portside promenade deck when Peterson, alone, emerged from the lounge and began walking forward. I had him in the viewfinder head-on, snapped the shutter twice, swung the lens seaward.

My heart beating rapidly, I climbed to the open deck, half expecting Peterson to come bounding up the stairs after me to try to throw the Nikon and perhaps me as well over the railing, even though his eyes had been focused out to sea. But Peterson did not appear, and I settled myself slowly into my deck chair. It was only a little past nine. Satisfied with the first action I had taken, I sat for a while until my breathing returned to normal, then read until ten, having to read some paragraphs twice, even three times, when my mind wandered away from the page to the perceived menace and malevolence of the man named Peterson.

At ten, I was emboldened to hunt for him again. I found him, with Pontalba this time, the pair of them stretched out in deck chairs, halfway along the port side of the promenade deck. Peterson's eyes were closed; Pontalba, eyes open but his face a blank, looked at nothing. It infused me with a certain measure of strength and confidence to realize that Peterson, for the duration of the voyage, was subject to the same constraints as any other first class passenger. There was no real scope for him to lord it over everyone else by being able to lead some kind of special, more luxurious existence.

Standing at the foot of the forward stairs I zeroed in on both reclining faces in profile, snapped off a half dozen shots.

"Whatever are you doing?"

Startled, I swung sixty degrees to the right, camera down, to look up into "Nicky Montaldo's" smiling face.

"Oh, good morning!" I said.

"Whose picture were you taking?"

"Didn't you see the porpoise out there?"

"Charles, you were pointing your camera straight down the deck at that nasty-looking old man."

I grabbed her hand. "Come on upstairs where we can have some privacy."

She was in slacks and a blue striped jersey, espadrilles.

No one had beaten us to it. Beside the deck chair I'd claimed there were five others, all empty. But Nicky didn't sit right away. She stood, hands at her sides, as though she might be on the carpet in the headmistress's office.

"You're going to ask why I wasn't where I said I'd be," she said. "It's because they keep me a virtual prisoner!"

I hadn't been about to ask her that but I said, "Oh, I'm sorry to hear it. But here you are, free again. Now, first things first. You called yourself Nicola—Nicky; the DeWitts called you Beth."

"I act. Nicky is a stage name and I prefer it."

"All right. Then who are the DeWitts? Your parents?"

"Of course not! Those two? They're my aunt and uncle. Not even that, really. I call them that because they like it, but they're really only friends of my late parents. My parents were killed in an auto accident in Italy."

She had pronounced "aunt" with a broad A.

"Where do you live? Where are you going?"

"You haven't told me near enough about yourself, and you promised."

We settled back in our deck chairs and I watched her curl towards me, speaking in a voice just above a whisper.

"Who is he, that man whose picture you were taking? A Russian, isn't he? And you're really with the CIA, aren't you? It's all right. I don't mind and I won't give you away."

"No, not true. Absolutely not true at all. I am what I say I am—a plain, everyday, garden variety public affairs officer. I concern myself with information about United States politics and culture, foreign policy, not Russian spies. But if I answer your question truthfully, will you still promise not to give me away?"

"Cross my heart."

"You have to promise me something else—to tell me more about yourself."

"I promise."

"All right, first of all, no, I don't think the nasty old man is a Russian but I really don't know what his nationality is. His name is Peterson, the purser told me that. That sounds Scandinavian but for some reason, some look about him, I don't think he is. I'd very much like to find out. Have you seen him up close?"

"Yes. He frightens me."

Excited and alert, I said, "He really does? Why?"

"He reminds me of someone who was very mean and cruel to me."

"Who was that?"

"Someone I don't want to think about."

She put her hands over her ears for a moment, took them away.

"I don't know when you came aboard," I said, "but just before I did, Peterson and that young man he's traveling with—whose name—last name—is Pontalba—both of them pushed in at the head of the line just as the gate opened. A very arrogant, unfair, antisocial, infuriating way to behave. They aroused my anger and my interest. Then I got a close look at Peterson and I've never seen a crueler face. He looked at me as though he could kill me—kill any of us—without batting an eye. Then in my hearing—deliberately, I'm sure—he made an insulting remark about Americans. He's the right age to have been a Nazi or to have worked for the Nazis in some country. This is all conjecture of course. Pure guesswork. But if he *is* a Nazi and has managed to escape prosecution up till now I'd like to nail him if I can. I've served in Israel. I've read a lot of books, documents, seen a lot of photographs. It's a subject that's never far from my mind. You saw me take his picture—I hope he didn't—I'm sure he didn't: his eyes were closed when I snapped the shutter. There are organizations that hunt for Nazis who got away. If I can do nothing else I'm going to send one of these groups at least one good photograph of him. They can compare it to hundreds, probably thousands of others, and take it from there. But I'd like to do better than that—at least find out his first name, what kind of passport he's carrying, where he's been recently, where he's going. As much as I can about Pontalba too."

Nicky smiled secretly. "Perhaps I can get to know *him.*"

"I have a feeling he doesn't care much for girls," I said.

"He's bi," Nicky said with an air of great knowledge and experience. "I've known boys like him in Cannes."

I was about to protest that she couldn't possibly know this when I remembered my own intuitive conviction about Peterson.

"Forget anything like that," I warned her. "If I'm right about Peterson, people like him are dangerous no matter where they are or in what circumstances—out of power, unarmed."

"When were you on the Riviera?" I asked, and got no reply.

"Nicky?"

"Yes?"

"When were you in Cannes?"

"Oh, why does it matter . . . summers ago . . ." Eyes open suddenly and grinning at me she said, "Charles, let's explore. I want you to take my picture. I want to take yours. When you develop the film, who knows what you might find in the background."

"I may have enough for one day," I said.

"But the camera lies, you know that. A good photographer needs to take a hundred shots to get one good likeness."

"Where are the DeWitts?"

"Playing bridge in the lounge with a dreary couple from Australia. Everything bores them, except bridge."

Avoiding only the lounge, we explored the outer passageways of the ship but did not run across Peterson or Pontalba anywhere.

"They're afraid of us," Nicky said.

"Hardly."

"Hiding in their cabins."

"Maybe they're playing bridge too."

"We'll find them eventually. They won't be able to escape us."

We parted. It was almost time for lunch.

Again, I brought a book to the dining salon but did not hide behind it quite so much. I saw Nicky with the DeWitts but she was seated with her back to me. I chanced a glance at Peterson's table and saw him eating heartily while he spoke in a low voice to Pontalba. Peterson wore a blue short-sleeved shirt open at the collar. The tan on his face and arms seemed a deeper hue. Now I noticed a plain gold ring on Peterson's right hand, a wristwatch on his left arm with an elastic metal strap. Sockless feet below the table were in blue canvas loafers. Pontalba was similarly outfitted in pink. Once, Peterson looked up, met my glance casually, looked back at his companion as though my presence had either not registered or had been put immediately out of mind. The normality, the ordinariness of this daylight shipboard scene set up a wave of doubt that crossed my consciousness from brain to gut, where it left a sensation of unrest. I did not consider myself a man with a notably suspicious nature or a busybody. If anything, there had been occasions during my career when I had been too trusting and had suffered for it. It seemed to me I was naturally inclined to give everyone the benefit of the doubt. What if Peterson was simply—and weren't the odds ten to one or better this was the case?—innocent of any major crime, or any crime at all except rudeness? What right did anyone really have to probe into his personal life, to hound him in any way?

Troubled, my conviction shaken for the first time, feeling something of a fool, I left the dining room quickly, went out on deck and paced along the rail, unsoothed by the balmy air, the monotony of the sea. Now everything came up in my mind quickly, accusingly, for review, and I was not the judge but the judged—and was found wanting, a failure in some respects some might say, lacking great success in others, damned with faint praise. I had a job, a career, and if I was very careful, made no more mistakes, kept my nose to the grindstone and had a reasonable amount of luck, I would be able to hang on to it until a pensioned retirement—at the minimum, ten years down the line. But it was no sinecure. I was subject to selection-out for staying too many years in the same grade, for being low-ranked two years in a row. So far I had not been low-ranked even once (a barbarous procedure, really; a certain percentage, no matter how competently they may have performed, had to be ritually stoned every year). But I had reached a grade level considered a great plateau crowded with too many other officers competing for too few spaces that opened up every year in the bottleneck leading to the next higher grade. I was never going to set the world on fire and I knew why—because I did not really want to. I lacked that kind of ambition. And I could never admit this to anyone. I had always, constantly, to feign ambition.

With Caroline beside me it had been easier. Attractive, vivacious, bright—academically, she was even better educated than I was; neither did she lack for common sense—she gave me many reasons to be proud of her and in public she drew out the best in me. There were times, at the end of what had seemed most successful work parties at which my immediate supervisor and the chief of mission had been present to take note, when it had almost seemed to me in my sense of satisfaction that I was truly ambitious after all. No, Caroline had built me up, not put me down. I was not brilliant but I was methodical. Though it was not expected of me, in time, at every post, I came to know as much about the country and the city and what was really going on there as any of the more glamorous political officers. I was as good a linguist as most and better than some. But my true, my deep, abiding interests lay outside my work, and without Caroline with me my work had suffered this past year. I had made mistakes, screwed up. My agency deputy director, out from Washington, had paid a three-day visit to the post and later complained, in writing, about the schedule I had laid on for him: "Unimaginative use of my time" were the words employed. Foolishly believing the country PAO in Delhi to be a sympathetic fellow, I had earlier mentioned the travel book I was writing on the side and in a letter the man in Delhi had cited that as one possible reason—an unnecessary distraction from duty—why the deputy director's Calcutta agenda had been less than satisfactory. Even now, my annual evaluation was being written to be sent to the selection board. And here I was more than likely chasing a wild goose across the Indian Ocean.

I slumped into a deck chair, closed my eyes, tried to empty my mind, dozed off, and woke with a start.

"Mr. McKay?"

An Indian deck steward was standing before me holding a folded piece of stationery.

"Message for you, Sah."

Hand-written and signed "Nicky" it said, "Charles, come to my cabin, #28. I have a little surprise for you."

I heard her respond to my knock: "It's not locked." I opened the door. She reclined on her bunk in shorts and a pullover and faced me just to the left of the door, her knees drawn up and feet together slightly to one side. Held between thumb and forefinger of her left hand, she was slowly waving a passport like a lure, back and forth.

"Peterson's," she said, smiling, immeasurably pleased with herself.

"Are you crazy?" I said.

She sat up suddenly and flung the passport at me.

"Get out!"

"What I mean to say is you've taken a big risk!"

"I never want to speak to you again!"

"Wait. Please! I'm simply amazed, that's all. Worried about you doing such a dangerous thing! And full of admiration! How did you get it?"

She giggled. "It was easy. The cabin steward keeps a duplicate set of keys."

"But his office isn't much bigger than a closet. If he was in there how could—"

"He wasn't there."

"But he must keep it locked when he's away."

"One has to know how to go about these things, Charles."

"How did you know the cabin number?"

"You ask so many silly questions. I followed them after lunch. All our cabins are quite close together after all."

"But do you know where they are now?"

"Playing ping pong."

"Ping pong!"

"You know. TOK TOK TOK," and she made more hollow clicking sounds with the top of her tongue against the roof of her mouth. "Now look at it and see what it is you need to know and then perhaps I'd best put it back." She slipped into espadrilles.

The passport had fallen to the cabin floor. Heart pounding, I bent over and nervously retrieved it.

Sverige. The Kingdom of Sweden. Arvid Peterson. Born in Göteborg, April 23, 1906. Businessman. Visas issued by Saudi Arabia, Qatar, the U.A.R. Immigration stamps from a scattering of countries in the Mideast and from India, Nepal, Burma. Some dates were blurred. At least once he'd entered India at Calcutta but the date was smudged. I wasn't able to determine where he had been most recently before India. All the visas had expired at least three years earlier.

"Here," I said with a dry mouth. "You're a wonder-worker. Now for God's sake hurry and get it back safely."

She plucked the passport out of my hand with a cocky little flourish, raised her eyebrows and said, "Wait for me here."

"No," I said, disappointed and frightened. "I'm not feeling well," and went out to the corridor with her. I was an accessory to this theft. If Peterson discovered it, linked me to it, the man would raise holy hell, probably succeed in getting me arrested by British authorities in the Seychelles, reported to U.S. authorities in Bombay, Calcutta. The affair might easily get into the news. I'd be dismissed for cause! And for what? A native of *Sweden*. False identity? What chance would I have of proving that?

I went to my cabin, left the door open, and sat on the bunk. A few minutes later she appeared in the doorway.

"Everything shipshape, Captain," she said, and started to enter.

"I really need some fresh air," I said, and she backed out far enough to let me exit, looking exasperated, and we went up to the open deck together.

3

We reclined side by side on the upper deck, stretched into the sun, borne southwest at a steady fifteen knots an hour.

"I was sent to school in Switzerland," Nicky said, eyes closed. "I hated it. I was the only girl from South Africa and made to feel some kind of freak. Why wasn't I black? Of course most of them knew better, but some were really incredibly stupid. My only friend was a Malaysian girl. I ran away once and got as far as Geneva before they hauled me back. I swallowed an entire bottle of aspirin but they pumped out my stomach and all I did was sleep for two days. Finally I was out of there and allowed to go to acting school in London. I loved it. I was on my own. Oh, I lived in a kind of theatrical boarding house and there were supposed to be rules and all that so mummies and daddies wouldn't fret, curfews and so on, but we did pretty much as we pleased and had a smashing time. Got to perform in some Shakespeare and modern plays—*As You Like It,* Pirandello, that sort of thing. Then I took a holiday on the Riviera and that started all the trouble."

She lit a cigarette, got up, and walked over to the railing, turned her back to it—stage business she'd seen in some movie, I thought.

"I met this prince from Muscat. He had tons of money of course, a Rolls, and swept me off my feet. I was sure I was in love with him and he said he wanted to marry me. I wrote to my parents and of course they were fit to be tied. A Muslim! Worse than that, a person of color! You can imagine. The fact he was of royal blood meant nothing to them. He might have been a Zulu for all they cared. They flew up at great expense, as they never ceased pointing out, and begged me to reconsider. I agreed to take a trip to Italy with them to think it over. The third day there we took a spin in a convertible Daddy had rented. Mountain road near Siena. I was driving. There was a collision and I was thrown clear. The car . . . fell two hundred feet. I blamed myself but there was nothing to be done. . . . I went back to France and married the prince in the town hall at Cannes. We'd have a Muslim ceremony later, he said, and we flew to Muscat. I'd been a complete fool not to realize he'd have other wives. It was horrible! I was a virtual prisoner. The other wives were spiteful and most of the time—when he wasn't having his way with me—my Prince Charming ignored me. I thought I'd go mad. Finally I was able to bribe a servant to take me into the capital to the British legation where I could contact the DeWitts. They came and took me to India for a rest. We spent the summer months in Kathmandu and Darjeeling, and here we are now going back. But there's nothing in South Africa for me, Charles. I hardly know anyone."

I didn't know if I could believe a quarter of it or any of it at all. I thought of a number of questions I might ask, but was afraid they might simply trip her up and then she'd be furious with me. She was wild, irresponsible, probably a liar, possibly psychiatrically disturbed, nothing but trouble.

"I wouldn't know how to advise you," I said lamely. "But you're young, pretty, intelligent. You'll make friends overnight."

Nothing I had said pleased her.

"I'm going to shower and nap in my cabin," she said, and hurried down the stairs.

Halfway through a page of my book something that had been chafing at the edge of my consciousness swam into view. I was pretty certain Arvid wasn't Swedish but a Latvian name.

I went into the bar at six, ordered half a bottle of red wine, then asked the steward, "Do you suppose it'd be possible to get some sort of sandwich in here in lieu of dinner? Not much of an appetite this evening."

The bar steward looked dubious.

"Not the usual thing, Sah. I will enquire."

The chief steward came out.

"Are you ill, sir?"

"No, no, not ill, just not terribly hungry."

"Only in your cabin would it be possible, sir."

"All right. Whatever you say."

I had to wait a long time for it and then it was a pretty dreadful sandwich, some kind of processed tinned meat with a peculiar aftertaste, but it filled me, and then I could read a while longer, stroll on deck, try to shake off my malaise.

No doubt people from the Baltic countries had emigrated to Sweden from time to time, though I was sure their numbers would have been severely restricted mostly to the professional classes unless industrial workers had been needed during certain years. The revolution of 1905 an omen, the stagnating Tsarist regime, the belief of educated Latvians that they are more energetic and efficient than Russians, might have sent Peterson's parents across the Baltic Sea from Riga to Stockholm and beyond. On the other hand, after World War I and the fall of the Romanovs, Latvia had succeeded

in becoming an independent republic—until it was annexed by the
Soviet Union in 1940, fell under German control, then was swallowed by Stalin again. In the twenties or thirties wouldn't it have
been natural for Peterson's parents to return to the homeland? Was
Peterson a Scandinavianized adaptation of a Latvian name? Of all
the anti-Semites of eastern, central, and southern Europe, the Ro-
manians, Lithuanians, and Latvians had been the most savage, out-
Naziing the German Nazis in their ferocious enthusiasm for exter-
minating Jews. The war over, the hunt for Nazi killers begun, what
more logical place to hide than neutral Sweden, if one could manage
to get there and be admitted, and who would have a better chance
at that than a Latvian born in Göteborg, once at least, possibly still,
under a dual arrangement, a Swedish citizen. Who would question
the very real motive of wanting to escape Soviet tyranny?

It was always possible, too, the passport was simply a forgery.
But surely if a hunted man wished to change his identity he would
become the complete Swede—a Lars or an Eric—not a Baltic Scandinavian hybrid.

But further speculation was useless at this point. I had to have
more to go on.

A. K. Ghosh and Peterson. Netaji Subhas Chandra Bose and
A. K. Ghosh and Peterson. Bose had probably been motivated
more by expediency than ideology in aligning himself with Nazi Germany and Tojo's Japan to form his Indian National Army during
World War II that he hoped would, but did not, drive the British
out of India. The British left anyway, under greater pressures. In
thinking of Ghosh, who claimed to have been a close associate of
the dead Netaji, I had focused only on Ghosh's reputation as a likely
drug dealer, not on any link to Nazis more than twenty years earlier.
But there it was, that possibility too, whose dimensions were unclear. Ghosh-Peterson—possibly the maharajah, some part of an
equation. And then I remembered that *I* was aboard this ship too,

the same ship on which Arvid Peterson was a passenger, because the Maharajah of Chittipore had talked me into it. But that made no sense.

I went back to my cabin.

A sorceress, Nicky was lying on my bunk smiling up at me.

"I won't ask how you got in here," I said in a sort of daze. "My question is, tomorrow can you get me into Peterson's cabin and Pontalba's?"

"Is that all you have to say?"

"Well, you see, what I'm saying is how amazed I am at the things you can do! And finding out who Peterson really is is extremely important to me."

Deflected, smile gone, she sat up, stood.

Just don't ask me to promise anything in return, said my silent voice.

"You *are* a stick. And I thought you were a *friendly* person," she said.

"I *am,* I am. I'd like to be your friend, Nicky, it's simply that— I'm really so much older than you are and when your family—my wife and children—are so far away, you worry about them, especially when someone, a man like Peterson, might be. . . . It's all I can think about. . . . But, no, I can't ask you to . . . get into Peterson's cabin. Forget that. You've helped enough already."

"I'll show you how," Nicky said, and then to my relief she left.

I had bad dreams. Not nightmares, but a nightmare might have been preferable; it would have waked me and given me a second chance at a restful night. The bad dreams simply ragged me till morning.

We met on deck after breakfast—I was carrying my camera without its telephoto lens—strolled together looking for Peterson and Pontalba, found them in deck chairs and, my God, Peterson was performing, shouting at a steward for failing to bring coffee quickly enough, giving the man a savage tongue-lashing. "How long must we wait, you ape? Until the end of the voyage? I intend to report you to the captain! You should be pulling freight wagons in Bombay, not serving gentlemen!" All during this tirade, Pontalba sat expressionless, as though he might be on some other planet. The steward, terrified, almost spilled the coffee, pouring with a shaking hand, but succeeded in completing this task successfully and making his escape. The fury I felt produced the flow of adrenaline needed for the job ahead. I took Nicky by the hand and led her quickly toward the door leading down to the cabin corridors.

"One thing I damn well intend to do is write a note to the captain defending that poor steward. The heartless son-of-a-bitch!"

Nicky hurried ahead. I rounded a corner into a right-angled corridor, and my heart sank. The door to the cabin steward's little office was open and light came from inside. But Nicky kept right on moving and stepped briskly a foot or so inside. Moments later she backed out with the steward following her, saying, "You are getting no water at all?"

"Not a trickle. I can't imagine what the trouble is. It was working all right last evening. Kind of you to have a look. I know how busy you are in the mornings."

She shot a quick look at me over her shoulder. As soon as the steward was out of sight, I stepped into the office, took two adjoining keys off their hooks on the steward's wall rack and made my way back in the direction I'd come. I was excited but calm enough and determined enough to move quickly and efficiently: unlocked the two doors, set the latches inside, reclosed the doors, returned to the steward's office and replaced the keys.

Peterson's cabin was the exact duplicate of my own. Passport in the top drawer of the little desk/dressing table. I opened it to the photograph, photographed that, and returned the passport to the drawer. Closet, luggage rack, under the bed. Clothes, toilet articles, elaborate scuba diving equipment, wet suit. No reading material of any sort other than a steamship ticket—Bombay-Seychelles-Durban. The Seychelles-Durban portion of the ticket was undated—open.

Bitterly disappointed, and the danger of being where I was a palpable weight that was turning into a sharp pain in my sternum, I went out, reset the latch, and locked the door again from the outside. Drenched in sweat, I had half-decided not to risk searching Pontalba's cabin, but steeled myself and went in.

The younger man's passport was on top of the dressing table. French. Fernand Pontalba. Né à Liban, Sept. 12, 1940. Immigration stamp reading Calcutta dated six months earlier. I snapped a photo of the photograph.

More elaborate scuba diving equipment and wet suit. Labels from a Paris sporting goods emporium. Identical ship tickets.

A copy of *Playboy*.

I fled—detected by no one—went to my own cabin and collapsed on my bunk.

I left a note under Nicky's door. "Can't thank you enough for your help. Not well. Slept badly last night and upset stomach today. Think I'd better stay close to my cabin. Might see you on deck later on."

It was all true enough. It simply didn't add that my indisposition also gave me an excuse to avoid her.

I did in fact spend most of the day in my cabin, dozing and reading, venturing out only to take a short walk on deck, during which I saw neither Nicky, Peterson, nor Pontalba. I did see the DeWitts from a distance and was greeted by wholesome Penny Graves and her healthy children. I skipped lunch. The cabin steward brought me clear soup and crackers, tea. I went to dinner early, saw no one I wanted to avoid, ate lightly, and went below again.

At 11:00 A.M. on the fourth day, a Wednesday, the S.S. *Nairobi* crossed the Equator. The ship was scheduled to reach the harbor at Mahé in the Seychelles at 9:00 A.M. Thursday.

On such a small ship any number of people, the DeWitts among them, had seen me and Nicky walking together, talking together on several occasions since the captain's cocktail party the second night out. I was not surprised, only apprehensive, to read the note delivered by a deck steward just before lunch: "Mr. McKay, I would like to confer with you concerning my niece, Beth. I believe it would be in your interest to do so. May I suggest we meet in the library at 11:30. Hugo DeWitt."

The "library," a small room at the rear of the lounge, had a narrow, open entrance but was mostly shut off from view by a bulkhead on the opposite side of which were shelves of books. Inside were only two chairs upholstered in brown leather. Mrs. DeWitt sat in one of them. Hugo DeWitt stood and motioned to me to take the other chair. He did not offer to shake hands and so I didn't initiate the gesture either.

DeWitt was a large, sleek man with thinning, carefully barbered hair, rimless glasses, fleshy features. His wife, unstylish, had a face like an axe. Compromising, I sat on the arm of the second chair and looked at Mr. DeWitt.

"Mr. McKay, let me begin by saying that as a consenting adult, my niece, Beth DeWitt, has the legal right to do as she pleases and my wife and I have no legal right to prevent her from doing as she pleases. Had she not just informed us she plans to disembark at

Mahé instead of continuing on with us to Durban as scheduled we would simply have overlooked the little adventure she has been carrying on with you and waited for it to come to an end tomorrow morning . . ."

My dander rose and I interrupted him with what sounded blustering even to myself, "Now just a minute here . . ." but DeWitt, his voice slightly louder, broke in, "I am speaking of my niece, not of you yet, sir, which I have every right to do. I wrote that it would be in your interest to come here, as you've done, and I will get to the reason why in just a moment. Now if you will allow me to continue. . . . My niece seems determined to take this step—either because of you or because she sees in you a means by which she can somehow remain in the Seychelles until some new whim strikes her. I pass no moral judgment on whatever relationship you have established with Beth, Mr. McKay. But I will do you the favor of making you fully aware of what you might be getting into. I don't know what she has decided to tell you about herself but I am quite sure, based on a great deal of past behavior, that it was fantasy, not the truth.

"She has very little money in her possession. She has no job, no profession, no skills. I am coadministrator of the trust fund set up by her father which is her sole means of support—"

"Excuse me," I interrupted, my tone more respectful. "Her father is deceased then?"

"My brother is quite alive," DeWitt said.

"Excuse me again. Please go on."

"Under the terms of this trust fund, in order to receive any allowance from it, Beth must reside with or travel with us or with her father's second brother and his wife."

"Is her father an invalid?"

"No, he is not. He quite simply cannot bear to live under the same roof with the child who shot his wife to death."

I received this information in silence. Then I needed to take a rather deep breath to speak again.

"Has she been in prison?"

"There was a hearing but no trial," DeWitt said. "Her attorney argued successfully the shooting had been an accident. A magistrate ruled death by misadventure.

"Before this tragedy she had quarreled often with her parents, with her mother in particular, over her totally amoral, irresponsible, destructive behavior. She had been married, had a child. The child was neglected almost from birth. Needless to say her ex-husband now has custody. She consorted with other men of all sorts, some of them known criminals. She has been diagnosed as a nymphomaniac but refuses psychiatric treatment. There are probably sufficient grounds to institutionalize her but neither her father nor I nor my other brother have been able to agree to take this step. Instead, for the past two years we have alternated in keeping a roof over her head. This era may be coming to an end. My wife and I have warned her we will not continue to give her money to remain in the Seychelles. Eventually, if she is judged to be indigent, the British authorities will deport her to Durban."

"Can't those same authorities be approached now to deny her entry on the same grounds?"

DeWitt paused before replying. "We do not choose to deal with the situation in this way," he said. "We believe she needs to discover the consequences of her own actions."

And I guessed, and did not blame them for it, that they had probably come to hope she'd live out one of her fantasies, marry a rich Arab or whomever, so they might finally be rid of her.

"What brought you to India?"

"The firm I represent has business interests on the subcontinent."

"I'm in your debt," I said. "I never believed her story. But the truth is a little more sobering than I might have guessed. . . . This is a small ship and we won't dock for another twenty-one hours or so. If you see me with Nicky—Beth, it'll only be because she's run me down. I don't want to—upset her unduly by snubbing her."

DeWitt signaled to his wife with his eyes and she got to her feet, not having said a word.

But Beth DeWitt was shrewder than I had given her credit for being. She did not dog my footsteps. On the contrary, she kept out of sight and gave the impression of avoiding *me*. Freed from the pressure of avoiding her, I began to think of her more kindly. I would not allow her to victimize me, I assured myself, but I pitied her. Her twisted life could only be miserable a good deal of the time, and was probably hopeless. I went to the lounge chairs on the upper deck, found them unoccupied, settled myself into one, and half waited for her to put in an appearance.

Suddenly, fifty or sixty yards off the track of the ship, a porpoise leaped from the sea, arced gracefully, and disappeared into a green swell, was followed by another and another, a school of them. And I did not have my camera with me.

And for the two hours I stayed on the upper deck Nicky/Beth did not appear.

Nor was she at dinner. The DeWitts sat at their table without her.

I was struck with pity, even sorrow, and concern.

Peterson and Pontalba conversed in low tones. Peterson did not browbeat his dining steward in any way.

The ship slipped on into the evening.

I read in the bar, sipped wine, when it was dark went out on deck and scanned the heavens. Stars, constellations, galaxies, were a kind of passion with me, though I did not pretend to be an astronomer. The continuity of their existence over eons, the continuity of their poetic names over millennia and centuries, were balm and solace on an ever-changing planet, and I looked now, searching the spangled skies for the Sails of Argo and the Southern Cross.

A tall figure stood alone in shadows at the stern end of the ship a deck-length away. Peterson? I could not be sure in the darkness at that distance and then whoever it was vanished through a doorway.

4

Low, heavily forested mountains rose steeply from a deeply indented, irregular coastline of coves and sandbars. A cluster of hump-backed islets lay off the port side; a quarter mile ahead off the starboard bow, the tiny, low-roofed capital of Victoria. The S.S. *Nairobi* was at anchor in the harbor.

British immigration officials in shorts and short-sleeved, tieless uniforms stamped passports in the ship's lounge. A launch brought disembarking first class passengers ashore: myself, Peterson and Pontalba, Beth DeWitt, the Sikhs, the Seychelleois family with ayah, the Australians, an elderly couple, grey and retiring as doves, who looked very French and spoke British English, a few other Commonwealth couples, twenty some persons in all. A more crowded launch transported steerage arrivals who, at a distance, seemed mostly Indian.

When she could get close enough to me Beth whispered fiercely, "I hate you, I despise you! You let them tell you all those lies about me!" I had nothing to say and turned away.

Victoria was ramshackle, not strikingly crowded, seemed sleepy and peaceful beyond a cheerfully animated marketplace. Immediately outside of town, tumble-down houses lined the narrow twisting road the hotel bus bounced along. I assumed there was poverty but I neither saw nor felt any evidence of seething discontent.

I had hung back as the little group lined up to board the bus so that now Peterson, Pontalba, and Beth DeWitt all sat ahead of me.

Four centuries earlier, pirates and traders had disturbed but had not put an end to the gentle sovereignty of the indigenous terns and tortoises. The intruders came and went and when they were gone, tranquillity reigned again. The islands had been sighted by the Portuguese in the fifteen hundreds but they had sailed on; the British seem to have been the first to land, in 1609, but another century and a half went by before anyone came to stay, to take possession—the French, with a boatload of African slaves. Half another century later the British took over, brought more slaves, though slavery was abolished in 1835. Indians, Chinese, Malayans came to trade and set up shop. Even then the archipelago did not get crowded. In 1966 the total population was about sixty thousand, most inhabitants settled on the largest island of Mahé. Most of the other 114 islands were still uninhabited. The giant tortoises, the terns, and birds found nowhere else had survived. As the bus reached the crest of the mountain and the road began descending one side of a green amphitheater towards the once again visible sea, this seemed to me the last earthly paradise. Above, blue sky was whitened only here and there by decorative banks and wisps of cloud. The temperature of the air was a dry, sweet seventy-six degrees. The tropical vegetation held the promise of a horticultural and zoological Eden.

There were, I had heard, two or three English-run guest houses

along this northwest coast of Mahé for those more conservative visitors who preferred greater isolation, but the Beau Vallon, on the
beach of that name, was *the* hotel, though its capacity was only
eighty, and at the moment, with the departure of some Kenyan
guests for Mombassa that day, it was less than half full. Most guests
were housed in simple detached cottages spread across a grassy,
sandy clearing in a grove of palms. The main building, a functional,
one-story structure of local wood on a stone foundation that blended
pleasingly into the surrounding foliage, housed a bar, kitchen, dining room for rainy days—dining otherwise was outside under a
thatched roof pavilion—lounge, office, storerooms, and a small
number of guest rooms. There were dart boards in the bar and
lounge, tables for card playing, a refectory table stacked with old
British magazines, a bookcase full of donated or left-behind mysteries, adventure novels, and popular love stories, more lounge
chairs on a wraparound outside verandah, and a second, smaller bar
just above the beach. Coconuts fell from tall palm trees. Rainbow
bands of songbirds visited, perched on tables, arms of chairs, railings, flashed off. Full pension—three meals plus cottage—worked
out to the equivalent of four dollars and nineteen cents a day.

I had been to Bermuda, the Bahamas, but I could not remember or imagine a more beautiful beach than Beau Vallon, a long,
wide arc of powdered-sugar sand that began a hundred feet or so
beyond my cottage and stretched in two directions past my range of
vision to blur into the mountainous coast. Along the back edge of
it, bending benevolently forward to provide shade when that was
desired, were palms and tacamahaca trees. A catamaran, its twin
hulls painted blue, was anchored offshore. Straight ahead, perhaps
twelve miles distant, rose the dark-green dream peaks of Silhouette.
North, a hundred yards or so, were smooth, granite rock formations
the height of temples, strangely shaped, some like sleeping prehistoric beasts. A few, a little farther out, rose from shallow water.

From a distance they seemed to present an obstacle course but not an impenetrable one. Sandy paths wound among them to more open beach.

A gentle surf frothed and beckoned. I ran into it, no pebbles underfoot to impede my progress or give me pain, plunged, came up through cool water of a marvelous clarity. Standing up to my neck I could see my feet below. Small oval fish darted around them but kept their distance. I climbed out and walked back to the few steps leading to the beachside bar. Beth DeWitt, in a one-piece black bathing suit, sat at a white table in between two men in bathing trunks. Both were muscular and deeply tanned.

My God, I thought. Did she simply wave her wand?

Nicky saw me and was suddenly all bright-eyed—and malicious—cordiality: "Charles, you must meet my new friends, the lost boys. They've sailed here all the way from Durban and eventually they're going on to the Maldives, Ceylon, the Nicobars, the East Indies, and Australia. They've asked me to crew for them. All we need is one more. Isn't that exciting?

"Charles and I are old friends from aboard ship," she explained.

I gave and received two firm hand grips and pulled up a chair.

They were Ivan and Kingston—called Stony. Ivan, about my age, was losing his hair; Stony, hair and brushy mustache prematurely grey, appeared to be in his early thirties.

Nicky was quickly helpful in a social sense. "Ivan's a compatriot, Stony is a fellow countryman of yours, Charles, I'll leave it to you to sort out which states. There, now you have it all, and I would like another cold drink."

A barefoot, coffee-colored Seychelleois boy in duck pants and a t-shirt brought lemon soda for everyone and a complimentary plate of coconut pieces. Ivan, Stony, and I paid.

I decided not to be the first to ask questions. Ivan, with his neat black mustache, mature manner, beginning of a pot, gentle brown eyes, solved the problem by asking genially, "On holiday from one of your diplomatic missions?"

"Consulate in Calcutta," I said. "I take it you've run into us before."

"Not here, no."

"And you?"

"I'm said to be in the banking business in Capetown."

"How long have you all been here?"

"A month, hasn't it been?" Ivan asked Stony, a rhetorical question evidently, since the latter didn't bother to reply and Ivan seemed satisfied with his own computation.

"Easy to see why you'd want to stay and stay and stay," I said. "Weather always this good?"

"This time of year."

Ivan had the comfortable air of an heir but I wondered if he might be on a leash, an allowance paid out in installments, a new installment not yet arrived. Stony? A poor black man or a rich white one might have a first name like Kingston. I broke my vow.

"What part of the States're you from?"

Stony's very pale blue eyes focused on me for a moment, then past me.

"Long Island. Nicky? Ready for a dip?"

Stony and Beth bounced to their feet and down the steps and ran across the sand.

I didn't want to be the only one left.

"Almost time for lunch, isn't it?" I said. "Think I'll shower and hold myself in readiness."

In the afternoon, I watched Peterson and Pontalba, reptilian in wet suits, goggles, masks, hoses, tanks, walking ponderously flipper-footed across the sand, climbing into a launch with an outboard motor and moving out and southward toward a mountainous point of land, and the far, deepest reef. I walked farther along the beach and had most of it to myself, swam again, for half an hour this time, soaked up twenty minutes of sun, back at the hotel studied a map of Mahé and the nearer islands, inquired about renting scuba diving and snorkeling equipment, one of two launches and a sailboat, transportation into Victoria (the small hotel bus made a round-trip run every morning and could be hired at other times), and where I could get film developed. I read, planned excursions, napped, showered again, and in clean shorts and shirt, tennis shoes, strolled down to the beachside bar at dusk. A British couple occupied one of the three round white tables, Ivan and Stony sat at a second.

"Join us," Ivan said.

"Enjoy your first day?" he asked.

"How could I not," I said, and sipped from the tulip glass of South African red wine the bar boy had just placed before me. The sun was setting behind the island of Silhouette, an extraordinarily magnificent vision of earthly perfection.

"The nearest reef?" I asked Ivan. "By boat the only—"

"Did I tell you what Reynaud said?" Stony asked Ivan. "She can wash dishes. 'I can't keep a dishwasher more than a month.' "

"Don't imagine she's ever washed a dish in her life," Ivan said, then turned to me. "You were asking about the reef."

"If by boat's the only way to get—"

"I don't suppose she knows anything about bookkeeping, either," Stony said.

"Boat, yes, there's no road," Ivan said. "You can come out with us."

"Very nice of you," I said, and watched Nicky crossing the coconut grove toward the beach. Tanned, in white, Nicky looked particularly alluring. Stony, still self-possessed, nonetheless avidly watched her approach. Ivan, smooth, experienced, no doubt persuasive, maintained greater detachment.

Now they all sat in a circle in the last of the sunset, Nicky holding court like some perverse Wendy with her "lost boys." (No question who was cast as Captain Hook, but who was Tinker Bell—Pontalba? And who Peter Pan, or did Ivan and Stony take turns?) Each of them very likely planned to try to take her to bed and I had no doubt she would come across, one at a time or more than one at a time, but Ivan and Stony might live to regret it. The question arose in my mind: Should I warn them against her? Did I have a duty—or a right? No, after all, I'd survived. I expected they would too. No, I'd mind my own business and see what was going to happen.

Lights had gone on in the main building. Peterson and Pontalba came out, stood for a moment under a light on the verandah, then walked down the steps and along the sandy path to the beach, Peterson in slacks, Pontalba in shorts.

"Hey, Ivan, you know what?" Stony said. "You're a lot cuter than that Frenchman. I'll bet if you tried you could turn the old Swede's head."

Ivan simply sat on, unperturbed.

"I don't know for sure they're that way," I said, surprising myself. "The thought crosses your mind, but the younger guy reads *Playboy,* if that means anything."

"Why don't we find out," Nicky said. "Stony, couldn't we pretend you're Swedish on your mother's side? You could start a conversation easily. You've never been to Scandinavia but you've always wanted to see your mother's ancestral homeland. What's it like and so forth."

"Nicky, that's not a very good idea," I said sternly.

"Charles doesn't like it because he doesn't think Mr. Peterson is really Swedish at all," Nicky said.

"Nicky," I said warningly.

"Let her talk," Stony said.

Already furious with Nicky, I stiffened angrily at this intrusion.

"Certain things said in confidence happen to be in question," I said.

"I think we might drop the subject," Ivan said, soothingly but no less firmly, and his words produced an effective period of silence, broken only by the ordering of fresh drinks.

"My father was in Calcutta during the war," Ivan said to me. "He used to carry on fondly about a club run by some Russian."

"Boris!" I said. "Boris has a hotel in Kathmandu now, complete with The Yak and Yeti Bar. The 500 Club was turned into an apartment house. It's just down the street from where I live. . . . I'm sorry I wasn't old enough to have been around in those days. British, other Commonwealth troops, Americans, Nationalist Chinese, White Russians. And at least one representative of the Polish government-in-exile. Black American jazz orchestra playing at the Grand Hotel. Teddy Weatherford. A few traces of all that left here and there, handful of White Russians, other European exiles, mostly British and Indians who remember. But Calcutta's still a city with character, for all its ills. You should go."

Though I found Ivan an engaging fellow and had accepted his invitation to sail to the reef someday, I decided that I would now reestablish the fact that I was an independent party of one, definitely not one of Beth/Nicky's lost boys nor beholden to them exclusively for company during my short fortnight in the Seychelles.

"Believe I'll wander on up," I said, and pushed back my chair.

In the evening I played darts in the upper bar with a British army major, retired, and a young, taciturn Rhodesian farmer. Ivan, unaccompanied, joined us after a while.

"We'll be going over to the near reef in the afternoon tomorrow," Ivan said. "Fairly shallow there. No need to bring anything, we have extra equipment. Ever done any diving before?"

"Never."

"Simplicity itself at this level."

"I warn you. I'm no sailor."

"No need to be. Ferryboat ride over there."

"Two weeks?" I said. "That's impossible. I'll be leaving before then. No way to get them done sooner? I'd be glad to pay extra."

"I can try to have them in one week, sir," said the Indian gentleman behind the counter, his general store a jumble of comestibles, beverages and other provisions, hardware, nautical supplies, toys, decorative artifacts, postcards.

"I'll think about it," I said, and left the shop without leaving the roll of film.

I had planned to mail one set of prints to myself in Calcutta and a second to Caroline in Washington for safekeeping, and to keep a third and the negatives with me. Conceiving of these precautions with their espionage implications had half embarrassed me. Now, midway through talking to the store proprietor something else had occurred to me. What would the photo processor discover and puzzle over? Most of the roll unexposed. No scenic shots of the islands. A half dozen shots of the same person either with his eyes closed or glowering and not looking into the camera, or as the subject of a passport photo. One other person, also with eyes closed and in a passport photo. Police and counterintelligence agencies have their informants in such public places who are retained and paid for being alert, on the job. Wouldn't anyone think to turn over copies of such curious photographs, complete with the name and hotel of the photographer, to keep in the good graces of their employers? These same employers, British government officials, would—theoretically—be on my side—but only if Peterson was in truth someone other than the man he pretended to be. There might be less heroic and savory motives for surreptitious photography. Those shots of Peterson and Pontalba together. Blackmail? Was taking someone's photograph without their knowledge and permission a felony, an actionable offense?

The shuttle bus back to the hotel wouldn't depart from Barclay's Bank for another hour, time enough to pick out gifts for Car-

oline and the children. Choice was severely limited if I stuck to my
determination to send only indigenous products, no Hong Kong
blouses, no Taiwan toys. Not entirely satisfied but resigned (I was
reminded of my grandmother's Victorian dressing table), I finally
selected tortoise-shell combs inlaid with mother-of-pearl for Caroline and Meredith, a collection of cowrie shells for Richard (a
printed card gave their scientific name and a brief history of their
use as coin in southern Asia and on the Guinea coast of Africa),
and arranged with the shopkeeper to have them wrapped and
mailed. Just getting packages from far-off places with strange and
pretty stamps would be exciting for the kids.

Abruptly, it occurred to me to send Caroline something else.
I walked to the Post & Telegraph office down the street and standing
at a chest-high counter drafted a cable:

CAROLINE, THIS UTMOST URGENT. DETAILS WILL FOLLOW IN
LETTER. WHAT CAN SWEDISH EMBASSY CONTACTS UNEARTH ABOUT
ARVID PETERSON, BORN GÖTEBORG, APRIL 23, 1906. SWEDISH
PASSPORT # 017298R. ANY POX RECORD? CABLE REPLY SOONEST.
LOVE CHARLIE.

POX was wire service jargon for police.

Immediately I felt, first foolish, then apprehensive. Was it li-
belous to send an open cable implying possible wrongdoing? I re-
wrote it, making it shorter in the process:

CAROLINE, NEED CABLED REPLY SOONEST. INTERESTED PARTY
TEL AVIV. ARVID PETERSON, BORN GÖTEBORG, APRIL 23, 1906.
SWEDISH PASSPORT # 017298R. LOVE CHARLIE.

Caroline would find this second message more puzzling but
would also put two and two together and get on to it just as quickly.

It still made me nervous, but I sent it off.

Mummers twirl as the carnival parade of marvels streams past, fans are flourished as the masked ball whirls. Blennies, Gobies, butterfly fish and parrot fish, fish fantastic, dazzling their decoration, colors, shapes; yellow, orange, Chinese and cinnamon red, violet, powder blue; banded, striped, patched, marbled, diamond crosshatched, polka-dotted, leopard-spotted; ovals, lozenges, random blots, flat, puffed, streamlined, fish with spikes and feathers, horned like unicorns and bulls. Transparent, luminous, phosphorescent; X-ray images, boy-imagined space ships from long ago Flash Gordon days; golden, blue-lipped angelfish; trigger fish, orange-striped chartreuse; pajama cardinal fish with great red eyes, red spots on scales of antique gold. Creations most whimsical and fanciful from the hand of God as sculptor, painter, magician, *maquilleur,* and clown.

I float on the surface face down, goggled, breathing through a bobbing tube, fill my lungs with air, dive into the sunlit sea to the edge of the reef, to hills, ledges, grottos, caverns, to coral shaped like warped megaphones on wind-up Victrolas, like glazed skeletons of pine trees, above fields of tendrils, waving tentacles of pink anemone, starfish—and up, up, quickly, quickly! from a depth a bit too far, to gulp in air beside the catamaran just as Nicky rocks the boat, springing up and away from it to dive back into her mermaid's lagoon.

Sailing back, I ask Ivan, "When do you plan to go on to the Maldives?"

"We're in no hurry."

Evasive answer, even a mild put-down: not your business, is it? I think Ivan doesn't want to commit himself to anything.

"Ever see any sharks around here?" I ask, to have something to talk about.

"Not I. They're around. I've heard no stories."

"Good. I know they get a worse press than they deserve, but I'd just as soon I didn't have to check this out for myself."

The afternoon is ending. A distance off we can see Peterson and Pontalba on the beach. Leaving Pontalba behind, Peterson, brown, lean, muscular, strides, lopes into the surf, arcs into the waves and begins swimming out with long, powerful strokes.

On the beach, Seychelleoise girls cruise and flirt. One or more of them have sand-sculpted a naked woman with graphic details, limbs spread invitingly. Small boys run alongside and trample on it but the girls only laugh and giggle.

Days and nights passed. I spent them on the beach, above the reef, in books, at the bar, alone or with the others, mostly watching, listening, in dreamless sleep and in slumber crowded with images of the past. In the evenings sometimes I walked long distances along the moonlit beach, past the few other more isolated inns. One was built on a bluff at the edge of the forest above the beach. Once, I saw a man looking over the railing of an open terrace and remembered the man on the deck of the S.S. *Nairobi* I did not think was Peterson, and remembered the man ill in his cabin, the man the purser and Penny Graves thought might be going home to die.

My holiday was half over. Nicky came to me in a secluded pathway between the granite rock formations.

"I was only teasing, I haven't given away your secret," she said. "Will you lend me fifty of your American dollars?"

"All right," I said. "I'll give you that much. But what are you going to do when I go back to India? Can you get money from your new friends?"

Very quickly she turned tense and gloomy.

"Ivan has it but he's tight-fisted."

"Stony doesn't have it?"

"Not much. He owns the boat but he's short of cash. Then let me have enough for a month. I helped you, didn't I?"

"I think you ought to go back to Durban."

"I might as well die!"

"Look. Now you've got enough to live at the hotel another twelve days. As for more, I'll have to think about it."

She stepped forward and put one hand on my crotch, kissed my lips with an open mouth. I stepped back, half reluctantly.

"Nicky, it's broad daylight."

"I'll go to your cottage."

"Nicky, you don't have to do this. I still have to think about whether I can help you anymore. I have to check my finances. Believe me, I'm not a rich American. But let me get the fifty dollars. Give me fifteen minutes. I'll meet you in the lounge."

I walked off, not looking back.

It wasn't a question of money. I could give her enough for two months and not miss it all that much. No, I really did have to think about it.

After dinner, Reynaud showed movies in the lounge, one British, one American, cartoons. Beth and the lost boys went. I walked on the moon-soaked beach barefoot, listening to the surf, sat at the beachside bar drinking wine and looking at the deadly stone fish in the glass jar, mossy yellow-green like a giant toad, and went to bed early, needing Nicky to have come to my cottage that afternoon but at the same time, shivering, not needing her at all. I lay awake, pondering.

The DeWitts, by telling me the truth about Beth, had put me in their debt. I might repay it by staking Beth long enough for her to sail away to another Neverland with Ivan, Stony, and whatever other crewmen they might find here. But what would that be letting them in for? A potentially murderous situation. All they knew about her and all they cared about now was that she was pretty, and wild. Who had screwed her already? Stony, no doubt. Probably only Stony so far. They didn't know that in her own way she was more dangerous than Peterson because her record was known.

Without funds, Ivan and Stony might sneak her into their beds—for the night—until Reynaud caught them at it and put a stop to such unpaid double occupancy. She'd sleep on the beach and cadge and steal. With her lock-picking skills, probably learned from some Durban second-story man, she'd be able to jimmy into Reynaud's storeroom a few times until he discovered the theft and named her as the prime suspect. A thief and a public nuisance, looking dirtier and more disheveled by the day and less and less appetizing to Stony and Ivan, she'd be abandoned by them and held in Victoria until she could be deported. The DeWitts would be stuck with her again, but maybe she would have learned by then either to behave herself or be shut away somewhere. She could save herself or hang herself but at least she would have the choice, more than most would have.

I could always tell Ivan about her *and* give her more money, but that would only delay the inevitable, assuming someone like Stony cared that she had shot her mother. Ivan had the most money and probably the most sense, but also probably not absolute veto power. Stony owned the boat and could decide who traveled on it, who slept on it, if he wanted to live dangerously.

On that thought I fell asleep and woke with it still in my head, and made my decision.

"We're planning a cruise to Silhouette on the weekend," Ivan said. "Nicky's been begging us to take her there. Two nights. We've anchored off one beach there before but never been inland any distance. You're invited. The major and his wife and our Rhodesian friend are coming along too."

"Sure," I said. "I'd like to go. My time is almost up."

I hoped that with fifty fresh dollars in her pocket Beth DeWitt would wait at least a few days to ask for more again. But only hours later she cornered me as I crossed the palm grove toward the beach.

"I can't do it, Nicky," I said. "I'm sorry. I've given you all I can give you."

Thwarted, enraged, and speechless, she ran off to her cottage and slammed the door behind her.

5

There had been a pattern starting at breakfast. Peterson would appear first, then ten minutes later Pontalba, a late sleeper or morning dawdler apparently, would saunter in and unfold his napkin. Then they would leave the dining pavilion together. Sometimes they left for the far reef in the morning, bringing lunch with them evidently, and did not return until dusk. Sometimes they spent the morning on the beach and went out to the near reef after lunch when no one else was there. Before dinner was the only other time I had seen them separated, and not for long. Pontalba had appeared once or twice at the bar in the main building, then Peterson had joined him five or ten minutes later. They never patronized the beach bar nor socialized in the main bar after dinner. How they spent their evenings I could only guess.

But if the spirit or the flesh is receptive, a few minutes are enough.

The first indication was seeing Peterson heading out to the reef alone Wednesday afternoon. Pontalba indisposed? But at about

3:00 P.M. Pontalba seemed in excellent health as he and Nicky passed behind my beach towel, speaking French, and strolled on down toward the temple and beast-shaped granite boulders, where they went out of sight.

On board ship Nicky had called Pontalba one of a bisexual type she had known at Cannes and implied that if she felt like it she could seduce him. Out of fear of provoking Peterson to some kind of dangerous violence, I had warned her to lay off. Nicky's motive now was clearly revenge against me. But what could she hope to accomplish except to enrage Peterson—to upset my timetable, put a crimp in my plans. But I had no timetable and I had no plans. I had photographs of Peterson and some scant information about him and chances were that was all I could expect to get. Experienced Nazi hunters could check it out but I could probably do no more. But maybe Nicky was unwittingly doing me a favor. Peterson had proved himself to be a choleric individual, aroused to fury over nothing, a deck steward's alleged tardiness. What would he do and what might he reveal as a result of Pontalba's perceived betrayal? Clearly Nicky, having already flaunted her wiles before me, would flaunt her conquest before Peterson. If, of course, Peterson's and Pontalba's relationship was actually what it might be but which I had publicly questioned. And in so doing, I now thought, had probably been naive. Could anyone seriously imagine that pair to be merely, let us say, business associates so affluent they could travel thousands of miles just to go scuba diving together in one of the more remote spots on the globe? Peterson had money, undoubtedly, but Pontalba had all the earmarks of a kept Parisian hustler, spawn of some French soldier and Lebanese mother, bored with his paramour—the one thing he never displayed was the slightest interest in, let alone affection for, Peterson, who was twice his age—and chafing under his confinement to such a degree he would risk Peterson's wrath by consorting with Nicky at least as long as a walk on the beach. And I knew very well Nicky would not let it stop there if she could help it.

That evening Pontalba appeared in the same loose group that included Nicky, Ivan, Stony, the major and his wife, and the Rhodesian farmer. Peterson was nowhere to be seen. Ivan seemed amused. Stony hid his feelings behind his mustache. Nicky, speaking fluent French, was teaching Pontalba—Fernand as she called him—how to play darts. I joined them and we formed two teams of four each.

Peterson's power over Pontalba was evidently limited—once again, assuming he really exercised power. The Frenchman was probably impervious to blackmail. Or maybe they *were* in business together. Drugs? Shades of A. K. Ghosh again. I hadn't checked for false bottoms in their suitcases. There would be a market for drugs in South Africa as there was everywhere. And they had spent many months near major sources of supply.

I left them all after a while, tired of darts and conscious that my nights on this beautiful island were numbered and that I did not want to waste them indoors. I went out and walked down the path to the beach. Peterson appeared on the steps leading up from the sand. On a post hung a lantern light. For a moment I felt almost sorry for the man—but not when I saw his expression, suffused with vicious ill will, and when I remembered his insulting remark aboard ship about Americans, his cruel treatment of the deck steward, the racist epithet he had hurled at the man, and when I viscerally remembered my suspicions, even convictions, about his origins and past. Vindictiveness rose in me and when I passed close to him I looked at him with all the contempt I could summon into my face. He passed behind a glare of pure hatred but said nothing. My heart pounding, I turned to look at his retreating figure, leaving the path before he reached the lights of the main building, and disappearing into the darkness.

Thursday evening, Reynaud the innkeeper called me away from the outdoor pavilion in the middle of my dinner.

"You have an overseas telephone call."

"My God," I said aloud.

Caroline's voice traveling down from the satellite, mine traveling up, were not quite coordinated—replies were delayed by several seconds and sometimes collided with repeated questions asked too soon, and words here and there faded, were lost—but it seemed to me later our strange, disjointed outer-spatial conversation suited the information Caroline had to tell me.

"*Charlie? . . . Darling, you have a ballpoint ready? . . . Swedish embassy being too cozy to be useful. . . . This . . . comes from home office . . . correspondent I know. Two and a half years ago leftist magazine in Stockholm published nineteen . . . no, not fourteen, forty-one . . . photo of subject not in uniform but with Nazi officials in Riga,* them *in uniform. Nightclub scene. Enjoying themselves . . . indictment brought. . . . No, negative.* Wasn't any. No *indictment, got that? Lawyers argued subject had been unwilling . . . at occasion innocent in itself. Before war he'd been official, now had to eat. Claimed he was virtual prisoner himself. . . . You still there? . . . He's businessman. Svenska-International Incorporated. Machine tools. Spends most . . . his time traveling. Now . . . Charlie? . . . This could be clincher. If we're cut off, call me back. . . . Photograph came from international Jewish agency. And they've found something else.* Recently. *A few months ago . . . you still with me? . . . subject's signature on document certifying list of people, all Jewish names, community leaders, duly received at quote processing. . . .* Processing. *And distribution center unquote. December, nineteen forty-one. I have a copy. Read that last part back to me. . . . OK. Bureaucratic language . . . might mean anything in another context. But similar document has been accepted as evidence in West German trial. Defendant . . . Latvian auxiliary police, and what they did is documented . . .*

"Charlie, be careful *do you hear me? . . . British authorities handle it. I love you . . ."*

I didn't want anything else to eat but I went back to the pavilion to look at Peterson. He and Pontalba had gone. I wandered and then drank wine. It still took me a long time to get to sleep but finally I fell off for a few hours.

Peterson and Pontalba did not appear for breakfast at all. Both the hotel launches stayed up on the beach until the major and his wife took one out. Then I saw Peterson climb aboard the shuttle bus to Victoria. Pontalba wasn't with him and I didn't run across him or Nicky anywhere all morning, nor in the dining pavilion at lunch. Peterson didn't show up either. The second launch remained up on the beach.

The catamaran was due to set sail for Silhouette at four in the afternoon. At three-thirty, I locked my cottage and strolled to the beachside bar. Ivan and Stony were there.

"It seems Fernand will be joining us," Ivan said. "I've been outvoted."

"I've got a bet going," Stony said, looking directly at me with his washed-out blue eyes. "Don't you think it might be fun?"

"Why should I think that?" I said. "I think it'll be too crowded with me along too."

"You might have a point," Stony said, and that settled that, then and there. My face flamed, but I was more relieved than disappointed. I'd come this far and didn't really need another island except to have this splendid view of it, in comfort. And who knows, in crowded conditions over forty-eight hours, whether I'd be able to restrain myself from taking a poke at my fellow countryman. And I would not be able to monitor Arvid Peterson's behavior from an island a dozen miles away.

If the Swedish government was being super cautious, reticent, what would this colonial British administration be? I certainly couldn't count on them taking any immediate action, doing any more than suggesting to London that London query Stockholm. Peterson would be long gone to South Africa.

The catamaran was equipped with an inflatable, motorized Zodiac raft for use from beach to boat and a little past four o'clock, watched by me and other patrons of the beachside bar and the Seychelleoise girls and small boys who began gathering every afternoon at this hour, the crew of two and their five passengers climbed into the raft and Stony started the engine. Not long afterward, canvas climbed, fluttered, flapped, and billowed in a light breeze and the catamaran moved slowly out to sea in a northwesterly direction. Less than an hour later it could no longer be seen.

With seven out of only twenty hotel guests gone, the dining pavilion was mostly empty and particularly quiet. A table of four, three tables of two, another single besides myself, an elderly British woman, all widely scattered as if to emphasize our separateness and aloneness. Peterson's table was empty. But he came in then and sat alone, and truth sat invisibly and silently between us.

He had been thirty-five in 1941, after the Germans drove the Russians out of Latvia. He'd been some kind of an official before and he was an official then, who relaxed in nightclubs with his supervisors, who signed papers that certified neatly, efficiently, that X number of Jews had been rounded up. Twenty-five thousand had disappeared in the woods outside Riga that December, shot by the Nazi *Einsatzgruppe* A and Latvian auxiliaries. The luckier early ones who would die quickly and would not have to wait to die in the camps. Thirty-five, a signer of papers, a bureaucrat, but thirty-five is quite young after all, and imagine the logistics of disposing quickly of twenty-five thousand people, certainly not an easy task to complete. Many days must have been required and many willing hands. Did he take part personally in that final action? But there would be other opportunities, the great Warsaw ghetto roundup of '42 in which Latvian battalions participated.

I stared at Peterson in fascination and revulsion but he took no notice of me. I waited until he had dabbed his mouth with a napkin and had left the pavilion. Then I went into the bar and began to work out the best way to proceed.

It seemed to me that finding the document with Peterson's signature on it was a *major step in a process* but not yet enough—not at least for British authorities in the Seychelles. Not enough for them to detain Peterson on any solid grounds. I was almost sure they'd have to have authorization from London and would not get that without a specific request from Sweden for extradition. Peterson had lawyers who'd gotten him off the hook before. Even now I could see them challenging the purport of the document, questioning whether the Peterson who signed it might not be another man entirely. I could be wrong, but if I went to the British police and they told me they could do nothing now except message London about the matter then my hands would be effectively tied as well.

But what could I do alone? I was twenty years younger than the man, not as tall, but I thought stronger. But what other resources did I have? What was needed was an Israeli commando team backed up by boats and aircraft!

There were Israeli missions in Africa, South Africa included. Ivan and Stony had sailed their catamaran all the way from Durban, just the two of them, and might be adventurous enough to provide transport if they believed that Peterson was a war criminal. Mombassa was a long way but considerably closer than Durban. The idea was wild but not crazy. When were they due back from Silhouette? Sunday, unless their expedition palled or soured and they came back sooner. But maybe not until Monday. Tuesday, the S.S. *Nairobi* was scheduled to dock at Victoria to take on passengers, one of them me, for the return trip to Bombay.

I couldn't simply leave and let him get away!

What time was it in Washington?

It took Reynaud an hour to get a line through to Caroline's office.

". . . Can you read me some of the names on the list? How many are there?"

". . . *fifty.*"

"Fifty? Five zero?"

"*Yes . . . leaders.*"

"Are there other lists?"

". . . *looking for them.*"

"One may be enough. Please start reading. I need them all."

"*Applebaum . . . Bermann . . . Bronshtein . . . Byk . . .*"

If Ivan and Stony wouldn't help me kidnap him then I would leave copies of this list everywhere—under his plate, in the launch he rented, haunt and hound him and force him into a corner. I would nail a list to his door. I would follow him everywhere, everywhere he went. There was no easy way he could get off the island. If he rented a fishing boat it could not go far. It would have to return or leave him on some other island and then I'd know where he was and would follow him there. I'd cable my office in Calcutta and tell them I was taking leave of absence in order to stay another month. I'd wait for the S.S. *Nairobi* to return on another roundtrip from Bombay and follow him to Durban if that's where he would try to go, and keep him in sight until people from the consulate of Israel could take over from me. I would not let him get away!

"*. . . Caro . . . Cohen . . .*"

Out of some extrasensory perception and memory that left me almost dizzy with the absurd possibility of it, an irrational notion came racing past.

"Caroline, have you looked at this list before, studied the names?"

". . . *the what?*"

"*Names.* Is this the first time you've really looked at them?"

"*Yes.*"

"Then skip to eff."

". . . *Samuelshon . . .*"

"No, *eff.* Eff as in Friday. Eff as in *Friedland.*"

There was such a pause I called her name twice before her voice
came down again.

"*How did you know!*"

"I didn't know. I guessed."

"*How . . . it be?*"

"Why couldn't it be? It is. There it is. . . . You once told me
those Polish friends of Stefan in Vienna might know more about how
the Friedlands were betrayed, but you'd been too upset before you
left for Italy to remember to contact them. Call them now."

". . . *ten years ago . . . don't remember their names.*"

"Call MacKenzie. He'll know how to reach them. If you find
out more, call me back. Otherwise I'll try to get back to you on
Sunday . . ."

I didn't have all the names but I had enough to start. A few at
a time would be even more effective than all of them at once. One
drop at a time. And I had the most important names of all now. I
knew. Now I knew. By themselves they would be enough.

Lack of sleep the night before had caught up with me. I
stretched out in my clothes around 8:00 P.M., slept until past 11:00
and woke with the illusion of being refreshed and alert. By daylight
I'd be punchy again but there was no help for it; I knew I'd be up
for the rest of the night. I washed my face in cool water and went
outside. There were no lights in any of the cabins, there was only a
night light, an unshaded bulb, above the rear entrance to the main

building. I crossed the grove of trees to the beach and walked down past the two launches and the sailboat pulled up onto the sand, down to the great boulders, spectral in the moonlight. Beyond them I walked for half an hour and saw no one, retraced my steps to the paths between the huge granite rock formations. It was not quite 1:00 A.M. now and my legs were tired. Just before the canyon exit one of the rock temples leaned back a few degrees like Pisa's tower and there was a ledge on the lower end of its canted side I could sit on, half-comfortably. There I rested, hidden in shadow but with an open view of the beach as far as the hotel boats and beyond. After a time I slipped down to the cool sandy path and leaned back on one elbow and forearm. I thought I might lie back and try to sleep a while but I waited—and saw Peterson in swimming trunks cross the sand and push the sailboat into the rocking surf. He waded behind it, climbed aboard, and began paddling out. Within ten minutes it was difficult to see the boat at all, but I thought he had the sail up. Then everything was blotted out.

Reynaud still fumed in the reception area outside his office over the theft of his boat, as he had been doing off and on since breakfast, but he did not ask me if I had seen anything and I volunteered nothing. I was sure Peterson had gone to Silhouette to try to bring back Pontalba and it didn't matter to me whether he succeeded or not, he'd have to come back and I'd be waiting for him. It would take him at least until noon even in the fair wind that snapped the furled Union Jack against the flagpole on the hotel grounds. To kill time and keep awake I took the shuttle bus into Victoria and looked at the yachts and fishing boats in the harbor until it was time to come back for lunch. I swam and jogged and swam again and sipped coffee on the terrace of the beachside bar and watched the sun descend. On my own notepaper I drew up a dozen copies of a partial list of names in alphabetical order—A through C.

A Seychelleois boy of no more than ten came up the beach from the direction of the temple rocks and stopped twenty-five yards from the edge of the terrace.

"McKay!" he called.

I waited for him to come closer. Instead, he waited for me to walk down to where he was standing, then skipped aside a few yards to keep his distance.

"You go to reef," he said, his treble voice both shrill and harsh.

"What?"

"You go to reef." It was a command.

"Which reef?"

"Near reef. You go."

"Wait a minute. Who told . . . ?"

I made a grab for his arm but he was too fast for me. He ran as fast as he could into the grove of trees and I didn't follow.

I signed up for one of the launches and rented flippers, simple snorkeling equipment, and a bowie knife in a leather sheath. Reynaud waded out behind the boat and waited until I had gotten the outboard engine started and was headed correctly toward the shallow reef. Once I lowered my head for a moment and fell into a five-second sleep. With pounding heart I shook myself out of it and kept my eyes on the rocky shoreline ahead.

Reynaud's sailboat bobbed empty in the cove. It was anchored there and its sails were furled.

Alone above the reef I floated.

A long, wide bank of clouds slid closer, obscured the setting sun. Haunted and uneasy, I saw the cloud shadow below me, felt the slight drop in temperature. Their colors muted, their decorations blurred, schools of oval fish, as flat as paper cutouts, seemed to flutter, rotating slowly like mobiles.

Then, two and a half fathoms below me, through the clearest

water in the world, I saw the fathom-length shape, one foot wedged in the entrance to the grotto, come to rest on the edge of the eighth continent—for the lunged creatures of the world like Arvid Peterson, the wondrous and perilous continent of death.

Frightened and dazed, disoriented by death, by this death, of a man who had caused more of it than might ever be known but whose own I had no reason to predict or expect, sky and sea tilted and swayed and I grabbed the sides of the boat to keep my balance. I looked away from the cove to find a steadying horizon.

Quiet. Only a little wind now, a far-off sound of surf.

Fifty yards along the coast sat a lone man in a motorized launch like mine. He seemed a kind of apparition, either because I had not looked in that direction until now or because he had just appeared. He stood, his back to the sun, so that it was difficult to see him clearly, yet by standing he seemed to want to make himself more visible. He wore a kind of desert outfit, slacks and a bush shirt of faded khaki it appeared from that distance, that once might have been a uniform. I stood too. I stood because he was standing. Neither of us called out or broke the silence in any other way, neither of us raised an arm or hand in any gesture of recognition. But he knew me and in awe and sorrow I knew him. Not risen from the dead, because I did not believe in that for mortal men; not by any miracle. I might believe in miracles but I did not believe I would ever be chosen to see one. Not miracle but return, thousands of miles from where he had disappeared, not to banish ten years of mystery, of fading hope and loss of belief, but in this surreal moment of amazed connection to create ever more of it. I knew only that *I* was part of the equation too, that he knew I knew that I had seen justice finally done, and that I would never betray him.

Sun-dazzled, I sat again, looked down at the floor of the boat to make the reeling stop. When I looked up again, he was gone.

Caroline telephoned a second time. Of the Polish couple in Vienna, one had died but his widow remembered. In the 1940 Lithuanian capital of Kaunas, where Stefan and Helena had gone to assist Polish refugees, Stefan met with a Latvian diplomat he had known in Stockholm during Stefan's brief diplomatic career in the 1920s. The Latvian agreed to escort the Friedlands to Riga to board a Swedish ship. Stefan trusted him especially because he had been born and bred in Sweden. That was the last Stefan saw of them. The Russians reoccupied Lithuania. In June that year, Stefan was arrested by the NKVD, accused of "subversive activities"—which translated into helping refugees to escape. In the charges were accurate details that could only have come from someone who had known Stefan in Kaunas. Only after Stefan's release from captivity in 1942 was he able to determine that the Friedlands had never reached Sweden. Latvia was German—enemy—territory then and after the war a Soviet republic. There was no way to locate the ex-Latvian diplomat who had probably betrayed them all.

"I still don't have all the pieces," I said to Caroline, "but listen to me—the situation has been resolved. . . . *Resolved.* . . . There's no danger now, do you understand?"

I didn't tell her what I'd seen and I wouldn't until I knew as much as it was possible to find out. There was no need to upset and confuse her now, not over this broken line.

"*Listen,*" she said. "*I'm coming to see you! . . . you get back. I cooked it up. Latching on to Codel flying to Tokyo, Bangkok, Tehran, Tel Aviv, Paris. Capitol Hill on the move. Capitol Hill is my beat, right? We're refueling in Calcutta. I'll skip Tehran, Tel Aviv, pay . . . own way . . . Paris . . . have a week with you! . . .*"

"Stony has turned himself in," Reynaud said. "Nicky is dead too."

"Say that again!"

They had all been sleeping on the beach. Disturbed by something, Stony, who had been next to her, awoke and saw that Nicky was gone. He could make out Reynaud's sailboat moving away offshore. Alone, Stony pursued it in his catamaran, only caught up when Peterson had reached the reef off Mahé. Peterson tried to fight Stony off with an oar but Stony had an oar of his own and greater strength. He boarded the sailboat. There was no sign of Nicky. Peterson may have smothered her before he ever set sail from Silhouette, then in deep water thrown her body overboard. Peterson tried to kill Stony, too. They fought for several minutes until Stony finally got an arm lock around Peterson's throat that Peterson couldn't break and Stony held it until Peterson ceased to struggle. Stony was afraid no one would believe his story. He dumped Peterson's body over the reef. He wondered where he could hide. Then he realized hiding would only make him look guilty when he was not guilty of anything. He secured the sailboat, returned to the catamaran, and sailed it around the island to Victoria.

That was a summary of Stony's deposition under oath.

6

A majordomo led Caroline and me down a long carpeted corridor hung with large photographs under glass of Indian gentlemen in Western morning dress or ceremonial satin and brocade from another age; old lithographs of Calcutta in centuries past. The majordomo had barely touched the ornate brass handle of a heavy door when it was flung open silently by a second bearer and we were ushered into a spacious, dark-paneled study softly lit with many lamps, furnished with four deep sofas and at least half a dozen club chairs, a profusion of inlaid chests and tables, and overlapping antique Persian carpets on the parquet floor. On the walls, more photographs, paintings. High glass cases were filled with all manner of treasures—ivory, jade, and ancient Chinese ceramic wear, an exquisite T'ang horse that men might kill for, and quite possibly had.

In his customary leggings and tunic, but turbanless, white-haired, the maharajah waited for us on his feet. He was scarcely more than five feet all.

"Mrs. McKay, so good to see you again after all this time."

The maharajah was almost lost in the enormous chair in which he sat, his tiny, polished, custom-made English shoes not touching the floor, drawing occasionally on his long Cuban cigar and regarding us with a pair of shrewd, merry eyes.

"As you know, there are many networks of people in this life," he said. "Your foreign service has one—which overlaps those of diplomatic services everywhere. I'm sure you've also heard mention of an international gay network, which is what brought Peterson to us, and later, Pontalba. There is a network of aristos too, growing rather smaller every year, but still viable, to which I also belong. It was in the aristo network I'd met Stefan in Europe in the thirties, and as you know during the war here we were allies and colleagues for a few months after his wife died. Six months ago he appeared at my door, quite alive and on the trail of Peterson.

"In November of '56, in the home of a dispossessed noble family of Győr—a couple in their eighties—he had managed to hide from both Soviet troops and the Hungarian secret police. He had located the wife of that violinist—Kovács, isn't it? Getting her out of the country, however, was no longer a viable possibility. But she was safe and would survive. But Stefan knew he himself could not survive long without identity papers, real or forged. He was as experienced in these matters as one can be. From his hiding place he telephoned the Swedish embassy in Budapest. Speaking only Swedish, he persuaded a diplomat at the other end—I believe he was able to establish mutual friends—to come to Győr with a new Swedish passport and an official stamp. He provided fictionalized biographic details. He had extra passport photos in his wallet, a natural precaution for a stateless person. Already he was successfully assuming the role that would get him out of Hungary into Sweden in March of '57. The Swedes were naturally conscious of the Wallenberg tradition—helping the innocent to escape from tyranny and death. The new Hungarian regime under Kádár, clever, pragmatic, had more important things to do than harass citizens of a useful neutral country. Still dressed as a *West* European, looking the part, speaking Swedish, and Russian and Hungarian with a Swedish accent, and accompanied by a Swedish diplomat, also of noble birth, Stefan had no difficulty making his way to Budapest. After a suitable interval as a guest of the Swedish embassy, when life in Hungary had returned to some semblance of normalcy and foreign airlines were flying regularly into and out of the country, Stefan, with an official escort, could one day quietly depart.

"As a free man in neutral Sweden, why did he not reveal his escape to friends in Germany, Austria, France, many places? He had been bored and restless in Germany, bored with less imaginative relatives in France and England. Through his wife he had come to love the world of the theater, of illusion. It was a relief, it was stimulating to simply let well enough alone for a while, to stay in the new persona he had had to adopt to survive. Under the circumstances, wouldn't you have been tempted too? A new life, a new lease on life, as though one had perhaps shed ten years of it in an instant to recapture a certain measure of youth?

"There was work for him as a translator and advisor in the Swedish foreign ministry, a flat. He fit perfectly as a frequent guest in beautiful country homes that would remind him of the manor house and estate he had lost, and Stockholm has great charm, at least in the summer months.

"Then one day on the street, at a distance, he recognized Peterson, whom he believed had led Jewish friends to their death or had killed them personally, whom he believed had also betrayed him to the Soviet NKVD. He had been looking for him for eighteen years.

"But he had no documentary evidence and Peterson, a Swedish citizen, had acquired power and influence in the business world. An international Jewish agency was more than willing to sift through thousands of photographs, to compare them with current photographs of Peterson, some even in newspaper files Peterson had been bold enough not to avoid."

"We know about the evidence that was uncovered," I said. "First, that photograph."

"And so you know that it was not enough. Peterson was still free. But looking over his shoulder now. His business was one that all along took him regularly to the Mideast, to South and East Asia. Several months after the failure to bring an indictment against him, Peterson left Sweden on an extended trip to Cairo, a haven for Nazis on the run.

"Legal means suspended, possibly exhausted, Stefan took leave of absence and went to the Mideast himself, not directly to Cairo but to Tel Aviv and Jerusalem. He had done refugee work in Palestine after the war and had become friends with Israelis who now held influential positions in government, the military, intelligence. They were able to confirm Peterson's residence in Cairo, even to pinpoint the location of Peterson's apartment. Stefan went on to Cairo by way of Cyprus, waited and watched. To confront Peterson on the streets of Cairo seemed impractical but there came a day when Stefan was able to follow him on a jaunt to the Gulf of Aqaba, where scuba diving is said to be the finest in the world. Peterson had taken up the sport. And this was not his first trip. He knew the terrain as Stefan did not, caught sight of Stefan and got away. He did not return to his apartment. By the time an Israeli agent was able to track him down again, the agent could only report that Peterson had left Alexandria on a Swedish vessel bound for Calcutta."

The maharajah disappeared behind a cloud of blue smoke, and reemerged.

"Stefan returned to Stockholm to regroup his forces. For one thing he was running out of money. He needed to return to his job for a while. And now to think in terms of seeking other kinds of help. It took almost two years of patient searching for the Jewish agency to discover something else—Peterson's signature on that document, the list of names—with the Friedlands' names among them. What had Peterson done? Under some pretext prevented the Friedlands from boarding that Swedish ship, that was clear. A 'mixup'? 'Overbooked'? While they waited for another ship, would they not be most comfortable among the Jewish elite of Riga? Then the Germans arrived and the trap was closed.

"But stymied once before, Stefan could see Peterson's lawyers pouncing on the apparent impreciseness of that document. Again, the law's delay. A quarter century of delay. Assuming Peterson could even be located. Assuming he could even be extradited.

"But what would Peterson's reaction be if confronted with this document by Stefan himself? Peterson alone in some primitive setting, without the protection of his suited attorneys with their umbrellas and spectacles and briefcases?

"What Stefan had to tell me about Peterson was shocking but not entirely surprising. I had never found Peterson attractive. But when one belongs to a persecuted minority one offers hospitality and assistance to brothers in distress, overlooking personality flaws insofar as that is possible. But when Peterson began an association with A. K. Ghosh and did not heed my warning to stay clear of the man I began to keep my distance. I think Peterson's role with his legitimate firm was becoming precarious—long absences, not enough profitable performance—and that he needed the income he could get by providing Ghosh with certain logistic services—the cover of his firm. This went on for considerably more than a year. He was in and out of India. Occasionally our paths would cross. I had not completely banished him. He was out of the country when Stefan arrived. Stefan would have to wait. Pontalba was around by this time.

He'd followed the Hashish Trail to our doors. An attractive young man in his way, though often sullen. But he did not occur to me as any sort of factor. That would only come later.

"I must note that Stefan had not come to the house here. He had sent a note by messenger that he was staying at Haratunian's boarding house where he'd put up in '45, and asked to meet me at some discreet location of my choosing. There is an old fellow I look in on from time to time, completely potty, who lives in a ruin of a house on the edge of the city, set in a large overgrown garden. Stefan and I arrived separately and were not seen together, of that I am sure. Yet when Peterson returned to Calcutta he came to me obviously agitated about something. Stefan told me later he had seen Peterson by accident—from a distance on a crowded street. He berated himself for his carelessness in allowing this to happen. It seems likely Peterson had also seen Stefan or thought he might have. It was enough to frighten him away. He'd been once to my palace in north Bengal. There is a guest lodge on the grounds. He asked if he might stay there a while to write his memoirs. I feigned doubt, some reluctance, then agreed, provided he engage his own servants, buy his own food. I said I had no vehicles to put at his disposal. But in the town are hire cars and he traveled often—to Darjeeling, Kalimpong. He climbed mountains. And stayed away from Calcutta.

"At first, Stefan considered confronting Peterson in Chittipore but, as my staff reported, Peterson moved around too much. One never knew exactly where he might be. Moreover, Stefan did not want to subject me in any way to difficulties with the authorities.

"In the meantime the monsoon season was upon us—rain, dampness, hot and sticky days. The farmer's joy but less so the town dweller's. I happened one evening to notice how fretful Pontalba had become, fretful and bored with India. I mentioned this to Stefan with the additional thought that perhaps Peterson might be equally fretful and bored. Could we somehow make use of this natural phenomenon?

"Pontalba was only one of many fancy boys like him who came our way. A Californian would have done just as well. An Australian. Pontalba just happened by instead. Stefan thought of Peterson's apparent passion for scuba diving. And one is not able to scuba dive in the Himalayas or in the forests below. The idea was to turn an indolent Riviera beach boy, who had barely snorkeled in his life, into an ardent would-be scuba diver. What followed naturally from this concept was that some island in the Indian Ocean would be necessary and a small island would be a far more practical setting than this vast subcontinent.

"I obtained glossy magazines and books with beautiful color illustrations of scuba divers in the cool depths of coral reefs and left them around to browse in. I spoke of the joys of this sport in which, to tell the truth, I have never indulged. Then, as if inspired, I offered to take Pontalba to Seychelles, though that would not be possible until late September; until then I would have to be in Chittipore attending to district business, mending political fences. But late September would be the ideal time to go to the islands anyway. In the interim, why didn't Pontalba come with me to Chittipore where life would be somewhat more comfortable during the monsoon weather? He accepted with alacrity.

"Stefan and I couldn't be sure that what we'd planned would work. If not, we'd have to think again. Peterson would first have to return to the guest lodge. Obviously he did. I had no doubt he would find Pontalba attractive. Tibetan and Nepali boys speak only rudimentary English, if any at all, and are not always the most scintillating company.

"I then announced that, alas, my official duties would prevent me from making the trip to Seychelles after all. But I would not renege on a promise. I would pay to send Pontalba there. In a great burst of the generosity for which I am noted I offered to buy Peterson's ticket too. You tell me he had the tickets rewritten from round-trip to one-way—all the way to South Africa. Our idea then was

even more successful than we'd imagined. Pontalba and scuba diving weren't the only incentives for Peterson to make the trip. Safety
seems to have been another. A new haven.

"Pontalba was told nothing, not asked to do anything. Stefan
would play the situation by ear.

"You were an afterthought, Mr. McKay, a final touch. You
could be a witness to justice. And Stefan felt the need of that. He
knew of course you were stationed here. Worldwide diplomatic lists
are available in every foreign ministry. And he was hardly surprised.
In the foreign service one serves at many posts. He had met you at
one. It was no coincidence to run across you in another a decade
later. The wonder was that this had not happened sooner. And Stefan had a special regard for you both. Mrs. McKay had been writing
the story of his life when he disappeared into Hungary . . ."

The maharajah looked at Caroline. "He had fallen in love with
you, my dear. I don't know if you were aware of that. He thought
not. Fallen in love for the first time since the death of his wife more
than a decade before. And had considered declaring himself. And
then realized, he said, what an act of selfishness that would turn out
to be if you accepted him—to be sooner than you imagined burdened with an old man for some of the most active years of your
life. No, he could not do that to you, not allow you to blind yourself
to that inevitability."

Caroline shot me a marvelous, unhesitant, beautifully timed
look of reassurance.

"The stage was set for the final act," the maharajah said. "You
followed my suggestion and bought a ticket to Seychelles rather than
Penang. Stefan would stay in his cabin as an invalid."

"And went out on deck only late at night," I said.

"Ah," said the maharajah. "Did you think you recognized
him?"

"I wondered, no, I didn't even wonder, I simply couldn't be-

lieve it. I rejected the notion as pure illusion. I thought I saw him
again one evening on the island and this time I did allow myself to
wonder, at least for a few minutes."

"Perhaps he intended that, to begin to prepare you psychologically.

"Ideally, he wanted to bring Peterson to Israel to stand trial.
But being physically able to do that seemed unlikely. The idea of an
ambush, a summary execution, was abhorrent to Stefan. For the
sake of his soul he needed to confront Peterson face to face, both
of them alone, to confront Peterson with the evidence of his betrayal
and his crimes. It seemed there could be only one outcome to such
an encounter—a struggle in which one of them would perish.

"That this American—this 'Stony'—actually was the instrument of Peterson's death was of course an accident of jealousy, mad-
ness, retribution Stefan could not have predicted or counted on.
Stefan never intended to seek your assistance or involve you directly."

"Yet willy-nilly I set the thing in motion," I said. "If I'd given
Nicky that extra money she asked for . . ."

I knew, too, it was better that I hadn't.

I remembered the story of Stefan, a prisoner of the Gulag,
swimming in the river Dvina to break up logjams. But now, wherever he was, he was sixty-three years old and Peterson had been
three years younger and I remembered the sight of Peterson swimming powerfully off the beach at Beau Vallon.

"You haven't seen him since?" I asked.

"No, and I don't believe I will again, do you?"

How had he left Mahé? I was reasonably certain he had not
been aboard the S.S. *Nairobi* back to Bombay, yet it was always
possible. But British-India liners also operated between Durban,
the Seychelles, and Karachi. There were freighter routes to Kenya,
Mauritius, Réunion. Private yachts and charter vessels had been in

the harbor at Victoria on the three occasions I'd seen it, and I did
not believe it would take Stefan very long to be invited to join whatever voyage was in the offing, to Aldabra or the Comoros, to Madagascar or the Mascarenes, and on to anywhere at all.

Caroline and I went up by air very early in the morning. The
flat green paddy fields of Bengal spread below. The sun appeared.
In a few minutes we were over East Pakistan, East Bengal, and
turning north. Long veins of rivers, water everywhere, reflecting the
sun.

Gauhati, where we landed after a ninety-minute flight, was a
dusty frontier town of a hundred thousand, busy, small traffic jams
in the market area, a river port—two-story warehouses along the
Strand Road, river steamers and barges tied up along the muddy
bank, chests of tea and bales and burlap sacks of other stuff piled
on the wooden wharves—and the river was the Brahmaputra, great,
wide, and swiftly flowing down from Tibet. Bhutan was less than
fifty miles north where the foothills of the Himalayas began.

Outside the town limits our hired car with driver began to climb
and twist. Steep, terraced hillsides, bamboo forests, banana and
pineapple groves, an elephant hauling logs, buffaloes in the rice
paddies, and around a bend in the road came a brown old man in
a loincloth, wizened Mongoloid face under a conical straw hat. He
walked with a stave. Other Khasi tribesmen trudged along with
sackloads of wood and brush on their backs, the straps of the sacks
around their foreheads. Some Khasis believed their origins to be in
Mongolia, but they speak a language akin to the Khmer of Cam-
bodia. In any case they have lived in the hills of Assam for many
hundreds of years. They had been heavily Christianized by Welsh
Presbyterian, Baptist, and Roman Catholic missionaries and had a
high rate of literacy, but some families still lived deep in the forest
and worshiped trees and snakes. Every so often there were rumors

of ritual murder—some Khasi found in a clearing with slivers of bamboo driven up his nostrils.

We drove into Nongpoh, a market village, almost all of it along the sides of the main road, a few tea shops and a dozen or more stalls piled with fruit and vegetables. From here the road was one-way and traffic was scheduled. We had to wait until the down traffic had cleared. There were striped crossbars like those at a frontier. Waiting here was interesting. We had never minded it. A truckload of army troops—all turbaned, bearded Sikhs—browsed along the fruit stalls. Our driver went to get a cup of tea. I bought some small sweet bananas and a pineapple. The merchant who sold them to me hacked off the outer bark of the pineapple and I sliced it with the large blade of a Swiss army knife. It was almost too juicy. We had to stand outside the car and lean over to eat it. Our driver came out of the tea shop just before the striped barrier went up.

Only six cars had come down from Shillong during the thirty minutes we had to wait. It wasn't a very efficient system and there were plans to widen the road. I'd be sorry to see it happen. The merchants of Nongpoh would be even sorrier.

The air turned noticeably cooler as we climbed. There were huts, little houses along the road with thatched roofs interwoven with yellow flowers. The road twisted almost continuously. The forest grew thicker, the trees taller. The sky clouded and sheets of rain drove across the car. Our driver turned his windscreen wipers on, shut them off when it dried. Now it was chilly and we kept the windows up. We entered another area of driving rain and then drove out of it. We might have been in Bavaria or Scotland or on the Blue Ridge Parkway in Virginia. The higher we drove the less tropical it seemed. Below us and to the right was one end of a large lake that widened and turned on all sides in a green, misty ring of hills. It looked as though it had been there since the dawn of creation, but was man-made, five years old, the reservoir of a hydroelectric project. The road widened considerably, went over the top of a broad, concrete spillway, and cut through the hillsides. Deep valleys and some piney summits were below us. We were almost to the top. In a few minutes we crossed a narrow bridge over a rocky stream and entered Shillong, altitude 4,200 feet. The houses looked almost Norman or Alsatian—crossed wooden beams, clay walls painted white—earthquake architecture—with faintly Chinese roofs, peaked and curving up at the rain gutters, above the eaves. The Khasi men on the streets wore thick woolen scarves, Scottish tams, the women long skirts and a kind of poncho.

Shillong was less picturesque than Darjeeling, less grand than Simla, but had a unique charm of its own. There were no magnificent mountains to look at beyond but the higher hillsides above the road opened on to some of the world's loveliest countryside.

We drove through an open market, almost a caravansarai, little Tibetan ponies loaded with packs, open sacks of grain and rice, hand scales; Khasis, Tibetans, Bhutanese—the Tibetans and Bhutanese with their faces from another planet. A little whipping wind, whirls of dust; jingling bells when the ponies moved.

The Pinewood Hotel sat on a hillside. Dating from the 1920s, it was a rambling wooden building with cottage annexes stepping down the hillside behind it. The road up passed through the gates of the governor's mansion and past a little lagoon with rowboats, over an arched Chinese bridge, and up an avenue of tall trees. Our cottage had a bedroom and bath and a little sitting room with a fireplace. There were thick woolen blankets on the beds.

We were the only Americans. There were three British couples, one elderly, two young with their extraordinarily apple-cheeked children.

In the afternoon we took the hired car, sans driver, to Captain Hunt's.

White houses with red roofs were scattered up and down the

hillsides. Every time we had come up here we had wondered which house Stefan and Helena had lived in during the last months of her life. The road climbed to about six thousand feet, as high as it would go, curved through parklike forests that opened into meadowland. Fruit trees lined the road. The sky was blue, the air clear. Hills rose above and beyond deep valleys. Khasi villages, like those in Andorra on the other side of the world, were stony, gloomy, but redeemed by their setting. We were only a few miles from a forested escarpment that plunged straight down to the sea-level plain of East Pakistan. At the top of the escarpment was Cherrapunji, which vied, during the monsoon season, with one of the Hawaiian islands for the distinction of being the wettest place on earth. We drove over there for a few minutes and it seemed like the end of the world.

In the village of Mawphlang we parked in the yard of a substantial wooden house, painted green and bordered with flowers. Through a heavy wooden door at ground level we walked into a little pub, almost but not quite a replica of country pubs in Ireland or England—bar, stools, tables, chairs, supporting beams, all of heavy wood, worn smooth. Captain Hunt, retired, and his Khasi wife made their own whiskey, beer, cherry brandy, plum brandy. It was one of our favorite places anywhere. We ordered cherry brandy, served in thick pony glasses. I ordered two bottles to bring back with us. It was delicious and, we knew, had a delayed-action kick. We sipped slowly.

Caroline clinked her glass against mine.

"Thank you," she said. "I needed this. You always know what I need."

After India, after a tour in Washington, I was assigned to West European posts, capitals where Caroline could pursue her career as a journalist, as an analyst of international affairs. We invested in an apartment in Strasbourg and rent it out except when we're in residence, usually during the month of August. When the time came, I retired in Washington. Meredith and Richard have their own families now. Caroline continues her career. Perhaps you've seen her syndicated column in one of the twenty or so U.S. papers where it regularly appears. I'm working on my third book of travel memoirs. When Caroline needs to move around we journey together. Naturally these days we've made several trips to countries in Eastern Europe, Poland included. We've never seen Stefan again, have never heard from him or anything about him and have never expected to. He'd be eighty-eight this year if he's still alive, quite possible. Poland is once again independent of alien control for the first time in half a century. We'd like to think he's there if he's anywhere, living out his life in the place he loved the most, or resting beneath Polish earth. But we've avoided asking about him. It seems to us by our silence we can not only best respect his wishes but keep his life alive, if not the man himself.

Printed in the United States
2813

9 780595 094516

Praise for *Voyage of the Turtle*

"A marvelous account, a mix of travelogue and scientific research that is never less than fascinating."
—*Seattle Post-Intelligencer*

"Safina assembles a dossier of intriguing information. . . . His book thrums with fascination where he explicates the evolutionary and ecological distinctions [of Leatherbacks]. . . . Characters he portrays are rich and complicated."
—*The New York Times Book Review*

"His account, filled with prose that is often graceful, weaves science and history into a chronicle of his adventures with the people who know, or seek to know, turtles best."
—*OnEarth*

"Yes, this book is another paean to charismatic megafauna—to the "most mega" among the sea turtles, the leatherback. But Carl Safina brings to this potentially predictable subject a tone that is lyrical yet not oversentimental, a perspective that is scientific yet full of wonder. . . . Fascinating and moving."
—*Conservation in Practice*

"Carl Safina is a rare breed of writer who doesn't just do research to get the story, but enters the story and lives it. With its indomitable research, *Voyage of the Turtle* is an exquisite blend of history, biology, politics and adventure. The result is a fascinating narrative that will appeal to a reading public beyond mere turtle huggers."
—*Rocky Mountain News*

"Carl Safina is like some extraordinary astronaut who goes into space and comes back with fantastic tales of other planets and the creatures who inhabit them. Except that the marvelous planet is our own. This is a story of stoicism and wonder that will make the oceans seem that much richer to all who read it."
—Bill McKibben, author of *Deep Economy*

"That remarkable voice for the marine realm, Carl Safina, reveals the riveting tale of that most extraordinary creature, the Leatherback Turtle, overlain with the drama and hope of the battle for its conservation. No naturalist or planetary citizen can hope to be complete without *Voyage of the Turtle*. A fabulous book."
—Thomas E. Lovejoy, president, The Heinz Center for Science, Economics and the Environment

ALSO BY CARL SAFINA

Song for the Blue Ocean

Eye of the Albatross

VOYAGE OF THE TURTLE

VOYAGE OF THE
TURTLE

In Pursuit of the Earth's Last Dinosaur

CARL SAFINA

A JOHN MACRAE / OWL BOOK

HENRY HOLT AND COMPANY   NEW YORK

Owl Books
Henry Holt and Company, LLC
Publishers since 1866
175 Fifth Avenue
New York, New York 10010
www.henryholt.com

Distributed in Canada by H. B. Fenn and Company Ltd.

Library of Congress Cataloging-in-Publication Data
Safina, Carl, 1955–
    Voyage of the turtle : in pursuit of the Earth's last dinosaur / Carl Safina.—1st ed.
    p.   cm.
Includes bibliographical references and index.
ISBN-13: 978-0-8050-8318-7
ISBN-10: 0-8050-8318-9
1. Leatherback turtle. I. Title.
QL666.C546S24 2005
597.92'89—dc22   2005055023

Henry Holt books are available for special promotions and
premiums. For details contact: Director, Special Markets.

Originally published in hardcover in 2006 by Henry Holt and Company

First Owl Books Edition 2007

Designed by Kelly Too

Printed in the United States of America
D 30 29 28 27 26 25 24 23 22 21

Para Paxita y Alexandra

I am affected by the thought that the earth nurses these eggs. They are planted in the earth, and the earth takes care of them; she is genial to them and does not kill them. It suggests a certain vitality and intelligence in the earth, which I had not realized. This mother is not merely inanimate and inorganic. Though the immediate mother turtle abandons her offspring, the earth and sun are kind to them. The old turtle on which the earth rests takes care of them while the other waddles off. Earth was not made poisonous and deadly to them. The earth has some virtue in it; when seeds are put into it, they germinate; when turtles' eggs, they hatch in due time.

HENRY DAVID THOREAU
Journals, vol. 7

He had no mysticism about turtles although he had gone in turtle boats for many years. He was sorry for them all, even the great trunk backs that were as long as the skiff and weighed a ton. Most people are heartless about turtles because a turtle's heart will beat for hours after he has been cut up and butchered. But the old man thought, I have such a heart too.

ERNEST HEMINGWAY
The Old Man and the Sea

CONTENTS

GRATITUDES

This book owes its existence to the generosities of people who took me into their working world, and of those who supported mine. I wish to thank, deeply, the dedicated, courageous scientists and conservation workers worldwide whose efforts are the reason we still have sea turtles. Some of the best among them generously allowed me into the field, sharing decades of insight and hard-won scientific understanding, providing entrée to the magic and mystery of seldom-seen realms. They are true professionals who make the difficult look easy. By helping me they have graciously shared themselves with you. I hope I have done some justice to them and the miraculous animals they love with the full force of their intellect and passion.

For believing in this book I thank my editor, the extraordinary Jack Macrae, who shows us all how it's done; publisher-fisherman John Sterling; and my fine agent, Jean Naggar. Bonnie Thompson, the world's greatest copy editor, catches my mIstakes. I thank also Alice Tasman, Supurna Banerjee, Raquel Jaramillo, Kelly Too, Kenn Russell, Richard Wagner, and Sharon Pochron. Jon Luoma made the excellent maps with rare craftsmanship and artistry.

This book has been supported in part by a senior fellowship at the World Wildlife Fund, U.S., during which I have greatly benefited from the helpfulness, camaraderie, and logistical support of Scott Burns, Kim Davis, Gilly Llewellen, Kathryn Fuller, and, at WWF Indonesia, the amazing Tetha Hitipeuw. Further generosity that made possible this book and its necessary travels, as well as the work of Blue Ocean Institute, came from the Wallace Research Foundation, David and Lucile Packard Foundation, John D. and Catherine T. MacArthur Foundation, Gordon and

Betty Moore Foundation, Curtis and Edith Munson Foundation, Norcross Wildlife Foundation, West Marine, Evan Frankel Foundation, Greenstone Foundation, Streisand Foundation, the Moore Charitable Foundation, the Nature Conservancy, Susan A. and Donald P. Babson Charitable Foundation, Alexander Abraham Foundation, Swiss Re America, Patagonia, Western Pacific Regional Fisheries Management Council, Vervane Foundation, United Nations Environment Programme, Spa Adriana Aveda Salon, and Atlantis Marine World. I extend special gratitude to Julie Packard and Robert Stephens, Jocelyn Wallace and H. B. Wallace, Robert J. Campbell, Geoffrey T. Freeman and Marjie M. Findlay, Randy Repass and Sally-Christine Rodgers, Andrew Sabin, Robert and Birgit Bateman, Jocelyn Sladen, Ann Stevenson Colley, Judy and Ennius Bergsma, Averill Babson, Peter and Jessica Tcherepnine, Nancy Abraham, Jason Roberts, Josephine A. Merck, Peter Matthiessen, Henry A. Jordan and Barbara McNeil Jordan, Mr. and Mrs. Rick Burnes, Burton Lee, Doug Mercer, Toni Ross, Jud Traphagen, Richard Miller, Lawrence and Rita Bonchek, John McGillian Jr., Michael I. Freedman, Doris Cadeux, Rodger S. Rickard, George Denny, Elliot Wadsworth, Mr. and Mrs. David Deming, Deborah Gary, Bob Steneck, Dawn Navarro, Jeff Spendelow, John D. Lowry, Mr. and Mrs. Eric Wright, and others to whom I am deeply indebted.

For hundreds of millions of years, turtles swam in a world without people, and in the peopled world they remain unaccustomed and too often unaccommodated. It could not be said of us that we are accustomed to a world without turtles. Yet now, through the darker side of our human genius, we can envision that day coming. But the brighter side of that same vision can correct our foolishness. This is the creative force behind all the key people in this story, a small group making their mark in a big, unruly world. They helped me to see, sharing wide ocean horizons and sandy paths along dark surf, my steps lit mainly by the light of their vision for a longer future and more humane world.

In the last few years, satellite tracking of ocean animals has revolutionized our understanding of how they use the planet. Some of that work is reflected in this book. All the work is collaborative, but the main researchers whose tracking work informs this book include Scott Eckert, Peter Dutton, Scott Benson, Laura Sarti, Jim Spotila, Frank Paladino, Mike James, George Shillinger, and Barbara Block. Their research has been funded in part by the Alfred P. Sloan Foundation's Census of Marine Life, through its Tagging of Pacific Pelagics (TOPP) program.

For major assistance in the field and in gathering information I am deeply grateful to Sally Murphy, Sandy Lanham, Tom Murphy, Kelly Stewart, Chris Johnson, Larry Crowder, Martín Hall, Monica Goldberg, Charlotte Gray Hudson, Abiraj Rambaran, Kirt Rusenko, Llew Ehrhart, John Weisample, Blair Witherington, David Godfrey, Leah Schad, Capt. Richard Baldwin, Al Segars, Phil Maier, Franklyn and Alice d'Entremont, Jim Crawford, Arthur and Justin Jacquard, Ram Myers, Blair and Bert Fricker, Karin Forney, Lisa Grossman, José Parra, Rodrigo Rangel Acevedo, Hoyt Peckham, Chris Pesenti, and Kama Dean. Wallace J. Nichols largely started turtle conservation among Baja fishermen and introduced me to Gordo Fisher and many whom I met in Baja. Bryan Wallace undertook to act as my guide, companion, and interpreter in Costa Rica; were it not for Bryan, I might have met only turtles.

I thank also Karen Eckert, Marydelle Donnelly, Colin Limpus, David Whitaker, Dick Rice, Dennis Sammy, Sabeena Beg, Dean Bagley, Josh Reece, Eliza Gilbert, David Addison, Mark and Mora Shartzies, Karyn Fein, Julia Byrd, Sophia Chiang, Kyler Abernathy, Mark Dodd, Megan Thynge, Pilar (Bibi) Santidrin Tomillo, Maria Teresa Koberg, Xavier Miramontes, Carla Miramontes, David Maldonado, Jeff Seminoff, Letey Gamez and the staff of the sea turtle station at Agua Blanca, John La-Grange, Gary Paul Nabhan, Tim Means and Baja Expeditions, Sebastian Troëng, Thierry Work, Kelly Newton, Stori Oates, Erin LaCasella, Tim McLaughlin, John Dutton, Bruce Robison, Baldo Morenovic, Bill Wardle, John Douglas, Lee Bradford, Heidi Gjertsen, Manjula Tiwari, and the Baja-focused organizations ProPeninsula, Groupo Tortuguero, and Pro Caguama. For additional information I thank Jeffrey Polovina, George Balazs, Carol Reeb, Andrea Ottensmeyer, Paula Kullberg, Connie Murtagh, John Turner, Mike Salmon, Stony Brook University's Alistair Dove and Malcolm Bowman, Russell Dunn, and Steve Dishart of Swiss Re America, as well as Eric Chivian, Paul Epstein, and the Harvard Medical School Center for Health and the Global Environment.

I acknowledge also the Hawaii Longliners' Association and those Atlantic U.S. long-liners and fishers in Central America, Australia, and elsewhere who are changing the way they work in an effort to reduce sea turtle deaths on their fishing gear.

And I salute the people worldwide who have sacrificed and risked much toward the survival of sea turtles. The good news is: they are too many to list. Just a few of the brighter stars whom I have not yet mentioned include Peter Pritchard, Karen Bjorndal, Allan Bolten, Rod Mast, Mike Weber, Deborah Crouse, Jaques Fretey, Jack Frazier, Brendan Godley, Pam Plotkin, Selena Heppell, Jeanette Wyneken, Maria and Guy Marcovaldi and Gustave Lopez and their Projecto TAMAR in Brazil, Randall Arauz in Costa Rica, Dimitri Margaritoulis in Greece, George Hughes in South Africa, Kartik Shanker in India, and numerous other tireless luminaries whose difficult, dedicated work helps maintain the living ocean for us all.

The steadfast Mercedes Lee, Myra Sarli, Eric Gilman, Carrie Brownstein, Mary Turnipseed, Leslie Wayne, and Trudy Sulli of Blue Ocean Institute provided—as always—important logistical and administrative support, information, and encouragement during my travels and long bouts of writing. I thank also Rainer Judd, Jennifer Chidsey, Richard Reagan, and Sunita Chaudhry.

Patricia Paladines provided tea and sympathy throughout. She supported—and would have been well within rights to have welcomed—my long absences to distant shores and seas.

Most important, my uncles Tony and Sal Aragona and my father, Carlo Safina, took me fishing that day, so long ago, when from the sea came the awesome head of an astonishing creature—my first Leatherback Turtle.

One note on style, and a travel tip: I capitalize species names, partly out of respect for living things, but mainly so it's clear in all cases whether the adjective is just descriptive or part of the name, because not every green turtle is a Green Turtle. The most accessible and comfortable place I came across for travelers interested in seeing Leatherback Turtles nesting was at Grande Riviere, on the north coast of Trinidad, where I enjoyed a comfortable night at a lodge called the Mt. Plaisir Estate Hotel. I'd also recommend the Nature Seekers in Matura, Trinidad, as described herein, or getting involved in an Earthwatch project in a place like Playa Grande, Costa Rica, described later in this book. Seeing is supporting; the world awaits.

SETTING COURSE

There exists a presence in the ocean, seldom glimpsed in waking hours, best envisioned in your dreams. While you drift in sleep, turtles ride the curve of the deep, seeking their inspiration from the sky. From tranquil tropic bays or nightmare maelstroms hissing foam, they come unseen to share our air. Each sharp exhalation affirms, "Life yet endures." Each inhaled gasp vows, "Life will continue." With each breath they declare to the stars and wild silence. By night and by light, sea turtles glide always, their parallel universe strangely alien, yet intertwining with ours.

Riding the churning ocean's turning tides and resisting no urge, they move, motivated neither by longing nor love nor reason, but tuned by a wisdom more ancient—so perhaps more trustworthy—than thought. Through jewel-hued sultry blue lagoons, through waters wild and green and cold, stroke these angels of the deep—ancient, ageless, great-grandparents of the world.

Earth's last warm-blooded monster reptile, the skin-covered Leatherback Turtle, whose ancestors saw dinosaurs rule and fall, is itself the closest thing we have to a living dinosaur. Imagine an eight-hundred-pound turtle and you've just envisioned merely an average female Leatherback. It's a turtle that can weigh over a ton.

Pursuing such a creature requires traveling through time as well as across space. To fully understand the Leatherback and what it means to people, I traveled with those who still worship it, those tracking it with satellites, and those whose valuation of sea turtles merely reflects their own lust and cravings. Such travels bring you face-to-face with animals, villagers, fishermen, and scientists who've staked their whole lives to the species' tumultuous fortunes.

Of course, one must also travel with the creature itself, one-on-one. To follow the Leatherback is to experience the vast and magnificent oceanic realm that is the sea turtles' theater on Earth, encountering whales, sharks, tunas, and the gladiator billfishes that share the stage and play their roles. It is to hear the ancient whispering wisdom of these creatures' long histories of survival.

My main motivation, as always, was to explore how the oceans are changing and what that means for wildlife and people. To travel with the Leatherback is also to explore a critical dichotomy of the changing oceans: the Leatherback—that gravity-generating centerpiece of our narrative—has declined 95 percent in the Pacific during just the last two decades. Yet the good news is that in the Atlantic, sea turtle recovery is the mode, with some populations growing exponentially. Many people are now working to carry this success into the Pacific.

Nowadays seven sea turtle species stroke the ocean. In descending size they are: Leatherback, Green, Loggerhead, Flatback, Hawksbill, Olive Ridley, and Kemp's Ridley. (No one seems to recollect what riddle "ridley" refers to.) They swim warm and temperate seas worldwide, but Kemp's is restricted to the North Atlantic, and the Flatback dwells only in Australian waters. Sea turtles are big animals. Even the smallest adult ridleys pull the scale to eighty pounds, and adult Greens and Loggerheads sometimes reach over four hundred pounds (close to two hundred kilos). But the heavyweight among heavyweights, sumo champion among turtles, is the Leatherback, whose average weight is more than twice the Green and Loggerhead's maximum—and its record weight, five times as heavy.

Leviathan the Leatherback made science's acquaintance in 1554 when Guillaume Rondelet, a French physician, introduced it in his *Books on Marine Fish, in which True Figures of the Fish are Presented.* The Leatherback's Latin name, *Dermochelys coriacea,* means "leathery skin-turtle." That skin is a dark blue-black with whitish pointillist spots, like an Australian aboriginal painting. Its back, that thick, resilient shield, bears seven longitudinal ridges, in form very much like the streamlined, friction-shedding denticles covering the skin of sharks.

Though the shell is turtles' signature design feature—and all sea turtles except the Leatherback live within rigid shells—Leatherbacks have, in a sense, no shell. Their ribs do not meet or fuse but remain an open lattice-work. Rather than a hard-bone carapace shingled with scaly scutes, the back forms over a jigsaw mosaic of thousands of small, thin—only a few millimeters—bones, overlaid by a thick matrix of oily fat and fibrous tissue. The belly consists only of a fragile, narrow oval of bone that's filled in with an expanse of heavy fibrous tissue several centimeters (more than an inch) thick. Rather than a domed back meeting a flat belly, the whole animal is rounder, more barrel-shaped. In different languages the Leatherback's names refer to its shape. In the Caribbean, for instance, it's sometimes called Trunk or Trunk-back.

Of the Leatherback, superlatives abound, inter alia: Leatherbacks are the fastest-growing and heaviest reptile in nature, the fastest-swimming turtle, the most widely distributed and highly migratory reptile, and the only one that can be called "warm-blooded." In this and other respects, they seem halfway to mammals.

As a species, the Leatherback ranges more widely than any animal except a few of the great whales. As individuals, probably no whales range farther. How could they? Leatherbacks cross entire ocean basins, and then crawl ashore to nest. No whale can do that. And Leatherbacks dive deeper than whales. Certainly no land animal, including humans, can call so much of the world their native habitat and home. Leatherbacks range through tropical and temperate seas to the boundary realms of Arctic and Antarctic regions. That wide range, and their multiplicity of nesting sites, should make them extinction-proof. But they have their vulnerabilities.

I traveled with Leatherbacks and other sea turtles along the Atlantic seaboard of the Americas, from South America to the Canadian Maritimes, then in the Pacific from Central America north to central California and west to New Guinea. Leatherbacks everywhere are telling us that since the time hungry dinosaurs were a sea turtle's worst problem, it's been a shrinking world. Their mute plea, as they attempt to carry on as always, is that we will understand, while there's time, the connections within this water-bound planet. This ancient mariner who has seen both the fall of dinosaurs and the dawn of humankind, this master navigator now, ironically, needs us—the only creature who ever posed its species a mortal threat—to chart a path to its future.

Poet laureate Billy Collins says poetry should displace silence, so that before the poem there is silence, and afterward, silence again. A sea turtle, suddenly appearing at the surface for a sip of air, displaces water. And afterward, water still. This is the turtle's poetry, a wordless eloquence stated in silence and, in a moment, gone.

PART I

ATLANTIC

Current Major
Leatherback
Nesting Sites

ANGELS OF EDEN

Trinidad

"Welcome to Matura," the night-darkened sign had said, "Home of the Leatherback Turtles." From the sleeping village on Trinidad's northeast coast we drive a jungle-curtained dirt road sparked by fireflies. Scott Eckert, his face framed by a short, graying beard, grips the steering wheel as we bounce along the ruts and roots of a place he loves. Rain-forest trees silhouetted by a half-moon line the sky. Above, a see-through veil of cloud is scudding across the lunar wedge. Where forest yields abruptly to palms dancing in the warm breeze, surf rumble overtakes the trilling jungle.

Rounding a turn and arriving finally at the beyond of nowhere, I'm surprised to see school buses parked around an open-sided rain shelter. If we've left the world behind, so have about 150 other people—many teens and children among them—hoping also to see a giant nesting sea turtle.

Coming immediately to greet Scott is a slender, dark-eyed twenty-five-year-old man named Abiraj Rambaran. He works with the group Nature Seekers, which organizes these outings. Youngest of tonight's Nature Seekers is eight-year-old Chantel, whose braids emerge from under a red baseball cap. She's with her grandmother Savita. On the dark beach the mist in my light beam comes thick with the sea's scent. A stiff breeze is blowing.

When Christopher Columbus got here he thought he had found the portal to Eden. He'd dedicated his third voyage to the Holy Trinity, and when he sighted a large island with three peaks—Trinidad—it seemed surely a sign. Columbus wrote, "God made me the messenger of the new heaven and the new earth . . . and he showed me where to find it." In the Gulf of Paria he found the sea freshening. An overwhelming sense of miracle must have attended an island bearing such obvious signs of heavenly guidance and a sea turned to freshwater. Columbus apparently believed Earth was "shaped like a woman's breast," with the Garden of Eden where the nipple might be and a great river flowing from it. Columbus's crew had never seen a river the size of the Orinoco, and its ocean-diluting flow convinced Columbus that the Garden of Eden lay near at hand. Columbus named the large landmass Tierra de Gracia—Grace Land. We call it South America. Columbus thought this realm was God's paradise on earth.

Above an ocean black but for the foaming surf, distant lightning flashes. Four people are patrolling somewhere on this miles-long beach for nesting giant Leatherback Turtles.

Last night, no turtles appeared. High wind and high surf discourage turtles from approaching shore. Leatherbacks are heavy enough to come down hard, so they tend to stay away when the surf is cracking wild. Tonight's surf remains rather heavy, with a rolling roar and foamy breakers. Most Leatherbacks arrive here before two A.M. It's already midnight, and no turtles.

Scott optimistically incants, "Any minute now."

Rain begins. I pull up my rain-jacket hood and turn my back to the wind. Heavy rain also keeps turtles off the beach here; they don't like muddy, brackish water flowing from the rivers. Abiraj says, "Normally, the beginning of turtle season is the dry season. Usually the beaches are very wide then. But this year it's been raining the whole time, very bad erosion. I've never seen weather this strange."

The beach is squeezed between a restless sea and the coconut palms and dense jungle. Where high-reaching surf pins us against the vegetation, we time the wave's retreat and then run before the next wave. One of these breakers could knock a person down. Rough and dark as the surf is, we proceed carefully.

A volunteer patroller greets us with news of an arriving female, far down the beach.

Her tractorlike track leads from the surf up to dry sand and shadows, revealing her whereabouts. The sight of her is sufficiently astonishing to strike a deep gasp into my ribs. The word *turtle* is vastly inadequate for this dark monster, breathing before me like a sudden remembrance of a world before memories.

Her proportions impress me as surreal, counterfeit, yet so imposing as to banish all doubt of the fact of her. Most of her shell is dusted with sand, making her look sugar-coated, an eight-hundred-pound confection, long as a man and thigh-high. Lying like a just-crashed saucer from the other side of darkness, with those huge splayed flippers, she seems wondrous as a fallen angel. She seems impossible.

Lured and shipwrecked by the hazards of maternal devotion, she lies quietly marooned. From the exertion suggested by her groundbreaking tracks, from the weight and gravity of her—and merely that she has paused, exhausted, atop the incline of the beach—her arrival seems an act of defiance, a tribute to everything that rises and persists against all reason.

Soon, her stillness stirs. She begins the odds-defying task she was born to perform. She brings her front flippers up and forward like the wings they are to her, twists them like propellers, and chops down vertically, straight into the sand. Now her wings are shovels, sand plows. She pulls back sharply and flings a shower of beach behind her. Thus she begins her "body pit"; this is how she clears the site and settles down, embedding herself into deeper, moister sand.

Each female encounters a different set of challenges every time she hits the beach. She may come in where the beach is too steep; she may come on the wrong tide; she may arrive where the beach is too narrow; she may ascend to find a wrack line obstructed with drift logs and trash—or a man with a machete.

I'm grateful for the moonlight. She's a *surprisingly* leather-bound beast: no scales, not on flippers, head, even shell. There isn't that turtle-hardness. Her wide, winglike foreflippers, each three-quarters her body length, span fully eight feet or so. Very different are her rear flippers: palmate like hands, for sculling and ruddering. A bridge of soft skin conjoins her rear flippers and her short tail like one integrated assembly. Notwithstanding its long meridian ridges, her back is smooth as the taut skin it is. The rear of her "shell" attenuates to a narrow, projecting point, serrated like the blade of an aloe plant. Her head and neck are massive, the size of a soccer ball.

Getting down onto my belly in the sand, my chin resting on clasped fingers, I am low and dark, still as a beach log. A few feet away and toward her rear, I don't seem to be disturbing her at all.

She deepens the pit by flinging sand with powerful strokes of her oar-like foreflippers—showering me—then clearing and pushing additional sand with her rear flippers. Her shoulders flex as she pivots closer and the ridged leather-bound shell pauses very near me. She stops and blinks away thick, gelatinous tears. She inhales, then continues chopping farther into the beach and flinging back more sand.

In the water she was weightless and buoyant. Here she suddenly weighs nearly half a ton. Her exertions reflect unaccustomed inner pressures. Every few minutes she rests for a few deeper, heaving breaths, opening her mouth slightly while drawing in a bucketful of atmosphere. Two strong, hard structures protrude from her upper jaw like large canine teeth, while the point of her lower jaw rises in one sharp, upward-projecting fanglike point that fits between the two "canines." Her entire shell rises as she breathes, her rear legs lifting her body like a bellows so air can enter. Each inhalation is a sharp gasp, each exhalation a deep gurgling hushing gush of air.

When her body pit is deep enough to settle her into moister sand, she stops using her foreflippers and rests.

Now, with her rear flippers flattened to surprisingly wide spades, she throws sand until she has a foot-deep hole directly under her tail. Her motion changing again, she next begins carefully lifting palmfuls of sand from the deepening chamber, depositing them gingerly alongside her. She's doing this with her *rear* flippers, cupping them like hands in mittens, her work unseen and flawless, the work of a blind watchmaker. Quite unlike the stiffened front flippers now helping anchor her in place, the manipulations of her rear flippers are dexterous beyond imagining. They have the exquisite sensitivity of an elephant's trunk.

I wriggle in closer. She alternates—one scoop of sand with the right rear flipper, then one flipperful with her left—pivoting her body slightly with each alternation so she can deftly maneuver each flipper into the hole. She's creating a perfectly cylindrical chamber, surprisingly deep, remarkably round. Strikingly, each time she reaches in, her flipper enters the hole with perfect delicacy, never knocking sand from the edge or sides. Nothing in human experience is so skilled while so unlearned.

Two Nature Seekers arrive. We exchange quiet greetings. They radio that a group can be sent to see this turtle ("She done body pittin'; she ready to lay de eggs now. Ovah") and continue along down the beach.

Now the hole is about the depth of one whole rear flipper. She again changes technique: reaching in, lifting a cupped flipperful of sand, and flinging the sand outward and forward with a quick snap. It's a tricky motion and an improbable maneuver.

She's alternating movement and deep gasps of air, her breathing so labored it's audible above the surf's thunder. She steadily digs this cylinder for half an hour—reaching, pulling, flinging, alternating, reaching, pulling—and now she's slowing, resting more, taking deeper breaths.

I hear voices and turn to see people who've found her track from the sea, moving toward us in the dark.

Now with one flipper she is touching, gently and sensitively, the chamber's interior. With her flipper tips she widens the bottom into a flared flask. Methodically, meticulously, delicately, she curls the fingers of her mitten, shaving one side of the chamber's base with the tip of one flipper, then using the other, flaring the flask that will receive her eggs. Finally one rear flipper is just dangling, waving in the hole, unable to reach more sand. The chamber is fully as deep as my arm is long.

Two dozen people of widely varying ages arrive, all Trinidadian, led by eight-year-old Chantel and her grandmother Savita. They come amid whispers of astonishment. Chantel sits silently in the sand next to me. Grandma Savita quietly directs the whole crowd behind us, to reduce visual distraction for the giant turtle. Many sit. Scott and Abiraj stand well off to the side.

When all have settled, a boy perhaps seven years old asks, "What is *that*?"

Grandma Savita replies, "That is the turtle."

The perplexed child reassesses the giant before him and responds, "*That's* a turtle?"

Carefully Savita directs her small, dim flashlight to the turtle's posterior. The whole crowd leans forward, their attention directed to the egg chamber.

The people have come with school or church groups from distant villages. Many are repeat visitors. They belie the stereotype that locals in developing countries lack interest in nature.

After a pause of perhaps two minutes come those long-anticipated first eggs. Two fall at once. I quietly move to give others a good glimpse of the eggs filling the chamber. When, in her next exertion, three eggs fall from her into the chamber, it draws gasps from the crowd.

I wonder about our disturbance. But this crowd is the turtle's best insurance against anyone coming to kill it. In the world as it is, this intrusive, admiring crowd is the price a turtle pays for living. Before Nature Seekers was formed in 1990, poachers killed roughly half the turtles coming to lay eggs in Trinidad (for meat or the ten gallons of oil they can yield). Nature Seekers has shown nesting turtles to seventy-five thousand people in the last ten years, with the numbers increasing. Now nearly everybody in Trinidad knows about their giant, endangered sea turtles. Poaching is much diminished. Nature Seekers is part of the Wider Caribbean Sea Turtle Conservation Network, a driving force behind sea turtle recoveries in the Caribbean region.

Each time her tail flexes she pushes out two or three, sometimes four eggs at a time. They seem a little rubbery and a little papery. Turtle eggshells aren't brittle like birds' eggs; they're something between leather and parchment. Incubation takes about two months if the sand is cool, perhaps six weeks if it's hot. During that time the fertilized cell's DNA code reassembles the yolk into a sea turtle.

Grandma Savita murmurs to the assembly, "If you want to touch the turtle, photograph the turtle, it will be okay now." You'd think egg laying would be the most sensitive and critical part of the nesting process. But while laying, Leatherbacks seem as if in a trance.

In the twenty years between 1980 and 2000, the Leatherback Turtle lost an estimated 70 percent of its worldwide population. One study saw this decline in only fourteen years; it estimated that Leatherback numbers plummeted from 115,000 adult females alive in 1982 to fewer than 35,000 by 1996. A Leatherback's two main problems are drowning in fishing gear and getting its eggs taken by people, mainly for food and supposed aphrodisiac powers.

Because the decline is steep and deep, the World Conservation Union considers the species "critically endangered." But Leatherback fortunes appear quite different in the two main oceans. Good records over several decades from its major rookeries in the Caribbean, Malaysia, and Mexico and detailed records from Costa Rica since the early 1990s tell this clearly: the Pacific Leatherback has crashed from an estimated 90,000-plus adult females living in 1980 to fewer than 5,000 by the threshold of the new millennium, down 95 percent. Conversely, Atlantic Leatherbacks seem generally stable, with some populations clearly increasing now from former lows.

Scott says, "We've definitely got more turtles compared to what people saw in the 1970s through '90s." About six thousand different individual females annually use several Trinidad beaches for nesting. Scott reports, "Trinidad's going up; Guyana and Suriname seem stable. The northern Caribbean and Florida population is growing exponentially."

The skin on her rear flippers is very soft; through it you can readily feel the long, fingerlike bones. Her head feels smooth. Her neck and shoulders are thick, soft, warmer than the sand. Her back feels unyielding under the normal pressure of a human hand; but if you move your finger sideways, you can push the skin over the underlying bones.

Scott says these bones are like little interlocking pieces about an inch in diameter. "If you pressed her shell with the flat of your hand, you would actually see the outline of those little bones," he notes. "It's like a jigsaw puzzle under a drape." The Leatherback's "shell" is often described as rubbery, but to me it feels more like a smooth, dense pad, like a foam mat. Scratch it with your fingernail, and it'll bleed.

When about seven dozen billiard-ball-sized eggs fill the chamber, the first of two dozen much smaller "eggs" fall from her. These strange small yolkless "eggs" have no embryos. Only Leatherbacks lay them, and it's not clear what their function is. They may provide air space at the top of the nest, stabilize its humidity, protect against fungus or insects, or provide elbow room for the unusually long-winged hatchlings. Even the experts don't know.

Each Leatherback averages seven nests in a breeding season, about ten days apart. Though averaging an undistinguished 65 to 85 eggs—in the Pacific and Atlantic, respectively—Leatherbacks' frequent nesting yields seasonal totals of 450 to 600 eggs, making them the egg-laying champions. (Other sea turtle species nest two to four times, laying about 100 eggs per clutch.) Quite probably, Leatherbacks can produce more offspring in a year than any reptile or mammal; they leave birds in the dust.

The world's most intrepid reptiles, Leatherbacks prefer ruggedly pounded shores. They like an open-faced, coarse-sand beach with a steep approach fully exposed to direct surf. Such dynamic beaches tend toward change, and many Leatherbacks lose nests to erosion even in good times. Because their beaches are not reliable, they put their eggs in different baskets. "One night they'll nest here," says Scott, "next time, two kilometers down the beach, or twenty kilometers up that way." Why would Leatherbacks want a steep, treacherous beach? Possibly their immense size makes it important to avoid getting stranded in extensive shoals if the tide recedes while they're ashore. Leatherbacks here like to emerge on flooding tides, when the water comes closest to the nesting sites.

Laying completed, she begins pulling sand down onto her eggs with her rear flippers, covering them up. Splaying each rear flipper into a paddle the size of a tennis racquet, she presses this sand in place. She wields these flippers carefully, patting the sand with the dexterity and seeming sensitivity of a hand in a mitten.

Can she have any sense of what she's done? What mental experience motivates her through these motions, producing eggs she will never even see, hatchlings of which she almost certainly has no inkling? All the activities have to be performed in exactly the right sequence, for exactly the right duration—no more, no less—and with exactly the correct effect. Can she have any idea of the *why* of any of this? How could she? Doing all this must satisfy an urge, perhaps as do our own appetites and bodily urges; humans know that feeling of being driven by something other than reason. I look for analogies, but there seems no exact parallel in human experience for what might be going on in this turtle's mind. If there is, then the turtle understands more than I credit her for, and that is entirely possible.

Now, finished patting, she suddenly makes three vigorous power thrusts with her front flippers, throwing sand backward. From ten feet away I can feel the deep thuds on the beach as she swings her flippers forward and *slams* them onto the shore, pulling back big loads of sand, obscuring her precious deed.

She rests, her throat pumping heavily as she pushes and pulls air in and out of her. Something catches Scott's eye and he moves in closer, saying, "See this?" A big pink streak goes around her shoulder and armpit, right where the skin is softest. "She might have taken a hook here in the shoulder, and then the line wrapped around her there. Or it might have been longline or lobster gear, but that's a classic fishing-line scar."

One of our entourage adds that he saw a turtle that had swallowed a section of fishing line with several hooks. "She had line all wrapped around her, going down her throat and hooks coming out her rear end."

Scott comments, "These old girls really do run the gauntlet out there." He estimates that Trinidadian gill nets alone tangle five hundred to six hundred turtles a year, and he's beginning to work with fishermen. Of those caught, some are released alive; some drown. Some get taken for meat or oil. Once when he tracked nine Leatherbacks from here, four got tangled in nets—three fatally—before they'd even left Trinidadian waters.

Scott applies disinfectant to the spot he has chosen for attaching a metal tag. He shows us where: "You don't want it in this soft skin at the base of the flipper. You want it out a little farther—here. Then it won't scrape the side of her body." The U-shaped clip goes snugly around the flipper's trailing edge. A sharp, triangular metal "tooth" is designed to come through the flipper into a hole on the opposite side of the tag, and fold securely with help of a clamping tool. "Make sure you have the point facing up when you apply the tag, so there's nothing sharp facing her body when she brings her flippers down along her side."

Scott applies the tag. I flinch as the metal tooth pierces her. The turtle reveals no reaction. It might bother me more than it does her; tagged turtles often return to the same beach. Surely it's a vast improvement over killing her for meat.

Watching her, and the people, I'm reminded of humans' strange range of treatment of other animals, our deep capacity for kindness and our equal one for cruelty. Each comes naturally, and each is learned in like measure.

She begins creeping forward, then stopping, turning her whole body this way and that while hurling large amounts of sand to all points of the compass, waving her arms like a child making snow angels. Then she turns and creeps forward a little farther, and flings some more. Not everything airborne is sand; a few coconuts go flying too. Slowly she obliterates the nest's location until, in the churned sand of a small landscape of bulldozed beach, it's impossible to see where, exactly, her eggs lie hidden.

Her throat flushes pink with exertion.

About an hour and a half since she first chopped into the beach, her motions change yet again. She stops thrashing, and now there's no question that she's headed to the sea. Each pull on her oars propels her forward. She heads straight down the wet part of the beach. Each thrust closes the gap between her and the highest reach of the waves, until finally the waves begin washing around her.

When she was in the pit I didn't appreciate the massiveness of her girth, because one thinks of a turtle's belly as flat. Here on hard sand her enormous thickness is suddenly apparent. Stand next to her, and you realize that this barrel-shaped turtle's back is several feet from the ground.

The swirling suds sweep the sand from her, leaving her shining like a polished stone. Suddenly she is a sleek, dark animal, regaining the cool relief of her weightlessness. The next wave pushes her backward a little, and the following wave pulls her into the sea, almost impatiently, and she is simply gone.

As she strikes homeward toward two thousand miles of blue universe, one impression recurs: *she succeeds, deprived of rational thought, as she has succeeded for one hundred million years.* Meanwhile I can only stand and spin the wheels of my vaunted reason.

We have word of *three* turtles widely separated farther along the beach, and we strike in their direction. Approaching the first I see, I realize it is dead. Its skull bears compound fractures, as from a series of sharp blows. It's an arresting shock with an overwhelming stench.

Scott says, "This was poachers." Leatherback adults don't really have natural predators on beaches. "Not anymore," Scott remarks, then gives it more thought and adds, "For a while, their ancestors probably had to contend with *Tyrannosaurus rex* lurking behind the dunes."

Savita says, in her lilting Trinidadian accent, "One turtle is nuttin'; I remember as a child, dis was a prime slaughterin' place. Now, to find turtles killed like dis, it's very rare. Now people see de turtles more for tourism, and as representing Trinidad."

Down along the beach, a turtle in the surf summons my attention like something darkly whispered. She pauses. A wave hits her and explodes, as though slamming a boulder. She has emerged where the beach is unusually steep *and* unusually narrow. If she had arrived farther up or down the shore, she could have pulled herself past the wipe of the highest waves. But here the beach is so pinched between sea and jungle there is no sand above the tide line. A wise turtle would lumber back into the sea and come ashore elsewhere. Instead, she shoves up the short steep beach to where it abuts the vegetation. She has turned, facing the ocean. Her foreflippers and head are on wet, hard sand. Surely she realizes, in that very successful three-ounce brain, that this is *not* the kind of place a turtle is supposed to dig. But she begins digging. A wave presents its foam just inches from her massive head.

Hands on hips, shaking her head in disapproval, Savita says, "Dis is really sad. Before, it was a good hundred yards to de water. I've never *seen* de beach like dis. Now I don't know what deez poor turtles are going to do. Is dis going to continue?"

The beach isn't what the turtles expect. Part of what's going on may be the rising sea level. Part is weather and lunar cycle. The moon, waxing toward full, pulls the tide higher up the beach each night. The surf is running such high laps it's undermining the overhanging palm trees, licking the jungle vegetation, and washing out nests, scattering eggs. Parts of the beach now lean at a thirty-degree angle, some spots have a knee-high step cut into them. Certain conclusion: this nest is doomed.

People say this is the way it is with Leatherbacks. But people have been studying them for only thirty years out of over one hundred million. During these recent years, the sea level has been rising, and almost every casual discussion reveals that people have never seen these beaches so eroded.

A wave wets her head and flippers—and the next wave swirls into her egg chamber. Even as the upper hand of each lapping wave slaps her face, she begins laying. Knowing how turtles accomplish such unfathomable and hazardous crossings of space and time to come here, it's disturbing to watch her squander her fertile fervor in so unsuitable a place. Had she landed fifty yards down the beach she might have salvaged this endeavor. Had she landed right here last year, she might have had no problem.

Savita admires her: "Dis one very nicely colored. Very nice spotting."

Scott remarks, "She's a little girl, kind of small—." She might weigh as "little" as five hundred pounds. But this might be the first time in her life that she's come ashore. Maybe her judgment reflects inexperience.

Savita, Scott, and I confer. We can't simply pick up this colossal beast and move her to a better spot. But her eggs—we *can* move those.

Meanwhile, our misguided turtle finishes laying and begins her covering motions. But because the swirling water washed much sand into the chamber, her eggs are mounded so near the surface that her patty-caking immediately begins breaking them, splattering her rear flippers with yolks. It's a mess.

Other eggs are getting washed out of the nest. Grandma Savita and Chantel begin handing eggs to me and Scott; we hold our shirts out like aprons to receive them. We'll rebury them someplace safer.

Meanwhile, another turtle who'd also started digging within the reach of oncoming waves does the sensible thing and returns to the water with her eggs still inside her.

HOWLER MONKEYS ROAR THE DAYBREAK'S THUNDER. AFTER A NIGHT filled with great beauty and bewilderment, I am somewhere in the outer orbits of exhaustion when we quit the beach at the pink of morning. Is

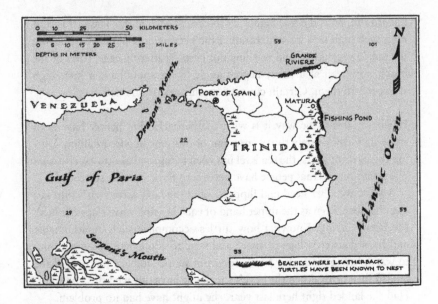

this when the night ends or when the day begins? It depends on whether you're a turtle, and I'm almost too tired to remember. Bats piercing the shadows of dawn above a stream give way to loftier day-patrolling kites, and we jounce deliriously toward town.

Matura, Trinidad, population two thousand, appears a typical tropical mix of tin-roofed shanties, downcast wooden houses, and aspiring, uninspiring, perpetually unfinished cement-block homes. Much of the population—too much—appears to be children who roam the roads as do the chickens.

Abiraj has graciously invited us to be his guests in the home he is slowly completing. Though Abiraj lives "alone," the house is anything but lonely. A tree frog resides in the shower; a couple of bats hang out under the high tin roof; and a hand-sized tarantula, with pink feet, seems to feel comfy and at home on the drapes. Of the tarantula, Abiraj says simply, "He's been all around the house for about two months—on the dining-room table, in the kitchen. . . ." Neither of us considers removing the hairy beast to the great outdoors; why spoil the amusement? Even with the tarantula, the living room remains safer than outside. On the road nearby, an auto has flattened a Fer-de-Lance, among the most devastatingly venomous of snakes.

While rain pelts the tin roof that keeps our indoor wildlife and ourselves happily dry, we sleep much of the day.

. . .

BEHOLD THE TURTLE. ITS REGISTERED TRADEMARK, OF COURSE, IS THAT shell, arguably the most astonishing armor in the history of life's many splendors. The top, or carapace, usually forms from expanded ribs fused with one another and with the spine. Large scales called scutes, covering the carapace, are made of keratin, like heavily reinforced fingernail. The belly, or plastron, forms of bones unique to turtles, not modified from ribs.

Turtles are ancient but not primitive. That body plan derives from a lengthy line of reptiles that evolved increasing defensive and structural plating. Achieving a shell like that requires extensive bodily rerigging that doesn't evolve overnight—moving the shoulder inside the ribs, for example, and devising a way to breathe through lungs locked within a pair of hard plates. Such a radical makeover takes what turtles had: time.

The earliest known turtles appear in deposits from the Triassic period 220 million years ago. Their origins remain uncertain, their immediate progenitors debated, but they were by then already fully formed and widely distributed. Things then were, in a word, different. All of the world's land formed one conjoined supercontinent, Pangaea. By around 200 million years ago, when dinosaurs stood poised for their main reign during the Jurassic period (which rumbled until about 145 million years ago), the first seagoing turtles had developed.

What makes some turtles *sea* turtles is fairly obvious: sea turtles are turtles that live in the ocean. Their limbs have been transformed to flippers and could be described as winglike or finlike. One living turtle, the Diamondback Terrapin of the United States' eastern and southern coasts, inhabits brackish bays and estuaries. It has feet rather than flippers and is not a sea turtle. One freshwater turtle has flippers; it's not a sea turtle either.

Three different groups of turtles entered the seas, one during the Jurassic and two in the following period, the Cretaceous. Some fared better than others, and various sea-swimming turtles flourished, wrote their stories, and went extinct over the long pages of evolutionary time. Their most-visited theme and cautionary tale is of specialized forms that couldn't survive a world of change.

Sea turtles in body forms we'd easily recognize first stirred water a little over 100 million years ago. Neither the Mediterranean Sea nor the North Atlantic yet existed; India was on a course to collide with Eurasia (its fender damage would be the Himalayas); Australia remained attached to Antarctica; Arabia was part of Africa; and North America,

Greenland, and Eurasia were joined. Despite the appetites of giant sharks, plesiosaurs, ichthyosaurs, and mosasaurs (and partly *because* of the selective pressures of predators), those ocean turtles flourished into four families and numerous species.

One family spawned Archelon, the biggest turtle ever. An average adult Leatherback, at 800 pounds and with a wingspan of perhaps 8 feet, is a hard-to-believe turtle. Archelon weighed about 6,000 pounds (2,700 kilos), with flippers spanning 16 feet (4.9 meters), and a body 15 feet long nose to tail, including a yard-long head that wielded a beak like a giant eagle's. Archelon would have filled a fair-sized room. It must have shaken the beach and dug like a steam shovel.

Scientists believe that an asteroid struck Earth 65 million years ago near the Gulf of Mexico and the present-day Yucatán Peninsula, creating a global climate catastrophe that swept away the dinosaurs and pterosaurs, the ocean's dreaded mosasaurs and plesiosaurs, mollusks like the spiral-formed ammonites (whose polished fossils flourish in gift shops), various of the sea's phytoplankton types, and many mammals and birds—all told, perhaps 85 percent of Earth's species. Sea turtles took it, and survived. But with casualties: Archelon's family and one other succumbed.

Two sea turtle families survive today: the several hard-shells make up the family Cheloniidae, while the family Dermochelyidae now contains the modern Leatherback alone. Leatherbacks split from hard-shells a long time ago, around 100 million years. After Archelon's family died out, the Leatherback family radiated into at least six species, as though taking their vacated jobs.

Earlier Leatherbacks had bonier shells and flatter backs. As Leatherbacks evolved, their shells got thinner and the bones beneath smaller and more numerous, increasing their flexibility. But the Leatherback family, in turn, also got downsized, possibly because of competition from newly evolving ocean mammals.

Only two species of Leatherbacks entered the Pleistocene and faced its ice ages. Only one emerged. So the modern Leatherback survived conditions that extinguished other Leatherback species about a million years ago. All Leatherbacks living worldwide today are genetically so similar that even the modern Leatherback probably came within a flipper's length of extinction, surviving in one small population, most likely in the Indian Ocean, then reradiating from that lost tribe of refugees.

·   ·   ·   ·

ONE OF THE GLORIES OF ANY BEACH IS THAT IT IS ALWAYS AT THE END of the road. Abiraj, Scott, and I return surfside a couple of hours before sunset. In daylight we can see that this is not a beach of glistening sands and tropical idyll; it's a wild place where the sea and the land both end and meet, a place of friction, contest, and clashing identities.

In one eroded spot where waves have cut a shelf into the beach, turtle nests washed out of the bank are scattered along the strand line. These eggs contain stilled near-term embryos, three-quarters of the way toward hatchlinghood.

Responding to my queries about rain, erosion, and the rising sea level, Scott says, "Beaches come, beaches go. Sea turtles have experienced lots of climate changes; some have gone extinct and some have survived to the present day. If the change is slow enough, the turtles may shift to new areas. But," he adds, "the key words are *if* and *may*." The global sea level rose something like eight inches in the last hundred years, due both to melting ice and seawater expansion caused by warming. The rate of rise is ten times faster than that during any time in the last three thousand years—in other words, during most of civilization. Turtles could adjust. Can people? And how badly will turtles be caught in the squeeze between beachfront development and rising tides?

Overhead, vultures slide effortlessly along the drafts, cruising the miles-long beach. They're drawn here partly because of these scattered eggs. But only partly. The beach is littered with wrack lines of palm fronds and drift logs and coconuts and some trash. Several vultures are poking their heads into a plastic trash bag as though entering the carcass of a dead animal. Scott says, "I'm noticing a lot more trash on the beaches—not just here, but wherever I go." I see a few bottles, pieces of plastic, part of a fishing net, and discarded chemical light sticks used to attract Swordfish to the baited longlines. But I've seen much worse.

Abiraj says the cooling from this afternoon's hard rain will likely trigger some hatchling emergence. I'm looking forward to seeing baby turtles.

When their time comes, little turtles begin scratching against the inside of the shell with a point atop their beak. As in birds, this "egg tooth" will fall off soon after hatching. Siblings synchronize, pipping through the shell within hours of one another. Then they rest for a day or so, still in their sandy nest, absorbing yolk, straightening out, readying. Meanwhile, egg fluids drain away, creating space. Unlike birds, they hatch into a dark, humid world of sand and squirming siblings. The activity sets the whole brood in motion, the little turtles working in stints lasting several hours, alternating with resting. The upward assault can take several days' effort. From first "pip" of the egg to emergence at the surface can take three to seven days, averaging perhaps five. The top hatchlings scrape sand from the roof, and all the others dig through it. As the sand trickles down, they are raised up, the brood and the floor of the nest rising together. Sticking with the group makes things easier. Left-behind stragglers may take twice the time, and singles who don't keep up often become entombed. When the brood reaches just below the surface, the sinking, settling sand creates a telltale depression. Agitation prompts activity, but heat inhibits movement. Thus if they near the surface during daylight, they stop, waiting just beneath the surface for the sand to cool, signaling that night has fallen and the surface is securely dark. On many beaches the sand doesn't begin cooling until ten P.M. or so.

But a cooling rain can fool some hatchlings into thinking it's night, time for safe emergence. Then off they go.

We might have already missed some action. Ominously, the sand carries the impressions of many splayed feet—vultures' feet. Scanning all the footprints, Scott says in a concerned, hushed voice, as though thinking aloud, "Jeez, this was mayhem."

Reappraising the vultures overhead, Abiraj says, "You see—the vultures know."

Scott adds, "They must have hit the hatchlings very hard today."

Down the beach a ways, half a dozen Black Vultures are gathered around a depression on the sand. Two hatchlings are just emerging, and the vultures see them instantly.

One grabs a hatchling. Another does likewise. You expect vultures to feed on death, not deliver it.

Abiraj runs ahead, arms waving, chasing the birds, who flap heavily away. One hatchling is on its back, its neck and shoulder torn partly open, moving but mortally injured. Another is dead. Five little Leatherback hatchlings emerge, one after another, their timing during our protective presence rather fortuitous. They are charcoal-colored, with whitish dots lining the ridges of their backs and flippers, as though they're bejeweled with little strands of pearls.

Half a mile down the shore seven Black Vultures and two Turkey Vultures suddenly plane down to one spot as another brood commences graduation.

We head toward them rapidly on the powdery sand.

Every little while along the beach we find a hatchling with its head and foreflippers missing and its shell emptied like a squeeze purse. Near one vulture-trod nest we find about a dozen such emptied hatchling husks.

Scott has never seen such intense predation here. "The way they're just tearing heads off and eviscerating them and leaving the rest—they could demolish whole broods like that." Scott adds agitatedly, "I wouldn't normally begrudge a vulture an occasional meal, but this seems out of control."

By the time we approach, vultures are shredding hatchlings, tearing heads off to get their bills inside the shell, eating just the good parts. One Turkey Vulture is trying to chug down a whole turtle. It can't quite swallow it, and a smaller Black Vulture saunters up and takes possession. Its audacity goes uncontested, indicating these vultures are well fed indeed.

We arrive and dig the nest, finding only one surviving hatchling left behind. Lucky mistiming. Like a homing pigeon, it makes a couple of orienting circles, then scrambles to gain the uncertain sea.

It enters the water with unflinching courage—or, at least, without pause or hesitation—then pops up a few feet away in the turbid water just beyond the foam. It'll be confronting new challenges solo.

All those vultures continue sliding in the updrafts over the palm trees, patrolling in the cushiony air. They look lazy but they're vigilant, and not slow. Now the action shifts back up the beach where we just came from: two dozen down-spiraling vultures mark another brood of hatchlings entering a world too eager to receive them.

All the vultures corkscrew to the beach. Through my binoculars I see a frenzy of tiny flippers churning up through the sand amid the legs, splayed toes, and monstrous bent-over heads of hungry birds. Most are getting picked off as they emerge. The vultures string out down to the waterline, finishing off hatchlings dashing seaward.

We arrive to chase them off. They move indolently, some taking dinner to go and continuing to peck and worry the writhing hatchlings they have carried. They land only about fifty feet away from us, looking baleful.

My justification for interfering with nature: this isn't natural. The number of Leatherbacks is lower than normal because of humans, and the number of vultures is higher than normal because of, well, humans. The more people, the more garbage, the more vultures.

Having survived their first half minute now in the world aboveground, twenty-eight newly emerging hatchlings who don't question my justifications are valiantly making their way to the waves that reach for them and withdraw, reach and withdraw, as though coaxing. The hatchlings dash through bits of cast-up seaweed and down the wet-hard surf-zone sand.

It's only about twenty yards from the nest to the water, yet they get a little strung out. I'm hoping I can adequately shepherd all of them, but I'm holding off several intent, alert, highly competent vultures.

The hatchling turtles hurtle seaward, full of vigorous energy, scrambling down the beach. Even on sand, their first motion is a rowing stroke, both front flippers so long that on the pull it lifts their entire little body off the ground, almost like a child on crutches. The hatchlings' hind flippers also spread, then pull closed, further propelling them. Their little palm-sized bodies rising and falling, they undulate up and down the miniaturized hills and valleys of the beach on their long wings, like a small flock of birds with flight confined to two dimensions.

A sea turtle's first "swim"—through sand—is perhaps the hardest of its life, and luck counts for more than skill in this first beach assault. Nothing about their worldly entrance presents ease. Their moist little blue-gray eyes quickly cake with sand. The rutted tracks and pits from adult turtles present major obstacles. Some hatchlings flip over in depressions. They right themselves. Some are forced to detour around a palm frond or log. They persevere.

The benefits of getting to the water fast suggest why some turtles might nest relatively low on the beach: the trade-off between keeping your eggs safely high and having your hatchlings emerge safely closer to the water.

One hatchling overturns and seems stuck. It's tangled hopelessly in a small snarl of fishing line; its exertions to free itself have enmeshed it beyond hope of its life. Already afoul of fishing gear before it reaches the sea!—what a world have we made. On my knees I carefully work it loose and send it along. But as I straighten up I realize that the vultures, exploiting my distraction, have rushed in—picking off hatchlings I'd counted safe. When several of the hatchlings attain the water, finally beyond vulturine reach, from nowhere a Black-Hawk streaking across the foamy surf plucks a paddling hatchling not ten feet from me, terminating its first harsh swimming lesson. From the moment the would-be turtles appear in the world, they are granted scant leeway.

I resume playing traffic cop to birds and turtles, holding the vultures away with a stern hand while waving the hatchlings toward the sandy on-ramp of the wide blue highway. As each hatchling hits the firmer, wet, wave-tamped sand of the surf zone, it gains speed, as though it's done this before.

Each sliding pane of water lifts hatchlings from the sand like a spatula lifting cookies off a tray. They begin swimming vigorously toward the horizon. Some get pushed backward and overturned; they right themselves with the next oncoming wave and are gone as the green ocean engulfs them. The drive so apparent in returning females is already evident in departing hatchlings.

So well oriented are they from moments after they emerge that a question presents itself: How do hatchlings know which way to go? They can't see the sea when they first appear, because they emerge in the slight depression of their imploding nest. They beeline seaward anyway. How?

A few pelicans are holding in the wind overhead. Through binoculars I gradually realize that the pelicans diving, now joined by three Magnificent Frigatebirds, are catching—hatchlings. I see them snatch several. They fly lazy, intent circles, and occasionally zoom down for a baby turtle that had already set course away from such a dangerous coast.

Hatchlings come out of the box fully equipped, switched on, powered up. Moments after emerging from the sand of their nest, usually in darkness, they are oriented and traveling toward an ocean they cannot see. The usual sea-finding cue is visual (in experiments, hooded hatchlings can't orient). The main trigger is brightness, normally leading away from dark jungle shadows and dune silhouettes, toward the open sky above the ocean. The darker and more natural the beach, the darker the shore and more starlit the sky.

Upon feeling their flippers lifted by the surf, they start swimming and at the same time dive, which puts them in the undertow and pulls them seaward beneath the incoming waves' foaming chaos. When they pop up a few yards from the beach, they immediately orient into the oncoming swell; that's the surest way to leave the beach. (In experimental tanks they swim randomly if the waves are turned off.)

That first scramble down the beach and out to sea, so full of kinetic hustle, begins their so-called hatchling frenzy. When the swirling sand of the foamy surf gives way to bottomless dark water, the hatchling swims with an intensity intended to break it away from the coast, just as burning rockets must break Earth's gravity before achieving the relative tranquillity of orbital drift.

While paddling away from the beach, into the swells, they lock onto a seaward heading, apparently using their ability to orient to Earth's magnetic field. They maintain this offshore heading after attaining distances where shifting winds alter the swells' angles and make them useless for sensing direction. The hatchlings remain locked onto that offshore heading long after they've left land far behind them and as out of sight below the horizon as the sun at midnight.

"Frenzy" swimming lasts from one to several days as the hatchlings continue pushing away from shore, swimming without rest all the first night and throughout their long day's journey into their second night. They're getting away from the coast's denser populations of ever-hungry seabirds and fishes, squeezing a few extra points out of the odds against them.

Out in open blue water, by perhaps the second day their frenzy relaxes to "postfrenzy" swimming, while they continue heading offshore. Nights, they rest. But Leatherback hatchlings, already full of their signature restlessness, continue swimming nearly half the night.

After about eighty hours their yolk is completely used and they need to find food without becoming food. For cruising fuel, they'll begin eating things like tiny larval crabs and shrimp and small jellies. They swim for hours, resting occasionally with flippers flattened along their sides to look less detectable or delectable. Then they continue swimming, and they swim and swim and swim—for about a week.

So mysterious are their nursery kingdoms that for decades, scientists referred to this phase of their lives as "the lost years." But only the scientists were lost; the hatchlings were at home. We still have much to learn about locations and durations of juvenile turtles. In the Pacific, we're still pretty lost. As fast as the baby turtles write their stories, the endlessly shifting sea erases them.

But now we know that their main survival ploy is to find floating seaweed like Sargassum. In the North Atlantic, at least, Hatchling Central is the great slow-swirling gyre that is the "eye" of the ocean's massive cyclonic currents—the Sargasso Sea. Like mythic children who've fallen into magical transporting dreams during their solitary quests, the hatchlings' headings put them into the realm of ocean currents that carry them off to regions rich in food. Out among big drifting mats of seaweed, they become part of the weeds' thriving community of animals that hide and abide under its leafy cover at the sea's surface. There the tables lie set with jellies, shrimps, snails and their shell-less cousins the pteropods, salps, worms, amphipods, fish eggs, sea horses, crabs, fleshy stalked barnacles, baby octopuses, edible vegetation, colonial animals such as hydroids and bryozoans, and, ironically, insects blown far from land and fallen not to earth but to ocean.

Most sea turtle types follow this broad pattern. For, say, Loggerhead Turtle hatchlings leaving the coast of the southeastern United States, their route will take them straight into the Gulf Stream, and the stream transports them north and east until it spins them out into Sargassum-weed rafts whirling slowly toward the Azores, off Portugal, then down past the Canary and Cape Verde Islands, slipping by the unseen coast of West Africa. Fair numbers of young American-hatched Loggerheads enter the Mediterranean, where in some locations they constitute up to half the Loggerheads caught in fishing gear. By the time they're headed west again, back toward North America to settle down as shellfish hunters of the continental shelf, elapsed time spans years, sometimes a decade.

Hawksbill Turtles are out there too, before moving to crystal coral reefs—what's left of them—at the relatively tender age of only about three years, and settling down to a long life of eating mainly sponges, anemones, and sea cucumbers. Kemp's Turtles, hatched in Mexico, may ride weed mats in the Gulf, or get swept out past Florida, into the Gulf Stream. Greens, those mostly vegetarian slow-growing turtles, as babes prey on pelagic snails and small jellies.

Leatherbacks are, well, somewhere. Where, exactly, has been called by Scott Eckert "one of the great mysteries of sea turtle life history." All we know is that as hatchlings they swim seaward for about a week. Then they give humanity the slip; their first few years remain a complete mystery. When they start turning up, their shells already about two and a half feet long (seventy-five centimeters), it's because they're getting snared in fishing gear.

Other species begin moving inshore and back onto continental shelves, where they shift their foraging attention to the seafloor, searching out sea grass or crabs or shellfish, according to their kind. They're not mature yet, but they've outgrown the near-shore predators and can come back along the continental margins, where more abundant food facilitates faster growth. Wayward and wandering, a Leatherback never forsakes its peripatetic youth, never leaves the open ocean for a more settled lifestyle.

As everywhere in the great sprawling exuberance of nature, none of this is as pat and patterned as presented. Exceptions abound, and turtles turn up surprisingly at times, coming earlier, staying later, or traveling farther than expected. But if you know this general pattern—beach hatching followed by offshore open-ocean youth, adolescent and adult life foraging on continental-shelf seafloors (for all species except the Leatherback and Olive Ridley), then lengthy migration to a nesting beach every few years—you know what scientists spent decades unraveling. You're already standing at the shoreline of the Isle of What Is Known, facing what Isaac Newton called that "great ocean of truth, lying all undiscovered before me."

With the sun now casting long shadows, a dark body breaks the nearshore swell. When the Leatherback lifts its head, a tourist says, "My God." Another big turtle roils the surface a quarter mile away, one long flipper flailing the air before biting back into the water. I sense many turtles biding their time till darkness.

Imagine the last stage of approach after long migration. Swells that had been constant for miles begin piling up on the shallows, and soon the turtle is swept forward near the crest of a wave whose abrasion with the seafloor breaks it into surf. Slowed a little by the undertow, the turtle continues swimming, until the next breaking wave delivers her ashore and recedes, stranding her in the world of friction and gravity. As subsequent waves reach for her, she begins chugging beachward.

Quite unlike yesterday's wild surf, tonight's swell is placid as moonlight, the waves molten. Shortly after sundown word comes of a truly gigantic turtle down the beach, and among Leatherbacks, that's saying something. Nearing the appointed place, I discern a dark crowd of people gathered quietly around a digging female.

Her sand-filled tears are so thick they drip like jelly, yet the corners of her large eyes remain caked with grit. The guide, Marissa, explains: "When you see de tears in her eyes, she not cryin', just excretin' de excess salt from her body." In sea turtles and seabirds, glands near the eyes that filter and discharge salt allow the animals to drink full-strength saltwater without dehydrating—and thus live in the sea. These glands are seemingly evolved from the same tear glands that evolved in another direction to bathe our eyes in salty fluid. Fishes and marine mammals handle salt with their kidneys. We, of course, cannot deal with saltwater, and people adrift on the ocean are most likely to die of thirst.

As usual, Marissa says that no flash photos are allowed until egg laying has begun and the turtle is fully committed. Our turtle raises her head for a deep inspiration of air, and rests. Then her eggs begin to fall.

At just this moment of her most intimate contact with the Earth, our flashes set off a paparazzi fusillade. As photographers attack from different angles, one local woman raises her hands in self-defense, and Marissa halts the assault.

Scott notices something disturbing: running across the turtle's shell is a pronounced crack. I feel the edge of it with my finger. It is healed over. Scott says it looks like a machete scar; fishermen sometimes hack turtles out of their nets.

These turtles, marked by fishing lines, scarred by machetes, emerge ashore to confront more people. The world must indeed seem crowded with humans.

The turtle is now heavily gulping air. And well-intentioned people are stepping forward to touch her flippers, her head. Our crowd tonight has a lot more children; they marvel at stroking her, feeling her leathery back. And despite our intrusive curiosity, it's all done gently and respectfully.

This turtle is extraordinarily massive; just the "hand" parts of her foreflippers are about three feet long, fully fourteen inches wide top to bottom. Her shell measures five and a half feet long (168 centimeters). The biggest turtle Scott ever measured clicked in at 172 centimeters, so this is pretty near the max. Girth: over four feet (125 centimeters). Estimated weight: five hundred kilos (eleven hundred pounds). "This is an enormous turtle," Scott pronounces.

As the turtle fills her chamber and cakes the sand atop it, Marissa tries to steady one rear flipper enough to read a tag. The turtle is very active and Scott steps in to help. The tag tells us she's previously nested in French Guiana.

I'm hoping that while we, the people, are crowding these turtles, other turtles are laying in dark privacy somewhere, beyond cameras, beyond the reach of human caring—or human craving. For 99.9 percent of the time Leatherback Turtles have lived on Earth—give or take—no human had yet drawn a breath. Times have changed.

A hundred yards beyond us, a dark turtle is headed up the beach like a cloud shadow. One of the patrols has just reported another Leatherback emerging from the surf, and near that, according to one of the rangers' radios, is a fourth digging female. Scott points behind me, saying, "Look." I see a great dark spot in the white foam, another behemoth emerging. That's an impressive lot of turtles.

Tonight Scott has a satellite transmitter to deploy. While a selected turtle is laying, Scott readies a harness consisting of three straps that will go around her like a big plus-sized belt and suspenders. The "suspenders" run through two soft, flexible plastic tubes to prevent chafing of her shoulders or neck. The transmitter, about the size of my shoe, is bulbous in front, narrowing to a streamlined point in the rear, a rather fish-shaped affair whose flat bottom is affixed to a mounting plate. The harness is flexible and elastic, coated with antifouling paint to ward off the drag of barnacles and whatnot; it's held together with a metal link designed to rust and let the whole harness come apart after the transmitter battery expires in about a year.

Scott has already tracked several Leatherbacks from Matura. Their travels are breathtaking: From the Caribbean one swam up past Canada's Grand Banks and east to the Flemish Cap—essentially the middle of the Atlantic—then on to the Azores, the Cape Verde Islands, and Mauritania. Another, swimming against the Atlantic Equatorial Current, continued to the Bay of Biscay, between France and Spain, and then to the Cape Verde Islands, off West Africa. Thousands of miles.

Why do Leatherbacks range the oceans? To feed and to breed. These are their two main motivations, as with most of us. But with Leatherbacks, the best places for each of these things are thousands of miles apart. In between, they may be fasting and living off their fat the whole time. Feast and famine. For Leatherbacks, that's life on a grand scale.

All sea turtles commit long migrations between nesting beaches and foraging zones. But "long" is relative. The Flatback, a comparative homebody among turtles, lives its whole life along the north coast of Australia. Leatherbacks and Loggerheads venture across entire ocean basins, continent to continent. Often they travel essentially straight courses over hundreds of miles, even when swimming across currents. Turtles don't flock along flyways in the sea. Each captains its own ship, running its own routes.

While she is still covering her eggs, we pass the straps around her and affix the transmitter plate to the suspenders atop her back. The attachment is made before she has fully concealed her egg chamber. Scott wants the straps snug and secure, but loose enough for easy motion.

This turtle's particularly beautiful head bears lovely marbling on a deep bluish-green base. Her back, flippers, and head are all speckled. The pointillist pattern on her leather-upholstered shell and a very bold series of white spots that form a dotted stripe down her tail enhance an aboriginal Dreamtime look. And upon her head the bright central pink spot unique to

Leatherbacks contrasts markedly with the dark-skinned outline. That pink spot is situated right over the thinnest part of a Leatherback's skull, beneath which sits the light-sensitive pineal organ. It would in theory be possible for a Leatherback, using just day length and an internal clock, to calculate its global position.

Scott and I are still fine-tuning the fittings when she starts moving forward and down the beach with the relentlessness of a lava flow—inexorable, uncontainable, unyielding, unstoppable. Slow though she is, she hurries us to her pace. Scott works rapidly and efficiently. Someone's light beam hits her eye and she closes her lids. It's almost ten P.M. when she touches the water's edge.

We wish her well. Scott remarks, "It'll be so exciting to see where she goes. I've seen them do the most *amazing* navigational things. One came off the Flemish Cap and beelined for the Canary Islands. Now, that's what, three thousand kilometers across open ocean? If you laid a straight edge over her track on the map, you couldn't have done better yourself using GPS and satellites. You look at those tracks, and their capabilities blow you away. Then you realize—fishing off Iceland and Africa can affect the turtles on this beach."

That remark makes the world seem both oddly small and strangely large at the same time, because Iceland seems a world removed from this warm beach, with its palm shadows and tropic breeze. And it is. But to be a Leatherback is to be perpetually on the move from one world to the next.

Caribbean-nesting turtles clearly go east. No Leatherback from West Africa has yet been found in the northwest Atlantic or in Canadian waters; they likely go southwest toward waters off Argentina and Uruguay. Scientists suspect that hundreds of Leatherbacks transiting the Gulf of Guinea perish in fishing gear. Longlines there snag Olive Ridleys and Leatherbacks at likely the highest rate yet recorded: as many as ten Leatherbacks have been caught in a single set of a line. (Even the average of just over one turtle per thousand hooks—about one per boat per day—is high.) Longlines are fishing lines up to sixty miles long (one hundred kilometers), dangling hundreds or thousands of baited hooks. Baiting, deployment, and retrieval requires up to twenty hours of work. For certain cold-water species fishers sometimes set them on the bottom. But of concern regarding turtles are longlines set to drift for hours through warm and temperate seas, targeting tunas, Swordfish, sharks, marlins, and Mahimahi (a.k.a. Dorado or Dolphinfish). They're largely responsible for depletions of Swordfish, marlins, and sharks, and they certainly catch turtles.

One Year's Travels of 3 Leatherbacks
after nesting · Tracked by Scott Eckert

A large, dark spot in the surf is much too big to be a turtle. We're discussing the possibility that it's a log when we realize we're looking at *two* turtles coming ashore almost shoulder to shoulder. Scott's never seen such a thing.

Another turtle begins lurching ashore forty yards to our right, and two more an equal distance to our left—*five* turtles emerging in one hundred-yard stretch. The beach at this moment hosts sufficient turtles that the tourists can be fully occupied while most of the turtles nest undisturbed.

Scott says, "This boggles my mind. All the good work on the nesting beaches seems to be paying off." In the 1980s, he remembers, the situation for Atlantic sea turtles looked pretty bad. "Now we can envision sea turtle survival. Things can change. Sea turtles are resilient creatures. If you figure out what got them in trouble, and deal with that, and you're prepared to keep at it for twenty years, then the turtles themselves will do the rest. They will. We've already seen it with Kemp's Ridley, with the Hawaiian Green, and it looks like we might be seeing it with the Atlantic Leatherback. This is what gives me hope for the Pacific."

Suddenly a nearby nest spews another wave of baby turtles. Several dozen emerge together, like ants swarming from a log—except, of course, that these are not ants but endangered hatchling dinosaurs. They quickly orient and scurry directly to the ocean, this time under cover of bird-free darkness. And though a few stumble, *this* time every one easily paddles into the sea under its own native powers. For the males, the short dash to the ocean is the only time they will ever feel land in their entire lives. For those females lucky enough to have entire lives, the burden of bringing the next generation ashore will, years hence, fall to them.

Not fifty feet away, another Leatherback begins ascending while an earlier turtle, finished and descending, passes so closely that the two chugging creatures must alter course to avoid a slow-speed head-on collision. Just down the beach I can see another flinging sand in the moonlight.

This night is truly extraordinary, a slow herd of ancient elders emerging from the coal-dark ocean as from the shadows of Earth's past.

And finally, with most people having gone, I sit alone on a log watching one ancient monster. Here in the magic, I'm loving her presence, the look and heft of her, her movements in the pit, the great plowing travel of her immense foreflippers, the raising of her head, her pulsing throat, the way the moonlight gleams off her tears and her marbled skin. I'm also digging the darkness of the shoreline, the jungle trees against moving clouds, the pinpricks of starlight, fireflies in forest shadows, the curling heave of lazy groundswell, and the rumbling snore of waves unfurling. It's not that everything is right with the world—far from it. But this is a good moment. These turtles cannot right the world, but they can put that world off to the periphery a little while, while I savor the miracle.

In the dreamlike drift of the smallest hour, I'm also thinking about those smallest turtles we watched leaving the beach today, putting the fast world behind them and pitting their whole future against the vast ocean. They have no choice. The odds against them even getting to the sea is one set of odds beaten, and it's quite an accomplishment. But that's just a turtle's first hurdle. In those dark undercurrents of existence, in this black ocean, where are they swimming? Where will they be when their first day dawns? Where a year from now? How many—if any—will make it to their first birthday, or their fiftieth, or beyond? So many simple things are unknowable.

The children of Nature Seekers may be the first humans to see one of these hatchlings again, weighing half a ton, hauling herself up on her mother's shore, near her birthplace and the sloping beach that launched her to the sea. Or perhaps a fisherman will see her first.

The hope born of uncertainty constitutes its own state of grace. And what is glowing in me now among this herd of hulking reptiles is a sense of odds beaten, of life triumphing, of recovery brought by a rare and improbable change in human values that *has* actually happened and is happening more each night—proven by the sheer turtle tonnage upon this shore.

Scott comes over, breaking my reverie to say it's time to hit the trail. He's just seen several more pairs of turtles arriving shoulder to shoulder, and is happy. We come upon one more dollop of darkness ascending the beach, from whose path Scott clears some driftwood.

He says, "Let's just sit and enjoy this turtle. I don't get to do this often enough."

It's a while before we walk down the dark beach, enveloped in the surf's rhythmic growl, toward the road at the dawn of civilization.

WEIGHT OF THE WORLD

The graves of turtles fill the cradle of civilization. From earliest cultures to the present day, people have both victimized and venerated turtles, their motivations ranging from the highly practical—food and implements—to the deeply mystical. Nearly sixty thousand years ago, humans in southern Africa were tossing turtle bones into their trash heaps. People along the shores of the Persian Gulf seven thousand years ago also left turtle bones in their middens, as have many others. Later, ancients from Arabia and the Mideast to China left records clearly indicating organized trade in turtle meat and shell. In Oman, human graves contain turtle shells more commonly than any other animal's remains. In Thailand, too, people sought burial with sea turtle remains, indicating significance and esteem. Later, in Mesopotamia, sealing stamps and palace walls bore turtle images. In the eighth century B.C.E., the citizens of Aegina struck the first coins of European Greece in honor of Aphrodite, goddess of sexual love and beauty. (On U.S. money we get dead politicians.) One side of the coin showed a sea turtle, sacred to the goddess. Two thousand years ago the most commonly traded item throughout the Indian Ocean was Hawksbill shell, perhaps the world's oldest luxury good and quite possibly the most important motivator in "globalizing" trade. In the Americas two thousand years ago, people traded Hawksbill shell as far inland as Indiana and Ohio.

Turtle icons, turtle stories, and mythic turtles abound around the world. Sometimes they instruct through fables, like this from Palau: A fisherman noticed a large Hawksbill—a true prize. Without pausing to anchor his canoe, he dove, and after a great deal of struggle, he surfaced with the turtle. But his canoe had drifted far away. He let go of the turtle but could not catch up to his canoe, and had to swim back to his village, exhausted and embarrassed, with neither turtle nor canoe. Moral: those who try to do two things at once often accomplish neither.

Turtles left their mark in stone carvings, cliff carvings, ceramics, and parchments. They loomed large in Central America, where, among many representations and references in art and cosmology, the Mayan god of thunder, mountains, and Earth's interior wears a turtle carapace, as did the lightning god Yahui of the Mixtecs and Zapotecs in what is now Mexico. The ancient Maya appear to have conceptualized a circular earth as a great turtle afloat in a sustaining sea.

In many cultures turtles, seemingly designed by nature as load-bearing creatures, bore the world. Turtles of astronomical proportion supported the world in India, China, Japan, and North America. In many cultures turtles assisted the world's very creation. In the Hindu religion a giant turtle bears the entire universe, which is re-created every 4.32 billion years, when Vishnu transforms into a turtle. Anchored firmly in space by force of omnipotent will, Vishnu-as-turtle bears on his back the cosmic churn from which gods and demons remake the world. Vishnu's turtle avatar remains creation's keystone, supporting a huge elephant, who in turn hoists the world.

The earliest description of what seems a Leatherback was written around the year 200 by Aelianus, a Roman, whose apparent confusion may simply reflect how magical and miraculous the world must have seemed to any traveler or receiver of news from afar. "There is also a monkey in the Red Sea, not a fish to be sure, but a cartilaginous beast, lacking scales. . . . The rest of its body is encased in the same manner as the covering of a turtle. . . . Its body is broad like that of a ray, with the result that you might say it was a bird unfolding its wings. When it swims, it seems to fly . . . and is spotted."

Pliny contributed his usual misadvice to sea turtle lore. This man deserves to be forgotten for getting just about everything wrong. But he is both too amusing and too much a reminder of how wrong yet confident-sounding people can be (I say that confidently). He tells us that the Indian Ocean produces turtles so large that dwellings are built from a single shell, while in the Red Sea people use turtle shells as sailboats. Of their use more locally, we learn that turtle flesh, mixed with frog flesh, is excellent against salamander bites. For baldness and every sort of ulceration of the head, turtle blood answers. Earache? Turtle blood mixed with woman's milk. Flour and vinegar with turtle blood cures epilepsy. Rinse your teeth with turtle blood for a year and they will be pain-free.

Shortness of breath? Turtle blood again. For colic, you don't want to know. Collect turtle blood in an earthen vessel never before used, and you're ready to treat shingles, warts, and erysipelas (an acute bacterial rash sometimes accompanied by vomiting and fever, a.k.a. Saint Anthony's fire). Now let us move on to turtle bile, for: clearing the eyes, reducing scars, and calming tonsils and all problems of the mouth (especially malignant sores) and the testicles, also angina. Pus-filled ears? If you're listening, you can guess by now that you want turtle bile mixed with vinegar and the shed skin of a snake. Or, if desired, first cook the turtle in wine for a long time and use the broth instead of the bile. For eye problems, mix the bile with honey and smear it on. If you wish to dye your hair, use sea turtle bile mixed with woman's milk. Did I mention that the bile is also good against those pesky salamanders? Feet got you down? Choose ground turtle shell mixed with fat, wine, and oil to cure foot ulcers. The overardent lust of Roman swains is easily cooled by scraping turtle shell into their drinks. (Oops—what if turtle really *is* an aphrodisiac?)

Sea turtles who will aid people, and people magically transformed into turtles and vice versa are themes common across the Pacific. Japanese fishermen working in Hawaii at the end of the nineteenth century scratched Japanese characters into turtles' carapaces, then set the turtles free in the belief that turtles so treated would guide them back to land should they be lost at sea.

Natives of places as disparate as Mexico, Fiji, and New Guinea have rituals for calling turtles, either for hunting or veneration. On many Pacific islands, turtles had magic powers, special cleverness, or were considered sacred and godly. Ceremonies and taboos governed the butchering, distribution, and eating of turtle or reserved these activities for high-ranking men. Failing to share a turtle might be punishable by exile or death. As recently as 1974 in Palau, the remains of a butchered turtle that had not been brought to chiefs for distribution drew a three-week proscription against using or eating anything from the sea, a punishment that applied even to U.S. government employees, Peace Corps personnel, and a Jesuit missionary. Other government officials were warned to stay away for the duration.

Two weeks after the Chinese New Year, villagers of the P'eng-hu (Pescadores) Islands offer sacrificial images of sea turtles to their temple deities to ensure peace, prosperity, and good fortune. For three days, the temples are crowded around the clock with worshippers praying for favors, seeking guidance, or showing appreciation for wishes granted. Rice cakes made into sea turtles are the most common offerings. Others include turtles fashioned from gold and coins. Money is sometimes burned. Coastal people of Taiwan retain a deep and widespread devotion to the goddess Ma-tsu, guardian of fishermen, ocean travelers, and all who live near the sea. And an Associated Press story reported as follows:

Hong Kong (August 13, 1999)—Authorities have freed an endangered sea turtle that drew thousands of worshippers to a temple on a fishing boat. Government officials confiscated the green sea turtle last week from the temple of Tin Hau, where it was worshipped for its supposed magical and protective powers. Worshippers of Tin Hau [Ma-tsu], or the Goddess of the Sea, accused the government of insensitivity. "They totally insulted my religion," said Leung Yau, who runs the floating temple on a remodeled boat moored at a typhoon shelter. Fishermen caught the baby turtle four years ago and decided to raise it. They soon discovered it had special powers and brought it to the temple, Leung said. "Before a typhoon or bad weather, it would flap its flippers furiously and make us all wet, as if it was warning us not to go to the sea," he said. "The turtle belongs to Tin Hau and was given to us to protect us."

Despite millennia of veneration and commerce, sea turtles have been an astonishingly poorly understood group. Many basic facts about species, nesting grounds, and behavior were debated until very recently, and some remain undiscovered. As recently as 1959, a Leatherback seen off Soay, near the Isle of Skye, Scotland, not only made headlines but was debated even in scholarly literature as a possible sea monster. One nearly hysterical witness said, "Petrified we stood and watched as it came closer and closer . . . like some hellish monster of prehistoric times." The artist's rendition manages to picture a sea serpent (what else?), even though both eyewitnesses drew pretty fair pictures of a Leatherback above the waterline, and the second witness's sober description includes some keen observing ("When the mouth was opened . . . I could see tendril-like growths hanging from the palate"—the projections used to retain jellyfish). The point is, no one said, "Oh, that's a big turtle, maybe a Leatherback," because in many untropical places people were still utterly unfamiliar with sea turtles. None of the major Leatherback nesting grounds was known to science until the 1960s and '70s. Scientists did not know until the 1960s that egg-incubation temperature determines a turtle's sex. In the 1970s scientists were just discovering that sea turtles migrate. As late as 1988, the idea that Caribbean-nesting Leatherbacks journey to temperate latitudes was considered unproven. Into the mid-1990s the origin of juvenile Loggerheads in Mexican waters remained unknown; the nearest known breeding ground was Japan—more than ten thousand kilometers (six thousand miles) distant—and because some researchers considered such migratory feats almost impossible they continued searching for undiscovered sites in the New World. One noted, "A trans-Pacific migration would greatly exceed the known geographic scale of marine turtle migrations." (In just a few years, tag returns and satellite transmitters would blow that apart, showing that Japanese and Australian Loggerheads indeed swim the Pacific Basin coast to coast and that almost all sea turtles are masterful seafarers.) Into the 1990s almost nothing was known of sea turtle hatchling whereabouts from the moment they left the beach until they showed up as platter-sized juveniles; for several species we still know essentially nothing. Even into the 1990s, researchers only conjectured that female sea turtles often return to lay eggs on the beach where they hatched (DNA evidence now appears convincing).

More than halfway through the twentieth century, scientists argued over whether three types of sea turtles were really distinct species (remember, there are only seven species worldwide). As recently as the 1960s, scientists disputed whether Kemp's Ridley was a true species. No scientist had ever seen one laying eggs, so some thought Kemp's must be a hybrid. The mass-nesting marches of both Ridley species, involving tens of thousands of turtles coming onto beaches together during daylight, were apparently unknown to science until amateur film footage of Kemp's Turtles mass nesting, shot in 1947, finally found its way into the hallowed halls in 1960. Australia's Flatback Turtle was unknown to science until the 1880s, and for a century thereafter scientists also debated whether it was really a separate species. As recently as 1996, debate raged over the so-called Black Turtle ("raged" if you studied Black Turtles): Was it a distinct species or a race of the Green Turtle? (Genetic analysis shows they're just a darker shade of Green.) That at least some individual Leatherbacks make round-trips from feeding grounds to breeding sites and back again to the same general feeding area wasn't confirmed until 2005. And, rather remarkably, in 2005 a scholarly paper noted, "Some debate exists about whether juvenile turtles are simply passive drifters or actively swim against opposing currents." Now satellite tracking has confirmed the probable: juvenile turtles go into and across the flow if they feel like it. Science marches on. But the point is, turtles reveal their secrets slowly, and many remain locked "twixt their plated decks."

Put a cookie-sized turtle into the ocean and years later it comes back to say hello. To reach adulthood, a hatchling must grow to thirty times its hatching length. When her belly first grinds ashore and feels gravity's grip and the weight of what she's achieved by surviving to maturity, a Leatherback has multiplied her hatchling weight six-thousand-fold. Age to maturity remains uncertain, perhaps twelve years in Leatherbacks and as early as seven years in Kemp's. Green Turtles and Loggerheads may not lay their first eggs until they've got thirty-five years or more of survival under their belts. Their longevity remains uncertain; science has not been involved long enough to see full life spans, and the number of breeding seasons in the life of a female remains likewise uncertain. The longest known Leatherback nesting career, that of a South African female, spanned eighteen years. Most researchers seem to think sea turtles can live at least two decades after maturing, so a sea turtle's life span likely falls into the forty- to sixty-year range. Some undoubtedly have lived far longer, especially when the world was safer for them. Like returning salmon, sea turtles generally breed at the place of their own origin. A creature returning to a pinpoint target after as much as three decades at sea is one of nature's most stunning navigational and homing achievements. Somehow turtles know how to get there. But what they find might surprise them. Nowadays ten years can change a beach's back border from jungle to Jacuzzis.

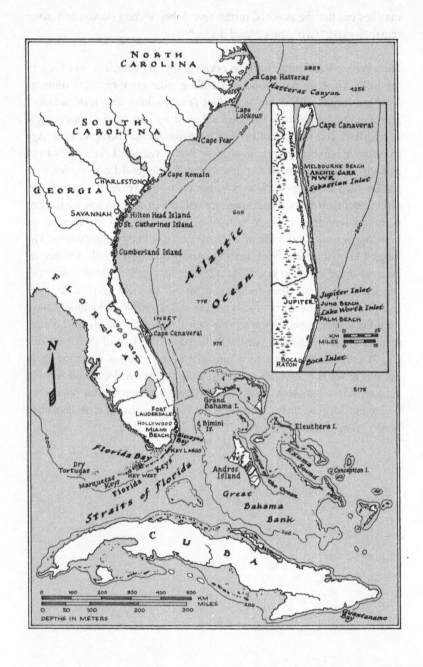

MOONLIGHT IN THE SUNSHINE STATE
Florida

Juno Beach, Florida, with its oceanfront high-rise condos and hotels, is a very different seascape from Trinidad's jungled beaches. But the street signs picture turtles, and the parks and shopping malls are named after sea turtles. Loggerhead, Green, and Leatherback Turtles still use the beach. Juno Beach is, in fact, Leatherback Central in Florida.

But nesting's been slow. "It hasn't felt like summer yet," says Kelly Stewart. "We're averaging under one Leatherback a night." Kelly's many sleepless nights searching for Florida Leatherbacks will earn her a Ph.D. at Duke University—if more turtles start showing. Dark-haired and energetic, Kelly says, "There's increased nesting in Florida. We want to know how many Leatherbacks are coming, how many clutches they're each laying, how often, what's the hatching rate. We want to track where they're going between nestings, what kind of habitat they're hanging out in, and migration routes. And genetic relationships to others in the Caribbean. That's all maybe ambitious, but"—she smiles a little shyly—"those are sort of our main objectives."

Kelly continues: "In the early 1990s there were about two hundred nests in the whole state. Suddenly it spiked up to four hundred, five hundred, a thousand. It's been hovering around five hundred to eight hundred. It seems to be going on throughout the Caribbean, numbers spiking."

At sundown we fuel an all-terrain vehicle and Kelly puts a small red flashlight around her neck. Kelly and her colleague Chris Johnson will be running the beach between Jupiter Inlet and Lake Worth Inlet at Port of Palm Beach. About twenty-four kilometers, fifteen miles or so.

First priority: place your bet. Where will a Leatherback show up? I say, "Two A.M. on the north end."

Chris is going north. Kelly takes the south half and me. We carry tags, pliers for said tags, tape measure, Betadine and blood-sampling equipage, ice for blood samples, a GPS unit, a cell phone in a waterproof bag, a camera, extra fuel.

I'm sitting on our ATV's equipment rack as we approach the beach. Kelly kills the headlight because turtles dig darkness. The night is warm with breeze enough to banish bugs. We turn south in the night, running the dark sand at a restrained pace. As she drives Kelly often stands—for miles at a time—alert and on the lookout. Constant vigilance pays; Kelly's never hit a turtle.

The first several miles of beach are quite dark, because we're riding alongside MacArthur State Park. Southward, the dark visages of distant beachfront high-rises ascend a sky backlit by human ingenuity. Kelly says there are two reasons the buildings look dark: half the inhabitants are snowbirds now flown north for the summer, and ordinances require keeping lights out for the turtles.

Much of the beach has long steplike sand escarpments three to six feet high, where waves have taken out swaths of sand. These are hazardous to any ATV driver inattentive in the small hours. Kelly says that most years, at this season, the beach is flatter, the water calmer. But this year, higher winds wrought erosion later into the season. Three years ago engineers pumped extra sand onto a three-mile stretch of this beach; this "scarpiness" may be the ocean yet carving away sand pumped along the tide line.

At ten P.M. we almost zoom past a Loggerhead obscured in a wrack line marbled with the shadowed camouflage of cast-up seaweed. Kelly stops in the turtle's track and checks: "Yeah, she's laying." But Kelly is studying only Leatherbacks. We continue.

The beach seems devoid of other human life. Yet the sand bears sufficient footprints from the daylight hours that Genghis Khan's hordes might well have swept through carrying beach balls and boogie boards, leaving the beach as pitted as the surface of a golf ball.

MacArthur Park ends at a complex of three seventeen-story condos, followed by a gated community with a few hundred homes. With their drapes closed and outside lights off, all the buildings look so dark they seem almost empty. This is "lights out for turtles."

I ask Kelly if it's brighter when it's not turtle season.

"*Ohhh* yeah. You could play volleyball all night all the way up this beach. Those condos look like they're expecting an invasion by sea, with security lights shining on the beach all night long. You go out there in November—*huge* lights. But when the turtles do invade, it gets pretty dark."

Lights discourage mama turtles from coming onto the beach, and they confuse hatchlings. When proliferating beachfront high-rises began shining huge floodlights on the beach in the 1980s, new residents found hatchlings in their bushes and elsewhere hatchlings shouldn't be, and little turtles by the hundreds were getting squashed in lit parking lots. Troubled, residents sought an ordinance. Now residents expect to extinguish their outdoor lights from June through October. There is no state law, but twenty counties and forty-six municipalities have lighting laws, encompassing 95 percent of Florida's Loggerhead and Green Turtle nesting areas. The ordinances say, basically, Because artificial light harms sea turtles, you should shield, lower, turn off, change, or redirect lights so they're not visible from the beach during sea turtle nesting season. It's pretty much that simple.

A while along, a middleweight Loggerhead is covering her nest. Her track proves that a sea turtle can climb a five-foot bluff of loose sand. We wait and watch her half-plummet, half-ski back down that loose scarp to the lapping lip of sea.

At midnight, as I run another year up the flagpole, Kelly sings a heartfelt if perfunctory "Happy Birthday." I request a matched set of Leatherbacks, no gift wrapping necessary. Kelly responds, *"Two Leatherbacks! That's a tall order, considering we've been averaging fewer than one a night."*

We pass a series of well-darkened ten- to twelve-story buildings stretching more than a mile. Sited right on the beach, their concrete footings stand in some cases not more than sixty feet from the high-tide line. I'm thinking, "With big-time money like this invested, you can bet they'll take the beach before the beach takes them."

And sure enough, several of the buildings are fronted by large cement aprons—essentially a concrete beach, impervious to human footprint and turtle flipper alike.

Here a Loggerhead has just turned away after hitting a different barrier: beach chairs. Prime nesting habitat is prime sunbathing habitat. And though there's a light ordinance, ain't no beach-chair ordinance. Chairs block about 20 percent of the beach here. Kelly says the hotels and condos are unwilling to move the chairs back even fifteen or twenty feet. On the Greek Island of Zákinthos, where hundreds of thousands of tourists annually enjoy all-night beach parties, resort owners so resolutely resist accommodating the turtles that the European Court of Justice has found Greece negligent in its stewardship of nesting sea turtles. One creature has no choice and no voice; the other chooses to act deaf and say no.

At two A.M. we motor past two standing women gazing seaward, wrapped only in the breeze. Kelly yells back to me, "They're crazy. I'm freezing."

At the south end of the beach, right at the inlet, a major hotel corporation is erecting a five-building condo complex. What are they thinking? How can they keep their basements from continually flooding? What about hurricanes?

At two-thirty Kelly's cell phone rings. Chris has a Leatherback. He's way up on the north part of the beach, about twelve miles from us. I win the bet. Kelly says, "Ready to zoom?" We slow only once, to avoid an armadillo.

When we arrive at the dark, still-digging turtle, Chris greets us with the words "It's Beatrice." Serial numbers are fine, but Kelly and Chris give their turtles names.

Kelly says, "Last time we saw Beatrice"—she knows this off the top of her head—"was April twenty-ninth. That's when we first flipper-tagged her. We haven't seen her since. The timing means between then and now, she's nested twice, somewhere."

Tonight Beatrice will get a permanent identity via a tiny internal tag, plus a satellite transmitter. The internal tag is a glass microchip the size of a grain of rice; it reacts to an electronic stimulus by reporting its individual serial number. It's called a Passive Integrated Transponder, or PIT, tag, and it stays for life.

Kelly and Chris have tracked several other Leatherbacks by satellite, and Kelly says, "Aires went to Canaveral, Charleston, Hatteras, then in September she went east. She spent the winter and the whole next year wandering around the northern part of the North Atlantic Gyre. Then in January, February, she looped around, then started coming down." Her last transmission: off Charleston. "We're hoping she's coming back to nest. So far *all* our transmittered turtles went north and stayed coastal till they got to Hatteras, then hung out there for a couple of months, presumably eating Cannonball Jellies. A couple headed out into the central Atlantic; one ended up off the west coast of Africa. Others went to Canada, to the Grand Banks."

• • •

I continue north with Chris. The road rubs right along this northern stretch, with public parking along its length.

In our first mile we find two Loggerheads. Chris is monitoring them and he notes their tag numbers, then asks me if I've ever felt a Loggerhead's nose. "They're soft and squishy," he says. He's right! Chris expects about fifty Loggerhead Turtles tonight. By season's end, this five-and-a-half-mile stretch of beach will get perhaps a thousand Green Turtle nests, five thousand Loggerhead Turtle nests, and maybe seventy Leatherback nests. Chris enthuses, "It's become a thousand-nest-per-mile beach—pretty cool."

Our progress gets abruptly halted by a hundred-yard-wide seawall. With the tide high, the Atlantic meets the twelve-foot wall directly, waves slapping concrete. No beach. We have to drive up onto the road and around the building. Turtles can't drive. When the tide is lower Chris often finds turtles stopped by the wall. This kind of "armoring" is used where erosion poses acute threat to buildings. It's how turtles and even the public can get squeezed out between real estate and the sea.

Chris is scanning with a nightscope, hoping one of these nights he'll catch a poacher who recently dug up three nests.

"We see some amusing things," Chris says.

I can imagine.

In the scope's ghostly green image we detect only one stroller and two fishermen, and watch one Loggerhead emerging. Chris's scope imparts an air of clandestine activity. We're not just watching this turtle, we are *spying*.

Chris remarks that all the Leatherbacks and Greens look the same to him but the Loggerheads all look different. "Different kinds of things growing on the shell, different barnacle patterns; some have a head that's extra-wide—huge." Suddenly Kelly's voice crackles from the radio, calling from the south with a Leatherback ascending.

"Happy Birthday," says Kelly. "You got your matched set." A big fresh track goes only up the beach. We follow to a dark mountain of muscle, settled in and digging.

Kelly says, "Carl, meet Georgia. She's a big girl." Georgia's the most massive turtle ever on this beach. Kelly's Leatherbacks' shell lengths average 151 centimeters; the curve of Georgia's back spans 168 centimeters, five and a half feet (not counting head, neck, or tail).

The only thing short about Georgia is the last third or so of her right front flipper. It's missing. I'm thinking shark bite, until I notice two pink scars at her other wrist—line tangling. Her intact flipper is 125 centimeters long, over four feet. Georgia finishes and begins moving from her nest. Though it's her right limb that's shortened, she tends to veer left when crawling, as if accustomed to compensating for her abbreviated flipper.

Kelly knows her turtles well enough to anticipate, on any night, who's due to return to lay their next clutch. Tonight Georgia was on her mind, and Kelly's also on the lookout for Hydra, who's a couple of days overdue. "We met Hydra two years ago. But when I saw her a week and a half ago, she had raw, bleeding wounds with thick white tissue, her head was badly scraped, and the top of her shell was shaved off. Her shoulder had an oozing wound with so much dead tissue she really stank."

Watching Georgia maneuver on her disfigured limb, listening to Kelly, I'm already getting sad on my birthday, though it hasn't even dawned yet.

Kelly speculates, "Maybe there was a hook or something caught up in Hydra's shoulder, with line trailing. Maybe every time she raised her flipper the line would abrade across. Every time she went like *this*"—Kelly raises one shoulder—"it would abrade more, shaving off little bits."

"Are there others?"

"Sedna has a mass in her shoulder that feels like a hook, with the eye on its shank and everything." Delphinia had terrible deep wounds and abrasions as though from ropes or fishing gear; she returned healed, though heavily scarred. "Pesca came once, last year. When we got close, we realized she was tangled in heavy longline monofilament, attached to a large hook embedded in her shoulder. She'd swallowed a lot of the line, and—this was horrible—the line went all the way through her and was sticking out of her cloaca, which was, at that moment, dropping eggs into her nest. We cut lots of line and removed the hook. We hoped that the rest of the line would work its way through her body and be expelled." They equipped her with a satellite transmitter and monitored her travels for several months, only to lose her signal east of Canada's Grand Banks, where there's intense longline fishing.

The momentary silence between us begins to unspool into a wordless lament. Kelly adds, "About one out of every four or five of our Leatherbacks has line scars from fishing gear."

This disfiguring and wounding, so unnatural and frequent, so unjust to innocent animals, tangles my mind in their suffering. And many turtles also swallow plastic, mistaking it for food. In one study, nearly half of adult Leatherbacks had plastic in their guts. Of Leatherbacks found dead here and autopsied at Juno's Marinelife Center, 70 percent have digestive tracts blocked by stuff like Mylar balloons and trash bags. One arrived ashore with a sheet of plastic emerging from her; only after someone pulled and pulled, and finally yanked a trash bag out of her, could she lay eggs. Is this the only thing we give generously and abundantly to nature, such pain?

The curl of dawn is just pinking the sky when, spent, we quit the beach. In an earlier dawn in the late 1960s, I had headed offshore from a marina in Brooklyn, New York, on a fine fall day. I was fourteen and in awe of the seafaring skills and oceanic knowledge of my uncles Sal and Tony, but actually we ventured only a few miles into the Atlantic; you didn't have to go far to catch Bluefin Tuna in those days. We were bobbing at anchor within easy sight of Highlands, New Jersey, steadily tossing pieces of fish into the current astern, and I was wound with anticipation of a heavy fishing rod suddenly bending under the frightening power of a great fish. I was gazing with a child's eyes into the infinity beneath us when suddenly, as though conjured by my sense of the ocean's limitless possibilities, a strange sea beast appeared at the surface about fifty yards off our stern. It was a creature sufficiently large to break the sea into whitecaps across its back. I was thinking it looked like a Volkswagen floating just under the surface when it raised a surreally huge head, drank a deep breath of air, and withdrew. I was still frozen in disbelief when one of our rods dipped and strained. But it was no speeding tuna. The line slowly arced across our stern and my eyes widened as I witnessed a turtle of impossible proportions. Our line was wrapped around its long, waving flipper, and as it began to angle away my uncle Tony screwed the reel's drag tight enough to part our heavy line. Thus ended my first awestruck encounter with the greatest turtle on Earth, the Leatherback, tangled in fishing gear.

Is this really the same beach? It's Saturday morning, and Kelly and I can't find a parking space at Jupiter Inlet Park. This beach beloved by turtles at night is by day a different beast, populated north to south, inlet to inlet, by people from condos, hotels, and private residences local and afar. Everyone—we're on the beach now with *hundreds* of people—wants a piece of beach to love. In this same sand that now bears the weight of innumerable oiled sun worshippers lie turtle nests, also incubating by the hundreds. It's hard to tell what's more improbable: that so many people live with turtles or that so many turtles live with people. I ask why this trampling is not catastrophic for turtles, and Kelly responds thus: "Well— I don't know." She adds, "There doesn't seem to be any real problem from beach blankets and chairs and people walking, except—the spikes from beach umbrellas would not be good in a nest."

IN THE BIBLICAL GENESIS, GOD'S FIRST UTTERANCE CREATED LIGHT. That's how fundamental light is—to people. Before light, more fundamentally, was dark. Our great-grandparents saw nights vastly different from what we see. For billions of electrified people, the light with which we flood each tide of darkness is drowning the stars.

Just past sundown I'm standing among two dozen Girl Scout Brownies on the beach in Boca Raton, Florida. We're here to release a dozen hatchlings earlier found disoriented and dropped off at the Gumbo Limbo Environmental Complex's "sea turtle hatchling box."

Impresario Dr. Kirt Rusenko is a tall, wiry, mustachioed scientist in his early fifties. With a Ph.D. in protein biochemistry but tired of lab work, he started volunteering at the Marinelife Center of Juno Beach, then landed a job here monitoring sea turtles' nesting and people's compliance with lighting ordinances. Government-granted authority makes him the turtles' ambassador to landlords, a statesman of the art of light.

Kirt gazes upon the Brownies and me, assessing our readiness. The girls, little hatchlings in their own right, are eager. We are facing the ocean waves. As the girls stop giggling, we begin.

Kirt reaches into his bucket and places three hatchlings on the sand. They head not straight seaward, but southeast. One must even be restarted. Their misorientation was immediate and predictable. Kirt comments, "Better than usual."

A little girl chirps, "I saw them go in th' *ocean*."

Kirt produces the next hatchling, asking, "Are you gonna name this one?" and letting the girls admire the baby turtle cupped in his palm.

One mother sardonically advises, "Don't get attached."

Kirt releases hatchlings three or four at a time until they're no more—all gone. The delighted girls and mommies thank him, leaving Kirt and me.

Of the hatchlings' imperfect performance, Kirt says, "It's unbelievable how strong their attraction to light is." Why hatchlings go to light is well known: the lightest area of a natural beach is usually the horizon over the ocean, the darkest the dunes or jungle. So going toward the light should get you quickly to the water. "When we do releases," Kirt adds, "they sometimes crawl toward white sneakers, white pants, or if we have a white bucket—." Kirt has seen a photo of three hundred turtle hatchlings charred in the ashes of a bonfire.

Monthly, Kirt monitors the night lighting here—porches, windows, landscaping and street lighting. The next day he calls people, reviewing their lightscape, sometimes bulb by bulb. Kirt adds, "It's not a matter of sea turtles versus safety and comfort. You can light your path; just make sure turtles can't see it."

Until the last instant in biological time, human-generated light amounted to scarcely a spark in the dark, merely a way to peer into each other's smudged faces. Moths to flames notwithstanding, wildlife didn't notice much of anything. Not until electricity, in just the last few generations, did we find a way to banish the night and light up Broadway. Now, more than two-thirds of the population of the United States and half the population of the European Union cannot see the Milky Way. In many cities, lights mask all but the very brightest stars.

Tonight as we begin traveling Boca's beach in Kirt's four-wheel-drive golf cart–like vehicle, waterfront condominiums stand dutifully darkened. One high-rise building, strikingly dark, shades the beach from night's brightness. Its paint is nonreflective, its windows tinted, and most of its drapes are drawn. "It's been a good condo," Kirt says, in a tone usually reserved for praising a worthy dog. "That's how we like to see them. It's the only big building on the beach that has never had disoriented hatchlings in front of it—and it's had lots of nests."

Farther along, in contrast, another high-rise has a light glaring as though left on absentmindedly. Brightness comes so easily that it takes effort and forethought simply to allow midnight its darkness. Now night itself has trouble falling.

At the next building, Kirt notes, "That new fluorescent at the end has to go." He explains, "A lot of people don't realize it's not the *light* that's the problem, it's the *wavelength* of light that matters. Turtles' perception of light gets really bad at wavelengths beyond five hundred and fifty nanometers. That's yellowish into red. We can see it, but most turtles basically can't." Or, at least, they don't respond to it. Hatchlings are least attracted to yellow or red light sources—such as might misleadingly come from a rising or setting moon or sun. Simply, then: artificial light visible to a person on a beach will cause problems to turtles unless it's red or yellow.

There's an efficiency question too. Only 10 percent of the energy used by an incandescent bulb produces light; the rest is lost as heat. Light is sometimes measured in lumens. Per watt of electricity, incandescent bulbs produce 20 lumens, mercury-vapor bulbs give off 60, fluorescents produce 100, high-pressure sodium puts out 140, and low-pressure sodium bulbs shine with 200 lumens. With these other bulbs you can get the same brightness while using much less electricity.

Kirt points. "That doorway light there? Those fixtures have turtle-friendly shields, but to save energy they put in a fluorescent bulb that sticks out, so I've gotta ask them to use a compact fluorescent that won't show." Kirt adds, "Luckily, I have no problem talking with condo managers. They're friendly. They know there are fines, but it's not a confrontational thing."

Farther along, Kirt says, "This building's good. All those are energy-saving yellow bug lights. In the past we had hatchlings going to their lights, but turtles really can't see this type very well."

Several adjacent buildings are dark from within, but because they're *angled*, their walls reflect lights from the streets behind them. Kirt comments, "Just because of this reflected light, there's almost no nesting here." To a female turtle, illuminated sand looks more like an ocean horizon than like land. She wants a dark dune with a darkly broken sky behind it, as it looks on a natural beach backed by jungle. Even a little light inhibits females from emerging. Even reflected light constitutes the unbearable lightness of buildings.

Nowadays, most of Florida's sea turtle nesting action happens at four beaches between Boca Raton and Cape Canaveral that differ from adjacent sites only by being dark. The east coast of Florida is the world's most important nesting ground for the Loggerhead Turtle, so merely doing nothing about the light of night on this populous coast would devastate one of the world's most important turtle shores.

Anyone planning alterations or construction on the beachfront must get Kirt's comment on whether it's up to ordinance standards for turtles. Options abound: install timers and motion-detector switches, turn lights off, reduce their number, lower their wattage, hide them, shield them, recess them, lower them, aim them down so you can't see them from the beach, or change their color. "It's nice to be ahead of things," Kirt comments. "I can say, 'If you do it this way, there won't be a problem.' I don't have to count dead turtles first. The condo owners now call and say, 'We're gonna do such-and-such; what kinds of bulbs should we use?' To me, that shows it's finally working."

Morning. We're returning to document last night's nesting and hatching by reading the tracks in the sand. We make the rounds as in a maternity ward. An adult Green Turtle's track indicates a new nest. Raccoon tracks are all over it and though they drilled a few test holes, they failed to find the eggs. That's why turtles are messy while covering; it conceals the exact location of their treasure chamber. Kirt surprises me by saying Raccoons are concentrated in unnaturally high numbers in the parks—where garbage bins keep their numbers subsidized. In the condos the garbage is all locked away. In terms of shadows and densities, the "natural" parks are less natural than the high-rises.

Kirt sprinkles powder on this nest, saying, "This habañero pepper is the hottest thing going." How hot? Peppery hotness is described in Scoville units, a measure of capsaicin, the chemical that activates pain receptors and makes peppers taste "hot." Tabasco sauce rates 5,000 Scoville units. Kirt's habañero pepper powder burns in at 250,000 Scoville units. "It's really good stuff—except when it's windy and you get it in your eyes. Even if you're digging up a nest much later, sometimes your forearms will start to burn. It really deters mammals, but it doesn't seem to bother turtles at all."

Another nest has fire ants penetrating the egg chamber. They don't chew through eggshells, but when a hatchling makes a hole in the shell, the ants invade, stinging, biting, and devouring the baby turtle, leaving little turtle skeletons. Kirt has just the potion: on the ants' busy trail he sprinkles a poison that they'll take back to their nest. They immediately begin picking up the dooming hors d'oeuvres. These nests contain the Red Imported Fire Ant—the "ant from hell" (*Solenopsis invicta,* for "invincible"). Having invaded the United States from Brazil before World War II and spread mainly in shipments of suburban nursery plants and sod, red fire ants occupy most of the southern United States, where they cause $1 billion in damage annually. A queen may produce fifteen hundred to five thousand eggs per day. Freed from the parasitic fly that keeps them in check back home—that's one reason invading species often get out of control—in the States they achieve densities ten to fifteen times higher than in their natural range. They're aggressive in extremis, and their stings form blistering sores. Not only are they hell on nestling turtles and birds, they attack crops, kill young livestock, attack farm-workers, and *protect* pests such as scale insects, mealy bugs, and aphids, which produce a sweet excretion called honeydew that the ants use for food; the ants then transport such "ant cows" to new feeding sites. They even damage irrigation systems, air conditioners, traffic signal boxes, telephone junctions, airport landing lights, and electric pumps for oil and water wells, wherein they chew electrical insulation or cause short cir-cuits. They've spread to Puerto Rico, New Zealand, and Australia. *Invicta* was intercepted at California agricultural inspection stations about once every three days between 1990 and 1996. In 1998, it finally got a piece of the Golden State. Persistence pays. Next stop: Hawaii.

Kirt has marked each nest with stakes and colored tape, so an easy glance reveals the whole season's nest locations. Here's what I'm notic-ing: more nests lie in front of the condos than in the park. Let me repeat that: more turtles have laid eggs in front of the condos than in the parks.

"That's testament to the lighting ordinances. Like I said: they're work-ing." Boca has the highest turtle-nesting density of any urban area in the country. The parks used to be the best place for turtles. Now the parks, with their long stretches of low dune vegetation and the glow of the city behind them, are becoming some of the worst places for light. Compared to low dunes, the dark shadows of brooding condominium complexes do a better job of shading the beach and blocking light. So a lot of turtles are nesting in the shadows of individual condos. "To me," Kirt says, "that's the first step in losing them entirely. First, the parks will get too bright, then, with urban sprawl expanding northward . . ."

We see where a brood of hatchlings emerged, but instead of dashing to the sea, the tracks from this nest lead landward. Kirt puts his cheek on the sand right at the nest stake. The nest is situated line of sight to a sea-wall with two fluorescent lights. Kirt mutters, "Earlier in the season we asked them to turn them off and they did." But now, despite the morning sun, we can see that those lights are on.

Under the lights turn the curlicue tracks of several hatchlings. "This stinks," Kirt says bluntly. "Well—I'll call the manager again."

Other tracks from the same nest lead toward a bright light from a building across the street. The tracks take a one-way trip, vanishing into the grass. It's distressing. But Kirt says, "This is uncommon now be-cause of the ordinances." He straightens and adds, "Fixing this is as easy as asking someone to change a light bulb. I'd rather deal with this anytime."

I'm about to see what he's alluding to. On a flat area are lots of little turtle tracks so loopy and directionless that even Kirt cannot find the nest whence they came.

"This," Kirt comments ominously, "is sky-glow." In the past, if there was a problem all the tracks went straight to a light source, like we just saw. They wouldn't wander around in circles. Kirt mutters, "This is a whole new ball game. It's chaos."

When a hatchling turtle emerges at the surface, its eyes are half an inch above the sand and its most immediate cue is the overhead sky. And when the sky is sending mixed messages, it confuses hatchlings about the single, simple question a questing hatchling must correctly answer: Where's the sea?

At night on the beach here, if you squint and scan slowly around the compass, north, south, east, and west—a blur of the world as I imagine a baby turtle might see—it's not the ocean horizon that seems brightest but the glow from town, lighting up the clouds. When the beachfront lighting ordinances were designed, no one thought lights in town could trouble nesting turtles.

Kirt illuminates the problem: "Just a couple of years ago, that glow was not as wide, certainly dimmer. High-pressure sodium was the main kind of bulb for city lighting. You could look south toward Miami and see an orangey glow in the sky. That wasn't too bad. Now the city glow is getting whiter." Boca put in several blocks' worth of 170-watt metal halide lights. "You'll see it; it's bright enough to take the paint off your car."

I saw it. On the streets of Boca Raton, each pole bears three brand-new fixtures. Some shine light upward as well as downward, illuminating buildings as well as streets. It's a nice effect—if you're not concerned about turtles or stars. Or sleeping; they're shielded on the sides that face buildings, so as not to flood people's bedrooms. But enough escapes sky-ward that it sets the clouds aglow, easily visible from the beach.

Kirt says, "That glow in the sky is why most hatchlings head not straight east into the ocean but instead begin crawling in different directions."

When I'd noticed that the north sky seemed particularly bright, Kirt had answered, "That's a whole strip of car dealers, a couple of miles up the highway."

Once you look, escaped light is inescapable. Light emanating from Boca Raton's streets, stores, and homes, and all the way down to Fort

Lauderdale (about twenty miles south), erases the shadow of night from the bellies of clouds, turning them into reflectors of the busyness below.

The glowing sky is the ever-advancing halo of humanity. About a third of all outdoor lighting is wasted by illuminating the atmosphere, costing more than $1 billion annually in the United States alone, according to the International Dark-Sky Association, whose motto is *"Carpe Noctem"*— Seize the Night. Wasted with the electricity is the six million tons of burned coal used to generate that electricity. The consequences include everything from global warming to wandering turtles.

Kirt, looking down and shaking his head, says, "This is the year of wandering. The increase in this kind of disorientation is so sudden—. It's good you got to see this. This is all actually pretty new to me, and I'm still a little confused by it myself."

We finally locate the nest; it's just twenty feet from the tide line— nearer the water than almost any other on the beach. At this proximity the hatchlings should have reached the sea in half a minute. Instead, the little tracks strike out in all directions, their perfect navigation system jammed by a few sparse photons, their sure-flippered ability disfigured into mere blundering, their legendary innate certainty frayed into confusion. It's heartbreaking to see such finely tuned instincts so disrupted by something so insubstantial as a diffuse glow.

We count the tracks emerging, then walk the tide line, tallying how many crossed it and got in, and how many are missing in traction.

With eyes to ground and notepad in hand, Kirt comments, "A lot are missing."

Some of these brave little tracks head directly away from the water, into the dunes. Others, further burdened with unearned penalty, pointlessly parallel the shore for a long trudge through dry sand—rather than simply turning into the nearby sea.

"This paralleling is something we see more and more; I guess the natural ocean-horizon light is counterbalanced by the town's glow, and they're just going down the middle, torn between two opposing forces."

We ourselves consequently wander among the spaghetti trails that should have been short, straight, seaward. Normally, in their brief rush to water, hatchlings traveling together would prevent a predator from picking off too many of the brood. Safety in numbers. Not here. Separated, lost hatchlings afford a predator leisure for a thorough meal. Night heron footprints amid the confusion suggest the first and final fate of some.

One set of little tracks crosses a set of fox prints, then, having avoided the fox by luck of timing, it gets rutted in a wheel track. Eventually wandering to the dune grass it loops, turns seaward, loops again.

"When they start circling, trying to get oriented," notes Kirt, "it's because the closer to the dune and vegetation the hatchling gets, the more into the shadows it goes, where it can sense the ocean. But once back out on the open beach, under the glowing sky, they get 're-disoriented,' going in circles."

The tiny track we're following finally makes a long sweep across the beach, angling slowly seaward. Another wandering hatchling track intersects this one just a few paces from the high-tide line. Here both could have turned handily into the water, but merely drifted toward the surf.

Hope: once dawn stirs, the sun emerging from the ocean reasserts itself as still the brightest thing in the sky. Hatchlings surviving a night of wandering this beach will—if they have enough energy left—turn toward the sea. Despair: by then gulls are patrolling, pelicans' bellies are growling, fish can better see.

Finally, this track is obliterated by the smoothness of high tide. Our hatchling reached water. If it survives the next two decades, it may return here, searching for a dark reach of beach.

Kirt checks his GPS: point of entry was fully 225 yards from the nest. Hatchlings have a certain amount of fuel to get them out past the surf and into the ocean and to the Gulf Stream. They also emerge dehydrated and needing water. "At least," Kirt comments, "this one went in." A few other tracks are still plugging and plowing along through the dry sand.

Several hundred feet farther, three more cross the high-tide line into the wave zone. Glancing up, Kirt explains, "Now, see, this building right here is nice and dark at night. When these hatchlings got in its shadow they quickly oriented."

Where the last hatchling finds the sea, Dr. Kirt announces, "Nine hundred and seventy feet." That's how far this little guy trudged from a nest only a few paces from the water—wandering all this way just to find darkness on a summer night.

Walking back to the nest, we cross other sets of tracks that took between sixty and two hundred yards to reach the water, rather than the twenty feet required.

Think of an adult turtle lucky enough to have lived decades, undertaking arduous migration, laboring up the beach and perfectly exerting all efforts necessary for nesting; her nest survived raccoons, foxes, ants, and weather, and then the hatchlings struggled up, emerged on cue in cover of what should be darkness—only to get all screwed up because now clouds glow.

"Yeah, well," Kirt says deflatedly, "this isn't even a bad one. Most of these made it to the water eventually."

Farther north, at Red Reef Park, Boca's densest turtle-nesting area, nests are packed into the sand at the rate of one every few steps, marked by Kirt's stakes and flagging. This park has a thirty-foot-high dune, with tall Australian Pines that darken the background and shadow the foreground. Mother turtles like this spot.

We see two fresh Green Turtle crawls, leading to new nests. We also find two new Green hatch-outs. I'm bracing for more heartache, but here all the turtle tracks scramble straight to the water as if on a tight little raceway—just like they're supposed to.

Kirt explains, "That really high dune, those big Australian Pines break up the skyline and cast shadows. So it's almost like a condo—."

The park beach is almost as good as if it had a *condo*! I've lived to see high-rise apartment buildings become the standard for habitat quality.

"Plus, they haven't pumped any new sand on it recently, so it's a narrow beach. Almost like natural."

It's nice to think something is almost like natural in an era of artificial beaches, artificial lighting, alien trees, and dazzled turtles.

In one park, six years ago sand was pumped ashore to make the beach about three hundred yards wider. That made the streetlights visible from the beach, above the vegetation. Nest density dropped from sixty nests to eleven. The next year more turtles nested, but sixteen hundred hatchlings became disoriented. Seventy-five percent never found the ocean. The following year the power company adjusted the lights' angle; disorientations dropped to twelve hundred hatchlings, and 25 percent died. Then Florida's transportation department removed the light poles and installed light-emitting diodes embedded in the road, wholly invisible from the beach. Kirt takes me up to the road to look at them. They're flat lights in the road itself, like aisle lights in a movie theatre. A sign says, SEA TURTLE LIGHTING PROJECT AREA. Kirt informs me, "After they installed these, hatchling misorientations dropped to zero."

We stop to check a Loggerhead nest, hatched from the foot of the dune. To me, the tracks look perfect. With the expertise of a true aficionado,

Kirt appraises them: "Still a little wider apart than they should be, but very good, pretty straight into the water."

We ramble homeward. Dr. Kirt Rusenko sees darkness simply: "It's so easy to fix. And cheap. For one hundred million years, that area over the ocean horizon was the brightest part of their sky. We just have to do a few things to help these animals. Most people are interested, and they're nice about working on the lighting. People wave to us on the beach. We used to see nests where *all* the hatchlings went directly inland because of glaring lights. We rarely see that anymore. It's a lot nicer than it was ten years ago. I'm happy about it."

AN ENDANGERED FLORIDA SCRUB JAY LANDS ON A MAN'S HAND, TAKES the offered peanut, and carries away its prize. The generous hand belongs to Llew Ehrhart, professor emeritus of the University of Central Florida. Around here, everyone calls Llew "Doc." Doc has a broad face, a kindly manner, and speaks with the thoughtfulness of professional science and the patience of a committed teacher.

Florida's coastline from Melbourne Beach to Wabasso Beach is a crucial habitat for Loggerhead, Green, and Leatherback Turtles. More Loggerheads nest in Florida than probably anywhere in the world, and more Loggerheads nest in this stretch than any other beach in Florida. Since 1980 Loggerhead Turtle numbers have roughly doubled. On this stretch they lay about fifteen thousand to twenty thousand clutches annually. Each year about a million hatchlings leave this shore. And Florida's Greens skyrocketed from three hundred nests in 1982 to more than twenty-five hundred in 2002. Most Leatherbacks nest farther south, but they began arriving here regularly in 1994. The last five years set records for Leatherbacks locally. This stretch now accounts for about 10 percent of the state's total.

Although Loggerhead nest numbers have declined for the last few years, Doc says the turtle numbers overall show the beginning of recovery. And for nesting Leatherbacks and Green Turtles, there's been "unassailable increase; the growth is exponential."

It might or might not be coincidental that this stretch includes the Archie Carr National Wildlife Refuge. In the 1950s Carr almost single-handedly invented modern sea turtle biology and conservation, and turned the tide for Atlantic Green Turtles from the path to extinction to the road to recovery. His books remain classics, and his students are leading scientists. Decades after his death, Archie Carr remains the sea turtles' patron saint. In the 1980s the federal government began patching together undeveloped land here, and the resulting twenty-mile quilt constitutes the Archie Carr National Wildlife Refuge.

It's an odd sort of wildlife refuge, interspersed with houses and small businesses, certainly not a wilderness. The main road along the beach is two lanes, heavily trafficked, strip-mauled, dotted with motels and expensive homes whose mailboxes are held at the curb by gaudy plastic turtles. Among all this are open areas running a quarter or a half mile or more, as if to remind us what an island looks like. Here the scrubscape looks as some might say God meant it to be—and others would say it's their God-given right to improve. A string of very large identical beachfront homes, still under construction, exemplifies the latter. As you go south from here, you'll find more development, more people. And each year development and people creep northward. Everyone knew getting this refuge together was a race against time.

Loggerheads use more than thirty beaches in Florida, but this refuge gets about one-fourth of all their nests. Many beaches would suit for digging, yet turtles use very few. Where they nest, they often do so in heavy concentrations, yet leave adjacent miles of coast untouched. What makes some beaches attractive to turtles? One guess is that only a few beaches lie near currents that can promptly take hatchlings into good nursery feeding and hideout habitats. At all others, hatchling survival would be so low that turtle populations could not get established. Most turtles nest on or near the beach from which they hatched. They've had millions of years to figure out which areas are good, so any beach that works is important to turtles. You can't scare them away and expect them to simply settle elsewhere, like a flock of pigeons.

Doc adds, "This is the densest turtle-nesting area in North America, yet it's also very heavily used by residents, surfers, sunbathers, and fishermen. People can live with endangered species. These are the same turtles that in other parts of the world are vanishing due to people. So it can be done, and it's being done—right here. But it doesn't mean there aren't big questions on the horizon for turtles."

Perhaps better than anywhere else in Florida, Melbourne Beach exemplifies coexistence between people and sea turtles. But it's got, as they say, issues. In broad strokes, at issue is a struggle over sand and seawater. As the world warms and sea levels rise, the beach begins adjusting. People try to freeze its contours. The face of sea-level rise is chronic erosion.

Doc understands erosion; his field station recently suffered the consequences of a breached seawall and he had to move his lab. Now the beach there has a seven-foot sheer drop where the ocean removed a chunk of sand like someone lifting a hundred-yard slice of cake from a plate.

As beaches shift and sand moves away, property owners seek to replace it. In the Orwellian speak of coastal engineers, pumping sand onto a beach is called "nourishment." To compensate for rapid washout, they pump extra sand right along the shore, making the first part of the beach higher and the rest flatter than natural.

Would a turtle care? "In the first year," Doc says, "more than half the females that emerge from the surf turn back without nesting. We think turtles are looking for a steep beach." A steep beach might indicate less chance of flooding. "In the second year the shoreline adjusts and nesting returns to about normal—if they use good sand."

Beaches here get artificially rebuilt every five years or so. Rebuilding one mile of beach requires about one million cubic yards of sand, at five to six dollars per cubic yard. U.S. beach rebuilding costs about $150 million annually. Taxpayers pay for it, and where the houses get washed away, taxpayers pay for rebuilding houses, including some very expensive oceanfront mansions.

After repeated pumping, rock or clay remains; the seafloor runs out of sand. Lacking sand for its beach, Broward County, Florida, plans to— I'm quoting here—"set up small experimental beaches of ground-up glass bottles." For over half a million dollars two beaches will be given what officials promise will be the look and feel of sand. "No—I hate it," said a sunbather named Rosi. "I like it natural." County officials will have to deal with troublemakers like Rosi, but they acknowledged, "It may be difficult to get the public to accept ground glass as a substitute for sand." They said with enough "education" (funded by taxpayers) it could be done.

Doc adds, "As long as we're going to have jetties and storms and ocean currents, people are going to demand more sand. If you bring in *good-quality* sand, you can increase hatching success." For nesting, all sea turtles require beaches with deep, loose sand. Moisture and temperature need to be right for eggshell function and embryo development.

"But," Doc excepts, "the engineers and the county officials absolutely refuse to talk about one indisputable fact: sea level is rising. They're trying to draw a line in the sand on beaches that continually change. Can't be done."

Just fifteen thousand years ago (practically yesterday in sea turtle history) sea level was 350 feet lower than today. Florida was thrice as big. For most of history, the shore was not where it is now. And during most of the future, the same will apply. Shift happens.

To turtles, the slow sloshing of coastline is a nonissue. If there were no houses here, it would merely be a shoreline dancing at a turtle's tempo. Nesting turtles care only that the sea meets the shore and that night means darkness. For a couple of hundred million years this humble set of requirements posed no hurdle. The recent end of such reliability, and the contests between turtle nests and human nest eggs, are nowhere more evident than here on Florida's Atlantic coast.

Global warming is accelerating the sea level's rise, the sea level's rise is accelerating erosion, erosion is intensifying calls for putting the beaches back where they just were or armoring them with walls or concrete. Llew paints some hard economic reality by saying, "Unless politicians do something about global warming, home owners wanting to try to keep those houses will be demanding sand or building seawalls—higher and higher, for generations."

The sea level is now rising at a rate of about a foot per century. But it's not quite as though the sea level will rise like water in a tub with a drippy faucet, eventually wetting the edges of, say, Manhattan and giving people time to move a few parked cars, strengthen some seawalls, and adjust. The flooding will likely first hit during storm surges, creating an enormous, expensive, deadly mess. New Orleans has had its experiment. Right now, there's one-chance-in-a-century of a ten-foot flood where I live, the Long Island and New York area. By 2090, because of sea-level rise *alone* (not counting increasing hurricane strength caused by warming waters), floods will reach those same contours once every thirty years on average, if the scientists are right. (And so far they're turning out right more frequently than the politicians and global-warming naysayers are, because they're scientists, not ideologues.) When the sea level rises a bit over three feet, lower Manhattan will flood every other year. That's three hundred years away at the recent rate, but the most extreme prediction suggests a meter-plus sea-level rise in this century. That's unlikely, but because I live on Long Island in a house eight feet above sea level, I find this all very interesting, indeed. Things can happen sooner than predicted. In mid 2005 the New York Academy of Sciences Web site quoted the head of the U.S. Geological Survey as saying that New Orleans probably won't exist one hundred years from now. That was three months before Hurricane Katrina.

After sundown, Doc Ehrhart and I go for a walk down the beach. There's no town here, no sky-glow, and a combination of local ordinance and pride makes beachfronters keep their lights out for turtles. The turtles oblige by emerging near the houses and the silhouettes of motels.

Two shadowy figures are descending a hotel's stairs, carrying a little red light. On any night from mid-May through August, you can stroll this beach and see dinosaurs laying eggs.

Doc's abrupt "Watch out!" saves me from tripping over a Loggerhead Turtle on its way back to sea. On a beach this dark even a big turtle, its shell dusted with sand, merges with shadows. She dramatically picks up her pace, verily trotting seaward with a gait that alternates like a pond turtle's; it's not the rowing breaststroke of Green Turtles or Leatherbacks.

In Florida you can trip over Loggerheads. In most of the world they're quite rare. To find Loggerheads at similar densities, you'd have to go to the place on the Arabian Peninsula where the sun first rises, an Omani island named Masirah. In Florida, Loggerheads dig close to seventy thousand nests in a good year. Recent information suggests that Florida and Masirah account for around 70 to 90 percent of the world's Loggerhead nesting, but Masirah seems to be declining, with problems from fisheries, beach lighting, egg collecting, beach driving, and so on. The most temperate-nesting sea turtle, Loggerheads nest on certain beaches northward to the Carolinas, and on beaches scattered as far north as the Mediterranean, as well as south to South Africa. On Pacific shores, Loggerheads nest only in Australia and Japan. Their Pacific population has crashed like the Leatherback's. All this makes Florida special.

When we find a Loggerhead digging with all her heart, we halt a circumspect distance away, because a disturbed Loggerhead may quit mid-clutch, leaving the chamber uncovered and a trail of fresh eggs in her fleeing track. It's evident that this Loggerhead is a beast different from the Leatherback. Quite unlike a Leatherback's sleek and living skin-coat, her hard, flaky shell is fuzzed with spongy growth like an old dock piling. In that wet fuzz, a sparse galaxy of phosphorescent organisms is twinkling on and off. Extraordinary.

Over twenty-five minutes, she labors through twelve dozen eggs, nearly two dozen more than average. All the while, Doc delivers an impromptu lecture. "If your nests are subject to tropical storms, inundation, washout, you'd better evolve a way of laying a lotta eggs. Sea turtles lay a *lot* more eggs than any other reptile. This turtle will probably lay six hundred eggs this season. Land turtles don't come close. Snapping turtles lay about a dozen eggs at a time." While speaking, he gazes admiringly upon the turtle. "Just think of the energy it takes to make all these eggs. And in about twelve hours she'll get another progesterone surge, and all the ova for her *next* clutch will burst from her ovary wall. Then she's gotta yolk up another hundred-plus eggs. It's incredible they can marshal so much nutrient-rich stuff in such a short time. I mean, yolk is pretty expensive stuff. Hard to believe she can spend such bodily resources tonight and *then* come back in just two weeks with another big, expensive clutch like this. To yolk up a hundred eggs in thirteen or fourteen days, she's gotta just draw on her reserves like crazy."

Because all this nesting depletes her body so much, a sea turtle almost never nests two years in a row. She needs time to replenish her reserves for making those hundreds of eggs. Food scarcity—as during Pacific El Niño years, for instance—will cause breeders to defer an extra year or more. Better conditions leading to higher ocean productivity can foretell heavier nesting.

Ehrhart and a colleague, John Weishampel, have been struck by studies detecting changes in seasonal timing across North America and Europe—forests greening up earlier in spring, summers lasting longer, birds nesting two weeks prematurely and shifting their migration tempos. So they looked at Doc's dates of turtle arrivals over a couple of decades. "And sure enough, we discovered the turtles are coming earlier," Doc says. Local May sea temperatures have warmed about a degree and a half Fahrenheit (0.8 degrees C), and the turtles' median nest date has shifted—fully ten days earlier.

"What it means," Ehrhart ventures, "depends on whether turtles' environments change in synchrony with their premature nesting." If the males' hormones don't change at the same rate as the females', egg fertilization could suffer. If the sand gets drier, it could depress hatching. Or, Llew considers, "If the sand gets hotter, or turtles nest earlier but the sand remains cool, that would affect the male-female ratio." Like most turtles and lizards, sea turtles don't have sex chromosomes. Their sex is determined by temperature during the middle third of incubation. Warmer temperatures produce females. Nests in the shade of trees, or early in the season, or late, or from different latitudes produce different sex ratios. A multiday rainstorm that cools the sand can change a beach's gender ratios. In Florida, Loggerhead nests produce about 90 to 100 percent females. South Carolina and Georgia Loggerhead nests produce 60 percent females. So even though their main population is in Florida, if the northern ones die out the whole coastwide population could lose its males and go extinct.

In a few places, sand temperatures are verging on lethal for eggs in turtle nests. According to Australia's renowned sea turtle expert Colin Limpus, "Over thirty-three degrees Celsius [91° F], you get abnormal scale counts, spinal curvature, stunted hatchlings, impaired locomotion. And no males." He was telling me this at a conference, and was talking mostly about his part of the world. A lot of nesting beaches there have had their beachfront shade trees removed. In Malaysia, Sarawak, and Thailand, where beaches are getting hotter, well-meaning workers compound the issue by moving eggs to save them from poachers and putting them in hatcheries sited on the hottest parts of the beach, exposed to full sun all day—producing perhaps exclusively females and lowering overall hatching rates. "When eggs fail to hatch," Limpus notes, "the people often shrug and say they must have been infertile."

Ignorant of the facts, the Loggerhead we're watching finishes her task, performs her rituals, and returns.

IN MIDMORNING ANTICIPATION OF THE FLORIDA SUN, DOC EHRHART ties his hair in a kerchief under a broad-brimmed hat and we pile into pickups, pulling three boats toward Sebastian Inlet's boat ramp. Doc's beat-up Whaler is thirty years old and, as he proudly points out, rather ugly. We have two turtle-catcher boats and a third boat that will function as a floating field lab.

Indian River Lagoon, between Melbourne Beach and the mainland, is an expansive bay, green and breezy. Our main company is two Royal Terns whose vision pierces the glare for a glimmer of dinner. You can see houses and moving traffic along the far shore, but the major agriculture is low and invisible.

Doc has been studying juvenile turtles living in the lagoon. Before he began this study, Doc knew that people caught turtles here until they'd nearly disappeared. In 1886 one fisherman took twenty-five hundred Green Turtles here. A few years later, he caught only sixty in a year's effort. Pressure continued for decades, until Greens almost vanished. On a whim in the 1970s, Llew decided to dunk an old turtle net he'd found. And on that day, his life took on a sweeter aroma, for, as he puts it, "If I hadn't caught that one little Green Turtle on the first day we tried it, I'd probably still be studying skunks."

We travel about four miles into the lagoon. Motoring slowly, we stream overboard our 1,500-foot-long (460-meter) turtle-catching net. A buoy every thirty feet hangs it like a curtain. The talk is all from fieldwork—the time they caught a big gator; the twelve-foot sawfish, now vanishingly rare.

Turtles need air, so at all times both catcher boats tend the net like web-walking spiders. It takes about twenty minutes to check the net's full length. On our second pass we find our web tensed taut—and the net serves a platter-sized, twenty-pound Green Turtle, flippers flapping. It has a beautiful young head and a pretty, shiny shell patterned with gorgeous starbursts. A very clean, lovely little turtle, it's about five or six years old. Turned on its back, it quiets.

Its finely serrated jaws would make good weed clippers. All turtles lack true teeth, so the cut of the jaw reflects the luck of the dietary draw. Greens are basically vegetarians. Their diet supports very slow growth, and Green Turtles first breed at around age twenty-five in some regions, as late as age forty in the western Pacific—possibly the longest time to maturity of any animal.

The other boat crew scores a Loggerhead and holds it up for my benefit. Its yellowness contrasts with our Green Turtle. They're about thirty yards away, but Doc Ehrhart says, "That turtle's about fifty-six or fifty-seven centimeters, seventy pounds."

One might reasonably assume that the lagoon's young turtles are locals. Not so. Turtles here are as likely to have hatched hundreds of miles away as just up the beach. Doc and his colleagues' genetic studies reveal that young Green Turtles here originate throughout the greater Caribbean, Mexico, Costa Rica, Suriname, Brazil, Aves Island, Ascension Island in the mid–South Atlantic, western Africa's Guinea-Bissau, and the Mediterranean Sea, as well as Florida.

Our net next arrests a Spotted Eagle Ray, of wingspread perhaps four feet across. Number of poison spines at the base of its whipping tail: five. Doc reaches for a pair of pliers and says to me almost apologetically,

"We do remove the spines—they're just too dangerous." When it's safely defused and untangled, we release the ray and garner another small Green, which flaps vigorously, slapping its shell in frantic circumvolutions. Those flat flapping flippers are a sea turtle's most striking specialization. They contain the same bones as our limbs, but the long limb bones lie shrunk and shortened, while the bones of the wrists and ankles have expanded and flattened. Fingers and toes are almost absurdly elongated, forming about half the flipper's length. The front flippers become lift- and thrust-developing propulsive wings—no longer just pond paddles. The rear, idled, merely steer. Powering the front flippers, pectoral muscles occupy more than a third of a sea turtle's internal body area, comparable to the thick breast muscle of flying birds. Like the wing of a bird or an aircraft, the foreflipper is curved on top, flat on the bottom. As molecules of the medium flow past a flipper or wing, they must spread out slightly to cover the longer distance of the curved upper surface. That creates higher density beneath, pushing upward and creating lift. In a sea turtle's downstroke, their flippers are usually twisted so that they're nearly vertical, the leading edge facing down and the "top" of the flipper facing forward like a propeller blade. As the turtle pulls its flippers down, the generated "lift" comes from behind, pushing the turtle ahead.

We locate a lemony Loggerhead whose shell is fouled like the hull of a neglected boat. Moving in its shell growth are scary-looking little praying mantis–like "skeleton shrimp"—amphipods—and other minimonsters a-movin' and a-wigglin'. Unlike the stateliness of an old, mossy tree, this shell seems, well, it seems infested. It's creepy. Greens don't get this way. Leatherbacks certainly don't. This Loggerhead has different kinds of specialized barnacles living on its flippers, its shell, even its tongue and the roof of its mouth. Over one hundred species of small animals and plants ride Loggerheads. Some things that grow on Loggerheads have things growing on *them;* some eat other hitchhikers. No man is an island, but most Loggerheads are.

Unlike the go-along Greens, Loggerheads remain unhappy whether on belly or back. Righted, they try climbing the boat's gunwale. Doc instructs, "Don't let it get out—but don't let it bite you, either." Loggerhead Turtles' shell-crushing jaws can have a colorful effect on fingers. "Loggerheads," pronounces our professor, "are the junkyard dogs among turtles." They eat, for instance, whelks and mussels. Anything that eats shellfish finds itself competing with humans as clam boats and scallop dredges turn the seabed into a factory floor. Along the U.S. Atlantic seaboard, Horseshoe Crabs are among Loggerheads' preferred foods. People don't eat Horseshoe Crabs, but they've been depleted for eel bait, to catch depleted eels.

We deliver our captives to the third boat, our floating lab, which, at anchor, waits with six people ready to weigh, measure, tag, examine, document, and release the animals.

A little while along, we catch a Green Turtle presenting moderate "paps"— fibropapilloma tumors. Whitish grape-sized tumors encumber its shell margins, foreflippers, armpits, and groin. Doc's seen much worse. Cauliflower tumors often overgrow the eyes of afflicted turtles and interfere with their ability to find food. This mysterious disease, almost unknown before the 1980s, now affects various sea turtle populations in different parts of the world. It showed up in 1982. In three years, half the turtles in this lagoon had tumors.

Doc says "The only place we haven't found it is up around Port Canaveral. And—guess what—tides flush the heck out of that place. In places like here, storm water, sewage, pesticides, fertilizers, and all that agricultural crap coming down—." The more pollution, the more tumors. It's unclear why these tumors began appearing around the world during the 1980s and '90s. A pleasant surprise of the last few years is that the disease can regress in the wild. Affected turtles have later reappeared greatly improved, even recovered. Ten years ago its rapid expansion posed a great threat, yet its spread now seems to have slowed, and in many places perhaps halted. Where this disease is headed is anyone's guess.

Three slashes into the armor of its back like chain-saw cuts in tree bark indicate a serious boat-propeller strike, wounds so deep you can see the membrane of this Green Turtle's body wall moving as it inhales. The width of that membrane is how close to fatal this wound was. Doc says, "This will probably heal. They're amazingly tough animals."

Green Turtles nest upon the shores of eighty countries and swim through the waters of about 140 nations as they range the world's warm waters. Their two largest nesting grounds are Caribbean Costa Rica's Tortuguero National Park, and Australia's Raine Island, with present-day annual averages of twenty-two thousand and eighteen thousand nesting females, respectively, digging roughly one hundred thousand nests in each place during good years. People take eggs at nearly half their worldwide nesting beaches, kill females at a quarter. Half the populations suffer accidental losses in fishing gear. Half are targeted for netting by people in various countries who eat Green Turtles. In Southeast Asia, people eat about one hundred thousand Green Turtles annually. Hunting remains significant off Nicaragua's Caribbean coast, along which you can see women on the street selling turtle stew from big steaming pots, and turtles on the decks of boats and in the backs of pickup trucks. Some poaching continues even at Tortuguero.

Doc Ehrhart says, "I don't think people realized Green Turtles were pretty close to blinking off the screen in Florida. We had only thirty-two nests one year. The commercial turtle netters were going out of business for lack of turtles when the Endangered Species Act was passed in the early 1970s." Then things turned around, he says. "By about 1990, conservation measures resulting from the Act finally gained traction. Green Turtles started recovering. They went from under a hundred nests most years to as many as twenty-five hundred nests statewide in the last few years. It's actually exponential now. What did it—in *my* opinion—was that the Act made it illegal in the U.S. to take turtles for their meat and eggs. There will always be poachers, but basically, the Endangered Species Act made people stop killing turtles on purpose. For Florida's Green Turtles, that's what did it."

Meanwhile, members of the U.S. Congress, led by California Republican Richard Pombo, have been working hard to revise the Endangered Species Act. By limiting what kinds of science can be used—no genetics or computer modeling, for example—and by putting people with commercial interests like logging and grazing and real estate on teams writing species recovery plans, and by a host of other requirements, such as mandating payments to landowners, their amendments would so change the Act that Democratic congressman Sam Farr called their bill "a gun to the head, an attack on America's great heritage." In fall of 2005, the Republican majority in the House of Representatives passed the Pombo bill.

A tiny sea horse falls from the net into the boat like an elegant living question mark. Here in Florida there is a magnificence in people's compassion that causes porch lights to go dark, giving room and consideration to ancient elders. But we are less amazed that turtles come than that turtles *still* come. In our bones we know what belongs. Buildings heightened, nights brightened, and beaches hardened are discordant. There is not on such altered shores the feel of how it always was and always can be. In our hearts we fear what's ahead. Sense of place and deep connection yield to the magic-robbing dread familiar to those in desperate love: that the object of our affection may cease returning, may somehow—through our failure to consider or to act, or simply by time's changes—be driven away forever. Here under high-rises the palpable dread is that push may come to shove, that seawalls will come up before home owners go down, and that in any further skirmish with the colonies of strange apes so capable of loving the shore to death, turtles may lose.

There is in the tender peace here a want of assurance, a sparseness of confidence that all's right with the world. This is to say, I worry about the turtles. But so do enough others that there is some comfort. One person worrying is desperation; a worrying group sows seeds of hope. Here people keep their lights out for turtles and ride with bumper stickers announcing, TURTLES DIG THE DARK, and put up shopping centers named Loggerhead Plaza. It certainly could be much, much worse—and elsewhere is. True, there is something diminished about turtles amid highrises and beach chairs. When a turtle comes ashore on a beach backed by dark jungle and a night buzzing the infinite potential of living nature, magic arises in the seamless meshing between the living thing and the setting that created it. Magic is the simplicity of rightness. Where ocean and land confront each other and dance their dance, negotiate their borders, an animal can come ashore for one hundred million years and find no disappointment. It finds the night secure in its darkness, the slope of the shore's shoulder poses the proper challenge, the very sand particles feel right; all systems living and non conspire toward the furthering of life, because the animal has been sharpened on the whetstone of this world. When a beach is yoked to a job it wasn't meant to do, or the land is forced to work, the magic ebbs. But here an accommodation is being struck, and this is the surest proof that it *is* effective: turtles come. A few years ago, the total number of Leatherback nests in Florida reached five hundred; the *next* year it was over nine hundred. At an international scientific conference Kelly Stewart and Chris Johnson recently delivered a paper titled "An Explosive Increase in Leatherback Nesting in Florida." That counts.

LEATHERBACKS AND CANNONBALLS

South Carolina

Like sacred Egyptian icons passing below us, six White Ibises bestow on us the lofty sensation of gazing down upon birds in flight. We ourselves are wafting smooth as a swallow in the soft morning haze of a lazy South Carolina Tuesday, savoring the view afforded by small aircraft—high enough to sense the minds of birds, low enough for intimate peeks at revealing details. The cloying plumes of pulp mills are rising to our right. We hook left, putting the brown clear-cuts behind us.

Soon we're over a mosaic of wooded islands inlaid into emerald marshes, grouted with wriggling creeks, spanning expansively toward the coastal contour. The verdant sprawl of a blossoming summer, languid and luscious, stretches to the planetary curve.

Sharing her views as we speed toward the ocean is Sally Murphy, South Carolina's official "sea turtle coordinator." For two decades Sally Murphy has probably worked harder than anyone to save turtles off the U.S. Atlantic and Gulf Coasts from their largest source of human-caused mortality in the Atlantic: drowning in shrimp nets.

Today Sally and her crew are heading out over the ocean to count Leatherbacks that pool offshore here in late spring. (Kelly Stewart's Florida Leatherbacks, for example, tend northward after nesting, often stopping off South Carolina.) Sally's also done a lot of work with the Loggerheads that nest on her state's shores. Her southern voice comes through my headphones. "See there? That's Cape Romain. Still the most significant Loggerhead nesting north of Canaveral, Florida." This slightly cooler region hosts only 6 percent of the coast's nesting Loggerheads but produces most of the population's males. "Lotsa Raccoons, so we've been moving nests to hatcheries."

If the North Atlantic Ocean's turtle species are stabilizing or recovering, fair thanks can go to Sally, and colleagues countable on one hand. But Sally won't acknowledge success. Despite her achievement in the twenty-year fight to require turtle escape doors in shrimp nets, Loggerhead nest counts here are declining. When Sally started surveying in the early 1980s, Cape Island had twenty-six hundred Loggerhead nests; now annual numbers have fallen to well under eight hundred.

Sally's eyes don't leave the plane window. "Oh, look"—she points— "there's a Loggerhead crawl." The track rises from the water to a disturbed patch of sand, then arcs back into the tide. Sally translates: "That's a textbook crawl. She nested. Sometimes, especially early in the season like this, turtles crawl but don't dig." A few moments later she adds, "There's another good crawl—and pig tracks."

Because shrimpers have, in fact, been required to have turtle escape devices in their nets since the early 1990s, I ask what's caused the recent decline of nesting Loggerheads. Is it natural die-off of older adults? Nest-robbing Raccoons and pigs? Erosion? A combination?

Sally immediately responds, "No, no, no, it's *fishery* die-off. If you want to look at the effects of turtle excluders in shrimp nets, start in 2003—not in the mid-nineties, when they were first required."

I'm about to ask for clarification when Sally, drinking in the view, observes, "It's really fall-down gorgeous in this early-morning light."

It is. The sun hasn't yet floated far from the horizon, and a golden, angled light is coating the coastline.

Sally's in the air a couple of times a week. She flies different surveys to count turtles nesting and turtles swimming, and washed-up turtles no longer doing either. Her husband, Tom—also a state biologist and an expert on endangered birds like Wood Storks and Bald Eagles—is with us today.

It's gonna be a blue-sky day. Our plane is a thirty-year-old, newly refurbished twin-engine, six-seat Aero Commander Shrike. Wildlife law enforcer John Madden, our pilot today, is wearing his gun in a shoulder holster. Rounding out the crew is DuBose Griffin, who recently earned her master's degree in environmental studies.

Readying to strike out over water, Madden says through the phones, "Safety check: we have life jackets, and a raft between the seats."

Sally's only response is "Your gun's pointin' right at us here in the back seats."

Outside, where all is safe and calm, marshes yield to a series of sluggish, muddy-mouth rivers spaced by long-running sand beaches, where ragged breakers of silty gray-green surf massage the shoreline.

We don life vests. Sally distributes small canisters of compressed air designed as emergency backup for scuba divers. We cross the surf, and slip out over the sea.

Today we'll span the ocean off South Carolina, between its water borders with Georgia and North Carolina. We'll be counting turtles along two transect lines: one inshore at 1.5 nautical miles from the coast, the other at three nautical miles.

A light southwest wind is chipping flecks into the ocean's flinty surface, turning the sea below into a sparkler field. The pea-green near-shore water is ribboned with brown mud plumes crawling from the river mouths like giant Anacondas headed for a swim.

Eyeing the GPS display, Tom announces formally, "Okay—coming up on the start of the transect."

The ocean is goose-bumped with dozens of fishing boats. Near and distant, they ply the silvered sea, plodding calmly, their picturesque outriggers spread wide, their dragging nets raising comet trails of mud, scoring the shallow seabed they scour for the ocean bugs we savor as shrimp.

Shrimping season has been open in federal waters but closed in state waters, inside of three miles from shore. Today is opening day in state waters, and boats have streamed in to take advantage. Impressive. Many boats are local, but many come from as far as the Gulf of Mexico—and the Gulf boats are *big*. With freezers aboard, they can stay at sea up to six weeks, dragging their much-bigger nets. Locals call these big boats "slab" trawlers, and they started fishing here in numbers only in the late 1990s. Many of the Gulf-boat operators are Vietnamese Americans, often with entire families aboard. Tom says over the phones for my benefit, "These big shrimpers up here from the Gulf 've gotta tow nets twenty-four hours a day to make a profit. At night, they often do six-hour tows; most any turtle that gets stuck in the nets then drowns."

Before the early 1900s, fishermen caught shrimp mainly with seine nets pulled by hand in the shallows. Trawling for shrimp really got going after World War II. Nowadays the fleet's concerted net power strains the newly opened waters for any and all shrimp. So intense is their collective catching capacity that after the first few days of the season their capture rate will drop significantly and the out-of-state boats will withdraw. But for now, while there are a lot of shrimp, there are a *lot* of boats.

DuBose announces, "Leatherback, at the surface." I'd assumed that spotting huge turtles from the air would be easy, but somehow I fail to see the giant blue-black Leatherback.

Tom marks his clipboard, affirming, "Got it." He adds that when he came out in his boat last week, big Cannonball Jellies were concentrated here. A Cannonball is a substantial creature, weighing about two pounds. Leatherbacks here eat almost nothing but these jellies. Certain crabs and other creatures reside in the jelly's bell, adding nutrients.

Sea turtles' similarities whisper shared ancestry. Their differences speak mainly of survival by divergent livelihoods. Each species uses the ocean differently. Collectively, their diets span a rather astonishing range of extremes that include some of the world's least-edible life-forms. Greens graze grass, Loggerheads crunch crabs, the Ridleys mainly munch crabs, shellfish barnacles, fish eggs, snails, worms, and gelatinous salps and sea squirts. Flatbacks forage for sea pens, other soft corals, and sea cucumbers. But: Hawksbills and Leatherbacks eat stuff that would kill most other animals. Hawksbills range the world's warm-water reefs, where they specialize on sponges—not the soft ones in your bathtub, but types whose bodies are laced with toxins and supported by lattices of glass spicules. Leatherbacks, meanwhile, dine placidly upon venomous jellyfish, to whose stings they appear immune. (I once saw a Blue Shark engulf by mistake one of the Leatherback's favorite foods, a Lion's Mane Jelly; the shark instantly rejected it as though it had bitten a flamethrower.) Perhaps the Pleistocene's last Leatherbacks found themselves facing increasing food competition in a world ocean shrunk by frost, and survived the ice by eating fire, adapting to hot-stinging jellyfish because few other animals could handle them.

"When a Leatherback approaches a big jelly," says Tom, "it gets about this far from it, then it opens its jaws—*Pop!*—and just sucks it in. Then they'll close their throat and shoot two jets of water out their nostrils."

Jellies are mostly water, so it takes a lot before a Leatherback is ready to signal the waiter for the check. They forage day and night. Small, fast-growing Leatherbacks reputedly eat roughly their body weight daily. Leatherbacks stuff in enough jellyfish to fuel their powerhouse partly by glutting an extraordinary gut; their esophagus runs from their mouth to the back of their body, then loops back again three-fourths of the way up to the head before entering the stomach. It's basically a long internal take-out bag. Lined with stiff, backward-pointing spikes, it lets a Leatherback who's found a food patch pack in a lot of jelly.

People in China and elsewhere also eat jellies. A few boat owners have found jelly-fishing more lucrative than shrimping. Tom says, "They get dried, shredded, and used in a few different recipes—."

Sally's summation: "Catching the food of an endangered species—it should be nipped in the bud."

The large shrimper below has ten dolphins prancing in its mud trail, snatching net-killed fish. Sally announces another Leatherback on her side of the plane. I had not seen the first Leatherback, but this one I do see, like a shining black pearl in pea soup.

DuBose follows immediately with "*Caretta,* just staying on the surface." I'm wondering why they call Leatherbacks "Leatherbacks" but Loggerheads by their Latin name *Caretta.* I should easily see it. But I strain.

"See? Right there off the wingtip?"

I search the glimmering whitecaps. Though the animals are large, it's a big ocean, and the view is restricted to a relatively narrow band of vision below. Whitecaps hamper it, as does incessant glare. And we're at nine hundred feet, moving now at about 140 miles an hour. But only I need excuses; the professionals are spotting turtles.

As we come even with Hilton Head Island, DuBose announces another Leatherback.

I remark that there are a lot of turtles. Sally comments that most of the Leatherbacks have actually moved on. Three weeks ago, on May 7, they saw a record 190 Leatherbacks, an astonishing number.

"But what we're seeing today is still a very unusual concentration of Leatherbacks," Tom hastens to add.

"There were years," says Sally, "when even on our best days we didn't see densities like today's."

There were, in fact, entire decades. From 1850 to 1980 South Carolina recorded only eight Leatherbacks. In the early 1980s an aerial survey from Cape Hatteras, North Carolina, to Key West, Florida, located one Leatherback every *three hundred miles*. Three weeks ago, during their record-setting survey, Sally and Tom saw twenty-eight Leatherbacks in one nine-mile stretch.

Was there a sudden real increase in turtles, or did they become more concentrated because of a sudden new concentration of their food? Tom says, "There was always Cannonball Jellies here. They were here well before the big Leatherback increase."

Cannonball Jellies can at times be incredibly abundant. But their density also varies a lot. "When we want density estimates," Tom says, "our survey vessel pulls the net for half an hour. Then, by hand, we count every jelly. We might catch ten, we might catch eighteen thousand. It's that variable. Our vessel once got into a patch of Cannonballs so thick that in ten minutes the net completely filled, the cables snapped, and we lost everything."

Sally admits, "We first assumed the turtles stopped here in spring migration after nesting. Then we found out the Leatherbacks here include juveniles and males."

Tom adds, "Some people still think these Leatherbacks are just migrating north. Not in *these* numbers. And transmitters show some traveling south to get here. This is now a major concentrating area."

This has become one of the Leatherbacks' few lush feeding oases in the sparse Atlantic. Here these long-haul winged horses of the deep can stop, rest, and, by grazing through fields of animals that are mostly water, put on enough weight to push ever forward.

"In the early eighties, when we started counting dead turtles washed up on our beaches," Sally says, "we found plenty of Loggerheads. No Leatherbacks. Leatherbacks would have been drowning in shrimp nets and washing up too—."

Tom finishes, "Leatherbacks just weren't here."

"Then in '87, '88, we saw, like one, two. But *then* in '89—really suddenly—people started seeing them washing up, swimming in the ocean—. It was like they came saying, '*Here we are!*' "

Sally acknowledges increases in some Caribbean Leatherback populations. "But they arrived here so suddenly I don't think what we saw was just because of more turtles. I think they were spending their time where we couldn't see them, then they moved, and we started seein' 'em."

And the reason is?

"North Atlantic Oscillation," declares Sally.

Tom laughs. He's not convinced.

Sally holds firm. "When the western Atlantic was beginning to warm up, we started seeing Leatherbacks inshore."

Imagine a vast mass of high-pressure air spinning clockwise west of Africa, and low-pressure air spinning counterclockwise up near Iceland. Envision these counterspinning masses as meshing gears whose teeth pull all air eastward. The relative strength of those air masses oscillates like a seesaw; when the high is stronger than usual, the low is deeper than usual. This state rates "positive" on the oscillation index. The increased pressure difference shoots more air, faster, through those gears. This causes remarkable climate changes: warmer, wetter winters in the eastern United States, longer growing seasons in northern Europe, colder and drier winters in northern Canada and Greenland, and less monsoon rainfall in India. It creates higher eastward-flowing winds, and sends stronger winter storms across the Atlantic Ocean—and it pulls them up onto a more northerly track. Such rough, storm-wracked winter seas in the eastern Atlantic diminish the single-celled plants called phytoplankton that make up the sea's drifting pastures. Swarms of sixteenth-inch crustaceans called copepods graze these pastures. Copepod numbers have dropped around 20 percent as the plankton has thinned. Because copepods are the main food of larval fishes, the food-chain reaction delivers repercussions to fish populations. Jellies eat copepods *and* larval fishes, so eastern Atlantic jelly numbers, too, have dropped.

The strength of the oscillation relates to sea-surface temperature, and it seems increasingly likely that human activities are playing a significant role as greenhouse gases from burning oil and coal force warming of tropical sea-surface temperatures. And, indeed, a startling feature of the North Atlantic Oscillation over the last three decades is its morphing into a positive phase of unprecedented magnitude and record-high positive values, especially since the winter of 1989—immediately prior to Sally's starting to see all those Leatherbacks.

Sally emphasizes the point: "The intensified east-flowing winds speed up the whole North Atlantic Gyre. That shifts the Gulf Stream northward, bringing it closer to our coast. Or, maybe," she speculates, "Leatherbacks that had gone to the east side of the ocean looking for jellies were disappointed and came back west. I don't know. I do know warmer water in the last few years has coincided with us seeing more Leatherbacks."

The point is, vast processes, conditions thousands of miles away, and possibly even human activities may be affecting what we're seeing today. Several Leatherbacks that Kelly Stewart tracked from Florida came straight here to South Carolina, lingered awhile, then headed north. And we know that the population is increasing. Another thing we all know is what Tom now underscores: "This is probably the densest concentration of Leatherbacks anywhere in the world these days."

· · ·

We get to Georgia's border, swing out to three miles, then hook back north along the imaginary transect line. Looking shoreward from the invisible line demarcating "state" and "federal" waters, the density of boats is so distracting, I cease seeking turtles and begin counting vessels. One-two, three-four-five, six-sev-eight. . . . We hardly need the GPS to know where the state line is. Boats are *so* crowded inside the line, the outer boats *are* the line. Inside the boats' wheelhouses the skippers are all looking at monitors showing their vessel instantaneously tracked by GPS satellites and screen-plotted on electronic nautical maps delineating the state-federal boundary. They know exactly where they are, with pinpoint precision.

The plane's shadow trails us on the sea's surface. The water is only twenty feet deep. One boat's nets are stirring a particularly heavy-looking plume of mud in the sea, like the smoke from a coal-fired loco-motive, as it plows up the seafloor. Another shrimper, hauling its gear, is trailing a flock of diving terns like a white lace veil. They, too, are living off leavings. The mingled muddiness of river water and so many drag plumes makes the ocean look swirled, like a marble cake. Much of the sea is the color of heavily creamed coffee. From the air, a Loggerhead or Kemp's is colored like lightly creamed coffee. Spotting one in here will be tough, and the Kemp's are often small.

Kemp's Ridley evolved from Olive Ridleys about four million years ago, when the Isthmus of Panama closed and a population of Olives got isolated from the rest of Ridleyhood. Kemp's breeds only in the Gulf of Mexico, mainly at one beach. Juveniles wander the eastern seaboard north to about Cape Cod Bay. Their small, wide, disk-shaped shells give them an unusu-ally small turning radius and spinning ability, a distinct advantage in run-ning down their main prey: crabs. (Anyone who has tried to catch Blue Crabs while snorkeling knows that being able to spin 180 degrees would be a great advantage.) They also eat mussels, scallops, and whelks.

Kemp's was unknown to science until the 1880s, when a Florida fisher-man, Richard Kemp, sent one to a Harvard reptile specialist. No one had ever seen this kind of turtle nesting, and for the better part of the next cen-tury many considered it a hybrid, the "bastard turtle." The search for its nesting grounds preoccupied several scientists until 1960. All failed. In the 1940s, though, a young pilot named Andrés Herrera became tanta-lized by rumors of sea turtles nesting in a huge group somewhere along the Gulf of Mexico, sometime between April and June. With a friend as photographer, for twenty-three days he flew a 145-kilometer stretch of coast. Their reward: surf, sand, and sunlight. No turtles. On day twenty-four the photographer didn't feel up to going, and Herrera decided to make one more flight, solo. The turtles must have known the photographer was on the ground, because they rewarded Herrera with an almost unbelievable sight: tens of thousands of emerging sea turtles. Turns out Herrera had a movie camera. Astonished and ecstatic, he filmed turtles coming, going, digging, laying, and covering. He filmed a beach covered with an estimated *forty thousand* turtles—and people collecting *piles* of eggs. Scientists didn't know where these turtles nested, but other people did (and no one will ever know how many turtles might have nested there fifty or a hundred years earlier). Deeply satisfied, he showed his film to family and friends—then shelved it. That was in 1947. Meanwhile, the late, great Archie Carr searched for nesting Kemp's Ridley Turtles, in vain, in Florida, Mexico, and Central America. Dr. Henry Hildebrand was also hunting. He heard about Herrera's film in 1960, after it had been collecting dust for thirteen years, and turned his hunt toward finding the footage instead of the flesh. One can only imagine his jaw dropping as the flickering projector conjured the shaky black-and-white camera pan of a Mexican beach wall to wall with Kemp's Ridleys, and people standing atop turtles whose very existence as a reproducing species many scientists had long disputed.

By the time scientists got to the beach, the eggers' legacy was apparent. Not forty thousand turtles but two thousand remained. Scientists got into gear, conservationists raised the cry—and locals continued digging eggs. Conservation workers could save only about a third of them. Within the next two decades, by the late 1980s, their plunge would put them within three hundred annual nesters of crashing to zero. Kemp's bastard, the turtle practically no one knew or cared about, was finally famous for being one of the dozen most critically endangered species on the planet.

There were under six hundred adult females in the ocean, and shrimp trawls were annually killing five thousand Kemp's, including males and juveniles. But then the other side of human nature kicked in, commencing beach protection and the long fight to mandate turtle escape devices in shrimp nets. The egg-saving effort began sending twenty to thirty thousand hatchings into the sea annually. A yearly population decline that was running 10 to 15 percent in the 1960s flattened to 2 to 3 percent by the mid-1980s. This probably saved the Kemp's from extinction during that decade. Meanwhile, conservationists battling to fix the other problem—shrimp trawls—were nearing initial success.

With exponential surges during the 1990s, Kemp's Ridley Turtles increased more than tenfold from their mid-1980s low point. In 2002 they staged their first mass nesting, or arribada, in decades, and half a million Kemp's hatchlings now venture seaward each year. It's been one of the all-time greatest turnarounds for any of the animals queued up at death's door.

Sally gripes, "You can't see the brown turtles in water like this." A few minutes later she adds with satisfaction, "But you can still see the black ones; there's another Leatherback."

I count fifty-one shrimp boats in just my wedge of vision.

DuBose calls to Tom, "Another Leatherback, at the surface." Having not seen the last Leatherback, neither can I pick this one from the whitecaps. DuBose points and says, "One more Leatherback."

I crane, searching the shining wrinkles hundreds of feet below. She guides my view: "See the little black dot? *There*." I try to follow her finger, bumping my headphones against the glass. She sits back, saying, "It's too far to see now." Back to scanning, she consoles me: "That one was really far." Then she abruptly calls, "Leatherback, underwater."

I actually see this one, a dark smudge with wings, beneath the surface.

"Here's the trick for Leatherbacks," instructs Sally. "You train your eyes to block out anything that's not black. The whitecaps. Anything floating. You just look for something black. And you don't just gaze; you work your eyes continuously, searching up and down, near and far. And you pay attention—the whole time."

That's hard to do, partly because the sheer number of boats remains so distracting; I've already counted over 150 shrimpers.

Past Winyah Bay the water clears noticeably. With satisfaction, I finally point: "There's a Leatherback." Sally pats my knee and gives me the thumbs-up, leaving me feeling flushed with renewed self-worth. When DuBose spots another Leatherback, I see this one, too; perhaps I'm getting the knack of it.

Tom announces this outer transect's last segment, which will take us to the state border. Sally narrows her eyes and calls, "There's another Leatherback." Looking like a black almond with wings, it appears still, splayed. It could be dead, but when it sculls and takes a breath of air I realize it is basking peacefully, letting the sun warm its wide, dark body.

DuBose points out four Cow-Nosed Rays: brown, distinctively diamond-shaped. I'm still watching when she announces, "*Caretta*—just diving."

Sally sights a Leatherback almost directly below, and *this* one I see very nicely, its head up in the sparkle. Four minutes pass—eight miles of shimmer and our droning engines—and more shrimp boats. I proudly find a Leatherback under the surface far from the plane, a blurry smudge like a dark droplet in the sea. After that we spot two more, both in the path of an oncoming shrimper.

Among wildlife biologists—just as with indigenous hunting peoples—the company of wild animals produces a deep sense of well-being and connection that feels spiritual. But here the boats induce tension. Their intense fishing power alters the options for everything trying to survive below. The most counterintuitive aspect of shrimp fishing is here most obvious: shrimping is about a lot more than shrimp.

The turtle sightings now quicken into an extraordinary flurry of Leatherbacks: one every ten seconds or so; there must be three or four per mile. All of us are spotting them, and it continues like this for several miles. Even Sally and Tom, who have seen more Leatherbacks from the air than anyone on earth, are saying "Wow!"

Throughout the spectacle: boats, boats, boats, smearing their trails like garden slugs. I tally my notes and realize that for every turtle we've seen, there've been about six shrimp boats. That's not the same as saying boats actually outnumber turtles. We can easily see boats; we are certainly missing turtles, especially those far from the plane or underwater when we overfly them. But watching the boats' lazy, inexorable progress, I wonder whether many of the turtles and rays we're seeing will become intimate with the inner panels of a shrimp net before the day is out. How could they not?

Sally, shaking her headphoned head, echoes my thought. "Look at all these boats. You can bet some turtles are having their day interrupted."

Even with now-mandatory turtle-escape devices (in vernacular lingo, turtle excluders, or TEDs, pronounced "teds") in all shrimp nets, turtles still get into nets before they go through them. When the net first engulfs them, they try outswimming it. As they tire, they fall back farther and farther in the net. Eventually they hit the device's grate and go out the escape flap. By the time they come to the surface, they're sometimes exhausted. Bottom-dragged nets and dredges targeting flounder, squids, scallops, and other creatures can also swallow turtles. Because such boats often tow their gear for hours before hauling it to the surface, entrained turtles can drown. Carcasses still wash up from time to time, the cause of death unclear. Sally has seen Leatherbacks entangled in crab-trap lines. She's also seen turtles wash up from natural causes.

Nonetheless, the saga of turtle-escape devices along the eastern United States is mainly a story of hard-won success. And no one's succeeded harder than the woman gazing out the window.

By the late 1970s, with sea turtles officially listed as endangered and causes sought, federal researchers estimated that shrimp nets in U.S. waters each year caught forty-seven thousand turtles, drowning twelve thousand of them. In the early 1980s the federal government's National Marine Fisheries Service developed a cagelike trapdoor device that allowed the escape of 97 percent of turtles and zero percent of shrimp. Problem solved. One last hurdle: it was cumbersome, and shrimpers hated the device, hated government regulation, hated the very idea. Because the Fisheries Service has always seen its job more as an official promoter of commercial fishing than the public's steward of ocean creatures (even though conserving is the best thing for fishing, long-term), the feds asked mere voluntary use of the turtle-escape devices. All but 98 percent of shrimp boats quickly adopted the device. That was round one. Round one lasted about a decade. Drowned turtles continued washing ashore.

In 1986 a shrimper named Sinkey Boone showed a grate and trapdoor designed to get rid of Cannonball Jellies. Cannonballs would hit the grate and slide out the trapdoor, while shrimp passed through the grate into the end of the net. His "Georgia jumper" had been a jealously guarded secret. Sally immediately realized: a similar shunt could let turtles escape.

One hundred thousand dead sea turtles after the government first recognized the problem, and with environmental groups such as the Ocean Conservancy and others pushing hard, the Fisheries Service in June 1987 published regulations requiring that shrimp nets off the southeast U.S. and Gulf states carry "turtle-excluder devices" (TEDs), to take effect several months hence.

Shrimpers began reaching for their telephones. One month later the U.S. Senate delayed the regulation; the great state of North Carolina sued the U.S. Commerce Department, further slowing any turtle-protection regulation; Louisiana sued to void the federal regulations, lost, and so passed a state law making it illegal for state agents to enforce any federal regulation requiring turtle-escape devices in shrimp nets.

Sally had started counting turtle nests from the air in 1980, and by the mid-1980s it was obvious that South Carolina's Loggerheads were in serious decline: down 25 percent in seven years. Citing her data, Sally said, "We can't wait for the feds; we need TEDs now." Thinking an effective, fishermen-devised turtle excluder could navigate shrimpers' resistance to government-designed devices, Sally lobbied hard for adaptation of Sinkey Boone's Georgia jumper to keep turtles out of shrimp nets. With Sally pressing, South Carolina's Wildlife and Marine Resources Commission in 1988 passed regulations requiring turtle excluders in shrimp nets—but only in the state's waters, within three miles from shore.

For her pains and considerations, shrimpers hung Sally in effigy. South Carolina's shrimpers sued not once but twice, fighting all the way to the state supreme court. The turtles won, and the rule went into effect in late 1988 against continued howls from the state's shrimpers.

South Carolina's shrimpers' main gripe was "We're the only shrimpers in the country that have to pull these things" (indeed, in the world). They had a point. Louisiana's lawsuit had effectively delayed any federal regulations. The U.S. Congress further delayed turtle-excluder regulations pending amendments to the Endangered Species Act. Those new amendments included an eight-month waiting period before any federal regulations could require turtle-excluding devices in shrimp nets in federal waters; the wait for state waters was twenty months. Assuming the earlier-estimated drowning rate of one thousand turtles per month, Congress had just used the Endangered Species Act to condemn thousands of endangered turtles to early mortality.

Those doomed turtles made a last visitation prior to final departure. In autumn 1988, hundreds of dead turtles washed ashore on Florida beaches, prompting that state to pass emergency regulations requiring turtle-escape devices in its waters. (When Sally's colleagues attached transmitters to twenty-five drowned turtles at sea, fewer than one in four washed up, and only 13 percent were actually found by people and reported. The fraction reported is what everybody talks about, but they're just the shell of the problem.)

In 1989 Louisiana sued again to preclude federal regulation. This again delayed the feds, and this delay allowed South Carolina shrimpers to get themselves a law exempting them from regulations stricter than federal rules. Since there weren't any federal rules . . .

With the dog chasing its tail and turtles drowning, the U.S. Commerce Department and its Fisheries Agency finally straightened out and implemented federal regulations on July 1, 1989, requiring that shrimp nets pull turtle-escape devices.

This halcyon peace persisted precisely ten days. Then, slowly, hell broke loose. First, the Coast Guard announced that it needed to check on a "sea-grass problem" with the excluders (enforcement suspended). Ten days further, regulations went back into effect—there was no sea-grass problem. Gulf shrimpers immediately blockaded harbors, disrupted navigation, and engaged in minor violence. One can almost hear the bullhorns: *The fedril guvmin—is tramplin' owuh rights!* Louisiana governor Edwin Edwards said, "Perhaps some species were just meant to disappear. If it comes to a question of whether it's the shrimpers or the turtles—bye-bye turtles." (He was later imprisoned for fraud and corruption, but I believe he was being earnest about turtles.) After two days of shrimpers' shenanigans, the U.S. Commerce Department, its Fisheries Agency ever uneasy about regulating the fishing free-for-all it was born to promote, again genuflected to the cheeky willfulness of the fishing industry, and suspended the regulations.

Now environmental groups sued. They argued that—tirades and tantrums notwithstanding—shrimpers were taking public resources, and the public had a legal right to demand that in the course thereof, endangered species be protected from further harm. They won. A federal judge instructed the commerce secretary to issue turtle regulations, "to become effective immediately."

The secretary complied. But, ah! The secretary's new rule gave shrimpers an essentially unenforceable cream-puff choice: you can either use turtle excluders *or* check your nets every 105 minutes.

The conservation groups took another opportunity to visit the courtroom. Meanwhile, in April 1990, the National Academy of Science's National Research Council issued "Decline of the Sea Turtle—Cause and Prevention," which emphasized that "for juveniles, sub-adults, and breeders in the coastal waters, the most important human-associated source of mortality is incidental capture in shrimp trawls, which accounts for more deaths than all other human activities combined."

Federal regulations finally went into effect a month later. The numbers of turtle carcasses washing ashore immediately diminished and stayed low all summer. But from September through the end of the year, they hit record highs. Why? Because in typical behind-the-curve fashion, the long-sought regulations required turtle excluders only from May through August. Turtles that had survived the summer, thanks to TEDs, were drowned in the fall, thanks to feds.

Turtle-escape devices were finally required year-round in 1992.

Not really. The federal government made the regulations mandatory, but gave itself two years to implement them. On December 1, 1994—twenty-four years after the Kemp's Ridley Turtle received endangered-species status—regulations mandating that all shrimp trawls from the Carolinas to Texas have turtle-escape devices actually went into effect.

"The shrimpers in the Gulf went nuts," recalls Sally with a twinkle of something like nostalgia. "They were sayin', y'know, 'This is overregulation!' 'Get big government off our backs!'" But the new requirements held, and they quickly resulted in record-low turtle drownings.

Only one species was still having problems with shrimp nets—the Leatherback, which had recently begun its mysterious influx. *Their* carcass-count hit new record highs, with dozens washing up along Georgia and South Carolina in 1991 and 1992. For Leatherbacks, turtle excluders just didn't work; the escape opening was nowhere near big enough.

"When TEDs were first certified for use in the late 1980s," Sally says, "the openings were really big, and they worked. Even for big Leatherbacks. But the regulations didn't say how big the opening had to be!" And shrimpers, concerned about keeping shrimp rather than losing turtles, started tying the openings smaller and smaller. "In '92, when it finally became obvious that you needed to state a dimension, somebody—it certainly wasn't me—wrote into the federal regulations a width of thirty-five inches and a height of only twelve inches. Well, that's ridiculous. Adult turtles are not going to get through twelve inches. In the Gulf, it was only *ten* inches—way too small for adult Loggerheads or Greens. It only worked for juveniles and for Kemp's Ridleys. For Leatherbacks, it wasn't even close.

"I was getting really frustrated. I started pitching a fit with the Fisheries Service over the openings because we were getting egg-carrying adult females dead on the beaches every summer. I couldn't track down who said the openings should be only ten or twelve inches, or why—but it drove me crazy. Our Loggerhead nest numbers were still going down and we had dozens of dead Leatherbacks washing up. Meanwhile, people kept asking us, 'When are we going to see the effects of the TEDs?' I said, 'You aren't, because *the opening's too small.'*

"So I went on the beach all night for nine nights, and with volunteers we measured eighty-nine nesting Loggerheads. *Every one* of the nesting females had a body deeper than twelve inches. Nine percent were deeper than sixteen; some were twenty inches. Well—*duh!* Now, in the ocean ninety percent of turtles are juveniles, but nearly half of washed-up carcasses had bodies deeper than twelve inches. Well, that tells you most smaller turtles were getting through the TED openings, but a lot of others were getting stuck and adults were still drowning. So *that's* why breeders continued declining *despite* the use of TEDs."

Unwilling to solve the problem by simply requiring large enough escape openings, the government did nothing for three years. Eventually the federal people instituted a complicated, expensive, high-maintenance trigger: if aerial surveys detected more than ten Leatherbacks along fifty nautical miles of transect line, the feds closed the coastline out to ten nautical miles, in blocks of one degree of latitude (sixty nautical miles), for two weeks, for boats that did not voluntarily have a Leatherback-sized TED. What could be simpler, right?

In late 1999, Sheryan Epperly and Wendy Teas of the National Marine Fisheries Service published a report, "Evaluation of TED Opening Dimensions Relative to Size of Turtles Stranding in the Western North Atlantic." (In the arcana of turtle lingo, "stranding" means washing up dead.) It concluded: "A reduction in mortality in exactly the size classes not fitting through the TED openings would result in the greatest annual population multiplication rate. A reduction in subadult and adult mortality from drowning in trawls would benefit all species and subpopulations of sea turtles. To decrease the mortality on large turtles caused by trawling, the opening dimensions of TEDs need to be larger." Their final suggestion was for "adopting the 'leatherback' modification for all areas and all times, which would allow the exclusion of turtles of all sizes, including leatherbacks."

Translation: Hole's too small.

For the next four years their own agency further dithered with its ponderous policies of partial temporary closures and voluntary use of Leatherback-sized turtle excluders. Clumsy and expensive as it was, the policy resulted in fewer Leatherback drownings, but it was far from perfect. In May 2000, Sally and Tom started hitting the trigger on almost every flight. When they saw their unprecedented twenty-eight Leatherbacks in nine miles, the federal agency responded with a two-week closure; but when needed repairs forced the plane to miss the next survey flight, the feds ended the action, reopening the area. "Right after that," Sally remembers, "we started getting all these dead Leatherbacks and Loggerheads on our beaches.

"*Four years* after their own staff's report highlighted the problem, the feds intended to enlarge the height of the opening to just sixteen inches!" Sally remembers with persisting amazement. "I told 'em, 'That would just create a different problem!' I wanted it fixed once and for all—which is why I went on my rampage to get TEDs big enough for Leatherbacks."

In 2002, from May 5 to May 19, ninety-three Leatherbacks washed up dead on Georgia's beaches. On May 20, South Carolina again flexed its leadership. This time with shrimpers' endorsement, the governor signed legislation requiring TEDs with twenty-inch-high escape openings. In a typically excruciating yet incomprehensible combination of speed and ineffectiveness, four days later the federal Fisheries Service required Leatherback-sized turtle-escape devices, but only from Cape Fear, North Carolina, to St. Augustine, Florida—and for only the next thirty days.

Not until August 2003 did the federal government require Leatherback-sized turtle-escape devices in shrimp nets along the U.S. East Coast and Gulf of Mexico.

That this quarter-century delay was utterly needless would be proven later, when many shrimpers grew devoted to TEDs because of the work they save by keeping not only turtles but a lot of trash and other unwanted things out of the catch. It was never really about the devices; it was always more about habit and not wanting to be told what to do.

Sally adds, "The summer of 2003 was the first you could really call 'with TEDs.' Twenty-odd years after we started working on this, adults can finally get through the hole. So we'll see."

Reasons for hope? Sally says, "Kemp's Ridleys are increasing at about ten percent a year." That's a meteoric rise for a species that had by the mid-1980s become so vanishingly rare it was widely considered hopelessly doomed. "Kemp's are much smaller, and their generation time is less than half what it is for Loggerheads. Time will tell if the big TEDs'll turn it around for our Loggerheads," Sally notes, adding brightly, "but suddenly—finally—we don't see many nice, big, adult females washing up dead on the beach. That used to just break my heart, going to the beach and finding a beautiful, big old turtle maybe fifty or more years old, loaded with eggs, not a mark on her, except she's dead.

"Those big TEDs have made a huge difference with our nesting females while they're in our waters," she acknowledges. "Three years ago adult female Loggerheads made up more than a third of the carcasses; this year we had only one adult. And especially considering how many Leatherbacks we see swimming, what's remarkable now is how *few* Leatherbacks we see drowned anymore."

But Sally isn't ready to go sentimental. I ask her whether in all these fights she's ever felt personally at risk. She replies, "In the early days, I'd go down to the docks, and the shrimpers'd rant and rave for about twenty minutes. Then they'd calm down. At a hearing over the Leatherback TEDs they cussed me for forty-five minutes. One said he'd be mailing me an envelope with white powder. Someone else asked if I owned a gun for self-defense. They're the world's biggest crybabies. And our department people are such wusses to allow people to talk like that at public hearings. But that's the last time I'm gonna take it. Twenty years is enough."

Sally's still feisty. But I make a prediction: someday Sally will be able to look herself squarely in the mirror and say, "Yes. It worked."

Sally's done her part. A lot of people in conservation groups, government, and even the fishing industry fought alongside her. But I believe that in the fight to end turtles' drowning in shrimp nets, no one stayed with it as continually and doggedly through the long haul, slow and steady as a racing turtle, as Sally Murphy.

Sally has left plenty for the rest of us to do. Still to be accomplished: getting turtle-excluder devices into use in trawl fisheries throughout the warm-water countries of the rest of the world, solving turtle mortality on longlines and in gill nets, and stabilizing the planet's climate.

When I spot a *Caretta,* Sally acknowledges it with the words "Big ol' pretty brown Loggerhead."

In our tour along imaginary lines we bump into North Carolina's make-believe airspace. Here, though the air continues, we will not proceed. Sally adds, "Cape Hatteras is a major departure point for Leatherbacks and Loggerhead Turtles going north. We have no idea what happens after they leave Hatteras. No one's looked."

Defying curiosity, we turn and head inshore. Thus far we've seen a gratifying 46 Leatherbacks. Of shrimp boats: 213 so far.

Flying alongside a stretch of coast that looks primordially wild, Sally comments, "Just look at that; it's the prettiest beach in the state. This part of South Carolina is the 'blank spot on the map' that Aldo Leopold talked about."

In *A Sand County Almanac,* Aldo Leopold's classic book about humanity, landscape, and the "search for a durable scale of values," Leopold resonantly asked, "Of what avail are forty freedoms without a blank spot on the map?" He would never have imagined that half a century after his death one could fly a portion of the eastern seaboard of the United States and find the human footprint falling most heavily not where he'd directed his famous essay "The Land Ethic," but rather upon the ocean, in the insatiable latticework of boat wakes crisscrossing the sea.

Sally sights another Leatherback just as it dives in jade-green water.

"Got it," Tom says crisply as he glances at the GPS and marks his form.

So it continues, for a few more miles. At one P.M. we click through the last position of the transect, and turn homeward over the green South Carolina coastline and its salt marshes, treed islands, and ribbony meandering creeks. Sally tells me that some of these protected wild coastlands were plantations. "In those marshes," Sally says, "you can see the former plantation impoundments where they grew indigo, rice, and cotton. This was once freshwater cypress swamps, almost all the way to the ocean. Those impoundments were all hand-cut and hand-dug," she adds, leaving unspoken all that those words imply. This plantation's slave shanties still stand, plainly visible, as though even nature doesn't want to claim them.

When the runway rises to bite our wheels, we've logged 465 nautical miles, an amazing 55 Leatherback Turtles, and a mind-altering 344 shrimp boats. The co-occurrence of so many turtles and shrimp boats would, in the years before Sally, have been followed in the next days by dozens of dead turtles washing up on the beach. In many parts of the world that kind of thing still happens. But not so much here anymore; not since Sally's gotten her Leatherback excluder.

"These flights hurt my back," Sally says stiffly as she climbs out of the plane. "People think this sounds like fun, but I tell 'em four hours of plane spotting is like eight hours in a dentist's chair. You have to be paying attention *every second,* your eyes sweeping up and down, up and down, at all that shiny water. When I come off this plane," she puffs, "I am *exhausted.*"

EVOLUTION HAS NOT FREED TURTLES FROM THE SURFACE. THEY MUST breathe, and if forcibly submerged too long, they drown. Turtles trapped in a shrimp net for fifty minutes should be fine upon surfacing. Following ninety minutes' forced submergence, however, their blood oxygen falls to essentially zero; high levels of lactic acid are by then circulating in the bloodstream, and a turtle runs a 70 percent chance of being dead or comatose when it hits the deck. Turtles brought to the surface alive at this point will hyperventilate for half an hour, yet their blood will remain acidified for up to twenty hours. Even with less than half an hour's submergence, a turtle's blood can remain acidic for more than ten hours. So it's not enough for a trawled-up turtle to get a few minutes of air before taking another prolonged dunking. It needs longer relief to survive.

Sea turtle diving involves two main features: systems for storing, using, and being miserly with oxygen during extended dives; and a backup if the oxygen runs out.

In just one breath sea turtles can exchange up to 80 percent of their air (in humans it's about 10 percent). They can completely flush and refill their lungs in a few breaths, requiring just two or three seconds. Then while holding their breath, sea turtles are exceptional at thoroughly stripping oxygen from the air in their lungs, depleting it to levels barely detectable with instruments.

Sea turtles dive night and day, spending up to 95 percent of their time underwater. Often they'll let out one single explosive exhalation just before appearing, then burst through the surface, inhale a single deep breath, and disappear again. Of course, basking turtles may stay topside for hours. Leatherbacks spend more time—20 to 45 percent—at the surface.

A sea turtle's average dive might range from barely three minutes for a migrating Leatherback traveling just below the surface to half an hour while foraging. But they can stay submerged an hour at a time, longer on occasion (in cold weather, Loggerheads and Greens sometimes hibernate at the bottom for weeks).

Sea turtles can dive as deep as the most deep-diving seals and whales. While the Kemp's reaches a maximum depth of only about 150 feet (30 meters), Hawksbills surpass 300 feet, Greens nearly 400, Flatbacks 500, Loggerheads 800, Olive Ridleys 900 feet. Most great whales reach 300 to 1,500 feet, Emperor Penguins reach 1,500 feet, and several seals get to 3,000 feet (roughly a kilometer).

As deep-diving extremists, Leatherbacks shrug off all other air-breathing animals, leaving them gasping far behind. Blowing past them all, the Leatherback drills as deep as 3,900 feet (1.2 kilometers). Though such dives are rare, their record depth surpasses by about 200 feet the deepest known dives of Sperm Whales.

At that depth, the pressure has gone from under 15 pounds per square inch at the surface to about 1,800 p.s.i.—roughly 120 atmospheres. In such cold and dark, under pressure beyond imagining, the chill alone would probably stun other turtles. A human would implode like bubble wrap. At around 300 feet, a turtle's lungs collapse. This deep squeeze may explain Leatherbacks' flexible shells—defense against cracking during the deepest dives. Their air gets pushed into their cartilage-reinforced trachea. This protects turtles from "the bends," because gas can no longer be forced from the lungs into the bloodstream. (A diver gets the bends when, during rapid surfacing, dissolved gas forced into the blood under high pressure while at sufficient depths begins forming fizzing bubbles in the blood as the pressure eases nearer the surface. Bubbles lodge in joints and elsewhere and expand, causing excruciating pain, damage, paralysis, and sometimes death.)

Like humans when diving, most turtles use oxygen directly from their lungs. Deep-diving Leatherbacks face a problem: If your lungs collapse, how do you access your oxygen? Leatherbacks' answer is to predissolve their oxygen reserves right into their blood. They can actually load more oxygen into their blood and tissues than into their lungs. Deep-diving mammals do the same, and often exhale to *empty* their lungs just before diving so they don't have to fight the buoyancy of internal air. Consequently, Leatherbacks and some seals have smaller lungs than you'd expect. To pack oxygen into their blood, Leatherbacks have the highest red-blood-cell density among reptiles, a density similar to mammals'. Loggerheads, which use oxygen from their lungs while diving, can carry 25 percent more oxygen per kilo of lung tissue than Leatherbacks' lungs can carry. But Leatherbacks can load more than two and a half times as much oxygen into their blood and tissues than can Loggerheads.

With the lungs of so little use while disconnected from the atmosphere, a question of economy arises: Why pay the expense of pumping blood through the lungs? As soon as a Leatherback submerges, its heart rate slows by about a third and stays slowed until the animal surfaces. At times during a dive, its heart might beat only once per minute.

Leatherbacks have much larger hearts than other sea turtles. In what at first appears to be a faulty cardiac system, freshly oxygenated "red" blood coming from the lungs can partly mix in the heart with deoxygenated venous blood returning from the tissues. In a person, such a major heart defect would seriously limit activity. But most humans neither gain their living nor maintain survival by diving deeply into the sea while holding their breath. And so what would be a serious heart defect in a human is a survival adaptation in a sea turtle. There's no point in sending blood to lungs that are devoid of oxygen, so might as well skip the lungs, pass the blood through the heart wall from one chamber to the next, and pool it all together. The pooled blood being shunted away from the lungs and through the heart chambers continues circulating to the other tissues. Thus deoxygenated blood is "recycled," allowing muscle cells to mine even more oxygen from it. When the turtle surfaces, the shunting port closes and the heart again sends depleted blood to the lungs to be reenriched with oxygen. Though not unique in this ability, a Leatherback uses its lungs less while diving and dives deep more often. Consequently, compared to other sea turtles, Leatherbacks have the most developed heart-shunting mechanism.

Size matters. The bigger an animal's body is, the more blood it has, but the lower its metabolic rate. So if you're big, you have more blood but proportionately less oxygen demand. This generally allows larger animals to dive deeper than smaller ones, and is a distinct advantage for animals that store their diving oxygen in their blood. Loggerheads, relying on lung storage, run out of oxygen in half an hour. Leatherbacks have more than twice the time. The duration record for Leatherbacks is in fact sixty-seven minutes, for a turtle that had gone to about 120 feet (37 meters) and stayed there during the dive.

That's how they pack and conserve oxygen. If that fails, their emergency backup is a brain capable of surviving oxygen starvation. Mammals like whales and scuba divers become quickly debilitated if they run out of brain oxygen. It stops all electrical activity in a few moments, like someone shutting down a fuse panel and turning out the lights, and it causes death in minutes. Sea turtles depleted of oxygen can keep their brains alive temporarily by anaerobic glycolysis. Anaerobic respiration is your body's backup generator. It's a way of continuing to supply cells with power when your body lacks sufficient oxygen for the usual chemical reactions. It is less efficient, and it produces blood buildup of lactic acid, which must be disposed of later. (Anaerobic respiration causes the ache in your legs after an extended all-out sprint. But it has survival value in emergencies—better aching legs than getting caught by the hyena.) Mammals can use anaerobic respiration in peripheral muscle, but not their brain. Sea turtles can turn their brain metabolism rate down so its demand can be met anaerobically. Dull wit beats dead wit. But we all have limits.

SHROUDED IN THE FOUR A.M. DARKNESS, THE SHRIMP VESSEL *BILLY B* lies peacefully, its outriggers folded prayerfully, its nets tied high off the deck in the warm Low Country breeze. The air wafts the rich, fertile fragrance of vast marshes. Black ebbing water flows slowly through the shadowed pilings, swirling lazily around the boat's quiet hull, causing it to rise and fall as in restful sleep.

Already aboard: crewmen Deon White, in his thirties, and Boyce Garrick, twice his age. Boyce appears tall, square-jawed, silvered, wrinkled, and weather-leathered. Deon seems almost painfully taciturn, a speak-only-when-spoken-to sort of a man, like a harsh father's oppressed boy, a deck shadow quiet as a cat among the ropes and riggings.

Our scheduled meeting time was four A.M., and at 4:07 the captain's lateness is much remarked upon by Boyce.

Skipper Richard Baldwin walks up briskly at 4:08, saying, "I'm runnin' a little late today. Didn't want t' get outta bed. Slapped the clock around a little."

Nothing during the rest of our day will explain, or even suggest, any reason for tight scheduling, punctuality, or an early start. But I'm happy to be here before the sun floats up, to see the world reconfirmed, then move awhile in angled light, before midmorning bleaches the colors pale.

With no motion lost, Baldwin awakens the engine. Boyce and Deon drop the dock lines and Baldwin nudges the seventy-five-foot, thirty-six-year-old *Billy B* into the streaming current.

In the wheelhouse, Richard Baldwin's face is softly lit by the screen lights of radar, sonar, loran, GPS, and a chart plotter with a wireless mouse. "When I was a kid, we had a radio. That was it. To navigate we'd plumb the depth with a lead line, and we'd run, say, for ten minutes at twenty-eight degrees until you hit fifteen foot of water, then you hadda turn and run southeast—I mean, it was more complicated." He reconsiders a moment, and revises, "Actually it's more complicated now, but the machines do all the work. Anybody can run a boat now."

He's underestimating the required skills. Baldwin's hand-controlled searchlight beam, hazed with the night's misty moisture, finds the marshy banks bordering the channel. "It's a dark night tonight." There's a shoal in the mouth of this creek. "This's the Ashepoo River, we're comin' into."

Baldwin's atomized beam strikes numerous bobbing floats. "These here're all crab pots." Stimulated by our dim halo of light, small fish are jumping like silver raindrops in the running tide of the muddied Ashepoo.

Baldwin, about five foot six or seven, stocky but not what you'd call heavy, is a second-generation shrimper. "Started helpin' my daddy when I was 'bout twelve. Got outta high school 1974, been shrimpin' since. I never did anything else. Got nothin' to compare it to."

That's almost entirely true. With his father, Baldwin also used to hunt alligators (illegally), and dig turtle eggs (illegally). "My father used to send me with a pillowcase to dig up eggs. Some of the black families used to eat turtle eggs, too. But now that they cost ten grand, they're too expensive for me." He winks. Taking turtle eggs was illegal in South Carolina even before the Endangered Species Act, but the Act made it very costly.

Dearth of comparative employment notwithstanding, Richard knows what he likes about shrimping. "We get to see the sun rise every morning. Other jobs, you got to clock in. Then again," he says with a thoughtful nod, "lotta times we got to work weekends. I have worked thirty days straight before, in my younger days. Nowadays, I don't ever work more than about ten days in a row. That's about as much as I can take. But I like tryin' t' figure out where shrimp'll be; try to be the best guesser out here."

Baldwin calls to his crewmen, "Okay, we'll put the doors on the outriggers." To me he explains, "We always do this here where it's calm." He takes the boat out of gear, but the ebbing tide urges the hull farther along in the current.

I leave the dark pilothouse for the well-lit work deck, where squealing winches and two silent men control the workings of things. Each side of the boat has one long boomlike outrigger, and the boat shudders as they lurch slowly downward toward the horizontal. Each outrigger will pull two nets. Deon and Boyce attach to the nets the "trawl doors," heavy wooden devices framed in heavier metal, which will keep the net mouths planed open as they plow over the seafloor. Once attached, a winch raises the "doors" from the deck and cables pull them toward the ends of the now-lowered outriggers. Each net, currently awaiting deployment, is equipped near its bag end with a turtle-escape device—the TED—a slanted grate through which shrimp pass but turtles are arrested so they can find their exit to freedom.

We continue downriver surrounded by forest-bordered marshes with so few lights anywhere in view that it might as well be a hundred years ago. Baldwin lives in a part of the state so rural his home is forty miles from the nearest town. On the eighteen-mile-long road to the dock last evening, I passed in that whole distance an equal number of Copperhead snakes and automobiles: two of each.

Even with the misty air, the Milky Way remains visible; it's that dark here. Deon and Boyce sit quietly in the darker galley, their invisible presence revealed by their cigarettes, glowing like indicator lights. Of his standby deckhands, Baldwin remarks, "Boyce has been with me ten years. That black guy, he just started. I still have to tell him everything."

We motor through a cut connecting the Ashepoo and South Edisto Rivers with the Intracoastal Waterway. Officially called Fenwick Cut, it's still "the gov'mint cut" to locals. Baldwin narrates: "When this channel was dug, in the late 1940s, the blacks living on the south end of this peninsula were just cut off from the whole world—just like that. No bridge. They didn't receive any compensation, or *nuthin'*."

The lights of Edisto Beach sparkle into view. Captain Baldwin orients me: "That's the back of the beach. You can see the beachfront is dark; that's 'lights out for turtles'—for them nestin', y'know. There used to be streetlights all along there. They're off because of Sally's campaign for the turtles."

We slide out the South Edisto Inlet at five-thirty, entering the ocean as first light begins painting outlines on dark clouds. For just a few moments the fleeting sky holds the day's maiden blush of pink.

With the dim silhouettes of several other shrimp boats within a mile or two, we slow to a crawl, then drop our nets alongside in a process so complicated with lines, ropes, and winches that I can't fully follow it. Things are in hazardous motion: drums turning, cables moving, ropes snaking through pulleys and across the deck. A hang-up or tangle could easily mean an ugly injury.

A deep red-orange ball acquires the horizon, flooding the ocean with its tide of light. We deploy each outrigger's two nets, total four. Each net has its planing "door" to keep the net mouth open and a "sled" to keep the net running straight. We begin our slow plowing prowl, dragging the nets along the seafloor at two knots, like a leisurely walk. One small sampling net, called a "try net," runs ahead of the main trawls. It can be quickly hauled and redeployed to help the skipper understand what his other nets are likely catching, and whether to haul his catch or consider moving elsewhere.

"We gonna try going around the edges of the shoals," Baldwin announces. Shrimp prefer mud, not sand, he explains. "This is a good little mud-bottom spot, right here."

We amble along in thirty feet of water. This leisurely stroll isn't exactly Bering Sea crabbing, but nature can be deadly here, too. A water spout—a seagoing tornado—recently caught and rolled a shrimp boat near here, killing the skipper's wife.

While the nets work, Baldwin has a little time to talk. A lot of time, actually, to talk. "We had a good year last year," he begins brightly.

Oh? What makes a year better for shrimp?

"Here, anyway, you gotta have the right weather June, July, and August. The shrimp spawn in the ocean in spring and then the postlarvae swim up rivers to the heads o' the creeks. It can't get too hot in the head of the creeks where the young shrimp develop. Water temperature don't need to get up into the nineties too long. You gotta have mild weather, and you gotta have rain. I think that's the main factor for what's gonna be out here to catch in the fall. You got t' get rain, steady rain, y'know; two, three inches a week. And a too cold winter can kill most of the overwintering shrimp. Mild weather.

"We catch mostly White Shrimp, good two-thirds. That's the money. Brown Shrimp, price is usually lower, quality ain't as good; they don't freeze so good. They're smaller, sixty to the pound. White roe're around twenty-six, twenty-seven to the pound. Right now early on, May, we're catching mostly White roe-shrimp. June, July, and August we catch Brown Shrimp, then we'll catch White again right up to January. Then do boat maintenance for a couple of months."

Captain Baldwin turns a tad cranky on the issues affecting his livelihood. To oversimplify, these might be binned into two categories: American meddlers and foreign meddlers. "One thing all shrimpers agree on: we believe we are more endangered than any turtles. Environmentalists, they love to hate shrimpers. But biggest thing affecting the shrimper right now—is the price. Biggest problem's imports; got the price down. China, Vietnam, Indonesia, Ecuador, y'know—Third World countries, mostly. Labor's cheap. Started dumpin' imported farmed shrimp a few years ago. And they got the weather; some of those countries, they can do two crops a year. Cut our price in half. If we don't get the price o' shrimp back up, I'd say we got but a couple o' years, or this thing—just ain't no way. Costs too much to maintain these boats. Price of fuel this year— ain't no way. We went from about fourteen hundred shrimp-boat licenses in 1980 to about four hundred this year. Out of Edisto there used to be seventeen boats; now there's two.

"I'm lucky, I've got the store at the dock. Retail, I can get forty or fifty cents more a pound. These big guys that have to sell through the dealers, I don't see how they're gonna make it."

When TEDs became mandatory, U.S. shrimpers got Congress to pass a law prohibiting import into the United States of shrimp from other countries *unless the country requires their boats to use TEDs in waters harboring turtles.* (Savor the irony.) The Department of State originally interpreted the law to apply only within the western Atlantic and Caribbean, but environmentalists won a federal court ruling requiring the law to apply worldwide. In 1996 several Asian countries brought a case against the United States to the World Trade Organization. The United States lost. The WTO said the States had to accept shrimp from countries not requiring turtle devices in trawls. In 1999 televised protesters in turtle costumes focused on this as evidence of the World Trade Organization's anonymous business-at-any-cost rise to influence. But on appeal, the United States won. It had initially lost the case not because it sought to protect the environment but because it discriminated among World Trade Organization members. It had provided countries in the Western Hemisphere—mainly in the Caribbean—technical and financial assistance and longer transition periods for using turtle-excluding devices. The World Trade Organization called upon the United States to implement its policy more flexibly and to provide technical assistance to all nations requesting it. The case remains widely misunderstood; the outcome actually affirmed the wider goal of protecting natural resources. Regarding the appeal, the World Trade Organization itself affirmed, "Countries have the right to take trade action to protect the environment and endangered species. The WTO does not have to 'allow' them this right." Would they have overturned the earlier ruling even if the people in the turtle suits hadn't gotten worldwide TV coverage? My guess is: probably. But I did like the costumes, and the watchdog spirit behind them.

The United States okays shrimp imports from various countries, many of which export farmed or cold-water shrimp that pose little threat to turtles. Australia is now doing a good job, but elsewhere, where the U.S. policy should help sea turtles, compliance is spotty—even where the United States is pitching softballs. In 2005, Costa Rica failed even a pre-announced dockside inspection by U.S. officials. Trinidad and Tobago also failed. Yet both countries are extremely important to turtles. India, with the largest Olive Ridley population remaining in the Eastern Hemisphere, and trawl-drowned turtles washing up at the rate of ten thousand annually, failed. And Indonesia failed, too, though it has the largest remaining Leatherback population in the Indian and Pacific Oceans.

Nations that don't jump through the U.S. hoop remain free to export to any other country. Except for Australia, the money, enforcement, and will that would make shrimping turtle-friendly is scarce. Indeed, Costa Rican ocean advocate Randall Arauz sent this around the Internet: "I have conducted investigations in every country in Central America, and none of these nations' shrimpers are using turtle-excluder devices, either." Yet after "determining" that "their sea turtle protection program is comparable to that of the United States," the U.S. State Department recently certified shrimp imports from Belize, Colombia, Ecuador, El Salvador, Guatemala, Guyana, Mexico, Nicaragua, Panama, Suriname, Thailand, Nigeria, and Pakistan. The department also certified sixteen countries whose cold waters aren't home to many sea turtles, places like Argentina, Denmark, Iceland, and New Zealand. "Eight nations and one economy," in the State Department's tortured terms, also made the cut because their shrimp fisheries are supposedly small-scale and hand-powered or their shrimp are farmed: Hong Kong (the "economy"), China, Jamaica, Peru, Sri Lanka, and others.

Whether or not these countries' shrimping practices will wipe out turtles isn't Baldwin's concern; his worry is that they'll wipe *him* out.

Baldwin is silent for a moment, and I scan the water through the wheelhouse windshield. The handful of other boats in view look pretty in the morning sun, their outriggers like arms opened to receive whatever bounty the sea might bestow. In the silence between us, I wonder whether Baldwin is musing further on the luck that has, in fact, allowed him to survive and stay at this. His next comment suggests luck's limitations.

Baldwin says, "My son used to come out a lot. If I'd've encouraged him, he mighta gone into it." Wistfully, as if repeating a conversation he's often had with himself, he adds, "When I get my youngest kid out of the house, I'm gonna think about quittin' shrimpin' too."

You hear of such generation-breaking decisions whenever you talk to people who've earned their bread from forest, farm, or sea. The pain and worry weighs on people's hearts without relent, clouding lives in the ominous overcast of an approaching storm whose intensifying whirlwinds draw strength from globalization, shortsightedness, greed, provincialism, and the old-fashioned mismanagement that denies natural limits. These tempests have grown to shrieking gales, blowing away livelihoods, dashing lives onto the rocks, scattering children and communities to all points of the compass.

Not that shrimping hasn't also created problems. Shrimpers, managers, and conservationists have long clashed over sea turtles, fishes, and other sea life swept into the small meshes. Baldwin's daddy fought bitterly against the idea of the government forcing him to use turtle excluders. Baldwin's own skepticism about fisheries management lurks just below the surface, like a waterlogged tree trunk in a boat channel. He complains, "They manage this ocean like it's a pond. Ain't no way. There's too much water out here. They don't know what's out here."

There was a time when Richard Baldwin was against the turtle huggers, too, and his take on it is interesting. "I don't remember ever catching more than three or four turtles a year. If they wasn't doin' well, unconscious, we used to turn 'em on their back, thump on their chest a little bit, and leave 'em alone on the deck. Usually they'd come back to life. I brought a lot of them back like that. My whole thirty years shrimpin' since high school, I prob'ly caught, y'know, just three or four that I know for certain drowned. Majority of them, you leave them back there, they'll come back to life.

"What started all the controversy—back around '76, '77—they suddenly said you couldn't leave 'em on deck anymore 'cause they got the Endangered Species Act. They could fine you if they found a turtle on the boat. Well, that kinda made it so we had t' throw 'em right back. That couldn't do any good for the *turtles!*

"Sally came to one of the first meetin's. She was young and fiery. She stood up in front of prob'ly two hundred shrimpers, said we was butcherin' all the turtles. She was feisty. She's got nerve. Said we was all murderers. That's prob'ly the first time we really started hearin' about problems with turtles." He shakes his head and smiles at the memory of them as adversaries, continuing, "I don't have a problem with Sally anymore, but I'll tell you what—some shrimpers *still* don't like her.

"South Carolina," Baldwin continues, "was the first state that come up with a law requirin' TEDs. When they first come out, they were these big, heavy box-shaped things like a cage you put in your net, with a door that flipped up like this. Then they had the soft TED, and if you dragged one net with it and one illegally without, you realized it clogged with grass and stuff and lost thirty, forty percent of your shrimp. We couldn't survive that. I was president of the Shrimpers Association at that time. We staged a big protest in Charleston. Two hundred shrimpers.

"I can't tell you *how* much money the feds wasted developin' somethin' that didn't work." (Sally can: $4.5 million.) "Fishermen actually come up with the one we use, like we're pullin' now. Called the 'super shooter'; the bars come down on an angle like this. Grass and stuff hits those bars, it slides along on that slope and goes on out. I don't think they cost you much shrimp loss at all.

"I was one of the biggest ones fightin' turtle excluders. But now I'm satisfied with them. Now—I told this to Sally—I'd drag TEDs whether I had to or not. It's more efficient. They let out a lot of the big stuff—trash, horseshoe crabs, and like that—that we used to catch. I've caught Leatherbacks with the smaller TEDs, but these new big Leatherback-size TEDs we hafta pull, they'll let even crab traps out. Plus Leatherbacks, of course. You don't want all that big stuff in there, beatin' up your shrimp, crushin' 'em. With TEDs, your shrimp ain't gettin' all squished by junk, so when you go to sell 'em, they look better."

Baldwin takes a pinch of tobacco, reaches for the radio mike. He raises the skipper of a nearby boat. They gab a little about the weather, the catch rate, the price. When he hangs up the mike, I mention that I've heard of some dead turtles still washing up; has he heard of anyone still fishing without the turtle devices?

"They'd be fools. See, the way I look at it, someone that does somethin' that don't go along with what we can do to protect turtles is jeopardizin' our own industry. Y'know. I'm sure there's people there that don't pull 'em, or don't pull the legal ones. They're cuttin' off their own throat, the way I see it."

He takes another pinch and adds, "But if there's a lotta boats in an area, maybe turtles are getting' into nets too many times in a row, just get too exhausted. Y'know. If another boat catches 'em right away, then another, maybe it could finish 'em."

Throughout the world's warm-water areas, shrimp fishing kills large numbers of turtles—possibly hundreds of thousands annually. But most kinds of fishing gear also snag turtles. Scallop dredges catch turtles. Just from New Jersey to North Carolina, between July and November in recent years, heavy metal scallop dredges have annually caught well over seven hundred Loggerheads, killing nearly five hundred. A new rule will require the dredge entrance to have chains that will let scallops in but keep turtles out—so simple and easy. Often the merest motivation can solve the problem. In Cape Cod Bay, Leatherbacks regularly tangle and drown in lobster gear. Gill nets and longlines, of course, kill turtles.

Baldwin adjusts our course slightly, straightens up a little, and continues with a fresh breath: "Everyone blames shrimpers. But by us pullin' TEDs, there's more turtles out here. The more turtles you got, the more you have other kinda tragedies, y'know—boats runnin' 'em over more, people hookin' 'em, and stuff like that; gettin' caught in crab-trap lines, eatin' Styrofoam, eatin' plastic, and like that. It's not all *shrimpers*. Turtles got to die of something. If people weren't here there'd be dead turtles around, anyway. The only reason you don't see dead people around is 'cause we bury 'em."

Our boat has already attracted several Laughing Gulls, a few Royal Terns, and a couple of Bottlenose Dolphins, working their accustomed day job of following our muddy wake, nabbing fish that are injured or escaping or dumped.

At six A.M. Boyce starts cooking breakfast: shrimp, gravy, and grits. Captain Baldwin says with enthusiasm, "Boyce is a good cook; he could be a chef."

The food sure smells good. And it *is*. It's a treat, this excuse to eat shrimp.

Immediately after we've finished breakfast, Baldwin calls for the crew to check the try net. The birds jostle for position. The net contains a galaxy of sea stars, a constellation of small crabs, a flatfish called a Hog-choker, a couple of three-inch croakers, a pocketful of sand dollars, and eight plump shrimp about six or eight inches long. The shrimp go into the basket. Picking up a wide broom, Deon pushes all the rest of the catch out the scupper holes into the sea.

One shrimper calls Richard on the radio, mentioning that he's just released a turtle from his try net. Because they are towed for much briefer intervals, try nets under twelve feet wide needn't have turtle-escape devices. "One guy in Georgia," Baldwin says, "had a sixteen-foot try net—didn't have a TED in it. Coast Guard took two tons of shrimp from him. Cost 'im eight grand worth of shrimp, another fifteen grand in fines."

Baldwin approves, but the Coast Guard is not, among shrimpers, universally embraced. "Coast Guard boards a boat—say there's fifteen shrimpers in the area—everybody picks up and hauls ass. Nobody wants to get boarded and have them do all their nit-picking, have them tell us our flares are expired or they don't like how our wiring looks or there's oil in the bilge." He turns to look at me. "You ever seen a boat's bilge didn't have some *oil*? They were on my boat *four hours* once waiting for some guy to get helicoptered out because they didn't believe my TEDs were legal. What money I was gonna make that day, I was on the verge of makin' when they arrived. But by the time they realized I was legal and they left, the tide was all wrong and I was some pissed off."

The try net comes up again at seven A.M. It has quite a little array of sea life, but only two shrimp. Baldwin complains that there's not much tide right now, and the wind, from the west, is wrong too. "West wind'll pull 'em up along the beach."

How would wind going one way make shrimp go the other way? "When the wind is from the west the surface water is going seaward but the water on the bottom has got to be runnin' west to replace it, pullin' 'em shrimp in."

We're slowly heading toward another shallow bank, marked by a line of breakers though several miles offshore. Lines of Sandwich Terns, with their elegant little frilly caps and yellow bill tips, are resting on our rocking outriggers while our net does their work, balancing with tilting bodies so synchronized they look amusingly choreographed. Laughing Gulls in full breeding plumage—red bills, sleek black heads, and eyebrows nicely lit with white—likewise ride prettily perched on our cables, enjoying this life of leisure, laughing all the way to the bank.

At the bank we find five other boats within a mile or two. Baldwin sits with his legs up on the wheel, steering with his feet, spitting his chew into his coffee cup, gabbing on the radio. Life is good. The skippers mainly chat about pecuniary matters, from the price of fuel to escalating health insurance.

By ten o'clock we've covered an area only a mile and a half long and a mile wide, but have gone up and down and up and down and up and down it, dragging the seafloor like oxen plowing, back and forth through the sunken aisle between two shoals, dispassionate assassins of shrimp.

We haven't yet checked our main nets, but the try net's scant results leave Baldwin shaking his head, knowing meager reward likely awaits— so far. We might yet hit a pocket of shrimp that Baldwin missed yesterday and the day before and the day before that. And that all the other boats have missed. His comment: "I'd say we'd be lucky to get two bushels today."

Idle during hours of net towing, Deon and Boyce sit silently at the galley table, eyes on a soundless television.

Apropos of nothing and everything, Baldwin suddenly asks if I've seen the film *Forrest Gump.* "When those shrimp hit the deck, you could tell they hadn't just caught 'em. Those are dead shrimp. And I'll tell y' what, *The Perfect Storm?* That looked pretty fake, too. Those guys shoulda respected the ocean—and kept an eye on the weather."

At ten-thirty, after we've watched the sea morph from the pastels of dawn to a midmorning mirror-ball, Baldwin further slows. Boyce and Deon leave the galley for the deck, and soon the winches complain of pulling the main nets. The doors emerge to meet the outrigger ends, and ropes winch the bags of each net closer to the hull. Amid a near-deafening clanging of machinery, terns and gulls dive excitedly for the few fish spilling through the net. Big, buff Bottlenose Dolphins that have been following the nets' porous progress now slice in alongside, swirling the cloudy water. They pick off a few already-injured morsels with as little exertion of their husky muscular bodies as if they were eating popcorn at the movies. Like the thousands of other dolphins who rely on shrimp trawls, they know the best is yet to come.

And now, the moment of universal anticipation in all fishing: first glimpse of the catch. In commercial fishing, this is also the money moment. The machinery clangs like a cash register and fishes flash the silver of coin. The winches pull the first net from the sea, and soon the bag of the net is hovering over the deck, pregnant with its glimmering payload. Captain Baldwin tugs the drawstring that opens the bag that dumps the catch that hits the deck that disappears under a shimmering metropolis of diverse marine creatures—very few of them shrimp.

The little hill of seafloor citizens spreads until it reaches its angle of slippery repose. Crabs begin walking from the bright mound of gasping fishes. No one even thinks about getting any of these humble glitterati back into the water before they die. They get the compassion you'd afford a just-dumped pile of gravel.

With all four nets on deck, I stand amid a lot of dying sea life. I'm glad I enjoyed our breakfast of shrimp this morning before I saw the nets come aboard. One very, very lucky ray flaps its way directly out the scupper and into the ocean, like a lucky random shot on a billiard table. No guarantee about tomorrow.

Deon puts aside a few small dead sharks. Family eats 'em; wouldn't want to see them go to waste. Then he and Boyce, on low stools, begin combing the catch. Once you get the blinders on and look past everything else, you see there *are* plenty of shrimp—if plenty means one out of, well, let's see: in a random sample that I kick out of the pile with my foot, I count 139 animals, of which 21—about 1 of 7—are White Shrimp. The other expiring creatures include juvenile Spanish Mackerel, drums, croakers, a species of fish unimaginatively named Spot. Stomatopods (a.k.a. mantis "shrimp," or squilla). Jellies. The juvenile sharks Deon *doesn't* want range from newborn pups under a foot long to about ten-pounders—including the unusual semi-hammerhead called Bonnethead, several of those. Sponges. Crabs. Bryozoans. More crabs. Sea stars. Herring. Additional crabs. Lizardfish. A juvenile sea robin of some kind. Juvenile Bluefish. Squid. A flat and silvery high-headed fish called a Lookdown. Another of the flatfish called Hogchoker. Silver Sea Trout and sand dollars. A sea biscuit. Urchins. Burrfish, Butterfish, and a Butterfly Ray. Anchovies. Cutlassfish. Harvestfish. Many individuals of a couple of species I'm not familiar with. And the 21 shrimp. Another sample culled with my shoe brings 4 squillas, 1 jelly, 1 squid, 1 crab, 71 small fish, and 4 White Shrimp.

Of all types of fishing gear, shrimp trawls stand alone at the top of the list for lowest ratio of desired target catch (shrimp) to unwanted bycatch (everything else). And among shrimp trawls, tropical shrimp fisheries lead the worst, generating a higher proportion of discarded ocean life than any other fishery type. Board a shrimp boat in Trinidad and get ready to see fifteen pounds of marine life killed for each pound of shrimp kept. About the best it ever gets is one-quarter of the catch discarded. What's killed includes—in the United States alone—billions of juvenile fish like snappers and groupers, which could otherwise grow up to take their place in the sea, support other fisheries, and feed people.

Shrimp farming now produces about half the shrimp that people eat. If anything, it's usually worse than shrimp fishing. It destroys natural coastal habitats to construct shrimp-raising ponds, killing not just wetlands and wildlife but also, occasionally, protesting poverty-stricken fishermen pushed out of the place where they'd been scratching out their living. A very few shrimp farms use shrimp-pond water and shrimp waste products to grow an edible vegetable crop. Such models of efficiency should be standard, but they account for a tiny fraction of shrimp produced.

Waste is in the eye of the beholder. Even here and now, virtually everything on deck is edible. Virtually no one in America wants to eat virtually any of it. Virtually all of it will die before the shrimp are picked out and the brooms sweep it under the carpet of the sea.

Aboil astern, the leisurely dolphins exhibit their superior intelligence by seeing our waste as a beautiful thing. They seem pleased and appreciative when hundreds of pounds of swept-overboard fish begin dropping from the scupper, becoming their supper. A couple hundred excitedly screaming birds likewise press in. The gulls and terns must think of shrimp boats as bird feeders. The dolphins must see our nets as seagoing feed bags. If so, their perceptions are more accurate than our delusion that the boat is shrimp fishing.

And this is shrimping at something approaching its best. In addition to turtle excluders, these shrimpers' nets must now include small open frames that provide an escape opportunity for the entrained fishes. Fishermen call such bycatch-reduction devices either "birds" (from the acronym BRDs) or "fish eyes," because they are openings to facilitate fish escape. The TEDs let out various larger fishes, like sharks, big crabs, and bigger rays— and turtles, of course—and the BRDs let out about 20 percent of the fish swept up by the net. Together, they can reduce the incidental kill by about 70 percent, according to Sally. Baldwin's estimate differs. He says, "The BRDs get it to about fifty percent—at best." Despite such reductions, on average in South Carolina, about 25 percent of what lands on deck is kept. Three-quarters is swept.

Though it was clear by the 1990s that shrimp trawls were killing and wasting billions of juvenile finfish—snappers, mackerel, sea trout, and others—the federal government shuffled its feet until 1997 before requiring bycatch-reduction devices in the South Atlantic. It crawled on all fours until 2004 before requiring them in the entire Gulf of Mexico.

And yet the United States has perhaps the world's best-managed shrimp fishing. Likely nowhere else combines requirements for turtle-excluder and bycatch-reduction devices with good enforcement. Without these things there'd be two to three times as much by-kill here as there is.

That Baldwin's TEDs and BRDs allow the *escape* of 50 to 70 percent of the marine life the net sweeps in seems amazing when I look at the animals twitching and gasping on deck. It seems to me that the price the ocean pays for our affordable shrimp dinners is still too high. That's not to mention the damage shrimp nets cause to the seafloor in some places, especially where corals grow. For these reasons, I don't buy shrimp.

I am well enough whipped to righteous anger, when, at eleven A.M.,

Baldwin announces, "It's a lot cheaper to go to bed than keep doing this. We're going in." The bushel and a half of eight-inch shrimp Deon and Boyce have culled is not enough. With fuel so expensive, at this rate he can't make a day's pay. To earn decent money he needs around a thousand dollars' worth of shrimp, about five or six bushels. This time of year he's looking for ten or twelve baskets a day; in the fall he likes to see twice that. He says he's not coming out tomorrow, either; he'll wait for the wind to shift.

Done? No more tows? No more pulling the try net? But—I'm enjoying this! I like the slow pace, the Laughing Gulls and porpoises, the rocking outriggers with their raggedly capped retinue of Sandwich Terns, how pretty the boats look plying the swells. It's nice. I'm having fun. If we weren't killing so much stuff we don't want, there would be something approaching idyllic about it.

There exists a West Coast shrimp called the Spot Prawn. Until a few years ago, they were often caught with trawls that killed between seven and seventeen pounds of fish for each pound of shrimp. But now, instead of dragging nets, fishermen must catch them with traps that kill one-fiftieth to one-eightieth as much marine life. I'd like to see that; I'd love to see shrimp fishing without brooms sweeping piles of dead fish overboard. I'd happily go back to buying shrimp, and these panhandling dolphins and loitering seabirds would regain their wild decorum, and those of us aboard, our dignity.

I sense that the dolphins, birds, skipper, and deckhands stand together of one mind on the subject, arrayed in opposition to my point of view. And while I can only intuit the disposition of dolphins and the brains of birds, I can query our captain directly. What does our skipper think about all the fish and other life we just dragged up?

"I don't think it's a problem," Baldwin says flatly. "Been doin' it thirty years, and I don't see where the fish we catch are any more, any less than there ever was. Over the whole season we try to run a pound of shrimp to a pound of bycatch. If we were catching a lot of Red Snapper, Striped Bass, Redfish, sea trout, or other fish like that, I could see where it would be a problem."

But, Baldwin continues, "It's better for us, y'know, if we don't have to deal with fish on deck. Some guys, they'll put extra panels in the net. One thing I do is pull a bigger webbing in the bag; lets out a lotta the small ones. There's also what they call expanded mesh; it goes right in around the TED. It's big mesh. They say more fish can get outta that. I've never tried it. Prob'ly lose more shrimp. As far as ever comin' up with somethin' we could drag here and catch just pure shrimp, I don't think so. If they did, I imagine once we got used to 'em, we would like it. Like TEDs."

We're steaming toward the inlet, back toward the pretty channels and those expansive green marshes that will ease our reentry to land. Most of the birds and dolphins know the show's over for today. This chuck wagon is headed for the barn.

While the noon sun reflects harshly on the ocean, Baldwin reflects humbly on his profession, offering this: "People've said how shrimpers are destroyin' the ocean and all that. Well, we drag the same place year after year. Some boats been doin' it sixty years. Y'know what I mean? I been doin' it all my life, and I haven't seen where what we catch has gone down. I mean, at times, we run into Spots or Croakers that load the deck. That's the way it was when I started, that's prob'ly the way it'll be in another hundred years from now. And what we catch ain't wasted, neither. I mean, those seagulls look like they're starvin' to death, sometimes. What if we didn't come out? Now, if we went back and there wouldn't be nothin' there, I could say, well, we done killed it, y'know?"

Cleaning up in the galley, Deon takes the pot of uneaten grits and motions to see whether anyone wants more. Like most of what we've caught today, it goes over the rail. Getting comfortable with waste can keep a person poor. When he makes the same questioning motion with the pan of uneaten shrimp, I indicate that I'll save them from the same fate.

We may disagree honorably about all the other incidental catch, and the want induced by waste. But at least this fishery, after all the years of fighting, lawsuits, protests, and Sally's holy rage, finally has a solution to its turtle problem. After two decades, we have achieved over turtles a meeting of the minds. It's been a long journey, requiring a painful stretch for Baldwin and his fellow shrimpers. They've had to change their values and worldview, more than those who grew up with toy turtles beside their crib. Meanwhile, Baldwin and sea turtles struggle to survive the shrimping customs of other nations. No doubt the future will hold other unexpected challenges, requiring further adjustment. Perhaps the next big adjustment will be for those who love turtles to learn to love shrimpers. Turnabout seems fair play.

Taciturn since his last remarks about the discarded fishes, Baldwin reboards his train of thought on a parallel track: "Now, TEDs? There's no doubt we need 'em, with the boats coming out here now, the size of 'em and all that. Without TEDs, I don't think turtles woulda gotten wiped *out*, y'know, *extinct*. Not in *our* lifetimes. But there would be less of 'em without us pullin' TEDs, there's no doubt." Captain Richard Baldwin looks philosophical for a moment. "But shrimp trawlin' destroyin' the ocean?" he asks rhetorically. He answers himself softly, saying, "I couldn't agree with that."

I AWAKEN AT FIRST LIGHT AND VENTURE ONTO DECK TEN MILES AT SEA. Against a western sky still indigo with night, towering blue thunderheads pile high enough to catch a gleam from a yet-unseen sun. The languor of a long rocking swell is broken by jolting bolts of lightning sizzling silently through clouds too distant to send thunder. The only sound's the rhythmic hiss and slosh against our bow.

With the day poised to emerge from its own dream and a swollen moon still visible in a paling sky, Captain Jeff Jacobs turns our stern to the first sliver of sunrise, slows *Lady Lisa,* and calls, "All right, go ahead."

Our deckhands let the sampling nets on each side of the boat slip beneath green waves to seek the seafloor fifty feet below. The earliest shimmer of morning lights our wake as we begin towing slowly toward the coast, barely visible in the distance on this hazy, lazy morning. This deeper shipping channel off Charleston appeals to turtles, so this is where we will "fish" for them.

Our research crew includes lead scientist Phil Maier, from South Carolina's Department of Natural Resources, veterinarian Al Segars, research assistant Julia Byrd, and veterinary students Karyn Fein and Sophia Chiang. Al and Phil are both large, broadly built guys. Phil paid his dues in the North Pacific during the late 1980s as an observer on a Japanese drift-net boat targeting Neon Flying Squid (yes, they make prodigious jumps and use their "wings" a bit like flying fish). "They're about as long as a person is tall, and have a buttery flavor. Delicious, if you ever get the chance—." He remembers those nets snagging birds, salmon, various unwanted fish, numerous Blue Sharks and Salmon Sharks, and even seals. Al is a wildlife veterinarian, often summoned at odd hours to crisis scenes such as multiple whale strandings. Julia, twenty-six, is putting her childhood love of sea turtles toward a master's in environmental science and policy. Everyone wears shorts and T-shirts or tank tops. The women seem upbeat and friendly, but Al warns me, "They're not shy; if our nets raise a two-hundred-pound turtle they'll knock you out of the way."

We're pulling shrimping-type trawl nets, but with much larger mesh to let most things through, including shrimp. And because we want to catch turtles, our nets of course lack the turtle excluders that shrimp nets must have. Shrimpers must now avoid turtles in their quest for shrimp; we are avoiding shrimp in our quest for turtles. So we'll be catching turtles at the same rate a shrimp boat without turtle-escape devices would. In most of the world, shrimp boats still fish this way. Our main difference: to avoid risk of drowning any turtles, we're checking the net every thirty minutes.

This is one of the world's few studies of turtle abundance in the ocean. Almost everywhere else, abundance is judged by trends on nesting beaches. Most turtles in this area are Loggerheads. They're the only species on this side of the Atlantic showing a clear decline in nesting females during the last two decades. So this should be interesting.

South Carolina's Loggerhead nesting has clearly declined—down 60 percent since 1980, from five thousand nests per season to under two thousand. Most researchers believe that's because, in the years before the law required turtle-escape devices, too many turtles drowned in nets. As the oldest turtles die off, the ones that should now be maturing to replace them are missing. Result: a decline in breeders.

With sympathies evident in his tone of voice, Captain Jeff asserts, "When shrimpers hear turtles're declining? They don't believe it. Shrimpers're seeing more and more turtles; they're seeing turtles all *over* the place."

Al helps me understand a key distinction: "On the beaches all along the southeast U.S., nesting *adult* Loggerhead numbers *are* down significantly in the last few years. But this study's mainly about juveniles." You can't count juveniles on beaches; they don't come ashore. Loggerheads first mature at twenty to forty years old. Around twenty-five is average. "We're trying to understand how many juvenile turtles are out here now," Al continues, "so we have some idea what to expect with the breeding population in fifteen or twenty years."

Phil comments, "And we might be able to pick up on any problems with juvenile survival early enough to do something."

Al adds, "Or, say if global warming kicks sand temperatures up a couple degrees, many beaches could start producing all females. If we don't keep checking juvenile sex ratios, we might not know what's happening until they're no males. If we had to rely only on nesting data, we wouldn't know of a problem with males until nesting females start laying unfertilized eggs that don't hatch."

Although the escape openings were too small for adults until recently, for over a decade the law required turtle excluders that were big enough to let juveniles escape. So: Is there a group of juveniles out here that have survived in good numbers because of turtle excluders and will start maturing a few years from now, pushing the nesting population higher?

Al ventures, "My gut feeling? Yeah—there's a whole bunch of juveniles out here that *have* survived because of turtle-excluder devices."

They call this the shipping channel for a good reason: steadily coming and going loom gigantic container ships. We have to dodge them, working in the clear mile or two before the next comes plowing through. They seem inhuman and ominous, like some natural danger of geologic scale—a lava flow, perhaps. There is no reasoning with them, no communicating, even. They are incapable of changing course to avoid us. We must simply steer clear, operating among them as we might among towering icebergs, at our peril.

To dodge one oncoming freighter, we begin hauling our nets a few minutes early. From the stern of the boat, Julia throws a grappling hook to pick up a line (that's the "sugar line") connecting ropes ("lazy lines") that run the length of each net from its mouth to a big ring ("the elephant ear") attached to the net's bag end. Pulling the sugar line into the boat puts the lazy lines in reach. We pull them to winches that hoist the bags along each side of the boat and then onto the deck. The whole idea is to get the net ends and their catch into the boat without pulling the entire net aboard. This eases redeployment because the bags can simply be dropped back overboard.

Our nets hit the deck with a few sea stars and sand dollars, a Horseshoe Crab, a Smooth Butterfly Ray and a Southern Stingray ("Watch that tail!"), and several small Scalloped Hammerhead Sharks with those wild-eyed dreamboxes. Among this mélange we discover a seventy-pound Loggerhead Turtle. When the more perishable gill-breathing catch is released, the turtle commands attention. Phil and Sophia hoist the lemon-headed Loggerhead into a kind of wooden rack that slants it head-downward. Resembling a gothic torture device, it actually calms our patient.

But then, as if suggesting that my first impression of a torture rack wasn't far off, one of the students moves toward the turtle with a needle, saying, "We're vampires, we like to get blood." It's my first brush with aspiring veterinarians. As if nothing should cause alarm, Al simply explains, "There're two muscles that kind of lift the head. If you go just lateral, either side—." He demonstrates by palpating with his fingers. "You can feel—get some gloves on so you don't transfer any bacteria to its skin— you can feel this muscular ridge that we use for a guide. Then you go about a third of the way between the shell and head. That's the vein." I can feel it.

Karyn sterilizes the site with Betadine and draws several vials of blood for later analysis. They'll look for indicators of immune-system health or stress, determine the turtle's sex (by testosterone level; juvenile turtles sport a unisex look), and measure concentrations of toxic contaminants such as DDT derivatives, PCBs, dioxins, and other unnatural things.

"With the blood work," Al says, "we're asking, Do toxins undermine a turtle's ability to fight infections and stay healthy?" Checking the turtle's skin, mouth, and eyes for any wounds or smudges of oil or tar, Al continues, "We've found that the closer these animals are to industrial discharges—Charleston or Savannah or wherever—the higher their blood-contaminant levels. But you know," he adds, "many times I'll make a presentation about contaminants in turtles, and people in the audience will naively think that contaminants show up *only* in something that lives somewhere dirty. People think, 'Well, I don't have mercury or any of those contaminants in *me*.' They've never thought about it. They're just playing golf all the time or whatever. I'm talking about audiences in, say, affluent retirement communities. They're stunned to hear that because they eat crabs and clams—the same things turtles are eating—they *also* have all these toxic chemicals. And actually," he notes, "over time, these contaminants accumulate more in people than in turtles, because we're higher up the food chain."

We've added variety to turtles' menus, worse than the junk-food we serve our own hatchlings. Though so robust to shark attacks and boat strikes as to seem indestructible, sea turtles are sensitive to chemicals. They don't know how to avoid oil slicks, and inhaling at the surface exposes them to fumes. They often forage where converging currents concentrate food along with floating trash, oil, and tar balls, eating things they shouldn't. Off Florida, 65 percent of Loggerheads examined in one study had tar in their mouth, esophagus, or stomach. Youngsters thus fouled sometimes starve. Exposure to petroleum can damage their skin, blood, digestive and immune systems, and salt glands. Fewer red blood cells means less oxygen to muscles, affecting diving performance and foraging. Getting exposed to crude oil can shut down a turtle's salt glands for up to two weeks, meaning a turtle in the ocean could die of dehydration. In a Japanese study, twenty-six of thirty-six Green Turtles (72 percent) had consumed plastic sheets, rope and line, foam, rubber, and/or cloth. Of fifty-four juvenile Leatherbacks in Mediterranean waters, 80 percent contained tar, paper, polystyrene foam, hooks, lines, or net fragments. Other studies returned similar results, because the sea is the great mixer. Of fifty hatchlings captured at sea off Florida, a third had eaten plastics and synthetic fibers. Turtles can absorb toxins from plastics. Eating plastic and latex (as from balloons mistaken for jellyfish) also interferes with the absorption of real food. Other effects can be subtler.

Phil writes an identifying number on a slate and takes the turtle's mug shot for the file. The turtle slaps its flippers. The researchers bustle around like a pit crew. They will affix a transmitter. Although Leatherbacks require a harness, other sea turtles' shells are hard and dead as fingernail, and can take glue. Julia presses a prepared transmitter into place, and epoxy oozes out around its base.

An hour or so after the turtle first joined us, the researchers carefully lower it to the water on a sling, not for the turtle's benefit—a turtle can be simply dropped the short distance to the water—but to protect the instrument. The transmitter costs close to four grand; a year of satellite-data downloading costs an equivalent amount. Phil says, "It'll be really exciting to see where they go. We think in winter they move to the edge of the Gulf Stream, or go south—but we really don't know."

On the next haul-back, no turtles; but when we check again, two turtles surface in the portside net. Phil comments, "If you compare turtle catch rates from the 1970s and 1980s to catch rates now, it looks like about a tenfold increase."

Tenfold?

Phil pauses, then affirms, "There are a lot more juvenile turtles out here now than twenty years ago, a lot more than expected. That's the most important thing we've learned."

Al adds, "Even though the TED openings were too small for adults until recently, juveniles have been benefiting since 1990. But," he cautions, "until we see that increase showing up as more breeders on the nesting beaches . . ."

"That's the real acid test," Phil agrees.

I'm at the rail when a turtle surfaces alongside, takes one quick breath, and dives as though into the maw of our oncoming starboard net. A few minutes later another turtle surfaces, seemingly guaranteeing us at least one capture.

But the nets arrive devoid. The taunting turtles have reminded us that even a sea full of young turtles makes no guarantees.

These larger juvenile turtles spend much of their time in the warmer southern waters. If they venture north, most stay on the continental shelf. But as Sally had said, "Cape Hatteras is a major departure point for Leatherbacks and Loggerheads going north. We have no idea what happens after they leave Hatteras. No one's looked." I'm going to have a look. I'm going to depart the coast too, far to the north and far from land, leapfrogging from here up past the Canadian border. My first stop will be more than a hundred miles offshore, and if I don't catch up with Leatherbacks there, I'll head farther north, into cold water no Loggerhead could withstand, in search of what it takes to be a Leatherback.

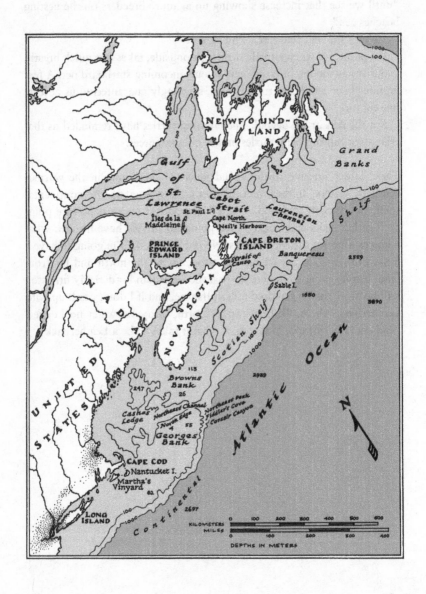

ON THE EDGE

Georges Bank

Franklyn glances aloft, then seaward, then aloft again. "Is that a fish or a shark?"

Abeam of us, fifty yards off, two light-colored fins are etching the surface like glass cutters. The dorsal is pointed, and now we see the tail is stiff in a way most sharks' tails are not. Up in the bridge, Arthur begins spinning the wheel. But from high in the crow's nest above, Jim directs, "Not yet. Run past it, *then* turn. Come at it downswell."

Franklyn is already out in the tip of the stand extending twenty feet from our bow over the water, looking calm, harpoon rigged and resting.

We turn, boat and Swordfish, two of the ocean's most self-assured top killers, approaching each other. We're executing a strange ambush in the form of a direct approach. Surely it hears our hull, but the Swordfish has no natural predators the size of our boat. It has on many occasions snapped up wounded herring around Humpback Whales our boat's size as the whales strained pools of water from schools they'd engulfed.

At about five to six knots we're rapidly closing the gap. The bruise-purple Swordfish makes no course alteration and in no way reacts. Its bill astonishes me with its length and breadth. Franklyn had told me, "You don't look at the bill. Don't look at the eye. Don't look at the tail. You look only at where the dorsal fin meets the body. That's your *spot*. If you look at anything else, you miss."

I'm looking at everything, and in the normal pace at which seconds unfold there seems inadequate time fully to take in so unlikely a large creature of such strange beauty. Franklyn remains relaxed, harpoon in hands. Suddenly and momentarily he is poised directly over the fish's back, traveling nearly past the Swordfish when he thrusts into the *spot,* driving his bronze harpoon head deep into flesh.

Nothing of what I expect ensues. No explosion of water. No lashing of the rapier bill, no counterthrust or desperate backslash. No yelling. The stricken fish merely turns sideways as though stunned, its steely side and the blank gaze of its enormous eye flashing upward. Franklyn has driven the harpoon so deep into the animal's thick back it has made a wound in its belly.

The point detaches from the shaft and the fish angles downward, pulling six hundred feet of rope and buoys attached to the dart deep within. We will pick it up later, when it's safe to do so.

It is sufficient commentary upon the state of oceans that in all my years on the world's seas, this was the first free-swimming Swordfish I ever got a good look at—and it had less than a minute to live.

Franklyn straightens the harpoon pole's violently bent tip, attaches another point, and resumes his wheelhouse vigil. There's no high-fiving or congratulating; everyone's back on station immediately. The understatement is remarkable, considering that, in their months ashore, all these men seem to speak of is their incessant obsession: swordfishing.

"Ha! We was just talkin' about you," Franklyn had said a few months ago when I'd phoned. I hadn't seen him since briefly meeting him two years earlier. "Isn't that somethin'? It happens a lot, you know; Alice can be talkin' about our daughter and—*ring!*—she calls. Or I can be thinkin' about a friend. My father used to walk up to a stranger and say, 'You look like you must be from Massachusetts'—or Maine or someplace— and he'd be from there. I don't know what's going on with that; sometimes I think it's just because we're swordfishermen."

Dispel all doubt about whether Swordfish harpooning is a bit spooky. Among peoples making their living as hunters, this is a kind of superhunting, traversing a thousand square miles of blue ocean to find a slender, blue nine-foot-long fish during the brief interval it is dozing off a meal at the surface. It is needle-in-a-haystack odds banked against your mortgage. So you'd better be not just good; you'd better be a bit supernatural about it. Superstitions, rituals, a sense of the Almighty—and truly expert skill and knowledge—make fish thud the deck. For these fishermen, to catch a Swordfish is to be part of what lives and to receive what is granted to men, to make contact with something profound and spiritual. Franklyn intones, "A harpooner has to have soul. He sees the awe of God's creation."

. . .

Joel Troy is a beefy, fifty-two-foot-long, twenty-one-and-a-half-foot-wide offshore lobster boat. A forty-foot-high crow's nest and a twenty-foot-long harpooner's stand extending forward from the bow enable it for hunting. Swordfish harpoon boats resemble their prey in profile: the fish's tall dorsal fin and long bill are reflected in the high mast and elongated stand.

Arthur Jacquard owns the boat and his son Justin—early twenties—works with him, but on swordfishing trips Franklyn d'Entremont, fifty-nine, master swordfisherman of near-legendary local repute, is de facto captain. He calls the shots as to where the boat will be, its search pattern, when it will change hunting locations, and other key decisions. He's brought Jim Crawford, a peerless fish spotter who spends all his time in the crow's nest looking for fins. Jim seldom accepts offers from anyone but Franklyn, citing this reason: "Other guys don't know where the fish will be. They just follow Franklyn and a couple of other people who know how to find them." Jim's a stocky man—early fifties, bushy mustache. He gives me a square look and says, "You ever been out to Georges Bank before? Place is *alive.* I'm a wanderer, but this is my home, out here, looking for fish." Whether fishing, cooking, even laughing, Jim's demeanor seems imbued with a heightened awareness, as though he is yearning to be right where he actually is, as though a fishing trip is for Jim one long sacred meditation from which he sucks each moment's marrow, each interaction's essence. Jim's presence is pilgrimage.

This is in fact my first trip to Georges Bank, one of the biologically richest places in the ocean, and the Leatherback's gateway to important northern foraging grounds. Getting here isn't easy, and I'm fortunate to come with people who know the place with intimacy. It's probably not so much that anyone who harpoons Swordfish had to be a fanatic about it as it is that only fanatics remain. Anyone who could take it or leave it or saw it as a job, they're off the water. These people *need* to do it. It reminds and reassures them of something about the world and who they are. At this stage, it remains less meal ticket than metaphor. The deep crow's-feet rimming Arthur's broad face crinkle to a smile as he comments, in French-tinged English, "I take all the money I make lobstering and I spend it swordfishing." The oyster farm on which Jim staked his future was just wiped out by an introduced disease called MSX that reached Canada after festering on the mid-Atlantic coast. Despite that, or perhaps because of it, Jim says, "Swordfishing means more than money to me now." Franklyn, in his slow, almost rhythmic cadence, says simply, "For me, swordfishing is like going to church." Speaking in the past tense about the thing we're doing this very morning, Franklyn adds, "It was a pretty basic fishery that called on the ability to hunt—not like setting out hooks or dragging a net. And it hasn't changed. In fact, it's become *more* basic without the airplane." When Swordfish began declining, boats often hired planes to spot them. Now there aren't enough fish to support a plane. "We're back to fishing like in the days of the Romans," Franklyn says with dramatic flourish. "Same damn thing."

There's virtually no harpooning anymore in U.S. waters, nor in most of the rest of Canada. Last of a breed, these guys are true masters at a dying craft. Swordfish harpooners are just about the last people on earth who engage big game with a hand-thrust spear. They follow a long series of peoples whose hunting cultures have gone extinct, withered to oblivion as they drove their prey to depletion or the world changed around them, inter alia: mammoth hunters, buffalo hunters, coastal whalers, Inuit sealers, Maori moa hunters, Masai lion hunters, Chumash Swordfish dancers—and these Swordfish harpooners. High priests in a vanishing act. Last men standing. Same damn thing.

Having run overnight from southwest Nova Scotia, we greeted the dawn more than a hundred miles from land, the sun revealing only water in all directions. I'm on the cabin roof. Franklyn alternately positions himself here or out on the stand, or inside the big-windowed pilothouse, where he monitors the radio chatter, sonar video image, sea-surface temperature, and the boat's satellite-fixed computer-plotted position. But more than the space-age electronics, his whole life has steered him here. "When I was a kid," Franklyn says, "all the ladies would listen to their marine radios, so we always knew if the fish were on the peak of Brown's Bank or the corner of Georges or wherever. And we would set up cardboard boxes and make believe we were swordfishing, and I'd be the striker." And so, a half century later, he remains.

Arthur and Justin are fifteen feet above me in a cramped plywood flying bridge. Ten ladder rungs above their heads is Jim in the crow's nest, a swinging seat with a snug torso ring—the most sun-desiccated, windblown spot on the boat, forty-five feet above the crinkling swells, the wagging mast lurching him around for ten hours a day. Jim looks for fins, but he specializes in seeing fish underwater. Among the three aloft, Jim is truly driven. Swordfish haunt his mind. Hyperattentive as a hunting dog, he aches to spot a Swordfish. Seated within his padded ring, he is a study in attention-surplus disorder, his neck craning constantly, searching far, wide, close, across the sea's surface, down into the near depths. At any moment might appear a fin or a streak of color from a fish capable of falling within grasp, or slipping from view through the ever-dancing glare of diamond-studded water.

We're over Georges Bank's northeast tip, the edge of Northeast Channel, but the slopes and coves lie hundreds of feet beneath our hull. Yet those seafloor contours bring us here, as they draw fish, birds, sea mammals, and turtles thousands of miles across featureless water. Life in the open ocean concentrates at the edges of things: edges of water masses and currents, ridges of drowned mountains, and the canyons and rumpled, slumping edges of the continental shelf. Georges Bank has them all. Though land has fallen far below the blue horizon, these submerged slopes of the shelf edge are where the great ocean first rubs shoulders with the great continent. We're here to exploit the living abundance born from this charged flirtation.

Franklyn is surprised to see the water surface temperature here has risen to 61 degrees Fahrenheit. A couple of hours ago we'd started searching in water 59.2 degrees. A few degrees—even a few tenths—affect the distribution of ocean animals. Just last week, down on Georges' south side at Corsair Canyon, they'd found much cooler water. "We had warm water just coming against the shelf, but cool water on the bank, with a sharp edge to it," says Franklyn, sounding a little dismayed at the change. The Swordfish were on the cold side. "The first fish I stuck was in water fifty-three degrees. That's pretty damn cold." He adds, "There was a ton of feed on the edge, but the fishes' stomachs were completely empty; they were just arriving on the bank." While Franklyn found Swordfish on the cold side, boats two, three miles away in the warm water were seeing turtles. "My brother Alvah was there. Here, talk to him."

Franklyn picks up the radio mike. We raise Alvah—we can see their boat—and he says last week, yeah, really quite a lot of turtles. "Leatherbacks like I haven't seen before. Just off the edge of the bank, mostly."

We cleave through yards-wide mats of rockweed from the north, and gulfweed from the south, strung along the border between great waters.

In this grand meeting two big pieces of the ocean's moving mosaic are encountering each other, the deep ocean rubbing the continental skirt. The bluer offshore waters and the greener bank-edge waters seem poised but hesitant about mingling, reluctant to lose their identities in each other.

Franklyn says only, "We need it colder and a little green. You can't approach fish as well in this clear blue Gulf Stream water."

We've developed an escort of seabirds: a couple dozen Greater and Sooty Shearwaters, skimming like little albatrosses just over the waves. They're long-distance migrants, summering here while winter scours their breeding islands in the far South Atlantic and around Cape Horn. Wilson's Storm-Petrel, abundant here, nests along Antarctic shores.

The sea surface has dropped to 57.7 degrees. That's just what Franklyn wants. Franklyn's keeping our boat just over the cooler side of the abrupt temperature gradient. Swordfish—and everything else—will concentrate along the seams of this frontier.

Water boundaries like this are a little like the moving front of a forest fire. On one side of a wildfire lie ash and cinders, fuel spent and the fire cooled; on the other side stands untouched fuel. The wild burn flares in the front, where combustion meets new fuel. In the sea, the blazes of life are one-celled microscopic plants called phytoplankton that need nutrients and light—fuel and ignition—and one place they get stoked is where deep nutrients rise into the light. On the slopes of a bank like Georges, one water mass brings nutrients from the dark deep—the new fuel—up shallow enough for light to ignite photosynthesis, that genesis process whereby green plants use the sun's energy to fuse carbon dioxide and water, producing sugar. (The convenient "exhaust" is breathable oxygen that makes Earth capable of supporting animals, including us.) The sugar then powers the plant's use of the newly available nutrients for self-assembly. The plant growth starts the food chain. Out here in the open ocean, the bluest, clearest, prettiest waters are emptiest of life, but the greenest host the mother of wet food chains. In the blue ocean, the wildfire burns green.

And I've never seen water of such verdure so far from shore. This conflagration is both cradle and crucible to existence in the sea. In the ocean, everything that gets eaten by everything else eats phytoplankton, and the color of this water attests to its living richness. Think of its greenness as money in Georges Bank. Those requiring additional evidence should immediately direct their gaze to starboard, about a mile off, where a whale is lofting its flukes skyward as if in hallelujah to the heavens, using its massive tail's weight in air to pile-drive its body to the food-filled depths. There it will sieve from the water for nourishment a few million tiny animals that have eaten nothing but green cells all their short lives.

Yet that's not to say that all sea creatures spend most of their time in green water. Camels need food and water, but their home is the desert. Likewise, many ocean animals are adapted to meager waters. They're the oceans' camels, traveling long distances across watery deserts. They include Bluefin, Yellowfin, and Bigeye Tunas, marlins, Swordfish, the large whales, certain sharks, albatrosses, shearwaters, and others. Some sea turtles also fit the profile, Leatherbacks foremost. But all camels must recharge at the oasis, and that's why so many big, migratory animals will be converging here on Georges.

A vast, sleek Finback Whale surfaces just a few yards in front of our boat, and we ride through its "footprints" of tail turbulence roiling the sea behind it. Distant geysers flag additional whales. Quite literally ranging from the microscopic single cells to the largest animals ever to have lived on Earth, this place *is* the food chain. That's why Leatherbacks, Swordfish, and all the rest come here. The feast is no picnic, no bucolic frolic; it's full of violent annihilation. So it's logical that in these canyons of life and death the regular stalkers include the most fearsome predator of all time, and it's here—in the wheelhouse and up in the crow's nest, and behind the notebook.

Franklyn, scanning, assesses: "The weather is plenty fine for seeing fins."

Out of the whole year, this early-summer concentration lasts just a few weeks. As summer advances, the warm water now against the slopes streams over the bank, the temperature edge dissolves, the water-mass boundary dissipates, and all this life will disperse over the wide shoal shelf. The fish and turtles will spread invisibly farther north and east and, in autumn, migrate out. That's why many of these animals are large; the oases form and fade, and body size means fuel capacity and a long-distance ticket. Last week conditions were excellent; this week conditions remain good; next week, if a strong blow mixes the edge, everything may be rearranged. So the crew will fish now, and hard.

The friction at the edges of the currents has driven little slicks here and there and collected more mats of weed and some trash. I spot a large yellowish jelly—a Lion's Mane, Leatherback food—like a smudge of rust pulsing through the sea.

The water temperature is back up to 61 degrees. We're off the edge of the bank, with three to four hundred fathoms of water floating our boat as we weave along the continental slope. As we slide back up the slope, cozying up the bank's shoulder, the water cools about one degree and green blotches appear on the sonar monitor—big schools of small fishes in mid-depths beneath our hull. Franklyn says, "These fish are all on the hundred-fathom contour right now."

This curtain of life along the edge is the bank's lunch counter. Smaller red blotches suggest individual larger animals—including perhaps Swordfish or tunas or a turtle. If you're on deck and can't see the sonar monitor or temperature gauge, use the old-fashioned method: look for the seabirds, or maybe a basking sunfish, or just cruise along the slicks and weed patches marking borders of the realms. Stay on the side where the tint is greenish.

We circle back toward where we harpooned the Swordfish, looking for another. Our string of buoys is moving slowly forward, making little wakes. Six hundred feet below, the struck Swordfish is laboriously towing the gear as though carrying its cross.

Unlike virtually every other fishery, here there is no accidental catch. If you don't want it, you don't stick it—no undersized juveniles, no unmarketable species, no seabirds or mammals, no turtles. Before long-lining, harpooning was clean, selective, and sustainable in ways long-lining has never figured out how to be. But still, harpooning is designed to kill some of the most extraordinary of the sea's creatures. One can only hope the Swordfish is somehow incapable of feeling the torment we've inflicted as it bears its strange burden of rope and floats. The fish will tow until the combined exhaustion, suffocation, and blood loss kill it. Loss of speed alone deprives it of oxygen. There is no fighting the great gladiator as in the old days, when each fish took a deployed boatman on a "sleigh ride" before he wrestled it to the surface, killing it with lance stabs to the heart and gills. In those days Swordfish sometimes turned the table, bursting through dory planking, hurting men despite the cast-iron stove plates they sometimes sat on. These days, the gladiator dies alone in a sphere of darkness, hundreds of feet beneath the sparkling surface.

Out of that glinting glare, a hundred Common Dolphins streak toward our boat like elegantly etched tracers, their sleek, effortlessly pumping bodies swarming playfully into the bow and wake waves. When their heads break the surface their blowholes open with the precision of engine valves, infusing their warm blood with atmosphere sufficient for carbureting the next moments of lyric motion, and in the same fluid movement they resume streaming along under the surface, trailing a long fizz of bubbles.

Converged into close quarters along this edge are thirteen other Swordfish-hunting boats. The radio chatter mixes English and Acadian French. We maintain a position easternmost in the pack, closest to the sun. We pass another drift line of weeds, and several floating milk containers that appeared after breakfast.

Our engine drones as we pace the edge and the hours mount. Anything moving in the water draws these men's attention the way small twitching objects fascinate kittens. An Ocean Sunfish, imprisoned inside the daze of its quarter-ton man-in-the-moon body, waves that big, dark, triangular dorsal that so scares bathers along northern beaches. Jim yells, "Lucky nobody eats them, or we wouldn't be seeing many of *them*, either." We eclipse the sunfish, which continues waving, as though saying, "I don't know why you say good-bye; I say hello."

Our boat abruptly turns, and the adrenaline rush that hits me says this is tribal big-game hunting in a way that's psychologically primal. From the tower Arthur is calling, "I've got either a fish or a shark." But it's so obvious to Franklyn that this is a shark that he looks to the mast several times, saying, "Are we looking at the same fins?" It's a Blue Shark—a large one—with dorsal streaming and that wobbly tail, enjoying the warmth at sea level.

Half an hour later a Manx Shearwater courses by on whip-and-glide wings, likely headed in this season toward Great Britain. By late morning most birds are bobbing on the sea. Two sitting storm-petrels, spaced just so, look like two upright fins. Part of the game entails squinting twice at a lot of petrel pairs. Yet of real Swordfish—or Leatherbacks— no further sign.

Getting antsy, Franklyn checks with other boats. Only two have struck fish. The water is 64 degrees now, and Franklyn grumbles, "The water down here is too warm, too mixed, and too spread out." With warm water streaming in over the bank here, parts of the temperature edge are already dissolving. The Swordfish and Leatherbacks so evident last week, stacked up along the gradient, are dispersing into summer pasture. "Last week everything was buzzing from here to the Hague Line," asserts Franklyn. "There were so many porpoises it was hard to see a Swordfish. And the sunfish—still some here, but most have moved up onto the bank."

Franklyn decides to pick up our fish while he considers a move. When we passed our gear earlier, the front float was underwater, and Franklyn commented, "Man, that fish is really pulling." Now the buoys bob inertly, the line hanging. Justin grabs the flag and the floats and places the rope in a hydraulic lobster-trap hauler. The taut line comes in looking wavy in the undulating surface.

The night-blue fish is still alive when the enormous trunk of its body looms into view. Nearly spent, it describes a slow, shocked half circle. Franklyn sinks a gaff-hook as Justin ropes its tail to a winch, which deposits the great fish on deck. Expressing approval of its size, Justin says, "I guess!," his general, all-purpose affirmation. A larger animal than it first appeared, it's about two hundred pounds. The long broadsword extending half the length of the body, its raked, rushing sweep of rigid fins, and the wide, stiff span of its sickle tail make the fish appear larger still. Justin says to me, "You don't see that every day in New York, do you."

The strangely beautiful creature appears misplaced not only on deck, but in the present. While a turtle or shark, ancient as they are, appear contemporary by their classic designs, the Swordfish looks wondrously relict from times of old, like a knight with a jousting pole appearing at the train station.

A Swordfish is a hypodermic creature, the most audaciously endowed of the sea's rhino-armamented fishes, leading with its weapon every moment of its life. In its natural role it is hunter and hunted, its double-edged sword by turns attacking and defensive, its natural demeanor often aggressive, usually confident, always aware of the blade preceding it. Universally in the sea and among fishing people, the Swordfish is rightly regarded dangerous. (I know a man who saw a hooked Swordfish leap over the rail of a longline boat and pin a fisherman to the wooden wheelhouse through his lung. Franklyn says that once while trying to find a leak that threatened to sink the boat, they discovered a Swordfish bill thrust through two and a half inches of wooden hull. In 2005 a ninety-pound Loggerhead Turtle was found swimming "with obvious difficulty" on the surface of the Tyrrhenian Sea off Italy; it had a small wound in its shell and veterinarians discovered twenty-three centimeters [nine inches] of Swordfish bill broken off inside the turtle, which recovered.)

Most surprising about the sword is how well the animal wears it. Snatch a unicorn's horn and the next person would see a normal horse. But you can't disarm a Swordfish; the sword is fundamental to the head—it's no after-market add-on. In fact, the whole body seems designed around that bill. With its high scimitar dorsal fin so far forward and its wide-shouldered weight gathered up behind that staggering dagger, this is a ballistic dart of a fish, a stiletto animal. Yet overall the strangeness derives from not just its obvious weapon but also its elephantine jaw and startling eyes. Those huge blue-green, dark-water eyes occupy an astonishingly large proportion of its head. Their size emphasizes the creature's vision investment for hunting deep and at night. Its strange lower jaw closes to a seemingly mismatched fit; the jaws don't clench. Its pointed lower jaw appears too small and narrow against the wide, broadly overlapping base of the flat bill, like putting an adult's sandal sole to sole with a child's, as though maxilla and mandible derive from two creatures of different sizes. The lack of teeth suggests a Swordfish's expectation that anything meeting those deficient jaws will be either pacified or blade-slashed to bite-sized bits. The fins are fibrous and fixed, neither spiny nor retractile as in marlins or tunas, nor leathered as in sharks. Just before its tail, each side of its body bears a stiff, wedgelike horizontal keel, for eliminating water resistance and drag on each side-to-side propelling stroke. Only amid the spectacular diversity of the ocean can a large predator be so unusually configured. But with these seemingly strange components the Swordfish packs a design and business plan that has kept it profitably at the top of the food chain for something like fifty million years. Fact is, it works.

Justin slits its throat. A gushing stream of blood stains the deck as the fish begins a prolonged, slow-twitching shudder that lasts minutes, its skin changing from blue to brown. The fish's bodily trunk, so surprisingly supple in water, lies on deck more like a log than a carcass. Despite its overall stockiness, its belly is subtly pleated with room for fattening out, this newly arrived migrant having settled in for a summer of feeding that she will not get. A stomach containing four dozen Short-Finned Squid and six or eight fish attests to a predator adept at feeding itself. The ingested fishes, already chemical-peeled by digestion, include herring, what look like young Conger Eels, and some larger fish, maybe hake, weighing perhaps four or five pounds, already a little beyond recognition.

Justin puts the Swordfish's beating heart on ice. "They taste *awesome.*" This is the only edible part of a Swordfish that fishermen usually have access to. They can't just cut a ten-pound chunk; that renders the rest unmarketable, and no one seems prepared to cut up a fish that could be sold for more than a thousand dollars. Justin can't remember the last time he had Swordfish steak; he thinks it was eight years ago.

Franklyn deliberates our next move. Jim pours himself a cup of tea and suggests, "How about across the channel—tip of Brown's." He gestures toward an unseen piece of open ocean thirty miles away as though he is pointing to a shop awning across the street.

Franklyn considers, but decides instead to work around the corner of Georges Bank until we are over a massive thumbprint in the seafloor the fishermen call Fiddler's Cove. Franklyn is betting that most of the fish that were here last week are still finding it profitable and remain, rather than having moved up to Brown's Bank. And he's also betting that where the cove's walls are steepest, the surface temperature may still retain a well-defined edge. If Swordfish and Leatherbacks think, this is how they think. If they don't think, they act as though they think like Franklyn.

With the sun just past high noon, our satellite map plotter tells us we've arrived at Fiddler's Cove. Nothing much changes on the surface; it's water, water everywhere. But to ocean animals such features are as obvious as mountains rising from plains.

We turn to put the sun behind us, working the unseen slope. The sea here is likewise tinted green. We're not alone; a few other boats have pegged their luck here, working the cove in long ellipses a couple of miles across.

We pick up the radio chatter of long-liners, unseen at the far edge of the vast patch of clear, blue 70-degree water that has broken off from the Gulf Stream and is spiraling oh so slowly toward Georges. They're focused at the moment more on Bigeye Tuna for lucrative export to Japan, where businessmen will disappear the big fish bite by bite, piranha-like, helping relieve the distant Atlantic of life.

Time pools like drops of water. The engine growls on. The moon is pulling a pucker of ocean, and we cross the silver-ribbon riffles of a tide rip, where subtle wavelets on the shimmering surface are the only suggestion of a tidal current now stampeding up the steep slope below, fueling the living power plant that mints the sea's currency.

A minute or so later a Finback Whale erupts from the depths like a great, steaming volcano of muscle. Franklyn scans intently; he's often seen Swordfish near whales. He grins at me. Even after forty-five years of commercial fishing he's feeling how great it is to be here. During those decades he's dragged for groundfish, dredged for scallops, set bottomlines for Haddock and Atlantic Cod, trapped lobsters, hunted Swordfish with harpoon, and also long-lined for Swords. A lot of what he saw in other fisheries—wasted fish and piles of dead juveniles—made him stop. After a few quiet minutes Franklyn suddenly says, "It's damn good to be here. Years ago in the cancer ward, all I could think about was swordfishing—thank you, Lord." No longer grinning, he adds solemnly, "I don't know why God takes the good. I guess he wants me to harpoon a few more fish."

It's the warmest, laziest part of the day, the best time for seeing Swordfish. But Franklyn comments, "There's a lot of ocean, and only a few fish. But—you never know; you *neh-verr* know."

While porpoise and bird sightings grow scarce, Jim's attention remains abundant. Each time I glance at Jim in the crow's nest he looks as though he has just seen something, craning his neck, torquing his body around, looking out, looking down. I try to emulate his attentiveness. It's a good time for seeing turtles, too, and if there's one in range I'm pretty confident we'll see it.

Suddenly Jim yells, *"Hard to starboard! Hard to starboard!"*

I glance in time to see the flukes of a Humpback Whale withdrawing massively in the distance. Closer, several hundred yards, a sunfish crashes an enormous pancake flop. All this I see. I *don't* see what Jim is pointing to.

A quarter mile off, Jim sees inches-high fins. Now I see them. At such remarkable distance, it takes a while to ascertain it's a Swordfish. Franklyn hurries onto the stand, moving with the suppleness of a much younger man. He grasps the harpoon and glances toward Jim, offering, "Good eyes—for an old fart."

We'll intersect the fish perpendicularly. Putting the stand in exactly the correct spot over a swimming fish at precisely the right moment requires considerable skill. The harpoon pole is only twelve feet long; the striker has one shot at a moving fish from a moving boat, and must thrust the point deep enough to prevent its pullout during the struggles.

In the fatal geometry now unfolding, we head straight, the fish heads straight, and the vectors intersect so flawlessly that as we cross the fish's line of travel Franklyn is directly over its head. It's as though the fish has offered itself and something predestined is playing out.

Franklyn hits the Swordfish so hard it turns sideways, drifts stunned a few moments, then, with the seeming serenity of a clean miss, the fish merely rights itself and angles down, wagging slowly out of sight.

Jim calls, "Right *on!*" Arthur shifts into reverse to back away from the harpoon line and Justin scrambles to the deck to manage its deployment. The detached harpoon point is connected to the six hundred feet of line coiled in a big plastic basket, ending with the string of three buoys tied a couple of fathoms apart—a lobster buoy and two basketball-sized inflated floats—and then the "high-flier," the upright pole with its radar reflector of diamond-shaped aluminum. The buoys absorb the Swordfish's most violent movements, helping foil it from wrenching out the dart. Fifty feet from the harpoon point are several heavy links of chain, the additional weight making it difficult for the fish to remain upright, the stress and drag helping kill it.

Satisfied with a perfect shot and the certainty that this Swordfish can do nothing to free itself, Franklyn sings, "There's a joy in my heart . . ."

When Justin hurls the high-flier we circle around our just-deployed gear. Its bright buoys are making cheerful chevrons through the surface, a picturesque abstraction of the grief and struggle deep below. In the fish's heart, there's a barbed bronze dart the size of a belt buckle.

Since hitting that last fish—forty minutes ago now—we've been pacing an area about two miles across, betting that there's another fish here with our name on it.

Franklin notices that the water temp's up to 65 degrees, and makes a face. He grumbles that warmer water makes Swordfish more skittish. Sure enough, when a nearby boat sends its striker hurrying into position, the fish sprints to the depths and the striker steps down.

Franklyn directs Arthur to circle toward them. Jumpy or not, he's hoping their fish will resurface—within our reach. If Franklyn thinks some fish—or a single fish—are in an area, he will often circle as though they must inevitably surface to offer themselves. And, often, they do.

Jim shouts, *"Starboard! Three o'clock!"*

Arthur cranks hard right.

Jim yells, "Perfect! Five boat lengths. Two o'clock." Its stiff tail and sharp dorsal are up at fifty yards.

Franklyn grasps the harpoon.

"One o'clock. Three boat lengths. Straight ahead now."

The fish withdraws beneath the glinting glare.

Jim narrates: ". . . should be in the sun going right; let's just give a minute here . . ."

I'm squinting into a patch of sea glistening like shards of glass.

Franklyn watches like a cat at a mouse hole, calm yet poised to pounce. Arthur has one hand on the wheel and the other at the throttle. We wait to the tempo of long swells.

The other boat, stopped a quarter mile away, likewise waits for a fish its crew regards as theirs.

Right where I am scanning, the fish suddenly fins out. Arthur's shift lever grunts the boat into a forward stalk.

The fish scarcely flinches.

Jim coaches, "Steady, steady. Come around to put the sun behind." Arthur takes the boat on a wide semicircle.

The fish turns away, and its fins stream ripples.

Arthur swings the boat until we are directly following.

Jim calls, "Just like that, Arthur. One boat length ahead. Give it some power." The boat comes on steadily, about twice as fast as a person walking.

Mildly alarmed, the fish withdraws from the surface and increases its pace.

Arthur pushes the throttle a little—a chase—but the fish easily angles down, slipping our grasp.

A moment later Jim yells, "Straight ahead—underwater." The Swordfish reappears, bright blue, just subsurface. Time coils as Franklyn comes over the fish and tenses. Arthur slows the boat just a bit to allow more opportunity to aim, and when Franklyn thrusts, the fish is just inches beyond the jab. It vanishes in a burst.

Franklyn's thrust would have struck if Arthur hadn't altered the timing; that's my take. But there's no recrimination. Franklyn looks to the bridge with a big grin, saying, "So many times I've seen that tail flex and wished I had that power."

Franklyn directs Arthur to make another circle. But Jim suggests that we stop screwing with this fish: it got away from the other boat, too, remember. Franklyn comments to me, "A Swordfish does what it wants." He calls aloft, "Okay, let's find another."

At a little before eight P.M. the men decide the fishing day's over. We've had the stand over three fish, struck and caught two, cleanly missed one.

When I express astonishment that the men can find their buoys after hours of drifting, even when they have several fish out after sundown, Franklyn says, "It's no problem, really." With his finger on the map he explains, "If you know you've dropped the flag here, and you know the tide's coming in, you know where it will be in a few hours. And if the tide has changed, you know it'll be over here, seldom more than five miles away, though occasionally as much as eight." To me, flags drifting in the dark five miles away would seem hopelessly lost, especially when other people have gear out and on the radar everyone's gear looks alike. To Franklyn it's in a day's work. He shrugs.

His marked-up map shows written-in fishing areas: Northeast Peak, Fiddler's Cove, the Whale's Tail, and so on. But most striking about the map is that the entire edge of the continental shelf has been leased to oil companies, and—though both the U.S. and Canadian sides of the bank are under drilling moratoriums—these lease boundaries are charted, as though someone wants everyone used to the idea. Needless to say, oil companies want the moratoriums ended. In rare anger, Franklyn boils over: "On Brown's Bank, the area they want to drill is exactly the area that spawns our whole lobster fishery. If there's a spill, it'll kill our fisheries. But they don't give a shit. They're so hungry for this oil and gas stuff, they'd like us out of the way—the goddamn bastards."

We locate our high-flier and haul our fish. Franklyn intones, "We'll thank the Lord for today's two, and hope for two more tomorrow."

At about nine-thirty the sun finally melts in the red west. No one will stand night watch; there's not enough shipping traffic out here to worry the fishermen. For safety we move about four miles from most other boats, shut our engine, and everyone turns in. Through the night we drift and dream.

Morning dawns in a fog cocoon so misty it quickly dampens my hair and shirt. We can hardly see the water, let alone a fish. So breakfast— bacon, toast, pancakes, tea, fried potatoes, eggs—gets stretched till ten o'clock.

While Jim commands the stove, the galley talk turns political. The Canadians are curious about government in the States. They fail to grasp how a person can lose an election yet become president. I fumble to explain the electoral college. Most Canadians can't understand it; does it not make a mockery of "one person, one vote"? And in an election where one person clearly won, why didn't the citizens rise up when on a party-line split the Supreme Court stopped the recount in Florida and handed victory to the loser of the vote, a member of the majority's party? Why do Americans tolerate election stealing? And why are prescription drugs so expensive? Why no national health insurance?

With the odd comment "She can *cook!*," Jim suddenly delivers a big plate of food under Arthur's nose. Though Arthur's proportions could understatedly be termed "hefty," he gives me a look as if to say, "How am I going to eat all this?" But I have confidence in him. His sensible strategy for the dilemma: first pour enough syrup to thoroughly soften the pancakes confronting him, as though bombing a beach before invasion. Franklyn says to him, "You've got Aunt Jemima by the balls."

Franklyn, in the helm chair with his plate in his lap, is eating pancakes and sausages while watching the radar. He points with his fork, mumbling something about other boats out in the fog. Franklyn suddenly asks about Hillary Clinton, saying, "I don't understand why people hate her; she's just an educated woman."

Jim finally sits down before one large pancake from which he has removed the center, and proceeds to flood that center with more syrup than I've ever seen a human put on a plate. In the syrup tsunami the pancake is suddenly and catastrophically awash, mortally inundated, in imminent danger of sinking. *Mayday! Mayday!* Jim engulfs this hazardous situation with the no-nonsense alacrity of a seasoned veteran.

At ten-thirty the fog really shuts down; I can't even see the whole boat. Franklyn complains. But he wants to be at the edge just in case. We'd drifted up onto the bank during the night, and so, guided by satellites and radar, we penetrate impenetrable fog until the sonar again shows schools of fishes hugging the bank's sloping shoulder. Here we slowly motor while Swordfish pierce our imaginations with fins slicing up through mist-smoked daydreams. Radar reveals two dozen vessels cruising within two miles, hazardous in such white-out fog. Franklyn gripes.

In the fog our hawk-eyed hunters are like hooded falcons, the whiteness their darkness. Invisibility suspends routine like snow on a school day, allowing people to try different roles. Jim is in the stand, practicing stabbing foggy water. He complains, "It's a tough time to learn to be a striker, with so few Swordfish left."

Franklyn recalls, "My first chance to get on the stand was when I was about nineteen and the striker missed three in a row. I hit the next thirteen in a row." Franklyn ended the trip having struck fifty-six Swordfish.

Justin is sitting alone on the back deck, pencil and paper on his lap, working out a tune on his guitar. Arthur opens a bag of chips and a soda, and we idly munch while blundering through our fog-bound blind-man's bluff. Why we're even cruising eludes me, but Jim says, "Maybe we'll stub our toe on a Swordfish today."

Franklyn adds, "You gotta believe in help from God."

With no visibility, the radio is lively. The talk is of fish and fog, and then someone mentions seeing turtles yesterday—the brown ones, Loggerheads. Another responds, "I saw the big dark one; shell's kinda longish, with ridges." A Leatherback. Someone else: "Yeah, there were great big Leatherbacks yesterday off the bank in the deep of that little canyon, four or five hundred fathoms, right where we stuck that fish." Someone else reports seeing a Leatherback thirty miles east of here, over a chink in the southern end of Brown's Bank. Today, of course, no one's seeing anything.

Franklyn shares, "One foggy day, we didn't see a thing until a quarter to five in the evening. By the time we quit for the day we'd seen thirty Swordfish, stuck twenty-five of them."

Jim remembers days in the 1970s when he had up to five Swordfish in view at once, and had the luxury of picking the bigger fish. "Big" fish then were really big because they had more chance to grow. Jim was on one trip that had fifty-one fish averaging 333 pounds *dressed* weight—no head, guts, or fins. That means the fish averaged well over four hundred pounds whole weight. On another trip forty-seven Swordfish dressed out at 341 pounds, meaning an *average* live weight of 443 pounds. "That was in 1976," he says. Numbers like that are unheard of now, and few fish live long enough to get that big.

Franklyn adds, "Anything under a hundred pounds back then, you wouldn't try to catch. It was dishonorable. But on longlines I killed little pups." Franklyn made about half a dozen trips as captain of a long-lining boat during the mid-1970s. His photo album keeps the image of his young wife, Alice, holding by its bill, with one hand, a Swordfish whose tail barely grazes her belt. He says, "They can't get big if hooks kill them *that* size." Jim mentions seeing—and I've seen this too—hundred-pound shipping boxes that each contained the bodies of *several* Swordfish. Long-liners consider a Sword hitting the hundred-pound mark a nice fish; they call them "markers." Most Swordfish that size are juveniles. Not surprisingly, harpooners resent getting only 10 percent of the quota while the government gives the rest to long-liners; they'd prefer to see long-lining banned.

Infer no personal attacks when I relay that long-lining has helped reduce Atlantic populations of Swordfish, various sharks, marlins, and certain tunas by roughly 90 percent since around 1960, when long-liners started proliferating. The most pessimistic possibility is that the great gladiator's long decline will continue until the fish are gone. But, in fact, things have begun improving. After conservation groups sued over high catches of illegally small fish and high-profile chefs boycotted Swordfish in the late 1990s, governments cut the Atlantic fishing quota and the United States banned long-lining from large southern areas where young Swordfish concentrate. Though fiercely contested by commercial longline boat owners and their lobbyists, the closures have saved enough juveniles that more young Swordfish are now evident off the coast, a definite upturn, the beginning of something like a recovery. What's odd is that the fish don't seem to go near shore anymore, and many commercial fishermen haven't seen one in decades.

What's the biggest secret to being a good swordfisherman? Jim says, "Having faith." Franklyn answers, "Having patience." Justin pipes, "Having Franklyn." Sometimes you look at that huge eye, and it looks up at you—you'll miss. Some guys, they see a fish and just go straight at it; that's wrong—you want the sun behind you; you don't want to be staring into that glare, so take time to come around and line up right. You want the boat positioned between swells. If the fish seems nervous, circle it to confuse it and make it stop moving. If the fish moves in a circle, steer for the center of the circle. If the fish is intersecting your path perpendicularly, steer for the tip of the bill, not the middle of the fish. If a fish reappears next to you while you're idling, *don't* put the boat in gear; let the fish move off some distance, because the "clunk" of shifting will alarm it. If the fish is underwater when you're coming over it, it's not where it seems because of diffraction; aim below the belly, and you'll hit it in its back. If the harpoon strikes one in the head it'll go berserk, slashing that bill, slashing, slashing. Hold the pole with your fingers *around* it; never thrust with your palm on the end of the pole, because if you strike bone or the boat dips hard, it can snap your wrist.

At five-forty we stumble over a ghost with both fins out, waving us down in a little patch of silver water that seems almost to float in cloud. Jim sprints into the stand; the fish sprints back into our dreams. One ghost in the mist. Hours of boredom punctuated by twenty seconds of excitement—that's the whole day. It's not 1976; we won't see thirty fish between now and sundown. On Franklyn's biggest day ever—he'd struck over *fifty* Swordfish—the deck crew got so exhausted from striking, hauling, and dressing that the lookouts stopped calling out the fish they continued seeing. One season, he harpooned over six hundred Swordfish. For a few moments Franklyn's life is passing before his eyes. Then he says, "It's the stories that keep the blood circulating."

Jim observes, "Stories keep us young, but they also make us old."

Fog darkens to velvet. Fade to black.

At seven Franklyn rouses me from my bunk. Visibility is opened, measurable in some miles, and our boat is amid several Right Whales, with their characteristic smooth-margined all-dark tail flukes and unfinned backs. Victim of many wrongs, Rights remain the most endangered whale in the North Atlantic. Beneath an entourage of shearwaters and storm-petrels they propel the big blunt prows of their callused heads, shooting white gusts of breath, rolling their massive backs, tipping tail flukes to the sun.

Arthur stumbles from the wheelhouse, digging out a cigarette from what he claims is the last carton he'll ever buy. Canadian cigarette packages carry informative labeling: "Warning: Each year the equivalent of a small city dies from tobacco use. Estimated annual deaths in Canada: Murder 510, Alcohol 1,000, car accidents 2,000, suicide 3,000, tobacco 45,000." Arthur lights up what may be one of his last smokes. Canadian cigarette packages also carry actual photographs of diseased gums, and this caption: "Warning: Cigarettes cause mouth disease. Cigarette smoke causes oral cancer, gum diseases, and tooth loss." Here's another one: in letters almost as high as the brand name, it says, "Tobacco use can make you impotent." Finer print elucidates: "Cigarettes may cause sexual impotence due to decreased blood flow to the penis. This can prevent you from having an erection." Apparently, Canada's bureaucrats see their job more as protecting the public from the excesses of greed than protecting greedy excess.

Jim uncases his thirty-year-old sunglasses, carefully unwraps their soft cloth and towel padding, polishes them, looks through them, and polishes them again. "Your eyes are the bait," he says. "They bring you the Swordfish." As he goes aloft Jim tells me, "I hope you goddamn spot a Swordfish on your own today—make us some money!" I tell him to spot me a goddamn Leatherback.

. . .

By about nine-thirty, we're fishing in a surprisingly dense group of vessels, many with less than half a mile between them, concentrated in an area four miles in diameter. Any Swordfish brave enough to wave a fin would incur rapid detection. The fleet is working over a substantial hill in 115 fathoms just off the bank's Northeast Peak. It's connected to the rest of the bank by a ridge 150 to 300 fathoms deep. These hundreds of feet above, tide running over that jutting knee roils the surface with stipples and white caps. That tide is forcing deep water up over the ledge, closer to sunlight, and despite the ocean's blue-sky reflection, if you look down into the water you can see that it carries a jade tint—that green-fire filament. As the current compels huge volumes of deep stampeding water to squeeze and hurry over the submerged ridge, everything in that water— plant cells, swarms of ant-sized copepod crustaceans, little shrimplike krill, mackerel, herring, squids—gets concentrated. An oasis of food in a desert of water, it's worth the trip for the biggest, hungriest animals in the sea—the warrior hunters, the big stuff: tide-bucking tunas, turtles, whales, and boats.

Outside this crowd, there is not a vessel visible, but those right here are getting in one another's way. We could motor five miles and lose the competition—but we wouldn't catch anything. One boat waits for a fish it had seen. When it resurfaces, another boat steams in and nails it. Franklyn says, "It's very aggressive now, because there are so few fish and so many bills to pay." He adds, "You need a place like this to yourself."

That'll never happen. But this is also a neighborhood, a big watery hunting encampment on the rolling prairies of the blue sea, a small floating village. Evidence: a big harpoon boat comes alongside—menacingly close, it seems to me—asking whether we can spare a cup of sugar. Their crew calls out thanks for the airborne pound bag of sugar one of them catches. They've also been setting bottom-lines, and in exchange for the sugar, several freshly iced Haddock come flying over our rail, drawing profuse gratitude. Jim calls down, "Our pork stays frozen tonight!" Amen.

Morning blurs to the dazzle of afternoon. Most birds are resting. Most of what's in the air is chatter. One boat reports seeing "not much, just whales." One skipper reports seeing two turtles, "but the other kind, not Leatherbacks."

News of an extraordinary catch comes through the receiver: a huge female Shortfin Mako Shark. Estimated weight: one thousand pounds. In her stomach: remains of "at least three, maybe four small Swordfish," the largest about seventy pounds, everything except their swords and tails, "about a hundred, hundred and fifty pounds of very fresh flesh." Of all the sea's creatures, only large makos carry any reputation for hunting Swordfish, and they do so spectacularly, materializing as a blue streak from below and with one devastating strike severing the Swordfish's tail, suddenly disabling both propeller and rudder. Few interactions in nature so cunningly and precisely apply so much savage power, turning such a well-armed and aggressive predator as a Swordfish into merely helplessly bleeding meat. One fishermen recalls that his father was about to harpoon a Swordfish when a mako zipped in and cut its tail off. The man gaffed the crippled Sword and hoisted it aboard, leaving the mako running mad circles, no doubt wondering what alien abduction had occurred.

The air has surrendered all motion, and this sea has fallen into the slickest kind of tranquil that ever obtains upon open ocean, with swells so long and gentle they rock like a cradle. Such flat water is our accomplice, a betrayer of fins.

Jim checks in from the crow's nest, yelling down, "Not much going on. A few sunfish, that's it."

Franklyn calls up, "There's plenty of time. You *neh-verr* know. It's early," he adds. "Some people, they don't see a Swordfish by four o'clock, they get discouraged."

Jim responds, "They don't have it."

I ask Jim again to at least find a Leatherback. He nods affirmatively.

We come over a deep slope where the depth changes a hundred fathoms in half a mile, causing surface tide rips that fairly boil. Soon the sea surface seems livened by an extraordinary congress of mammals. Virtually every time we take a sweep around, our view captures dolphins slicing or leaping, or Pilot Whales slow-rolling their high-dorsaled black backs. A Finback Whale bursts suddenly to our left from someplace deep, rolling its heft and blowing stacks of steam. Another huge Finback and her calf surface almost directly ahead of our bow, so close that the mother gives an extra-deep kick with her flukes to put a wider comfort zone between us.

Franklyn says, "To see the life, that's what gets me. Why the hell come here otherwise? I thank the Lord for letting me be here once again."

Jim yells, "I can smell 'em here."

Franklyn agrees conditions are "finest kind." With the intonation of a patriarch, he says, "It's important to believe you're going to get them. I know some are gonna show, anytime." People who fished with Franklyn decades ago still tell stories of him working one small area for hours until Swordfish started rising, then banging out more fish than did less persevering captains who'd left in search of wetter waters.

Arthur suddenly slows the boat. Franklyn takes the stand, but sees nothing. He looks to me, and I reply with a shrug; neither of us sees whatever prompted our pause. We look to the crow's nest. Jim shrugs too.

Franklyn calls up, "Arthur, what did you see?" Arthur's not sure; Justin thinks he saw a Swordfish. The sea seems dotted with dolphins in the near distance. Franklyn looks up questioningly. A couple of minutes pass. Franklyn leaves the stand, muttering to me under his breath, "If you're an experienced swordfisherman, you don't slow the boat because you've seen a porpoise splash." He goes into the wheelhouse.

Suddenly Jim yells, "Eight o'clock! I've got a fish underwater. Let's go, *let's go!*"

Franklyn again scurries into the stand and poises the long shaft. Jim calls out tensely, "Two boat lengths ahead. Under the surface. Come more to port—ten degrees port." Arthur's response is not immediate, and Jim yells, "*Port,* Arthur."

Arthur steers port.

"Okay, good. Now look close. Look close. Do you see it, Arthur?"

Arthur is saying no, he doesn't see it; none of us does. Only Jim sees a fish.

Jim says, "Okay, just a touch to starboard. Underwater. Not far—two boat lengths."

Still no one sees it.

"One boat length. Straight ahead. Slightly to port. Have you got it yet, Arthur?"

Arthur hasn't seen the fish; he's just steering as instructed.

"Half a boat length!"

How is this possible? Half a boat length from a Swordfish and no one except Jim—not Arthur or Justin in the tower, not me on the pilothouse roof, not even Franklyn out in the striker stand—sees anything?

Jim yells, "Look close, *close*—six feet down."

Arthur suddenly calls, "Okay, I got it," as a large sky-blue Swordfish materializes practically under Franklyn's feet.

It's big, and Jim yells, "Nice *fish!*"

The animal rises until its fins barely scratch the slick, transparent surface.

Arthur puts the stand directly over its broad back.

The fish adds a touch of speed and starts pulling away.

Franklyn sweeps the long shaft forward and decides the creature's final moment. Struck deeply, the big fish careens, its silver side flashing like a sudden distress signal. Arthur clunks the boat into hard reverse.

Justin, dumbfounded, says, "Jim is *awesome*, eh? Seeing that fish underwater like that?"

Franklyn, all grins, says approvingly, "Jim's an underwater man." He congratulates Justin for having first spotted the fish, after all.

A Swordfish spends its life underwater, often deep. Yet these fish, having decided to bask near the warming sun, usually fail to make the one familiar move that could save their lives—simply angling down. And now, like the others, this fish, heavily wounded, makes that move too late, weaving downward, emptying the basket of its hundred heavy fathoms of line.

The hunter in me, who has killed many fish, shares the excitement and enjoys the adrenaline. And though the nature lover is relieved to be just a spectator in this venture, there is something else I like. The extraordinary performance of these Neolithic hunters is enveloped in the Great Mystery of vast nature and long tradition, imbued with the spiritual tone Franklyn and Jim evoke. Yet I most admire their plain skill. These guys make their own luck; then, at excitement's crucial height, they summon a calm that slows the unfolding moments. There is no posturing or pretense. This is as direct and honest as it gets. You look for a fish. If you see a fish, you go to it and try to stab it. If you miss, the fish swims away. No one is trying to create a false impression; no one can. There's no room for self-delusion. Everything is plain and in the open. Bluffing, manipulation, and exaggerated claims—epidemic on land—can't find a fingerhold in something this authentic.

It's turned into a fine day, and the crews are killing Swordfish. About three hundred yards away, Franklyn's brother Alvah sticks a fish, and his victory pose—harpoon shaft in both hands over his head—could as easily have come from a band of mammoth hunters. Sitting in a swinging seat in the striker's stand, Franklyn is feeling avid. Closing on sixty, he remains youthful, his eyes frequently a-twinkle with a mischievous thought, a little scratch-and-win grin just below the surface. Franklyn seems illuminated from within by the joy derived from living on stolen time. He has made a living killing the sea's creatures. He has made a life by overcoming addictive tendencies and cancer and realizing that what hasn't sunk him is what keeps him afloat. So he's more buoyant now. Franklyn's holiday flags are always hoisted. More than perhaps anyone I've met, he appreciates each day lived as a miracle granted. More the mystery is why the majority of us drift in a fog of distraction when, right over our heads, the sun shines.

We cross a weed line whose depth is dotted with drifting Moon Jellies, *Aurelia*. Surely nearby must lurk a Leatherback. Bobbing in the drift line we see not a turtle but several recently discarded motor-oil containers and foam cups. These crews feel no need to have garbage bags aboard because just outside the pilothouse window is the world's largest dump. Yesterday Arthur threw the plastic bag from a loaf of bread overboard. When Franklyn mentioned that turtles mistake plastic bags for jellyfish, Arthur looked surprised. Likewise gathered in the jetsam bob several half-deflated party balloons from distant celebrations, also looking rather like jellyfish, drifting like Leatherback bait.

Rarin' to Go comes alongside, her one-armed skipper and Franklyn's brother Alvah anxious to have an in-person word with us. Less than a mile away they just came upon a large Leatherback. "Biggest turtle I've ever seen," Alvah says. "First I thought it was a life raft. At least fifteen hundred pounds it must have been; looked eight feet long. We circled it before it dived. So keep your eyes open. Over there."

Two hours later only one thing remains abundant: Jim's patience. And when Jim yells, it's because a quarter mile away the sea is pierced by two fins that do not belong to a shark.

As we close, the fish makes a bad decision: it turns toward the boat. When the stand is about to slide over it, the Swordfish displays further poor judgment, flexing its body to pirouette away from the boat directly beneath Franklyn, giving him a moment to drive the shaft extra far in. The Swordfish receives the harpoon so deep it instantly loses equilibrium and all coherence. Arthur reverses and Justin pays line as usual, but the fish never moves. The drag of the chain pivots the fish's body, and its broad bill pierces the surface, wagging unconsciously in the swell, like a flag waving belated surrender.

Franklyn turns to us and yells, "I felt a crunch, as though I was breaking bones."

Jim calls tightly, "Justin watch out; keep your feet clear of that rope in case the fish wakes up."

The fish does nothing. Franklyn says, "Now, Carl, you've seen it all. That's one for the book."

So ends the hazard-filled life of one of the sea's more violent citizens. Mere minutes past a career as a great predator, the javelin fish thuds the deck, senseless. Its great body flexes slightly, life still draining. Its color has rapidly changed from midnight-blue back with silver-flash flanks to a bronzing on the way to gray death.

Arthur tells Justin to slit its throat; until then a violent slashing from that double-edged sword remains possible. Justin appears hesitant. He moves in with a knife, deems it inadequate, then trades it and steps back in as the fish starts a slow, methodic thrash. Justin delivers the coup de grâce, and now the fish begins beating that great bill against a deck plate as it dies in a widening pool of its own blood, its huge body flexing, its gigantic eye jiggling each time the bill and tail slam the deck.

It vomits up some fish and squid. In the time it takes the blood to coagulate to the thickness of red paint, the fish stills. Its light-sensitive chameleon skin is now oddly patterned as though tattooed with everything that has just touched it, including the braid of the harpoon rope across its face. The fish seems lifeless, surely brain-dead from blood loss. Yet when I lay four fingers on its flank, its rippling sensitivity to touch is fine and exquisite. No surface of the human body is capable of quivering so responsively. It's eerie.

The creature begins a shuddering death rattle, its great fluid-plumped eye twitching. As the Swordfish shivers, deep indigo refloods its skin with living color, and the flanks and belly shine silvered as though its life is flashing before its big eyes as it swims through great, warm, sunlit waters somewhere far away.

As those big eyes hint, Swordfish are visual predators. Swordfish need excellent eyesight and fast response ability, yet they often hunt at night or deep, where everything is dim as starlight even during daytime. (In 1967 a Swordfish struck the research submersible *Alvin* at a depth of two thousand feet, got its bill stuck in a joint, and was hauled to the surface—where the researchers and crew ate it.) The cold at those depths also slows reaction times and degrades vision. But in addition to its lethal bayonet, a

Swordfish carries a secret weapon concealed inside its skull: a unique muscle that burns energy yet creates no movement, its sole role to generate heat for warming its brain and eyes while it's hunting in frigid depths, giving it superior vision and an advantage over cold-brained prey. This strange muscle's cells lack the proteins that contract to cause movement. Instead, it converts all the energy it uses into heat, like an electric clothes iron. The difference between typical muscle and the Swordfish's head heater is a little like the difference between a coal-fired steam engine and a coal-burning stove. This motionless muscular furnace is embedded in fat that both insulates and fuels the heater. By warming blood flowing into the brain and behind the eyes, the Swordfish can maintain those crucial organs at temperatures up to around 27 degrees Fahrenheit (15° C) higher than the surrounding water. The cells of an eye's retina collect light; then nerves send signals to the brain at periodic intervals, like the shutter in a movie camera. Low temperatures slow the retina's "shutter speed," causing the brain to wait longer for each optical signal. A Swordfish's eyes can distinguish more than forty light flashes per second at 72 degrees Fahrenheit (22° C), but only five flashes if the eye is chilled to 50 degrees Fahrenheit (10° C). The difference is a bit like a movie in which seven out of eight frames are missing. A hundred meters down, warm eyes give a Swordfish ten times sharper eyesight than if its eyes were as cool as the water. Dim light also decreases the eyes' "shutter speed." At about 500 meters (1,640 feet), the dark erases the warm-eye advantage. So Swordfish seldom go there. Other billfishes also have this organ, but in the Swordfish it's most developed. The Swordfish's strange head-warming muscle gives it access to more of the ocean, and to food supplies that lie beyond the reach of other hunters. In the sea, warmer heads prevail.

When a Swordfish needs to rewarm its whole body and digest, it moves upward, coming to bask at the surface, within harpoon range.

A butterfly flutters over the deck, 110 miles from land. Late afternoon. Our search resumes, mine for a Leatherback, theirs for Swords. Justin calls out a splash, but Franklyn corrects him: "Porpoise."

A while later Justin calls, "I just saw a splash that was no damn porpoise." This dubious news is sufficient to send Franklyn to the stand. A whale dives a quarter mile away. Franklyn asks Arthur to cruise over and stop on the whale's roiling "footprints." We're idling when Jim's magic eyes kick in again, and he yells, "Swordfish! Underwater right here! Don't move the boat, Arthur."

I look down and am confronted by a large Swordfish nearly the color of milk chocolate, casually zigzagging about six feet down. Still wearing its deepwater camouflage color, it must have just risen from far below.

The Swordfish moves off, and Jim says, "Okay, Arthur, now go ahead and follow it."

Arthur pushes the throttle forward, puffing a black diesel belch through the exhaust pipe atop the wheelhouse. We follow the fish toward a large patch of floating weeds.

The fish goes down, and even Jim's underwater eyes can't pull it. We stop. Jim cranes his neck all around the boat, like a hawk atop a pole. He says, "Come up. Come up. Come up." A minute passes.

Two. The boat rocks.

Three. The swells roll.

Four. The sea shimmers.

Five. Another boat arrives, hoping to steal the fish they know we're waiting for. Jim and Franklyn curse the other crew, whom they know well.

Jim says, "Okay, let's just motor off a ways, maybe he'll show."

No sooner do we get under way than Jim yells, *"I got 'im, got 'im, got 'im! Two o'clock, two hundred yards."* Franklyn starts toward his position, but Jim quickly retracts: "Nope, different; that's a shark. Blue dog. Sorry."

The real Swordfish suddenly breaks the surface, arcing slowly right.

Arthur makes a steering correction that swings Franklyn behind the fish, which becomes alarmed. As the stand comes directly over, its fins submerge and it spurts forward. It's eight feet below the surface and headed away as Franklyn again looms over it. Just as Jim yells, "Not yet," Franklyn *throws* the harpoon. Swordfish strikers never throw the harpoon unless it's really last-ditch. It's a marginal shot, and Franklyn's had to compensate for the distortion of light underwater by aiming where the fish appeared *not* to be.

There is no flash of the creature or any indication of contact, and when the harpoon's splash clears, the fish is out of sight.

Jim calls, "Did you hit it?"

Franklyn nods deeply. But on deck Justin holds the slack rope for a couple of seconds until it tightens and he confirms the unstoppable pull of a diving fish on it. Jim gasps, *"Damn—he did it!"*

Franklyn is displeased, saying, "I should have waited another second. It'll probably pull out. Don't know how the hell I hit that one. I hit it in the gut, and if it gets away it'll die." Justin finishes paying out the rope and hurls the buoys and high-flier.

The air cools, the light changes. As the sun nears the horizon, whales are much evident. Each time I scan the great circular stage that has become the world, I see a blow, a dark arching back, high flukes—sometimes two, three. Franklyn peeks at me from behind the pilothouse, nodding approval. Here where people once harpooned whales, harpooners simply watch them. Times change.

Franklyn says to me, "Glad you came. *Jesus,* I'm glad you came; it was the right place and the right trip. Finest kind. I'm glad we stayed out today." And then he pats me on the back, and this makes me feel accepted in an unexpected way.

We find our first flag and begin hauling the line. This is the big fish Justin had spotted when Franklyn didn't believe him; the one Jim relocated underwater. Jim comes down from the crow's nest for the first time in twelve hours. The only time all day that Jim has given his eyes anything like a rest were the brief, intense moments when Arthur was bearing down on a fish and Franklyn was about to dart it and Jim was just watching the action unfold. He's either been looking for Swordfish or looking *at* Swordfish every moment since climbing to the crow's nest this morning. When his feet hit the deck he says to me, "Great day, eh? Great to be alive."

It's a thought I hold as I gaze upon the dead Swordfish looming into view. Our biggest fish brings hoots of enthusiasm. Arthur gets a gaff-hook in the fish while Justin loops a rope around the flared base of its tail and winches the animal aboard, ripping one gill cover as it comes over the gunwale. He guides the fish onto the deck, then bleeds it in the usual way. When the fish seems dead, Justin touches it with his toe. Its huge tail comes up, then whumps the deck. It looked big in the water, and it is big. Jim says, "That's one of God's creatures, boy."

This fish's overall length exceeds ten feet. From fork of tail to point of lower jaw this animal measures ninety and a half inches, just over seven and a half feet; its bill, five inches wide at its base, adds another three feet, one inch; its crescent tail spans thirty-eight tip-to-tip inches wide; the dorsal stands eighteen and a half inches high; its hard-to-escape eye is fully three and a half inches in diameter. Weight? Jim tilts his head and estimates, "About three hundred and thirty pounds."

Justin says this fish is worth some bucks. Jim, nodding thoughtfully, takes the toothpick from his teeth and assesses, "Probably about two grand."

This fishery can be profitable on only one fish per day. Few forms of fishing can make that claim. Last trip they had nine Swordfish for the trip with dressed weights (no heads or guts) totaling 1,768 pounds. The per-pound price was a fishermen-pleasing $6.75. Bills are paid off the top. From what's left, each crew member gets 20 percent; the boat also gets a 20 percent cut. (That is to say, the boat owner takes 40 percent of the profit.) Franklyn says a couple of fish usually pay for fuel and the grub. Food for the trip costs $450. The last trip consumed 710 gallons of fuel, costing $1,100. So this one fish may take care of expenses.

Justin puts on a pair of overalls and boots. He cuts the pectoral fins, then relieves the carcass of its tail and its dorsal, like a logger limbing a tree. Next he cuts through the skull base. Grasping the bill and lifting upward, he snaps the formidable head from its body. Justin chocks the trunk of the fish so that it lies belly up. He slits the belly and gathers out the guts. Franklyn says admiringly, "Lots of crews, they use saws and axes and all this stuff. Look at Justin go with just a knife. He knows what he's doing."

Its stomach contains forty-two Short-Finned Squid, plus half a dozen fish that are probably Silver Hake, as well as a mackerel and a few herring. The squids are whole, the fishes slashed in half. Its stomach is also rather densely populated with a parasitic worm of some sort. Justin reaches into the blood pooled in the body cavity and retrieves the harpoon dart. Once he frees the entrails, the machinery that ran the fish is tossed overboard, whipping the shearwaters and fulmars into frenzied feasting.

Meanwhile we've reached the second set of gear, its line still bearing the weight of that chocolate-colored victim of Franklyn's last-ditch throw. Franklyn has directed that this lightly hit fish be hauled by hand, not winch. The fish comes up through a cloud of the first fish's blood. Still barely alive, it is feebly opening and closing its mouth, its sturdy fins twitching. Indeed, the dart under the skin is embedded only shallowly in muscle. This fish measures 107 inches with sword, nearly nine feet. It bears an old scar as from a pulled-out harpoon.

Jim falls promptly to cutting the second fish. He flashes me a grin. He's happier than a pig in the stuff that makes pigs happy. Our perimeter buzzes with the shearwaters' squeak-toy squabbles. They follow in our wake and clot into big rowdy bunches when something juicy goes into the water. They pull apart the guts and recycle the squid.

Recounting the day—how Jim saw the big fish deep, how Franklyn killed a fish instantly, how we stopped for a whale and saw that chocolate-colored fish, how Franklyn should have waited one more second rather than throwing, but how the dart held—goes on throughout dinner. They speak of the old days when there were so many Swordfish that hauling, cleaning, and icing continued well into night. Jim says there's nothing worse than working into darkness after a long day. Agreed, nothing worse. They speak of fishing and boats, of memorable fish caught or missed, of boats rolled and righted, of boats that sank because the captain overloaded them in the days when it was possible to catch too many fish. They remember those whose ashes are scattered on Georges Bank. They chuckle over boats reported overdue by anxious girlfriends whose men merely had no intention of coming in while the weather held, and of "channel fever" at the end of a trip, when with land in sight you start counting the time to the dock in minutes—"And the impatience doesn't come from your head." All this talk suits me. It bonds and helps burn the images to memory.

In the last little while a weather front has appeared in the southeast, heavy with cloud, suggesting that maybe as early as tomorrow, maybe the next day, the weather will turn the edge of Georges Bank into a Swordfish sanctuary for a few days. More Swordfish will move in here, and they'll find the food plentiful, the competition surprisingly sparse. Next time a south wind blows hard, warm water will push over the bank, and everything concentrated here will fan out and move on into the summer ripeness of mid-July. The harpooning season will be history.

Because of the forecast, half the fleet has swung their bows north for the ten-hour ride home. Because of the weather, half remain. In wind marginal for fishing, a rain squall pelts us. They're calling for scattered showers and thunderstorms. Franklyn announces, "Okay. Just like they do at Alcoholics Anonymous, we're going to make this a group decision." Not much of a decision, it seems to me. Ocean addicts all, we unanimously elect to stay and see what morning brings. I haven't gotten my eyes on one of those offshore Leatherbacks yet. And if the sun dawns on a fair sea, the last twenty-first-century mammoth hunters will be back along the edge, with their best eyes aloft. We'll take it one day at a time.

ANIMAL MAGNETISM

A sea turtle's life is a continuous series of migrations between distant feeding and breeding sites. One migration cycle, from breeding to feeding realms and back, often takes years. And unlike the familiar, well-patterned north-south migrations of birds, individual sea turtles from the same nesting beach may travel in different directions, ending up thousands of miles apart before returning to the same shared breeding ground. Therefore, staying oriented during months or years of traveling across an ocean so seemingly featureless as to numb a human mind is for turtles a constant, acute need.

Satellite tracks that remain essentially straight for weeks leave little doubt: turtles know where they're going. Sea turtles possess the same five senses we do, and add others. Out of water, their vision is blurred, like ours within water. Their smell is acute, helping them not only in food finding but also in homing in on nesting beaches. For major navigation, they can detect Earth's magnetic field and develop a "map sense" of where they are compared to somewhere else. (They may get lost, though, if you catch them and move them. So their sense of where they are may partly depend on their maintaining a continuous record of travel, as when we venture from our hotel and back in a new city.) Leatherbacks—again uniquely—have atop their otherwise dark, opaque heads that pink translucent spot above the thinnest part of the skull. Perhaps literally a window to the brain, it may facilitate the pineal gland's processing of light and day-length information, which could be integrated with their biological clock to help the animal assess its geographical position.

Many animals possess what, to us, are extrasensory abilities that let them know where in the world they are. They can orient, act appropriately, and navigate to a target thousands of miles distant. Birds use several sorts of cues, including stars and possibly patterns of polarized light. For shorter distances, some use scents, as do sea turtles and salmon nearing their breeding grounds. Certain mammals, many birds, reptiles, frogs and salamanders, fishes, insects—even some bacteria—can sense and use magnetic forces. These creatures possess the capability to respond to minute magnetic-field changes. How they do it remains, for us, somewhere beyond the horizon. But after decades of slow discovery, scientists are accruing some understanding.

Earth's magnetism arises from the conversion of mechanical energy to electrical energy—same as an automobile's generator—as molten iron oozes through Earth's deep fluid core. Several aspects of the field vary over the planet's surface. The magnetic field's "inclination" varies with latitude, meaning that magnetic-field lines intersect the planet's surface at reliable, consistent angles, ranging from zero degrees at the equator (parallel to Earth) to ninety degrees at the magnetic poles. Another feature is field intensity, which also varies in a consistent way over the planet's surface.

The long-term consistency is important because it provides fixed cues (despite flips in the field every few million years). Animals appear to use the magnetic field differently than a human-made compass, which merely aligns with the magnetic poles. Magnetic inclination and intensity lines make a grid of sorts. While wavy and not neat like lines of latitude and longitude, they form a unique combination at any given location. (This is a little like loran lines, which radiate from central broadcasting points but intersect to form unique combinations specific to any location, allowing loran receivers to identify their own position.) So the information is there.

Turtles can use that information. In indoor-pool experiments where computers can generate Earth-strength fields of varying inclinations and intensities, Ken and Catherine Lohmann presented Florida Loggerhead hatchings with magnetic conditions mimicking different places in the North Atlantic. Normally, baby Atlantic Loggerheads head directly into the huge, slowly pinwheeling Sargassum-weed-filled gyre stretching across much of the North Atlantic, and stay in it for a decade or so.

In the experiments, when exposed to a magnetic-inclination angle normally found on the northern boundary of the North Atlantic Gyre, the hatchlings swam south-southwest. If they reacted that way in nature, they would put themselves back into a more central location in the gyre. Exposed to an inclination angle found on the southern boundary of the gyre, they swam northeast (which, again, would put them back into a more central location in the gyre). When exposed to a field strength normally encountered off the Carolinas, they swam eastward—toward the gyre. Exposed to a field strength normally encountered off West Africa, they swam west—sending them, again, back toward the gyre. Exposed to inclinations found well within the gyre's central core, they didn't do much.

What I find stunning is that little hatchlings spring from their eggs as fully functional global-orientation systems, with multistage, self-correcting programming to get and keep them properly situated over the next span of years, all booted up and running within their first minutes out of the sand. When they leave the beach for what, to us, is a great unknown, they don't even need to know what to do; it comes with their autopilot.

Eventually, they turn back toward a shore hundreds or thousands of miles away, where they will breed. If female, they will likely ascend the beach they hatched from, and with that link their chain of being will become the circle of life.

Many of their nesting sites are tiny, isolated places. Homing works in reverse, too, as some species, after breeding, go back to familiar feeding spots on particular reefs or sea-grass beds. For such precise targeting of feeding and breeding sites, they need to know where they are relative to important places—using either an internal map or directions for getting from where they are to where they need to go. Exactly how animals acquire and sense such directions has been called "one of the most enduring and intriguing mysteries of animal behavior."

Scientists have two main hypotheses about animals' magnetic perception. One is that magnetite crystals interact with the nervous system to create an internal magnetic compass. The other is that some animals can see magnetic fields. Animals might use either or both. To see magnetic fields, some light—even if very faint—would be necessary. Yet even in total darkness turtle hatchlings in laboratories can orient and reorient to magnetic fields as they are experimentally shifted. So it appears that turtles have at least some nonvisual way of sensing magnetic fields and achieving magnetic orientation.

Sea turtles, bees, birds, salmon, and other species possess magnetite crystals arrayed into minute bar magnets. Studying how they work is difficult. In trout, certain magnetite-bearing cells in the snout connect to a branch of a particular nerve called the trigeminal. In a bird called the Bobolink, magnetite in the beak also receives a branch of the trigeminal nerve. This nerve responds to changes in magnetic-field intensity. So we seem to be getting close to understanding how animals build functioning compasses. We may someday understand the fine and exacting internal mechanisms and structures by which turtles and other animals achieve senses of orientation and navigation we ourselves wholly lack.

For now, we must content ourselves with pressing on along the migration route, hoping to catch up with the Leatherbacks that have already moved on, headed farther north.

NORTHEAST OF SUMMER

Cape Breton Island

You'll seldom read "sea turtles" and "frost" in the same sentence, but there you go; last night's forecast allowed the possibility. And when I step out into the bell-clear morning, Blue Jays ring through crystal.

A village of trim, colorful little houses backed by deep forest, Neil's Harbour lies at 47° north latitude near the northeast corner of Cape Breton Island, which itself lies in the northeast corner of Nova Scotia. Only three days ago it was still August, but the sun, seeming prematurely stooped toward winter, already shines diffusely on a place that feels northeast of summer.

Coastal Canada is a long reach from anything lush or sultry—or even particularly warm. No tropical languor here. This isn't a place you associate with sea turtles, and indeed the hard-shelled Greens, Loggerheads, Hawksbills, and Ridleys all remain in our distant wake far south or far offshore. This distance north, this deep inshore, in a class by itself as usual, only the Leatherback penetrates. The soft-shelled Leatherback is most hard-core.

Animals migrate for one reason: they need something that's somewhere else. The two main "somethings" are feeding or breeding. Here, it's food. Leatherbacks brave the Canadian cold because this refrigerator is stocked with jelly—Lion's Mane Jellies and Moon Jellies—at concentrations worth a five-thousand-kilometer (three-thousand-mile) swim. In some parts of the Leatherback's northern feeding range, the continental shelf is packed with food at densities of one meal per square meter. That's a lot of jellies.

At the wharf a sliver before seven A.M., the sun remains low and golden, the ocean flat. The sky, a September pale blue, floats light clouds.

Though the calendar retains nearly three weeks of summer, the air's autumnal tautness conjures the imminence of change.

Rows of big round crab traps ring the tiny harbor, where the sign at Victoria Fisheries Co-op features visages of American Lobster, Snow Crab, and Swordfish.

Like everyone else who sails from here, Captain Blair Fricker hasn't seen a Swordfish in years. The declines the Georges Bank harpooners complained about seem to have completely eliminated Swordfish on these inshore grounds. Notwithstanding, our scientific ringleader, Mike James, nods toward our captain, saying, "To look for Leatherbacks, go with an experienced Swordfish harpooner—they're the ones who see everything." Mike is a Ph.D. candidate from Nova Scotia's Dalhousie University, tall, blond and blue-eyed, loquacious and convivial.

Blair ignites *Wide Awake III*'s engine, and the loud, tooth-rattling diesel begins warming as we prep for departure. In his mid-thirties, Blair is wearing a green cap, a green slicker, green rubber boots.

An older, well-weathered fisherman walks over to help read the sky and send us off. He's a chipper, talkative old fellow, living partly in the cocoon of memory and partly in this crisp morning. As he's untying our dock lines, he comments, "When I was a kid out swordfishing with my father—around 1950, say—we didn't see turtles but maybe one a year. By the time we quit, we might see five or six on the same day. I'll tell you one thing: there's lots more turtles than there used to be. Swordfish, of course, well—. But turtles? You bet!"

Sounds good. We shove off and *Wide Awake III* peels from the wharf. Well-worn and unadorned, our thirty-foot workboat is decidedly no-frills. Everything about this vessel seems downsized, built with the narrowest or lightest-gauge materials, from its small wooden striker's stand extending only about ten feet from the bow (originally for swordfishing, now integral to catching turtles), to the light plywood of the deck and wheelhouse, to outer pilothouse handrails seemingly insufficient for the weight of men, to the aluminum bridge frame, rising only about ten feet off the water, whose seams cry out for reinforcement and a heavier gauge of pipe. I'm happy to mark the presence of a life raft, because while the boat impresses me as adequate for a day trip in fine weather, the mere possibility of getting caught in one of Cape Breton's god-awful gales sends me a shiver of fright.

Cheerfully discussing today's prospects, Mike says, "You really can sense when a pulse of turtles moves in. Sometimes it's overnight. But they don't stick around; a week later they'll be gone." Mike presumes that Leatherback movements are tied to movements of jellies, but unlike elsewhere, you don't really see jellyfish at the surface here. The only jellies you're likely to see here are already in the jaws of a Leatherback that has dragged one up from deeper water. With the water now as warm as it gets, the jellies are as big as they come. (They're annual animals; winter's cold kills them.) "I'm talking about some gargantuan jellies," Mike says. "Lion's Manes with a bell like a garbage-can lid, with tentacles long as the turtle." Lion's Mane Jellies, in fact, get incredibly large, maxing out with bells over seven feet across (two meters) and tentacles reportedly trailing as much as 250 feet (seventy-five meters). They are the world's largest "true" jellies (i.e., members of the phylum Cnidaria, which includes corals and anemones, wherein tiny venom-filled cells harpoon prey—and sting swimmers). Lion's Manes, Moon Jellies, and some of the other big stinging Leatherback fodder belong to a class called Scyphozoa. They develop after budding off from a bottom-resting life stage, usually in late winter (jelly life cycles are different from what we're used to). The bud becomes a free-swimming medusa (a.k.a. jellyfish), which spends spring and summer trolling for zooplankton and growing. After a maximum of about eight months they attain their most impressive heft; they spawn, then die.

Nobody knows precisely what the jellies are doing here. Extrapolating from the turtles' dive data, it seems the jellies swim at depths of 40 to 150 feet (12 to roughly 50 meters). Trivial distances when you think about it; a walk across a lawn can be farther. But because mere water is so impenetrable, really, to mere humans, Leatherbacks travel inside an envelope of unknowns. How they find food in depths beyond light penetration: unknown. How well they see, smell, or hear underwater: unknown. How they sense and use currents: unknown. Life span: unknown. Habits of juveniles: unknown. Distribution and behavior of food: unknown.

Leaning casually on the boat's gunwale, Mike comments, "That's something I really like about this work: discovering the basics of these animals. A turtle transmittered in Juno Beach, Florida, this spring is here in this area right now. We've seen Leatherbacks here that were tagged nesting in Trinidad, Panama, Costa Rica, French Guiana, and Suriname. We're pulling Leatherbacks from all over the western Atlantic. The picture that's emerging is: we're discovering a critically important feeding area."

In late spring, Leatherbacks come straight into Canadian waters from the south, then work northeast. That doesn't mean they're easy to find— as I learned on Georges Bank. The Scotian Shelf is also wide, its turtles often dispersed. Mike once spent twenty-one consecutive days off south- west Nova Scotia without seeing a turtle. "Imagine how depressing . . . ," he chuckles. "Then I moved up here—and things were different."

Geography makes the difference. Between Cape Breton Island and Newfoundland, the Laurentian Channel plows a massive seafloor gouge through that 150-mile-wide shelf. When the sea level was a few hundred feet lower than today, this was the mouth of the great river we now know as the St. Lawrence. Turtles follow the shelf edge's sharp northward jag along the channel, eventually finding themselves where the continental shelf is narrowest in all of Atlantic Canada—within twenty miles of Neil's Harbour. Mike proclaims, "It's really unique to have the shelf edge so close to shore."

But that's not the whole reason they're here. Mike explains further: "Leatherbacks pool here in Cabot Strait because the shape of the land means they can't go much farther—and there's a lot of food here." Once turtles swim this far, Newfoundland largely blocks continued northward travel and, because torrents of river water dilute the Gulf of St. Lawrence, prime Leatherback habitat pretty much ends here. Jellies concentrate here because the waters are enriched by deep channel water, which bathes the shelf edge, and by nutrients from the St. Lawrence River flowing out the gulf. The combination of attractive factors aggregates, amasses, and accumulates Leatherbacks until, by late summer, the place fairly swarms. These guys have seen between two and three dozen Leatherbacks in a sin- gle day, an almost unbelievable number of sightings for a boat lacking air support. "Bottom line is, this area probably has a higher density of Leatherbacks at this time of year than anywhere in the world," Mike says, adding, "You'll see what I mean—if the weather holds."

Our roaring diesel shakes and rattles our vibrating hull as we roll into a mild oncoming swell. We steer straight into the early sun on an ocean as level as these waters get—but the forecast has already deteriorated; winds are to strengthen this morning rather than hold their breath till af- ternoon. To the south rise the Cape Breton Highlands, their distantly forested slopes blued in early light. The world feels wide open and ex- pansive here, civilized yet uncrowded.

But the hand of humanity has fallen heavily in even these waters, as elsewhere. Though it's still the single-digit days of September, no other boat plies the wide sea. Cape Breton's fishing fleet already lies dormant, tied to the dock or hauled out for winter, victims of scarcity, seeking nei-ther sustenance nor pleasure. For turtles, that tragedy has one positive side: unlike New England or the Grand Banks, here in the late summer and fall there's no fishing gear or trap lines for Leatherbacks to tangle in. Mike observes, "This is a haven for them, a safe place to feed."

Like a Jurassic butterfly net, our turtle net—a five-by-six-foot rectangular frame on an eight-foot handle—lies readied. Its netting, cleverly rigged with Velcro ties, will detach from the frame under the strain of the world's largest reptile, forming a purse-stringed bag cinched around the monster, affixed to the boat by a length of substantial rope.

We plan a ten-mile run, to where turtles appeared yesterday, and we all move into positions advantageous for spotting swimming animals. Rather hazardously, there's no deck ladder to the bridge; you have to inch your way around the pilothouse with your boots on the edge of the boat, then step up to the roof, then step up again to the unpainted ply-wood platform of the flimsily framed aluminum bridge. It's easy and safe as long as the boat is in the harbor, tied securely to the dock.

For all our engine's sound and fury, our little boat is plodding forward at only about eight knots, perhaps ten miles an hour. So loud is the diesel that it plunges us into silence, canceling conversation, isolating us from one another despite close proximity.

For many long minutes we proceed to the rattly roar of the burdened diesel and the slap and splash of bow-cleaved water. An hour out, I see a glinting white fleck on the horizon suggestive of a bird, and my binocu-lars reveal a flock of perhaps two dozen Northern Gannets, wheeling, sweeping back their luminous nearly-six-foot wings, and falling in spec-tacular high-plunging dives, raising small geysers of glistening spray.

A three-masted sailing ship appears on the horizon, looking stately and placid and antique, well fitted to moving upon a sea surface void of com-pany, within sight of a landscape so innocent of human structure, so dom-inated by forests and rugged headlands. It might as well be the ghost of a ship that etched its wake here four hundred years ago, when vast herds of big Atlantic Cod cluttered the seafloor beneath our keels. That was the most valuable, most important fishery in the world, drawing nations across the ocean, fueling their hemispheric ambitions, the arc of its history summed up by the absence of fishing boats on so fine a morning.

Nowadays the legal fisheries here are lobstering, snow-crabbing, and a modest quota for Atlantic Halibut. Yelling over the engine, Blair says that since the drag-netters were banned from these waters, the halibut seem to be increasing—a lot of little halibut around, "little" being ten pounds in a species that can exceed a quarter ton. People fishing for halibut now do so with lines perhaps five miles long, carrying thousands of baited hooks and sunk to the bottom. This area has been closed to codfishing for a decade, although boats fishing halibut are allowed a ton a week of incidentally caught cod. Then they're supposed to stop fishing. But Blair, still shouting, reveals that to keep fishing for halibut, "a lot of the boats cut their cod in half before tossing them overboard, to make sure they sink, so the patrol plane doesn't see them." Lobstering runs May 15 to July 15; fishermen may keep as many lobsters as they catch. Snow-crabbing spans July 15 to September 15, but crabbing is limited by individual quota. This year Blair caught his annual crab quota in nine days.

After the fishing season the water looks void as Day One. The fishermen do no recreational boating. No one seems to own a sailboat, and there's essentially no rod-and-reel fishing. Blair has a hard time imagining that in Cape Cod Bay there are enough recreational boats that they sometimes hit turtles. He's seen a photo Mike has of a Leatherback that looks like it went through an egg slicer, but it's a stretch for him to picture what that many boats looks like. Recreational boats—people out on the water simply for the fun of it—you just don't see that around here. What does everyone do most of the year? Blair explains: "Drink beer, watch movies, chase women." Since Neil's Harbour is more a settlement than a town, and since Blair, with a shrug, estimates the population at "maybe four hundred," I imagine that translates mostly into beer and movies. Blair also hunts Harp Seals during winter, shooting them on ice floes or in the water. I hesitate to ask, but he says, "Most of the ones shot in the water float, especially early in the season when they've got a lot of fat on them." They're skinned for their coats—the furs go mainly to China; the rest gets discarded.

At around eight-thirty, Blair eases the throttle. The engine's rattling roar growls down, sending a thrill of alert anticipation: we're in the area. We've reached the range turtles have been in, about eighty fathoms of water under the sky.

Instinctively we begin searching, and though we can finally hear, we fall silent. We scrutinize the wrinkled blue sea, scanning just-arisen whitecaps. Blair spins the small wooden wheel to swing us northwest, putting both the climbing sun and the rising wind behind us, easing the squint, gentling our progress afore a following sea. We're throttled way down, crawling along, walking speed, the three of us hunting from the plywood platform of the bridge. In shafts of bright sun the sea from this vantage appears green. When the sun exits offstage behind curtains of cloud, the ocean turns a very dark blue.

The distant island of St. Paul pierces the horizon, a place notorious for rough waters and forbidding cliffs. Blair intones, "No one lives there, but a lot of people have died there." Mike comments that one of his transmittered turtles is now foraging near there. Far ahead, about twenty miles up the coast, rises Cape North's thousand-foot profile. Just past the cape, a long line of unusual clouds occupies the horizon like the heralding headlands of a heavenly continent. Blair once thought heaven close at hand there indeed, when a wave destroyed the boat he was in.

We begin making quartering zigzags, partly to cover a wider swath, partly to keep the diesel's nauseating exhaust from continually enveloping us.

A loon flies by, heading south, fleeing winter while it's still summer. I zip my jacket against the cold. Despite the date, I'm wearing three top layers, my regular pants covered with fleece pants, and calf-high rubber boots. Leatherbacks ply these waters mostly between June and October. But—I find this astonishing—they have now been sighted in Canadian waters every month of the year. "Low numbers," Mike clarifies, "but there *are* a few here in winter." Off Newfoundland, one Leatherback was seen swimming in water freezing up, slushy with ice. Mike's unnecessary comment: "Maybe we're underestimating their body-warming capability."

Hundreds of miles south of here, Loggerheads, Greens, and Ridleys get stunned and immobilized by cold—sometimes fatally—if trapped in bays when autumn waters dip merely below 50 degrees Fahrenheit. To stop a Leatherback you have to hit it with a lot more cold. They've been seen swimming around icebergs in the Barents Sea in saltwater 0 degrees Celsius (32° F). Mike has a photo of a freshly dead Leatherback loaded onto a snowmobile, surrounded by snowdrifts. It looks surreal, superimposed, like a researcher's joking Christmas card. Chanced upon in Northumberland Strait in January, it was probably having difficulty finding its way back out when it was finally overcome, long after cold would have fatally clenched a lesser turtle.

Among reptiles, Leatherbacks possess unparalleled ability to penetrate bone-achingly cold water. Leatherbacks have been seen off Iceland,

Alaska, and Norway, beyond the Arctic Circle at 71° north latitude. And there exists a soapstone carving from Baffin Island's Cape Dorset, on the north side of the Hudson Strait (65° N), of what appears to be a Leatherback that must have overwhelmed its Inuit discoverer with awed wonder. Before overfishing demolished the Bluefin Tuna, North Sea fishermen netted the magnificent fish as far north as Norway, and occasionally found a Leatherback in the net along with them.

Mike has never seen a juvenile Leatherback up here with a shell smaller than a meter in length. The smaller turtles can't take the cold. The bigger and rounder a body is, the better it conserves heat. That's why Leatherbacks are the most cylindrical turtles. It's also why Leatherbacks *grow* large—to go where no turtle can and exploit a cold-water food source unavailable to cold-blooded reptiles. (Uniquely among turtles, for fueling rapid growth Leatherbacks' bones are tipped with thick cartilage, packed with blood vessels supplying nutrients. Same as mammals'.) The Leatherback is apparently the world's heaviest wild reptile (captive Saltwater Crocodiles notwithstanding). The largest Leatherback ever recorded, a male washed ashore in Wales in 1988 after tangling in whelk trap lines and drowning, weighed just over a ton (916 kilograms). Its foreflippers, tip to flipper tip, spanned nine feet (277 centimeters). Nose to tail along its belly it measured eight and a half feet (259 centimeters). Why be so massive if you're only eating jelly? Size gives Leatherbacks the widest distribution of any animal in the world except *some* of the great whales. For migratory animals, size is time, and time is distance. Large bodies can store enough energy to go from one feeding oasis to another across long stretches without food. If you're really big you can cover big distances. If you're an anchovy, you can't cross an ocean to get to the next patch of food; if you're a Leatherback, you can.

After exactly one hour's searching, Blair claims credibly that he believes he's just seen a turtle—ahead, couple of hundred yards.

I don't see anything.

He guns the groaning engine and we move closer.

When we arrive on the spot, I see—nothing.

Mike says, "Turtles here often dive five to seven minutes; the other day we waited fifteen minutes for a turtle that eventually surfaced."

Wait we do. We turn into the whitecaps and creep forward, trying not to let the wind drift us too far. Blair is sure he saw something, "Either a turtle or a seal, but I've not seen many seals here."

When, after fifteen minutes, no animal shows, we break off the search. Mike believes Blair saw a turtle. Sometimes, they just give you the slip.

Half an hour later, White-Sided Dolphins appear, running in and out of the surface as though stitching their way across the sea.

We turn southeast again, but plunging into what has built to a white-capped chop will not do, and a few minutes later we are again swung northward, working downsea.

At eleven o'clock I notice two small, grayish Red-Necked Phalaropes, their necks already winter white, sitting on the water amid the rocking waves and whitecaps. These small, delicately featured tundra-nesting shore-birds look utterly improbable upon the open ocean. Yet here they spend their winter, as though toughing out an undeserved punishment.

The engine drones along, the boat rocks on, and after a while I must remind myself that if I close my eyes I'll never spot the first turtle.

At eleven-thirty Blair discovers an Ocean Sunfish basking on its side, awash—several hundred pounds of life, looking more like a reflected full moon than a fish. Twenty minutes later, Blair sights another fin. This is no sunfish. There's a dorsal and a tail—and the tail is stiff. Blair guns excitedly toward what might be the first Swordfish he's seen in years.

Blair killed his last Swordfish in 1986 and hasn't even seen one in a decade, but so extreme is his addiction that not one or two but *three* harpoon poles remain aboard, including one all rigged with dart, line, and buoys attached, ready to go should he see another Swordfish before he dies. Blair's always searching for a Swordfish, as though trying to find that lost piece of himself, and he might have just scared up a ghost.

But I can see that optimism is interfering with his vision; the first dorsal is rounded, certainly a shark's. Most likely here are Blue Sharks, but with the stiff tail I'm seeing, this is no blue dog. The makos, Great White, and the gigantic Basking Shark have stiff tails. Coming upon it, we recognize the latter. This awesome beast is fully fifteen feet long, probably a couple of tons, and Blair says, "That's the smallest Basking Shark I've ever seen."

In this sea of half-ton turtles, a fifteen-foot shark can be "small."

As the boat approaches, the juvenile giant drifts dreamily downward, its dark shape eventually seeming to spread and merge among the sea's shadows, like dark ink dissolving.

Blair is disappointed. "It's a pretty sad thing nowadays for a fisherman like me; you go out on the ocean and the endangered species is here, but the Swordfish is gone." He adds, "And we've been out all week and seen, what, one shark? We used to see fifty or sixty sharks a *day*. Makos, Blue Sharks, Porbeagles... Once the long-liners started, they went down real fast. I guess it's the same all over now." Directing a surprise question to me, he adds, "Is that what you find?"

I nod. I find much the same all over. I do. But if there are more turtles here than fifty years ago, that is hope enough for now. Fifty years from now, the children of these men may yet have stories of Swordfish and sharks, *and* turtles, but that depends on whether we accomplish what it takes to merely let the ocean do what it knows how to do.

An hour further into our search we hear a sudden crack followed by a metallic *clunk*. Two of the four welds on the flimsy-looking tower have suddenly broken, and we have to scramble off the bridge before it collapses and dumps us either overboard or onto the deck. Our search so ignominiously aborted, we hurry home to call the welder.

HARD-DRIVING RAIN HAS TREES SHAKING TO THEIR ROOTS, AND THE welder hopes to get to our bridge frame this morning if he can. With no weather and no welder, we're marooned.

I find the cottage Mike's renting. Mike's landlocked Ontario boyhood spawned his interest in freshwater turtles, and he arrived in Nova Scotia expecting to start research on the threatened Blanding's Turtle. He soon caught wind of tantalizing rumors: ocean fishermen claiming they'd seen live Leatherbacks. Mike got fascinated, but most scientists didn't believe sea turtles lived here, and no one supported him. Leatherbacks were considered extremely rare strays in Canadian waters; Nova Scotia and Newfoundland combined had fewer than eighty officially documented occurrences in the century-plus since 1897. Those that got this far—the thinking went—must be hopelessly lost, doomed. In 1981 one scientist wrote, "There is no proof that Leatherbacks that come this far north actually find their way south to breed again."

Mike says, "I didn't know how to get near it." Researchers dismissed him with comments like "Sea turtles live in the tropics—go there." But he thought, "Do I really want to work on pond turtles before I at least talk to fishermen about the ultimate turtle?"

He talked, and fishermen talked back. With a small grant from the World Wildlife Fund, Mike drove all around Nova Scotia one summer, stopping at over three hundred fishing wharves; conferring and conversing, tacking up LEATHERBACK WANTED posters at docks, fish plants, and waterside coffee shops, and asking fishermen to be on the lookout for sea turtles; he distributed lots of point-and-shoot cameras. Mike remembers, "We said to fishermen, 'Most people don't believe sea turtles exist in our coastal waters. Prove 'em wrong.' " Within days, the phone started ringing. He had well over two hundred sightings that first season, many with confirming photos.

Mike next ventured to the annual International Sea Turtle Symposium, where his new proof that Leatherbacks were regular summer inhabitants of Canadian waters immediately surprised the scientific community. The conference afforded Mike sudden access to top sea turtle researchers. "I knew Scott Eckert was *the* name for satellite-tracking Leatherbacks, so I was chasing after him, trying to get his attention for a few minutes." They discussed tracking males—something you can't do from nesting beaches.

Mike adds, "Mind you, I still hadn't even *seen* a Leatherback. But after the meeting Scott Eckert sent me a transmitter." Next, Mike needed a plan for capturing half-ton turtles in water one hundred fathoms deep. He recalls, "Fishermen said, 'You'll never get near one'; 'You don't *want* to go near one'; 'They'll bite'; 'They'll tear your arm off!' " But Mike decided to try.

Things started slowly, but he'd been hearing of turtles off Cape Breton Island. So Mike arrived in Neil's Harbour with the Jurassic net strapped on the roof of his car, asking people to help him catch a turtle. "Everyone thought I was crazy," he says. "Some still do." But someone directed him to Blair Fricker and his brother Bert. "After they stopped laughing," Mike remembers, "they said, 'Sure.' "

They were going halibut fishing the next day and told him to meet them at the boat at three in the morning. On the way there, Mike got pulled over at a drunk-driver checkpoint. The policeman took one look at that huge net on his roof and concluded the obvious: Mike was a nut. But insanity is both legal and a defense, so Mike eluded arrest. That first day out, he saw five turtles: "My first good looks at live, swimming Leatherbacks. I was floored."

As we sit down at his computer Mike is saying, "We originally imagined Leatherbacks migrating into Canadian waters during a certain time of year via a certain migration 'corridor' along which they all moved, then exiting our waters again at a certain time of year, again via a corridor—a regular, orderly migration."

I'm envisioning turtles moving through the sea like birds along a flyway. "What I'm going to show you on the computer here in the next little while is, that's not really the case. So—." Mike waves his cursor, and an ocean full of spaghetti appears on the screen. "Okay, these are the active tracks for all eleven devices we put on turtles this year." As an aside he notes, "They're all still working, which is encouraging." He clicks his mouse to pick out one track, and displays it on the screen. Mike explains, "So here's one, for instance, who, as of five thirty-one this morning, is at 41°31' and 65°31'—about the latitude of New York City but way offshore, on a path toward Bermuda."

Mike's fastest Leatherback covered 120 kilometers (75 miles) in a day. "You never see that while they're foraging here. You only see that kind of movement in the first burst, which gets them off the shelf." Then they usually go thirty to fifty kilometers a day.

Mike studies the southbound track and says a little abruptly, "The Leatherback is a *totally* different animal in the south. They don't dive the same way, they don't surface the same way. You'll see in a moment."

He clicks a graph onto the screen. "Here's data from one of our tracked animals. In these northern feeding areas, it's spending a quarter of the day right at the surface. Then, look, it goes down south, and—this is still the same Leatherback, believe it or not—it's not a surface animal *at all*—only one to three percent of its time at the surface. You'd never be able to catch them at sea there; you'd never see them, because they're almost always underwater."

I pull my chair a little closer to the computer screen. In the 1950s Dr. Archie Carr tried to see where turtles go by attaching helium-filled balloons to females leaving the beach. If he were sitting here right now, he'd be slack-jawed.

"Here on the foraging grounds, its dives average twelve minutes or so. The instant it leaves the northern feeding areas—look—*totally* different diving behavior: most dives at least thirty minutes underwater. That doesn't mean it's deep all the time. During migration they swim for long periods just a few feet under the surface.

"Traveling farther south, it begins diving deeper. Here in the northern foraging areas, it's spending quite a bit of time in shallower dives, average maybe between twenty and thirty meters. Then in southern waters, it occasionally goes very deep—like this dive—to four hundred and fifty meters."

I look at Mike. That's fifteen hundred feet of crushing cold and blackness, a depth that would be instantly fatal to a person.

He just shakes his head, saying, "I can't explain that."

I ask what they do at night.

"Our data shows little difference, day versus night."

Males and females?

"Males make marathon migrations similar to females. Converging near nesting areas is probably the best way to meet females." In the gentle, placid life that is a sea turtle's, lovemaking is the roughest thing they do. Males chase and grab, biting, trying to hook on with the longer, curved claws on the leading edge of their front flippers (except the clawless Leatherback). An unimpressed female may twist and resist, covering her portal with her flippers or diving to the seafloor. Other males attempt to charge and dislodge. Females are usually receptive just a month before egg laying, and for a day after laying each clutch. If the female accepts and the disturbance is minimal, the male curls his extra-long tail under her shell and, with his penis protruded, injects his sperm into her cloaca. Their hours-long embrace probably led to the widespread belief that consuming turtle parts enhances sexual performance. Females store sperm until they ovulate. Both males and females mate with multiple partners, and it's not unusual for hatchlings in the same clutch to have different fathers.

Mike noodles around with the computer mouse, teasing out individual tracks on the monitor. "We do have two in the Gulf of St. Lawrence at the moment, near the Madeleine Islands. There are still several around St. Paul; several we tagged in July off southwest Nova are now up here."

Mike shows one from last year, saying, "This turtle here really surprised me." He sits back while I study the track.

From Nova Scotia it headed south, passing east of Bermuda, then turned into the Caribbean, went around Cuba, swam north at the edge of the Gulf Stream until it cut in to the shelf edge seventy miles off New Jersey around Hudson Canyon, then continued working farther and farther north through New England.

Mike summons another track to the screen. "Now, here's a gigantic male whose travels are highly unusual—the only one we've ever seen doing this. We transmittered him right off here. He went up into the Gulf of St. Lawrence, around Prince Edward Island. But then he made three attempts to go south through the Strait of Canso, which used to be open water until around 1960, when it was closed by a lock. There's no free water flow anymore. Well, this turtle swam right to the causeway three times like it was expecting to go through. And then he just hugged the coast as though looking for an accustomed shortcut. He finally left and went to the Caribbean."

Mike goes back to the squiggly track lines that scrawl their unimaginable journeys across the ocean map. "Look, here's an interesting track: this turtle made this *big* migration from here past the Caribbean, swinging out about five hundred miles off northern South America, turning back north, passing Bermuda, and coming straight around Cape Breton Island and into the Gulf of St. Lawrence. After summer here, it went straight back down the middle of the Atlantic Ocean."

But, it turns out, this is not unusual. People once assumed all Leatherbacks coming and going from Caribbean nesting areas migrated along the United States coast. Mike's found otherwise. His departing turtles strike straight south across deep, open ocean, then turn into breeding areas. "After nesting," Mike explains, "they truck back up across deep mid-ocean, not the coastal United States." Leatherbacks from the Caribbean also appear in British waters at this same time of year. Possibly some African nesters may be there too. "But," emphasizes Mike, "what I really think is: individual Leatherbacks return repeatedly to the same foraging areas. Based on what we've already seen, I don't expect animals we tag here to go to Europe in a different year.

"Bottom line is," he adds, "every animal we've tracked, this has always been their final northern destination. When they're done feeding here, that's it for feeding in the north. They're headed out; they're leaving for the year. And it looks like if you're a Canadian-foraging Leatherback, you're gonna come back to Canadian waters."

An animal this big needs food to keep going; how are they finding concentrations of jellies? Mike raises a finger as if to say "Glad you asked," and calls up a track of an animal doing two big loops off the Northeast Peak of Georges Bank at the mouth of Northeast Channel, right where it meets the edge of the shelf.

I look at the track and wonder why it's doing this.

Mike says, "So you look at the behavior, and you wonder *why* it's doing this." The next click displays a map showing sea-surface temperature. "See him riding up and around the edge of this warm ring of water? We've also seen them around edges of cold-core rings."

The rings are broken-off chunks and filaments of the Gulf Stream, whirling toward the continent like slow-motion cyclones of water. We saw this on the slopes of Georges Bank. The friction between the colliding warm and cool water masses helps concentrate food along the boundary. There the blue ocean meets that green tint, visible to experienced fishers and photographic satellites alike, detectable to certain seabirds by scent

One Year's Travels of 2 Leatherbacks
from Nova Scotia • tracked by Mike James

from leagues away, as Serengeti Wildebeest can smell rain from great distances across the vast vault of dry sky. Soon come other animals, who further link and lengthen the food chain—jellyfish, squids, and small fishes. And we've experienced how they in turn draw the appetites of dolphins, whales, tunas, and, of course, Leatherbacks—and Swordfish.

"And *that's* why Leatherbacks get tangled in longlines set for Swordfish," Mike concludes. At the northeast portion of the Grand Banks called the Flemish Cap, where the cold Labrador Current collides with the Gulf Stream, the fronts of sharply contrasting warm and cold water spark food concentrations so attractive to both Leatherbacks and Swordfish that longliners there have at times averaged one Leatherback Turtle each time they set their fishing gear.

When Mike displays the travels of twenty-seven turtles, all together, the confetti of their tracks coalesces into a little more scientific magic. I *see* what their vast travels are about. And here it is: a very few fronts are sufficiently reliable to hold food enough for long enough to draw turtles across an ocean. Like desert watering holes, these feeding "holes" are the destinations. All else is open road, a furrow in the dust, a fingernail scratching through water on the way to something big.

Those few big ocean-feedlot foraging hot spots are: right here in Cabot Strait, the deep continental slope waters between Georges Bank's northeast peak and the southwest Scotian Shelf, the Grand Banks, a lesser area south of Cape Cod, and—in early spring while Canadian waters remain frigid—off South Carolina and Georgia (where I flew with Sally Murphy). For the western half of the North Atlantic, that's about it. The only other destinations are breeding grounds. In between, they're constantly migrating.

"Our turtles cover the whole western Atlantic," Mike confirms, "but as you can see, all they mainly care about is the water north of 40° and their breeding areas. So, in Canadian waters, you get turtles pooling off Georges Bank, then working north and east—feeding, feeding, feeding—then out, south."

Across long, hungering distances of empty water, a handful of ocean oases draw the sea's nomads, those great wanderers striving to survive from one watering hole to the next in the great frenzied chain of being: turtles and fish and seabirds—and people.

Mike makes a few clicks and his screen again displays the western North Atlantic Ocean. But this time the noodles of turtle tracks are gone;

this map has polka dots. Mike explains, "This shows longline effort." Each dot represents a fishing boat's longline deployment. Each deployment: a line about thirty miles long with a thousand or so baited hooks, usually set to drift overnight. Much fishing concentrates in frontal zones 75 to 125 miles or so offshore, where the drowned underwater skirt of the continent plunges to the deep ocean basin along its ruffled edge. So numerous, overlapping, and dense are the polka dots that they make one big smear along the edge of the continental shelf all the way up the map, a swarm representing millions of baited hooks.

Mike displays more data. "This shows turtles caught per million hooks set for Swordfish and tuna." From the shelf edge off the mid-Atlantic states to southern New England where turtles are migrating, the boats catch a few tens of Leatherbacks per million hooks. But on the Grand Banks, a destination where turtles feed for months, Mike points the cursor, saying, "See? Hundreds of turtles per million hooks. That's just Leatherbacks." *Click.* "Look at Loggerheads—thousands of Loggerheads per million hooks." Mike concludes, "In the west Atlantic, Grand Banks is *the* hot spot for turtles getting snagged in fishing gear."

Long-lining for tunas and Swordfish started in the late 1950s and began spreading worldwide around 1960. Japan and Taiwan each take about 30 percent of the global catch. No other single nation catches more than 7 percent of the longline total. Worldwide, pelagic longlines catch 85 percent of Swordfish landed and more than 60 percent of Bigeye and Albacore Tuna taken annually, totaling more than 680,000 metric tons. Their catch rates have declined precipitously over the last decades, but the number of boats working skyrocketed in recent years.

Every day, forty nations' tuna and swordfishing boats stream four million baited hooks into the world's warm water on one hundred thousand miles of line—1.4 billion hooks a year. That's not counting boats in the chilly albatross latitudes, targeting toothfishes (sold to you as "Chilean seabass") or cold-water halibut or various cods, or small-scale warm-water boats, which add many millions more hooks.

Into this minefield glides a turtle. Even averaging one mile an hour, a turtle can swim three hundred miles in under two weeks, passing over, around, or through a lot of fishing gear in major Leatherback feeding and migration areas worldwide. The Atlantic's Leatherback-frequented Grand Banks and the Cape Verde Islands are both fishing hot spots. Turtles commuting to the Pacific's most important remaining Leatherback nesting rookeries, on New Guinea, must also go through a particularly dense gauntlet between Indonesia and the Philippines. After nesting, Pacific Leatherback turtles swimming east to North America must enter another fishing-gear gauntlet in the central equatorial Pacific. A turtle that is supposed to swim for several decades has ample opportunity to run afoul.

Getting caught doesn't necessarily mean getting killed. A 2004 study by Duke University researchers estimated that after growing large enough to run afoul of longline fishing gear, the average Leatherback or Loggerhead will likely get caught every other year of its life. The Duke scientists concluded that longlines annually arrest about fifty thousand Leatherbacks and a quarter million Loggerheads. They weren't sure how many get killed in the Atlantic, but estimated that in the Pacific over four thousand Loggerheads and about two thousand Leatherbacks die this way. More Leatherback and Loggerhead Turtles are killed each year—many of them juveniles—than dig nests.

The lines also snag mammals. But how many oceanwide, and whether it affects overall numbers, no one yet knows. Around Hawaii, just as one example, longlines catch several dozen mammals a year. These include both common and little-known species, including the Short-finned Pilot Whale, Blainville's Beaked Whale, the False Killer Whale, Risso's Dolphin, Bottlenose, Spotted, Common, and Spinner Dolphins, and Humpback and Sperm Whales. This is nothing like the drowning of several hundred thousand dolphins a year in tuna nets in the name of "tunafish" sandwiches between the 1960s and 1980s. But I find it distressing, as if the ocean is a fishing-gear spiderweb.

As we've seen, many of the turtles surviving the encounters bear visible testimony. A few more clicks and Mike launches a photo gallery. As the first image opens, Mike says, "When we saw this animal, its head was pulled over to the right. We captured it and found it had a longline hook embedded in his shoulder and had actually swallowed sixteen feet of the fishing line. We were reluctant to pull on the line too hard because we didn't want to do more damage. But when we did pull, it came right out."

This reminds me of Kelly Stewart's Juno Beach Leatherback named Pesca, who also had a hook in her shoulder and had swallowed a lot of line. I ask if Mike's ever seen another like that.

"One other had an embedded hook in its shoulder. We see a lot of scars around their heads and shoulders and chafes on the leading edge of their shell, from entanglement. I'd say we see that in, maybe, fifteen percent of turtles."

Mike comments on Leatherbacks' well-known propensity to tangle in lines and ropes: sailboat moorings, fishing lines, lobster-trap buoy lines—everything. If they get one flipper wrapped they seem to panic, sometimes winding the line very tight, or wrapping a figure-eight around themselves. Sometimes they start dragging a lobster trap and it tangles other traps until, dragging all that stuff around, they drown. He's heard that in New England there's so much gear it can't be easy for a Leatherback to swim through it all.

Mike clicks open another photo. "This particular animal had tangled well over one hundred feet of quarter-inch line. If they can get free and their limbs are alive, they appear to heal really quickly. If they've been tangled tight a long time they can lose a flipper." He clicks to an animal missing its entire left front flipper and comments, "She's alive."

A Leatherback surviving with one front flipper seems unbelievable, like a wild bird surviving with one wing.

Mike looks thoughtful for a moment, then offers, "I can only guess that the rear flippers can be very powerful rudders." Looking at the image again, he continues: "She seemed healthy. But without that flipper, nesting is out of the question for her. And you can see white scarring around the base of the one remaining flipper and her neck. So she was probably pretty looped up." Still staring at the photo he comments, "She's probably lucky; probably an animal like this would usually die."

Among dead, washed-up Leatherbacks, Mike sees a *lot* of entanglement. He adds, "As long as rope is flexible and can be coiled—which is what rope *is*—it can tangle a turtle. It's not easy to solve; no one wants to catch the animals, but fishermen want to make a living—and that's a fair goal, too." He notes, "There's a lot of goodwill around Atlantic Canada among fishermen towards Leatherbacks; they'll usually take the trouble to release them unharmed if they find them tangled, and try to make sure they're all right."

I'm glad to think this. But turtles can't rely on Canadian goodwill if the gear is the killer. Fishing needs more than good intentions; it needs invention. It needs new techniques, new tools, new motivation.

How many turtles die after release remains unknown. A Loggerhead and an Olive Ridley bearing deeply ingested hooks lived at least 458 days and 193 days, respectively, until their transmitters stopped reporting. So some survive for extended periods; no doubt others do not. In

2001 the U.S. National Marine Fisheries Service assumed that up to half of released sea turtles died of hook wounds and line damage, and that U.S. Atlantic longlines therefore killed about 150 to 500 Leatherbacks per year. But the estimate was obviously rough, and new fishing techniques can change the death rate, reducing injuries and improving after-release survival. Where skippers are using new hooks and release techniques designed to avoid turtles and help snagged turtles survive, turtles that are caught on longlines seldom arrive at the boat dead. For instance, on U.S. Atlantic longline trips in 2001 and 2002, federal observers on boats experimenting with new techniques to reduce turtle deaths tallied over three hundred Leatherbacks and nearly three hundred Loggerheads caught; only one of each came up dead. In a Brazilian study, by contrast, 15 percent of the Loggerheads and 10 percent of the Leatherbacks were dead on arrival.

WE'RE GOING TO GAIN A DAY WE DIDN'T COUNT ON. THE FORECASTED all-day windy rain actually abated by noon, and by three o'clock the newly refabricated tower is back from the welder and on the boat, nicely reinforced. Blair's brother Bert has joined us. We have about five hours of usable light, and we intend to squeeze the most from it.

Barely five minutes out of the harbor, a chunky sunfish the size of a car hood greets us like a big round animated welcome mat, just another hallucination conjured from this ocean of jolly giants, another wonder from underland. Five minutes later, a second wags an oddly bent fin at us. Sunfish so soon suggests heightened chances for a turtle. We're getting stoked.

We speak approvingly of the nearly slick ocean, the lifting but still solid cloud cover making the sea lighter yet glareless. For a fuller description of these conditions, see the word *perfect*.

Yesterday we had to try to find a blue-black turtle in a blue-black whitecapped sea. Not easy. Today we have to find a blue-black turtle in a silver sea that lies calm as a nicely made bed. Mike proclaims, "We'd see a turtle's head in *this*."

The sky and clouds gleam with the kind of dramatic poststorm light that appears only over open water. The changeability of such magnificent illumination lends immediacy to the moment. It's the kind of light and air that lets you forget you are anyplace but here, makes you feel you're everywhere, reminding you how exquisite is the opportunity from such air to draw breath.

I'm sitting on the cabin roof; the other three guys are on the bridge just above my head. By the time we're out about seven miles we've stopped seeing much of anything and I'm starting to wonder if we're actually anywhere or nowhere, and whether we should have stayed buddied up inshore with the giant sunfish. At least there was a little life there. Then I see something dark in the water ahead and look up to the people above me. They already see it. The boat turns toward it. Suddenly its head comes out, followed by a black back.

A seal.

We begin seeing little patches of "nervous water" where schools of small fish—"Those're mackerel"—are pressed to the surface by their own fear of what lurks unseen below. Their ancestral fears of sharks and Swordfish are getting them uptight for no reason. Some run crazily away as the boat approaches. If they had any sense they would receive humans as liberators, since we are the enemies of their enemies. But they do as well not to trust us.

A Greater Shearwater glides in and slides below the surface in a patch of ruffling water about fifty yards in diameter. Soon another shearwater, traveling alone on the wide sea, sails into view. Yesterday nowhere to be seen, these wandering cousins of albatrosses arrived overnight, riding the hurricane remnants that so unsettled our skies during the night and morning. Also new today and likely gone tomorrow, a Wilson's Storm-Petrel flutters nearby, foot-pattering and half-hovering in its busy plankton pickings. I enjoy the birds' transient company and our shared sense of quest.

After forty minutes of continual water and changing sky, Mike shouts and points. The glimpse I get is both momentary and instantly unmistakable: that blue-black watermelon of a head withdrawing, followed by a deep boil as it massively vanishes.

Bert scrambles into the striker stand with the Jurassic net. Mike hurries behind him, stationing himself in the bow, holding on to the rope that purses the net. Blair idles the vessel in the windless calm.

Six minutes.

Bert says, "He must have found something to eat, or he'd be up by now."

Ten minutes.

Bert calls up to Blair, "You don't suppose it could have surfaced in water this slick without us seeing it, do you?"

Sixteen minutes.

Muttering, Bert lays down the net and climbs back to the bridge. Blair puts the boat in gear.

For people who are still carrying harpoons in readiness for the Swordfish they haven't seen in a decade, this strikes me as uncharacteristically short on patience. I'd have stayed another ten minutes.

But there is method. Mike explains, "If you stay in one spot and the animal is moving north, as they usually are right here, by the time it decides to surface you may miss it. So we're just trying to creep north, hoping it comes up where we can see it."

I must look skeptical, because Mike acknowledges, "But that one kinda looked like it was headed south, so . . ." He adds, "We'll work this area thoroughly. There's at least one turtle here. There should be others."

A soft, stippling breeze summons light rain. Soon there's rain enough to dissolve the coastal headlands that minutes ago rose so startlingly. The day ebbs from dreamy to dreary as my hopes for a turtle fade with the light.

Ten minutes later Blair shifts abruptly into neutral; he thinks he's seen something. We scan intently ahead, abeam, and aback. After a few minutes Blair has bumped the boat back into gear to continue when, almost before I realize it, I shout, "Right here! Right here! Eleven o'clock, fifty feet."

Well before I've gotten all that verbiage into the air the boat is already moving up on the animal.

It vanishes.

But in less than a minute, it resurfaces, even closer. Bert and Mike are scrambling into position.

Blair calls, "You ready?"

"Yup," Bert says intently.

There the turtle is, straight ahead, raising that big dark mechanical-monster head and the broad, ridged shield of its back.

We creep forward. Bert calls, "A little closer, Blair."

As the stand sneaks up over the creature, Bert plunges the net directly before the animal. It startles, and in the next half instant the monster is diving through the hoop. As the turtle snaps the net away from the frame, Mike tightens the cinching rope.

"*Pull! Pull!*" Bert calls. "Don't let 'im get under the boat!" There's a moment of confusion in clearing the rope from the net frame, but it is handled with fast, efficient motion and no yelling.

Bagged, the turtle thrashes.

"Good-sized turtle," assesses Bert. Its much larger tail says male.

Mike agrees, "He's not small."

Commentary: A fifty-pound Snapping Turtle plucked from the sweep of a great continental river would be called huge, gigantic, a monster; its strength would be much remarked upon, its danger to digits and limbs emphatically forewarned. Here, a turtle of eight hundred pounds is termed, with a slight shrug, "not small." The human mind recalibrates all relationships relative to the familiar, risking perspective in the balance. Benefiting from *my* relative unfamiliarity, thus awestruck as usual, I'm thinking it would do this turtle's size some injustice to call him enormous. In fact—let's just say it—this turtle is absolutely colossal.

Mike offers, "Here in the north where they come to feed, they're about a third heavier than at the nesting beaches." By the cusp of autumn the turtles have waxed fat, with rolls of flesh thickening their necks and tails. Maybe that's why this one looks so big even compared to those I've seen nesting, while they're at their "skinniest"—though even the smallest nesting Leatherback is a tank.

The guys lash the net alongside such that the great and awesome creature that has so astonishingly captured us lies safely in the bag, able to breathe easily. Even in the net he continues his swimming motions, occasionally raising his head and ejecting two fountaining jets of water from his nostrils, followed closely by a *whoosh* of spent air.

Bert allows that this turtle is in fine shape, gleaming and seemingly without scarring. Mike agrees, "Really clean." With a scanner resembling a clothes iron, Mike searches for an internal transponder tag.

Few people get to see a Leatherback Turtle, and almost no one who gets to see a Leatherback ever gets a glimpse at its underside. But now I can report that the belly of the beast is mostly light with dark markings. As I move in tentatively for a close look at the animal, Mike reassures me: "They never try to bite."

I reach down and, fully recognizing the privilege, stroke his smooth, cool, immaculate skin. The turtle cannot be said to be enjoying this, as is suggested by the bits of jellyfish leaving his mouth. But whether this is because he is very upset or simply because we caught him with his mouth full, I can't say.

Further minor indignities are imminent. From the trailing edge of its winglike forelimb Mike takes two pencil eraser–sized plugs of flesh for DNA analysis, to help determine origin. These go into a vial with a fixative agent. A trickle of blood washes away in the seawater. No worries; there are almost no sharks left here. Bert affectionately pats the creature's marbled head.

Next Mike implants a tiny transponder tag into the massive propelling muscle of his right shoulder. But because detecting these tags requires the special instrument, Mike also affixes standard flipper tags.

We unlash the net. As the meshes loosen, the turtle—still bagged in the ballooning webbing—opens his wings enough to resume swimming, generating a problematic forward thrust. Mike and I attempt to turn the turtle head-downward by hanging on to his rear flippers, hoping to let the net fall forward and away from our animal. Though laborious, a little strange, and not very successful, this allows Bert and Blair to maneuver much of the increasingly loosening netting past his whipping flippers and around his head. The turtle comes up snorting jets, and Blair cuts the last strand of webbing from the clenched W of his serrated jaws.

Released, the turtle resurfaces calm and close, gasps and pauses afloat, looks at me, then waves his big wings like Pegasus and removes himself from the company of men. Total elapsed interruption of this dinosaur's workday: twelve minutes.

I congratulate Blair, Mike, and Bert for seamless teamwork. Beaming with satisfaction, Mike urges, "Let's find another, while the water's calm."

The wondrous creature we've so improbably met resumes his intangible life. Carrying on as always, he'll dive, heading down from light green to darker water. He'll linger for some suspended interval, hunting his stinger-filled food. Then the backdrop will again brighten, and deep light shafts reappear. He'll blow bubbles just before reentering the atmosphere, so that by the time his head breaks the surface he's ready to inhale. His world is light to dark and back to light, a blank screen of blue and green and sun shafts that light his way to air. He inhabits a world elemental, spare of sights and sounds. But somehow he acquires information enough to find his way, and sustenance sufficient for fueling his grand enterprise.

To the profound mystery, honesty compels me to add a truth about his existence: it's very repetitive and usually pretty boring—at least from our perspective. For vast distances in the open ocean, the visual is numbingly devoid, like traveling inside a blue tarp. With so little happening visually, everything is rhythm. Rhythm of stroking, rhythm of diving and resting, rhythm of breath expended, breath regained. Stroke and propulsion, the flow and resistance of water. Stroke. Diving deeper, deeper still. Stroke. Stroke. Darkness and the squeezing tons of water upon the chest; minutes expended, breathing suspended; ascending, lighter, lighter, reexpansion and pressure relaxing; bubbles exhaled, bursting into moonlit air, another day slipped into night. *Gasp.* Stroke and propulsion. Stroke.

Morning blueness and the dancing sun shafts. Stroke. Transit and dive, rise and transit. Into the great flow, across the great stage, through the oceanic universe and the currents of time.

Underwater, a Leatherback looks really big; they have a lot of presence. They stroke with just their front flippers; they use their rear flippers only as rudders. Once they start to move, even though their flippers are barely sculling, you can't keep up with them. When you see how effortlessly they swim, how efficient they are, it's quite startling. Absolutely everything about how they move is completely smooth. Even when they change direction, it's part of one fluid motion without pause. They look over their shoulder at you, and if they decide to take off they don't sprint; they just plane away, turning downward and going deep. They'll let you touch their shell, but the moment you touch their flippers they're gone. They're bluish underwater. And that spotting pattern is awesome camouflage. They get a little ways off and begin blending into the background. It's not even that they disappear into the gloom; it's that the spotting makes them seem to disintegrate before your eyes.

Leatherbacks cannot stop traveling. If captured and placed in an aquarium, a Leatherback won't stop swimming. And eventually, against the wet glass, it'll abraid itself to death. They don't recognize barriers. They never realize there are limits. In the ocean, they just go and go.

It's already about six P.M., and the light is getting a bit tricky. A floating piece of wood draws more attention than it deserves from our turtle-trained eyes. Suddenly Bert guns the boat forward.

I look up to the bridge.

Blair yells down, "Another turtle!" He climbs down and scrambles to the stand, readying the net. The turtle, meanwhile, vanishes.

We drift.

Ten minutes later Bert says, "Some *long* dives, eh?"

Mike says, "Light's fading. I think we've lost 'im."

Blair stands expectantly.

Bert calls, "It's gonna get dark on us, Blair."

Blair is unmoved. But a minute later, admitting that night will come, he rests the net and climbs down off the stand. We turn to cover the fifteen nautical miles between our bow and the harbor.

I'm down on deck, hooded against the spray and staring at grizzled whitecaps, when the boat turns sharply to port and abruptly guns. On the bridge Blair is pointing straight ahead as Bert scrambles into the stand and Mike readies the rope.

The creature is difficult to discern, traveling underwater in the low sun's glare, beneath the chop, about a hundred feet ahead.

As we close, the turtle is still swimming just subsurface. Blair places Bert right over the animal, matching its speed so that Bert is looking straight down at the turtle as it's swimming before our bow. When the turtle bursts for its next chunk of air, Bert has the net right over it, and in an instant the perfectly centered turtle slips through the frame and into the mesh bag.

Mike whoops. Blair yells, *"Pull! Pull! Pull!"* as he shoves the boat into reverse to help snug the bag down around the turtle.

This turtle has a flipper tag. That means it has a history. So Mike wants additional measurements, which requires getting this behemoth aboard. I've got my fingers clenched into the net. Bert has the net's rope. Waves bang our hull; the chop is making things difficult. Mike lowers a large hinged stern ramp, Bert puts the rope into a block and tackle, and the giant turtle begins what must seem to her a surreal assisted crawl up a steep, slick, plastic beach. Getting her up requires all our best heaving and grunting, until finally she is lying atop a plywood work platform, dripping a puddle of seawater. She smells like fresh oysters on the half shell.

She defecates a watery coffee-colored liquid, and from her throat comes a similar-looking liquid that convinces me the handling has given her an upset stomach.

She shocks me by making a soft roar, a guttural gurgle. Suddenly her entire body expands with newly inhaled air.

The tag is on her left rear flipper. Mike reads the serial number, T13708, and bursts, "It's from Trinidad! It's from Matura! Which is *crazy*, because it's the only nesting beach I've ever been to." Mike bubbles, "This is *great!* Oh my God!"

Less than thrilled are several gulls who'd gathered around our drifting vessel, expecting this crab boat would be discarding old bait. Experience can leave you hungry in a changing world. Sometimes you learn the wrong lessons.

Oblivious to disappointed gulls, Mike puts a new tag on her right rear flipper, right over a scar where she'd lost a tag. She's got a palm-sized half-moon missing from her left front flipper, as though bitten by a small shark when she was young. Sea turtles need big shoulder muscles for pulling, and so retracting head or limbs within their streamlined shell is a comfort denied. Result: an armored ocean creature vulnerable to shark attack. It's not unusual to see a turtle with a telltale half-moon snatched from a flipper. But turtles' blood has ten times more fibrinogen than humans', so it coagulates rapidly, quickly stanching bleeding, often allowing them to survive the loss of a limb.

Mike next raises our turtle's tail and inserts a temperature probe. He comments, "Glad this one's female; males' tails are so much more muscular it's extremely hard to do this."

I'm not surprised a turtle might resist; this is not the thermometer you've got in the medicine cabinet. This anal probe is well over a foot long. Now comes some interesting data: her body temp is 77 degrees Fahrenheit (25° C), much warmer than the sea-surface temperature of 62° F (16.5° C) and well above the much cooler depths into which she's been diving. Even shallow dives would be taking her to about 57° Fahrenheit (14° C), deeper dives correspondingly chillier. Cold-blooded reptiles need not apply.

Ranging from the tropics to beyond the Arctic Circle, Leatherbacks can maintain body temperature between 77 and 84 degrees Fahrenheit (25° C–29° C) even in waters as cold as about 41 degrees Fahrenheit (5° C). Such temperatures would in minutes chill a human to death and kill other sea turtles. One book calls the Leatherback "more like a reptilian whale than a turtle." They've evolved solutions to various environmental challenges almost as though they're honorary mammals. Leatherbacks' metabolic rates, though not as high as a mammal's, are three times what you'd expect from a reptile. Perhaps they're still evolving.

Leatherbacks generate heat, then conserve it through a combination of large body size, insulating tissue, and circulatory plumbing. They generate body warmth through special heat-generating tissue, digestion, and the action of their muscles. To avoid losing that heat to the ocean, they have several things going for them. One, sheer size. Being big has a lot to do with being here, and being here owes a lot to being big. The bigger an animal gets, the less surface area it has for every unit of body weight. A smaller proportion of body surface exposed to cold water means it takes longer for its body core to cool. This is why small Leatherbacks remain in warm latitudes until they grow big enough. And that's probably why Leatherbacks grow much faster than other sea turtles—to get big enough to quickly start venturing to their main sources of food.

Leatherbacks both conserve and generate heat. They have two kinds of fat layers: an outer white-fat insulating layer like the blubber of marine mammals and a layer of brown fat full of blood vessels. The brown fat is special. Mammals and at least some birds that endure cold winters have similar tissue; it generates heat. No other reptile has anything like that. One white-fat layer insulates their core organs, and another pads their neck against the cold, like a scarf. Leatherbacks' circulatory system can shunt blood flow either away from the skin for added heat conservation or to the skin for cooling. That's why the skin of a Leatherback's neck flushes pink while she's nesting. In cold water, they close their shunts and keep more blood deeper in their tissues. Mammals have the same response, which is why you feel the chill when you first dip into a cool pool or the surf but then "get used to it" while you're swimming. It's why human swimmers' skin often gets pale in cool water.

A Leatherback's flippers are the only thin part of an otherwise massive beast, the only part likely to get quickly chilled by immersion in cold water. To deal with this, two adaptations: One, at the base of each limb a Leatherback has a countercurrent heat exchanger, to keep the heat in the body core and the chill out in the flippers. It's a closely packed bundle of about seventy veins and twenty arteries. The outnumbering by fine veins, which carry cooled returning blood coming from the flippers, helps ensure that they will capture all the arteries' heat on their way back inside the body. The arteries will thus send already-cooled blood into the flippers.

Leatherbacks also possess a highly unusual chemical resistance to the effects of cold. In most animals' muscles, chemical reactions occur faster at warmer temperatures, slower at cooler temperatures. That's why your fingers feel stiff and clumsy if they get chilled (think of trying to tie a knot with very cold fingers). Green Turtles' muscles, for instance, work more efficiently at warmer temperatures, as you'd expect in any animal. But even if a Leatherback's flippers get chilled, it can continue swimming just fine at temperatures that would impair, and even stun, tropical turtles. In Leatherbacks' swimming muscles, the cells' metabolic reaction rate remains constant even if the muscle itself goes through wide temperature swings ranging between about 40 and 100 degrees Fahrenheit, or 5 and 38 degrees Celsius. Further, Leatherbacks' flippers don't freeze at temperatures that freeze the tissues of other reptiles or mammals (because of special lipids). This uniquely consistent level of muscular performance might help medical researchers learn ways of fighting degenerative muscle diseases. That's one more reason Leatherbacks are good for the world.

In sum, even while swimming in subpolar regions, Leatherbacks are pretty impervious to cold. The combination of large size, heat generation, thick insulation, blood-flow regulation, and cold-resistant chemistry allows Leatherbacks to stay cool on a hot beach and warm in a cold ocean. A similar combination of heat-conserving body plan and size— called *gigantothermy*—probably allowed large dinosaurs to live in habitats including the polar regions.

So the exceptional Leatherback is both dinosaur and whale, with a hint of long-winged, long-distance albatross. The 1973 research report announcing the discovery of Leatherbacks' heat-exchange system noted somewhat reverently, "Not only can they generate a striking temperature differential between their body core and the external environment . . . but they have the two classic adaptations of birds and mammals for retaining body heat, namely, an insulating layer of fat and a countercurrent heat exchanger. . . . Leatherbacks, of all reptiles, are the most similar to the birds and mammals."

We loosen the netting. With us pushing, she slides down the ramp, detonating a big splash and disappearing in a veil of fine bubbles. When she bobs up, I walk onto the striker stand and Bert maneuvers me directly over the turtle, affording me a perfect view of her massively effortless, fluid flight. Reflected light makes her seem to glow softly in the green water. She sculls through the tide looking almost as effortless as an albatross aloft in a thick breeze. She angles deep and away. Bert says, "We'll leave her go now, eh?" But the turtle has already made that decision.

In fading light only three miles from the harbor, my gaze fixes like a pointer's. That telltale black melon appears between the waves. "Turtle!"

Bert cranks the wheel hard over. The Leatherback lingers obligingly at the surface. It's chomping a pie-sized Lion's Mane, and not daintily. Tentacle fragments and chunks of jelly bell litter the water.

The last turtle seemed gigantic. But now the mind is forced to recalibrate, because this turtle's size strains the eye-mind connection.

Mike turns to me excitedly, yelling, "*This* is a big one!"

Blair resorts to prayer, calling, "Holy Lord!" Most turtles' backs are awash when they're at the surface. Her body is so thick and high it looks like a steamer trunk from the *Titanic*.

Scarcely is Bert readied when the giant is almost under his feet.

Female. She dives.

The murk of night is rising like a tide of darkness, the third-quarter moon already risen in a sky gone red before bedtime.

But two minutes later Blair shouts "Eleven o'clock! Thirty yards!"

No time to waste. Blair calls down, "I've never seen one *this* big."

As we slide upon her, Bert centers the net right before her nose. The approach was perfect and the placement is perfect. But this turtle can hardly fit. She hits all sides of the frame on her way in, her head and shoulders knocking the netting loose.

Bert hardly needs to be yelling, *"Pull! Pull! Pull!"* Mike is pulling mightily but isn't getting that netting around her, so Bert and I rush to help him.

Mike grunts. "She's a *boat*!"

Our pulling and the boat's backing up, plus the turtle's continued attempts to swim, which move her forward, slowly succeed in sleeving this sea monster.

Mike nods appraisingly, saying, "This one's a bruiser. Wow." Staring at our beast he adds, a little solemnly, "I reckon if we weigh this one, we'll break the record." He glances at the ramp and the weighing device and block and tackle, thinks a moment, looks back at the turtle, and voices the assessment we're all independently arriving at: "No way."

That last turtle was enormous and we got her up the ramp with our best exertion, but there was never a question about whether we could bring her aboard. There is similarly no question in our minds that bringing *this* turtle aboard is, quite simply, not possible.

"Good thing we're getting paid by the pound," Blair chuckles.

Mike adds in an awestruck hush, "Look how *wide* she is."

Bert's just shaking his head.

"I'm sure," Mike pronounces solemnly, "this would beat the 2,019-pound record Leatherback that washed up dead in Wales."

Mike is trying hard to see if she has flipper tags, but she's essentially immovable. You don't just pull on the rear flipper of something this gigantic and get a look. You pull and nothing moves. You might as well be pulling on the boat's rudder. Plus, it's getting dark. We're all leaning over the side of the boat with our fingers clenching the webbing, pulling, trying to maneuver a one-ton turtle. She's doing a better job of maneuvering us. The boat is gently rocking, our arms are getting wet, and waves hitting the hull splash us in the face, leaving our hair dripping. Technically, we've caught her, but we're not fully in control of the situation.

As far as we can tell, her flippers bear no tags. Mike strains his reach to get the electronic tag scanner into position to search for an implanted transponder tag. When the reader malfunctions due to an exhausted battery, he curses, then says, "Sorry for the swear." How very Canadian.

With a new battery, Mike detects no tags. This monster reveals no hint of her whereabouts during any of many decades. Where and when did she hatch? Who else may have seen her?

Getting her length requires snaking the tape measure under the netting and along her shell. This is more difficult than it should be, because she is so neutrally buoyant that her body does not respond as quickly or fully to a rising swell as does our boat. So we are sometimes forced to let go our grip on the net when a swell lifts our boat. But eventually the boat, the swell, and the turtle meet just right, just long enough for us to get a good, careful measurement. Carapace length, scientifically measured, is 168.5 centimeters, a little over five and a half feet. Add about two feet for her head. Though her carapace is only a little longer than those of the two biggest turtles I saw in Trinidad and Florida, she's strikingly more massive. None of us can reach across to measure her width, so Bert measures the distance from her back's central ridge to her shell's edge, then doubles it to approximate her width. She is about 132 centimeters wide, nearly four and a half feet, wide as a rowboat.

We have before us a *turtle* whose head, tail, and shell would overextend each edge of a four-by-eight sheet of plywood. Based on the impression that her flippers look twelve feet wide, I conservatively estimate their span at eight feet. Mike estimates nine feet.

Almost to himself, he adds, "I bet she's been nesting for the last fifty years." Truly this turtle is a veteran of an immense life journey. It's possible she was already swimming the sea before pesticides, plastics, and longline fishing boats became part of the everyday survival challenges to sea animals everywhere. Based solely on size, this turtle must be near the end of a natural life. How did she get past all the nets and lines, the egg collectors and poachers? What brushes with death has she survived? All we can know is that she has lived large.

She bellows a snort.

The moon is now lighting a path across the sea. Our deck lights are glaring. It's a little after eight P.M. Mike applies an internal transponder tag and scans it to make sure it's working. Onto his scanner screen appears number 132332652. Mike applies metal clip tags to her rear flippers as Mars rises in the southeast. Last, Bert acquires the tissue samples that may tell us more about her origins after she's gone than we've been able to learn in her presence. Then Blair announces, "Okay now, we're gonna need everyone's help getting her freed. Watch that flipper, eh?"

She jets some water out her nostrils and pulls a deep drag of air. We relax the cinching on the net end and begin to widen the opening and, with great difficulty and considerable dampness, work the netting around her flippers and up toward her head. The freer she gets, the more difficult she's making it—and the wetter. When she works her two front flippers out she twists with massive thrusts and much flung water as she turns clear of the net.

Mike, delighted with all her superlative extremeness, is giddy. She comes up again, looking just unbelievable. This one has so much of her back in the atmosphere that she does look like a rowboat, riding pertly on the waves.

Bert throttles forward. Our bow turns toward the lights of the harbor and village. The view shoreward is of shadowed slopes and forested coast. Isolated within that span of coast, the sunset-twinkling lights of Neil's Harbour indicate homes linked to the Internet, with hot water, ice cream, and books. Bert opens a plastic container revealing pizza and soft drinks sufficient for all hands. Here on the continental shelf, among leathery reptiles and with a hint of long winter in the air, we're suddenly having a sundown pizza cruise. This works for me. We clink our cans—here's to turtles—and suck the sweet, diesel-perfumed air. We are still amid the realm of giant Leatherbacks, giant Basking Sharks, giant Ocean Sunfish. May our affections for such monsters help resurrect the other giants, the Swordfish, Bluefin Tuna, and Makos, and save them from the jaws of the most frightening predator.

The western clouds leave space enough to admit the last sunlight, and what on the sea was silver is now softly shimmering pastel pink. We head toward highlands robed in the day's last remnants.

Mike, still shaking his head, says, "I really don't think I'll see another turtle that big."

PART II

BETWEEN OCEANS

THE VIEW FROM TURTLE ISLAND

Creation stories from many corners of the Americas converge on the conclusion that a turtle created the world. Because there is no central text, every tale spawns a new version nearly each time it's told. Like Greek and Roman gods and modern-day celebrity worship, these stories are rich with characters bigger than life yet plagued by human qualities: jealousy, rage, sadness, generosity, need. One of the things I like about these stories is that instead of relegating the magic of creation to a remote god working from a distance and holding his magic in heaven, as do the Western monotheistic religions (Christianity's sly polytheistic pantheon notwithstanding), they seem to better imbue the immediate world and all its characters with a sense of the miraculous.

In parts of North America, it seems that in the time before humans existed on Earth, a sky chief uprooted a great tree, making a hole. His wife looked into the hole and saw stars glittering in the darkness. Curious, she leaned too far—and fell. Down and down and down through the stars she fell. Animals swimming in the great waters of the world below looked up. They quickly held a council and decided that Loon and Duck must break her fall with their soft wings and that upon Turtle's broad back she must rest. While Sky Woman slept exhausted, Beaver, Otter, and Muskrat dived into the cosmic sea, bringing up bits of mud to coat Turtle's back. The soil on Turtle's back grew and grew, and the world increased rapidly in size. Streams appeared, and trees, shrubs, grasses, corn, and other plants sprouted. When the woman woke, she felt cheered, and blessed it all. Thus this world, riding as it does on the back of Great Turtle in an infinite sea, is Turtle Island.

...

Others took a different approach to explaining the world. The story they started took centuries, and in many ways it is a creation story that will not end.

Pythagoras seems to have first reasoned and written that because the sun and moon are round, and the shadow of Earth during an eclipse is round, Earth, too, may be round. That was cutting edge science twenty-five hundred years ago. About two thousand years later, so the story goes, a young Christopher Columbus noticed that the tops of ships' masts appeared over the horizon before the ships themselves, and deduced a spherical world and the possibility of voyaging to the East by sailing west.

By the time European sails filled with wind were heading west and south, the world's warm and temperate seas were still filled with sea turtles, whose numbers probably ran to billions. It's quite likely that for every sea turtle alive today, there were, within historic times, a hundred. Just within the last century, many populations have declined 90 percent.

The living abundance in the oceans at the starting line of modern times can scarcely be imagined this late in the day. Christopher Columbus's second voyage, in 1492, gave us, for instance, this snapshot: "In those twenty leagues . . . the sea was thick with turtles . . . so numerous that it seemed the ships would run aground on them and were as if bathing in them." On May 10, 1503, during Columbus's fourth voyage, he came in sight of, as his son Ferdinand penned, "two very small and low islands, full of turtles, as was all the sea about, so that they looked like little rocks." They named them the Tortugas, Turtle Islands. Later renamed the Cayman Islands, they harbored possibly the largest Green Turtle rookery within historic times. Such sights clearly conveyed the impression—*always* mistaken—of wildlife inexhaustible. Aboriginal peoples had already depleted some small nesting populations. But that was nothing compared to the coming European onslaught. In the Caribbean, especially, turtles took it hard during the colonial era. Soon after European settlement, Green Turtles—the preferred species and a staple food for ship crews and arriving colonists—became targets of a trade so intense and thorough it triggered a wave of local extinctions at important nesting grounds.

In 1610, a Bermuda settler noted that *"on the shores . . . Turtles, Fish and Fowle do abound as dust of the earth."* In 1620, only eleven years after its colonization, Bermuda was already so depleted that its assembly enacted a law protecting younger turtles, possibly the New World's first conservation legislation:

> ### An Act agaynst the killinge of ouer younge Tortoyses
>
> In regard that much waste and abuse . . . by sudrye lewd and impvident persons . . . who in their continuall goinges out to sea . . . snatch & catch up indifferentlye all kinds of Tortoyses both young & old little and greate and soe kill, carrye awaye and devoure them to the much decay of the breed of so excellent a fishe . . . therefore . . . from hence forward noe manner of pson . . . shall pesume to kill or cause to be killed . . . any young Tortoyses that are . . . Eighteen inches in the Breadth or Dyameter.

The penalty was fifteen pounds of tobacco (half went to government and half to the informer). In spite of this early protection of young turtles, slaughter continued, and by the late 1700s the waves of breeders trickled to a few drops and then ran dry. Bermuda's nesting Green Turtles were essentially gone by around 1800 (though a few survivors lasted into the 1930s). After the "dust of the earth" was turned to ashes, people continued catching sea turtles visiting Bermuda waters. Bermuda finally granted turtles full protection in 1973—two centuries late. (Releases of hatchlings in the 1960s and '70s have so far failed to establish breeders.)

In 1655, with the British colony in Jamaica needing meat, the admiral dispatched one of his ships to the Caymans for turtles. From that day, the Caymans became a killing field for nesting females. One Edward Long wrote of the turtles, "It is affirmed, that vessels, which have lost their latitude in hazy weather, have steered entirely by the noise which these creatures make in swimming, to attain the Cayman Isles. . . . In these annual peregrinations across the ocean they resemble . . . herring shoals. . . . By the gracious dispensation of the Almighty . . . when the fruits of the earth are deficient, an ample sustenance may still be drawn from this never failing resource of turtle, or their eggs, conducted annually as it were into their very hands."

Faithful to a fault about a place that had worked for millennia, generations of Green Turtles returned to beaches that had broken their promise. During nesting, May to September, turtles coming to dig nests found themselves turned onto their backs on the beaches; their flippers, for the first time in their long lives, unable to gain the purchase of either water or sand. By 1670, forty sloops from Jamaica were taking turtles year-round. Outside the nesting season the boats pursued and hounded them in their feeding grounds among the shoals and sea-grass flats and cays. Each time the sailors lifted their glasses to ring in the New Year, another thirteen thousand turtles had gone to feed Jamaican settlers.

By 1711, with Caribbean turtles showing an exhaustion that Columbus and his men could never have envisioned, the government of Jamaica enacted a law prohibiting turtle-egg collection from any island belonging to Jamaica, including the Caymans. It was never enforced, either on the beaches or in Jamaica's markets. Turtle was Jamaica's main meat, and permanent settlers lived and worked on the Caymans, mining the ancient mariners.

In the late 1700s, the Caymans' Green Turtles finally buckled. Only a few turtles crawled from the sea to lay doomed eggs on the Caymans each year. Eight or nine boats still hunted for Jamaican appetites, but now they sought their turtles mostly around Cuba's southern cays.

By 1830, Cuba was depleted, and the focal point of Caribbean turtle hunting shifted to the coast of Nicaragua and Honduras. By 1900 hunters had largely depleted those areas; in the next decades they turned to Pacific Mexico.

Originally, Caribbean Green Turtles numbered in the tens of millions, perhaps several hundred million; likely far more than the number of American Bison before the New World heard its first gunshot. They've never substantially recolonized the Bermuda or Cayman rookeries, and nowadays Caribbean colonies hold only an estimated 5 percent or less of their pre-Columbian Green Turtle numbers.

Nonetheless, all seven species of sea turtles made it through the twentieth century and into the twenty-first century. The question is, Will they make it out?

Sea turtle expert Jim Spotila summarized some estimates of original adult turtle populations worldwide: Of Green Turtles, six hundred million. Half a billion Olive Ridleys. Tens of millions of Loggerheads. Four or five million Hawksbills. Leatherbacks probably numbered one to five million worldwide.

Most species today likely stand at fewer than 5 percent of those numbers. Today we derive relief hearing that Kemp's Ridley Turtles have increased from 300 females to 2,500. That hard-earned relief is warranted. But backlit by past numbers of perhaps 500,000 Kemp's Ridleys, it's a pale shadow.

Turtles once played an important role in ocean communities. Nowadays, their scarcity is more significant. Sea-grass beds that would once have been grazed short by Greens have become overgrown and diseased. Hawksbills' main food in the Caribbean, a sponge called *Chondrilla nucula*, is now overgrowing coral reefs and in Belize has been called "one of the major threats to corals." Caribbean specialists Karen Bjorndal and Jeremy Jackson derive a "very conservative" estimate of 540,000 adult Hawksbills in that region before Europeans arrived, but about 27,000 today. Bjorndal and Jackson conclude, "The virtual ecological extinction of sea turtles in the Caribbean must have resulted in major changes in the structure and function of the marine ecosystems they inhabited." Leatherbacks eat jellies, jellies eat fish larvae, and fish larvae grow into fish that people eat. So fewer Leatherbacks means more jellies, which means fewer fish. Are the numbers significant? No one can say; there are no turtle-filled, fish-filled oceans left to compare with. The point is that under the sea, out of sight, various sets of dominoes are falling.

There's no question that turtle populations were once much higher, but the trends are important. As we've seen, Florida's Greens, nearly gone by the 1980s, now annually dig as many as 2,500 nests—an exponential increase. Caribbean Greens have greatly improved from the lows of the 1970s and '80s. On the east coast of Mexico, Green Turtle nest counts have risen from only a couple hundred nests annually in the 1980s to nearly 3,000 clutches now. Greens on Costa Rica's Caribbean side have increased massively, quintupling between 1970 and 2004 at the famed Tortuguero beach, where up to 37,000 female Green Turtles now annually dig more than 100,000 nests, depositing about 10 million eggs—possibly the largest Green Turtle population in the world. They've increased despite some continued poaching of both eggs and adults, and jaguars preying on a few dozen nesting females annually—and despite hungry Nicaraguans annually taking about 10,000 Greens of various sizes from their waters to their cook pots.

The main message about sea turtles in the Atlantic is that, despite a bumpy ride, in the last few decades they're generally doing much better. That's not true in the Pacific or Indian Oceans.

For one thing, most sea turtles nest more frequently and lay more eggs in the Atlantic than the Pacific. Leatherbacks nest roughly every other year in the Atlantic and every four years in the Pacific. Leatherback clutches average eighty-five eggs in the Atlantic, sixty-five in the Pacific. Similarly, female Green Turtles nest every two to three years in Florida and the Caribbean, whereas in the Pacific they grow more slowly, mature later, and nest every four or five years. Likewise, Loggerhead Turtles return for nesting every three years in the Atlantic, every four in the Pacific. That's probably because the Pacific's vast intercontinental distances produce sparser food. For Leatherbacks in the Pacific, the difference means only about three-quarters as many eggs in each nest and half the number of nests during a life. In difficult times, that could have real consequences. And with fisheries, beach development, and egg poaching, these are difficult times.

For example, various Green Turtle populations in the Pacific, Indian Ocean, and Mediterranean are down 30 to 98 percent in the last few decades. The main Pacific and Indian Ocean bright spots are places known for conservation: the Galápagos (stable), Australia (up by around 50 percent), and Hawaii (tripled since the Endangered Species Act kicked in). Throughout Southeast Asia, people eat about 100,000 juvenile Green Turtles annually, an unsustainable rate. (People also eat many kinds of land and pond turtles in parts of Asia. *Ten million* turtles like the now-endangered Three-Striped Box Tortoise get traded into China annually. Turtles are now wiped out near human population centers, and half of Asia's ninety turtle species are endangered.) Nowadays the Indonesian island of Bali hosts perhaps the world's largest centralized sea turtle slaughtering place, with as many as 20,000 Green Turtles brought into the markets annually. Boats scour the sea for up to two months for enough turtles to fill their boats, hunting them as far away as Borneo and Sulawesi. The pressure threatens nesting populations over a large region. The trade is deeply rooted in tradition and custom, and you can see how difficult it is to just say "Stop." Balinese Hindus hold turtles sacred—but eat them. The mainly Muslim turtle hunters are not allowed to eat turtles—but can kill them. For weddings, pregnancies, cremations, temple purification, teeth filing (not filling), and other ceremonial rites of passage, any proper Balinese host wants turtle on the table, signaling wealth and prestige. They say it is part of being Hindu. (In India, where Hinduism originated, turtles are not religiously sacrificed.) One boat captain argues that his business benefits the environment because turtle hunting keeps his employees from their previous occupations: piracy and reef fishing with explosives. One of his men says that until he became a turtle hunter, he often threw fifty homemade bombs into the sea each day, blowing up corals, so that he could rake up the dead and dying fish that appeared at the surface. "If there is another job that can provide enough income for me, I will change jobs," he said. "But for now, I can only catch turtles." One former turtle hunter found work at a turtle-breeding center in Bali. He says he is haunted by the image of turtles being butchered. Like everything about its life, a turtle dies slowly, often remaining alive and moving well after its throat is slit and its shell opened. "It's a torture to the sea turtle," the former hunter said. "Maybe if it could speak, it would ask for mercy."

There's good reason to believe Leatherbacks could actually vanish throughout the Pacific and Indian Oceans. Leatherbacks had disappeared from India before 1930 and declined to near zero in Sri Lanka by 1994. The few Leatherbacks that had nested in Australia went extinct in the 1990s. And the Leatherback's former western Pacific fortress, its Malaysia population, fell from thousands in the 1950s to survivors you can count on one hand today. Malaysia was home to 10,000 to 15,000 adult female Leatherbacks. Of that total, 3,000 females nested annually, laying several million eggs. Of those, local people took nearly every egg—for fifty years. Partial protection and artificial incubation came late and at the wrong incubation temperatures, resulting in either all females or sterile intersex individuals. When those animals returned years later, their eggs didn't hatch. New trawl-net fishing nearby in the early 1970s coincided with a sudden further nesting decline of 20 percent per year. That tailspin accelerated to 30 percent annually with the introduction of forty-mile-long Japanese drift nets, plus mortality from gill nets and fish traps. In recent years the nesting count has fallen as low as two females for the whole season. The population has essentially been eradicated. New Guinea's northwest tip, with about 500 to 1,500 females nesting annually, constitutes Leatherbacks' last stronghold in the whole span of the Pacific and Indian Oceans. It too appears to be declining, from rough estimates of 1,400 or so turtles in the 1980s to perhaps half that now—severe, though certainly not the free fall of other places.

The eastern Pacific fares no better. In 1990 about 1,400 individual female Leatherbacks nested on Pacific Costa Rica's most key beach. A decade later only about 100 returned, and by 2005, under 50—a decline of about 97 percent. In the early 1980s an estimated 75,000 female Leatherbacks used Mexico's Pacific coast for nesting. By the late 1990s, as few as 250 remained—a decline of well over 99 percent. (That early 1980s estimate was quick and rough, but even if it was overestimated by a factor of ten—which is highly unlikely—the decline is still 97 percent. And there's also the possibility that it was underestimated.) At one Mexican beach where thousands of females nested in the early 1980s, two decades later only four females used the beach.

Atlantic Leatherback populations, by contrast, stand far stronger. The 2,600 adult females that nest on Central American beaches appear stable or only slightly declining. Leatherbacks using the northern Caribbean (1,100 adult females), Florida (250 females), and Brazil (50) are all increasing. Gabon and Congo on Africa's west coast host the world's second-largest Leatherback population, with about 10,000 females. (These are estimates of total living adult females that use those beaches in their nesting years, not annual nesting female numbers or annual nest numbers. Each female takes several years off between nestings, but in a nesting year lays about seven clutches.) Africa's west coast still also maintains significant nesting populations of Loggerheads, Olive Ridleys, Hawksbills, and Greens. Villagers in some areas kill two-thirds of nesting females for food, while along one stretch of Ghana's coast local people worship the turtles, which respond by nesting at high densities. West Africa's Leatherbacks seem stable in recent years. The world's largest current Leatherback nesting population, around 14,000 adult females, stretches from Trinidad to French Guiana. Leatherbacks come ashore more densely at their Trinidad nesting sites than at any other beach in the world.

Given what we know collectively, globally, about the fall of turtle populations, their continued declines in many places, their obvious vulnerability, and the difficulty of reestablishing them once major populations vanish, two things remain remarkable: One, in most of the world people continue to kill adults, take eggs, and deploy fishing gear as if there will be no tomorrow. Two, people working to protect sea turtles are actually succeeding. Some populations are recovering. The list of recovering populations is not trivial: In the western Atlantic, certain Green, Loggerhead, Hawksbill, and Leatherback populations, as well as the Kemp's Ridley Turtle, are more abundant now than in 1980, with, as we've heard, some populations increasing exponentially. In the eastern Pacific, Olive Ridleys are recovering after decades of overexploitation. We will hear more as we drop into the Pacific. These facts show that some people never learn, but others do, and that what people do, good and bad, matters.

WORLDWIDE, FIFTEEN MILLION PEOPLE FISH COMMERCIALLY. THE MOST dangerous occupation, fishing kills workers at rates eighteen to thirty times higher than national averages of on-the-job deaths. The fish they land are worth about $80 billion annually at the dock. But depletion from overfishing marginalizes the profits, and mechanization is reducing employment. Many longline boats operate on thin margins or take losses. The average U.S. Atlantic and Gulf of Mexico longline boat loses $7,000 annually.

Into this picture stroll conservationists, usually pale and plump, asking—nay, often demanding—that fishers use new and unfamiliar gear, rerig their boats, or change their hook styles. Or stop fishing. But shutting down Hawaii-based long-liners would cost sixteen hundred jobs, for instance. So politicians would likely oppose any proposal to eliminate the industry.

The courts offer a different route.

Peaceable though they be, all sea turtles currently pack the punch of the U.S. Endangered Species Act. Whenever a species that goes by the title "endangered" or "threatened" might be affected by an action of the U.S. federal government, the U.S. Fish and Wildlife Service or the National Marine Fisheries Service must issue a "biological opinion" saying whether the activity is likely to "jeopardize the continued existence" of the species. If so, officials are supposed to lay out steps toward eliminating the jeopardy. Solomon in his glory could only have hoped for such wisdom.

But neither the U.S. government nor its citizenry is Solomon, so disputes arise. The game is usually played like this: the government tries to squeeze out the narrowest, rosiest interpretation, while conservation groups try to force a sweeping assessment that takes every problem into account. In the case of Hawaii long-lining, the Fisheries Service issued no fewer than five biological opinions between 1985 and 1998. Each had, shall we say, issues. In 1985 the service considered the fishery out to only two hundred miles, and issued it permission to "take" 50 Loggerheads and 50 Leatherbacks and to kill 25 of each. In the legalese, "take" means, basically, mess with in any way, including catching and releasing. Due to crashing fish populations on the U.S. East and Gulf Coasts, many boats moved to Hawaii in the late 1980s. Their influx prompted another biological opinion. Again the Fisheries Service constricted its geographical view, issuing the industry permission to "take" 25 and kill 1 each of Loggerhead, Leatherback, and Green. When the Fisheries Service finally recognized that the industry was operating over a huge swath of ocean extending hundreds of miles from Hawaii, its 1993 biological opinion determined that the fishery would not "jeopardize the continued existence" of turtles—over the next twelve months. That time restriction is a no-no, but the service was hoping to either buy time or pull a fast one. Its officials were pushing other envelopes, too—they jacked the allowed "take" to 752 turtles, including the mortality of a precise-sounding 299.

Emboldened perhaps by getting away with it, the service's 1994 biological opinion increased the authorization to 849 turtles annually, including 129 lethal "takes." In 1996 sea turtle specialists were already sounding the alarm on Pacific Leatherbacks and publishing papers indicating much lower populations than previously thought, trends that, if continued, clearly meant extinction in a few decades. The 1998 biological opinion concluded that the operation of the Hawaii longline fishery was, still, "not likely to jeopardize the continued existence" of the turtles. It upped its allowed "take" to 955, and okayed killing exactly 184.

The excruciating exactitude of those numbers reflects the out-of-touch world of government bean counters and the faux precision of official insincerity. Far better than such a circus of hollow policy would have been spending the decade looking for solutions to the problem of endangered animals getting killed. But apparently the Fisheries Service's idea of managing was simply to keep signing death warrants with increasing laxity—anything to allow the fishing to continue without inconvenience—and hope no one noticed.

People noticed. Several conservation groups sued. They argued that the latest biological opinion, with its confident finding of "no jeopardy" to sea turtles, a) broke with the logical trajectory of the scientific information, and that its authorized turtle take numbers were "arbitrary and capricious"; b) did not consider, as required, cumulative effects of other problems on the turtle population and did nothing to halt or reverse the endangered species' declines; c) ignored the government's own experts and its own official recovery plan; and d) further violated the law by issuing permits to kill endangered species when experts urged stopping such mortality.

On all four of these arguments, the court ruled in the government's favor and against the conservation groups. The judge agreed with the enviros on one small technicality: he decided that until the impact statement was completed and formally filed in the legal way, it would be appropriate to require a few things.

An environmental impact statement is a big project, usually running to many hundreds of pages of description and analyses, taking months or years to complete. The judge ordered the Fisheries Service in the meanwhile to start researching ways for long-liners to catch fewer turtles while fishing. He decided that all vessels had to start carrying line clippers, dehookers, and dip nets to ensure better turtle releases. And rather stunningly, he ordered the Fisheries Service to analyze what areas of the ocean could be closed to fishing with the most salutary benefits to turtles.

And so, in 1999, a U.S. judge's order closed about a million square miles of the North Pacific to Hawaii-based longline boats. The boats could no longer fish between 30° and 44° north latitude and longitudes 137° west and 173° east. Fishing was closed part of the year from 30° down to 6° north. Targeted swordfishing was altogether banned. With baits set shallower than tuna lines, at depths turtles frequent, Swordfish lines catch ten times as many turtles. Because the boats were also drowning about 3,000 albatrosses each year, the northern closure was a boon to birds too. Tangles of turtles and albatrosses dropped sharply.

Altogether, the vast closure left people gasping. Some of the conservation groups hoped it might be the beginning of a push for a successful worldwide longline ban, similar to the United Nation's global large-driftnet ban of the early 1990s.

But while a lot of things changed, a lot remained the same. Most Hawaii swordfishing boats either switched to tuna or took up bases in California and continued swordfishing. Boats from other countries remained unaffected. "We go out and fish side by side with the foreign boats," Long Nguyen of Honolulu told the *Los Angeles Times* when he moved his eighty-five-foot boat to California. "They eat turtles. We save turtles. So how come they can fish, and we cannot?"

In April 2004 the judge's injunction expired and the closures ended, but the rules changed. The government was allowing only half the number of swordfishing trips. It now required swordfishing boats to use large "circle hooks," baited with fish instead of squid. In Atlantic studies done during the Pacific closure, such gear reduced the Loggerhead catch nearly 90 percent and the Leatherback catch nearly 65 percent. Vessel operators and owners had to attend a special workshop and be able to use dehooking devices for turtles. A government-paid observer would be required aboard every swordfishing trip. And if observers reported a total of 16 Leatherbacks or 17 Loggerheads caught dead *or* alive, the government would shut Swordfish long-lining for the rest of the year.

The National Marine Fisheries Service had come a long way on this issue, far from its lazy 1998 permitting of 955 turtle captures and 184 killings. Now fewer turtles would be at risk. When the fishery reopened, those changes looked like a win. Kimberly Davis of the World Wildlife Fund said in a press release, "The strict new sea turtle protections offer a critical opportunity to prove that new methods of longline fishing are consistent with the survival of some of the planet's oldest creatures."

But the groups that had sued seemed bitter. They'd hoped the closure would become permanent, step one in a global long-lining ban, and they viewed the reopening—even with only half the fishing days allowed, the observers, mortality cap, and all the other new restrictions—as a setback. Further, they viewed groups who saw a conservation victory and supported the changes (groups like the World Wildlife Fund and the Blue Ocean Institute, both of which I'm closely affiliated with) as sellouts and stooges.

I saw the lawsuits as a necessary kick in the ass to a lazy, cynical government that can't seem to learn that managing commerce in wild plants and animals (living "resources") is mostly a matter of protecting the public trust and our children's options. But the groups who sued seemed—to me, anyhow—unable to see their own success.

"It's another example of the Bush administration manipulating science in favor of industry," said Todd Steiner, director of the Turtle Island Restoration Network, one of the groups that had sued. "These are hooks of mass destruction."

That rhetoric surprised me, because I was thinking this was one rare instance wherein the G. W. Bush administration *didn't* manipulate science in favor of industry or twist truth until it broke. I figured longlines were simply off Bush's radar, since all he seemed to know about the ocean was that it floated aircraft carriers and made oil harder to reach. (The Bush administration's hostility to science and the environment was unprecedented, and among many other things it had approved gas drilling on Padre Island National Seashore, the main U.S. nesting beach for the Kemp's Ridley. Then again, let's not forget that all those biological opinions allowing ever-increasing turtle kills had spanned the administrations of Ronald Reagan, George H. W. Bush, and Bill Clinton. Take-home message: blindness toward oceans is a bipartisan cause.

I think the reason the feds put a short leash on the longlines in 2004 was that the judge was watching, the enviros were watching, and the science had really changed. In 2000, the premier science journal *Nature* published a paper by Drexel University professor Jim Spotila and several turtle experts entitled "Pacific Leatherback Turtles Face Extinction." It graphed population crashes, cited high rates of adult losses, fingered longlines, and got everyone's notice. They estimated that Pacific Leatherbacks had crashed from 91,000 adult females in 1980 to under 3,000 in 2000. To reopen swordfishing, the Fisheries Service needed to do it in a way that avoided more lawsuits. It had to pay attention to new findings about both the turtles' status and fishing techniques that reduced turtle kills. Now, things were different.

Just as U.S. shrimpers fought turtle devices for years and then, once they had to live with them, demanded that every country be required to use them, these new restrictions got long-liners started thinking internationally, too. Of the circle hooks and the release tools, Kitty Simonds, executive director of the Western Pacific Fishery Management Council, said, "The sooner we find out this gear works, the sooner all of the other countries will accept it." The word for that is: *leadership*.

Here's why this matters: Hawaii has around 100 to 150 longline boats; the number is always in flux. That sounds like a lot, but it's a fraction— under 4 percent—of perhaps 4,000 boats long-lining throughout the Pacific. Japan has nearly 1,500 longline boats, Taiwan 1,800. China, Korea, Australia, Fiji, New Caledonia, French Polynesia, Mexico, Guatemala, Costa Rica, Ecuador, and Peru are some of the other countries longlining in the Pacific. At least some American conservation groups, scientists, and fishery managers are now setting their sights on the other 97 percent of the boats out there.

What the plaintiff conservation groups didn't seem to appreciate was how much they'd accomplished and what they'd started. Some continued suing and calling for a permanent end to longline fishing. What I don't think they fully realized was, as Duke University sea turtle expert Larry Crowder told the *Los Angeles Times,* "If you shut down the entire U.S. fishery, you don't solve the problem for the loggerhead and leatherback turtles. You can export new methods to other countries. You cannot export a closure."

Meanwhile Atlantic U.S. longline boats fishing the edges of warm currents were also getting into hot water over turtles. Government observers on Atlantic U.S. longline boats had dutifully recorded turtles hooked or tangled, and when the Fisheries Service added up the numbers they found that the boats were catching about 1,000 Loggerheads and 800 Leatherbacks yearly, killing up to an estimated (mainly guessed-at) half of them, including those released with bad injuries or swallowed hooks. The official government report said, "Noteworthy was that marine turtle bycatch estimated from observer data was significantly higher than that reported in captains' logbooks, indicating that an assessment method dependent upon the fishery's self-reporting has limitations."

Translation: "Fishermen are liars." Who knew?

Despite the fishing industry's attempts to cover up, it was getting hard to ignore a couple thousand dead turtles a year. The Fisheries Service was already in the throes of Hawaii's controversy. The Atlantic biological opinion in 2000 was a "jeopardy" opinion: "The fishery is likely to jeopardize the continued existence of Atlantic leatherback and loggerhead sea turtles." After decades of doing nothing, it was time for a solution.

Seek and ye shall find. The Fisheries Service's first stab at a solution: close a large part of the Grand Banks to U.S. boats. That section measured 56,000 square nautical miles at first and was later expanded to an area known as the Northeast Distant Area, something like 2.6 million square nautical miles, stretching to the Azores. Though U.S. boats take about 30 percent and 20 percent of North Atlantic long-lined Swordfish and tuna, respectively, they set less than 10 percent of the gear. The list of countries competing for slices of the Atlantic pie runs longer than the list of countries with Atlantic waterfront, including Taiwan, Korea, China, Japan, Russia, Brazil, Trinidad, Morocco, Cyprus, Venezuela, Mexico, Cuba, the United Kingdom, Bermuda, various Caribbean countries, Canada, Belize, France, Ireland, Portugal, Equatorial Guinea, Spain, and our dear friend Libya. Boats from these other countries remained free to fish wherever, and no doubt reveled in the reduced competition.

This time, the Fisheries Service had been forthright about its responsibility under the Endangered Species Act, had looked at its data, and had done what it could. So this time, it was the fishing industry that sued.

I am in the court in Boston as both sides present arguments to the judge. This time, the environmentalists are helping defend the government, like old pals. Monica Goldberg is an attorney with a conservation group called Oceana.

The courtroom is bright, surprisingly so, in a new building overlooking Boston Harbor and pretty boats at placid anchor. Today's only storm is gathering within the courtroom.

Of the two hundred or so U.S. boats that use longlines in the Atlantic Ocean, only about a dozen fish the Grand Banks region. But that dozen cause 75 percent of the whole fleet's Loggerhead Turtle catches, and 40 percent of the Leatherback run-ins. That's why attention is focused on that area.

The government lawyers have brought a poster-sized map showing the locations of turtle catches by long-liners. Each turtle capture of the last decade—whether the turtle was released alive or drowned—is represented by a colored dot on the map. The Gulf of Mexico has its share of dots, and the edge of the continental shelf off the eastern seaboard sports a case of measles. But on the Grand Banks the dots merge to a great festering rash, a red smear in the ocean.

A few fishermen sit on the benches in the back of the room. Their representatives wear suits. The fishermen wear sweaters, as do I. Each lawyer has one or two silently assisting coworkers, who take occasional notes or pass occasional suggestions.

As we wait for the proceedings to start, one of the Swordfish longliners says to me, "Other countries are already eyeing the U.S. Swordfish quota. If we can't catch it, they'll take it from us." Another says agitatedly, "We'll lose the U.S. quota to other countries because of these closures. At least with us, you have reasonable people. If it goes to other countries, who will enforce the rules?" He has a point there. For all its faults, the United States does a pretty good job of policing its regulations. Most countries can barely regulate their police.

The closure the fishermen came here to fight isn't the first. In the last several years the Fisheries Service has permanently closed large areas off the southeast states and the Gulf of Mexico to protect baby Swordfish. An area the size of Florida and another the size of Louisiana are closed permanently; one the size of Georgia and South Carolina put together is closed for three months each year; another about the size of New Jersey and Connecticut combined is closed each June. Those closures resulted from a lawsuit several conservation groups (including mine, which is why the fishermen know me) brought against the Fisheries Service because it was allowing continued fishing in nursery areas where long-liners discarded excessive numbers of undersized Swordfish. The discards were significant. In the five years before the closure, U.S. long-liners kept between 64,000 and 73,000 Swordfish annually, while killing and discarding an additional 20,000 to 30,000 because they were too small. In the first couple of years following the southern closures, the numbers of Swordfish discarded fell to about 13,000 to 14,000 annually, an improvement.

The long-liners fought each closure tooth and nail. At each step, they lost. And they're still stung by the bad publicity brought by celebrity chefs who vocally boycotted Swordfish until fishery managers reduced the catch quota. Now they feel more uncertain than ever about their future. They believe the Fisheries Service has been captured by environmentalists who care more about Swordfish and turtles than about people, and who have no idea of the realities of fishing in international waters where the United States is a minority member and anything it does unilaterally merely gives a gift to ravenous nations.

The judge arrives an hour late. "Excuse me," she says. "We've been selecting a jury since nine A.M. It's a very important—though very boring—process."

Blue Water Fishermen's Association lawyer George Mannina is allowed to open with his argument. The National Marine Fisheries Service has closed the Grand Banks area to U.S. boats because of the turtle catches. So the boat owners have sued to keep it open.

Point of clarification: though the Fisheries Service has closed the area, it has begun three years of research on new hooks and baits that might catch fish yet deter turtles. It has already hired these same long-liners to do the experiments—inside the closed area, and they're allowed to sell their catch. But the research won't be a permanent gig, and the fishermen want the area left officially open, not officially closed.

Their lawyer must convince the judge that the government closed the area arbitrarily, for reasons unsupported by science or law. He seems to believe it will be easy to show that.

Rather theatrically, Mannina evokes the story shown in the movie *The Perfect Storm,* and how hard his clients work to make a dangerous living. He makes a transparent attempt to bond with the judge by making reference to working moms with teenage sons.

The judge is a small, alert woman in her mid-forties with shoulder-length dark hair brushing her dark-robed shoulders.

Mannina, in his dark suit, wire-rimmed glasses, and finely brushed-back silver hair, paces and gesticulates, unfurling his argument. "My clients are not beasts, deliberately killing turtles. They do kill some," he concedes, "but not enough to jeopardize the species."

The government's rationale, he says, "has some surface appeal. But," he emphasizes, "it is a siren's song that leads to poor conclusions." He claims we can't tell what's really going on with turtles, because the science is too soft. And, he continues, the Fisheries Service is particularly concerned with the rather small northern Loggerhead population that nests from northern Florida to the Carolinas, but there's no legal basis for the government to single out this subpopulation.

His initial argument that this population is of no legal concern is scientifically nonsensical. But this is not a science meeting. His reasoning begins to shape up with the charge that the defendant—the Fisheries Service—is seeking to protect a group of turtles *not formally listed as a distinct, separate population under the Endangered Species Act.* (The whole species is listed as one unit; the government interprets that as meaning that all populations are of concern.)

The judge, listening intently, alternates resting her chin on her palm, asking occasional questions, requesting clarification of certain points, taking sips of water, and typing occasional notes into a laptop computer on her bench.

Mannina next addresses the Fisheries Service's finding that the catch by the dozen or so boats constitutes "jeopardy" to the continued existence of the Loggerhead Turtle.

Mannina says U.S. shrimp boats kill thousands of Loggerhead Turtles (this was before shrimpers' turtle-escape devices were required to have large openings), yet the Fisheries Service has said the shrimpers' catch causes "no jeopardy" to the species. Meanwhile, the "few hundred" that run afoul of longlines have provoked a "jeopardy" opinion. "It makes no sense," he concludes. Mannina sits.

But the Fisheries Service has a rationale, which its attorney explains is *not arbitrary:* it requires the shrimp boats to use devices in their nets designed to let turtles escape before they drown. Long-liners do nothing to avoid killing turtles—not yet, anyway.

The Fisheries Service's lawyer focuses on the major part of the U.S. longline fleet's turtle kills that occur in that blood-red smear on the map, around the Grand Banks. He reminds us that of the couple hundred American longline boats fishing the Atlantic, the mere dozen fishing the Grand Banks account for over 70 percent of all Loggerhead Turtle takes and 40 percent of all Leatherback catches. He holds up a poster-sized map for the judge. Mannina extends a hand to help him steady it on the tabletop.

The government's lawyer is younger, less forceful, less lawyerly, but the substance of his argument is also compelling. He points out that Mannina glossed over key items, such as those turtle-excluder regulations shrimpers must comply with. He focuses on the different ages and stages of a turtle's life and maturity cycle, and how killing them just before they reach sexual maturity affects whether the turtle population will likely grow or decline.

Next, supporting the Fisheries Service's closure, Monica Goldberg stands suited and straight-backed in her place, fingertips steadily touching the tabletop. She knows the fishermen are not bad people, she says, that they have the bad luck of just happening to kill endangered animals while they work, but that the law has certain requirements in a case like this. She argues that by closing this one area to these few fishing vessels, the service can fulfill its obligation to avoid jeopardy to the endangered species.

I cringe at the thought of the fishermen hearing themselves referred to as "these few boats." But Goldberg points out that the humans can move elsewhere; the turtles cannot. She explains that the northern nesting population is a critical producer of males to the species coastwide. Goldberg tells the judge she does not want to go into too much technical detail. But the judge, referring to the government lawyer's rather complex chart, which denoted statistics using Greek letters, quips, "Detail is fine; I'm into lambda." Her sudden informality prompts an unexpected laugh from everyone.

All the attorneys are doing an impressive job of arguing without notes. While Goldberg is speaking, the judge's clerk passes her a slip of paper. The judge reads it and asks, "Do you concur with the 'no jeopardy' opinion for the shrimp fishery?" Goldberg begins to respond while looking straight at the clerk, who averts her gaze.

Mannina is forceful in rebuttal, raising his voice, again emphasizing his claim that concern for subpopulations cannot be a basis for government action because those subpopulations are not separately listed. Mannina claims that because breeding females are only 1 percent of all turtles in the ocean, there must be 4.5 million Loggerhead Turtles in the Atlantic. Against such numbers, he argues, the few hundred turtles his long-liners kill are a tiny fraction of the population. He reemphasizes that the shrimpers pulled a "no jeopardy" opinion even though they kill thousands of turtles. "So *how,*" he demands, "can the few turtles the long-liners kill be considered to cause jeopardy?"

The judge responds, "You may have the better argument, but you can't just show there were other options the government didn't choose. The question is whether they have been arbitrary and capricious." She tells Mannina, "That's a very high standard you have to reach. You have to hit a home run here. Getting on base is not good enough."

Unruffled, Mannina says that by not using all of its data, the Fisheries Service was indeed arbitrary, indeed capricious. He argues that it was arbitrary to decide that long-lining posed jeopardy to the species but that shrimping does not.

All the arguments combined use one hour of our time.

Outside, as we hail a cab for the airport, Monica says, "I don't think he met the standard she was looking for. We'll see in a few days." About the fishers getting paid to fish while testing new techniques, and still getting to sell the fish they catch, she says, "It's a pretty good deal they're getting."

The fishermen might disagree. The uncertainty about the future must be emotionally draining. One fisherman, James Budi from Beaufort, South Carolina, walks over and says to me, "I read the section you wrote on long-lining, in the bookstore. I was so incensed by what I read in your book that I couldn't buy it, of course. But it's really a pleasure to meet you."

Embarrassed, I glance down and say, "That's very gracious of you."

The judge's decision was later summed in this headline:

JUDGE AFFIRMS LONGLINE FISHING CLOSURE

As in Hawaii, the North Atlantic closure had foreseen its own reopening, with the Fisheries Service stating that it would reopen the area if it could find a way to modify the fishing gear and keep turtle deaths down "significantly."

The results of those Atlantic long-liner experiments proved promising for turtles. The series of experiments sought a better mousetrap, a new combination of bait and hook style that would catch fish but not turtles. Most hooks are J-shaped. The usual bait is squid. The new bait is mackerel; the new hooks are sort of G-shaped and are called "circle hooks." The first time you see one, it's hard to understand how a circle hook can work. The point of the hook curls inward and points at the shank, then curls a little more so it's actually pointing a bit downward. If your straightened thumb is the hook shank (your thumbnail would be the hook's eye), and you curl your index finger in toward your thumb until the "point" of your finger almost touches your thumb's joint, that's a circle hook. Weird, eh? It's actually very clever. Instead of needing to pierce the flesh, it just slides into place, usually in the corner of a fish's mouth. Once positioned, that downward-curling point won't allow the hook to back out, and as the fish pulls that point digs in, and then the barb lodges. Circle hooks usually can't hook in the throat or gut. If one is swallowed, as the fish starts to pull away it will usually come back up like a steel ring, until that curled gap catches the corner of the mouth. Neat and simple. Because they seldom cause injury to the gut, throat, or gills, they've become popular with catch-and-release anglers. I've used them quite a bit for Striped Bass and Bluefin Tuna, and they work well.

Circle hooks reduced the Loggerhead catch up to nearly 90 percent, and caught about 65 percent fewer Leatherbacks. These statistics held only if the hooks were a large size, called 18/0. Using mackerel as bait resulted in the fewest caught Loggerheads. And while J-hooks snagged about half the turtles deep in the throat, resulting in many later deaths, 90 percent of the turtles caught on circle hooks had the hook in their jaw, where it could be removed without serious injury.

The Fisheries Service largely justified reopening both the Grand Banks and North Pacific waters in 2004 on the success of these experiments. It required that all U.S. longline boats fishing the Atlantic use only circle hooks, and further required boats to carry turtle-hoisting and hook-removal gear and to train crews. This is the work they should have been doing all along, helping clean up the long-liners' act instead of fronting for them, making excuses, and acting like the industry's agents rather than guardians of the public estate.

A year after the grounds were reopened, Mr. Budi wrote to tell me how he saw the events around the closure, the turtle-saving research, the Swordfish-conservation restrictions, the reopening of the Northeast Distant Area, and the new turtle-conservation mandates:

Personally, I'm delighted to have been able to work with all the parties involved, including turtle experts, biologists, statisticians, gear specialists and fishermen to reach the incredible turtle interaction reductions and improved safe handling that is now being promoted around the world. And as you know, the U.S. represents a minuscule portion of the overall pelagic longline effort in the world. The tools we developed make handling and release safer and easier for both turtles and fishermen. All U.S. longline boats are now required to use circle hooks, and I hope your current interest in turtles might lead you to promoting these aids internationally. We can only look forward to further improvements in all of the offshore fisheries once circle hooks become mandatory for all fishermen, not just U.S. pelagic longliners. By the way, an added advantage to our use of circle hooks has been an improvement in fish quality in that a much greater percentage of our catch is alive when landed. That translates into greater economic returns for the fishermen. And North Atlantic swordfish are successfully rebuilding: In the past several years we've seen record vessel landings with significantly larger fish. While our total harvest is still limited due to rigorous management controls, a burgeoning recreational fishery for swordfish speaks for a solid recovery. Certainly the rebuilding I brought to your attention in the Boston courtroom has continued, as you are aware.

Regards, J.B.

Ways to keep turtles and seabirds off longlines are spreading, through international conferences, skipper-to-skipper dialogues, and skipper-exchange programs like the one started by New Zealand–based Southern Seabird Solutions. As mainly U.S.-funded scientists work with fishing crews to test new hooks, different baits, and alternate fishing depths, conservation groups and management agencies like the World Wildlife Fund, BirdLife International, the Blue Ocean Institute, the Inter-America Tropical Tuna Commission, and the Western Pacific Fishery Management Council are looking for new things that work.

When long-liner captains complain that other countries have to be in this to win this, they're right. American environmentalists who think the United States can and should do the right thing and then work to export it—even if it takes a lawsuit to pop that lid—are also right. But how much time is left is another question. And from the moment your pursuit of turtles puts you on a Pacific shore, the answer seems to be: not much time, at all.

PART III

PACIFIC

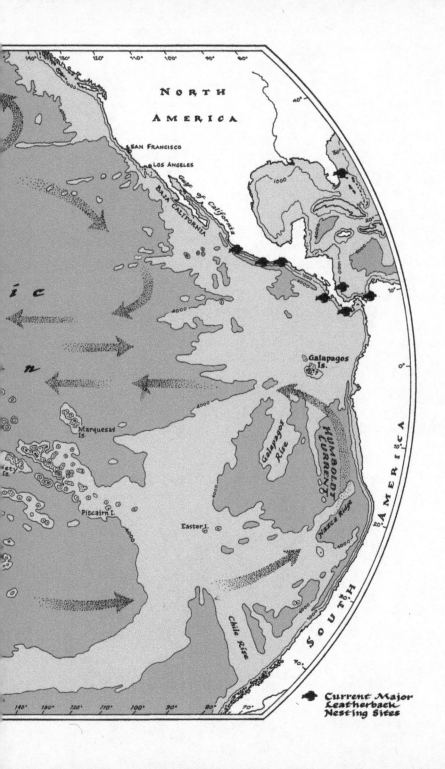

THE GREAT BEACH
Costa Rica

Playa Grande—the Great Beach—unfurls its graceful, mile-long sandy arc along a gentle indentation in Costa Rica's northwest coast. It's situated within a region—Guanacaste Province—whose acacia-dotted pastures and pleasant "Mediterranean" climate combine California and East Africa, attracting cowboys, shoestring travelers, and land speculators.

North and south of Playa Grande's sleepy enclave, tourist booms are gobbling beaches. Rumbles of development reach here as regularly as the sound of surf. Here the same dusty road leads both to the beach and to a few new fancy vacation homes, some still under construction. The forested strip along the beach whispers the portent conveyed by real-estate signs nailed to roadside trees.

Tension arises for three reasons. One, Playa Grande hosts the largest remaining Leatherback nesting population of any beach on the Pacific coast of the Americas. Two, whether the beach is really a national park or prime real estate for developers is a matter of intense legal dispute. Three, the Leatherbacks here, as all through their eastern Pacific nesting range up through Mexico, seem doomed to extinction.

Extinction on those beaches would mean no Leatherbacks in the entire eastern tropical Pacific and South Pacific Ocean—a vast swath of the world.

What I've sought to understand since starting my journey of the turtle is whether Leatherbacks and other sea turtles can really be stable or recovering in the Atlantic and crashing toward extinction in the Pacific. More to the point: If this is happening, what can be done to save turtles in the Pacific?

Here in Costa Rica, Leatherbacks are called *baulas,* Spanish for "storage trunk." Parque Nacional las Baulas, or Leatherback National Park, comprises one coastal mountain with no turtles, two mangrove estuaries with no turtles, and a beach called Langosta with almost no turtles anymore, and—*very* oddly—here at the main Leatherback nesting beach, the "park" is just a fifty-meter-wide strip along the high-tide line. The park's strange configuration reflects the deep split in how people view this ribbon of sand. For some, this beach is holy ground, absolutely critical to the survival of the Leatherback Turtle. For others, the beach would be just as pretty and relaxing, the waves as nice, without the turtles they've only heard about, who come in the night and disrupt their real-estate dreams.

And although this is the Leatherback's largest remaining nesting population in the eastern Pacific, "largest remaining" is relative. Frank

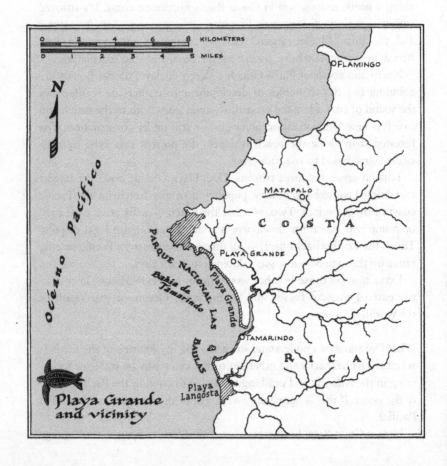

Paladino, an American scientist and professor, explains, "It's the height of the season, so about five or six turtles a night. It used to be closer to a hundred turtles nightly." Frank strongly favors a proposal that would widen the park. But doing so would engulf a couple of rustic lodges and new beachfront homes.

Frank is a dancing bear in a man's body. With his longtime research collaborator Jim Spotila, he's been working here since the late 1980s. Counting students and volunteers, about a hundred people come here to study Leatherbacks each year—more people, now, than turtles. "It used to be hectic as hell," Frank adds. "Now people patrol up and down, waiting for one to arrive."

When Paladino and Spotila arrived here in the late 1980s, they had to pay egg poachers for access to the beach. They'd be studying one nesting turtle while nearby poachers were taking eggs. When they finished their research for the night, poachers came and dug up their nests. The scientists didn't like it, but the poachers were in charge.

In 2000, Spotila, Paladino, and several coauthors shocked a lot of people with their article in the top-tier science journal *Nature,* entitled "Pacific Leatherback Turtles Face Extinction." They showed that in just ten years, the number of Leatherbacks nesting here plummeted 90 percent. For the entire Pacific, Leatherbacks declined from an estimated 91,000 adult females to fewer than 3,000—a 97 percent loss in just two decades. Viewed over the history of the species, it was as if Pacific Leatherbacks had been suddenly vaporized. "For all this to have happened over just twenty years"—Frank shakes his head—"it's incredible."

At midnight the sea is flat, the temperature mild, the waves gentle, their low rumble overlaid by insects answering from dark vegetation. The curling, unfurling surf gleams softly with phosphorescence, each breaking wave igniting a muted glow that fades before the wash runs its tongue up the beach.

As we're walking in the dark, Frank explains, "Open sandy beach like this is rare on this coast." Just around the headland to the north, for instance, the coast is armored by a fan of lava whose hard vertical bluff stands like a shield to repel the possibility of nesting turtles. "But this here"—Frank stops and spreads his arms—"it's what the turtles are looking for."

This middle part of the beach, where it's darkest, has the most turtle nests. Two miles to our south, where the coast curves seaward, stands a bright, shining town: Tamarindo.

"Can you believe those lights?" In the mid-1980s, basically none of that was there. What was there: nesting turtles.

At half past one, a sickle moon slices through papery clouds. Soon the sky clears sufficiently to reveal both the Southern Cross and the North Star. I hadn't realized, until this moment, that one sky could be so big.

Twenty minutes later I spot a dark smudge in the black sheet of water just above a withdrawing wave.

Over nine minutes, she crawls sixty feet to where her silhouette disappears against dark forest. We give her time to work in peace.

Scouts from two teams of licensed tour guides are patrolling the beach. One team brings tourists from those bright Tamarindo hotels. The other, from the town of Matapalo, guides tourists from the headquarters of this odd national park.

Another turtle is chugging ashore in the distance, the wet ridges of her back gleaming in the spare moonglow while the sea's sedate surf makes its muffled, rhythmic inquiries.

Sixteen tourists soon arrive with a uniformed guide. Many are young couples hand in hand; some are families with kids. About half are Costa Ricans, mostly from the capital, San José, for whom Leatherbacks are as exotic as for travelers from America or Europe. Halted by the sudden sight of the huge, dark animal, they stand quietly. His red light illuminating the egg chamber, the guide also stands silently. The turtle speaks for herself. A mother bends at the waist to match her son's height, arm around her child, watching as eggs fall into the magic chamber. The man next to me breathes, "Wow."

Tourist dollars are a strong motivator for keeping the turtles and protecting this beach. The miracle of life ought to seem motivation enough, but it's all about who's paying. At Playa Grande this season four thousand tourists will spend over $80,000 on park and tour fees. Add hotels and meals, and their local contribution—about $500 per person—tops $2 million. Trinidad's Matura Beach, where I first saw Leatherbacks nesting, received protected status in 1990. Now over ten thousand paying visitors come yearly to see the turtles there. In worldwide terms, where sea turtles are a major tourist attraction revenue is three times as high as where people mainly eat the turtles or their eggs. Moreover, turtles are declining in two-thirds of the populations where people eat them or sell their eggs. By contrast they're declining at only 15 percent of the sites where turtles are featured for tourism. That's not to say that all tourism is always good. Tourists can bring lights and disturbance. But well-regulated tourism seems to benefit both people and turtles. Yet here there's another factor many beaches lack: this beach is pretty enough to draw tourists all by itself; it doesn't need turtles to entice visitors.

When the laying ends, the tourists begin trekking back along the beach.

The turtle covers her eggs with the usual prodigious amount of flying sand and a few deep groans, throat pulsing, shell heaving, energetically plowing a figure eight and disguising the egg site, her exertion typically epic.

What she is doing accords well with the logic of deep time, yet what can be her sense of the *why* of this? I'd like to think she understands instinctively throughout this arduous ordeal that she is laying eggs, attempting to reproduce. But how could she? There can be virtually no chance that she has any idea of what she is doing, other than the *sensation* of it, the exertion of it, and the mysterious motivation to perform a series of behaviors for some absence of reason. Can something so intricate, so right, so strenuously crucial be accomplished as unthinkingly as scratching an itch? Is this ageless maternal wisdom merely an automatically performed program of sequenced behaviors? Is she not just motivated by but possessed by hormone levels, run by them the way timers and software switches run the cycles of a household appliance? If she feels or thinks anything, perhaps she's just delirious with exhaustion, confused by the strangeness of it all.

Frank, who has actually studied their hormone levels, thinks nesting turtles may feel conflicted. He's detected high levels of stress-related hormones while they're nesting. "After years in the ocean, their hormones are suddenly directing them to migrate toward this beach, to mate with males. Then they have these eggs shoved down their oviduct and shell gland, ready to go. They begin getting whiffs of land, and finally this hormonal urge to leave the ocean is just too overwhelming and they come out."

Any teenager has experienced the very strong hormone-induced motivations that we feel as urges. We share at least that with the turtles. Such impulses sometimes overpower human intellect, leading us into so much conflict we feel powerless to resist ourselves—hormonal incitement overwhelms insight, and behaviors flow. But we are always at least aware of *why* we are doing the things we're motivated to do. Aren't we? Maybe not. The hormones driving us toward reproduction are usually felt merely as impulses to perform certain behaviors. The acts yield a new generation, but that's not why we perform them. We perform them because hormones compel us; then hormones immediately reward our obedience with sensations of high excitement and intense pleasure. The hormones train us to want that pleasure again and again. Almost everything else we actually understand about those behaviors and their consequences, we must be taught. The connection isn't very intuitive, and some tribal peoples reputedly never equated reproductive acts with reproductive outcomes. How much more insight could a turtle have?

But even if a turtle's complex nesting routine is "just" a hormone-driven program, it's an astonishingly exact one, full of dogged perseverance, Olympian strength, and finely nuanced sensitivities, each applied in just the right way at just the right time in just the right sequence. Could hormones really drive all that integrated sequencing? Frank says, "Between behaviors—like between clearing the body pit and digging the egg chamber—one hormone drops as another begins surging. It's not until they're done, and the hormones are waning, that they start to again become aware of things around them. It's pretty cool."

Sounds almost human.

At nearly four A.M., the turtle turns, beginning to chug seaward with newly summoned—or newly injected—determination. The surf shines her shell, and in another moment she is lost to us. Meanwhile, in her sandy nest, the clock begins ticking on the future.

Walking homeward along the beach we come upon a well-known female, named Broken because she cannot dig an egg chamber. Broken isn't missing any part of any flipper, but something is wrong. Her left rear flipper's knuckles are swollen with rheumatoid arthritis; her right rear flipper seems also to hold abnormal bones. She can't really dig. Her flippers can't scoop. When she does bring up some sand, she usually hits the other flipper and drops it all. Broken might have been injured as a hatchling, perhaps grabbed by a crab or pecked by a bird on her dash from the nest. Or maybe she's seizing up with old age. Doubly cursed, this poor arthritic creature also has trouble laying. She hauls herself up night after night for several days, seeking release of her precious eggs, yet for some reason is unable to unburden. Again and again, she climbs and thrashes out a body pit, expending efforts that, compared to the exertions of healthy turtles, must be even harder. Yet she's been using the beach throughout the season, and has managed to lay several clutches. The pattern has been this: after coming up repeatedly, she lays on the fourth night—in a chamber dug for her by human friends. This is her first night of a new nesting attempt, and despite our help, she leaves without laying.

We depart the beach as the day's first Howler Monkey booms from the forest, its roars mingling with the growling surf.

After snoozing for a few hours, Frank takes me for a little walk. Several White-Throated Magpie Jays fly across the road behind the beach, which is lined with houses—most for sale—and a few unbuilt lots, all for sale. Inca Doves send coos from the foliage.

Frank says, "You see how in front of the houses they've removed the vegetation?" There's raked sand under planted palm trees. Where beach sand was quarried for concrete, rocks show.

Frank grunts, "Turtles don't go there anymore." He complains, "If this place gets built up, Playa Grande will be lost to Leatherbacks. Just like Tamarindo. Just like Flamingo. Those were major nesting beaches. Those were—." He sighs with exasperation.

We begin walking back and Frank adds, "The thing is, none of the owners of these houses right here is Costa Rican. Most are Americans, in it just to see the values inflate so they can sell. Or they'll rent to tourists, but at those prices you won't find many Costa Ricans renting."

What was once the mouth of a small stream looks like a dirt parking lot sprouting weeds. The dirt also sprouts a Century 21 sign advertising—in English—FILLED AND READY TO BUILD. The gates on an adjacent house feature wrought-iron Leatherback Turtles. I hope they won't someday be the last Leatherbacks in Playa Grande.

By 10:30 A.M. the January heat is already oppressive. I park myself in a shaded patio chair. Frank cuts me a slice of watermelon and we sit listening to the breeze, the waves upon the beach, the resonant bamboo wind chimes. This all seems so relaxed, so tropical and lazy. Yet the whole enterprise is a race against time.

Frank opines, "If we don't get this beach secured within the next couple of years, the Pacific Leatherback Turtle will probably go extinct."

Playa Grande has two kinds of tides. One, ruled by sun and moon, ebbs and flows and brings the turtles. The other is the rising tide of humanity. Which will prevail on this small stretch of beach—and everywhere else—is the drama unfolding.

Team spirit walks onto the patio in the form of three men. If this beach gets salvation from real-estate developers, it will be largely because of these three guys and Frank.

Rotney Piedra, currently the Baulas Park director, arrived here in 1994. Mario Boza had been environment minister; he was the visionary behind Costa Rica's national park system. He'd originally invited Dr. Jim Spotila to visit Playa Grande in the late 1980s and consider doing scientific work here.

In his signature floppy hat, Spotila seems an unlikely crusader. A bespectacled, mustached man, late fifties, of medium height and modest bearing, he is soft-voiced, droll, and paternal toward his turtles and academic hatchlings alike. Upon arrival yesterday he playfully distributed turtle-shaped clay ocarinas to the graduate students, prompting from all an immediate noise more joyful than ever before heard from a chorus of turtles. It's easy to sense that, in a better world, doing science and mentoring his students would be his definition of pure satisfaction.

He tells me, "There is no other animal in the world that compares to a Leatherback. Other turtles are nice, but they're not Leatherbacks. A Leatherback is a truly regal creature; I think it's the most beautiful animal in the world. It's the biggest large wild animal you can walk up close to without getting attacked. They're certainly a lot like living dinosaurs, more so than anything still living on Earth."

Spotila was the first to sense the Leatherbacks' critical condition here and throughout the Pacific. In 1988 Playa Grande hosted about fourteen hundred individual female nesters. By the early 1990s the number was down to several hundred coming annually. Yet Spotila knew from tagging studies that turtles can—occasionally—stay away for up to eight years or so between nestings. Reasoning along lines ranging between intellectual caution and plain hopefulness, he thought that perhaps oceanic conditions like El Niño's surge of warm, food-sparse water might be keeping turtles in cooler, fatter climes, far away.

"So we were waiting for the big year," he recalls for my benefit, "waiting for a thousand turtles to come back. Well, by the mid-nineties, it was finally getting obvious—there wouldn't be any more years that big. Numbers were going down in a major way. If you put the numbers on a graph and draw a line through them, the line hits zero just a few years from now. In other words, if the decline continues..."

At an international sea turtle conference, Spotila showed that graph. Several other turtle experts objected. They said, "You can't say they're going extinct; a lot of complex things can be going on." Spotila responded, "I believe they're going extinct, because that's the numerical trend."

Like a line in the sand, that line on the graph turned out to be the challenge call on Pacific Leatherbacks. It was also Spotila's Rubicon, his transformation from pure scientist to conservation biologist.

Frank indicates Spotila with his chin, saying to me, "Jim's a visionary. He saw the problem earlier than any of us. People pooh-poohed him, but he's turned out right."

Park director Rotney Piedra chimes in optimistically. "Now with our protection, maybe we will see the difference in the future. I hope, because in Mexico, very low the nesting."

Frank explains, "Mexico in the early 1980s had tens of thousands of Leatherbacks, and three beaches that *each* had as many turtles as this beach had. Now they have virtually none. We, at least, still have a viable population; Mexico's seems almost finished." He reasons, "Mexican turtles and Costa Rican turtles go and live in the same ocean, so they likely face the same fishing threats. Why are there virtually none left in Mexico, and still some here? It's gotta be something on the beach that's different.

"Mexico's had very heavy egg poaching for longer, and it's much more Wild West there than here. Mexico's got lots of beaches that are hard to patrol, and dangerous. By contrast, this place here's been basically protected since the mid-1990s. We've also started a hatchery that safeguards eggs and puts out thousands of hatchlings per year. Maybe one in a thousand comes back, but I think we're at least slowing the decline. So," he sums up, "that's why this seems like the last beach in the entire eastern Pacific where there's a viable population."

This beach is critical *not* because Leatherbacks are so endangered here. It's critical because there are more Leatherbacks left here than on any beach in the eastern Pacific. Of a recently estimated thirty-five thousand living adult females worldwide, likely fewer than one thousand now nest in the eastern Pacific. The western Pacific has had its disasters, too. Other beaches have been lost to egg taking, disturbance, and development. So any thought of recovery relies ever more heavily on Playa Grande remaining suitable for nesting.

"That's the main thing," Piedra emphasizes. "To get the land where there are no houses. It is very expensive to buy houses. We would rather use money to buy land with no houses, where the turtles are mainly nesting now."

Frank notes, "If they can buy the dark part of the beach, the turtles will probably keep coming. But we have limited time."

Remember, limited time looks like this: in just the last twelve years this population has declined about 90 percent.

Yet even extinction wouldn't stop Frank. If the Leatherback goes extinct in the Pacific, he explains, "We'll bring eggs from the Atlantic and reintroduce them here. If you have the beach, you could bring Pacific Leatherbacks back from extinction. No beach, no turtles."

Spotila adds, "Fishing's also important. Florida had virtually no Leatherbacks. The state banned fishing with gill nets in the mid-1990s. Now they have more than five hundred Leatherback nests a year. We've gotta deal with the fishing internationally, and there are gill-net fisheries all along Latin America. But I agree, without this beach, there's no Leatherbacks."

I'm puzzled. Back in the early 1990s these guys put a lot of work into creating Leatherback National Park. The president signed the law in 1995. But if everyone involved realizes this beach is critical to the turtles' future, why is the park shaped so oddly? Why is there so little park in the park?

Mario Boza, the visionary, says, "The park was supposed to secure the beach two hundred meters inland from the high-tide line. But instead of saying 'from the beach landward two hundred meters,' it says, 'from the beach seaward two hundred meters.' It was just a stupid mistake."

Spotila says, "I think it was deliberate."

"Was a *stupid* mistake," persists Boza. "Was supposed to be, from the high-tide line, two hundred meters *inland*."

So the national park is mostly in the surf. This underlies almost all the real-estate trouble in Playa Grande now. But that happened in the 1990s. Why hasn't it been fixed?

"Because that's just one problem in the country," explains Boza. "And there are thousands of problems." And buying land to add to the park will require money the government doesn't have—national park or not. So while Spotila and Frank are trying to raise money for buying land through their nonprofit Leatherback Trust, Piedra is trying to chill building permits until things get resolved, and Boza's attempting to get the law repaired and the park expanded to include most of what hasn't been built on yet in sleepy Playa Grande.

Not surprisingly, some people don't like these men, so they tend not to walk the roads alone at night.

If the law had been worded correctly, the houses along the dune could not have been built. But now, they're there, more are under construction, and the rest of the beach seems headed that way. So it's also a race pitting fund-raising against construction and rising property values.

About the lack of government funding to get the job done, Boza, the former environment minister, seems a little frustrated. He says tourists annually spend a billion dollars; they're the biggest contributor to the country's economy, and most come to see nature and visit the country's parks. He adds, "When you see the numbers, you think, 'Okay—solved!' You'll just show how big a contributor nature is to the economy, and parks will be protected so tourists will continue coming to Costa Rica. It's all very positive." He wags his finger, saying, "Doesn't work that way. When you go to the Institute of Tourism and ask them for money to help the parks, they will say they have no money—even though they receive millions in tourist taxes. If you go to the Ministry of Public Works and say, 'We need good roads in the parks,' they will say, 'We have other needs.' Lawmakers still don't understand that protecting nature is protecting the chicken that lays golden eggs. How do you say that in English?"

"The goose."

"Yes! The goose. But—I'm very optimistic, because of the very high level of education in this country, the high level of public consciousness about the environment. These things are missing in many countries, for instance in Nicaragua."

I'm thinking of a small banana republic called Washington, D.C.

But isn't it unfair for the government to forcibly buy out landowners?

Without hesitating, Boza emphatically says, "We have hundreds— literally hundreds—of beaches in this country *ideal* for development. We are trying to protect, like, *four* beaches: Santa Rosa, Ostional, Cabo Blanco, Playa Grande—that's it. You either have vacation houses, condominiums, hotels, whatever—or you have a national park. You cannot have both. Simple, really."

He continues: "I have seen the faces of people when they see the turtles. To see a Leatherback dig the nest and lay the eggs, this is an outstanding phenomenon. To preserve this *precious* resource, we have to preserve this area. This is not done against private interests. It is in favor of public interests. This is the key point." He leans forward, tapping a finger. "Public interests—versus personal interest."

"What's scary," Spotila adds, "is that this beach is worth a lot more money with hotels than with turtles. The real question is, Do other species deserve to live, or not? If yes, you can build hotels—just not where the turtles nest."

There's an uncomfortable silence. Then Spotila sighs. "This is such a nice beach; you can see why people would want to have a house here. When I'm getting ready to come here, I just count the days till I can be on this beach with these wonderful turtles. It's just a real pleasure. It would be really great if the turtles weren't going extinct. A few years ago, when the lights from Tamarindo weren't so bright, you could have a really nice walk, feeling you were in the wilderness, at the edge of things. But it's still a pretty nice beach—there's still a lot to save here."

I ask, "What's everyone's prognosis?"

Frank's comment is "I'll at least go down fighting. I gotta say, though, I see momentum. I see a lot of people who care, coming together, rallying around. But we gotta do it now. There were fourteen hundred females here in 1988 and we have, like, a hundred turtles now. That's a real compeller."

Jim Spotila is silent for a moment in a way that is more than just quiet. A deep stillness comes over him, almost as if part of him has fled. Then he says softly, "We didn't set out to save turtles. It kinda crept up on us. We were doing science and there were lots of turtles. Next thing you know, you're still here, the turtles are disappearing, and one day you wake up realizing a lot depends on you."

THE TOWN OF TAMARINDO HAS PERHAPS TEN MAJOR HOTELS, LIKE THE Barceló, with a couple hundred rooms, a casino, the works. Boosting the tourist capacity are various surfer flophouses, numerous bars, an Internet café or two, and sportfishing charter boats. If you stand on the beach and look to the right, your eye follows the rocky shore to the shining beach of Playa Grande. To the people relaxing on the beach—surfers with their boards at ease, youths tossing a ball, women and children in the shade of palms—the idea is a holiday by the sea, not a diabolical plot against turtles who happen to be going extinct. I'd wager that not one person in this town knows that turtles nested here a few years ago, or that these rocks were covered by a beach of sand that now rises in the concrete of the hotels.

Walking the dusty road back in Playa Grande, I find opinion mixed. "They have to finalize their boundaries. It's hard to talk about sales when you don't know where the lines are going to be." That's the view of John Lahoud and Alicia Carvallo, two thirty-something Americans running Pura Vida Realty, a short walk from the turtle beach. "We really like the idea of an expanded national park, actually. Twenty years from now we wouldn't mind still having this nice little quiet place to live. Just tell us what's happening."

The hotel Villa Baula—Leatherback House—advertises itself as an ecological lodge on the beach. Manager Mario Araya and I sit on bamboo chairs next to a sunny flower garden. Speaking with a slightly formal cadence, he says, "Our establishment was founded on the idea of appreciation, and respect for, the natural environment. That the beach may remain dark and the turtles feel comfortable, we have kept our natural curtain of green vegetation in front. Our outdoor walkway lights point downward and are low-intensity. We don't want this lovely area to turn into another Tamarindo." Taking a sip of coffee, he continues, "If turtles went extinct, it would be a huge loss. Such a marvelous species. If this species known as the last dinosaur would return in their former numbers, this would be wonderful, good for everyone. But people come here for many reasons, not just turtles. If the turtles disappeared, the impact upon tourism would not be so great."

Walking back up the forested road, I stop at a small lodge whose proprietor is sweeping beneath a sign announcing, TURTLE TOURS. He introduces himself as Brandon. He's thirty-four years old, wiry, with large hazel eyes.

About expanding the national park to save the turtles, he begins casually: "Hey, I like turtles because they bring me some business. But I'm against expropriating private land for parks. I'm more important than a fuckin' turtle." A former member of the U.S. military, he says, "In America, the idea now is to profit by exporting all the blue-collar jobs. The whole fucking U.S. economy is selling itself off to the rest of the world for the lowest bidder. And of course I hate war." He looks at me. "So I'm here." He leans forward and in a faked whisper, confides, "But I fucked up—I moved to a place they want to expand a *national park*." He gestures with disgust, then adds, "You work hard for something, they'll take it away from you. Rotney, the park director? Him and me are like oil and water. He's trying to tell me what I can fuckin' do. My light a quarter mile from the beach scares turtles because it shines? If you don't see the world the way they do, you got problems. And why do they want to expand the park? Say a person who works at a bank in Canada comes and sees a turtle. They get educated: 'This many eggs, this big—.' Does that help the fuckin' turtles? I don't *think* so. I think the people doing the educating are just looking for a big check when that person gets home. If they're really interested in education, they wouldn't charge them. See what I'm saying? If they *loved* the turtles they'd leave them in peace, not tramp people all around them every night. So, man, don't lie to me. I wouldn't care if every turtle in the world died. Species die every day. I mean, what happened to dinosaurs?" He's been here thirteen months, he tells me. That's roughly a hundred million years less than the turtles have been here, give or take— yet he may, in fact, hang on more resolutely than the turtles themselves.

THE ODOMETER OF THIS SHUDDERING VEHICLE HAS TALLIED 314,000 kilometers, and the explanation offered is *"tiene muy fuerte."* Lurching, rattling, and whining along in a cloud of dust, our van sounds like it's relying more on *suerte* than *fuerte*—luck rather than strength. From roadside wires, elegant Scissor-Tailed Flycatchers and jaunty Great Kiskadees survey their realms. With the windows down we're immersed in the hot wind, freely circulating dust, the scents of banana trees, pigs, burned grass, and barbed-wired cow pastures. We shift into low and drive through a small stream, then up to an unpainted tin-roofed clapboard house.

The aged woman who is introduced as Godmother of the Turtles is one Doña Esperanza, a small, stocky woman with short-sheared hair and skin leathery as a turtle's. Standing in her worn-out T-shirt, with a coil of rope around one shoulder and a deep ancient scar on her shin, she looks like one tough cookie.

On a nail over the tiny table in the gloom indoors hangs a tiny plaque. Esperanza is sufficiently proud of it to lift it from its nail and show it to us, but she has never learned to read the words on the parchment. It's from the Ministry of Environment and Energy, recognizing her efforts on behalf of the turtles.

We go into her dirt yard, under a spreading mango tree. Doña Esperanza pulls out a cigarette, grips it in her mostly toothless mouth, settles into a chair, and slips out of her dusty sandals.

A little girl climbs into Esperanza's lap, sprawling over her small frame, causing Esperanza to stretch her neck to look over the top of the child's head. This, explains Esperanza, is her "granddaughter," salvaged from a nearby doorstep where she'd been abandoned as an infant.

Everyone knows certain things about Doña Esperanza: that her scars are from machete fights with poachers and that she has, more than once, flattened people with one punch. We're here to separate facts from the legend, by asking the legend herself.

"When I first moved to Playa Grande," recalls Doña Esperanza, "there were only three houses. I was twenty-eight." That was forty-four years ago. "My husband tended to land. He had a machete; that is how we earned money. Every Saturday we traveled on horseback to get rice, beans, and so on, meat—. Even in 1980, Playa Grande had no plumbing, no lights, no real roads. No one realized turtles were there. People eventually noticed the *Loras*"—Olive Ridleys, named *Lora* for their parrotlike face—"then realized *Baulas* came there too. We started trekking to the beach for eggs. Word spread. We ate just the eggs, not the mother turtles. People started coming from all over. That was the early eighties. There were no laws against taking eggs. We took all we wanted, back then."

She continues, "Usually you stayed until you got three or four or five nests. It is hard to carry all the eggs from a nest. But everyone came to the beach on horseback. You rode home with your eggs. They are very good for baking, making breads and pastries.

"Then, about twenty years ago, a new idea came. People began saying turtle eggs help arouse the men. Like Viagra." Soon a man with a truck appeared, offering money for all the eggs anyone could bring him. Sold in bars and sucked down raw, the largest turtle egg of all offered extra enhancement and macho appeal.

Esperanza's stepson Don Chico arrives, settling into an old dusty rocking chair. Only five years her junior and looking every day of it, with a slight cataract visible behind his eyeglasses, he's a small man with a body like taut canvas over a wire frame. Catching him up on the conversation, I ask whether turtle eggs boost male performance. He smiles slyly, making a fist and slowly raising his forearm. He says, "People thought the turtle eggs, also the clams, and certain fish are natural Viagra."

Esperanza informs me, "People now know it is not true, so there is less attraction to eating turtle eggs."

Chico counters this: "Some people still think so. A few still come here looking for eggs. I tell them, 'Not anymore.'" He recalls, "It was a very wild place. People coming to collect eggs also spent time clamming, fishing, looking for honey. This area was great for finding food. We had deer and guans. There were many more streams, more water to drink. Much forest has now been cleared for cattle. Then the water dries up and the deer and other animals run away."

"They call me the first park ranger," Esperanza recalls, "but it wasn't a park when I first started counting the nests. I can't write, but I can count. Starting in November, all night, turtles—a hundred and twenty, a hundred and forty, a hundred and fifty—every night for months. The beaches were left, I believe, without one single egg." The heaviest commercial take lasted about a decade. "When I understood there was concern for the turtles, I started riding on the beach counting tracks, watching over the turtles, trying to protect them. At first, the men did not like me. Many times, they threatened me. But by about 1988, 1989, everyone knew it had become illegal." When Boy Scouts arrived for camping trips, helping count and protect the turtles, the poachers started leaving. Esperanza continued the counts for ten years.

What about all these scars, including the infamous leg wound from the famous struggle with the poacher?

She laughs. A rooster answers. "Here is the story: We went to the estuary one day to catch fish called *Róbalo*. They are good-sized fish. We did not have hooks and lines back then. We had a pole with a nail, like a spear. A huge one came by. I hit the fish right behind the head and started yelling for my friend to come and assist me with it. 'I got one, I got one!'" Doña Esperanza pantomimes. "We took it back and cut it up and sold it. So we came back later with lanterns, thinking we'd catch more at night. We had our spears, and also machetes. I lit up the water with the lantern and three started coming toward the light and me. I was holding a mangrove with one hand so I would not slip on the muddy bottom. When one of them was right near me, I swung my machete." She reenacts her swing. "But because of the water the fish was not where it appeared, and I chopped my own leg. Very deep. They took me to the horse and put a tourniquet on my leg. We could not reach a doctor. No one had a car. So we put tobacco on it. And I was in bed for four months! And that is the true story." She chuckles, admiring her scar.

And what about the broken finger? I ask. "We have heard you punched a turtle-egg poacher."

Again she laughs. She displays the little finger of her right hand, healed at a startling angle. "My son-in-law, I didn't like. One day, he was yelling at my daughter. I came and"—she swings her fist through the air—"popped him one. I broke my hand—but he took off running." She laughs again. Apparently the pleasure has lasted long after the pain.

"I have had other fights," she adds, as if not wanting to leave the subject. "If they are looking for it, they will find it with me," she asserts convincingly. "One day, a woman came looking for my sister-in-law, who wasn't here. She was mad. She tried to hit me." She pulls her head back and raises her eyebrows to pantomime her surprise and her evasion of the blow. "What would *you* do? I grabbed her hair and with my head I broke her nose; then I punched her. That was another time I broke my hand. That was two years ago."

Veering through some memories, she continues: "I have been here a long time. There were many turtles. Then the biologists came. I think turtles are few because of the tags the scientists put in. I think the turtles don't like it, so they don't come back. That is what I think. We touched and stroked her when she came; we showed her *cariño,* affection. She likes that contact, that interaction. Now no one shows her any tenderness. Now when she is touched, they are marking her, tagging her, taking blood." Esperanza makes jabbing motions. "She is only touched in ways that cause her pain. And they take pictures with flashes, sudden and harsh." Esperanza opens and closes her hand rapidly several times, making flashing motions. "That, I *really* don't like. We never did anything like that to the turtles."

But then Doña Esperanza's voice softens, and she says, "In the beginning we never thought about whether taking eggs could make any difference. There were so many turtles. You don't think that because you take food off the shelves in a store, there might not be food someday. I am sad they are now so few. Yes, I took many eggs. I admit it. But then I quit to work for the turtles. We started simply, just a couple of us, bringing beans and rice and a little meat to the beach and sleeping in a tent. We collected rainwater. And we were turtle guards. It was so simple."

A HAND-PAINTED LEATHERBACK TURTLE HATCHERY SIGN HANGS ON A low wooden fence. Within, like an open-air beach garden, lie rows of little round protective cages bearing I.D. tags. In 1998—"pretty late into the crisis," as Frank Paladino says—the science team started moving most Leatherback clutches into the protective custody of this perimeter, redepositing them in hand-dug egg chambers.

Each nest in this hatchery is covered with fine-meshed insect netting to thwart a fly that lays eggs on the sand over a turtle clutch; its maggots dig down to infest the eggs. So many dangers. Raccoons and skunks, formerly uncommon, now have a year-round food source—garbage—and they've become plentiful. Dogs. With so few turtles and so many more mammals now, saving nests from predators, high tides, and all the hazards of the beach, and bringing them here, allows Playa Grande to produce roughly twice as many hatchlings as would naturally placed nests. The main thing you have to pay attention to is nest temperature, to make sure you're not producing all one sex. The hatchery puts out four to five thousand hatchlings per year.

Poaching took almost every nest until the early 1990s, but virtually ended with the establishment of the park. Now, about as many hatchlings are entering the Pacific here each year as in the early 1990s—when there were almost fifteen times as many nesting females but no park or hatchery.

Frank says. "We're hoping we'll start seeing here the same thing that happened in St. Croix." On that Caribbean island, twenty years of moving virtually every nest into protective custody caused the Leatherback population to balloon from under thirty females to about two hundred.

In Playa Grande, now half the nesting turtles are here for their first time. They're almost certainly the fruit of that protection. That would be great if it was the whole story. But about 15 to 20 percent of breeding females are dying annually, double the death rate of a stable population. Unless that rate changes, the population seems doomed.

Extrapolating from recent adult survival, Frank and Spotila have a hypothesis that can be stated in nontechnical terms: "We think they're getting whacked in the ocean by fishing gear. We don't have all the data to prove this, but that's what we think the problem is."

The business plan of long-lived animals counts on high adult survival—around 90 percent per year—to offset the many years to maturity and low infant survival. Populations with high adult survival are growing—for instance, Leatherbacks nesting on St. Croix. But a survival rate of only 80 percent or less means capital losses year after year, a recipe for bankruptcy, a long-term decline sliding toward extinction. And with Pacific Leatherbacks and Loggerheads, that's where we're at.

Turtles die for two reasons: natural and human causes. We know their populations can generally handle natural causes. We know they can't handle too much added mortality from humans. And we know, as I've mentioned, that their overall Pacific mortality is about twice what they can handle. We've seen that some people still eat them. Where they don't—in the United States for example—seafood's increasing popularity means more fishing gear in the water, more turtles running afoul of long-lines, gill nets, and trawls. They get caught in nets set for Swordfish, sharks, and tunas. The Pacific's major longline fishing nations, Japan, Taiwan, and Korea, collectively set over seven hundred million hooks per year on lines roughly thirty-five to fifty-five miles long (sixty to ninety kilometers), deployed from their thousands of boats. That's a lot of pressure. But is the current death rate all from the fishing gear? The overall death rate nowadays must owe something to all the egg poaching of the 1980s, which robbed the population of its youth.

I look over the nests in this hopeful hatchery. As more of the eggs produce hatchlings that return as young breeders, the population's overall mortality rate should improve. Can that improvement from young ones maturing outpace the decline from older ones dying, in time to prevent the population's extinction?

In the hatchery, sundown and the fresh whisper of night start the vigil. Sharing our interest in the nests but having more immediate motives, a family of Raccoons visits the hatchery fence. To say the little masked egg gourmands are not welcomed would be to greatly understate the greeting they receive.

In charge of the hatchery is a thin woman in a smudged T-shirt and yellow shorts, her dark hair pulled back. Her name: Pilar Santidrin Tomillo—we call her Bibi. She's from Madrid. A little while later, Bibi makes a round of nest checks with her little red flashlight and announces, "We've got hatchlings in two nests."

She tilts the screens up, plucking them out with the delicacy of a pastry chef, placing them softly in buckets. They weigh about fifty grams. Say a hatchling weighs two ounces soaking wet. For it to mature to an average eight-hundred-pound nest digger, its weight gain will have to be sixty-four-thousand-fold. At that rate, a human baby would level out into adulthood at about forty-five thousand pounds.

We wish to take the newly minted nestlings to their destiny without delay. As a moth knows nothing of flame, our hatchlings, knowing nothing of the sea, are nonetheless restless and impatient. One-in-a-thousand odds. Here we go.

With the little *tortuguitas* in buckets, we walk about seventy yards down the beach, picking a random place so fish don't learn to gather at one particular spot for nightly hors d'oeuvres. We stop on dry sand because the turtles' seaward march may aid them in storing in their brain information crucial for their eventual return, in the unlikely case any survive. We first push sand into nearby crabs' burrow entrances with our feet; in the next few minutes these crabs will not get a chance to pull hatchlings into their murdering chambers.

We tilt the dark buckets forward on the dim apron of sand, and in moments blackish shapes emerge. Some of the hatchlings appear slow in getting oriented seaward. It might be the lights from those houses north of the hatchery. They must seem bright to the baby turtles newly emerged from black nests, with eyes fine enough to be guided by starlight.

But they do soon get oriented. Rising and falling in the dimpled footprints of the day's surfers, the baby behemoths scamper seaward to wet sand and beyond, black turtles to blackness born, bearing themselves into the black sea. Within the confines of their nearly impossible prospects, we calculate the odds for their race.

They, however, bet everything on survival. Watching them, there is no sensing that these babes are among the last of their tribe, because by every action they reaffirm themselves, so avidly asserting their run at life. There is nothing downtrodden or depleted about them. Only we bear the burden of knowledge that the odds are so fearsomely against such vigorous innocence. Their energy matches that of hatchlings who emerged a thousand or ten million years ago, when these beaches rumbled with the thunder of hundreds of turtle mothers. They are the new generation, always the world's only hope.

Adult Olive Ridley Turtles sometimes come ashore by the thousands in the spectacular mass nestings called arribadas. But many come up alone—and here's one, just covering her clutch. This seventy-pound, yard-long turtle seems tiny compared to a Leatherback ten times her size. Her strikingly high-domed, helmetlike shell appears, of all things, petite.

She's so light she can't pack the sand well enough with her rear flippers, so she begins vigorously tamping down the nest with body blows from her hard belly, repeatedly rising and smacking the sand flat and snug. She shifts her weight to land a few blows from one side of her body, a few from the other. By comparison to her monster cousin, the Olive is a gymnast, her whole rear shell thumping the ground like a small tom-tom. She pumps her sandy throat and blinks.

She's got a 150-yard run to the ocean. Down the slope to the sea she goes, almost sprightly, her alternating gate a tortoiselike walk, wholly unlike the Leatherback's lurching breaststroke.

Frank comments happily, "Pretty cool." Each turtle he sees seems to reassure him that the world still makes sense.

By midnight, the first adult Leatherback has arrived. It's Broken, who keeps knocking sand into the hole that Jim Spotila is digging for her. Just when it looks like the hole is deep enough, she moves forward slightly, partly collapsing the artificial chamber. She doesn't lay.

Jim says, "This is only her second try with this clutch; she usually lays on the fourth night. I guess she's not quite ready. She needs a little more oxytocin, I guess."

It again seems alien that in this leathery machine such crucial acts are determined merely by levels of circulating hormones. But again the difference is skin-deep. The same oxytocin she needs to release her eggs is also manufactured by that old pituitary gland in the reptilian part of our own brains. During human birth it causes the uterine contractions of labor. It's used medically to induce or assist women's labor and cervical dilation. It is also released during intercourse, resulting in uterine contractions during orgasm; circulates at elevated levels in people claiming to feel love, friendship, bonding, or familial ties; and stimulates maternal care in humans and other animals. If given to animals, oxytocin induces virgin mammals to provide maternal care toward unrelated juveniles (they wouldn't normally do that). And when it's chemically blocked in real mothers, they lose interest in their own offspring. Infants suckling at the nipple stimulate the release of oxytocin into the bloodstream, where it causes milk to flood into the ducts of the breasts and sometimes causes mild uterine contractions during nursing.

Scorpio rises. I'm patrolling with a volunteer named Steve, a psychiatrist from Visalia, California, who signed up through the group Earthwatch.

We're on the south stretch of beach, walking wordlessly, listening to the black surf's white noise as Tamarindo blights the night with light. The town's effect on the eye is dramatic. It seems to catch your view, wiping out your night vision and washing out the fainter stars.

Having come to the end of our patrol perimeter, we turn back toward the darker part of the beach as someone on the Tamarindo waterfront begins setting off firecrackers.

Ten minutes to five. Up ahead, a digging turtle. Steve, who wastes few words, says, "To see them coming—like prehistory. And the shell with its ridges. Like triceratops." He turns to me and asks, "Have you felt them, how soft they are? How warm the skin around their neck? Beautiful."

We're waiting for her to finish her egg chamber and begin laying. Steve says, "Just listen. The breathing."

She emits a deep sound, a low bellow, almost cowlike.

My dim flashlight finds a recently healed scar four inches wide, a broad pink stripe wrapped around the base of her right foreflipper. The last time this turtle came up, this wound was really raw, with skin hanging. Now that it's healed, the scar tissue is thick. But she still has full use of that arm.

This time I'm the official egg counter. So I turn my cap backward, don a head lamp with a red bulb, and pull out my click counter. I wriggle in tight.

When laying, a Leatherback often keeps one protective rear flipper palmed over the hole. If you need a good count, you just hold her rear flipper to the side a little so you can get a little light into the chamber. It seems difficult the first time.

Holding the surprisingly soft—like buckskin—rear flipper, you can feel the fingerlike toe bones inside. Her big tail in my face, I'm tilted into the body pit as though about to slide into the egg chamber, illuminating things with my little light. The eggs smell like the ocean.

In ten minutes she lays eighty-four robust eggs. Some of her final, yolk-less "eggs"—that peculiar Leatherback phenomenon—are even odder than usual: they're pea-sized, and fused like melted marshmallows.

She finishes laying as the weaker stars begin fading, the world hinged between starlight and dawn. It's rare to be with a nesting turtle at day's dawning, when you can begin seeing color and details.

The gathering light reveals another pink stripe of scar, on her left front flipper where it joins her body. Was it luck that allowed her to join us, a fisherman's compassion, or the benefit of being "worthless"?

She gasps and thrusts, gasps and thrusts, flings and struggles, covering her work. Her eye is swiveling slightly as though she's dreaming, thick tears running like lava down the sides of her face.

One of the graduate students has joined us. He says, "Notice she's starting to perfuse there underneath, what we call the gular or clavicular region. They can use cardiovascular changes to help thermoregulate."

That is to say, she's getting hot, so she's blushing at her throat, where the air can help cool her blood. That's harder to see at night.

The day breaks warm with birdsong. Soon pelicans begin patrolling.

The sun comes to hover over the horizon behind us, but the tilted beach remains forest-shadowed even as strengthening sunshine gleams on the surf. An Elegant Tern pauses, dives, snatches a silver snack.

She's still covering when the first surfers and strollers come out. A young couple walk past, affecting world-weary indifference (a dinosaur—whatever). Next, though, a man and his small granddaughter stand duly halted by the monster. Watching, I imagine the little girl's fright at encountering a chest-high turtle, and years from now, perhaps, telling friends about her grandfather's reassurance, and wondering aloud whether such creatures remain in the world.

It is fully light when our mama gets her seawater face wash. She's been late, slow, and successful, and has escaped the tropic morning's full heat. The next wave lifts her, and with the rare advantage of daylight we can watch her pushing a bulge of water and moving just under the surface, much faster than a human swimmer, perhaps six miles an hour, leaving a rippling wake. Her great head comes up for another breath and she resumes traveling. A hundred yards offshore, in the curl of a wave, her body becomes briefly visible for one final glimpse, and the next time she raises her head it's the last trace of her. She's going home.

FOREIGN TOURISTS SEEKING A NESTING LEATHERBACK PAY FIVE DOLLARS to the park, plus a fee to the guide group that leads them to the turtle. There are two guide cooperatives, from two towns: Tamarindo, to the south, and Matapalo, to the north, a short drive over the hill. Local people on horseback still come and go from the square there, and roosters make more noise than the sparse traffic.

Idanuel Contreras, the head of the Matapalo guide cooperative, says, "Thank God for the turtles. If they keep coming, we have a good thing."

"In the past," vice president Laura Jaen says, "we saw turtles only as egg producers. Now we know the more effective way to use turtles for improving the human situation is to look after the turtles."

After paying the guides and covering their expenses, the cooperative gives the equivalent of about fifty dollars weekly to the local civic fund. A village meeting hall lacked toilets; turtle money took care of that. The elementary school lacked a fence to prevent children from running into the street; turtle money to the rescue. And then the church needed a public-address system.

Contreras removes his glasses and gives his eyes a rub. "The turtles—we are concerned," he begins. "Ten years ago, so many turtles—so different. We are doing what we can locally, but they are subject to pollution, fishing."

Laura responds, "It would break my heart if there were no turtles for my children."

ON THE WAY BACK TO PLAYA GRANDE, I FIND MYSELF AT A BULL-RIDING rodeo. There's food and a carnival atmosphere, a few drunks, not many tourists. I squeeze in atop the wooden wall of the ring with a bunch of locals.

The riders file into the ring with all the dusty pomp mustered by a small Wild West town. A man yelling over a distorting public-address system presents them in grandiloquent hyperbole, asserting that these bull-riding hombres represent *"the best spirit of humanity."* They take their bows and march from the ring.

A few minutes later the chute opens and a rider bursts into the ring on the back of a bucking bull. A belt cinched tight around the most sensitive part of the bull's belly prompts the discomfited animal's bucking and kicking. After the rider dismounts or gets thrown off—usually in less than about ten seconds, either way—dozens of spectators who have jumped into the ring taunt the animal, running up behind it and throwing soft-drink cups and pieces of trash and cardboard, then scampering up the walls as soon as the bull snorts in their direction. The bull is chased from the ring by a horseman, and eventually the next rider and bull burst forth.

One rider, thrown clear, lands flat on his back, his head glancing off the wooden side of the ring. Stunned and sprained, he clutches the wooden slats, and must be pried and dragged away. The last we see of him is his feet, disappearing through the gate where he emerged.

Meanwhile the bull trots the perimeter, scaring and scattering high-alcohol hecklers. Soon two people on horseback enter the ring, lasso the bull, and direct it into the corral. The taunters, who always approach from behind, do their most energetic garbage throwing after the bull is lassoed. They always retreat immediately if a bull turns toward them. Only the bulls maintain their dignity. Only the bulls' behavior really makes sense.

People have been on Earth in our present form for only about 100,000 years, and in so many ways we're still ironing out kinks. These turtles we've been traveling with, they outrank us in longevity, having earned three more zeros than we. They've got one hundred million years of success on their résumé, and they've learned something about how to survive in the world. And this, I think, is part of it: they have settled upon peaceful career paths, with a stable rhythm. If humans could survive another one hundred million years, I expect we would no longer find ourselves riding bulls. It's not so much that I think animals have rights; it's more that I believe humans have hearts and minds—though I've yet to see consistent, convincing proof of either. Turtles may seem to lack sense, but they don't do senseless things. They're not terribly energetic, yet they do not waste energy. Turtles don't have the intellect to form opinions about greed, oppression, superstition, or ideology, yet they don't inflict misery on themselves or other creatures. Turtles cannot consider what might happen, yet nothing turtles do threatens anyone's future. Turtles don't think about their next generation, but they risk and provide all they can to ensure that there will be one. Meanwhile, we profess to love our own offspring above all else, yet above all else it is they from whom we daily steal. We cannot learn to be more like turtles, but from turtles we could learn to be more human. That is the wisdom carried within one hundred million years of survival. What turtles could learn from us, I can't quite imagine.

JUST SOUTH OF THE FORMER TURTLE NESTING BEACH THAT'S NOW Tamarindo lies a beach called Langosta, still visited by a few turtles. We're walking there. The light and thumping of Tamarindo eventually fall away, and we plunge toward deep darkness in the black breeze under the wide gaze of a galaxy-crowded sky. The contrast is stark and startling.

I am with doctoral student Bryan Wallace and a twenty-year-old dreadlocked aspiring scientist named Roberto, from Costa Rica's Caribbean side. Roberto has worked with turtles since age five, first professionally, as an egg poacher. At age eight he switched sides voluntarily. He would dig nests in his usual poacherly way, then rebury them so other poachers wouldn't get them.

Roberto signals a halt at the wet shore of a shallow lagoon we must cross to reach Langosta Beach. He proceeds forward toward waist-deep water to retrieve a rowboat. As he wades into the dark water, his motion creates a phosphorescent trail.

"This," Bryan whispers, "is a bizarre place. Very different."

Starlight reveals the black wake of a smallish—four-foot—crocodilian approaching Roberto—either *Lagarto,* the Black Caiman, or *Cocodrilo* himself. When Roberto turns toward it, the animal submerges.

Where there's a four-footer, there could be an eight-footer. Nevertheless, after letting Bryan and me get into the boat, Roberto walks alongside, pulling us in chest-deep water instead of joining us and paddling.

We reach the other side of the lagoon intact, crest the dune, and suddenly confront a coast much wilder than any I expected. As far south as your eye can take you, the whole dark continental shoreline runs enveloped in velvet night. One sole dim pinprick of artificial light from a bulb or lantern visits us from a couple of miles away. From there a seemingly eternal darkness runs to a stark dark point. Beyond that, vision finds only ocean spread to black infinity, curling into the glittered vault of space.

Unlike Playa Grande's wide bowl of semisheltered coastline, Langosta directly fronts open ocean. Here the glowing surf thunders ragged and raw, a beach beyond the rim of civilization.

We walk south between an opaque forest and hissing surf. Deep in the dark of so wild a beach it's easy to feel spooked. Roberto has a couple of ghost stories; he says some turtle patrollers have seen glowing eyes here, and won't come alone.

In 1994, each night eight or nine turtles still arrived here on Playa Langosta; one night forty-eight came ashore. A decade later, they averaged one per night.

All this deep night, there appear to us no turtles, and that is by far the night's most frightening ghost story.

Just after dawn, Sanderlings are scurrying along the surf, mirrored in sheets of water. I stroll the strand, admiring shells, pleased to have taken form on so wondrous a planet.

While we patrolled, no turtles came; while we slept, the ocean's turtles all stayed away. Yet in this gloried morning the eye finds no thing out of place. If we fail the turtles in this deciding hour of their long run, the ghost story of the mighty Leatherback will be told every morning hence just like this: a smooth beach. Who would miss the Leatherback?

The end of a species comes as tranquilly as this gentle sunrise. There's no final struggle, no valorous last stand or terminal flourish. Just one final puff of breath, then mere absence. No creature mourns its own passing. The grief and the consequence lie solely with us, but few feel the loss. Hotels may rise and tourists come, admiring the sedate curve of beach, enjoying the seafood at face value, going home satisfied.

Several Ruddy Turnstones buzz the surf on low, nervous wings. On a wet tide flat a single Snowy Egret is trotting erratically around on its yellow-toed slippers, seemingly pursuing hallucinations, but actually chasing fish imprisoned like Flatlanders in a pane of water. Directly overhead slides the great dark crossbow of a frigatebird, reminding us that the way of the world is not peaceful. Even the coursing pelicans, with their lugubrious eyes and comic pouches, live by killing. They have no options. But they wield no malice. Since the first cell engulfed another to steal its laboriously synthesized sugar, Earth has been an unsafe place. Turtles lay hundreds of eggs because they're at the mercy of poor odds. But we who have named ourselves *sapiens* and human can seek wisdom and strive to be humane. Two identical ships, leaving the same harbor on headings differing by just a couple of degrees, will end long journeys on very different shores. We might yet adjust our course.

BY AN HOUR PAST MIDNIGHT ON PLAYA GRANDE, BROKEN, TRUE TO HER stricken, persisting, overachieving form, has returned for her fourth consecutive night. I imagine her as the last Leatherback, an ancient wrecked turtle on a beach stippled with human footprints, trying vainly to sow her race's final trace.

But thoughts of the Leatherback's demise are premature. Other animals believed lost have resurrected themselves. The Short-Tailed Albatross was believed extinct for two decades; likewise, Antarctic Fur Seals, who now again swim by the millions; and similarly many others whose simple, innate perseverance from one dawn to the next brought them back from the dead. And though Pacific Leatherbacks have crashed, they may yet crawl from the wreckage and survive. Though days of a thousand turtles using this beach are in the past, they may also await in the future. Several good reasons provide hope that things aren't as bad as they seem. No one really knows what's going on with the hatchlings that are out there, and whether they will—as in the Caribbean—begin appearing as breeders in good numbers in the next few years. The poaching here is under control and the hatchery program is boosting the survival of nests and eggs. And every few years more favorable ocean conditions prompt a "good year," bringing ashore many more females who'd been holding back. So the people here are waiting for a bigger year, with more nests for the hatchery. And new fishing techniques that can reduce turtle deaths are being spread to fleets along Latin American coasts and distant

Pacific islands. No one expects a thousand turtles again in the next year or decade, but good things may well start happening.

Here's one that may help: responding to a lawsuit brought by the Leatherback Trust and several environmental groups, Costa Rica's Constitutional Court recently ruled in favor of the Leatherback, suspending development within 125 meters (a little over 400 feet) of the beach. This will likely make a major difference toward preserving viable Leatherback nesting habitat here.

Broken's crippled rear flippers are waving lamely. Bryan Wallace is on his belly, tilted forward, energetically digging her a chamber. What a confusing species we are, by turns murderous and merciful, negligent and attentive, angels of both death and salvation. As I walk up Bryan says quietly, "She was already leaking when I found her trying to dig. I thought, 'Just drop them, please.'"

And so she does, finally. She, at least, has overcome all obstacles, answered her calling, done her best, received some needed help.

As I stand and turn seaward into the breeze, my attention refocuses from this one creature to the wider world.

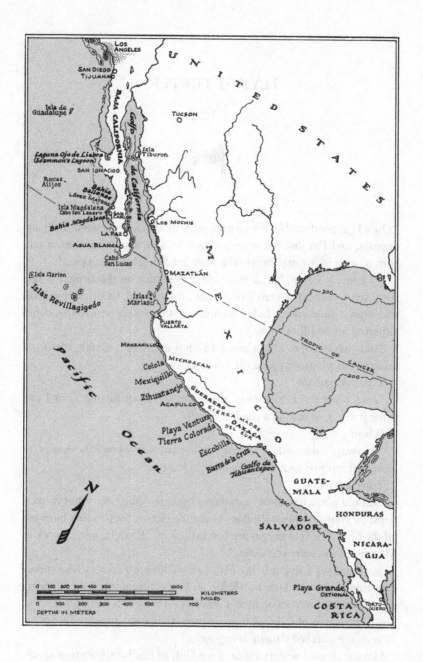

FLYING TURTLES

Mexico

"Once I get comfortable, the control panel disappears, the windshield disappears, and I'm just out here, seeing." So says Sandy Lanham, a tall, trim woman in her mid-fifties who loves her flying low and slow.

It's a lovely vision, but, already aloft, I'm stuck on the airplane's age: forty-seven years. The craft looks—well, it looks old, its original yellow-and-brown paint like a faded bumblebee (that insect which also defies expectations and flies anyway).

Sandy assures me, "No Cessna 182 has ever had a midair structural failure—no wings snapping off, for instance."

That's reassuring.

"And when the engine fails, the plane will keep gliding until I can bring it safely to rest on a road or beach."

When?

"Anyway," she adds, "the engine is new, and—you'll be happy to know—it has just enough hours on it to trust it."

Trust is good.

"An old plane has some advantages because—like, see, it has manual flaps; on younger planes the flaps have little electric motors that burn out all the time. The fuel gauges are just little floats. If you're gonna work in Mexico, this is what you *want*."

Sandy makes a living flying Mexican wildlife researchers who survey everything from plankton to whales. So I'm surprised when she suddenly says, "I miss a lot from up here. I mean, it's a surreal existence. Like, I've flown thousands of miles of turtle surveys and"—she turns to face me—*"I've never watched a turtle laying eggs."*

Having crossed seventy miles of the Gulf of California we turn south, floating in blue haze along Baja's massive coast and vertical red-rock desert. Soon we're twelve hundred feet over the Bay of La Paz, talking to the tower, preparing to land and rendezvous with our scientific director.

Laura Sarti's bandanna reins in her bushy shock of woolly hair. She works with Mexico's Environment Ministry, and last week she was in Papua New Guinea, helping train local biologists to count Leatherback nests from the air. This week she'll train me to do the same.

Our aerial census of Leatherback nests along Mexico's Pacific coast— from southern Baja to the Guatemalan border—will take us about ten days.

Laura has borne close witness to the Leatherback's Pacific plunge. "In 1993," she says in Spanish-accented English, "we saw the drastic decline of Leatherbacks. The trend is *zoom*"—she gestures—"down. Extreme down."

Last year's survey found Mexico's Leatherbacks at an all-time low. Word is that because of cooler water temperatures, more Leatherbacks are coming ashore to nest this year. Apparently this is a "good year." So Laura says it'll give us an idea of how many Leatherbacks are left.

How "good," we'll see.

We lift wheels from La Paz into midmorning blue sky and are soon overlooking undulating aprons of brush-velvet desert. We drop to two hundred feet—*low*—and begin surveying the lower Baja beaches. Small houses, resort villas, and trophy homes colorize the shoreline. Tracks of all-terrain vehicles riddle the beach. Many run circles and irregular designs. The visual distraction makes looking for turtle tracks more difficult. Laura complains, "With all these ATVs—"

The shore turns limestone-armored, stern and rockbound. Sandy evades a frigatebird. At nearly two miles a minute, at this low altitude the word *velocity* applies. The shore morphs to pink badlands, then limestone cliffs, followed by slumping boulders and scree tumbling to the sea.

The next long ribbon of sand beach also bears multitudinous tracks: SUVs, ATVs, POF (people on foot) walking their DOGs all leave their impression. But for miles, no TRTLs.

In Mexico Leatherbacks are called *Laúd*. Laura says the name derives from "an old kind of musical instrument." She sketches to show me. An oud is a stringed instrument with a big rounded body, usually associated with Arab culture. Add a head and flippers to *la oud,* and you have *Laúd.*

A flock of shorebirds explodes from the shoreline like a charge of shot.

I suddenly notice a depression in the sand, and immediately Laura says through the headphones, "That looks like a nest, Carl. An old one. We will count it." Two more Leatherback nests appear within the mile. We record nine more Leatherback nests, some very recent.

At Cabo San Lucas, high-rise hotels overlook yacht-crammed marinas. Mansion swimming pools jut from cliff slopes where private palaces perch. "Thirty years ago," Laura notes, "this was just a little fishing camp. All the coast here is used. All."

With a nod Sandy indicates four Gray Whales moving slowly just outside the surf. On the ocean several fishing boats are dragging trawl nets for shrimp. Laura says they've been required for the last decade to use nets equipped with turtle-escape doors.

Do they use them?

Laura nods decisively. "Yes. They use. But sometimes they are tying the opening shut."

But Sandy adds, "Some things have improved. During our first survey twelve years ago, some beaches had just a string of turtle shells and carcasses. We hardly see that anymore."

On the next beach, which is not built up, Leatherback tracks and nests begin appearing at a much higher rate than we'd expected. Laura tells us this beach will be the next to have hotels. "The governor says, 'What good is a protected beach if no one is enjoying it?'"

We skirt a headland and pick up again on the next frill of sand, till the next headland. So it goes. On for miles we scan unceasingly. Most of the time, we fly wordless for long stretches spanning leagues of shore: Sandy keeps the plane along the surf, Laura scans, I look and look, the engine drones.

Scanning bright reflective sand along gleaming surf strains the eyes. But Laura's attention never wavers.

The farther north, the fewer nests. This is *Laúd*'s northern nesting limit, because the winter sand temperatures are marginal here. On Baja's ocean coast, eggs hatch only if laid at the warmer ends of the season (October or March); midwinter Pacific winds deliver a fatal chilling to embryos. Nests on Baja's gulf side do only a little better.

By afternoon we've flown 350 miles along the irregular contours of this ragged coast, and we've logged 107 *Laúd* nests—far more than we expected.

Laura says, "Last year was the worst year in twenty years; we saw *zero* nests where we saw over a hundred today." In the next days we'll cover thousands of miles, and find out whether the luck of this "good year" holds.

THAT FIRST DAY IN BAJA SEEMS A PROMISING START THAT DIDN'T PAN out. Two days ago we flew a couple hundred miles of Mexico's west coast, from Los Mochis to Mazatlán—finding not one Leatherback Turtle nest. Yesterday, from Mazatlán to Manzanillo we found only twenty-seven nests, near the end of the day.

Today dawns with the anticipation of flying the best Leatherback beaches in the country, including the famed eleven-mile strand called Mexiquillo. As at Playa Grande, "best" is relative. In the late 1980s, Leatherbacks at Mexiquillo laid about five thousand nests; last year, just twenty-nine nests, the combined efforts of only four or five females. However this year, here as elsewhere, Laura's on-the-ground workers have reported sharply increased nesting.

But there's been trouble. Two months ago, armed men took an all-terrain vehicle from the turtle researchers who work the beach here. Two marines sent to retrieve it were shot, one fatally. Just this week, a policeman was killed during a gunfight on the road. Laura says local drug traffickers are battling drug traffickers from outside. The policeman's life was wasted "to send a message" about who's now in control.

Tension is high, the biologists frightened and confused. Laura says, "They are feeling alone, scared, very worried, but still working to save these sea turtles. No one knows they are there, but they are heroes."

This trouble is not the first. Several years ago, gunmen held up turtle monitors working the night beach at Mexiquillo, taking their ATVs and raping a conservation worker. Shortly thereafter, Laura herself was delivering two replacement ATVs when armed men stopped her truck on the road. Laura and two other researchers were lucky to lose only their truck, both ATVs, their money, computer, wallets, and identification papers.

We seem a very distant cry from the park tour guides of Playa Grande, or the Caribbean with its Nature Seekers taking church groups and tourists to be awed by turtles.

Laura has been in frequent phone contact with the distraught Mexiquillo fieldworkers during the last few days. She is trying to help arrange military protection and a visit. But when one of the researchers suggests that they should quit in protest if soldiers do not appear, Laura retorts, "I will respect your decision—but to *stay,* that is protest."

The recent troubles raise a question about today's air count. Drug wars, however, will not deter Laura. She explains, "We will do the count, and we will turn and count a second time. Then we may pass again." She adds, with what strikes me as misplaced enthusiasm, "They have very good guns, that shoot long-distance. But I think everything will be okay. If we see anyone, or we think there is any trouble, we will just go out over the ocean. Okay?"

Wheels up at ten A.M. The tower tells Sandy to remain above five hundred feet. Sandy affirms, then when we leave the airport's vicinity she drops to two hundred. This morning's ocean appears *tranquilo;* not a zephyr or cat's paw mars its surface. The air holds moisture enough to blue the mountains' contours. The water is slick and breathless; only a few small fishing skiffs break the calm pane of sea.

The main event, Mexiquillo, will come later. Trouble aside, Mexiquillo is one of several "index" beaches where on-the-ground workers monitor and tally all the nests through the season. So, for instance, if the air count at index beaches results in half the nests the ground workers eventually count, Laura will double her air counts for all beaches to estimate the whole country's total for the nesting season.

Meanwhile, the first twenty-five miles or so reveal 40 *Laúd* nests. Then Laura begins calling nests every ten to fifteen seconds. I check our position and record the nests in the notebook, tallying in the first hour 113 nests of the rare beast. Laura is pleased.

Suddenly the bright sand looks bombarded with nests—but not Leatherbacks'. This is Colola, the largest Black Turtle rookery in Mexico. (Green Turtles from the eastern Pacific look so dusky here they're called Black Turtles, remember.) I watch, astonished, as the beach streams past thoroughly pocked with hundreds and hundreds of Black Turtle tracks. Sandy jokes, "They sure mess up a nice beach."

Laura points out how to differentiate the species by their tracks. A Leatherback's massive chuggings lead up to a big churned area around their nest. Black Turtles—*Prietas* in Mexico—pock the scrawl of their irregular crawl with several "test holes." Olive Ridleys—here *Golfinas*—leave smaller tracks and one neatly covered body pit at their *nido,* their nest.

Turtle habitat ends when mountains meet the coast with spectacular three-hundred-foot sheer cliffs arcing into a stunning series of proud headlands, plunging granite, and scalloped beaches. Sandy gasps, *"Preciosa."*

When the coast relaxes, the infamous Mexiquillo looms into view. Sandy climbs to one thousand feet to check things out. She asks, "Who lives in this big mansion on top of the hill?"

"Nobody," Laura replies. "The owner was killed. Shot in the street."

Sandy says, "I don't see anyone or any trucks. Let's go back and do it."

Sandy dives into a steep circling descent. I notice two small Black Turtles bobbing in the near-shore sea—and the slick gleam of a huge Leatherback at rest in the swell. Laura spots an Olive Ridley. Lots of turtles here.

With plenty of advance notice to friend or foe, we drop along the beach. This beach has too many nests to call individually. Laura is silent, her forehead to the window, her cap situated backward, her finger constantly working the click counter. She says excitely over our headphones, *"Muchos nidos!"*

Just beyond the surf, I'm seeing adult Leatherbacks at a rate of about one a minute, one every couple of miles. By the time we reach the end of the beach I'll see twice as many Leatherbacks in the water as were using this stretch all last year.

Drug lords remain out of sight, but the turtle biologists come onto the beach outside their camp, waving energetically. They have written "S.O.S." in the sand. I'm sure they're only partly joking. Sandy takes us straight over, low, wagging her wings while we wave energetically at each other.

Just off the beach, stingrays are gliding the shallows, gangs of heavy-shouldered Roosterfish are patrolling, and there're a few small sharks—all here because hatchlings equal food. When one Roosterfish streaks up to take something in a fast blast of foam, I envision that a new cookie-sized Leatherback, headed seaward for the first time, has just had its brief existence deleted.

At the end of the beach Laura announces her count: 193. We run the beach again and get a nearly identical 186. Compared to last year's flight-survey total of 19, there are *ten times* as many *Laúd* nests. The Leatherback, beleaguered, is not yet vanquished.

But 200 nests—or even the ground team's total-season count of roughly 400 (compared to last year's ground-counted 29 nests)—is not the 5,000 of a few years ago. What ascends the beach these days is just the smoldering wreckage of what was. Whether the embers will reignite or be snuffed is a story yet to play out. Laura says, "Every time we get a good year, it is not as good as the last good year. Every bad year is the worst ever. This year is a good year—but it is the worst good year we've had."

Nonetheless, extinction is not as imminent—and not as certain—as it seemed last year. There's more to work with. A little more time to train fishermen, dissuade poachers, buy nesting beaches. A little more time for trying to save the Leatherback.

Laura had shown us computer graphs of sea turtle trends. They're decidedly mixed. Olive Ridleys account for Pacific Mexico's main improvement. From the 1960s to the 1980s they annually dug about 200,000 nests in Mexico. When a slaughterhouse that had killed turtles to make leather and other products closed in 1990, Olives started increasing sharply. Now they dig about 1.4 million nests annually on Pacific Mexico's beaches.

For Mexico's Pacific Green—or "Black"—Turtle, the last twenty years show low numbers and little trend, but in recent years they're up some. Inasmuch as *all* of Mexico's nesting turtles were doing poorly a decade or two ago, one might see the increases of two species as a trend turning positive.

The two nesting species in real trouble on Mexico's Pacific coast are the Hawksbill and Leatherback.

Pacific Mexico's Hawksbill population is now nearly nonexistent, under twenty nests per year. Occasionally toxic because of their toxic-sponge diet, thus seldom eaten by people, Hawksbill Turtles are nonetheless too beautiful for their own good. Hunted for millennia, their shells can be worked like plastic. In Japan, where Hawksbill shell—often erroneously called "tortoiseshell"—is referred to as *bekko,* the craft reached its pinnacle. Bekko processing got started in Japan during the late 1600s in the Edo era. Artisans and craftsmen transformed mere turtle shells into combs and hair ornaments beyond the means of average women, worn by wives of feudal lords and so-called high-class prostitutes. By the end of the nineteenth century overseas exhibitions featured the famed Japanese bekko products, including ornaments, jewelry, cigarette cases, model ships, and the like. In Japan I once saw a magnificent bekko rooster with a luxuriant ten-foot tail made entirely of Hawksbill shell, from perhaps dozens of turtles.

In 1977 most countries agreed to stop international commerce in

Hawksbills and their shells. They did this under a treaty called the Convention on International Trade in Endangered Species (CITES), the same vehicle that brought elephants the relief of banned ivory. Japan, epicenter of world turtle-shell demand, exempted itself. Japan imported roughly forty thousand kilograms of Hawksbill shell annually in the 1970s and "limited itself" to thirty thousand kilograms annually in the 1980s. One average-sized Hawksbill turtle yields about one kilogram of workable shell (most get caught as juveniles), so that's something like three-quarters of a million turtles in twenty years. In some countries Hawksbill populations thinned to the vanishing point. Japan belatedly, showing its characteristic grudge against nature, in 1994 closed its ports to Hawksbill shell. But, working with Cuba, Japan has repeatedly tried getting CITES countries to allow trade at least between Cuba and Japan. They've pushed this proposal several times, so far unsuccessfully. (In open defiance of another global ban, Japan continues killing increasing numbers of whales, driven by a misguidedly nationalistic identity, similar to America's insistence on wasting energy as part of its national character. The main difference is that in America almost everyone loves to waste energy while in Japan hardly anyone cares to eat whale meat, making it interesting to weigh which of those ironies is worse.) While many Caribbean countries are working to restore the region's sea turtles, Japan and Cuba's continued proposals encourage continued illicit killing and stockpiling in hopes of eventual reopening. Meanwhile, smuggling continues.

Laura's twenty-year graph of the Pacific Leatherback shows its now-familiar crash. Pacific Loggerheads nest only in Japan and Australia but visit Mexico in significant numbers. They're crashing too.

On the Atlantic side, however, the graphs look different. There's the Caribbean Green Turtles' rally and big increase. Also, as Kemp's Ridley recovers from catastrophic decline, the graph tracks the species' rise from its low of a few hundred nests annually between the 1960s and the 1980s to eight thousand nests now, and climbing. At this rate they could conceivably regain their historic numbers of tens of thousands of nests. And in parts of the Caribbean, even Hawksbills are increasing.

Of *Laúd,* Laura clicked open several graphs at once, saying, "Look at the Caribbean, look how the Virgin Islands Leatherbacks are increasing rapidly. Now, compare that to places in the Pacific, like, look—Malaysia, crashed. In the 1970s they had several thousand nests a year, too, just like Mexiquillo did. Now, they have, like—*pfft*—nothing."

* * *

Today, as we rise from Zihuatanejo airport over the ocean, Laura observes, "It is a very shiny day." We again expect some high-density Leatherback beaches, and we start racking up Leatherback nests as soon as we're over the beach—about one or two per minute.

Suddenly Laura adds, "Six dead Olive Ridley Turtles."

Sandy, looking down at the beach, says she hasn't seen turtle remains piled like that for a long time.

Ten minutes later we see another turtle carcass pleasing vultures. We skirt another headland and *Laúd* nests again start coming every mile or so.

Into my headphones Laura calls three dead Leatherback adults. Duly noted; positions entered. Something here loves death.

I ask Laura if she thinks all these dead turtles have been killed by people.

She suddenly turns from the window—breaking her concentration for the first time all week—and looks at me as if I can't be serious. Then she says, "Yes—of course, killed by people." She again turns her concentrated scrutiny to the beach streaming by below, adding, "This area is worse than Michoacán. *Muy broncos*—many rough people. They are lawless. They do anything they want. They kill turtles on the beach. They kill people in the roads. There are drugs and rebels. Is really bad here."

Five or six minutes later another dead turtle lies among a string of nests.

Laúd nests continue coming every mile or so. At two miles per minute, that keeps us pretty busy. Meanwhile, six big commercial shrimp boats are working the area. One of the boats has recently raised its net, and now it pulls behind it a train of seabirds squabbling over the many thousands of small fish a crewman is shoveling overboard. In Mazatlán a couple of nights ago, Laura's friend the wildlife geneticist Alberto Abreu had told us how shrimping is intensifying on this coast: "Too many boats, and the reason is, there's a crisis in the countryside: more new people, not enough new land. So the population is overflowing to the coast, fishing and drug running. These are not traditional fishermen. They are the type of person who does everything illegally. Their nets are catching turtles; some they sell, others they discard. In one week this year over fifty dead turtles washed up on the beach. Twenty-five years ago we thought we would save the world by working with turtles on the beach. Now I believe the key to conservation is eliminating the causes of poverty."

A few miles down the beach, four men and a boy, their horses waiting patiently, are digging *Laúd* eggs, near the remains of two adult *Golfinas*.

We seem to be flying fast, but the world is traveling at nearly 9,000 new babies per hour—more than 2 per second. Each year 76 million new persons reach Earth's surface. That's 2 million more than the recent populations of New York, Tokyo, Beijing, Rio de Janeiro, Mexico City, Moscow, Delhi, London, and Cairo combined. The rate will slow, but by midcentury, we'll still be adding 34 million new persons annually. The world's population will increase from today's 6.5 billion to 9.1 billion in 2050. The poorest, least developed countries will saddle themselves with almost all that new hunger and demand. But that pressure will look for relief in the world's less pressured places.

A few days ago I asked Laura what she thinks caused the Leatherback's Pacific flameout. Was it fisheries bycatch, egg poaching, killing nesting females for food, a combination—? Many environmentalists and some scientists believe increased longline fishing has caused the Leatherback's decline. The circumstantial evidence is largely in the timing; the crash coincided with sharply increased long-lining. And long-lining kills turtles, no question. Some blame increased netting for Swordfish off California and South America. Nets kill turtles, no question. Others think that what happens on nesting beaches is the main problem. So I wanted to know what Laura, who lives it, thinks.

Laura replied, "The *Laúd*'s decline was so sudden it had to be caused mainly by near-total nesting failure." Laura believes that starting ten to twenty years before the observed crash in returning adult nesting females, hatchling production fell to near zero as nest poaching became a long-term problem.

But people living here knew of nesting turtles for a long time, so how could catastrophic nest poaching have happened suddenly?

"Roads" was Laura's surprising reply. "In the 1960s, many new roads went into the states of Guerrero and Oaxaca. In the 1970s, new roads went into Michoacán. Suddenly, people from outside could easily get to the beaches to buy eggs, to sell in cities."

This sounds familiar. From the great forests of the Pacific Northwest to the coral reefs of Micronesia to New England's giant tuna to rhinos and tigers and bears, to turtles and beyond, a familiar pattern: when distant markets suddenly arrive offering new cash fueled by insatiable demand from outside, long-standing local use of nature intensifies to firestorms of overexploitation, and populations crash.

And, Laura added, "when the demand for eggs increased, often they killed the nesting female so they would not have to wait for her to lay."

Waiting for a female means risking you'll miss the next turtle. But since each turtle returns repeatedly to the same beach in the same season, and since killing an adult is equivalent to erasing all the eggs she would have laid in all the years she would have lived and returned, such poachers cut not just the turtles' throats but their own. More poverty results, a spiral of nature destruction, self-depletion, increasing desperation, and shrinking options. In the long term, crime doesn't pay. But in the moment, it can seem the best option.

Laura's conservation workers now protect all the most important Leatherback beaches in Pacific Mexico, plus some of the smaller beaches. Her assessment: "I would say that now we are protecting maybe seventy-five percent of the nests on the whole coastline. Of those twenty-five percent we are not protecting, I would say, yes—nearly all those get poached."

All sea turtles in every ocean once ushered from a sandy nest on a somewhere beach. They are among the few groups of animals that descended from land ancestors and reentered the ocean. Their last trace of land-oriented existence—the females' need to return to shore to lay eggs—is their Achilles' heel.

Antaeus, son of the earth-goddess Gaia and the sea-god Poseidon, was a giant whose extraordinary strength derived from contact with his mother, Earth. He became vulnerable—and was killed—when Hercules severed his contact with the ground. Substitute poachers for Hercules, and it's apparent that the Leatherback stands an Antaean beast indeed. Sever the leathery waterlord from contact with the ground by getting between a turtle's eggs and the sand, and—despite long-proven resilience—the mighty giant teeters.

A hurricane can wash away hundreds of turtle nests, destroying a year's nesting on an entire section of coast. But hurricanes do not destroy *each* year's nesting on *every* beach for *every* turtle. Only people pack that kind of fury.

Laura is fighting this human storm. Each time we land for fuel she returns cell-phone messages and makes necessary calls. Laura is a conservation field marshal, deploying biologists to the turtle camps and hatcheries throughout the country, reinforcing good news with encouragement, rallying shaky morale in the face of real danger and despair.

No one should expect Laura Sarti to save the Leatherback by herself. This shore of harried conservation workers, contested nests, and poached eggs seems an omelet of scrambled motives, where a mix of apathy, appetite, and affirmation will somehow determine the destiny of turtles and people.

Sandy suggests that it's not necessary to have hope all the time, that to carry you over short hopeless patches anger will do. Being acquainted with anger, I turn this thought over in my mind. I have accomplished things with anger. Yes, you can get places on anger, as long as you're not going far.

Past Acapulco the beach *looks* like the earlier stretches, yet this one runs without trace of turtles. We span long minutes of emptiness in silence that mounts to miles. Scenery streams: coconut plantations pattern the coastal plain; riverbanks host thatched shacks; and skiffs called *pangas* lie upon the sand.

At a place called Playa Ventura, Leatherback nests suddenly reappear—like an abrupt downpour. Laura calls them in groups: "One nest . . . five nests . . . one . . . six . . . nine, no, *twelve* nests . . ." Sandy works constantly to implement the simple two-button GPS "save current position" process—while also piloting—as I struggle to scribble the corresponding entries. Like this, nests whiz by for twenty-six kilometers, or sixteen miles, wherein the Leatherbacks have placed the faith of 250 clutches of eggs.

At Tierra Colorada, a small band of turtle monitors streak from their open-sided, grass-roofed camp, waving wildly in greeting. Unlike the S.O.S. at Mexiquillo, they've written *"Hola! We Want a Ride!"*

We zoom around small rocky headlands and on the next few beaches Laura clicks off 304 more nests. We also add 5 dead adult Leatherbacks whose reproductive output for this season might have been 20 or so nests—about 7 percent of the total there.

At one-thirty, when we land for a break at Puerto Escondido, I remove the heavy headphones and my ears resume their normal shape. Stiffly we disembark our cramped plane cabin. Our day's total stands at just under 1,500 Leatherback nests.

By the lowered standards of the last few years, that tally is impressive. It has actually exceeded our hope that in this "good year" Leatherbacks of the eastern Pacific could make this strong a show of their remaining reserves.

When, in 1981, renowned turtle scientist Peter Pritchard followed rumors of nesting Leatherbacks on Mexico's Pacific coast, he wrote, "We were unprepared for the abundance or wide distribution of the nesting." He estimated the breeding population at possibly over 70,000 individual females. But the many carcasses of freshly killed adult females indicated "a distressingly high level of poaching." It would be comforting if that was all in the past. But the continued killing of breeding females is disturbing. At this point, they really can't afford it.

We take a taxi into town. Because taxi drivers are the first line of insider information in any town, for curiosity's sake I ask the driver if he can bring us somewhere to eat turtle. "No," he answers. "We never bring tourists." Mexico first banned consumption of sea turtle eggs in 1927. Our driver gripes, "Turtle eggs are harder to get now. They now cost fifty pesos a dozen if you buy direct from a digger; in a restaurant, about a hundred and fifty pesos a dozen" (roughly U.S.$15). In 1972, Mexico declared it illegal to catch turtles or consume the meat or possess the skin, with certain exceptions. Our driver explains that he doesn't much like turtle eggs anyway. "I prefer the turtle's meat, sliced thin, sprinkled with lemon and dried for a day, then grilled." In 1990, Mexico placed a total ban on using any part of any sea turtle. "With tortillas and a little salsa—*that* is the best." In 1994, all sea turtles were protected under Mexican law. A decade later, our driver laments, "I haven't tasted turtle for a long time—about eleven months."

THE BEACH IS *PEPPERED* RIM TO RIM WITH NEST DEPRESSIONS, AND NO end in sight. This beach—Escobilla, in Oaxaca—isn't just Mexico's largest Olive Ridley Turtle nesting site; it's just about the greatest sea turtle nesting beach in the world. Only Costa Rica's Olive Ridleys at Ostional slightly outnumber these. During their periodic mass-nesting arrivals, or arribadas, about five hundred *thousand* Olive Ridley Turtles come ashore here over a three-day period. They collect outside these beaches for days until some cue triggers a mass landing like the assault at Normandy. Turtle grandmaster Peter Pritchard says, "If you haven't seen an arribada, you need to. To go to a beach where, anywhere you sit, you get hit by a turtle is very reassuring."

Arribadas remain in many ways mysterious. Only the two Ridley species stage mass nestings, yet many individuals nest singly. Before an arribada, turtles gather off nesting beaches for weeks before something sends them onto the shore. Scientists aren't sure what the cue is. Ridleys have scent glands no other sea turtles have, so it's probably a chemical message suddenly shouting, "Okay, let's go!"

Olive Ridley arribadas were apparently unknown to science until the 1970s. Though Olives nest along the tropical Pacific, Indian, and South Atlantic Oceans, they stage arribadas at only a handful of beaches. In the closing decades of the twentieth century, near-total egging and drowning in shrimp nets wiped out or depleted large arribada populations in Nicaragua, Guatemala, El Salvador, and elsewhere. The only place Olives now stage such mass nestings outside Mexico and Costa Rica is India's state of Orissa, where they perform arribadas at three sites. India's Olive Ridley populations have also declined sharply. India had 600,000 Olive Ridleys well into the 1990s, whereas the number is around 135,000 recently. Fishing boats dragging trawl nets near Indian nesting beaches kill large numbers of Olives—about 10,000 annually—yet Indian trawler captains have resisted using turtle-escape devices. Along the Indian Ocean people use turtles for meat, animal feed, aphrodisiac and medical potions, bait, and leather. In India and in Pakistan, villagers feed turtle eggs to cattle, camels, and goats. (In Iran, coastal people eat turtle eggs and use them as pain relievers and aphrodisiacs, and feed them to sheep and camels as well.) Olives nest in Malaysia, too, but, like the Leatherbacks there, their numbers have crashed, dropping from a quarter million nests to well under 200.

In the 1950s, likely over 10 million Olive Ridleys inhabited the eastern Pacific off Mexico. We fly right over the turtle slaughterhouse that closed its doors around 1990. This place was responsible for killing in the neighborhood of 80,000 Turtles annually. For a strip of skin along the flippers, over several decades starting in the 1960s leather processors killed several million adult female Olive Ridleys. Most of the leather went to Europe to become Italian shoes and the like. As a result, three of Mexico's four arribada populations fell apart. The only surviving mass-nesting phenomenon was here at Escobilla. By the late 1980s, the number of nesting females here had also fallen sharply. As soon as the slaughter ended, the Olive Ridley Turtles' increase was meteoric, quintupling in about a decade. Nest protection and hatcheries paid off, and the population has soared to nearly half a million females nesting annually. Seasonal total right here in recent years: 1.2 million nests. It's the Pacific's best sea turtle turnaround.

Even at midday several turtles are ashore, digging and laying. The densest nesting runs four or five miles. The idea seems to be safety in numbers, a synchronous invasion that overwhelms the opposition. If your nest is one of a hundred thousand, the local predators won't likely eat yours. But there's a snag: the turtles get in one another's way. So dense are they that these turtles now dislodge and break one another's eggs. The whole beach becomes so infected with bacteria, fungus, and insects that as few as one out of a hundred eggs here can hatch. Predators and scavengers hang around for weeks digging up eggs and preying on hatchlings. While solitary-nesting Olives achieve hatching rates around 80 percent, those exploiting the "safety" of arribadas suffer 90 to 98 percent egg loss. So arribadas seem like a good idea taken to a bad extreme. It might be that they're advantageous for a few years, until too many turtles get involved, after which the population wanes over many years for want of hatchlings. At that point, perhaps, a few solitary nesters may form the core of a new arribada somewhere, reinitiating a cycle. But no one knows for sure, because like many things about turtles, their time scales reach further into the past and future than the few decades during which biologists have studied them.

Meanwhile, local people see a million turtles in their backyard. Their eyes suggest that if the turtles are wasting their own eggs, people could better make use of them. Yet they are told that the turtle is still considered endangered. The problem, as Costa Rica has found by legalizing the taking of eggs from Ostional, is that any legal eggs in commerce provide cover for many identical-looking illegal eggs from endangered populations. This gnawing question—what is reasonable use of wildlife in poor countries?—poses difficulties as great as anything wildlife managers or conservationists face.

WHEN TOMORROW DAWNS, SANDY WILL NO LONGER BE ABLE TO SAY she's never seen a turtle laying eggs. A short while ago we arrived at the camp at Barra de la Cruz. Now we're on an all-terrain vehicle with Laura driving, streaking along the night wind, running the wet-packed sand alongside hissing waves. After being aloft all week, the wide powdery beach smells deliciously of vegetation and the sea.

This beach impresses me as a very remote place. I see no human-made light, not up or down the beach, nor back into the moonlight-shadowed hills. About a mile from camp a fresh track stops us. Up on dry sand, the turtle is already digging, well into her body pit.

Sandy's jaw drops. She whispers, "I don't be*lieve* it. I *don't* believe it." Without taking her eyes off the turtle, she murmurs as though narrating, "Think of it. She has wandered in weightless motion, flying through the water. All the while, all she knows is a world in motion. She surfaces to breathe, and the moon and stars are waving in the sky. After years in this deep, moving world, she drives herself to shore. And the sea beneath her shallows until that final wave retreats and she is stranded. Just imagine! Suddenly the moon overhead is stock-still, and the stars overhead are frozen in place. For the first time in her life, the world has just *stopped,* still as a photograph of a girl on a swing."

Sandy pauses, then says, "When you are coming down for a landing, there comes a moment when you look at the runway right under you and you know your landing gear is about to touch. You lift the nose a little and you anticipate that first bump of the wheels. If you've forgotten to put your landing gear down, you suddenly sense the runway a little too close under your belly, and the pavement comes up high into your windshield. And suddenly the propeller hits something hard it was never made to hit, and the plane screeches and skids to a stop and is stranded there. I imagine that's what it's like to be her right now."

Sandy and I both know we cannot cross that narrow strait separating the ocean of our own experience and the strange wild country of this other being. The blade of our thinking has hit something it was never made to hit.

The mystery is how we've all gotten here together. I think part of the answer is, we all share the same basic pilgrimage, each of us making our own separate offerings toward a future wherein life persists. That's really why we're all here. You can travel far on hope.

Laura surprises me by saying that if we don't take her eggs to the hatchery, poachers will get them.

I ask, "What poachers? There's no one else here."

Laura laughs. "They are here. Already, they know she is here digging. A man has already come with a bucket for her eggs. He said, 'Okay, you found her first.' There is a village, not far. And a path, there." She nods toward a cleft in the nearby dune that leads into the vegetative shadows. "They are like ghosts. You don't see them. But they are here. Always here."

And so Laura produces a large plastic bag and collects *la Laúd*'s eggs as they fall. The hatchery promises deliverance. The intervention nonetheless unsettles me. Eggs don't belong in hatcheries any more than poachers belong on beaches.

When the turtle has finished laying, she covers her empty egg chamber, suspecting nothing. She chugs heavily down the beach. Sandy accompanies her on hands and knees, her eyes riveted to the turtle's.

The moon-pulled surf is running hard and high. The very first wave that hits the turtle is big enough to float her off her belly, and she begins swimming as its receding waters suck her into the tumbled sea foam.

The turtle's head emerges in the moonlit surf before the next wave licks her away for good. Sandy exclaims, "That was fantastic! I *loved* that."

Laura drops Sandy and me off at 3:18 A.M. so we can spread our blankets on the beach and dream of giant turtles. Knowing there might be more Leatherbacks to save, Laura zooms back into the night. I'm tired, and in less time than it takes a Leatherback to disappear into the ocean, I vanish into my *sueño*, my dreaming. My dream is that the tribes of great sea turtles may increase.

BAJA

Behind a school in the Baja fishing village of San Carlos is a pile of four hundred turtle shells. In every coastal Baja community, one can find hundreds. Dr. Wallace J. Nichols estimates that people in Baja still eat thirty thousand turtles a year. Fishermen say that's low. When scientists put transmitters on ten Black Turtles, three got killed within the year.

Javier Miramontes, fisherman of San Carlos, has a story. "One day I had in my yard a turtle—a Loggerhead—that I had caught. I noticed something shiny on its flipper, like a metal clip. I looked closely. It had words and a number: 'Okinawa Aquarium Expo 532.' I put it on my key chain. We ate the turtle. It was on my key chain five years.

"Then I went to the school to see students make presentations for the community. One student had done a project about turtles. That student informed us that some scientists suspected our Loggerhead Turtles, here in Baja, are actually born in Japan and return to Japan for nesting. They suspected this because there were no other known nesting grounds in our whole ocean. But the student explained there was no proof, no evidence connecting our turtles with Japan. I reached into my pocket."

At that moment, the scientists had their proof.

Javier gave the tag to the teacher. The teacher e-mailed Dr. Nichols, an American conservation biologist who had told the students about their Loggerhead Turtles possibly originating in Japan. When Nichols checked his e-mail, he happened to be in Japan—at the same beach where the turtle had hatched. After hatching, the turtle had been held at the Okinawa Aquarium for one year, then released by school children. The delayed release had succeeded in growing the turtle past the beaks of birds and the jaws of many coastal predators who eat turtle hatchlings like snacks. But this success ended six years later, when the turtle's forward motion slowed as Javier's net stretched and began tangling. It was doubtless not the only turtle to go from the hands of Japanese kids to the soup pots of Baja.

Proof that Javier's Loggerhead was typical, not just lost, slowly accumulated. A flipper-tagged turtle from Japan showed up near San Diego. In 1995 a fisherman in Japan found in his net a drowned Loggerhead Turtle that had been tagged 478 days earlier, 10,600 kilometers away, in Baja, Mexico.

Further proof came in the form of Adelita. Adelita was netted off Baja's coast in 1986, when she weighed just eight pounds. She was held and studied in captivity for ten years. In August 1996 marine biologists Antonio Resendiz, Wallace J. Nichols, and Jeff Seminoff gave her a transmitter and slid her off a boat into the Pacific. Till that time, the tag on Javier's key chain was almost as much detail as anyone knew of how Loggerheads use the Pacific. Adelita's immediate response to freedom was to swim only as far as she had been able to go in her enclosure. She stopped and paused. Wild turtles never pause upon release. But when she resumed swimming she immediately headed west. All her food-finding and navigational instincts kicked in, and by December, she was off Hawaii. Fourteen months after release, she reached waters off Japan. There her signal stopped for two weeks; then the scientists received a set of transmissions indicating motion much more rapid than any turtle's swimming speed—on a course straight to Sendai, the nearest fishing port. Adelita had stunned the scientific world by journeying nearly twelve thousand kilometers, more than seven thousand miles, directly across the Pacific toward her ancestral breeding grounds. Her route was just slightly longer than the shortest possible direct distance between Baja and Japan. As a youngster she had crossed the ocean eastward and been stopped by a Mexican fishing net, after which she'd lived in captivity; given a second chance, she had headed home to Japan—only to again run afoul of fishing gear and, this time, lose her life.

Señor Miramontes no longer catches turtles. No longer fishes. Now he sells boating supplies and teaches school. He'd grown up in Sinaloa, on the mainland. When he was fifteen his father told him, "Our catch is not what it was. We are seeing the tips of the wolf's ears." Running from the wolf, the family arrived here in 1979. "It was rich here," Javier recalls. "With just three guys we could catch two to three hundred kilos of abalone. So many lobsters that no one was even interested in the shrimp. Now, with more and more fishermen and traps, this year—for the first time—our crab catch dropped. What we are trying now is to be careful with our scallops, to not overcatch. We are trying to have a new ethic for conservation. The younger fishermen are supporting this. People who used to poach turtles are giving that up and are supporting this. Reality has hit us in the face. After seeing such declines, we are learning."

Today San Carlos still has streets of sand, yard fences of fishing nets, numerous squatter shacks, and horses grazing vacant lots littered with plastic—the town is clearly short on cash. A large wall mural featuring a vivid rising sun, a whale, and a giant sea turtle is the brightest thing in town.

But in much of Baja, the mere suggestion that turtles ought not be used for food still strikes people as nonsensical. For many fishermen, releasing a turtle would be like taking a turkey out of the oven on Sunday and placing it in the garbage. For others, it's an accounting question: "The turtle is endangered? Okay; if I release it, who will replace that $150?"

NOT ALL THE PACIFIC'S JUVENILE LOGGERHEADS USE THE NORTH Pacific merely as a highway to Baja. Another chow-wagon realm lies far out in the open ocean, east of Japan. Ocean biologist Jeff Polovina and colleagues announced in 2005 that they'd found the hot spot by letting satellite-tagged turtles lead them to it. Much as the Gulf Stream sweeps along the U.S. southeast coast and moves offshore at Cape Hatteras at about 35° north latitude, the Kuroshio Current departs Japan also at about 35° north, then flows east toward the middle of the North Pacific. At about 155° east longitude it encounters a deep mountain called the Shatsky Rise, which splits the current into two. The turbulence creates large dynamic meanders, whirls, and eddies that mix the water, bringing up untapped nutrients, triggering plankton blooms, and making this region—eastward over the deep-drowned Emperor Seamounts to about the date line (180° longitude)—one of the most bountiful in the North Pacific.

Edges of ocean currents flow like vast rivers of the sea. But, lacking the discipline of riverbanks, their borders swirl with whirling rings and waving tongues of ocean miles across, often shifting with the seasons. In the first half of the year, the region's most productive span lies between 30° and 40° north latitude. During summer the region of greatest productivity shifts north, above 40° and outside the main current.

The turtles swim north and south as the seasons unfurl, tracking the edge of the sharpest gradient in plankton density. Loggerheads like to live where surface temperature and plankton concentrations change rather abruptly, near fronts where cool masses of water slide beneath warmer water masses, concentrating floating food. For a juvenile Loggerhead foraging the wide ocean, the menu includes open-ocean snails called *Janthina,* which float themselves on bubble rafts, and gelatinous By-the-Wind Sailors (known in polite company by their velvety formal name, *Velella velella,* also savored by *Janthina*), strange swimming predatory snails called heteropods, and familiar things like crabs and gooseneck barnacles clinging to driftwood. Turtles can swim faster and stronger than the currents flow, often searching into the current. If they find a place that pays, they may stay weeks or months in a particular front or eddy. When crisp edges of such fronts or eddies dissolve, as they often do in the heat of summer, the turtles may hike 350 miles (roughly 600 kilometers) to find the edge of cooler water and another front. Thus they stay mainly within sea-surface temperatures between about 60 and 75 degrees Fahrenheit (roughly 15 and 25 degrees Celsius), traveling to around 40° north in the summer, returning to 30° north latitude in winter, logging 1,200 miles (2,000 kilometers) round-trip, tracking their food. This camping trip may last their whole juvenile phase—decades.

Joining them in such migrations are other front-trackers, like squids, spawning Japanese Anchovies and Japanese Sardines, Albacore and Bluefin Tunas, Short-Tailed, Laysan, and Black-footed Albatrosses, and numerous others whose business cards identify them as either "predator" or "prey." Like Loggerheads, all these amazing animals use the Kuroshio Current's eastbound extension most of the year and shift their base camp north to the plankton front in summer. Collectively they make it one of the ocean's true hot-button regions, lit with life, all based on an accidental collision of a current and a drowned mountain and the stories that flow from that.

Everyone clues in to the same productivity, and fishing boat captains are no exception. They've long hunted tunas and other big ocean wildlife in this dynamic current and where it flows over the deep Emperor Seamounts. And it's in their gear that turtles catch trouble. Looking mainly for near-surface food, juvenile Loggerheads of the central North Pacific spend 40 percent of their time at the surface and forage almost exclusively shallower than fifty meters. The depth is important, because long-liners targeting Swordfish often set their lines in the depth range frequented by turtles; that's why Swordfish lines catch ten times as many turtles as do lines set for tuna. Fishermen often set tuna lines much deeper, one hundred meters or so. Americans drive the swordfishing market, consuming 75 percent of Swordfish caught worldwide. But tuna trumps in sheer volume; six out of seven longline trips target tunas, largely for Japanese sushi lovers. If it were the other way around and most of the world demand was for Swordfish, the situation for turtles would be worse than it is.

Different species exist mainly because they've evolved different jobs in the community. Loggerhead and Olive Ridley Turtles live in different open-ocean habitats that to us, without instruments, look much the same. In the Pacific, Olive Ridleys swim mainly south of Loggerhead habitat and in warmer waters. They generally stay between 8° north and 31° north latitude, between 23 and 28 degrees Celsius (73–82° F). Olive Ridleys inhabit broader regions of subtropical water, where, rather than looking for concentrations of floating food, they dive deeper than Loggerheads and spend more time underwater, searching for cowfish and gelatinous glow-in-the-dark pyrosomes (the name means "fire-bodies") and salps. They spend only 20 percent of their time at the surface and nearly half deeper than forty meters.

The kernel of a solution comes from learning what the turtles do, what the fishing skippers do, and putting it together to come up with something new.

THE FISHING VILLAGE PUERTO ADOLFO LÓPEZ MATEOS LIES NEAR THE mangrove-lined north end of Magdalena Bay. Across the bay from the busy shore where numerous small boats land and clean and ship their catch, the long, thin island called Isla Magdalena runs about twenty-seven sand-dune miles between its two mountainous ends, forming the vast bay on its inner shoreline, holding off the Pacific on its outer coast. We've brought an all-terrain-vehicle.

I'm with the lighthouse keeper's son, Vladdie de la Toba, and graduate student Hoyt Peckham of the University of California at Santa Cruz. They're working in some of the fishing villages, helping the people understand the plight of turtles—while the people help them understand the plight of, well, the people.

Here, the main turtle is the Loggerhead. Almost all of Mexico's Loggerheads hatch on Japanese beaches (a small added fraction come from Australia). The Loggerhead's Pacific numbers are plunging almost as badly as the Leatherback's. Only around one thousand to fifteen hundred Loggerheads still nest in Japan, and their numbers have dropped around 90 percent since the 1950s. Australia's Loggerheads are also threatened. Though the North Pacific Loggerhead Turtles nest in Japan,

Baja fishermen may largely decide their future. Many juveniles concentrate right off this coast. Gill nets now turn the turtles' ancient epic of migration and survival into a tally toward extinction. Much of the human-caused Loggerhead mortality in the entire North Pacific appears to be caused by boats working off this beach. Yet because juveniles outnumber adults by as much as one thousand to one, fishermen here still see Loggerheads regularly. Halibut netters have occasionally caught dozens of Loggerheads in one day. The fishermen say, "We catch so many—how could they *possibly* be endangered?"

The ocean's tide line is strewn with a tragic opera of former life, dominated by millions of thumb-sized Pelagic Red Crabs, resembling little lobsters. Running miles down the beach, they lie sun-dried in a band about two feet wide, to far beyond where your eye can see.

These wrecked legions—just the fraction that strayed too close to shore and got cast up—merely whisper of the swarms camped along this coast, drawing Loggerheads all the way from Japan. The crabs' center of abundance is right here off Magdalena Bay. That this excellent food concentrates a large fraction of the North Pacific's Loggerhead Turtles within reach of Isla Magdalena's fishing nets is one of the ocean's saddest coincidences.

After hatching in Japan, many young Loggerheads come to this region for what appears an extended stay of up to two decades. Here they swim, fatten, and grow until the urge to breed calls them back to Japan—or until the urge to breathe, ungranted, casts them onto this beach. Whichever comes first.

Vladdie, still in his teens, says, "I get invited to people's houses to eat turtle, but since I work with the *Caguamas,* I can't eat *Caguama*." I tell them, 'You go ahead and eat.' I don't have any right to tell them not to eat it. I just tell my fishermen friends, there's a problem with the *Caguama;* if you get a turtle, release it. They say, 'Some come up already dead.' "

When Hoyt and Vladdie first started working here, people in the scientific and conservation communities didn't know of this area as a source of Loggerhead Turtle mortality. Says Hoyt, "Last season, in four months, May through August, on this twenty-seven-mile beach we found about three hundred and fifty turtle carcasses." Nearly all: juvenile Loggerheads. Between his daily count and what he's learned from talking with fishermen, Hoyt estimates that eighteen hundred Loggerhead turtles are killed each year during the gill-netting season—by boats from around

López Mateos alone. This is more than any other known source of Loggerhead Turtle mortality in the Pacific. Hoyt adds, "When I realized that, I was flabbergasted."

After driving only a mile along the beach, we come upon the morning's first turtle. Its entrails are strewn across the Coyote tracks that dance a celebration of good fortune and sudden wealth. With such daily deliveries of discards from the human enterprise, this shoreline is prime real estate for scavengers, who must think the ocean provident indeed. Every few steps the sand is volcanoed with the burrows of beach crabs that likewise thrive best where death flourishes.

This turtle is undergoing the festering bacterial decay known as "cooking" under Baja's incubator sun—bloating, pieces of shell curling and flaking off, skin opening in places, releasing slow-bubbling rivulets of blood and fluid. And the impressive stink. A joy to flies, a promise to maggots.

Hoyt, who runs this beach daily, confirms, "This is from yesterday. They go real fast here."

A realization: each day we live and breathe, our immune system is the only thing holding off this riot of rot. Shut it down for a day in this heat, and you're a rancid milkshake.

Hoyt rolls the bloated turtle over. Its head drops, mouth open, flippers splayed, crucified. He sprays a mark of red paint on it; thus it will not be recounted when next he passes. Other unintended fishing-net victims lying nearby include a porcupinefish and a sea lion pup minus its head.

The next carcass is a Black Turtle. Gill-net fishermen here catch a weekly average of four turtles per boat. Nearly all drown. One boat reportedly caught seventy in one week. Hoyt says, "We never expected such a small-time, local fishery could have such impact on an entire species, oceanwide." Often set by small unlicensed boats, gill nets make minefields of many coasts worldwide. Their landed catch is usually undocumented, their accidental and discarded catch almost completely unknown.

Despite sparse information on their catches, it's safe to say the nets kill tens of thousands of turtles annually worldwide. In French Guiana a WWF monitoring team found twelve entangled Leatherbacks in a single net; only one remained alive. In Trinidad, where we saw that Leatherback with the healed-over crack in her back, hundreds of adult females annually die not just from drowning in nets but often because fishermen hack the turtles out of their webbing just to get rid of them. A Mexican newspaper, La Jornada, ran a story on July 22, 2004, reporting a shark net found off Oaxaca, with 125 dead turtles in it. The drift nets still used off California catch Leatherbacks and Loggerheads, and to reduce the risk officials there close certain areas in warm-water years, when more turtles are present. On the U.S. east coast, where gill nets set for Goosefish (sold as monkfish) can catch turtles, fishers have moved to stiffer mesh in the search for a solution. Even the nets used to encircle large schools of tuna, safe for most turtle species, kill over a hundred Olive Ridley Turtles annually in the eastern tropical Pacific. Discarded netting and floating rope also snarls turtles, sometimes fatally. I once saw an Olive Ridley tangled in rope in a floating mass of trash hundreds of miles offshore. We freed it. Worldwide, such out-of-sight tangles no doubt kill thousands of turtles yearly.

Another Loggerhead. It's a big juvenile—adult-sized, really. In terms of value to the population's prospects for recovery, this is the most important size, because it has survived its entire childhood and has its whole reproductive life before it. Except it's dead. This turtle was old enough to have earned free miles to Japan; instead it got a one-way ticket to Coyoteville.

The song-dogs did the dirty work of breaking out the stomach, then wisely decided against tucking into it. Hoyt unsnaps his pocketknife. "We thought they'd be eating the red crabs almost exclusively, because that's why Loggerheads migrate all this way. But look—see these fine bones and spines? They're also eating fish." He squints up at me, adding, "But turtles can't catch fish. They're eating fish out of nets. Sometimes you see them around the boats, waiting for discards. They hang around boats, they hang around nets—they end up like this."

They who live by discards die discarded. There's no free lunch.

A much older turtle carcass lies mummified in the desiccating sun. Its empty eye sockets must at times whistle lament into the winds and blowing sand. It had been hooked and wrapped in a local longline attached to a foam buoy almost as large as its shell. With diving impossible, turtle and buoy battled for supremacy until the turtle starved. The buoy remains firmly wound to the dried carcass.

Having already seen more dead turtles today than I had in my life as of yesterday, I am familiarized. The sight and smell are no longer strange, and that is the strangest thing. How quickly one becomes inured. It is an irony of human emotional mechanics that as tragedy builds into a confronting mountain of outrageous wrong, we become more accustomed, increasingly comfortable seeing it, able to discuss it calmly, when we should be raising a wailing like air-raid sirens. One of the world's great creatures is passing, here and now, carcass by carcass, and the fishermen

shrug, the politicians shrug, the priests grant benediction as always—
"What can be done? The people must eat."

A large dead sea lion has a hole in its back. Vladdie makes a shooting
motion—*Pow!* Sea lions are not popular with fishermen.

Our next guest at this beach party *de la muerte* is a dolphin. Rather,
was. Likely also a victim of nearby nets, it lies oozing, its sun-cracked
lips shrink-wrapped around grimacing teeth. A dolphin more hideous
cannot be imagined.

Fishes in this sunny morgue include the unpalatable Roosterfish, large
and magnificent when not crawling with maggots; stargazers; porcupinefish; and numerous other small, finned, thrown-away creatures brought
to you by your friends at The People Must Eat, Unlimited.

Up ahead is the telltale yellow hulk of another Loggerhead in the lapping
surf. When a little wave swirls around it, its head bobs.

Hoyt hooks a gaff in its flipper, hauling it from the water. Its shell
length is seventy-four centimeters (twenty-nine inches). Loggerheads begin nesting in Japan at about eighty centimeters; only about two inches
bigger. These larger dead turtles are mostly around twenty years old.
Their numbers are the result of nesting density two decades ago, a window on what was, like starlight that takes millennia to reach our eyes.
That they are dead is a window on what will be. These washed-up Loggerheads *are* extinction happening, the end of their population's days on
Earth. As with Leatherbacks, there is still time, but this situation needs to
get turned around soon. For a creature that counts its survival at a million
years times a hundred, a decline so fast and steep is equivalent to having
all our cities instantly nuked. It is their holocaust; we are its agent.

When we find two more, Hoyt's brow is furrowed, and I realize he
hasn't gotten used to this. He looks over at me and says, "To come out
here day after day and to see these huge carcasses of an endangered
species, it's..." He searches for the words. "It's fundamentally disturbing to me."

Hoyt marks the carcasses, then drags them up past the highest reach of
the waves, skidding them through the windrows of crabs that continue
down the beach like a red carpet of welcome. Amid the superabundance
of the food for which they crossed an ocean, the lifeless turtles rest.

We're behind schedule and racing a rising tide, so, like the Black-Bellied
Plovers and Whimbrels along the shore, we're flying now, Hoyt pushing

the speed needle past fifty miles an hour, tear-assing over the powdery sand in the sea breeze until we rise away from the beach, into the dust-dry spine of thorny, bone-strewn desert.

In low gear we jounce and bounce up over a mountain and down into a fishing camp called San Lázaro, tucked in under an arm of Magdalena Bay. Like several such camps in the Mag Bay estuary, it's a cluster of shanties used for weeks at a time by fisherfolk from places like López Mateos and San Carlos. It has the usual piles of fishing gear in various stages of use and abandonment. A truck, having earlier come down the same track, is packing and icing some scorpionfish, a few halibut, Corbina, Pacific Yellowtail, Garibaldi. No one keeps track of how many fish daily come out of such hidden little camps.

One arriving *panga* lands stingrays. Another, a load of baby hammer-head sharks. The activity draws the interests of thin dogs, small children, and myself. So small are these young sharks that, holding them by the base of the tail, the men can carry in each fist four to eight at a time. I'm guessing they unload sixty young sharks, about five pounds each. I am told that ten years ago here, a hammerhead often required two people to lift it from the boat. Those, I'm told, are now few.

Hoyt says the next camp, unreachable by road, is sited at one of his favorite spots in the world. So we ask a fisherman if he'll shuttle us over by boat.

Truly, the camp's setting can't be faulted. Leading to the nearby inlet runs a stunning smooth jade throat of water between green mangroves, necklaced with white breakers. Across the inlet, dunes run southward to a steep, corrugated landscape looking as though it has for centuries sat desperate for a sip of rain. A timeless place.

The beach is jumbled with critical equipment and trash—traps, buoys, nets, a solar panel, liquor bottles, a drum tidily holding empty motor oil containers. Children are splashing one another along the shore.

Hoyt says, "You'll just have to imagine how many turtles once lived here." Twenty-five years ago there were thousands of turtles in the bay. Fishermen say, "You'd see them all over the lagoon, nothing like today."

But one must remain positive or go home. So I reply to Hoyt, "We'll just have to imagine how many will live here in the future when your projects and the efforts of the communities all succeed."

This is a specialty camp, for shark fishermen. With no navigational equipment or radios, these guys venture forty or fifty miles offshore in open skiffs called *pangas,* usually staying overnight, running their sets of baited hooks like fur trappers. They've let Hoyt hop aboard with them. His report: "It's pretty spooky." Their anchored lines are marked by flags and buoyed by chunks of foam or empty plastic beverage bottles stuffed into used rice sacks. They catch sharks such as hammerheads, Threshers, Shortfin Makos, and Blue Sharks. They also tangle or hook several species of turtles.

Salted shark meat is hanging on ropes strung between poles, like laundry in Baja's pitiless sun. On the beach, fins are drying.

Manuel Lucero, who at around age fifty ranks as senior shark fisher, is coiling rope. He tells Hoyt they get about two dollars a pound for the meat. "It's quite a lot of work, you know, salting and drying." These fins? "Ah, yes, about forty dollars per pound."

Big difference.

"Sometimes, fifty dollars."

For two dollars, it would not be profitable. But at forty dollars a pound, it's mainly for their fins the sharks are killed. For shark fins, turtles get killed.

The dried shark meat stays in Mexico, where, called *machaca* and tasting like salted sawdust with a fishy smell, it's used in tacos. But the fins go "mostly to San Francisco, San Diego, mainly the U.S." In each bowl of shark-fin soup swim the ghosts of turtles. Shark-fin soup is beef or chicken stock thickened by the cartilaginous parts of shark fins. Largely for this, we have since the mid-1980s reduced many shark populations worldwide by roughly 90 percent.

Señor Lucero has been a shark fisherman for only about six years. Before, it was lobster, things like that.

Shark-finning is fairly new here. Last year Lucero caught two six-hundred-pound Great Whites. Everywhere else in the world where sharks have been targeted by modern fisheries, they've been depleted within about ten to fifteen years. From what I've already seen, I'm betting this will be no exception.

Lucero mentions that the fishing has been slow. He says hammerheads are particularly prized; their dorsal fin is so large. Admiring Hoyt's T-shirt, which sports several swimming hammerheads, Manuel calculates how much money he could make from the fins over Hoyt's heart.

A *panga* arrives with a fisherman and his little son, about ten years old. The boy wears a life preserver; the man wears bright orange bib overalls.

They were out overnight, far offshore, trusting their lives to their single outboard engine. They have a boatful of medium and largish sharks.

He unloads first a Shortfin Mako, that sleek, steely-sided, Swordfish-snapping meteor of the sea, one of the most exquisitely devastating animals on Earth. The mako's taut, magnificent corpse hits the wet sand with a thud. It's a juvenile female, perhaps 130 pounds (59 kilograms). Females don't begin breeding until they reach around 700 pounds.

Next the man begins muscling out the floppy Blue Sharks, dragging them from skiff to beach with a meathook. After them comes a second mako, about 110 pounds. A third might pull a scale to the 100-pound mark. The fourth mako would be called a "pup"—20 pounds.

The fisherman moves with the pumped, self-conscious posture of a man in a tough, dangerous trade, proud to be surviving and bringing home the prize, aware that people are watching. His work is a far cry from office cubicles. I'm sure that, having done a hard day's labor and killed big animals, he's got a certain adrenal feeling—a feeling I'm familiar with. It feels elemental and unchanged from the time humans were mainly hunters of large prey. But considering the fistfuls of baby hammerheads and these juvenile makos, we're likely looking at the winding down of this way of life. Whatever the future holds for this fisherman's little boy, I imagine his father's footsteps will grow cold and fade.

When the boat is empty, the beach holds ten Blue Sharks averaging seven feet in length and the four makos, their grinning rows of teeth gritted in the sand.

After sharpening his knife, the man begins severing the mako sharks' ocean-slicing fins, then separating their heads and tossing their guts into the lapping water.

The water around the skiff begins clouding with blood. It draws small fishes who nibble scraps in their own miniaturized savage frenzy. Twenty years ago, I'm told, so much blood in the water here might have drawn sharks.

The table begins piling with dorsals, second dorsals, paired pectorals and ventrals, anal fins, and tail lobes. Eight from each shark, times fourteen. Nine dozen fins.

By the time we get back to López Mateos, it's been a long and beautiful day full of dead turtles, dead sharks, dead fish, and sadness. As if to bring me back to life, the evening's first nighthawks try the air.

· · ·

GILL NETS THAT TANGLE TURTLES ARE OFTEN DEPLOYED FROM SMALL *panga* skiffs like this one. Capitán José Parra wears a salted mustache, a red cap, and a red bandanna to keep the sun off his leathered neck. His young deckhand Kuko is less than half his age, perhaps twenty.

Their nets are set ten miles or so from shore in water about 150 feet deep. With no compass, we follow a sun angle from the inlet. We have no life vests, no radio; the boat contains no flotation material. Plowing into oncoming swells, its well-worn fiberglass floor flexes and shudders a little worrisomely. The fishermen cannot swim, and are rather afraid of the water. When something in our single engine begins complaining, I realize we also have no tools. José stops and does something to the wiring with a fish knife. We resume.

After a little wandering in what should be the right area, we see the red flag on a buoyed bamboo pole that signals the anchored net's location. Kuko grabs the pole. He pulls and piles the rope awhile; up comes the anchor, then more rope. Pelicans crowd in on us for the inevitable discards before the net even appears.

When the net comes into view, the *capitán* helps haul. Almost immediately, a small California Halibut—five or six pounds—comes aboard. Its body follows the typical flat flounder floor plan, one side blank as an unpainted canvas, the other bearing both eyes together beside its mouth like a Picasso, with lovely dark-marbled skin. A few minutes later two more come aboard, followed by a Torpedo Ray. Next comes a spadefish with empty eye sockets. Some sea scavenger eats eyes first.

A scorpionfish, still very much alive, comes aboard with its gills flared defiantly, venomous spines rigidly erected in the hope of returning the favor. José stuns it with a club. It's edible. The net continues piling up. It is 240 meters long—nearly 800 feet. José has two such nets. One edge of each net is weighted to keep it resting on the seafloor, the other edge buoyed to hold it upright in the water like a curtain. Each nearly invisible net is one small brick in the Great Wall of Hunger with which humanity interrupts the travels of sea life worldwide.

Over several minutes the net brings a small halibut, a type of croaker called *Chano,* and a Pacific Porgy. Nearly twenty-five minutes of continued hauling raises a Cow-Nosed Ray about a meter wide wingtip to wingtip, three halibut, a triggerfish just under two feet long, and another porgy.

When we come to the end of the net, José backs up the boat and Kuko guides the net out over the bow as though someone's hit the reverse button on a video player—except, of course, that the fish don't go back into the ocean.

Halibut—the money fish—bring fifteen to twenty pesos a kilo, well under two dollars per pound. Other species go for as little as four pesos. On a good day José and Kuko get as much as one hundred kilos of halibut, but lately they've been averaging just twenty.

From the second net, a few hundred yards away, a small stingray is followed by a squat fish whose mouth bristles with needlelike teeth. This is a species of stargazer, so-called because in ambush it normally lies on the bottom with its eyes focused upward as if toward the heavens. It arrives crisscrossed with marks from struggling in the net. Its more natural markings are fine light-blue speckles on a night-dark background, like the starry night it eternally seeks. Capitán José says, "They have electricity." Actually, this comes as no shock: a type of stargazer lives in my home waters, and I have felt its sizzling tingle. José short-circuits it with a club, making it finally see stars.

Kuko pulls a Shovel-Nosed Guitarfish from the net, miming air guitar with it for my benefit. Everyone's a comedian. These things look like steam-rollered sharks morphing into stingrays. They're low-profile creatures the color of wet sand. But camouflage is no defense against José's invisible net. Barely glancing at the fish, Capitán José merely says, "Machaca," referring to that dried, shredded product made of the flesh of sharks and rays.

A discarded lizardfish immediately gets pouched by a pelican, but a tiny mouth-sized stingray, released alive, swims slowly away while the hungry yet wise pelicans demur.

Two more guitarfish and three more porgies get added to the floor of the skiff. The Torpedo Ray that's been lying quietly now begins a death rattle, flapping its wings emphatically for a piteous minute.

Two very small halibut come aboard, reminding us which species we are "trying" to catch. Of the next two guitarfish, one has a slightly different shape and markings. The fishermen joke that it's merely a different brand of guitar. The naturalist in me is compelled to inform myself that this is—let's find the right page in the field guide: ah!—a Banded Guitarfish. It joins the others.

The meshes bring in a Horn Shark. With a fistlike face and two hostile dorsal spines, it gets released. Two more halibut and four more guitarfish hit the pile, setting off a brief flurry of vain protest from the gasping mass. A little searobin, several more now-familiar fishes, and a husky Bat

Ray come aboard. In the boat the expiring fishes' gills are working hard, trying to breathe the insubstantial air, the exertion speeding their final expiration. When another stargazer joins them, its fixation on heaven seems foresightful.

The sudden appearance of a meter-long halibut, around twelve or thirteen pounds, insecurely tangled, causes Capitán José more than a little excitement. He fumbles to locate the gaff-hook before the day's most valuable fish escapes. When he does procure the fish, he turns proudly, hoisting the halibut in a classic fisherman's pose for benefit of my admiration, which I duly and truly display.

An ensemble of guitarfish are now strumming the deck at such high volume I wonder whether we're depleting the ocean of its song. We're fishing "for" halibut because of the price, but we're catching whatever hits the nets.

By ten A.M., the fishermen are done, and we relax awhile as the boat bobs in the swells. The nets are back to work. I am relieved that we didn't see the looming shape of a dead Loggerhead come up today. The fishermen splash themselves with seawater, then scrub their slimed overalls. Our mixed catch weighs perhaps two hundred aggregate pounds. We open crackers and some fresh fruit. Capitán José says, "It is the beautiful hour—the hour when we eat." He says it's also the hour of turtles; they like the warm kiss of sun, and now is when you'd start to see them.

I'M ON THE OUTDOOR DECK OF A LITTLE VILLAGE RESTAURANT, SEATED across from a man named after Saint Francis, patron saint of animals. He's known by his nickname, Gordo, and to him many thousands of sea turtles owe their deaths.

Gordo set turtle nets for about twenty years. With his thick, fleshy neck and a growth of silver stubble, he slouches in an open flannel shirt. He's heavy and disheveled, a shambling self-caricature, part junkyard dog, part lost puppy.

Having just spent six months in jail, Gordo is savoring his freedom, sort of. He seems chastened and a little stunned because the one freedom he most savored—to catch and sell turtles—seems to be off the table.

"It's really hard for me," he says, his voice surprisingly soft. "I'm used to money, and good cars." He has a large face and gentle eyes. "The fishermen's cooperative wants the worst for me. They know I'm a threat to the future of their children." (In 1997, fishing co-op members shot and killed a poacher raiding valuable lobster and abalone grounds near San Ignacio Lagoon.)

According to his own estimate, Gordo regularly caught more than a thousand turtles each year. What does a turtle catcher need to know?

"A good turtle catcher must know how to find turtles. This is not easy. They are very astute, one of the most astute animals in the ocean. Not just anyone can catch them. A person can set a net among a thousand turtles and catch none. You must know where they swim, how they swim, how they use the currents. I had to study them. I put many hours on my boat engine learning their ways. In summer, they come into lagoons to be in warm water for feeding. In winter, they travel toward the ocean as the shallows cool. You must know their routes.

"When I was a boy," Gordo says, "we all ate *Caguama*. It was normal, it wasn't a problem." In his father's footsteps, Gordo simply went into the business.

In May 1990, Mexico's President Carlos Salinas de Gortari made catching, transporting, eating, selling, and harming sea turtles federal offenses punishable by steep fines and jail time. That presidential decree changed Gordo's job title from "turtle catcher" to "poacher." Gordo didn't really become an outlaw; Gordo was *outlawed*.

But the decree didn't come with job counseling. And the turtles' changing status did little to lessen the demand for them. Turtle hunters like Gordo caught their breath and dove quietly beneath the surface, toward the back roads and greased palms of black markets that also handle narcotics and arms smuggling.

Gordo made crucial contacts with powerful, politically connected buyers in Tijuana and Ensenada, near the U.S. border. He shipped the turtles by truck or drove them himself, or he sent them by passenger bus, stacked alive on their sides in the cargo bins, their flippers tied behind their backs. It was all illegal, sure, but not difficult.

For a string of years, nobody denounced him, and he made good, easy money. Locals helped him. "Even the police assisted me," he brags, explaining, "To be a good poacher, first you must know how to control the authorities. All of them." He counts on his fingers: "The state politicians, federals, highway police, the army—. I have always worked in coordination with the authorities. They were all paid by the boss in Tijuana."

We interrogate him: How much can a live turtle sell for? "Anywhere from twenty dollars to over five hundred U.S. sometimes, a single turtle."

How are the military checkpoints negotiated? "Walkie-talkies and bribes, or using back roads at night." Were drugs involved? "Of course. Often as payment." And: Who buys illegal turtles? "Influential officials, politicians, drug lords, restaurants—who did you think?"

The mere illicitness of turtle boosts its attraction. It appeals to those who like to signal, "I am above the law." Sea turtle is the most emotional food in Mexico. It touches some of the most powerful motivators: danger, power, sex. Some still insist that turtle eggs give *mucho palo*—"much stick," or prolonged sexual readiness. Gordo says that if you drop a turtle penis into a bottle of white wine and let it soak ten to twenty days, the resulting aphrodisiac will sell for fifty dollars a glass. "I tried it once, with a good result," he reports.

The overall result of his life's work, though, has been less than salutary. Gordo's wife made her escape while he was in jail. And he has no savings: "I spent all the turtle money on cars, drugs, women." He doesn't look good for a man in his forties. He's got a few health problems, and his chain-smoking, drinking, and weight can't be helping. A few years ago, speeding across the bay with a boatload of turtles, he struck one of the Gray Whales that famously come to breed in San Ignacio Lagoon. The force threw him against the side of the boat hard enough to cause a permanent hip injury and a slight limp. It could not have been good for the whale, either.

Before his arrest, he'd gotten called for turtles for Holy Week. (Many Catholics forgo meat before Easter, and since turtles swim, they're thought of as fish, not meat. This convenient inaccuracy dooms many turtles in the name of Resurrection and Everlasting Life.) Gordo sent word, and his boys delivered fifty-seven turtles. Happy to have so many, Gordo began driving them to Tijuana. He took a back road and was surprised to come over a hill into an army roadblock. The soldiers asked Gordo what he had.

He said, "Nothing."

"Open the car."

"Will ten thousand pesos do it?"

"There are nine of us."

"Fifteen thousand?"

Silence.

"Thirty."

This they talked about. Their counteroffer: "You're under arrest."

Gordo believes that another fish camp tipped them off, to eliminate his competition in the turtle business. Or it might have been local fishermen who'd just gotten tired of Gordo. Legal fishermen in local cooperatives don't like poachers because, by definition, poachers take from their local waters turtles, fish, scallops, lobsters, and other things they're not entitled to.

The army also confiscated his truck.

This was Gordo's fourth arrest—always on turtle charges—but his first protracted prison stay. "In the past," he says, "everything was worked out in a few days because of my government contacts. But with the change in government, my former friends are out of power."

As Gordo cleans his ear with a toothpick I ask what happened to the buyer while he was in prison. "She has many sources and no worries. It is fixed for her all the way to Mexico City."

Gordo says she offered to pay his fine to keep him out of jail and on the road. "But that would have obliged me to continue with her. I decided I would rather be done with this business. Now I am better free— like the turtles."

But he doesn't sound convinced.

He takes another swig of his beer. "I don't know how I got so screwed," he says self-pityingly. "It is hard work cleaning lobsters all day, getting my hands scratched up for so little money. I know some of the biggest drug lords; I've sold turtles to them. But I prefer to suffer than to work for them."

Gordo seems decidedly torn about his future. The buyer is trying to get him back into the business. The attention is flattering. "She just called this morning, because I am really good at moving turtles," he declares, brightening with pride. And the idea is tempting. At present Gordo is making the equivalent of twenty dollars per day separating lobsters' meat from their shells. Selling turtles, he can be on the water and earn four hundred dollars per day.

Through a veil of cigarette smoke, he worries, "I don't know exactly what I am going to do. If I go back to jail... " Getting involved in turtles again could mean a much longer prison sentence. Gordo weighs his options: "In prison, you can get anything—drugs, prostitutes, cable TV— but," he says gravely, "there is always tension. You can go crazy from the pressure, the danger, the violence. Fights, stabbings—whatever they want. You don't have your friends, your family, your freedom. I decided in prison, it's not worth having problems and problems and problems."

Gordo adds that he did have some support during the time he was imprisoned. Family members visited. They brought him turtle soup.

With him out of action, Gordo says, there are more turtles in the lagoon.

That is the point, after all. But he seems to chafe at the forgone opportunity and the restrictions. "I was in my boat a couple of weeks ago. I saw a turtle and set my net. I caught thirteen turtles. But I kept only one, just to eat."

On paper, Gordo is a monster compulsively addicted to killing sea turtles. But when he's sitting there in front of you, he's a sad person with a problem to solve and limited options. If we want to let turtles live, we have to help him solve his problem. To deter him we must offer a way he can benefit from listening to our view of how the world is changing. That requires understanding his world and its practical constraints. Where there is adequate law and enforcement, one can report crimes to the authorities and fight opponents in court. For all the wide rest of the world—almost everywhere—our shared humanity is our only hope. Seeing people as enemies distorts them into something both bigger and smaller than they really are.

Gordo says he's broke. Today he had two hundred pesos after work. He gave some to a child and bought cigarettes and now has forty pesos left, about four dollars. "I'm not going to smoke anymore after this pack," he says as he pulls out yet another cigarette. He assures us that he is also quitting sea turtle trafficking. He has spoken publicly in favor of the ban. Gordo says he wants people to know he's changed. He wants to save sea turtles and set a better example for the younger generation. In a few minutes we will leave. I may never see Gordo again, but I know for certain that his turtle buyer will be calling.

THOSE DUKE SCIENTISTS WHO'D DETERMINED THAT WARM-WATER LONG-liners set 1.4 billion hooks yearly counted only bigger, sophisticated boats called "industrial" long-liners. They left out smaller, "artisanal" boats. But when you start moving south of the U.S. border, a funny thing happens: you find there are lots—*lots*—of small-scale boats. Many of them are long-liners and gillnetters using boats just twenty-three feet or so long, usually operated by only two people, whose catches seldom get recorded.

At a sea turtle conference in Costa Rica, I learned that that country now has eighteen industrial long-liners *plus* over five hundred smaller long-liners, collectively setting 70 million hooks a year. They mainly target Dorado, often called by their Hawaiian name, Mahimahi. The study that tallied 1.4 billion hooks wholly left out Dorado fishing, but boats chase these fish all along Pacific Central America and down to Peru. In Costa Rica the second most common animals in their catch, after Dorado themselves, are turtles. They catch 5 turtles for every thousand hooks. That's actually an astronomical rate. Japan's long-liners catch 0.1 per thousand hooks. Before the North Pacific closure, Hawaii-based long-liners were catching 0.07 turtles per thousand hooks. Subsequent restrictions reduced that to 0.002 turtles per thousand hooks, or one turtle per half million hooks. Dorado live near the surface. That's one of the reasons the lines tangle so many turtles, but most turtles caught by longlines targeting Dorado can rise and keep breathing. They can be released if the fishermen aren't too hungry. And they can live if they haven't swallowed the hook or been badly injured by it. That's where those circle hooks that almost always lodge in the jaw would come in handy.

A well-seasoned scientist with the Inter-American Tropical Tuna Commission, Martín Hall has become the circle hook's evangelist and patron saint. With a small entourage he's visited Pacific fishing communities from Mexico to Peru like a traveling medicine show, holding workshops, drumming up excitement over sea turtle conservation, and planting a cautionary tale—a subtle warning—about what could happen to their fisheries if Leatherbacks slide further.

The best word for the fishers he works with is *poor*. They inhabit a different world, as removed from boats with air-conditioned wheelhouses, exercise rooms, global positioning systems, and satellite phones as are donkey carts from BMWs. Their boats—virtually all identical—are those ubiquitous open fiberglass craft about twenty-three feet long called *pangas* or *fibras,* with a single outboard engine. That shell can seem a cell for men as each fishing trip becomes a short prison sentence of close confinement with the possibility of drowning. With ten ten-gallon plastic fuel containers they can fish a hundred miles offshore. Most have no navigational equipment; they travel along compass angles. Most have no radios. It's not for the faint of heart. Nor even for the courageous. It's just one of poverty's traps, a space your life occupies if you lack options.

There in the sun and wind far beyond sight of land they may remain a few days, baiting and setting their few hundred hooks, catnapping on the seats, and probably working to avoid thoughts of storm, motor failure, or the pirates who sometimes come for engines and leave fishermen to drift to their deaths. If the Dorado are close they can do day trips. But if they're far, or the fishermen decide to hunt tuna—hundreds of miles from shore—several *fibras* will hire a sixty-five-foot-long *bote* to tow them offshore for about two weeks, paying the *bote* 45 percent of their catch.

Into this struggle for existence Martín Hall, Ph.D., comes bearing strange new hooks and news of turtles' declines. Somehow he has to get these fishermen to believe him, share his concern, and make their own commitment. That's a very tall order.

But Martín is probably the only person in the world with a chance of pulling this off. A native of Argentina who has lived for years in La Jolla, California, while working for the Inter-American Tropical Tuna Commission, he knows players on all sides: government, fishing industry, conservation, science, management, and the poor fishing families he has come to speak with. He and his team must get the fishermen to try the new hooks and document their results.

The fishermen who lead these lives are unlikely to care about turtles just because it's the right thing to do. Nor will they try new kinds of hooks out of curiosity. "A hook is not much of an expense to an American fisherman," Martín tells me, "but in some countries a hook is worth five or six lunches." He says, "We need goals that bring people together, not goals that polarize people."

This kind of work must be done community by community, face-to-face. Martín explains, "In almost all cases, our knowledge of fisheries is pathetic. We don't know who's catching what, when, where. In most of Latin America, boats don't even have licenses, and enforcement for fisheries—it's nearly nonexistent."

How to approach it then? In most fishing communities, he tells me, the women are the civic leaders, making the economic decisions and having the future in mind. That's why families are important.

Martín looks Latin and speaks native-born Spanish and he knows what he's talking about. He has great compassion for the fishermen and their families, and armed with these elements and his scientific knowledge, he works the crowds with an earnest zeal that surprises me a little. I've known Martín for about ten years, and he doesn't always share environmentalists' views about the urgency of problems. He's a veteran, naturally methodical, a bit conservative.

But on this issue, Martín's convinced that the problem is critical. He says, "We don't need to study this problem to learn how much bycatch there is. We already know the Leatherbacks are declining fast, so the goal is no dead Leatherbacks."

From Mexico to Peru, Martín and several helpers visit fishing villages, holding meetings in dusty halls or under a canopy on the waterfront. In the first half hour Martín must convince fishermen that there's a real problem, it affects them, and they need to solve it. He conveys the scientific information, shows the declines, relates the studies showing how turtles get killed on longlines.

Though many issues are exaggerated, he tells the people, the evidence for the Leatherback's decline is very solid. Unlike, say, estimating the number of sharks in the Pacific Ocean, Leatherbacks come ashore, so you can simply count them. "These graphs are reality, these are real numbers. Some things are not opinion. If a soccer game is three–nothing, it's three–nothing. The score determines who wins and loses. It doesn't matter how beautifully one team played. The turtle data is the game score. The only thing that matters is if that score changes, if the numbers go up, and if the Leatherbacks start winning. At sea no one is checking you," he acknowledges, "but—you can't cheat this score. Other people are going to keep counting nesting turtles, and the only way to win is to change the score. The only thing that matters is those numbers." Concluding with a compassionate appeal to their self-interest, Martín tells the people, "If the turtle numbers keep going down—you are done. There is not a lot of time to find a solution for Leatherbacks. Leatherbacks can't wait that long. You fishermen don't have fifteen years. You don't have ten. You probably don't have five. Not only do things have to change, but they have to change in a time frame that is unprecedented."

The fishers already know that *Norteamericanos* have banned tuna caught in nets that drown dolphins, and they know the United States refuses to import shrimp from some countries because of turtles. So they know those crazy gringos are likely to do anything next—and now there's concern about sea turtles and longlines. They've heard the United States has shut some of its own fisheries to save turtles. They realize outsiders can stop buying the fish from fisheries that kill sea turtles. These possibilities are a real threat to the fishermen, and they quickly understand those parts of the problem.

But coastal fishers using three hundred hooks a night might catch two Leatherbacks per year, so it's hard for them to see that they're the main problem.

Martín tells them, yes, turtles are killed in other fisheries too, but that doesn't help you. Deal with your share of the problem. Don't waste time and energy blaming others. You can be leaders, your country can be a leader; this problem is solvable.

How can they start changing? Martín and his associates have brought bags and bags of circle hooks, thousands. And they have hook removers to give away, too.

Then, while his associates are studying the hooks' effectiveness in one country, Martín will move to the next and commence workshops there.

Ecuadorian tuna and Dorado fishers tested one large and one small circle hook. Tuna fishermen found that the larger hooks reduced turtle snagging by almost 90 percent, the smaller hooks by 44 percent. Dorado boats hooked 37 percent fewer turtles with the larger and 16 percent fewer with the smaller hooks. The chance of a turtle surviving capture is even better, because few swallow these hooks. Circle hooks reduced sea turtle mortality by 60 to 90 percent in the tuna fishery and 40 to 90 percent in the Dorado fishery, depending on hook size.

That's all fine. But the fishermen need to catch fish. The circle hooks caught about as many tuna as did J-hooks. But they caught far fewer Dorado—about a third less. That's enough of a problem that the fishermen will probably want their old hooks back.

Martín had just completed a workshop for Baja fishermen and was hurrying to South America. He e-mailed me from Peru: "We have improvement, but no solution yet."

It's a search for imperfect compromise. I'd prefer it if no one had invented long-lining, but the wisdom of working with fishermen is that the approach accepts the validity of each perspective—fishers', turtles', conservationists'—and engages the fishery in the conservation effort. If environmentalists pushed for a worldwide ban and lost—as I believe they would—long-lining could go on as always in most countries. Some countries are planning more long-lining, not less. So it seems important to keep improving it, making it as good as possible.

PUERTO MAGDALENA IS THE ONLY REAL SETTLEMENT ON ISLA MAGdalena. Hardly more than a large fishing camp, the tiny town's composed of a few dozen shanties. Today's festivity is a kid's soccer game, home team versus San Carlos.

San Carlos, López Mateos, Puerto Magdalena, and other poor communities where fishing rules everything are the hardest kind of place to make the case for protecting edible sea animals such as turtles. But then little fingerholds slip into the conversation: "Yes, as a child I saw turtles everywhere." You start conversations here as though scaling a vertical cliff. Many adults here have lived the experience of seeing turtles go from common to rare. *But*—they still see turtles regularly. They've also seen the fish, lobster, and abalones decline, so in a sense the decline of turtles isn't special. It's just part of how things are.

The town's only restaurant has lined its outdoor patio with turtle shells. The larger shells pain me particularly because they came from breeders. The smaller pain me because they didn't. One such shell—from a turtle eaten within the last year or so—is from a very large Black Turtle. It was probably fifty or sixty years old, and had probably made the nesting migration many times.

At this restaurant, a hand-painted sign features a turtle and the words PROTECT US. The sign is brand-new. Turtles are now off the menu here.

The son of a fisherman and a former fisherman himself, Rodrigo Rangel Acevedo grew up here. Now he's *coordinador* of Groupo Tortuguero, a sea turtle conservation network. "I never say, 'Don't eat turtle,'" he tells me. "I just tell them to be aware that turtles are in danger, that we're in a privileged place."

The soccer game breaks for halftime. Suddenly the tallest and most colorful sea turtle anyone's ever seen is riding slowly onto the playing field on an all-terrain vehicle, waving gaily. The brightly uniformed teams—and all the other kids in town—come streaming behind this most fabulous turtle. Parents line up with their kids for photos. For them, the turtle brings the magic of surprise and mystery; who is behind all this fun?! (Hoyt Peckham, he who counts drowned Loggerheads, is in the turtle suit.) Amid the display of youthful enthusiasm, a big friendly man from far away hands out forms asking kids to suggest a name for the giant turtle. Whichever name is suggested most often will win. And also, he says, it is important to take care of sea turtles, because they are having some troubles.

Eager hands crowd in for the exotic forms they can write on and hand back to this strange man from somewhere who has come with the giant turtle just to speak to them. It's gimmicky, sure, but it creates a friendly atmosphere for an important message. And now, even adults wish to have their photo taken with their arm around the multicolored turtle. No one wants to be left out.

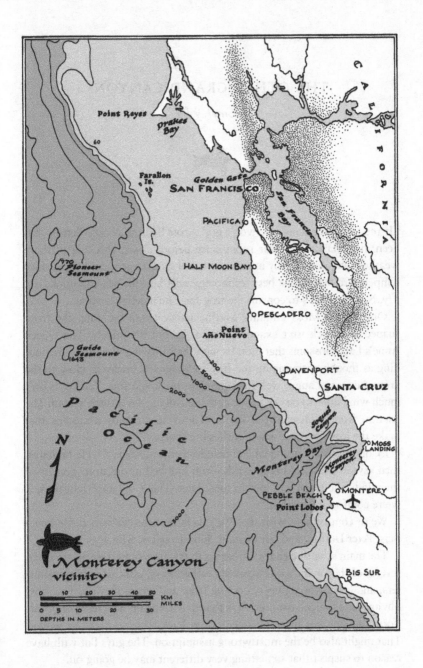

Monterey Canyon
vicinity

| 0 | 10 | 20 | 30 | 40 | 50 | KM |
| 0 | 5 | 10 | 20 | | 30 | MILES |

DEPTHS IN METERS

THE OTHER GRAND CANYON

Monterey Bay

"If the frog is dancing, we won't go," Scott Benson asserts. Benson has been in his laboratory war room since before dawn, checking offshore weather data, ocean-buoy information, and satellite-generated sea-surface temperature maps. The best technology tells him the sea conditions are iffy. Now he wants to consult the frog for a final determination.

Outside the Moss Landing Marine Laboratories building, the frog-shaped windsock isn't exactly doing a jig, but it's fidgety. The Queen Anne's Lace blossoms that bless us with their thriving weediness are nodding as though encouraging the frog to boogie. A breeze so close to the ground does not augur well for boating or turtle spotting. Ten knots isn't much wind unless you need to scan the sea all day for a turtle's head. The friction from a mere fifteen knots of moving air adds whitecaps that make the job infeasible where turtles are sparse.

"Conditions are not ideal," concludes Benson. "But..." He hesitates, then says, "We should take a ride—run like hell up north to get out of the wind. The plane will join us there later. That's my idea right now, if we're comfortable with it."

We're comfortable with it. "We" includes Scott Eckert, turtle geneticist Peter Dutton, and our captain, John Douglas, who goes by J.D.

The main scientific endeavor here is to try, over several weeks, to catch several of the Pacific's ever-scarcer Leatherbacks, affix satellite transmitters, and learn where they're coming from and where they go. The most obvious and logical assumption is that they come up here to central California in summer from Mexico and go back there to breed in winter. That might also be the most wrong assumption. The guys I'm with have reason to suspect that something very different may be going on.

. . .

Among the few harbors on California's rugged coast, Moss Landing stands as a last passing relic of Steinbeck's working waterfront, with old salmon trolling boats, sardine seiners, and funky cottages whose bright flower gardens balance the ruined warehouses and weedlots.

The view from its inlet seems typical—you're ashore looking at the ocean's surface—but actually it's an extraordinary place. The deep-sea tongue of Monterey Canyon practically swallows the inlet jetties. Just a few miles from the beach the water piles hundreds of fathoms deep— thousands of feet. Most undersea canyons lie many miles from the world's coasts. Monterey's undersea version of the Grand Canyon comes right to shore. The resulting productivity draws migratory wildlife to the canyon's bounty from hundreds, thousands of miles distant.

We load the boat with net and transmitter gear and leave the dock under a layer of cloud so low and dense it hides the tops of sailboats' masts. Fog's silver lining is usually that it accompanies calm winds and waters.

But today there's more breeze than we bargained for. And it's cool; I can see my breath. I'm wearing a weatherproof jacket over a sweatshirt, over a flannel shirt, over a T-shirt. But the damp still delivers chills. It's the last day of August.

A three-foot white-fanged chop confronts us as soon as we leave the harbor jetties. Our thirty-foot boat, *Sheila B,* has a square drop-down bow like a military landing craft, making it possible to slide big turtles aboard; it also makes the boat pound hellishly in a chop. And now we're pounding. J.D. is already expressing doubts about our chances of even seeing a turtle.

But Benson reminds us: we're heading to the bay's north end, where the landform should block this wind.

That sounded good in the lab. Out here on the foam-streaked ocean, the prospect of pounding up there inspires something less than enthusiasm. Further, the fog will likely keep the spotter plane grounded.

We travel a few miles offshore and hook north in deep water. You can know a lot about where off Monterey Leatherbacks should be, based on the conditions, the depths they like, the season, and where on the ocean the temperature breaks are. But you still have to simply come here and look and look and look. If that fails, cruise elsewhere and look more. If this were 1980, when—if the early estimates are true—Leatherbacks were perhaps twenty times more abundant, you'd be finding them. Now you want air support and you'll settle for blind luck.

Scott Benson, in his late forties, is, among us, the main expert on the central California ocean. He confides, "Predicting where in the bay they'll be is really about trying to piece together how animals here respond to currents, winds, temperatures. This is actually one of my more challenging gigs—but it's fun."

As on their other feeding grounds—as off Cape Breton, for example— Leatherbacks appear when the water nears 60 degrees Fahrenheit (around 16° C). That happens here at the very end of summer—around now— when the seaward winds stop blowing and that warmer water brushes in close.

Right now, we have just one small warm pocket off Davenport, where we're headed.

Benson's main challenge is that this isn't the Atlantic Ocean. Turtles seem so much rarer in the Pacific that motoring around in a slow little fishing boat, as I did off Cape Breton with Mike James and Blair and Bert Fricker, would be a waste of time here. And if the airplane gets up, it also won't find dozens of Leatherbacks, as Sally Murphy sees off South Carolina; most days it might find one or two. Finding Leatherbacks in these waters requires superior speed, persistent air support, and sophisticated daily satellite-generated sea-temperature maps.

It wasn't always this way, but the Pacific Leatherback's fortunes seem to be changing fast. As recently as two years ago this crew found a lot of turtles in Monterey Bay. They saw as many as four at once, and in only a week they had forty-five turtle-capture attempts (with no prior experience, they caught just two). Last year they were here three times as long, but got only ten capture opportunities (they caught three). Their catch ratio was skyrocketing as they gained skill, but the number of turtles they were seeing was plummeting.

But last year the offshore wind persisted, preventing warmer oceanic water from coming in. Maybe the turtles just stayed offshore. Is the apparent scarcity of Leatherbacks here really due to scarcity? Could it be simply ocean conditions—wind or El Niño—keeping them away?

Peter Dutton, an organized man with curly dark hair and a trimmed beard, has worked with turtles in the Atlantic and Pacific, North America, South America, and Asia. He's one of the more big-picture field scientists I've met. And he knows his answer. "The collapse people are talking about for Pacific Leatherbacks is real," he says with the matter-of-factness of someone who's come to grips with a grim diagnosis. He offers a comparison: "In the Atlantic, conservation programs got started earlier, and in a number of places they're succeeding; several populations are growing fast. The thing is: recovery is a numbers game. You need a certain proportion of adults to survive from one year to the next, but you also need eggs. In the Atlantic there's a lot of egg production now, enough reproduction to offset more adult mortality from fishing. In the Pacific, even if you protected every egg, you'd still be in trouble now because there are so few females and so few eggs."

Peter gets to the crux by saying, "A lot of people blame longlines for the Pacific collapse. And in the Atlantic we see a lot of adult females very beaten up with line scars, embedded hooks—. Yet where we've worked a lot, on St. Croix in the Caribbean, annual survival of nesting Leatherbacks is actually high, about ninety percent. And, because of twenty years of effective nest protection there, the population is growing rapidly. Now, for *eastern Pacific* nesting beaches, I've felt we've overlooked the role of egg taking. When I went to Mexico to work with Laura Sarti, a turtle would come up and a poacher would be on it, and the biologists would be pleading for one or two eggs for the hatchery. In the last few years, egg protection actually improved steadily, but that's only in the last few years.

"I think the collapse was caused by a one-two punch: first, years of egg taking on Pacific beaches robbed the population of new youngsters, leaving a hole. That put the adults out on a limb. Then in the 1980s something—most likely drift-netting—slammed the adults. Western Pacific, similar pattern and timing: heavy egging, intensified fishing, and turtles crashing. So I think it's misleading to characterize longline fishing as the *cause* of the collapse. That doesn't mean it isn't a problem now. The Pacific population is so low now that killing any turtle makes a difference. But I think the situation is not quite as bad as it seems, because for the last few years more eggs have been protected, so there're more hatchlings going out there. My gut feeling is that what we're seeing now is the population bottoming out from the bad stuff that happened in the eighties. There are very few females nesting, and that's a big problem. Still, if their nests can be protected and those hatchlings survive—I go by what I've seen in the last twenty years in the Caribbean—I think the Pacific Leatherback will start coming back."

As a teenage drummer in the 1960s and early '70s, I was a jazz lover in the rock era. My time was great, but my timing's often off. Coltrane died early, Miles got hard to hear, Maynard Ferguson and Buddy Rich were tearing up the place for small audiences, and when I heard people saying big bands were coming back, I wanted to believe them, too. Then again, big bands and turtles—apples and oranges.

The wind slackens noticeably, and whitecaps begin lying down like surrendering enemies. We're still heading toward that small pocket of warmer water that Benson found on the satellite maps.

We climb atop the pilothouse roof—where the cruising boat creates a raw wind—to scan for our quarry. Scott Eckert looks dressed for the South Pole, with waterproof jumpsuit, hood drawn down to his nose, and a life vest just for warmth.

Peter says this beats sitting in front of a computer.

Sinking my chin deep into my two upturned collars, stiffening with the cold of a Monterey Bay summer, I concur; though a computer would be warmer.

We begin intersecting large numbers of Sooty Shearwaters—flocks of hundreds that become *thousands,* all airborne in the lofting breeze. Over the next few miles shearwater numbers continue building spectacularly until perhaps twenty thousand Sooties are swarming the air around us. They've flown here from New Zealand, propelled by instinct we cannot feel, drawn across the Pacific by cues we cannot detect, to form this dense knot of fluttering wings and hungering voices.

Suddenly their flocks break, like we're coming through a cloud, and there are none—at all—for miles ahead.

The water temperature at the sea surface is 14 degrees Celsius. Too cold. We're looking for water closer to 16 degrees. With turtles now so sparse, we can't afford to look anywhere that isn't textbook. Benson climbs down to the cabin to ask J.D. to speed it up a little, to get us faster to that warmer pocket he saw on the computer.

I follow inside to get another jacket. Our captain is clutching a hand-warming cup of coffee. Right behind me Scott Eckert slides the door of the pilothouse open, steps in, slides it shut, and says, "Wow—I've gotta warm up." Peter comes in saying, "Man, it's cold."

Mind you, this is late summer. Mark Twain's apocryphal snub of this coast applies with a vengeance: "The coldest winter I ever spent was a summer in San Francisco."

Seas are still lumpy, everything looking gray-green. The surface remains blank, poker-faced, withholding.

Benson notices a couple of Pink-Footed Shearwaters. Compared to Sooties, their graceful glidings make them seem more like albatross: buoyant, effortless as good news.

They're a good sign. They prefer open-ocean waters. Their presence suggests that offshore water is pushing closer to shore, creating a narrower band of the water most suitable for turtles. Unlike on Georges Bank, this front is affected mainly by wind rather than the bottom topography, so it moves a lot. But our basic search strategy is similar: find the productive edge, get in it, keep working it. Most animals do the same.

The floating pieces of kelp make Benson happy too. "It shows that, in this area, stuff is being retained"—further evidence of front formation.

Scott Eckert calls, "Starting to see a few Moon Jellies, anyway." Peter Dutton adds that he just saw the first *Chrysaora* (pronounced cry-*sora*), also called Sea Nettle; it's the Leatherback's preferred lunch in these waters. Benson says to me, "This is right around our original sweet spot; we've had luck here."

There's another *Chrysaora*, about a foot across, a dancing mushroom trailing perhaps ten feet of tentacles armed with fire. Leatherbacks snack on them like hors d'oeuvres, but you don't want one of those across your face. Aboard working boats, the stinging *Chrysaora* is unanimously unloved, distinctively disdained. Crab fishermen sometimes coat their faces with Vaseline to protect against broken-off tentacles that come up stuck to traplines and flapping in the breeze. A scientist once opined to me, "I realize they perform an important role in the ecosystem, but to me they're just a pain in the ass." He'd gotten *Chrysaora* fragments in his eye—and their spring-loaded stinging cells continued firing randomly as much as a week later. The captain of a research ship I was on had gotten tentacles on his arm. Two days later his skin started peeling off.

We traverse a drift line just a couple of meters wide, marked by a dense collection of floating kelp-frond fragments. The water's slick on one side and wind-stippled on the other. When we go over it, the temperature changes a few tenths of a degree, indicating two abutting water masses. We cross the front, and—as through a gate into new pasture—Moon Jellies suddenly appear everywhere we look, one every two or three square meters. Another group of jellies called salps, clear fist-sized sacklike things with a bright pink gut, likewise come on heavy. And we're heavy into the *Chrysaoras*, too, about one for every boat length. "This is good," Benson says.

Jellyfish Wonderland lasts about ten minutes. When we cross another line of grass and seaweed, the Moon Jellies and the rest vanish as though to the dark side of the moon itself. The seemingly eternal sea's true constant is change, year to year, day by day, mile by mile, minute to minute.

Benson calls down from the roof, "It's now 15.2 degrees."

That's a shave under 60 degrees Fahrenheit. The water's warming. We begin seeing platter-sized baby Ocean Sunfish, one every ten minutes or so. Another good sign, Benson says, because they too indicate arriving offshore water. He considers them part of the "turtle community."

Everyone agrees there's a lot here; conditions have gotten pretty good. Only problem is, the turtles are now so scarce.

"I WAS AN INNOCENT FISH GUY. I THOUGHT THINGS WERE PRETTY straightforward," Bruce Robison is confessing as the 110-foot-long research ship *Point Lobos* casts its dock lines. "I've graduated down to jellies. They're a lot more interesting."

Robison, senior scientist with the Monterey Bay Aquarium Research Institute, focuses on soft-bodied animals living suspended in open water between the surface and one thousand meters in depth, around half a mile from the surface. His mind inhabits a deep-water world without firm boundaries, very different from the one most people—even most ocean scientists—experience. It's the world Leatherbacks ply during their deep dives—and it's another universe.

Robison has friendly blue-gray eyes set in a sea-seasoned face framed by gray hair and a salted beard. He's wearing a battered blue jacket and jeans. We're talking over coffee and tea at the galley table. The ship's interior walls feature photos paying homage to iridescent squids, crimson crabs, and a truly bizarre gallery of nightmarish-looking deep-sea fishes and jellies. Robison has been at the institute since its inception in the late 1980s and for a decade worked closely with its founder, David Packard. "He was tremendously invigorating to work with," Bruce remembers with obvious affection. "He wanted us to shake the constraints that usually keep science in a safe place. He'd say, 'If you don't fail sometimes, you're not reaching far enough.' David Packard was very curious, interested in all kinds of things, and he loved nature in many ways. He wanted us to advance the field. That's why we're here."

We're cruising through mild swells toward a site about twelve miles from the beach. The hull conveys the sway of slow progress. Getting there will take an hour and a half. The place we're going to is sixteen hundred meters deep (fifty-two hundred feet). Robison's focus doesn't include animals on or in the seafloor. The "midwater invertebrates" he's most interested in are soft-bodied, hardly studied. One problem with this work, Robison says, is there's very little to compare it to. "It's too new. We can't tell how fast things are changing or whether these communities are changing at all. There's almost no frame of reference."

The force of nets usually shreds and blows apart the many delicate lifeforms that rely on the dependable, gentle drift of water to support their fragile bodies. If you're interested in gelatinous animals and how they live in the ocean, you need a better plan.

So Robison began deep-diving in mini-submarines and using unmanned subs, or ROVs (remotely operated vehicles), to peek in on the deep. He's been coming out here a couple of times a week for eight years, and his work is truly pioneer biology. "When we first got a look inside Monterey Bay we were instantly overwhelmed by the richness. It wasn't what we were expecting at *all*," adds Robison, waving his hands as though banishing earlier assumption.

No one had ever seen this habitat so well before, and Robison and his coworkers made a series of discoveries that he sums up thus: "It became immediately apparent that all of that stinging goo that comes up on nets was *really* important.

"Any way you slice it, the ocean's midwater, between surface and seafloor, is the largest living space on Earth. It's got the largest animal communities on the planet, with the largest combined mass. To suddenly realize that the world's dominant animals are *jellies*—that's a strange feeling."

A Sperm Whale up ahead is only the second the skipper has seen in fifteen years. It draws a few deep breaths, and then—extremely slowly—arches its back, lifts its flukes from the ocean toward the sky, and lets the weight of its great black tail drive it like a spike.

A few minutes' ride ahead, two Blue Whales—the most massive animals that have ever lived on Earth, at lengths up to one hundred feet (thirty meters)—force their towering breath skyward, so startlingly high their columnar spouts appear detonated, expanding at their tops like big sheaves of wheat. Their gleaming backs are sky blue, their flukes shockingly broad compared even to the behemoth Sperm Whale. The Blue has always eluded me; now here are two of them in my binoculars at once. Thrilling.

Unlike Sperm Whales, who mainly hunt big squids, the mountainous Blues hunt some of the smallest animals in the sea, mainly little pinkish things half to three-quarters of an inch long, vaguely shrimplike, with prominent dark eyes: krill. The whales need a lot of food, and they find it right here on the canyon rim. Vast swarms of krill migrate up at night from the deep part of Monterey Canyon to graze the plant plankton near the surface. Currents drift many krill over the canyon's submerged rim, and when they try to descend for the day they find themselves in water only a hundred fathoms—six hundred feet—deep. So they become concentrated in great seething clouds near the seafloor. There, out of the daytime darkness along that edge, sweep the sudden bulldozer maws of whales.

The energy economics that make Blue Whales feasible are interesting. Blue Whales can afford to be so big because they shorten the food chain between sunlight-produced sugar and the biggest animal in the world to just one intermediate link: the krill. Krill graze on single-celled plants, then whales tap directly into all that energy. So in economic terms, krill are like extreme wholesalers, bringing sunlight-produced energy from phytoplankton straight to the top of the food chain without other ecological middlemen taking cuts. The krill operate on a one-year life cycle; an exceptionally old one might reach its second birthday. Live fast, die young, leave a Blue Whale. Whales can eat krill only because krill behave exactly wrong. By aggregating during the day in swarms, krill allow whales to go and get big gulps of food. If krill spread out, whales would not be able to eat them; they'd burn more energy than they could get. So why don't krill spread out and be safe from whales? Baldo Morenovic of the University of California at San Diego explains that the enemies of krill are many and varied. Rockfishes, salmon, mackerel, hake, flatfishes, some sharks, squids, sardines, and various seabirds eat krill, and a lot of jellies, particularly the big ones, kill krill. Krill are universal currency, Euros of the open ocean, cashable everywhere. All the other predators actually add up to much more predatory weight than do whales. Whales are the least of krill's problems. Against the legions of other predators small enough to pick off individual krill, being in a crowd is the best protection—safety in numbers. That's what whales exploit.

Work here enough years, I'm told, and you begin to know the neighborhoods of the bay, what you can expect, where, and when. Like everything, the Moon Jellies *Aurelia* and the Sea Nettles *Chrysaora* have seasonal peaks and valleys. Where do they come from? Bruce Robison doesn't know, but he poses a question for me: "Where in hell *would* they come from, anyway?" He's not sure they're coming *from* anywhere.

Chances are, the ones you see are from local polyps on the seafloor, waiting for upwelling to tell them it's their time. Chances also are that they can grow so fast it *seems* they're arriving from somewhere. "They're almost all water. It's really easy to build one of those animals. There's not much cost in terms of proteins or complicated structure."

Our skipper pulls the throttles back. We're here. The sea surface is an azure calm. Two lovely Black-Footed Albatrosses begin circling the ship as though visiting from my last project. For the moment we're just drifting in outer Monterey Bay, nearly a mile above the canyon floor. You can travel a mile across the ocean and not see any change. But travel one vertical mile into the ocean, and pressure, temperature, and oxygen change in ways so profound you pass through other realms like falling into a magic well. We're going to get a glimpse of that today.

Ventana (Spanish for "window") is the name of our remotely operated vehicle, now being prepped for diving. "Streamlined" is not the word that leaps to mind. Indeed, the ROV looks nothing like a submarine. It's a squared-off piece of machinery roughly eight feet by five by five, seven thousand pounds or so. Outside its housing are various arrays of lights, cameras, collecting tubes and suction cylinders, robotic grasping claws, propellant gear for six thrusters, and bewildering bundles of hydraulic tubes, lines, and wiring. *Ventana* also packs lasers for length measurements and sensors for oxygen, depth, temperature, chlorophyll, current, and distance traveled. *Ventana* works tethered to the ship, and with a depth range of more than a mile, to 1,850 meters, the spool holds about 2,500 meters of tether. The tether contains three layers of overlapping Kevlar protecting power wires and optical fibers that transmit data. It's critical that the ship never pull tight on the tether. Break it, two million bucks sink.

The cameras are perhaps the most important of all *Ventana*'s gear. There's a new scratch on a $5,000 lens. "When did *that* happen?"

"Last week."

"Damn geologists."

At a quarter after nine we unhook the tie-down straps and the crane operator lifts *Ventana* from the deck, immersing it in a blue-green sea. It drifts in the surface like a huge orange turtle, waves washing across its back. The pilot sends it down about ten meters to check its buoyancy. Satisfied, they initiate the dive.

Bruce says this is dive number 2,343 for *Ventana*. "More dives than all the other big ROVs in the world combined," he adds with dedicated pride. This will be *Ventana*'s first dive as a surrogate Leatherback Turtle.

The dive is to 1,000 meters, a bit over 3,000 feet deep. Robison's research plan: starting at 50 meters and then at 100, 200, all the way to 1,000 meters, *Ventana* will level out horizontally and travel at each depth for ten minutes at a one-knot crawl, logging video footage. Impressive as *Ventana*'s work plan is, Leatherbacks go deeper than we're going today. The greatest *recorded* depth is 1,200 meters (3,900 feet), three-quarters of a mile. (Leatherbacks wearing depth recorders dive past 700 meters, well over 2,000 feet deep, several times a year.) No one knows how much deeper Leatherbacks have actually gone. Twelve hundred meters sounds deep, until you actually see what the world looks like down there; then it seems *incredibly* deep. As we're about to see.

With *Ventana* headed toward exploration depth, Robison takes me into the control room, shut into the bow of the ship like a night-dark corner of the deep sea itself. Here four people work at two dozen dimly glowing video screens, communicating through headsets, digitally recording into the dive's video the human conversation about what's encountered. "So," advises Robison, "if you're about to say something really crude or offensive, be sure to speak up."

Ventana's pilot, Craig Dawe, in a gray shirt, doesn't speak of controlling or even driving *Ventana;* he talks of flying her.

So, what're all these screens? "This one with this little diagram against this grid shows *Ventana*'s orientation with respect to the ship. This one shows *Ventana*'s sonar signal, which can be rotated all around. See these little hits right here? Those show where the tether is right now." Cartoonlike diagrams on another screen show *Ventana*'s compass orientation, pitch and roll angles, and which lights are on. The other screens correspond to *Ventana*'s various cameras, showing views ahead of the craft and a view of *Ventana* itself. The ship can transmit and receive images between the control room and the Monterey Bay Aquarium, so visitors can see what the scientists are seeing, as they're seeing it. While such advantages of thus probing the deep seem obvious and many, pilot Dawe sees a few trade-offs: "Oceanography used to be done off the end of ships, worrying about falling over, drowning, being swept overboard by waves, getting caught in nets. Now we sit cooped up in the dark watching TV screens for eight hours, eating junk food."

· · ·

Fifty meters. Dawe stops *Ventana*. Ready to begin transect. Oxygen concentration: 2.14 milliliters per liter, already a lot less oxygen than at the surface, where it was 6 milliliters. Robison's voice comes through my headphones as smoothly as in a recording studio. "As we go deeper," he says, "watch the oxygen; it'll drop, then come up a little. Temperature will drop and flatten out. The salinity will increase." *Ventana* begins moving forward. And so, slowly from nothing, like the Dawn of Time, a whole universe begins assembling before my eyes. We're instantly into a bright galaxy of white flecks like stars coming at us and streaming past. This is constant.

What *are* the stars? It's called marine snow. It's stardust of life, wafting fragments and fine bits of things once living, echo signals from former lives, adrift in the ocean's vast space like radio waves from the Big Bang.

More prosaically: "It's mostly detritus derived from phytoplankton, mucus, body parts, feces—all kinds of junk," says the man with the eye for it. "It may take years to reach the bottom."

Is any of this stuff alive? Robison hesitates: Well, not quite, but it's covered with bacteria, "so the definition of 'alive' is fuzzy." Let's turn off the lights. See the bacteria glowing? That weak luminescence? Light generated by living things—bioluminescence—is very common throughout the sea. No one knows what most of it is for.

For Robison, this is as typical a start to the workday as sitting down at your desk with a cup of coffee, but I'm transfixed. The stuff we're seeing is actually drifting so slowly it's hardly moving, but *Ventana*'s motion makes everything stream past bewilderingly.

Yet Robison is offhandedly identifying the animals—and they're all strange: ctenophores (*teen*-a-forz), siphonophores (sy-*fon*-a-forz), the occasional medusa, larvaceans. Think of the basic animal body form—head, body, tail—and now forget it; we left that idea at the surface. Aliens streak through this galaxy like emissaries from the Federation. These creatures are so oddly configured that I'm having difficulty even seeing animals that Robison so casually identifies.

Bruce insightfully assists with, "Blobs, strings, dots, bullets—those are the four basic shapes down here."

Rudimentary as that is, it actually begins helping me see what I'm looking at. Okay: there's a string, pencil-thick and maybe a foot long, with a series of little swimming bells like chimes, spreading long, threadlike drifting stinger-laced tentacles.

Bruce says of it, "That's a siphonophore called *Nanomia bijuga*. They probably eat more krill than whales and salmon combined. They're extremely successful, extremely abundant, very important in the system. And"—a twinkle comes into his eye—"almost no one knows they exist."

Turns out there's a lot here I don't know exists. Many things down here I haven't heard of, or barely recollect hearing their names. I have no framework. Most days, I don't face such a steep learning curve. That makes this a good day.

Jellies, says Bruce, are "*vastly* more complex than we imagined, and much more interesting." Recall the Blue Whale's elegant two-step food chain. Here, instead of a "food chain," we have the "jelly web." For instance, a gelatinous group called tunicates—which includes larvaceans, salps, and doliolids—grazes on phytoplankton and marine snow. Doing the same are tiny, shelled crustaceans like copepods and krill and others. Predatory jellies like *Chrysaora* prey on both groups. "So you have the energy from phytoplankton going into these predatory jellies from two major channels." And to ratchet up the complexity, there are three main groups of predatory jellies here: siphonophores, ctenophores, and the typical bell-and-tentacle "jellyfish," or medusae. "And what happens?" Bruce asks rhetorically. "Siphonophores eat medusae and ctenophores. And ctenophores eat other ctenophores and siphonophores and medusae. And medusae eat siphonophores and ctenophores and other medusae. The intricacy of these predatory relationships is truly astonishing. Forget about a food 'chain'; they're all competing with each other and also eating one another!"

Everything here is boxes inside boxes. Ratcheting up the complexity further, there are, for instance, three groups of siphonophores. One group has no swimming bells—they can only drift; a gas gland keeps them from sinking. Another group has swimming bells but no gas glands; they must continually swim. The last group has both a gas gland to help them maintain buoyancy and swimming bells. They can control their buoyancy and move through the water. Some get extraordinarily large. "Some of the siphonophores we *commonly* encounter grow to be as large as forty meters long, well over a hundred feet," Robison notes. "That's right. We've measured them with the lasers. There're the longest known animals in the world."

Underline the word *known*. It doesn't take long to realize how complicated this all is, how far evolved, though we think them primitive. Jellies were the first animals capable of organized motion, and though that may seem rudimentary, I'm here to tell you that organized motion is pretty special. It characterizes my best days. But this also makes you realize how extraordinarily advanced are vertebrates like sea turtles and birds, with brains, multiple advanced sensory systems, navigational capabilities, instincts, *thoughts*—! I, for one, enjoy a sense of vertebrate pride. Someday, I predict, vertebrates will rule the world.

Ten minutes are up. End transect. Next, Dawe flies *Ventana* down to 100 meters. I get the feeling we're penetrating deeper into Life's subconscious.

Bruce says, "Okay, here's an active larvacean house. It's used to filter food. See the animal in there, feeding?" Within a roomy tent made of a fine self-extruded mucus veil, a tiny tadpole-shaped creature sits slowly beating to draw food particles into its parlor. As we're watching the larvacean, a single squid comes to hover like someone behind a reporter on TV, trying to get on camera. It blushes in the lens. Behind it, like pedestrians on a busy sidewalk, other squids are jetting along smoothly.

The familiar-looking squids are almost a relief amid the strangeness. Yet the larvacean may be a closer relative. Its tail possesses a notochord, the nervous-system's first inkling of a spinal cord, putting it in the classification phylum Chordata, same as vertebrates like us. Stranger, larvae of the clear jellies called salps also have a rudimentary nerve cord indicating a very ancient shared ancestry with vertebrates.

"When we were dragging nets, of course," Robison comments, "these super-fragile things shredded all apart. We had no way of knowing larvaceans were even here. There are billions of them, but they weren't discovered until the first submersibles, in the 1960s."

Robison is particularly interested in these guys. As larvaceans' houses clog with particles, they get replaced several times a day. The discarded ones sink relatively quickly, and Bruce believes they must transport a lot of carbon to the deep sea. "The total amount of carbon in these gelatinous things is huge, and their numbers have been grossly underestimated. That has implications for understanding a lot of things, including rates of climate change—and we haven't accounted for it. So," he postulates, "larvaceans may be helping save us from ourselves and the carbon with which we're burdening the atmosphere and ocean."

Carbon that reaches the deep seafloor is effectively removed from the atmosphere for thousands of years. Because we're releasing the vast carbon stores in fossil fuels like oil, coal, and gas, how and where carbon moves helps determine the rate at which the atmosphere will change, the world will warm, and the ocean's pH will grow more acidic and corrosive to shell-making animals and corals. Robison is studying this unaccounted-for source of carbon transport and measuring the carbon in larvacean houses, so he'd like some samples.

Even if carbon dioxide wasn't changing the climate *at all*, it would still be exerting an entirely separate worldwide effect: changing the ocean's basic chemistry, making seawater acidic enough to dissolve corals and many animals' calcium carbonate shells. The oceans are currently absorbing about one metric ton of human-generated carbon dioxide per year for each person on the planet. We're putting about a million tons of carbon dioxide into the air every hour. This rate of increase is beyond the range of natural variability, leading some scientists to refer to this time as the "no-analog Earth," because these conditions have never quite happened before. Atmospheric concentrations of carbon dioxide have been higher—perhaps twenty times higher before land was colonized by plants 400 million years ago, and three to ten times higher when the first Leatherbacks were evolving 100 million years ago—but never within human experience. Importantly, it's unlikely ocean pH was ever lower, because in the past when atmospheric carbon dioxide increased it did so slowly enough to give the oceans time to fully assimilate it; calcium carbonate sediments would have dissolved to neutralize acidified waters.

The most important implication is for the many animals, and even some algae, who make shells or support structures out of calcium carbonate. These include numerous photosynthesizing organisms at the food chain's base, as well as animals like sea stars and urchins, mollusks like clams and oysters, and reef-building corals. Crabs and lobsters make shells mainly of chitin (the same material as your fingernails), but reinforced with calcium carbonate. What keeps all these important calcium carbonate shells from dissolving is that, naturally, they live surrounded in seawater saturated with carbonate ions. But the cascade of changes caused by our mushrooming cloud of carbon dioxide causes progressive carbonate scarcity. Thus making shells will get much more difficult and energy-consuming. And once formed, the shells will begin to slowly dissolve. If atmospheric carbon dioxide doubles from preindustrial levels, corals and other creatures will suffer reductions in shell thickness and strength. (In 1750, the atmosphere's carbon dioxide concentration was about 280 parts per million; today it's about 380 p.p.m., and by 2100 it will likely be 1,000 p.p.m. if we don't reduce burning of oil and coal.)

If you reduce the ocean carbonate abundance by 30 percent—which happens when you double the carbon dioxide—coral growth will drop by 30 percent. The higher carbon dioxide levels go, the thinner the shells. The result will be reduced ocean productivity and widespread food scarcity for sea life because the base of the whole food chain will be affected; plus, weaker corals and reefs will be more vulnerable to storms—which are intensifying because of global warming caused by burning oil and coal. The Royal Society concluded in 2005, "Changes in ocean chemistry will present severe challenges to some of the components of these vast and important ecosystems. . . . Marine ecosystems are likely to become less robust as a result of the changes to the atmosphere and more vulnerable to other environmental impacts (for example climate change, deteriorating water quality, coastal deforestation, fisheries and pollution). Without significant action to reduce CO_2 emissions into the atmosphere, this may mean that there will be no place in the future oceans for many of the species and ecosystems that we know today. . . . Ocean acidification is a powerful reason, in addition to that of climate change, for reducing global carbon dioxide (CO_2) emissions. Action needs to be taken now to reduce global emissions of CO_2 to the atmosphere to avoid the risk of irreversible damage to the oceans."

Pilot Dawe maneuvers the collecting arm with his joystick, but there's interference. "Come on, squids, get out of here." He goes for a grab with a suction tube, but the thing is so light and insubstantial, the mere motion of the arm sends it swirling to pieces. A touch exasperated, Dawe says, "Honestly, Carl, we don't suck this badly; these larvacean houses are the hardest things we try to catch."

Several bizarre isopods come "walking" through the water using elongated appendages, like a spider on land. A gelatinous oval ctenophore looms into view with its surreally iridescent cilia beating shimmering rainbows, strikingly beautiful.

Bruce points out a thick-looking cylindrical salp. "This one we've seen before; it's a new genus and a new species that we haven't named or published yet. It stays strictly at mid-depths; other salps are vertical migrators."

More squids come curiously and companionably within the bright halo, hanging around the rig, sometimes staring directly into the camera lens. You would think that animals living in darkness would avoid lights. But the really strange thing is, some of these animals that live vampire existences, migrating toward the surface only at night, withdrawing during the day and seemingly eschewing natural illumination—are actually *drawn* to the floodlit vehicle.

As the next transect commences, at 200 meters, Robison suddenly says, "Ooh—look at that *Nanomia;* it's got a krill. Remember I said they compete with salmon and whales for these krill? Now you've seen something practically nobody knows about. Watch—it will straighten out and pull that krill into one of its stomachs." The krill-killer "nanos" are now abundant, drifting their stinging threads like tiny living longlines, helping make the world a more dangerous place. "And there's a chaetognath, an arrow worm." These peculiar worms are predators, too.

Robison says a little ominously, "There are giant larvaceans down here; some make huge feeding structures more than a meter across. They're a significant part of the landscape here." (Turns out giant, for a larvacean, is only about two and a half inches [sixty millimeters.]) "Ooh—see that? That was a little octopus."

Next, *Ventana* descends through an invisible boundary, departing from the upper open ocean, or "epipelagic zone," where significant sunlight penetrates, into the mesopelagic realm, between 200 and 1,000 meters, where the scant light is too dim and weak to support photosynthesis. The main difference is that up above, sunlight is available for one-celled algae and other plants to make food, while pretty much everything below either commutes to the surface layers at night for food or depends for sustenance on murder, the rain of corpses, and the gently falling marine snow.

We continue sightseeing while Dawe flies *Ventana* down toward 300 meters. At 220 meters the squids spook, vanishing in clouds of ink—as a large and decidedly nongelatinous Blue Shark comes nosing around like a beagle, very active despite a chilly water temp of only 47 degrees Fahrenheit (8.3° C). Possibly it senses an exciting electrical field around *Ventana* that it mistakenly interprets as evidence that *Ventana* is alive, and thus edible. Robison overlooks the shark as his eye is drawn to a cyclosalp, which—as anyone in this room can tell you—is a form of salp spiral-chained together with its own clones in the whorl of their aggregate phase.

Bruce suddenly says, "Oh, look: that's the prototype for the creature in the movie *Aliens*—this amphipod hollows out a salp or a doliolid and lays its eggs in them. When they hatch, they devour their host from inside."

Doliolids, Bruce notes, have the most complex sexual cycle of any animal on Earth—

"They'd feel at home in San Francisco," Dawe comments.

"—and boy, is it tricky. Basically, there are alternating sexual and asexual generations. Eggs and sperm combine in open water to form individuals who bud off other individuals who produce eggs and sperm. But there can be additional steps involved, some in parallel, some sequentially, including intermediate stages whose jobs are to feed the developing sexual generation, and others who will carry them about. What makes it even worse is that not all doliolids play by the same rules; some species have certain stages while other species do not. Getting your ashes hauled in Doliolid Town ain't simple."

Bruce says it's a wonder the doliolids can figure it out. But more amazing to me than doliolid libido is the biologists who were able to figure this out.

Out of the blizzard at 300 meters, we start seeing lanternfishes, a group named for their light-producing organs. They're probably here eating krill. "There's a giant larvacean's house, sinking." "Another chaetognath." "More 'nanos.'" It goes on like this. Most of these creatures are tiny, but Robison continues smoothly identifying organisms that to me mostly slide by in a blur. It's a little like a video game: identify it while it's coming at you. I can't help expressing my amazement at Robison's ability to name the blurs going by.

Dawe, with his headset on, looks over at me and nods.

But Robison says, "It's like anything—you develop an eye for it."

The "snow," those falling filings of life above, seems denser as we go deeper. I guess that makes sense. Past the lens slides a shrimp with really long antennae that look like skis, as though a pun for life amid the snow.

Between transects comes small talk about movies, car repairs, and things pertaining to life at the surface, on land, among humans.

At 350 meters the temp is 7.6 degrees Celsius, but the squids remain quite active. Why people thought dinosaurs had to be slow when they were widely presumed to have been cold-blooded is beyond me; look at how active at cold temperatures cold-blooded squids can be.

New transect at 400 meters. Oxygen 0.71, temperature 6.96 degrees Celsius.

Bruce introduces me casually to several "redheads," another kind of larvacean. "We were the first to identify them for science," he notes, "but it's still easier to call them redheads." Here also are many of the tiny dark crustaceans called copepods, among the most important animals supporting the ocean food chain.

The squids here include familiar-looking types and some very strange ones, such as a clear species. One little thumb-sized squid has one small eye and one big one. It also has light-generating organs with which it can erase its own silhouette by just barely illuminating its belly, matching any light from above and thereby obliterating its shadow. Why doesn't it have *two* really big eyes?

Bruce answers, "It's not known. We almost always see them oriented with the big eye looking upward. That eye has a yellow filter. Some bio-luminescent animals hide down here by lighting themselves just enough to hide their silhouette against the dim light from above. But with the proper filter you can see those organisms against the background. So the big eye is looking upward to unmask bioluminescent camouflage, and the little eye is looking out into the very dim light for either predators or prey. As you watch these animals in their own habitat, you begin to understand some of their bizarre shapes, like squids with weird eyes, things like that. But hell," he adds, "in most cases we *don't* know the answers yet. That's why it's so much fun."

Bruce says there are several types of transparent squids. "That's kind of easy to understand," he says, "but look at these shrimp." Their shells and bodies are mostly clear, with a blood-red digestive gland. He continues, "Imagine the extreme predatory pressures driving it to achieve transparency while having a hard shell. What a remarkable accomplishment."

Battalions of squids suddenly sweep in from dark nowhere like space raiders, carrying off shrimp, their long antennae trailing. Even Bruce exclaims, "*Look* at that—that's right out of *Star Trek*! *That's* pretty cool. I don't think I've ever watched them do that."

A very tiny squid with light-emitting organs around its eyes and a fin that looks like a whale's tail comes into view. I ask Robison what it's called. He scrutinizes it closely and answers, "I don't know. I've never seen an animal like this."

Here at 400 meters we also see a little larval fish, nearly transparent. At our approach it suddenly curls its body like a doughnut. Weird.

Not weird, Bruce explains: "Defensive curling mimics bell-shaped stinging jellyfish. It's a strategy that works in dim light. You don't see it up shallow, where a predator can see that it's obviously a fish, and you don't see it real deep, where there's no light left at all."

At 500 meters, oxygen is down to 0.44 and the temperature has slipped to 6.09 degrees Celsius. The background is the blue-black color of absolute night. Bruce says, "Ooh—there's that intensely blue little siphonophore. Those are amazing." We next meet *Atolla,* a very pretty medusa pulsing its reddish bell.

At 600 meters, we encounter a squid named for its beautiful black eyes, a spectacularly crimson-belled jelly, a small siphonophore nicknamed "rocket ship," and pink-eyed "opossum shrimp," who protect their young in a pouch.

On down to 700 meters. A Leatherback dives several times a year to greater depths. If you're a jellyfish feeder, and you're diving into dark, frigid water for the really deep jellies, how do you find your prey? Do you smell it? Turtles' brains have proportionately big olfactory lobes, so they probably do have a pretty good sense of smell. Or do you look for it? Because most jellies glow when disturbed, turtles might look for telltale glowing stuff. Perhaps that's why turtles are attracted to the chemical glow sticks swordfishing crews usually attach near longline hooks. The eye sockets of a Leatherback skull are huge compared to those of other turtles.

Here there's only 3 percent as much oxygen as at the surface. It's now down to 0.19; at the surface, it was about 6.0. Bruce announces, "We're now in the core of the oxygen-minimum layer." Oxygen concentration in the ocean is far less than in air to begin with, and there's less oxygen here than anywhere else in the ocean. What's weird is that below this zone, oxygen increases again.

What causes the oxygen minimum? Bruce states categorically, "All the explanations offered are unsatisfactory." One possibility: where the surface productivity is very high, as here in Monterey Bay, the "snow" from that high productivity is rather dense. As it slowly sinks it gets decomposed by bacteria and other organisms. They use up a lot of the surrounding oxygen. At the deepest place where there are still fair numbers of organisms, they scour virtually all the oxygen from the water. That most-depleted depth is the oxygen-minimum zone. The zone's thickness varies; it can be 200 meters thick in one place (as in Monterey Bay), 600 in another. Below that, conditions are so extreme, few organisms can survive. So there is less oxygen scouring and thus a little more oxygen in the water. Water moves mainly horizontally at these depths and extremely slowly; layers hardly mix upward or downward, so oxygen doesn't get widely distributed.

Here in that zone of strangulation lives the small but infamous *Vampyroteuthis infernalis,* literally "vampire squid from hell." Hyping it up quite a bit, Robison describes it as "a heartless, cold-blooded, bloodsucking predator."

To which Dawe mutters, "Easier just to say 'ex-spouse.'"

Not wishing to go to a topic with even less oxygen, I observe that there seems noticeably less life down here.

"You bet," Bruce says. "If you can adapt to it, the payoff is you gain a *lot* of protection from predators who can't breathe here. But not many animals can withstand the strain." The Vampire Squid, however, has a few tricks up its eight sleeves. They've evolved some radical adaptations, including very low metabolism that demands little oxygen, and large oxygen-grabby gills. Their blue, copper-based blood is more efficient at binding oxygen than any other squid's, and their ammonium-rich tissues closely match the surrounding seawater's density, so they stay neutrally buoyant without exerting energy swimming.

The Vampire Squid's got some enemies, though, even here. If you're an Elephant Seal, say, you don't care how much oxygen's in the water; you're holding your breath. Against the threat of diving mammals and the few other predators that can operate here even temporarily, Vampires have defenses. Their whole body can generate a bluish light capable of "cloaking" their silhouette. Because squids' usual defensive ink is useless in so dark a place, the Vampire instead emits a luminous cloud of thick mucus, a dazzling assault that lasts for minutes, allowing the Vampire to slip away in the blackness without needing to swim far or use much oxygen in the getaway.

Down at 900 meters, the oxygen is back up to 0.30, and the temp down to a flat 4 degrees Celsius (39° F); 99 percent of all sunlight that penetrates the ocean surface never gets this far. Bruce mentions a jelly-eating creature called an Owl Fish that has double retinas, "for scavenging light down to the photon level." Our own electronic surrogate eye on *Ventana* finds an eel-like fish from the genus *Serrivomer*, a voracious predator. Robison comments, "See how it's oriented head-up? Even here, its eyes must be able to gather enough light to see the silhouettes of prey, or maybe scan for animals who give away their presence by bumping into light-producing animals." Vampire, beware.

At 1,000 meters we've penetrated into the boundary between the mesopelagic and bathypelagic zones. Bruce says, "Here no light from the surface penetrates. It's every bit as black upward as it is down."

A different group of animals lives below here. The animals that live below 1,000 meters don't migrate up and down. Some are predators, but ultimately they all depend on the passive down-drift of the snow, the constant rain of detritus, the dust of life from the sunlit surface of the miracle planet, the blue curve of Earth.

With *Ventana*'s eye focused on one gelatinous creature, we pause. "Is that Big Ugly?"

"I don't think so. I think maybe it's Gumdrop, but it doesn't have the—"

It's a thick, meaty-looking jelly with a bell like a mushroom cap and tentacles thick as a squid's.

"Yeah, it's Gumdrop, after all," Bruce determines. Gumdrop's related to Moon Jellies and Sea Nettles like *Chrysaora*. "It's another new genus and species. George and Kevin are describing it for science for the first time, writing it up now."

Of another animal a couple of feet long, Bruce says, "Whoa, now what is *that*? It's a siphonophore, but I think this is a completely new one." Its tentacles are braided. "That's *different*. That doesn't happen."

Dawe groans, "Oh no! Not another new species, please!"

"Look how purple—. That's *really* different." For extra emphasis Robison turns to me and adds rhetorically, "Ever seen one of these before? Nobody has."

They decide to capture this anonymous creature, but Robison cautions, "No one who lives at three thousand feet is expecting any turbulence. Some organisms are so delicate that the lights alone seem to disintegrate them." Sometimes, even with a perfect catch, an organism can't be brought up intact because temperature changes are enough to destroy such wisps of life.

Pilot Dawe again maneuvers *Ventana*'s collecting arm. Each time the edge of the canister touches this animal, pieces of creature break away. He eventually maneuvers most of it into the canister, and shuts the lid.

Another siphonophore appears, part of its body like a clear rattlesnake rattle and the rest like a red feather boa. No one knows what species this might be, either, but it shows and goes.

And that's it. Today's space shot is done. A classic-rock CD goes into the control room music player as *Ventana* flies home and we relax. At 3:05 *Ventana* comes to the frothing surface, into the air and sunshine, like a great big Leatherback Turtle. Only difference is, today *Ventana* went only to 1,000 meters. Leatherbacks go to at least 1,200.

DARKNESS HAS NOT YET MET THE DAWN WHEN BENSON GREETS ME WITH, "We have a dead frog."

"Dense fog?" I play along.

"No, *dead frog*."

Despite the forecast for winds, the air lies silent and breathless as a wish. Taking the weather at face value, we direct our footsteps toward the boat without delay. Right alongside the dock appears a large, pulsing *Chrysaora*, prompting Peter to exclaim, "It's a sign! I feel lucky. Some unsuspecting Leatherback out there is gonna have a surprising day."

This strikes me as bold. As the boat's pulling from the dock Benson mentions that several well-defined fronts have formed in the bay over the last couple of days. There's a cold plume blocking warmer water from moving into the south bay. But the computer map shows a very well set-up warm pocket against the coast in the north, with water just about 16 degrees Celsius (61° F)—perfect.

We leave the jetties, with instruments glowing in the pilothouse, as a seiner riding alarmingly low in the water returns "belly full" from a night of sardine netting (sixty or seventy tons of sardines in that hull, removed from nature mostly to feed not people but farm animals. When next you eat meat, taste the ocean).

Dawn finds an ocean so calm we can see fish, probably anchovies, dappling the surface like raindrops. And the air is noticeably warmer. Things seem different today.

Less than a mile from shore we transect a dense patch of *Chrysaora*, hundreds visible in the early slant of light. Past a band of clear water, we're into jellies very thick, far more numerous and closer to home than last time. A couple of days ago, these animals simply weren't here.

For a while, any glance at the sea surface or down into the water reveals multiple pulsing jellies—ten at a glance in the sparsest patches, dozens in the thickest. For any Leatherback taking the trouble to get here, food would be superabundant.

Another difference: A few days ago Moon Jellies dominated. Today nineteen of twenty jellies are *Chrysaora*. These drifting assassins range in size from minis—three or four inches across the bell—to husky creatures with bell diameters of about a foot and a half.

Benson's wife, Karin, radios to say that she intends to get her airspotting crew off the ground within an hour. Things are coming together.

A big surface school of small fish—at least a third of a mile long and as wide—is attended by gulls, terns, and pelicans so full they're just sitting. A nearby Blue Shark's pale tail wags the leisurely zigzag of fat times.

Benson says, "This is starting to look like it did last year, when the turtles were in here."

Yet another difference today: the shearwaters. By the time we're five miles from shore, the shearwaters I've seen can be counted by making the peace sign. Where have *they* gone?

Ten Brandt's Cormorants in a ragged line are traveling north just above an ocean surface so calm it mirrors their images. A couple of miles beyond, we find perhaps three thousand Sooty Shearwaters all sitting firmly beneath the dead air. That's probably why we're not seeing them: there's no breeze to subsidize their glideful flight. Anyway, they're probably full. Motoring along, we see another fifteen thousand loitering, waiting for motivation and winds aloft to signal takeoff.

Where they sit, we see no jellies—at all. There can be swarms of jellies where no birds gather, flocks of birds where no jellies pulse; such is the patchy mosaic of the sea's varied neighborhoods. But somewhere through the streets of this liquid city strides a giant turtle. Its presence now seems palpable.

From the pilothouse roof we scan. At about eight-thirty, Benson calls to J.D., "Turn ninety degrees right, please; I may have seen a turtle." We bob for a few moments in the long, rolling swell, until suddenly up ahead appears something not only leathery-backed but white-walled: a floating inflated tire mounted on its wheel.

Karin calls again from the airport. Fog there, extending over the south bay, now has the plane pinned on the ground. Benson remarks, "Getting clear skies and calm seas together is like pulling a royal flush."

By late morning we're off Año Nuevo, but the water remains a cool 14.3 degrees Celsius. We continue north until, as we're approaching Pescadero, the water temperature picks up to over 15.

Ahead, a pod of Risso's Dolphins, a dozen and a half of them, break their glass ceiling. Their nearly whitish heads come up shining, heavily streaked with the scratches typical of their kind. We stop to watch, the boat settling into the surface. It's so calm and quiet out here that as their heads roll forward we can easily hear the *poosh* of their breathing. The stillness and the haze make me feel adrift in a world without borders, gone entirely fluid, the peacefulness so vast and fine it gets into my pores.

About a mile away, black backs bulge and roll against the overcast horizon. And then fluke, fluke, fluke, fluke; they lift aloft those startling T-blades, their own emblems of themselves. Humpback Whales.

The area where the whales have dived is marked by hundreds of wheeling shearwaters and pods of excited sea lions so densely packed they look like big mats of brown kelp. They're eating sardines the chickens and pigs won't get.

As we're traveling in for a closer look, eight Dall's Porpoises, chunky black-and-white animals, slice in stiff and fast, riding our bow wave like a police-car escort.

The density and diversity of life right here is breathtaking. Scott Eckert says what I'm thinking: "This water is good; everything is piled up right here." Clearly, the birds, dolphins, sea lions, and whales think being here is worthwhile. Gotta be a Leatherback here. We're getting revved.

The whales resurface together as though blowing the roof off the ocean, shoving their huge knobbed heads through the surface, followed by the curve of their knuckled backs. This is quintessential Humpback feeding, rare to see, the whales working hard, cooperating, herding fish schools into tight balls, then lunging through them with their gigantic jaws open and their pleated throats distended like Olympian pelican pouches.

When the whales smash the mirror, dozens of sea lions come porpoising in, diving to attack the small fishes milling in shocked confusion. Shearwaters continue streaming in, sifting into the water among them, landing momentarily before slipping through the looking glass and flying underwater into the charge. The whales, working concertedly like synchronized swimmers, fluke up and vanish again together.

We're waiting at the rail when a calf—twenty feet long—surfaces just off the bow. "Mom has to be close," J.D. intones.

Mama comes up suddenly with a roaring blow, gushing steam into cool air. Flexing a gray wall of flesh, her broad body resembles the hull of an overturned vessel. She's so close at hand we hear the water rushing off her body and the low, resonant inhalation as she floods her deepest passages with new air. She's bigger than the boat we're standing in.

She arches her back and lifts her big tail. She and her calf both pour themselves into the out-of-sight, leaving slickly roiled patches that slowly vanish as the sea repairs its texture and contours.

"That will be hard to top," exclaims Benson.

Eckert says, "Okay, make my day; next a Leatherback."

And suddenly we seem hot on the trail: a *Chrysaora* bobs up missing all its tentacles and oral arms and a pie-slice notch from its bell.

Peter laughs, "What's this *Chrysaora* trying to tell us?"

Benson singsongs, "We're going to find a Leatherback today!"

The plane is headed our way. And in a short while we get a visual on it. Now we have air support, and before long the plane radios a possible sighting.

Crackles the receiver, "We have a Leatherback. Ready to copy position?"

J.D. punches the latitude and longitude numbers into the GPS, and we're soon skipping along the surface at twenty-four knots while Scott and Peter ready the big hoop net. The distance is two miles, with the plane circling the animal at an altitude of four hundred feet.

When we near, Benson is in the bow with the hoop net, waiting anxiously.

The radio jumps to life again. "Animal is now one o'clock on your bow."

We proceed.

Karin instructs, "Okay, *Sheila B,* full stop." The plane can see the turtle before it surfaces and when it's traveling just beneath the waves. "Right starboard quarter!"

And now, finally, we see it at the surface—but briefly.

"Diving. Will inform when resighted," the radio promises, then goes silent.

After some minutes, Karin breaks the taut pause: "Coming up—"

Now the Leatherback surfaces *right here,* only about fifteen feet away. Not so fast. After a brief gulp of air, the turtle is gone.

After about one minute, the Leatherback surfaces again to our right. We've got a shot at it and we begin closing the short gap. The turtle slips under and planes away from the surface at a shallow angle—we can still see it. It turns and goes under the boat, seeming purposely evasive.

Another minute.

Karin radios, "Port side. Just below the surface. Twenty meters. Go slow. Ten meters. Very slow or you'll run over him."

The turtle surfaces directly ahead, and dives again. This turtle wants no part of us and will not stay up as we near it. Despite the boat, plane, satellite positioning systems, radios, the many people with innumerable university degrees and over a century of combined experience, this turtle is beating us at our own game. It's beaten worse odds before. It's a one-in-a-thousand survivor who wasn't born yesterday. And its slim-brained mind holds the accurate assumption that boats are bad. It wants us to get lost.

It bursts through the surface thirty feet ahead. One breath and it powers away.

After it repeats this pattern several times, Scott says the turtle is tiring. Skeptical, I begin timing its dives. Forty-three seconds . . . "There it is, there it is." Twenty feet away. One breath and down. Forty-six seconds . . . thirty feet to our right. One breath and down. Sixty-one seconds . . . straight ahead. Down . . .

This turtle is not tiring. It has hit a rhythm of breathing and diving it can maintain. It has a game plan and is sticking to it. We need to hope that just once, we can line up behind it just as it's surfacing, and get lucky.

Overhead, the plane drones circles.

Benson says, "Okay, I see it coming up now. This is good." He puts the net over it and—*misses!* Jogging left at the critical instant, the turtle deflected its head from the enveloping net. The hoop glances along its body as the Leatherback slides from reach.

That's okay, we say. As the turtle has persistence, we likewise have patience. But now that the turtle has been touched it has another plan: Lose this stalker. Suddenly trying to put real distance between us, it is now traveling quickly and changing directions. It takes its next breath fully seventy yards away, distance enough for a deep exchange of lung volume and a full recharge of blood oxygen. The air crew relays that it's gliding away on long power strokes. Now it kicks its evasiveness to yet another level. We have to make several hairpin turns to continue our pursuit. The turtle is surfacing about five times farther from us than before.

But with all the hard swimming and changing directions, the surfacing intervals are in fact shorter. It is—finally—tiring.

It surfaces forty feet ahead, and we close on it. Benson reaches—but the turtle knocks the netting from the hoop without getting bagged.

While he's resetting the net, the turtle repeatedly surfaces within reaching distance. Karin transmits, "He's toying with you." And then: "He's down again."

It's nearing three P.M., and the plane crew reports that the sun's glare is hampering their ability to maintain visual contact with the animal. Karin radios, "We can see the turtle only at certain angles now. We can't keep it in view." Pause. "Okay, off your bow, twenty meters left. Stay on that heading. Ten meters—coming up—step on it a little bit."

The turtle surfaces just out of reach. Karin calls, "Meow." The cat wants this mouse. Patience is stretching toward exasperation.

Leatherback crosses our bow, subsurface. Benson is intently focused, vigorously chewing a wad of gum, ready. The plane radios, "Heading to the surface. Good. Little left—. Go go *go go!*"

But Leatherback will have none of it and dives well ahead of Benson's reach. An hour and a mile and a half earlier, we thought we had this sucker. Over that time and distance, it's maintained its edge.

Karin's next transmission is a bit of a surprise. A big surprise, actually. "Hey," her voice crackles brightly, "we've got a different turtle! A hundred meters off your port bow."

We drop the first Leatherback like a hot potato. Everyone's silently relieved to have reason to stop following it without admitting that a turtle beat us.

When this new turtle resurfaces, Scott turns to me and says, "Did you see the size of this one? Holy smoke!"

This much larger turtle is naive to what's up with us. Our first approach of the new turtle is a very near miss. Karin radios, "Ooohhh, *so close!*"

It dives out of sight for a few minutes. We wait.

Karin calls, "Come ahead. Off your bow." When we come up on it, Benson turns and breaks the news that this turtle—is the first one! We never see the second one again.

Perfect angle. Perfect lineup. Go, Benson!

Benson strains to make a very awkward attempt just as the turtle executes an abrupt vertical dive. The net goes down and J.D. throws the boat into reverse. And suddenly the line comes tight, and very heavy.

But the turtle has one flipper outside the net, and it's thrashing. We're all bent over the side, trying to pull the net down and over that one loose, dangerously slamming flipper. Benson's cell phone slips from his shirt pocket, making a neat *plop* as it begins its long-distance fall to the bottom. When the turtle finally twists, spins, and burns downward out of sight, Benson curses loudly.

Maybe, I say, the turtle was hurrying to answer a phone call.

Six minutes pass. We're three miles from where we first met this turtle and the sun is angled into late afternoon. The plane has twelve minutes of fuel left before it must head landward.

It's nearly five P.M. and we've got a fifty-mile run home. We decide jointly to call it a day. J.D. turns the wheel for home and pushes the throttles forward. We spent a lot of time and money today, and we missed our chance. We feel a bit dejected.

We're running home at full throttle in a mood subdued when we nearly cruise right past a Leatherback chomping sloppily into a *Chrysaora* at the surface, sending bits of stinging tentacles and bell into the slow downward drift of snow that will be welcomed by the soft, mindless creatures of the deep dark below. We turn and stop, and the turtle is actually swimming toward the boat, trusting, inquisitive—a breath, a stroke, another gulp of air, another stroke closer. When it surfaces Benson slips the net right over it.

With a bit of strained heaving we welcome aboard the 750-pound female, and give her a free transmitter.

By the time we release her, it feels like a long day. It'll be two and a half hours to the dock. But now it will feel like an easy ride.

EACH LEATHERBACK THIS TEAM HAS TRACKED SOON LEFT MONTEREY Bay. Peter says, "They arrive here fat and they're constantly moving. We see them, and off they go."

But *where* their tracked turtles go stunned a lot of people. Everyone pretty much assumed that the Leatherbacks off California came from Mexico for the summer, then went back south.

But what Eckert, Benson, and Dutton actually found was this: all the Leatherbacks tracked from here headed southwest, and kept going past Hawaii. Apparent destination: waters around New Guinea—a swim of about sixty-seven hundred miles, or eleven thousand kilometers. Then, when Dutton and Benson went to New Guinea and put transmitters on nesting females *there,* more than half of them headed east across the Pacific, toward North America. One spent a few months within forty miles of the Oregon coast before heading southwest and passing Hawaii again en route. The fact that West Coast–foraging Leatherbacks are born in the sands of New Guinea and the Solomon Islands was one of the most surprising discoveries in the history of ocean ecology.

It means the future of Monterey Bay's turtles depends on Pacific countries' fishing practices, on Asian governments' logging policies near nesting beaches, and on how villagers in New Guinea treat nesting females and their eggs. It means that the number of nesting Leatherbacks arriving on Indonesian shores depends partly on California's gill-net regulations and Japan's long-liners. It means that the world is both bigger than anyone ever thought, and much smaller.

Before Scott Eckert, Peter Dutton, and Scott Benson tracked Monterey turtles to Asia, they'd had a clue of a connection. In 1995 Dutton began analyzing DNA of turtles caught on longlines by Hawaiian-based boats.

Like everyone, he'd assumed the Leatherbacks in the northeast Pacific were from the population that nested from Mexico to Costa Rica; it was logical to assume they'd go north in summer and south in winter. His first Hawaii-caught DNA sample indicated that the turtle had indeed hatched from an eastern Pacific beach. No surprise there. His next showed genetic markers not found in turtles nesting in Mexico or Costa Rica. Instead, they matched a few samples Peter had from Papua, on the island of New Guinea. He said, "Hmmm, looks like the Hawaii boats are catching fifty-fifty, turtles of eastern and western Pacific origin." That *Hmmm* was based on just the first two samples. Then came the real surprise: *every* other Leatherback sample he analyzed from North Pacific fishing boats, from Monterey Bay and the West Coast, even Alaska—about sixty in total—all originated in the far western Pacific. That first one, a turtle who'd hatched in the Americas, had been a fluke! For the first couple of years Dutton stayed surprised. When he went to Monterey with Benson and Eckert to see if they could find and catch Leatherbacks in the ocean there, they put transmitters on two animals. One transmitter failed after a few months. The other remained functional for two years, while the turtle crossed the Pacific. It didn't nest on that trip, but remained north of New Guinea, near the deepest point in the world's ocean, the Mariana Trench, before starting back east. "That convinced me, and my focus changed," Peter says. "Everyone was focused on Mexico and Costa Rica. I had to sell the idea that to conserve turtles in U.S. waters, we needed to work in places like New Guinea, too."

JAMURSBA *BELIMBINGS*
New Guinea

Warmon, New Guinea. We haven't walked two hundred yards before Peter Dutton notices the dark outline of a turtle in the surf. Lurch by lurch, the shadow climbs. Shadow into shadows, she vanishes against the black-velvet curtain of primeval forest. Rather than follow, we sit quietly, the natives smoking and chewing betel nuts, speaking their murmuring tongue, our voices joining the rhythmic *shuss* of surf. We let her begin digging in peace, before we get to work. This is some of the first scientific census work that's been done here. In just the last year it's become apparent that Warmon is a sizable Leatherback rookery that has been overlooked until now.

For an open-ocean beach, the sea is calm in the extreme, as though heavily sedated. The surf—if you can call it that—does not so much break as gently lap the shore, like a big cat with a slow-stroke tongue. The swell rises and falls as subtly as the breathing of a sleeping child.

All my life I've imagined New Guinea as among the wildest and most exotic of remaining wild lands. Our eight-hour boat journey here did nothing to dispel that fantasy. For 150 miles from the port of Sorong, we beheld a shore devoid of a single visible dwelling or even one line of smoke. What we saw was towering primordial forest and ridge upon ridge of layered mountains backed into churning clouds. Within plain sight of the beach, frothing frenzies of big Yellowfin Tuna were crashing chrome-plated flyingfish beneath mobs of screaming terns and frigatebirds. We saw not a single fishing vessel. The only sign of human presence was a rare figure walking the beach, as people here have for more than fifty thousand years.

We cruised until we approached this stretch of beach called Warmon. The Pacific's passivity let the captain simply back the boat practically against the beach, where it shrugged off a light surge as, carrying our bags and gear high, we stepped overboard and waded ashore amid tracks of Leatherbacks.

The massive and mountainous Bird's Head Peninsula makes up New Guinea's northwestern corner. We're on its north coast, just an eyelash below the equator. Taking in the vast forest, the uninterrupted sweep of sea and long, lonely beaches, this coast makes a deep impression as the most primeval of places. We're beyond reach of cell phones, beyond e-mail and the civilized world's news of bombs in London, beyond indoor plumbing, refrigeration, ice, toilet paper. The people have no land vehicles, no carts, no beasts of burden, no wheels, no shoes. Their feet grow massive and splayed from walking along beaches and through the forest. (They travel barefoot even on rare boat trips to far-away Sorong to meet with urban officials.) And if, on a long-trudging beach walk, your native companion strides out of sight ahead, he'll soon come walking back to see what's up, effortless as a swallow circling.

Those of us who fly in airplanes, those who skim upon the surface of the sea, and those who walk have converged together here for essentially one reason: in so many words, the turtles told us to come. They had something to say that could be said only in a place this elemental. So here we are, open to possibility, awaiting their counsel.

A place so wild has, above all, potential. In a place without roads, who can say where the road will lead? All options, good and bad, remain open. The people may or may not live the lives they were born to. The forest may or may not stand. Turtles might maintain or vanish. Technology, opportunity, education, and complication could come, or perhaps keep their distance another few thousand years—who knows? Strife could engulf. Peace may abide.

We would like to think we're a little piece of the peace we hope will follow. The turtles have convened us from around the world; our half dozen beach tents house an international team from the United States, India, Canada, and Indonesia, including native Papuans. This is the last significant surviving Leatherback Turtle nesting ground in the western Pacific. Conservation here is critical. But the local people have made it known: they too have needs.

We'd arrived an hour before sunset, and made camp high on the steep beach, pitching tents upon fine gray sand. Gecko lizards were calling

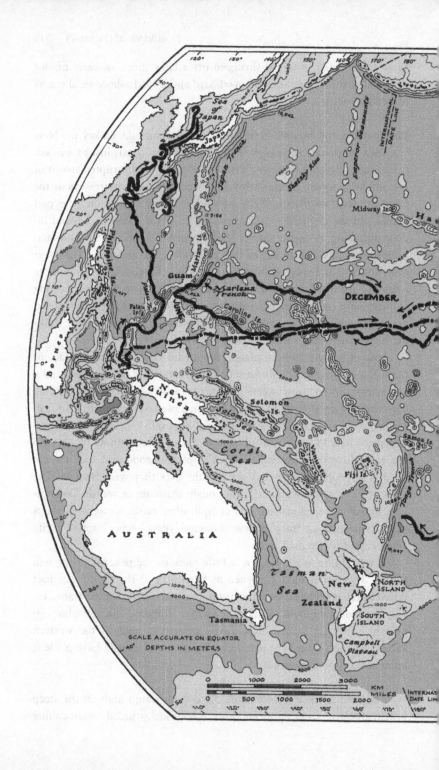

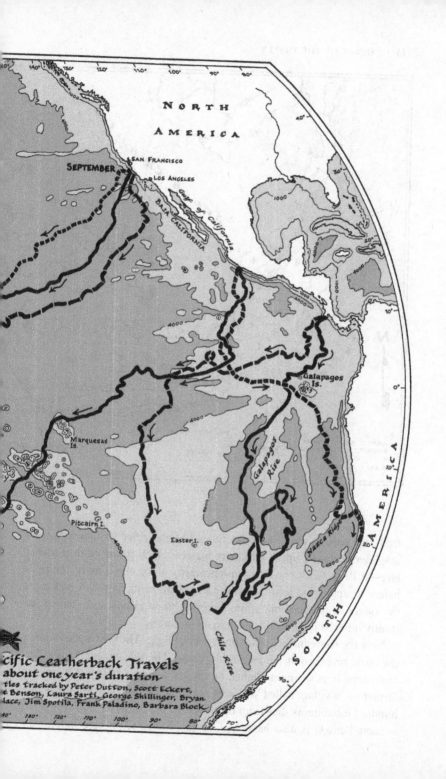

NORTH
AMERICA

SEPTEMBER ● SAN FRANCISCO
● LOS ANGELES

Gulf of California

BAJA CALIFORNIA

Galapagos Is.

Marquesas Is.

Galapagos Rise

Pitcairn I.

Easter I.

Nazca Ridge

SOUTH AMERICA

Chile Rise

Pacific Leatherback Travels
about one year's duration

Turtles tracked by Peter Dutton, Scott Eckert,
Scott Benson, Laura Sarti, George Shillinger, Bryan
Wallace, Jim Spotila, Frank Paladino, Barbara Block

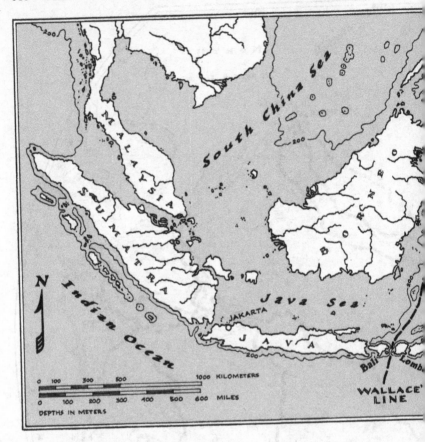

from the trees, as were insects sounding like electrified cicadas with their amplifiers cranked up. A strikingly massive black parrot with a scarlet face—a Palm Cockatoo—flew momentarily along the edge of the trees before disappearing into the great green swallowing forest. A racket on the ridges came from big white flakes of snow falling and melting instantly into the jungle: Sulfur-Crested Cockatoos.

Now the shoreline bears not one artificial light. The view up and down the coast reveals only unbroken blackness. The sole exception is a distant cargo boat's running lights, out at sea. I'm told that just five miles farther on, a village called Wau nestles behind the beach, with nearly one hundred inhabitants. But from here I see no sign of it.

Scott Benson is also here, and Tetha Hitipeuw, an able Indonesian

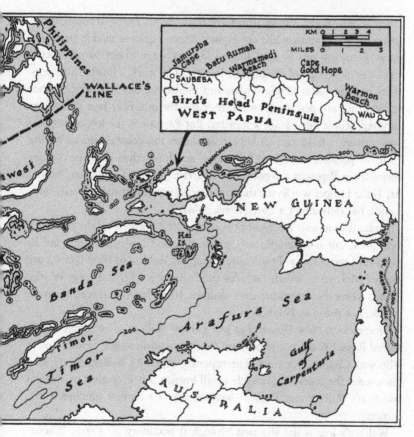

woman in her late thirties who works with the World Wide Fund for Nature. Meeting us was a small entourage of native people, several of whom, including Nimbrot Yeblo and Dorsina Jokson, have been hired to help monitor turtle nesting. At least an equal number of local people are here out of curiosity.

After waiting out a downpour at dusk, we began walking the beach under thick clouds in the darkest kind of nighttime. That was just a few minutes ago, but already I feel as though, today, worlds have been exchanged.

The planet's second-largest island (after Greenland), New Guinea is politically divided roughly in half and shared by two nations. The east is the independent country Papua New Guinea. The west, where we are, is called, confusingly, Papua (formerly Irian Jaya). Dense tropical forest covers most of Papua, while the highest inland peaks lie clad in perennial snow. Politically it's part of Indonesia, and we're about two thousand miles east-northeast of the capital, Jakarta. The world's fourth most populous country (after China, India, and the United States), Indonesia has regions that are densely crowded indeed—for instance, Java with eight hundred people per square kilometer. But Papua has the lowest population density in Indonesia. A U.N. map shows this coastal area as having "0 to 2" persons per square kilometer, and fewer than three per square kilometer in Papua as a whole. Her cigarette glowing in the dark, humid air, Tetha Hitipeuw tells me that the nearest settlement to our west, Warmandi, has only about a dozen households.

Papua is Indonesia's biggest province, with 20 percent of the country's land area, but demographically, culturally, and biologically it's unlike the rest of the country. Ethnically, Papua and the rest of New Guinea are part of Melanesia, which includes the Solomons, Fiji, and other nearby islands where the natives are dark-skinned, frizzy-haired, African-featured people, not Asian or Polynesian.

Biologically, New Guinea lies just east of Wallace's line, named after Alfred Russel Wallace, the brilliant (not to mention tough) field biologist who was Charles Darwin's contemporary and who independently also discovered the unifying principle of all known life: evolution by natural selection. Wallace and Darwin were biology's two first intelligent discerners.

Wallace's line is the sharpest biological boundary on Earth. It separates animals and plants of Asia from those of the Australian region. Two worlds. It's where monkeys end and tree kangaroos begin. Wallace's line lies between Bali and Lombok Island and between Borneo and Sulawesi, and hooks east south of the Philippines. During the Pleistocene ice ages, when sea level was hundreds of feet lower than today, the present islands west of the line were connected, all part of the continental landmass. Animals and plants from mainland Asia could walk throughout and flourish freely. But deep water separated that area from New Guinea, Australia, and their associated islands. Tigers, squirrels, elephants, pheasants, most other animals, and most seeds couldn't cross it—nor could kangaroos, opossums, or Australia's egg-laying mammals. That's why things are so very different on each side of that line.

Yet people crossed. For people to reach New Guinea and Australia, they had to cross a dozen straits separating these lands from Asia. Biologist Jared Diamond and others have speculated on the meaning this region's challenging water barriers had for human cultural evolution. Something momentous happened with humans between one hundred thousand years ago, when there were still no signs of art or complex tools anywhere in the world, and around forty thousand to thirty thousand years ago, when such things began flourishing in Europe. It's conventionally assumed that this cultural blossoming began in Africa or the Mideast, then spread. This vast assumption overlooks an inconvenient fact: physically modern humans reached Australia before they got into Europe—probably by sixty thousand years ago.

Momentous as a moon landing, breaching Wallace's barrier was "one giant step for humankind." No other large walking mammal had ever managed to crash the line. Nor had earlier humans such as Java man (*Homo erectus*), who'd gotten a waterfront view of Wallacea—the line's associated islands and straits—a million years earlier. During ice-age periods they could have walked as far as Bali. But getting farther required island-hopping. That meant watercraft. The island of Lombok is visible from Bali. (Many of Indonesia's seventeen thousand islands rise within plain sight of one another.) The first people to set foot on Lombok's shore, whether swept to sea on a crude raft or intentionally venturing, found a new, safe paradise without tigers, competitors, or enemies, and full of naive, delectable animals. The line also sits amid coasts bearing food-rich mangroves and the shallow-water fishes of the world's richest coral reefs. In whatever way people got across the first strait, their discoveries provided incentive for creatively adapting food-getting techniques and exploring further. Each small island offered the same. From each island reached, another would be sighted, which provided a stimulus for improving water-crossing craft. And success on each new island would eventually engender competition and tribal warfare—a cycle of incentives for advancing seafaring skills in search of untapped food and safe refuge.

While speculation about how humans crashed Wallace's line is fun, one hard fact still confronts us: people crossed open sea to Australia tens of thousands of years before there's any evidence for watercraft in the Mediterranean—or anywhere else in the world. So, sixty thousand years ago, the first New Guineans and Australians may have led the world in inventive technology, thus perhaps even art. Jared Diamond concludes this line of conjecture by saying, "Wallacea may have been the crucible of human creativity, and our ancestors may have crossed from ape-hood to humanity as they crossed Wallace's line." Having just crossed Wallace's line myself, I'm less concerned with whether that's precisely true than with the sheer pleasure of speculating upon the possibilities.

Though people have been here for sixty thousand years, sea turtles have likely been leaving tracks in these sands a thousand times longer. To further our understanding of where they go when they leave, we have brought three satellite-tracking transmitters and three "pop-up" data-archiving satellite tags. The transmitters track more or less continually whenever the turtle is at the surface. The pop-ups store data on diving depths, temperatures, and positions, then after a preprogrammed period they electronically disengage themselves and float free while beaming all their collected data to a satellite.

That Leatherback Scott Benson tracked to Oregon got her transmitter on these shores in July 2003 and swam across the Pacific to reach Oregon in October 2004. She then hooked southwest, past Hawaii, wintered, and was heading northeast again when her transmitter's battery quit, after 616 days. On her way northeast, she had passed several other turtles transmittered in Monterey Bay and heading southwest.

We're still waiting for the turtle we so easily found to start laying eggs. A turtle can become alarmed during her ascent or disrupted during digging, but once her eggs start falling she's usually imperturbable for the duration, do what you might. That's the "trance" researchers refer to, and that's when there's time to affix a harness and deploy scientific devices with scant risk of dissolving her resolve for nesting.

But when we move to inspect the shifting shadow, and our head lamps softly illuminate her posterior, we see she is having some inexplicable trouble digging. Her limbs are intact, but she's not positioning her rear flippers effectively. They're dutifully alternating strokes, just not cupping or picking up sand.

We decide to give her more time. Distant lightning flashes above the ocean horizon.

After half an hour with this turtle, no egg chamber is forthcoming. At about the time we give up on her, she gives up, too, going through covering motions even though she has not laid, but getting none of them quite right. Enough things go wrong with expensive transmitters; we want at least to start with a perfect turtle. *We're sorry you're having trouble tonight, my dear,* we tell her, *but we must move on.*

As we're all walking, Tetha tells me that the people living here are hunter-gatherers in transition. They set snares for wild animals and also tend scruffy little subsistence forest gardens, where they raise the starch-hearted sago palm, root crops like cassava and taro, and fruits such as bananas, papayas, pineapples, and several I wouldn't recognize. They raise some corn, cacao, and coconuts to trade for cash to buy things like cooking oil, rice, soap, sugar, and coffee. For meat they eat wild boar and deer (both introduced by humans), monitor lizards, opossums, wallabies, cassowaries, cockatoos, megapodes, and other birds. In a traditional ceremony, no longer practiced, a man called to the turtles to arrange a time for them to come ashore. But the people here no longer eat turtle eggs. A village we'll later visit has some mammalian "livestock" consisting of two small, ill-tempered wild pigs and two deer, all tethered in place. It looks like a diorama of the "dawn of domestication." Tetha explains that while wild boar are often sold for cash, people keep domestic pigs as wealth and for marriage payments, and that a woman might still suckle her own child at one breast and a newly acquired piglet at the other.

People exposed to the wider world (and our electronics, books, cameras, tents, malaria pills, and bug repellants certainly count as exposure) want more of what that world offers. Getting it requires money. Money originates as human energy applied to converting natural resources into products.

Logging companies like to wave money around. One of the indications that the world is overpopulated is that even in places with few people, forests are being destroyed because the demand from distant markets has become insatiable. New Guinea and the surrounding Melanesian archipelago make up the largest remaining wilderness region in Pacific Asia. Logging has already removed 97 percent of the Philippines' forests, the Pacific Northwest of the United States has lost 95 percent (much of it shipped directly to Japan as raw logs while American lumber companies blamed sawmill closures on environmentalists), and Sumatra and other parts of Indonesia were also heavily clear-cut during the 1980s and

1990s. With so much of Sumatra's wood now gone, loggers are eyeing the vast virgin Papua wilderness. Indeed, conflict over often-illegal logging and the official corruption that attends it has festered in parts of Papua for years, igniting violence and adding fuel to a long struggle for autonomy. A few miles from the main Leatherback beach is a small clear-cut, with a mud road piercing its way into the forest and, left on the beach, a few big chain-sawed logs that would block any turtle. It would be factually true to say that, in all this wilderness, those few cut-over acres are a tiny spot. But given what we know of logging elsewhere, that would be a little like a doctor reassuring a patient that she had only a very small spot of cancer in her right lung.

Exploiters seldom hesitate to pay cash commissions for exploitation. Even if the people realize the jobs will last just a few years, until the resources are gone, the present usually seems more compelling than the future. Conservation will have to compete financially. Conservation's disadvantage is that its funds are chronically tight.

Conservation's main untapped advantage—and it's a big one—is that it is more capable of caring about people and their natural endowment than cut-and-run loggers or mining companies who leave places ruined and people displaced from their own identities, dislocated from their futures. Up to now, most conservation groups' money has gone to staffing. Relatively little pays local people for conservation and protection. That could be overcome by redirecting funds, and by showing more investment-encouraging successes for both wildlife and people.

Many conservationists—myself included—don't like the idea of paying people to simply not destroy trees or wildlife. But when the competition is waving cash to cut the forests, ideology had better adapt, fast. In the United States, conservation is done through laws and regulations backed by enforcement and the courts. Very little of the planet works that way. In most places, what counts are custom, community, and the material aspirations of the local people. Some conservationists who've seen what does and doesn't work—people like Peter and Tetha and economists from groups like Conservation International—now believe that long-term conservation plans will have to include a package of benefits for villagers, with funding endowed by the biggest conservation groups and institutions like the World Bank.

Some of the local people here have already felt insulted that the world would look here and see the needs of turtles more than of the people themselves. Fewer than half have been to school; they want education for their children. They want access to markets. They want what other people have. They live in a beautiful place with more leisure and more priceless waterfront than they could ever use. But there have always been unquenched desires in paradise. The human heart will cast itself out of Eden every time, because it has needs heaven never addresses.

One of our local patrollers reports locating another *Penyu Belimbing*. (*Penyu* means turtle in Indonesian. The Leatherback here is called the starfruit turtle after the ridges on its shell; that's *Belimbing*.) She's in perfect shape but has nearly finished laying. We really need to find one that is still digging, because putting on the transmitter harness requires about the same amount of time a *Belimbing* takes to lay a full clutch.

Scott Benson has been here several times in the last couple of years, including the first few months of this year, and he knows what he's looking for. If he's going to work with a particular turtle, he likes to be fully situated, with all the equipment laid out, when her first eggs fall. Otherwise, while the crew is still adjusting the straps and fasteners, she'll begin covering, striking with those long-oar foreflippers and moving unmanageably. That doesn't work, and Scott is a perfectionist about the harness. Plus, the transmitters cost $4,000 each; the pop-ups, $3,500. Add personnel travel and the salaries of workers and you realize that the turtles that carry electronic devices come freely but their departure is very expensive indeed. We continue looking for just the right turtle.

The turtle-nesting pattern on this coast is unusual; they nest year-round. But the transmitters show that early-in-the-year nesters usually go south around New Guinea and don't travel as far. These June-July-August nesters that we're here to see are the ones that often crisscross the whole North Pacific, reaching the U.S. West Coast. Are these earlier and later nesters different genetic "stocks"? That's one of the many things Peter is still working on. As part of his federal job and its imperatives under the Endangered Species Act, he's deploying teams and funding conservation-related sea turtle research in North and South America, Asia, and Africa.

The reach and vision of the U.S. Endangered Species Act is a magnificent thing, high-minded and compassionate, one of America's greatest exports, able in its best moments to help preserve both nature and people's options. That's the idea and the ideal here. Peter has arranged for his agency—the National Oceanographic and Atmospheric Administration—as part of its Endangered Species mission, to make a grant of $20,000 to pay local people for patrolling the beaches, monitoring nesting, and protecting the *Belimbings* and their eggs from human appetites. In this place, that's big money, worth many snared pigs and cacao pods. Most importantly, it gives new value to the turtles, puts outsider-driven conservation on a competitive footing with outsider-driven exploitation, and helps the people. Tetha explains that the money is given through WWF to run all the research, monitoring, and nest counting. The idea is that if wildlife has value, people will keep it; otherwise wildlife and habitat will be cleared to make room for what pays.

Right now the turtle-grant money has gotten everyone's attention, but in a culture where community cohesion and sharing is fundamental and entrepreneurship foreign, the fact that some people are paid to monitor turtle nesting while others get nothing strikes people as unfair. Everyone wants a share. Those not on the payroll feel left out, and that's created considerable dissent in these tiny communities. Further, more than thirty people work as patrollers, so $20,000 goes only so far. One village even went "on strike" recently. And not long ago the few people here derailed plans to both extend logging and to create a national park. The struggle for autonomy means the people insist on inclusion in any planning process, no matter its goals.

Peter and Tetha realize that to make this work for turtles, they'll have to work with the people to devise a broader, long-term vision to make conservation valuable to the whole community, responsive to its needs.

The community's needs are many. Nearly all the locals have malaria that comes and goes; it can kill children and the elderly. But good health care requires money and an enlightened policy that sees health services not just for treating sickness but as part of a package for human betterment that could include education, conservation of nature, the ability to plan families, freedom of expression, and self-determination. Indonesia has struggled, sometimes violently, with various separatist movements and bids for self-governance, Papuans' among them. But I think any nation that offers such a package of dignity to its citizens would likely sow support.

Tetha had asked, "I was wondering, why is this creature's home also home for the poor?" In one sense, Papua's low population density is a great and valuable asset, not just because it affords space for other creatures to continue flourishing here as almost nowhere else in the tropics, but because a little money and effort, applied wisely, could go a long way toward helping the people choose the life they would aspire toward.

The people have heard of tourism, and think that perhaps outsiders— not just us—might like to come see their giant turtles, their intact forests, their resplendent birds of paradise. The conservationists are certain that ecotourism can't work here right now; it's too far from everything, too hard to get to, and it lacks every amenity. Yet schools, health care, and employing people for wildlife work—that's feasible as part of an overall regional conservation plan that seeks to secure nature while also benefiting the people materially. This is conservation's next frontier.

But what then? Health care brings population increase. Adding roads, transportation, a taste for manufactured goods, boats, and a need for services like outboard-engine repair will hitch them to a market economy capable of cashing their local resources such as fish, turtle eggs, and logs. Where does the next step on that route lead? The nearest modern settlement, Sorong, is a crowded, dingy port city. The boat that got us here from there had three outboard engines—not so we could go terribly fast, but because one or two of them would frequently quit. When that happened—and it happened countless times—we never stopped. Instead, a couple of young men opened engine cowlings and, in cramped positions amid fumes, flying spray, noise, kerosene-soaked rags, open fuel drums, and lit cigarettes, they started sucking on fuel hoses, wiping spark plugs, rinsing fuel filters, and even removing carburetors while a yet-roaring engine or two kept thrusting us toward our unseen goal. When all the engines were running on all cylinders, life was good. And in those brief stretches of time and space, only one thing seemed certain: good times wouldn't last long. The chaos of the outboards seemed emblematic of life in the developing world, and I was never able to say with certainty whether this modernizing life, with its crowds, noise, hazards, and tantalizing glimpses of the wider world, was better than living on a beautiful beach and tending subsistence gardens with no options and nothing else to do. To me, neither seemed quite desirable. But I think the die is cast and, however slowly, the modern world's allure inexorably beckons, the Rubicon perhaps already crossed. And so the challenge: amid inevitable change, try to do some good, attempt to discern a better balance. And be prepared to pay.

The next *Belimbing*—just a couple hundred yards farther—is not yet laying eggs when we find her. But she's got an abrasion on one shoulder.

The harness might rub it. Or someone might find the turtle and assume that our harness caused the abrasion—not good for public relations. Benson shakes his head lamp.

Though we locate several more turtles during the Warmon night, none is at the right stage, or in quite the right physical condition, to receive our tracking backpack and its expensive ornaments. Having just arrived from half a world away, I'm not in the right physical condition to stay awake all night. So in between turtles I catch a few power naps, lying on my back in the sand in the warm, dreamy air, letting the river of time lapse past while my companions continue flowing down the intertwining channels of conversation about turtles, people, and the fanning delta of possible destinies.

The forest edge at dawn begins ringing with the flutelike calls of friarbirds and unseen others. Famous birdwing butterflies, their flight strong and batlike, flit metallic tints and glints through sunlit patches.

Today we'll travel back west by boat an hour or so to a top-heavy rock the size of a three-story building standing just off the beach. We passed it yesterday on our way here. It's called Batu Rumah, Rock House. Picturesquely pinched at the waterline, it seems it could almost tumble off its pedestal. There we'll pitch our second camp.

A small, clear stream leaves the forest for the sea just a few hundred yards from the rock. Here a wooden house on stilts is the *Belimbing* Project's outpost, cooking shack, and gear storeroom. A fortyish woman and two shyly smiling teenage girls do most of the cooking. Other people here are locally hired turtle monitors. (*Local* is a relative term; the nearest settlement you could term a village, thirty-eight houses called Saubebah, is four hours from here by foot, five if your feet are white. You walk west along the beach for a few hours—there are some Leatherback crawls the whole way—wading several streams. When you come to a large and impassable rocky headland, enter the forest and climb the steep, narrow, and at times precipitous mountain trail. The vegetation is all big: big leaves, big vines, huge buttressed trunks, and filigreed giant strangler figs. You walk until you come to another stream and follow the path back to the beach; from that point the houses are visible.)

A dark heron with yellow feet lands where the stream meets the sea, and a Brahminy Kite, like a small, faded Bald Eagle, sails over while we're setting up. This being a sea turtle project, the first thing we want

to do after pitching the tents and having breakfast is get some sleep. We
have an all-nighter coming up.

After a supper featuring cassava, wild boar, and diced vegetables, we
strike out near sunset for a stretch of beach called Warmamedi. It's the
easternmost of three beaches collectively called Jamursba Medi, stretching between Jamursba Cape and Cape Good Hope, about eleven miles total (eighteen kilometers). The Warmamedi beach is under an hour's walk
from camp, but it proves challenging. The first half mile involves clam-
bering over, under, and around a stretch of big bleached tree trunks
slumped from the forest into the surf. Next in our obstacle course comes
a long stretch of water-slicked, wave-polished boulders where a walking
stick keeps me upright. Then we trudge a half mile or so, a good kilometer, through clean but very soft sand. Here the tracks and treadings of
Belimbings from recent nights suddenly become evident. Just off the beach
rises another large rock, from one angle looking, with almost spooky
precision, like a giant stone Leatherback.

The sand lies piled and pushed not just by turtles but also by wild
pigs, whose cone-shaped craters are necklaced by emptied, shriveled
Leatherback eggshells. Pearls to swine. Pigs don't belong on this side of
Wallace's line. People brought them. They are, by far, the turtles' worst
current problem here. On this nearly unpeopled island, pigs levy a
heavy toll. So saving the Leatherbacks here will entail making bacon. A
Japanese researcher tried erecting a low electric fence along the forest
edge, but you need miles of it, and falling branches are a constant problem. It's ironic that in most places too many people spell disaster for
wildlife, while here there are not enough people to eat the pigs that people brought. Pigs are so plentiful, I'm told, that all the wild pork you'd
want can be snared close to camp. No trappers bother coming even this
far. The local turtle conservation slogan might well be "Eat More Pork!"
Here, eating meat is good for the environment. Peter and Tetha haven't
heard about the Florida folks' habañero pepper powder to stifle snuffling
mammals, but I think it might rout the snouts, and I promise to put them
in touch with the Floridians.

Despite the tracks, this is not yet the main beach, so we keep walking.
Leatherbacks, like other sea turtles, mysteriously gravitate to certain
beaches. Two beaches lying adjacent, looking identical, might attract

very different numbers of turtles. Or two beaches that look *different* to us will both appeal to them. Warmon's sand was charcoal-colored; Jamursba Medi's is light and has a different texture. Perhaps the main thing is proximity to currents favoring hatchling survival. At any rate, of all the world's coasts, both wild and settled, only an extraordinary few beaches lure Leatherbacks. Of thousands upon thousands of miles of shorelines, this stretch and Warmon are the most important beaches for the largest surviving Leatherback population in the whole Pacific—this little pinpoint that you could walk in one day.

I'm not saying it's the only place; eastern New Guinea, the Solomon Islands, the tsunami-scoured Nicobars and Sri Lanka, and some other spots have a few, too. But these precious stretches of Jamursba Medi and Warmon have so far this year received about three thousand *Penyu Belimbing* nests. Nowadays, that's impressive. Warmamedi, which we're approaching, has the highest density of nests—and it's only about three miles long.

Getting to the main nesting beach requires skirting a bordering rocky headland, so we cut behind it into thick, dark forest. New insects and frogs immediately dominate the audio stage, and remarkable luminous mushrooms glow along the path. The while, we sweat most of the extra water in our bodies to the equatorial heat.

When we emerge from the forest, we've arrived at Warmamedi Beach. I switch off my head lamp and reach for my water bottle. The beach has been heavily worked by turtles.

Darkness has firmly befallen us. The canopy of night reveals dense sprays of stars, the sky nearly overcome with stellar presence and a Milky Way aglow with astral clouds in unspeakable silence. Soft galactic light suffuses sufficiently for foot travel and the detection of dark fresh tracks. Turtles could begin arriving anytime, so we just keep walking, looking for those big shadows.

Twenty minutes later, the night's first *Belimbing* lies like a boulder at the end of a dark track, just beginning to lay. She's clean and healthy-looking. Benson and Peter prep the harness and electronics.

Villagers here at first believed the transmitters were remote controls enabling Peter and Scott Benson to draw the turtles away—so they could have them. Locals had noticed the *Belimbings* declining right around the time scientists started appearing. Thus, scientists caused the turtles' decline. So Peter and Benson hosted several villagers on an exchange to California, searching for turtles in Monterey Bay and showing their transmitter tracks on computer maps. They explained that if they command a remote control, so does someone here at Jamursba Medi—because most Monterey-tagged turtles swim toward here!

With the harnessing nearly completed, Benson starts grunting dissatisfaction with its fit. The straps and rings, coated with extra antifouling paint to thwart drag-inducing algae and barnacles, are stiff and difficult to readjust. As the turtle begins unsettling herself, Benson decides to remove the whole thing. He doesn't want to risk sending her off with something ill-fitting. It's early; there'll be more turtles.

Our next turtle is a good and proper digger. Before she lays, two more turtles arise nearby. Soon there's a lot of digging going on. Benson says, "This is the way it is here; they all start coming around the same time."

By the time the crew finishes adjusting the harness and its payload, two additional *Belimbings* have arisen and are tossing sand. Night deepens as science marches slowly on.

By three A.M. there've been about eighteen turtles on the beach, but our timing has been off. For various reasons, we haven't been able to work with some turtles, and others have come and gone before we reached them. So we still have two transmitter kits.

Enter the local villain: the biggest turtle of the night is already wearing a harness applied by a Japanese researcher who was here recently. He's been in and out a few times, operating secretively. He's complained that Americans shouldn't be working in the western Pacific. It should be left for the Japanese. Peter's prior explanation, that he tracked turtles here from California, did not seem to blunt the man's objections. Americans should stay away from Japan's side of the pond, he said.

He'd have a case if this were Japan. But there's also a problem with this researcher's turtle. To carry a mere cigar-sized dive logger, he'd attached an entire harness. For one thing, the harness is designed for transmitters whose antennas need to be out of the water—and his dive logger did not need to be out of the water. For another, he could have clipped it to a flipper tag; he didn't need a harness. Worst, by far, is that his materials are all wrong. No antifouling paint; the turtle would eventually have been condemned to drag huge bunches of algae and gooseneck barnacles. Ill-fitting shoulder pads are made of a material that is already chafing her shoulders raw and a little bloody. And a strap-connecting ring not of flexible rubber tubing with corrodible connectors but *stainless steel cable*, is already abrading grooves into her back. It looks like he tried to copy from photos of the Eckert-style harness we're using, but the result is a big mess.

Luckily for the turtle and us, several locals paid by the Japanese researcher are here on the beach. He'd told them to look for turtles with his dive loggers coming to re-lay. (He wants the loggers back; they need to be retrieved in order for him to get their data.) We hand his men a pair of clippers, and they cut off the whole unholy muddle. But what if she'd returned two miles away? If his men were simply resting and we were busy with another turtle, all of us could have missed her. And how many others are there?

Through the night turtles continually arrive and depart. Benson searches for another perfect turtle in perfect physical condition at the perfect stage of nesting. One likely candidate costs us half an hour as we wait while she digs, digs, digs. But she quits without laying, and goes back into the Pacific.

As we are finishing our second transmitter deployment, the first pastel of day begins erasing the east edge of night. The sky blushes into a morning of such glory that upon reaching our tents all of us, even after a night of walking with only a few quick catnaps, want to sit on the beach and watch the light.

No boats ply the ocean, and when I ask why the locals don't seem to go fishing, Tetha tells me that the people living here came to the coast from the highlands, and they have no fishing tradition, no seafaring knowledge.

Elsewhere it's a different matter. South of New Guinea, off the Kei Islands (where, like Monterey Bay, deep water runs close to shore and upwelling nutrients produce pastures trolled by lots of jellyfish), native islanders are perhaps the only people in the world who specifically hunt Leatherbacks at sea. They've harpooned forty-five so far this year. They consider Leatherbacks their most sacred food. But like some other peoples who've used turtles for rituals, strict traditional constraints are vanishing, and the hunt is turning commercial. Tetha Hitipeuw and Scott Benson are working with the Kei Islanders on conservation and development. The hope is that if the islanders' hunting skills are put to use in catching Leatherbacks alive, for science, they might feel their cultural relationship satisfied nonlethally.

The Kei Islanders' ancient belief is that their turtles arose on the north coast of Papua, and Benson's tracking has confirmed that. They also believe Leatherbacks are their ancestors. Because the hunt for the sacred food is facilitated by the ancestors themselves, the islanders assume that Leatherback extinction is not possible. I hope they prove right about that too.

Tetha relates that just before I arrived, a Kei village chief had come here to Jamursba Medi at her invitation, to participate in the nest-monitoring and transmitter-tagging work. It was not only his first time seeing Leatherbacks nesting, but the first time he'd seen Leatherbacks where no person sought to kill them. Moved by watching them coming ashore and the people working with them, he told Tetha, "If this happened in Kei, people would say the ancestor has come, and has approached us." When he helped Scott Benson and the local folks here deploy a transmitter, Tetha heard him address the turtle as *Ubee*—Ancestor—and whisper, "Please do not go to Kei; you'll be killed. Try to go for another route so you'll be safe." He requested photos of him with the turtles, to show his people how the Papuans treat the Ancestors. He said, "My knowledge is that the Kei Islanders long ago came here to teach the Papuans. Why in this case are the Papuans wiser than we, not killing those threatened with extinction?"

Several *loomba-loomba*—dolphins—cruise placidly not far from shore. Within two sunrises of being here, I've completely lost track of day and date, though I do at least remember that it's July. Whooshing and buzzing wings herald an arriving group of Papuan Hornbills, like giant black-and-tan toucans the size of eagles. I love seeing them. Yesterday I saw a real eagle—a White-Bellied Sea Eagle with all-white head and smart white leading edges to its broad, massive wings—making a surprise appearance along the beach.

A butterfly with wings the size of my hands transits along the shoreline. Something very much like a mind seems to govern all these creatures. They do things that make sense, do what's appropriate, all of them seemingly knowing the right acts and actions to commit toward their survival, the butterfly and friarbird, turtle and sea eagle each nesting, resting, feeding, and breeding as need calls for. They all seem so sensible. Yet we have no real clue whether a butterfly, say, is even conscious. We have no reliable sense of the sentience of any being. Who can plumb the perimeters of consciousness for termites or turtles? Of what they do, how much are they aware? How much do they perform unawares? And what of the inexplicable and perplexing minds of such sentient yet nonsensical beings as we, so ruled and riled by superstition and rage? How much do we do for reasons we are not truly aware of, or that we falsely think we understand? What kind of imperfected work in progress is a mind like ours? If lesser beings may not be what they seem, what assurances can we grant about ourselves?

We recap the night. I'm guessing, considering the turtles we saw and the fresh tracks of those we missed, that more than two dozen Leatherbacks emerged from the Pacific onto Warmamedi sands last night. The official counters' tally is even higher: twenty-nine *Penyu Belimbings*, just on that one stretch where we worked and walked away the dark, hot hours.

At eight A.M. two men come into camp shouldering a deer whose legs and neck are tied with vines to a pole. Not only has it been snared—one ankle is peeled to the tendons—but it is still alive. It grunts and struggles until the men place it, still bound, pole and all, into the shallow stream. Though its nose and mouth are above water on the bank, in a few minutes it dies, seemingly of shock. About an hour later the men return with knives and whetstones and deftly reduce their victim to victuals. Theirs is a life of direct connections.

Later, after a jungle supper featuring the fresh venison and rice, we again walk the couple of miles to Warmamedi, again rounding the fallen trees, climbing over the slick polished slipping-stones, trudging through the soft sand and the glowing-mushroom jungle shortcut, out to the pig-pitted, Leatherback-laced beach.

At nine P.M. the first turtle gets our last transmitter pack. Moments after our harnessed lady enters the waves, she seems to reemerge from the water at the same spot, as if she's coming back for something she'd forgotten. But this is a new turtle. Not far away, two more are chopping into the starlight that overspreads this beach like linen. Their density instills hope that all is not lost, and augurs a better destiny for the *Penyu Belimbings* of Jamursba Medi.

I'm noticing something important: there are a lot of turtles here. Maybe, after all, the story isn't as simple as "Leatherbacks are going extinct in the Pacific." This *is* the Pacific. But I've just gotten here. So I turn to the expert.

Peter says, "Well, it's certainly a critical time, because most major Pacific Leatherback populations have certainly crashed. But"—he pauses—"there are important nuances. Malaysia, Mexico, and Costa Rica collapsed; the situation here along this coast is very different."

There may have been twice as many females here in the early 1980s. Nest counts here from the mid-1980s through the late '90s were a third higher than they were from 2000 to '04. That's cause for concern, but Peter says, "This is still a fairly robust population. Whatever might be influencing turtles, it's different here from what happened in Malaysia and what's happening in Mexico and Costa Rica."

In Malaysia, where the once-great population is virtually extinct, Leatherbacks endured fifty years of near-total egg taking. Scientists warned the people way back in the 1970s that they weren't putting enough eggs aside. The population started plummeting before they got serious about hatcheries, and then there were real problems with temperature fluctuations in artificial hatching boxes. On top of that, turtles had to run a nearby gauntlet of intense gillnetting that, according to Dutton, "really pounded them." At their main beach, a once-bustling ecotourism center with shorefront cottages, a museum, and a big statue of a sea turtle is now a vine-overgrown ghost town. The tourists hadn't helped, shining lights and disturbing turtles. Now the ghost town bears testament to a future lost for local people and turtles, caused by killing the goose and her golden eggs.

It's different here. Although boats from outside inflicted intensive commercial nest raids during the 1980s, taking away tens of thousands of eggs, that ended in the early 1990s. Local people also stopped taking eggs around the same time, when conservationists started working here. When Scott Benson is flying aerial surveys elsewhere in Papua, he sometimes sees people digging turtle nests; they wave to the plane. But here the conservation groups are paying local people to monitor nests, making eggs worth more alive. Says Tetha: it's that simple.

Peter adds, "There's still time here, but it'll be critical to take advantage of the time we have left, and get it right—because once a major population starts collapsing, y'know, forget it; you're talking about a hundred years to try to recover it. It's *so* much more work."

Should I infer that he's pessimistic about the collapsed Mexico–to–Costa Rica population?

"Well..." He takes a deep breath, then answers: "I refuse to believe the eastern Pacific Leatherbacks will go extinct. I keep thinking, 'The collapses resulted from bad things that happened in the past—the rampant egging, the drift-netting—and we're about to come out of it.' I keep thinking, 'Next year we'll start seeing their recovery.' I keep thinking—" He looks at me and laughs. "Maybe I'm delusional."

Peter gazes upward, as if searching heaven for the answer. But he's just trying to see if Scorpio has risen. It's actually difficult to see the constellations here; they hide among so many stars.

So then it's true: separate populations *are* faring differently. That forces me to reconsider the "curious fact" that lured me into all these travels: that in the Atlantic, sea turtle recovery is the mode, while in the Pacific, Leatherbacks and several others are careening toward extinction. But is that really correct?

It's not that simple. Having been here, there, and everywhere, I now appreciate what Peter called "the nuances." I've come to realize that not all Pacific Leatherbacks are equal. Malaysia's are virtually extinct. The eastern Pacific nesters, Mexico to Costa Rica, are crashing. But these turtles that journey between New Guinea and North America's West Coast remain rather robust.

That paradox spawns a key question: how can different populations in the same ocean be experiencing different survival rates?

As we walk the sand, I walk my mind through everything I've seen in all my travels. I'm trying to form an informed best guess accounting for everything I've learned.

There's a pattern: Each crashed population in the Pacific suffered decades of nesting failure resulting from intensive egg taking. Where they're still crashing, something is killing off adults in the ocean. Each recovering population has a couple of decades of egg protection under its belt and enjoys high adult survival. So there seems some link between egg survival on beaches and adult survival in the ocean.

What could be the link between them?

The biggest known ocean killer of larger turtles is fishing gear. Longlines are most widely considered the main fishing gear now killing Leatherbacks. On many beaches, nesting turtles attest to this with their entanglement scars, hideous injuries, and hook wounds.

But there's this contradiction: though exposed to the same fishing fleets while mixing throughout their foraging travels, different nesting populations are performing differently.

For instance, in the wider Caribbean, Leatherback numbers appear stable at some beaches but are increasing exponentially at others. St. Croix's Leatherback population is likely both the fastest growing and the longest studied in the world. As elsewhere, turtles nesting at St. Croix frequently bear clear evidence of entanglements. Yet, Donna Dutton and Peter Dutton and colleagues, writing in the journal *Biological Conserva-*

tion in 2005, stated, "Adult females are more resilient than previously believed to the hazards leatherbacks face at sea, as evidenced by the many turtles we have seen returning repeatedly to nest on St. Croix despite open wounds, scars from entanglement in fishing gear and other marine debris, and long-line hooks embedded in their flippers." Despite the obvious frequent run-ins with fishing gear, this population achieves annual adult survival of around 90 percent. Without fishing gear and the misery it inflicts, survival would certainly be higher. But 90 percent is high. High enough to bring the population back from the brink.

If high-seas fishing was the major factor driving their numbers, you'd think all populations that mix at sea should be doing equally well or poorly. Clearly that's not the case. Different nesting colonies are performing differently despite shared high-seas fishery exposure. So some are being driven by local factors. That could include locally intense fishing near certain nesting beaches. And remember, all recently crashed Leatherback populations have in common decades of nest failure caused by intensive egg taking.

So what's killing the adults? One possibility: old age. Populations are now crashing because egg taking robbed them of a generation of young adults that should be maturing to take the place of those reaching the natural end of their lives. No hatchlings back then equals no young adults now.

Like I say, that's one possibility. It's a strong one. That would make the needed link between intensive egging and high adult mortality. It would also explain the link between intensive egg protection and high adult survival: recovering populations enjoy high adult survival because years of nest protection and boosted hatchling production continue supplying a stream of young adults into the population. And this line of logic accounts for different population trends among nesting populations exposed to the same high-seas fisheries.

All of this suggests that what happens locally on beaches can be the most important factor. The World Conservation Union has warned that adult populations can seem stable for years while egging robs the next generation, but "when declines come, they will be fast, thorough, and long-lasting."

That's where my past travels and tonight's thinking lead me. This hopeful hypothesis seems to account for everything I've learned about the populations that have crashed, and those recovering. If it's right, even the crashed populations could get kicked into recovery mode solely by intensively protecting nests. This would buy time for the longer-term process of fixing the fisheries problems. The essentials have been set in motion: egg taking is under control at most major beaches, while fishery problems are getting increasing attention. (The United States is exporting techniques to reduce longline turtle bycatch, and, responding to a United Nations call that nations reduce their longline capacity 20 to 30 percent, Taiwan is reducing its longline fleet by 120 vessels.) In the world's fastest-growing Leatherback population, the *only* thing done to affect survival was saving all the nests, year after year.

So, this line of thinking accounts for almost everything I'd learned—but it doesn't account for things I don't know. If long-lining intensity is different in different oceans, it could change the picture and the prospects. During their long oceanic travels, the Leatherbacks that nest on the west side of the Pacific Ocean generally stay well north of those that nest in Mexico and Central America, so they're not exposed to precisely the same fishing gear. If Pacific Leatherbacks grow more slowly and take longer to reach adulthood than those in the Atlantic, their situation will be more difficult; we already know that in the Atlantic they nest more frequently and lay more eggs. These are among the important nuances.

But the main question remains this: Can local efforts on individual beaches affect the future of individual populations? The answer for the Atlantic seems a clear yes. But the question is most pertinent in the Pacific, where the situation remains critical.

While I was trying to sort this out by traveling, talking, walking, and thinking, someone was in an academic lab crunching numbers. A few months after I got home a colleague sent me a newly published study, which took a different run at basically the same question. It compared Pacific Leatherback mortality from long-lining to deaths from "coastal sources" like the killing of nesting females and the taking of eggs. The paper concluded with a bell-ringing statement: "The results clearly indicate that factors besides longlining are responsible for the majority of the leatherback's decline. . . . For both eastern and western Pacific leatherback stocks, eliminating longline-caused mortality will not prevent extinction. The coastal mortality must be eliminated or reduced for the stocks to recover." Those were the results of just one mathematical model, but I found it pretty interesting because it had approached mathematically a question I'd approached with personal experience and logic, and we'd both come out in a similar place.

There is other evidence, from other species. Costa Rica's Atlantic

Green Turtles surged following years of nest protection. In the Caribbean in general, where many populations are stable or increasing, egg taking has been largely under control in most places since the mid-1980s (thanks mainly to the Wider Caribbean Sea Turtle Conservation Network, Caribbean Conservation Corporation, and U.S. Endangered Species Act).

This is not to let fisheries off the hook. Fisheries kill too many turtles—not to mention too many fish—and that must be fixed.

But as Jim Spotila and colleagues wrote, "Egg poaching alone can drive a Leatherback population to extinction. Adding fishing mortality drives it to extinction faster." They did a computer simulation, too, and it indicated that even with modest fishing mortality, doubling egg and hatchling survival on the beach could allow population doubling in about forty years. They noted that "very high egg and hatchling mortality can devastate a Leatherback population more rapidly than low-to-moderate adult mortality; likewise a very high survivorship of eggs and hatchlings can counteract low-to-moderate adult mortality."

One other Indo-Pacific bright spot provides an instructive tale. The Turtle Islands of the Philippines and those of Malaysia lie within sight of each other. In 1972, the Malaysian government ended egg collection on their complement of the islands. Nesting females kept declining for fifteen years, then turned upward, and by 2001 nesting numbers finally exceeded those of the 1960s. It can be done; it takes patience, perseverance, foresight. As Green Turtle nesting in the Sabah Turtle Park grew from three thousand to ten thousand nests per year, tourism leaped 28 percent annually and now brings in a million dollars a year. Meanwhile, the people on the Philippines side continued overcollecting eggs, and their turtles have declined 80 percent.

Various lines of evidence converge on an important point: things local people can control on local beaches can, in many cases, bring turtles back. And have. Local control of nature and natural resources has a chance of working. All hope is local.

I know I'm ignoring important details. How will fisheries change? What will the wild card of increasing carbon dioxide do above and beneath the warming ocean's surface? Will turtle hunting in Southeast Asia destroy Australia's nesting populations or, as in other parts of the world, will people realize that turtles are worth more alive?

But the question I'm wrestling with is not What are all the problems?

(Answers to that question appeared in every country I visited.) The question I'm asking now is: Can we cause recovery?

I'm trying to sift through all I've seen to determine what we can do in our lifetime to take a situation that was broken when we got it and improve it a little. And the facts, taken together, make me hopeful.

All the senior professionals—Peter Dutton, Laura Sarti, Scott and Karen Eckert, Scott Benson, Sally Murphy, Jim Spotila, and Frank Paladino, for instance—they all work from hope. They're not the types to gloss over problems or look through rose-tinted lenses. Quite the opposite; they've been the first to sound alarms. They've felt despair and fought despite it. I've learned this by observing the real professionals who go the distance: You dodge despair by not taking the deluge of problems full-bore. You focus on what can work, what can help, or what you can do, and you seize it, and then—you don't let go. What they see, and what I've come to see, is the possibility of making things better. That's what hope is: the belief that things can get better. The world belongs to people who don't give up.

"One thing that's really colored my experience," Peter Dutton says, "is having stood on the beach at St. Croix, thinking, 'It's all over'—and being wrong. I mean, for a long time it was very discouraging. We sometimes walked all night, several nights in a row, finding nothing. We'd have, like, five turtles in a week. You start wondering if protecting so few eggs could matter. You begin feeling your efforts are meaningless; it can't work. Then, after fifteen years, you realize new turtles are coming—it's working."

In the twenty years between 1980 and 2000, St. Croix's Leatherback population mushroomed tenfold, from a low of about twenty to around two hundred females nesting annually, while yearly hatchling production ballooned from two thousand to fifty thousand, with no end in sight. So, yes, saving a few eggs year after year, protecting nests that would've been doomed, mattered.

Peter was also present when, in 1987, the Kemp's Ridley Turtle population hit its bottom. "That was also," he recalls, "really depressing. Again, night after night, no turtles. We'd sit in camp, saying it was just a short matter of time before the last female came." That turned out to be wrong, too. Almost everyone recognizes the turtle-excluding devices in shrimp nets for causing the Kemp's recovering trend, and rightly so. But an underappreciated fact is that intensive egg taking for the market was also a cause of the decline, and effective nest protection had already caused Kemp's numbers to begin nosing upward even before the shrimp-net escape devices became mandatory. And in Tongaland, KwaZulu-Natal, South Africa, thirty years of "vigorous protection" resulted in "lucrative tourism" as the number of female Leatherbacks nesting per season increased from a seemingly hopeless low of five to well over a hundred.

"I think, in the future," Peter says, "these sorts of turnarounds are what we'll be talking about with Pacific Leatherbacks. Egging is coming under control at the most important places, and if we prevent gill-net fisheries from expanding, and maybe achieve better control of long-lining," he says, "maybe within sixty or seventy years we'll see some good recoveries."

He adds, "In Mexico I stood on a beach with Laura Sarti while she was feeling that same despair, that emptiness for what was, that I had felt in St. Croix. But by the time I got to Mexico I also knew another feeling: understanding they *can* come back."

CHANT FOR THE ENCHANTED

The Leatherback is one of the few original sentient beings. That it is a kind of human is indicated by its propensity to shed tears, something only humans do. In ancient times, the sentient beings all communicated freely. At some point this ability was lost, but Leatherbacks remain fully capable of understanding songs and what is spoken to them.

The Seri people have for millennia lived in the upper Gulf of California. Their ancestral center of gravity is the large and rugged island Tahéjöc (Spanish: Isla Tiburón). As the Seri have long known, Black Turtle created land; Leatherback rose up to create Tahéjöc, its shell still visible as the mountains' serrated ridges.

A century ago, Western diseases and war reduced the Seri from about 5,000 to 110 individuals (a 98 percent decline, similar to the Pacific's Leatherbacks). Having recovered to about 750 individuals so far, they are still considered an endangered people. Yet the main thing about the Seri is that, fiercely holding to their language, land, and traditions, they have survived.

As Pacific Northwest tribes relied on salmon, and the Plains Indians upon buffalo, sea turtles formed the Seri people's nutritional, material, artistic, and spiritual core. Living on turtle-created land in a turtle-created world, the Seri relied heavily on Black Turtles for their single most important food and for leather, roofing material, and a wide array of implements and toys. The Black Turtle was their most economically important animal; the Leatherback, by far their most sacred.

No one sought to starve the Seri by destroying their turtles, as the U.S. government systematically destroyed buffalo to starve the Plains Indians. But turtle crashes caused by egging and commercial fishing have eroded the Seri identity and economy. Former hunters now carve turtles for tourists, like other traditional peoples who've become tethered to the unstable fringes of cash culture by the depletion of nature.

The Seri people traditionally honored Leatherback with a four-day ceremony spontaneously sparked by the sudden arrival of the rare turtle near their villages. No other animal commanded such veneration.

When a species crashes it may take down cultures grown enmeshed with it, snapping limbs off the human family tree as it falls, robbing the world of cultural complexity, leaving the human landscape simplified—leaving more of the world like all the rest of the world as the whole world grows increasingly the same.

But cultural values can survive by adapting, too. Experienced Seri turtle hunters are now working with scientists, who seek their help because the Seri have long understood things about sea turtle populations, movements, and food habits that science is only beginning to look at.

Because the species has never been a regular visitor to the Seri home waters of the upper Gulf of California, an arriving Leatherback would always trigger the abrupt interruption of whatever everyone was doing. Thus the Leatherback ceremony was unpredictable, timed only by the chance arrival of the Sacred One. A fisherman would notice, call the village, and everyone would assemble on the shore to sing the turtle in with special Leatherback songs. Some say Leatherback simply swam ashore in response to singing. Others say a fisherman would spear Leatherback in a flipper; then, aided by song, the turtle would lead them shoreward. Once on the beach, Leatherback stayed for four days, during which it was ceremonially painted, housed in a sacred bower built over it on the beach, and then sung back to sea.

The Seri know their songs have the power to communicate to turtles. Scientists will tell you that it certainly seems that way. "When you're out in a boat on a day when no one has seen a turtle, and an elder begins singing, and suddenly a turtle appears five feet away," ethnobiologist Dr. Gary Nabhan told me, "you feel there's some connection between these people and sea turtles that deserves respect." U.S. government biologist Dr. Jeff Seminoff remembers, "I went out with two of the great turtle hunters. It was a horrible day, cold, overcast, very windy, whitecaps everywhere, and they said, 'We're going to find Black Turtles.' I thought, 'I don't think so.' We went to one place they call Turtle Home. We get there and it's just blowing, rough as hell, and I'm wondering what we're doing here. Well, the two elders start singing one of the Seri turtle songs. And within *five* minutes, the rain stops, the clouds part, the waters calm. And—I'm not kidding you—turtles start appearing at the surface. I was astonished. But the Seri were just matter of fact about it: 'This is how we sing in the turtles—here they come.' "

Perhaps it's not beyond possibility that there's some connection the rest of us don't comprehend. Certain scientists and animal handlers seem to have a special rapport with the animals they study or care for. Dogs sometimes begin whimpering and shaking as their owner is dying. No one understands how trained "seizure alert" dogs are able to sense and warn their owners of oncoming epileptic attacks, sometimes hours before the owner feels anything. Professional naturalists often develop extraordinary skill in locating and understanding their study animals. So I listen to these descriptions with interest. They broaden my understanding of the range of human experiences with animals, they raise intriguing questions, and they're good stories.

A Leatherback visitation and ceremony was the Seri's most sacred happening. But the waiting time between Leatherback visits doubled each decade from the 1940s through the 1970s. In the 1940s, a Leatherback visited about every other year. In the 1950s, only two or three Leatherbacks presented themselves. In the 1960s, just one or two. As the Seri's most sacred animals grew scarce, their unique religious ceremony began fading from experience, then even from memory. The last full Seri Leatherback ceremony happened around 1980. By 1997 most living Seris had never seen this most revered being alive. A few elders decided to initiate the ceremony when someone found Leatherback bones and a shell upon the shore. A celebration over mere bones seemed a clear indication of something passing. Eight years later, when no Leatherback had visited the Seri in almost a quarter century, the elders decided that if *Moosnipol* could no longer come, they would send a delegation to *Moosnipol*'s last haunts, even if that means venturing away from the homeland.

Five hundred miles from the Seri land, near Baja's southern tip, we stand upon an isolated span of desert seashore. Cordon cacti prickle the horizon with raised arms. The place is called Agua Blanca. For the five Seri who've journeyed so far from home, this is unfamiliar territory.

The Seri delegation is led by seventy-three-year-old matriarch Cleotilde

Morales. Accompanying her are three young women in their early twenties. The three younger delegates have never been in an airplane, never before beheld the Pacific Ocean. Much Seri cultural knowledge is stored, handed down, and conveyed in songs, and Cleotilde is both a master singer and the daughter of a master singer—something like descendant royalty. Outwardly her status is marked neither by appearance nor pomp but simply respect and the deference afforded her. Her son, José Luis, explains, "My mother is a very important person because of the knowledge she has, in her stories and songs—knowledge she keeps within herself, things you can't put down in a book."

Joining this delegation are about a dozen people including conservationists, a few scientists, and one longline captain, convened by the Leatherback's powers and a shared mission. Mexico's Leatherback expert Laura Sarti is present. Notably, the hatchery operation here is funded by long-liners from Hawaii and California. Their motivation: "As long as the situation with turtles stays bad, we're gonna have problems."

Only six Leatherback nests have been found here this whole season, representing probably *one* surviving female using this shore. So the Seri—with the pragmatism of hunter-gatherers—rather than trying to bring a Leatherback ashore, will perform their Leatherback rite by paying homage to a hatchling.

Right now, one brood of hatchlings is emerging in a tiny hatchery shed at a two-room field station. Ancient turtles in incubators, traditional people venturing from their homeland, fishers trying to put a little life back into the ocean, and biologists who don't just study but roll up their sleeves are all changing their traditional ways, urgently hoping to facilitate continued existence. The change creates community, and at the center of this community, gathering all of us around it, simultaneously so powerful and vulnerable, is the Seri's most sacred animal.

The Seri see the Leatherback as sacred in religious terms. I see it as sacred in practical terms. The mystical view of animals holds a kind of wisdom not because it brings us closer to reality but because it brings us closer to survival. Veneration's robust power is that, whatever one's belief in the architecture of Heaven and Earth, a covenant of stewardship will light your path.

Cleotilde hands out sprigs of Desert Lavender to bless us and bring us into the spirit of what we are about to do. She herself holds a sprig of Elephant Tree. After a sea turtle brought earth from the bottom of the ocean and made the land, these were the first plants.

The sight of the first hatchling, the little *criatura*, the babe so tender for whom she has made this life pilgrimage, moves Cleotilde to tears. Because Leatherbacks don't nest as far north as the Seri homeland, it is almost certainly the first baby *Moosnipol* any Seri has ever seen. Cleotilde greets it with the familiarity one might show a close friend's infant. Her sense of familial relation interests me. Rather than it seeming superstitious or primitive, it's how I wish the whole world felt.

Flanked by the three younger women and with her hands raised, Cleotilde begins singing. She offers a song of love, and a wish for safety. Her song has a chanting sort of Native American tom-tom rhythm to it. Cleotilde's aged voice is neither sweet nor melodic but beautiful, as anything genuine is beautiful, a little frail but resonant with the long experience of a people who have seen, suffered much, and survived. Her singing feels rooted and bewitching. It's the voice of the human spirit, loosed into the desert like an owl at dusk.

When she is finished singing, we lay down our fragrant offerings. After this initial invocation, the Seri cease calling the turtle *Moosnipol* and begin addressing it as "Vulnerable One," *Xica cmotómanoj*. From now on they will refer to it only by this honorific, its name never directly spoken.

By noon the Seri are finishing a ceremonial bower of bowed branches, thatched with green foliage and colored ribbons, large enough to cast adequate shade on an adult Leatherback.

The Seri women are now arrayed in bright ceremonial blouses, long skirts, and broad red headbands. The younger women paint thin lines and zigzags across one another's cheekbones and noses—red and blue lines, blue diamonds, white dots. Cleotilde wears a pattern bolder, more striking. Everyone here must get painted. When my turn comes, I am surprised by the intimacy.

Cleotilde has made a rattle from an empty plastic water bottle enlivened with a few desert pebbles and painted with zigzags representing the jagged light of vision quests. She begins dancing a song around the bower. Then she sits quietly in the bright desert sun, the harsh light etching sharp shadows in her creased face, wisps of hair blowing in the breeze. Every few minutes, spontaneous as a wren calling from a cactus, she sings another song that lasts a minute or two, occasionally traveling around the bower. This is not done for any audience, nor are we even assembled. Her songs are not performances but incantations, sacred rituals and rites. Their value is apart from anyone.

This vigil of song and consecration lasts all day. After dark, in the halo of a fire, Cleotilde sings for anyone wishing to dance. Her companions set up a kind of giant Native American board game. With slices of thick cactus they make a circle roughly four strides across, and players toss sticks marked like dice to see how many spaces around this circle they will advance their pieces. As the hours pass in dance and play, our small crowd of strangers begins bonding into a group of friends.

Night yields to day. The steep beach stretches far south to ragged blue mountains. Northward the beach merely vanishes unbounded into the haze. Sometime during the night, about a mile down the beach, the adult Leatherback returned. For the young women gathered in awe, the colossal tracks are the closest they've come to the full-scale Sacred One.

Late in the afternoon, the biologists take the hatchlings from their sandy incubator, weighing and measuring each one according to the ceremony of science. We are going to release all but one. That one is carefully taken to the bower, where Cleotilde initiates it as the ceremonial individual. Traditionally, adult Leatherbacks received bold paint patterns, but Cleotilde anoints this babe with but a few white dots. According to the ceremonial plan, we will release the rest of the brood, but this one selected innocent will receive further demonstrations of devotion and respect for the next two days.

I'm thinking that if kept in the desert air for two days without access to the sea it might die. I imagine this would be disastrous to the ceremonial intent. No one has ever done a four-day ceremony with a Vulnerable One who was so utterly vulnerable. We are preparing to release the rest of the brood, and I think Cleotilde should initiate two, with one as a spare, for insurance. But I say nothing.

After leaving it in the bower for just a few minutes, Cleotilde removes the initiate so it may accompany us all to the beach while we release its brothers and sisters. As the Seri see it, we are brothers and sisters all, we are family, turtles and other humans alike. As a biologist who has studied evolution in books and in life, I see it essentially the same way.

Following Cleotilde, we proceed over the forty-foot dune separating the desert from the sea. Cleotilde carries the Vulnerable One in her hands, continually chanting and singing. The rest of the brood is being carried in a foam container. The sun, slipped to the horizon, is painting the desert and sky in changing pastels. The surf grows louder.

No sooner have we crested the dune than, just outside the waves, a Gray Whale unfurls a prayer flag of white breath. Cleotilde launches a whale song, and suddenly the whole scene feels aglow in magic.

Upon the sand we rest the container and its sacred brood. Cleotilde kneels and begins placing the little turtles one by one onto the sand, chanting a Leatherback song as they begin rowing down the steep beach. They move slowly, as though motivated seaward by instinct yet enthralled by Cleotilde's incantation.

Or maybe it's that, for me, the stream of time is pooling at the confluence of biology and belief, the junction of grief and hope. And in the air is something that bypasses hope, something that packs the force of prayer: the conviction that energy applied deeply and consistently, with sufficient faith, can redirect the future.

The hatchlings advance. A wave tumbles the vulnerable ones, which roll and right themselves. The next wave washes them back up the beach, a setback from which they merely resume marching forward. The following wave drags them down in the raking wash. No one ever said their lives will be easy, and nothing about their start in life suggests ease.

Three whales have now gathered just outside the surf, directly before us, quite as if assembled in welcome. I think this is just an extraordinary coincidence, but I feel chills. Cleotilde responds by discarding the script; she spontaneously releases her specially anointed one, that it may join its siblings and enter the sea at this auspicious moment.

Catching up to the last straggler, the little anointed one pauses as though still reluctant to leave the sound of Cleotilde's song. Yet while she chants, her hands wave encouragement toward its progress.

As the last little one commits itself to the infinite mystery, the nearest whale lifts its huge head from the water. It seems to be watching, as though checking to be sure that all are accounted for. It's so extraordinary—this gesture of the whale—so surreal, so tuned in to the spirit of the ceremony, that it raises the hairs on my arms.

The little ones have left us, slipping into the lacy whitewater and under the hem of the ocean, entering the great swim, never pausing to ask "what if," using everything they know, with all they've got. Life is mostly a story we tell ourselves, but in fact all our frenzy is but a quick dash toward the inner rim of a vast unknown, and no more than that.

. . .

Within the halo of an all-night campfire, food, singing, dancing, and laughter reach deep into the indeterminate hours. Much later, as we sit huddled in blankets in the chilly desert air, lulled by the rumbling surf, Cleotilde remains cheerfully alert, immune to cold. She is wide awake when first light silhouettes the blue-black mountains, backlights the cactus for miles around, and brings a thin, hopeful chorus from the desert birds. As the rising sun strides through night's finish line, Cleotilde presides over the ceremony's closing song, then leads us all in a final dance around the dying fire.

I wonder if this is the end of something ancient or the start of a future regained. I'm not certain what it is, but I know what it means: it means there truly is hope. Other peoples, other species, even other kinds of sea turtles—in situations as bad, sometimes worse—have recovered. Turtles have taught me this: Do all you can and don't worry about the odds against you. Wield the miracle of life's energy, never worrying whether we may fail, concerned only that whether we fail or succeed we do so with all our might. That's all we need to know to feel certain that all our force of diligent effort is worth our while on Earth.

Cleotilde gestures for us to array ourselves before her in a semicircle. She reaches into a bag at her feet and showers us with goodies ranging from beaded bracelets to noisemakers.

APPENDIX

A Few Places to See Nesting Sea Turtles

Dr. Karen Eckert of the Wider Caribbean Sea Turtle Conservation Network (WIDECAST) points out that tour operators are bringing nesting sea turtles and tourists into contact with increasing frequency. At some sites the interaction is well organized and sustainable, involving trained guides, visitor fees, interpretive materials, and "turtle-friendly" (and enforced) beach etiquette. At other sites the result has been harassed turtles, interrupted nesting, litter, beach fires, and trampled vegetation. The difference revolves around whether the program is part of a planned conservation or community development initiative or simply short-term profiteering. Dr. Eckert believes that well-planned interaction between visitors and nesting turtles can be a success story in nature tourism, integrating economic and ecological goals. For people interested in seeing nesting turtles with good guides in situations that work both for the turtles and the tourists, here are a few suggestions.

Florida has a variety of organized opportunities to observe nesting sea turtles (see http://myfwc.com/seaturtle/Education/2006_Watches_List.htm, and related very helpful map: http://myfwc.com/seaturtle/images/Turtle_Watches.jpg).

Earthwatch has several programs allowing people to assist on scientific and conservation projects with Leatherbacks, other turtles, and various wildlife worldwide (see http://www.earthwatch.org/results/turtles.html). The Playa Grande project described in this book on Costa Rica's Pacific coast, for example, involves Earthwatch participants, as does the Trinidad project. As mentioned earlier, Nature Seekers takes curious people to see nesting Leatherbacks in Trinidad (see http://www.trinidad-tobago.net/Article.aspx?PageId=11).

Programs recommended by the Wider Caribbean Sea Turtle Conservation Network include the Save Our Sea Turtles program in Tobago (www.sos-tobago.org/ecotourism.html#turtletours), and the Asociación ANAI Turtle Project at Gandoca/Manzanilla National Wildlife Refuge on Costa Rica's Caribbean coast (see http://www.anaicr.org/turtle/en/turtle_conservation_and_research.html; see also www.ptes.org/events/documents/costarica.pdf). Tortuguero National Park on the Caribbean coast of Costa Rica has the largest Green Turtle population in the Atlantic and perhaps the world, and also some Leatherbacks (see www.cccturtle.org, or www.turtles.org/ccc.htm). Elsewhere in the Wider Caribbean Region, high-quality, community-based turtle watching is available through WIDECAST affiliated programs in St. Lucia (Grande Anse Turtle Watch Group; www.tropicaltraveller.com/april-02/wildside.htm), in Belize (Gales Point Wildlife Sanctuary; www.toucantrail.com/Belize-on-a-Budget/Gales-Point-Village.html), in Grenada (Ocean Spirits; www.oceanspirits.org), and in St. Eustatius (Statia Conservation Project; www.statiapark.org/stenapa/stenapa_conservproject.html), among others.

That this is a Caribbean-heavy list partly reflects the success of conservation efforts in the wider Caribbean region in the last two decades. Such successes are worth celebrating. It is my hope that in a decade or two more and similar successes will be apparent throughout the Pacific and Indian Ocean regions as well. As I've said, seeing is supporting.

REFERENCES

GENERAL

Two excellent basic introductions to sea turtles are: Spotila, J. R. 2005. *Sea Turtles*. Baltimore: Johns Hopkins Univ. Press (from which I gleaned much information about basic biology, population trends, threats, and many usefully summarized statistics) and Gulko, D., and K. Eckert. 2004. *Sea Turtles: An Ecological Guide*. Honolulu: Mutual.

For a good general introduction to all turtles, see: Orenstein, R. 2001. *Turtles, Tortoises, and Terrapins: Survivors in Armor*. Buffalo, NY: Firefly Books.

Some more technical introductions are the multiauthored reviews contained in: Lutz, P. L., and J. A. Musick, eds. 1996. *The Biology of Sea Turtles*. Boca Raton: CRC Press. And the sequel: Lutz, P. L., J. A. Musick, and J. Wyneken, eds. 2003. *The Biology of Sea Turtles, Volume II*. Boca Raton: CRC Press.

Thoreau quote: Thoreau, D. 1984. *The Journal of Henry David Thoreau*, vol. 7, September 1854 to October 1855. Utah: Peregrine Smith Books.

SETTING COURSE

Rondelet's 1554 scientific description of the Leatherback, ably translated, including the engraving that appears in this book, is in: Rhodin, A. G. J. 1996. "Books on Marine Fish, in which True Figures of the Fish are Presented." *Chelonian Conservation and Biology* 2:287–302.

ANGELS OF EDEN

Lutcavage, Plotkin, Witherington, and Lutz explore various negative effects humans have on turtles starting on p. 387 in: Lutz, P. L., and J. A. Musick, eds. 1996. *The Biology of Sea Turtles*. Boca Raton: CRC Press.

Results from a 2005 workshop to assess Atlantic Leatherback status are at: http://www.cccturtle.org/leatherbacks/.

Pacific Leatherback status is described in: Dutton, P., et al. In press. "Status and Genetic Structure of Nesting Stocks of Leatherback Turtles (*Dermochelys coriacea*) in the Western Pacific." *Chelonian Conservation and Biology*. **Rough 1981 estimate of Pacific Mexico's Leatherbacks and world estimate is in:** Pritchard, P. C. H. 1982. "Nesting of the Leatherback Turtle in Pacific Mexico, with a New Estimate of World Population Status." *Copeia* 4:741–47.

Where turtles come from: Lee, M. 1994. "The Turtle's Long-Lost Relatives." *Natural History*. June, pp. 63–66.

Regarding mass extinction 65 million years ago, broad facts and links can be found at: http://en.wikipedia.org/wiki/Cretaceous-Tertiary_extinction_event.

Early extinct Leatherbacks and Leatherback evolution is in: Dutton, P., et al. 1999. "Global Phylogeography of the Leatherback Turtle." *Journal of Zoology*, London. 248:397–407. See also: Wood, R. C., et al. 1996. "Evolution and Phylogeny of Leatherback Turtles (*Dermochelyidae*) with Descriptions of New Fossil Taxa." *Chelonian Conservation and Biology* 2:266–86.

American Loggerheads in the Mediterranean: Laurent, L., et al. 1998. "Molecular Resolution of Marine Turtle Stock Composition in Fishery Bycatch: A Case Study in the Mediterranean." *Molecular Ecology* 7:1529–42.

Orientation is summarized in the review by: Lohmann et al., starting on p. 107 in Lutz, P. L., and J. A. Musick, eds. 1996. *The Biology of Sea Turtles*. Boca Raton: CRC Press.

Musick and Limpus summarize lives of juvenile turtles in their review on p. 137 in: Lutz, P. L., and J. A. Musick, eds. 1996. *The Biology of Sea Turtles*. Boca Raton: CRC Press.

Juvenile Leatherbacks' whereabouts: Eckert, S. A. 2002. "Distribution of Juvenile Leatherback Sea Turtle *Dermochelys coriacea* Sightings." *Marine Ecology Progress Series* 230:289–93.

Turtle catch rates in the Gulf of Guinea: Carranza, A., A. Domingo, and A. Estrades. Manuscript. "Pelagic Longlines: A Threat to Sea Turtles in the Equatorial Eastern Atlantic?"

WEIGHT OF THE WORLD

Ancient human uses of sea turtles: Frazier starting on p. 1 in Lutz, P. L., J. A. Musick, and J. Wyneken, eds. 2003. *The Biology of Sea Turtles, Volume II*. Boca Raton: CRC Press. More on cultural importance by Frazier: www.ioseaturtles.org/MeetingSS3/ MT_IO3_DOC08-3_Trad_use.pdf. See also http://oshadavidson.com/Turtle_Culture.pdf.

Palauan turtle fable: Richardson, J. 1993 "Sea Turtles in Folklore: The Turtle of Medatum-loket." *Marine Turtle Newsletter* 62:25–26.

Pliny and the translation of Aelianus is in: Rhodin, A. G. J. 1996. "Books on Marine Fish, in which True Figures of the Fish are Presented." *Chelonian Conservation and Biology* 2:287–302. More on Pliny and world cultural mythology is from: Minton, S. A., and M. R. Minton. 1973. Chapter 9, "Legendary Turtles," in *Giant Reptiles*. New York: Charles Scribner's Sons.

The originals are: Aelianus, C. [ca. A.D. 200] 1958–59. *De Natura Animalium.* 3 vols. Trans. A. F. Sholfield. Loeb Classical Library. Cambridge: Harvard Univ. Press. And: Pliny (the Elder). [ca. A.D. 50] 1938–63. *Naturalis Historia.* Trans. H. Rackham. 10 vols. Loeb Classical Library. Cambridge: Harvard Univ. Press.

Belief that turtles bearing etched characters will guide lost sailors: Collins, J. W. 1901. *Commercial Fisheries of the Hawaiian Islands: Report of Commissioner of Fish and Fisheries, 1900.* U.S. Fish Commission, Washington, DC: Government Printing Office, p. 393.

Palauan taboo: Johannes, R. 1986. "A Review of Information on the Subsistence Use of Green and Hawksbill Sea Turtles of Islands Under United States Jurisdiction in the Western Pacific Ocean." Administrative Report SWR-862. Honolulu: Southwest Fisheries Science Center, National Marine Fisheries Service, NOAA. February, 18–19.

Chinese New Year sacrifices: Balazs, G. H., I-Jiunn Cheng, and Hui-Chen Wang. 2000. "Turtle Sacrifice to the Temple Gods in the Penghu Islands of Taiwan." *Proceedings of the Nineteenth Annual Symposium on Sea Turtle Biology and Conservation, March 2–6, 1999, South Padre Island, Texas.* Washington, DC: U.S. Department of Commerce, NOAA Technical Memo. NMFS-SEFSC-443, pp. 98–110. With photos at www.balazs.itgo.com.

Leatherback as sea monster: Brongersman, L. D. 1968. "The Soay Beast." *Beaufortia* 15:33–46. Early discoveries of international migrations: Pritchard, P. C. H. 1973. International migrations of South American sea turtles: *Animal Behavior* 21:18–27. Also: Boulon, et al. 1988. "*Dermochelys coriacea* (Leatherback Sea Turtle) Migration." *Herpetological Review* 19:88. Additionally, a turtle that swam from the English Channel to Ascension in 1865 is mentioned in: Papi, F., and P. Luschi. 1996. "Pinpointing Isla Meta: The Case of Sea Turtles and Albatrosses." *Journal of Experimental Biology* 199:65–71. Round-trip migrations: James, M. C., et al. 2005. "Identification of High-Use Habitat and Threats to Leatherback Sea Turtles in Northern Waters: New Directions for Conservation." *Ecology Letters* 8:195–201.

MOONLIGHT IN THE SUNSHINE STATE

Nearly half of adult Leatherbacks have ingested plastic: Mrosovsky, N. 1987. "Leatherback Turtle Off Scale." *Nature* 327: May 28.

Darkness at night: Longcore, T., and C. Rich. 2004. "Ecological Light Pollution." *Frontiers in Ecology and the Environment* 2:191–98. And turtle nesting: Salmon, M. 2003. "Artificial Night Lighting and Sea Turtles." *Biologist* 50:163–68. Hatchling turtle disorientation: Tuxbury, S. M., and M. Salmon. 2005. "Competitive Interactions Between Artificial Lighting and Natural Cues During Seafinding by Hatchling Marine Turtles." *Biological Conservation* 121.2:311–16. Artificial light masking the stars: http://www.nps.gov/moja/pphtml/ subenvironmentalfactors27.html.

Comparing efficiency of different kinds of bulbs: Singapore Science Center. 2002. "Light Pollution: An Overview." http://www.science.edu.sg/ssc/virtual_ssc.jsp?type=4&root=140&parent=181&cat=182. Also: www.mme.state.va.us/de/hbchap8.html.

Fire ants: Allen, C. R. 2001. "Effects of Fire Ants (Hymenoptera: Formicidae) on Hatching Turtles and Prevalence of Fire Ants on Sea Turtle Nesting Beaches in Florida." *Florida Entomologist* 84:250–53. More on fire ants: http://tncweeds.ucdavis.edu/moredocs/solinv01.html. Also: Virginia cooperative extension: http://www.ext.vt.edu/pubs/entomology/444-284/444-284.html: And: http://www.rso.cornell.edu/scitech/archive/95sum/trns.html.

Turtles' response to lights: Witherington, B. 1992. "Behavioral Responses of Sea Turtles to Artificial Lighting." *Herpetologica* 48:31–39. Witherington and Frazer consider economic and social aspects of beach lighting and fisheries at: p. 355 in Lutz, P. L., J. A. Musick, and J. Wyneken, eds. 2003. *The Biology of Sea Turtles, Volume II.* Boca Raton: CRC Press.

Sand and beach nourishment: Trembanis, A. C., et al. 1999. "Comparison of Beach Nourishment Along the U.S. Atlantic, Great Lakes, Gulf of Mexico, and New England Shorelines." www.env.duke.edu/psds/docs.htm. See also: http://www3.csc.noaa.gov/beachnourishment/html/human/socio/change.htm. Costs and controversy of sand pumping: Jonsson, P. 2004. "Beach Brouhaha: As Coastlines Erode, Who Pays for New Sand?" *Christian Science Monitor.* October 19. Glass instead of sand: Fleshler, D. 2004. "Ground Glass May Ease Beach Erosion." *South Florida Sun-Sentinel.* May 22.

Information on Oman: Blair Witherington, personal communication.

Earlier turtle nesting in response to warmer temperatures: Weishampel, J. F., et al. 2004. "Earlier Nesting by Loggerhead Sea Turtles Following Sea Surface Warming." *Global Change Biology* 10:1424.

Florida commercial turtle catches: Witzell, W. N. 1994. "The Origin, Evolution, and Demise of the U.S. Sea Turtle Fisheries." *Marine Fisheries Review* 56:8–23. Also: Witzell, W. N. 1994. "The U.S. Commercial Sea Turtle Landings." NOAA Technical Memo. NMFS-SEFSC-350.

Biology and many references on Green Turtles: Seminoff, J. A. (assessor), et al. 2004. "IUCN Red List Status Assessment, Green Turtle (*Chelonia mydas*)." IUCN Marine Turtle Specialist Group.

Geographic origins of turtles in Florida waters: Bass, A. L., and W. N. Witzell. 2000. "Demographic Composition of Immature Green Turtles from the East-Central Florida Coast: Evidence from mtDNA Markers." *Herpetologica* 56:357–67.

Wyneken reviews locomotion at: p. 165 in Lutz, P. L., and J. A. Musick, eds. 1996. *The Biology of Sea Turtles.* Boca Raton: CRC Press.

Turtle tumors: Greenblatt, R. J., et al. 2004. "The Ozobranchus Leech Is a Candidate Mechanical Vector for the Fibropapilloma-Associated Turtle

Herpesvirus Found Latently Infecting Skin Tumors on Hawaiian Green Turtles
(*Chelonia mydas*)." *Virology* 321:101–10.

LEATHERBACKS AND CANNONBALLS

Loggerhead nesting declines: http://www.theturtleplace.com/research/
nesting.htm.

Turtle diets: Bjorndal, K., starting on p. 199 in Lutz, P. L., and J. A. Musick,
eds. 1996. *The Biology of Sea Turtles.* Boca Raton: CRC Press.

Kemp's Ridley story: Spotila, J. R. 2005. *Sea Turtles.* Baltimore: Johns Hopkins
Univ. Press. **Also:** Heppell, S. S. 1997. "On the Importance of Eggs." *Marine
Turtle Newsletter* 76:6–8. **And:** Lewison, R. L., et al. 2003. "The Impact of
Turtle Excluder Devices and Fisheries Closures on Loggerhead and Kemp's Ridley
Strandings in the Western Gulf of Mexico." *Conservation Biology* 17:1089–97.

**Turtles' responses to stress, and oxygen consumption of swimming versus
resting young turtles:** Milton and Lutz starting on p. 163 in Lutz, P. L., J. A.
Musick, and J. Wyneken, eds. 2003. *The Biology of Sea Turtles, Volume II.* Boca
Raton: CRC Press.

Leatherback diving record: Hays, G. C., et al. 2004. "Pan-Atlantic Leatherback
Turtle Movements." *Nature* 429:522. **Diving behavior and physiology and how
blood stores oxygen:** Lutcavage and Lutz starting on p. 277 in Lutz, P. L., and
J. A. Musick, eds. 1996. *The Biology of Sea Turtles.* Boca Raton: CRC Press.

Regarding diving of different marine animals, and physiology involved:
Schreer, J. F., and K. M. Kovacs. 1997. "Allometry of Diving Capacity in
Air-Breathing Vertebrates." *Canadian Journal of Zoology* 75:339–58. **The longest
Leatherback dive time:** Southwood, A. L., et al. 1999. "Heart Rates and Diving
Behavior of Leatherback Sea Turtles in the Eastern Pacific Ocean." *Journal of
Experimental Biology* 202:1115–25. **Leatherback heart blood-shunting:** Jeanette
Wyneken, personal communication.

Epperly discusses shrimp trawling, including the World Trade Organization, at:
p. 339 in Lutz, P. L., J. A. Musick, and J. Wyneken, eds. 2003. *The Biology of
Sea Turtles, Volume II.* Boca Raton: CRC Press. **The WTO's perspective can be
found at:** http://www.wto.org/english/tratop_e/dispu_e/distab_e.htm#r58.

India sea turtle trawling deaths: Pandav, B., and B. C. Choudhury. 1999. "An
Update on the Mortality of the Olive Ridley Sea Turtles in Orissa, India." *Marine
Turtle Newsletter* 83:10–12.

Regarding fisheries bycatch of turtles, see: National Marine Fisheries
Service. 1998. *Southeastern United States Shrimp Trawl Bycatch Program.*
Report to Congress. Washington, DC: U.S. Department of Commerce.
See also: Weber, M., D. Crouse, R. Irvin, S. Iudicello. 1995. *Delay and Denial:
A Political History of Sea Turtles and Shrimp Fishing.* Washington, DC: Center
for Marine Conservation (Ocean Conservancy). **See also:** Fletcher, K. M. 1998.
Bycatch Reduction Device Rule in Gulf. Sea Grant Law Center. Available at

www.olemiss.edu/pubs/waterlog/18.2/brds.htm. **And also:** National Marine
Fisheries Service. 2001. *Stock Assessments of Loggerhead and Leatherback Sea
Turtles and an Assessment of the Impact of the Pelagic Longline Fishery on the
Loggerhead and Leatherback Sea Turtles of the Western North Atlantic.* U.S.
Department of Commerce. NOAA Technical Memorandum NMFS-SEFSC-
455:1–343. **And:** Chaloupka, et al. 2004. "Modelling Post-release Mortality of
Loggerhead Sea Turtles Exposed to the Hawaii-Based Pelagic Longline Fishery."
Marine Ecology Progress Series 280:285–93. **See also:** Food and Agriculture
Organization of the United Nations. 2004. "Report of the Expert Consultation
on Interactions Between Sea Turtles and Fisheries Within an Ecosystem Context."
Rome, Italy, 9–12 March 2004. FAO Fisheries Report No. 738. Rome, FAO.
Regarding scallop dredges: Murray, K. T. 2004. *Bycatch of Sea Turtles in the
Mid-Atlantic Sea Scallop* (Placopecten magellanicus) *Dredge Fishery During
2003.* U.S. Department of Commerce, Northeast Fishery Scientific Center
Reference Document 04–11; available from: National Marine Fisheries Service,
166 Water Street, Woods Hole, MA 02543–1026; http://www.olemiss.edu/orgs/
SGLC/18.2/brds.htm. **For a global review of bycatch see:** Alverson, D. L.,
M. H. Freeberg, J. G. Pope, and S. A. Murawski. 1994. *A Global Assessment of
Fisheries Bycatch and Discards.* FAO Fisheries Technical Paper No. 339.
Rome, FAO.

   Plastic ingestion: K. Bjorndal reviews diet, including ingested pollutants, on
p. 199 in Lutz, P. L., and J. A. Musick, eds. 1996. *The Biology of Sea Turtles.*
Boca Raton: CRC Press. **See also:** Sarti Martinez, A. L., et al. 2000. "Assessment
of Leatherback Turtle." IUCN. www.redlist.org/search/details.php?species=6494.
Also: Sako, T., and K. Horikishi. 2002. "Marine Debris Ingested by Green Turtles
in the Ogasawara Islands." Japan. Proceedings of the Twenty-second Annual
Symposium on Sea Turtle Conservation and Biology. NOAA Technical Memo.
NMFS-SEFSC-503. **Also:** Guitart, T. J., et al. 2002. "Marine Debris Ingestion in
Loggerhead Sea Turtles, *Caretta caretta,* from the Western Mediterranean."
Marine Pollution Bulletin 44:211–16.

ON THE EDGE

   Swordfish bill in turtle: Flegra, B. 2005. "Gladiatorial Attack on a Turtle."
Marine Turtle Newsletter 110:8. **Swordfish attacking** *Alvin:* www.whoi.edu/
marops/vehicles/alvin/alvin_history.html.

   Warm eyes of Swordfish: Fritsches, K. A., et al. 2005. "Warm Eyes Provide
Superior Vision in Swordfishes." *Current Biology* 15:55–58. **And:** Fritsches,
K. A., et al. 2005. "The Effect of Ocular Heating on Vision in Swordfishes."
Pelagic Fisheries Research Program, University of Hawaii at Manoa 10:1–6. **See
also:** Goldman, K., S. Anderson, R. Latour, and John Musick. 2004.
"Homeothermy in Adult Salmon Sharks, *Lamna ditropis.*" *Environmental
Biology of Fishes* 71:403–11.

ANIMAL MAGNETISM

Information on orientation and magnetic navigation: Lohmann, K. J., and S. Johnsen. 2000. "The Neurobiology of Magnetoreception in Vertebrate Animals." *Trends in Neuroscience* 23:153–59. Displaced turtles getting lost: Hays, G. C., et al. 2003. "Island-Finding Ability of Marine Turtles." *Proceedings of the Royal Society of London B* (Suppl.) 270, S5–S7. Regarding chemical cues and scent: Grassman, M. 1993. "Chemosensory Orientation Behavior in Juvenile Sea Turtles." *Brain Behavior and Evolution* 41:224–28.

Magnetism and sea turtle navigation: Irwin, W. P., and K. J. Lohmann. 2003. "Magnet-Induced Disorientation in Hatchling Loggerhead Sea Turtles." *Journal of Experimental Biology* 206:497–501. Also: Lohmann, K. J., et al. 2004. "Geomagnetic Map Used in Sea-Turtle Navigation." *Nature* 428:909–10. And on magnetic receptors: Walker, M. M., et al. 1997. "Structure and Functions of the Vertebrate Magnetic Sense." *Nature* 390:371–76. And: Diebel, C. E., et al. 2000. "Magnetite Defines a Vertebrate Magnetoreceptor." *Nature* 406:299–302. Regarding "one of the most enduring and intriguing mysteries of animal behavior," see: Gould, J. L. "Sensory Bases of Navigation." *Current Biology* 8:R731–38.

Turtle migrations: P. Plotkin starting on p. 225 in Lutz, P. L., J. A. Musick, and J. Wyneken, eds. 2003. *The Biology of Sea Turtles, Volume II*. Boca Raton: CRC Press. Bolton's discussion of ocean versus coastal life stages begins on p. 243 in: Lutz, P. L., J. A. Musick, and J. Wyneken, eds. 2003. *The Biology of Sea Turtles, Volume II*. Boca Raton: CRC Press.

NORTHEAST OF SUMMER

Jellyfish densities: Hays, G. C., et al. 2003. "Aircraft Give a New View of Jellyfish Behaviour." *Nature* 426:383.

Leatherback foraging and movements: James, M. C., et al. 2005. "Behaviour of Leatherback Sea Turtles, *Dermochelys coriacea*, During the Migratory Cycle." *Proceedings of the Royal Society B* 272: 1547–1555.

Leatherback in Canadian waters: Cook, F. R. 1981. "Status Report on the Leatherback Turtle, *Dermochelys coriacea*." Committee on the Status of Endangered Wildlife in Canada, Ottawa; found at http://www.sararegistry.gc.ca/status/showASCII_e.cfm?ocid=177. Leatherbacks off Norway: Willgohs, J. F. 1957. "Occurrence of the Leathery Turtle in the Northern North Sea and Off Western Norway." *Nature* 179:163–64. Inuit turtle carving: Shoop, R. C. 1980. "Innuit Turtle Song: Leatherback Turtles Near Baffin Island?" *Marine Turtle Newsletter* 15:5–6.

The largest leatherback ever found and the plastic in it as a possible cause or contributor to death: Eckert, K. L., and C. Luginbuhl. 1988. "Death of a Giant." *Marine Turtle Newsletter* 43:2–3. That this turtle was first found tangled and alive and washed ashore dead an hour later is casually mentioned in: Davenport, J., et al. 1990. "Thermal Biological Characteristics of the Lipids of the

Leatherback Turtle: Evidence of Endothermy." *Journal of the Marine Biological Association of the United Kingdom* 70:33–41. **Additional measurements of largest Leatherback:** Davenport, J., et al. 1990. "Metal and PCB Concentrations in the 'Harlech' Leatherback." *Marine Turtle Newsletter* 48:1–6.

Female Leatherbacks' response to males: Reina, R. D. 2005. "Respiratory Frequency, Dive Behaviour and Social Interactions of Leatherback Turtles, *Dermochelys coriacea*, During the Inter-nesting Interval." *Journal of Experimental Marine Biology and Ecology* 316:1–16.

Global long-lining intensity: Lewison, R. L., S. A. Freeman, and L. B. Crowder. 2004. "Quantifying the Effects of Fisheries on Threatened Species: The Impact of Pelagic Longlines on Loggerhead and Leatherback Sea Turtles." *Ecology Letters* 7:221–31. **Regarding Hawaii long-liners and mammals:** Forney, K. "Estimates of Cetacean Mortality and Injury in the Hawai'i-Based Longline Fishery, 1994–2002," U.S. National Marine Fisheries Service, Southwest Fisheries Science Center. Draft, last revised November 4, 2003. **Survival of turtles with ingested hooks:** Polovina, J. J., et al. 2003. "Dive-Depth Distribution of Loggerhead (*Carretta carretta*) and Olive Ridley (*Lepidochelys olivacea*) Sea Turtles in the Central North Pacific: Might Deep Longline Sets Catch Fewer Turtles?" *Fishery Bulletin* 101 (1):189–93. **Estimate that half of U.S. longline-caught turtles survive:** U.S. National Marine Fisheries Service, Southeast Fisheries Science Center. 2001. *Stock Assessments of Loggerhead and Leatherback Sea Turtles and an Assessment of the Impact of the Pelagic Longline Fishery on the Loggerhead and Leatherback Sea Turtles of the Western North Atlantic.* U.S. Department of Commerce. NOAA Technical Memorandum NMFS-SEFSC-455.

Leatherbacks' blood coagulation characteristics: Soslau G., et al. 2004. "Comparison of Functional Aspects of the Coagulation Cascade in Human and Sea Turtle Plasmas." *Comparative Biochemistry Physicology B* 138:399–406.

Leatherback heat: Spotila, O'Connor, and Paladino on p. 297 in Lutz, P. L., and J. A. Musick, eds. 1996. *The Biology of Sea Turtles.* Boca Raton: CRC Press. **The Leatherback is "more like a reptilian whale."** Orenstein, R. 2001. *Turtles, Tortoises, and Terrapins: Survivors in Armor.* Buffalo, NY: Firefly Books. **See also:** Davenport, J., et al. 1990. "Thermal Biological Characteristics of the Lipids of the Leatherback Turtle: Evidence of Endothermy." *Journal of the Marine Biological Association of the United Kingdom* 70:33–41. **And see:** Goff, G. P., and G. B. Stenson. 1988. "Brown Adipose Tissue in Leatherback Sea Turtles: A Thermogenic Organ in an Endothermic Reptile." *Copeia* 4:1071–75. **Leatherbacks' countercurrent heat exchanger is in:** Lazell, J. D., Jr. 1976. *This Broken Archipelago.* New York: Times Books. **And:** Greer, A. E., et al. 1973. "Anatomical Evidence for a Countercurrent Heat Exchanger in the Leatherback Turtle." *Nature* 244:181.

A couple of nice summaries of homeothermy are in the online biology text *Kimball's Biology Pages* (http://users.rcn.com/jkimball.ma.ultranet/

BiologyPages/H/HeatTransport.html), and Wikipedia (http://en.wikipedia.org/
wiki/Homeotherm). For adaptations against cold in Leatherback Turtles: Paladino,
F.V., M. P. O'Connor, J. R. Spotila. 1990. "Metabolism of Leatherback Turtles,
Gigantothermy, and Thermoregulation of Dinosaurs." *Nature* 344:858–60.
Also: Penick, D.N., et al. 1998. "Thermal Independence of Muscle Tissue
Metabolism in the Leatherback Turtle, *Dermochelys coriacea*." *Comparative
Biochemistry and Physiology A* 120:399–403. And: Petruzzelli, R., et al. 1982.
"Regional Endothermy in the Sea Turtle *Chelonia mydas*." *Journal of Thermal
Biology* 7:159–65. As well as: Goff, P. G., and G. B. Stenson. 1988. "Brown
Adipose Tissue in Leatherback Sea Turtles: A Thermogenic Organ in an
Endothermic Reptile?" *Copeia* 4:1071–75. Freezing resistance of Leatherback
tissue is in: Davenport, J., et al. 1990. "Thermal Biological Characteristics of the
Lipids of the Leatherback Turtle: Evidence of Endothermy." *Journal of the Marine
Biological Association of the United Kingdom* 70:33–41. For comparison to birds
and mammals, see also: Greer, A. E., J. D. Lazell, and R. M. Wright. 1973.
"Anatomical Evidence for a Countercurrent Heat Exchanger in the Leatherback
Turtle (*Dermochelys coriacea*)." *Nature* 244:181.

THE VIEW FROM TURTLE ISLAND

One version of a Native American Turtle Island creation myth: http://www
.championtrees.org/yarrow/turtleisland.htm.

Initial New World abundance of sea turtles and Ferdinand Columbus quote:
Bjorndal, K. A., ed., on p. 184 in: *Biology and Conservation of Sea Turtles.* Rev.
ed. 1995. Washington, DC: Smithsonian Institution. Also: Long, E. 1744. *The
history of Jamaica, or General survey of the Ancient and modern state of that
island.* London: T. Loundes. Regarding Bermuda, see: Babcock, H. L. 1938. "Sea
Turtles of the Bermuda Islands, with a Survey of the Present State of the Turtle
Fishing Industry." *Proceedings of the Zoological Society of London (A)* 107:
595–601. Information on Bermuda including "Do abound as dust of the earth"
and "An Act Against the Killinge" can also be found at:
http://www.cccturtle.org/bermuda/conservation.htm. Original turtle populations:
Spotila, J. R. 2005. *Sea Turtles.* Baltimore: Johns Hopkins Univ. Press.
K. Bjorndal and J. Jackson evoke and estimate lost turtle populations starting at
p. 259 in: Lutz, P. L., J. A. Musick, and J. Wyneken, eds. 2003. *The Biology of
Sea Turtles, Volume II.* Boca Raton: CRC Press. Further impressions of early
explorers on numbers of Caribbean turtles including quote from Columbus's
second voyage: Jackson, J. B. C. 1997. "Reefs Since Columbus." *Coral Reefs*
16:S23–32.

Tortuguero: Troëng, S., and E. Rankin. 2005. "Long-term Conservation
Efforts Contribute to Positive Green Turtle *Chelonia mydas* Nesting Trend at
Tortuguero, Costa Rica." *Biological Conservation* 121:111–16. Leatherback
clutch sizes and nesting intervals in Atlantic and Pacific: pp. 16–17 in Spotila,

J. R. 2005. *Sea Turtles*. Baltimore: Johns Hopkins Univ. Press. **Hawaii Green Turtle increase:** National Marine Fisheries Service Endangered Species Division, Office of Protected Resources. 2000. "Section 7. Consultation on Authorization to Take Listed Marine Mammals Incidental to Commercial Fishing Operations Under Fishery Section 101(a)(5)(E) of the Marine Mammal Protection Act for the California/Oregon Drift Gillnet." Biological Opinion, October 23, 2000.

Rate at which land and pond turtles are eaten in Asia: Environmental News Service. 2003. "Endangered Turtles Vanish into Asian Cooking Pots." May 15.

Bali Green Turtle market: *Los Angeles Times*. 2001. "The Blood of Turtles Stains Bali." March 28.

Certain Leatherback population trends are discussed in the following: Malaysia's Leatherback plight is summarized in: Chua, T. H. 1988. "On the Road to Local Extinction: The Leatherback Turtle in Terengganu, Malaysia." *Proceeding of the Eleventh Annual Seminar of the Malaysian Society of Marine Science*. **Also:** Chan, E., and H. Liew. 1996. "Decline of the Leatherback Population in Terengganu, Malaysia, 1956–1995." *Chelonian Conservation and Biology* 2.2:196–203. **See also:** Chan, E. H., et al. 1988. "The Incidental Capture of the Sea Turtles in Fishing Gear in Terengganu, Malaysia." *Biological Conservation* 43.1:1–7. **Leatherbacks in Papua:** Hitipeuw, C., P. Dutton, et al. Submitted. "Population Status and Inter-nesting Movement of Leatherback Turtles, *Dermochelys coriacea*, Nesting on the Northwest Coast of Papua, Indonesia." *Chelonian Conservation and Biology*. **Leatherback numbers in the Atlantic:** Conference convened in 2005 by Caribbean Conservation Corporation at St. Catherines Island, Georgia. **Turtles on Africa's west coast:** Fretey, J. Undated. "Biogeography and Conservation of Marine Turtles of the Atlantic Coast of Africa." UNEP/CMS Secretariat, Bonn, Germany. www.oceansatlas.com/cds_static/en/biogeography.

Longline economics and cost of saving a turtle: Dumas, C. Unpublished. 2002. "The Economics of Pelagic Longline Fishing in the U.S. and Canada: A Brief Overview." E-mail: dumasc@uncw.edu.

Number of Pacific long-liners: U.S. National Marine Fisheries Service. 2002. "Biological Opinion on the Pelagic Fisheries Under the Fishery Management Plan for the Pelagic Fisheries of the Western Pacific Region." Silver Spring, MD. **Also:** Secretariat of the Pacific Community. 2002. *Secretariat of the Pacific Community Tuna Fishery Yearbook 2001*. Nouméa, New Caledonia: Oceanic Fisheries Programme. **And:** Brothers, N. P., J. Cooper, and S. Lokkeborg. 1999. *The Incidental Catch of Seabirds by Longline Fisheries: Worldwide Review and Technical Guidelines for Mitigation*. FAO Fisheries Circular No. 937. Rome: FAO.

Longline catch rates: U.S. Western Pacific Regional Fishery Management Council. 1993. "Statement Regarding Incidental Taking: Biological Opinion for the Pelagic Fishery Management Plan." Honolulu, Hawaii. **Also:** U.S. National

Marine Fisheries Service. 2001. *Final Environmental Impact Statement: Fisheries Management Plan—Pelagic Fisheries of the Western Pacific Region.* Honolulu: NOAA. The Hawaii biological opinions and lawsuit history came mostly as a personal communication from Eric Gilman of the Blue Ocean Institute. See also (note that the Center for Marine Conservation is now the Ocean Conservancy): *Center for Marine Conservation, et al. vs. National Marine Fisheries Service, et al.* 1999. Civil No. 99-00152 DAE. Order Denying Plaintiffs' Motion for Summary Judgment and Granting Defendants' Motion for Summary Judgment on Plaintiffs' Claims Under the ESA. Order Denying Plaintiffs' Request in Their Motion for Summary Judgment on Plaintiffs' Second Claim for Relief That an EIS Be Prepared Because It Is Moot and Granting Plaintiffs' Request for Injunction and Granting in Part and Denying in Part Defendants' Motion for Dismissal or, in the Alternative, for Temporary Stay of Litigation of Plaintiffs' Second Claim for Relief. *Center for Marine Conservation, et al. vs. National Marine Fisheries Service, et al.* 1999. Civil No. 99-00152 DAE. Order Setting Terms of Injunction. See also: Weiss, K. R. 2004. "Swordfish Fleet Must Stop Fishing to Save Turtles." *Los Angeles Times.* March 12. Quotes of Steiner and Simonds, see: Weiss, K. R. 2004. "Swordfish off Hawaii Are Again Fair Game." *Los Angeles Times.* March 31.

Atlantic longlines including comparison of observer data and captains' logbooks: U.S. National Marine Fisheries Service, Southeast Fisheries Science Center. 2001. *Stock Assessments of Loggerhead and Leatherback Sea Turtles and an Assessment of the Impact of the Pelagic Long-line Fishery on the Loggerhead and Leatherback Sea Turtles of the Western North Atlantic.* U.S. Department of Commerce. NOAA Technical Memorandum NMFS-SEFSC-455. Atlantic circle-hook experiments: Watson, J., et al. 2004. *Experiments in the Western Atlantic Northeast Distant Waters to Evaluate Sea Turtle Mitigation Measures in the Pelagic Longline Fishery.* Report on Experiments Conducted in 2001–03. Pascagoula, MS: U.S. National Marine Fisheries Service.

THE GREAT BEACH

Turtle economics and conservation tourism: Troëng, S., and C. Drews. 2004. "Money Talks: Economic Aspects of Marine Turtle Use and Conservation," WWF-International, Gland, Switzerland; www.panda.org. Global Green Turtle status and trends: Seminoff, J. A. (assessor), et al. 2004. "IUCN Red List Status Assessment, Green Turtle (*Chelonia mydas*)." IUCN Marine Turtle Specialist Group.

Decline in Leatherback numbers: Spotila, J. R., et al. 2000. "Pacific Leatherback Turtles Face Extinction." *Nature* 405:529–30. And: Sarti, L. M., S. A. Eckert, N. T. Garcia, and A. R. Barragan. 1996. "Decline of the World's Largest Nesting Assemblage of Leatherback Turtles." *Marine Turtle Newsletter* 74:2–5.

Estimates of annual adult Leatherback survival: Dutton, D., P. Dutton, M. Chaloupka, and R. H. Boulon. 2005. "Increase of a Caribbean Leatherback Turtle *Dermochelys coriacea* Nesting Population Linked to Long-Term Nest Protection." *Biological Conservation* 126:186–94. See also: Spotila, J. R., et al. 1996. "Worldwide Population Decline of *Dermochelys coriacea*: Are Leatherback Turtles Going Extinct?" *Chelonian Conservation and Biology* 2:209–22. And: Hays, G. C., et al. 2003. "Satellite Telemetry Suggests High Levels of Fishing-Induced Mortality in Marine Turtles." *Marine Ecology Progress Series* 262:305–09.

Rate and implications of Las Baulas hatchery output: Tomillo, P. S., et al. Manuscript. 2005. "Reassessment of the Leatherback Turtle (*Dermochelys coriacea*) Population Nesting at Parque Nacional Marino las Baulas: Effects of Conservation Efforts."

Numbers of Pacific long-lining boats and hooks: Kaplan, I. C. 2005. "A Risk Assessment for Pacific Leatherback Turtles (*Dermochelys coriacea*)." *Canadian Journal of Fisheries and Aquatic Sciences* 62:1710–19. For an estimate of Leatherbacks killed in western South America's fisheries: Eckert, S. A. 1997. "Distant Fisheries Implicated in the Loss of the World's Largest Leatherback Nesting Population." *Marine Turtle Newsletter* 78:2–7. See also: Kotas, J. E., et al. 2004. "Incidental Capture of Loggerhead (*Caretta caretta*) and Leatherback (*Dermochelys coriacea*) Sea Turtles by the Pelagic Longline Fishery off Southern Brazil." *Fishery Bulletin* 102:393–99. Regarding turtles and tuna seine nets: Inter-American Tropical Tuna Commission. 2004. Working Group on Bycatch, Fourth Meeting, Kobe, Japan, 14–16 January. Document byc-4-05a, *Interactions of Sea Turtles with Tuna Fisheries, and Other Impacts on Turtle Populations*.

Quick summary of the hormone oxytocin: http://en.wikipedia.org/wiki/Oxytocin.

FLYING TURTLES

"Extreme down:" Sarti, L. M., et al. 1996. "Decline of the World's Largest Nesting Assemblage of Leatherback Turtles." *Marine Turtle Newsletter* 74:2–5.

Mexican Ridleys, poaching and recovery: Fullerton, E. 2004. "Mexican Sea Turtles Massacred by Armed Poachers." Reuters. 30 January. See also: 2004. "Mexico's Olive Ridley Sea Turtles Make a Comeback." Reuters. September 17.

Bekko: Japan Wildlife Conservation Society. 2000. *Hawksbill Trade Revived? Analysis of the Management System of Domestic "Bekko" Trade in Japan*. Japan Wildlife Conservation Society.

World human population growth and migration data are from the U.N. at: un.org/News/Press/docs/2005/pop918.doc.htm. Populations of cities: infoplease.com/ipa/A0762524.html. Note that: in the least developed countries, the average woman gives birth to five children, compared to rates below two in many developed countries. (In southern and eastern Europe, fertility has reached below 1.3 children per woman, unprecedented in human history.) Half the population increase will come in India, Pakistan, Nigeria, Democratic Republic of the Congo, Bangladesh, Uganda, United States, Ethiopia, and China. Between 2005 and midcentury, the U.N. tells us, populations will "at least triple" in Afghanistan, Burkina Faso, Burundi, Chad, Congo, Democratic Republic of the Congo, East Timor, Guinea-Bissau, Liberia, Mali, Niger, and Uganda. If you haven't heard of some of these places, now's the time to check an atlas and get to know them, because they've heard of you. Hopeful immigrants will be arriving in the United States (1.1 million annually), Germany (204,000), Canada (201,000), United Kingdom (133,000), Italy (120,000), and Australia (100,000), mainly from China (333,000 leaving annually), Mexico (304,000), India (245,000), Philippines (180,000), Pakistan (173,000), and Indonesia (168,000).

Unprepared for the abundance: Pritchard, P. C. H. 1982. "Nesting of the Leatherback Turtle in Pacific Mexico, with a New Estimate of World Population Status." *Copeia* 4:741–47.

Olive Ridley arribadas and numbers in Costa Rica, Mexico, and Malaysia: See pp. 131–32 in Spotila, J. R. 2005. *Sea Turtles*. Baltimore: Johns Hopkins Univ. Press. **Also:** Karen Eckert, Wider Caribbean Sea Turtle Conservation Network (WIDECAST), personal communication. **Also:** NMFS Endangered Species Division, Office of Protected Resources. 2000. "Section 7. Consultation on Authorization to Take Listed Marine Mammals Incidental to Commercial Fishing Operations Under Fishery Section 101(a)(5)(E) of the Marine Mammal Protection Act for the California/Oregon Drift Gillnet." Biological Opinion. October 23, 2000. **In India:** Kartik Shanker, personal communication. **Feeding turtle eggs to camels and goats:** Groombridge, B., et al. 1988. "Marine Turtles in Baluchistan (Pakistan)." *Marine Turtle Newsletter* 42:1–3.

BAJA

The 1990s skepticism over whether Mexican Loggerheads could have hatched in Japan is portrayed by Bowen and Karl, starting on p. 29 in Lutz, P. L., and J. A. Musick, eds. 1996. *The Biology of Sea Turtles*. Boca Raton: CRC Press. Adelita's journey is at: www.turtles.org/adelita.htm. **Further information about cross-Pacific Loggerhead movements:** Nichols, W. J., A. Resendiz, J. A. Seminoff, and B. Resendiz. 2000. "Transpacific Migration of a Loggerhead Turtle Monitored by Satellite Telemetry." *Bulletin of Marine Science* 67:937–47. See also: Resendiz, A., et al. 1998. "First Confirmed East-West Trans-Pacific Movement of a Loggerhead Sea Turtle *Caretta caretta* Released in Baja California, Mexico." *Pacific Science* 52:151–53.

Loggerhead Turtles in Japan: Kamezaki, N., et al., "Loggerhead Turtles Nesting in Japan," pp. 210–18 in Bolten A. B., and B. Witherington, eds. 2003. *Loggerhead Sea Turtles*. Washington DC: Smithsonian Books. **In the same**

volume, for Australia, see: pp. 199–209, Limpus, C. J., and D. J. Limpus. "Loggerhead Turtles in the Equatorial and Southern Pacific Ocean: A Species in Decline."

Red crab distribution: Gómez-Gutiérrez, J., E. Domínguez-Hernández, C. J. Robinson, V. Arenas. 2000. "Hydroacoustical Evidence of Autumn Inshore Residence of the Pelagic Red Crab *Pleuroncodes planipes* at Punta Eugenia, Baja California, Mexico." *Marine Ecology Progress Series* 208:283–91.

Gordo: Nichols, W. J., and C. Safina. 2004. "Lunch with a Turtle Poacher." *Conservation in Practice* 5:30–36.

Loggerhead Pacific ecology: Polovina, J. J., et al. 2004. "Forage and Migration Habitat of Loggerhead (*Caretta caretta*) and Olive Ridley (*Lepidochelys olivacea*) Sea Turtles in the Central North Pacific Ocean." *Fisheries Oceanography* 13: 36–51. Also: Polovina, J., et al. Manuscript. 2005. "The Kuroshio Extension Current Bifurcation Region: A Pelagic Hotspot for Juvenile Loggerhead Sea Turtles." Loggerhead depth preferences: Polovina, J., G. Balazs, E. Howell, D. Parker, M. Seki, and P. Dutton. 2004. "Forage and Migration Habitat of Loggerhead (*Caretta caretta*) and Olive Ridley (*Lepidochelys olivacea*) Sea Turtles in the Central North Pacific Ocean." *Fisheries Oceanography* 13:36–51. Depth of tuna longline sets: Kaplan, I. C. 2005. "A Risk Assessment for Pacific Leatherback Turtles (*Dermochelys coriacea*)." *Canadian Journal of Fisheries and Aquatic Science* 62:1710–19.

Turtle mortality related to longline, scallop dredge, and gill net: James, M. C., et al. 2005. "Identification of High-Use Habitat and Threats to Leatherback Sea Turtles in Northern Waters: New Directions for Conservation." *Ecology Letters* 8:195–201. Also: Garrison, L. P. 2003. *Estimated Bycatch of Marine Mammals and Turtles in the U.S. Atlantic Pelagic Longline Fleet During 2001–2002.* NOAA Technical Memo. NMFS-SEFSC-515. Also: National Marine Fisheries Service, Southeast Fisheries Science Center. 2001. *Stock Assessments of Loggerhead and Leatherback Sea Turtles and an Assessment of the Impact of the Pelagic Longline Fishery on the Loggerhead and Leatherback Sea Turtles of the Western North Atlantic.* U.S. Department of Commerce. NOAA Technical Memorandum NMFS-SEFSC-455. And: NOAA. 2005. "Sea Scallop Gear Change Proposed to Protect Turtles." News release 2005-R114. Plus: Kotas, J. E., et al. 2004. "Incidental Capture of Loggerhead (*Caretta caretta*) and Leatherback (*Dermochelys coriacea*) Sea Turtles by the Pelagic Longline Fishery off Southern Brazil." *Fishery Bulletin* 102:393–99.

Fisheries effects on sharks: Baum J. K., et al. 2003. "Collapse and Conservation of Shark Populations in the Northwest Atlantic." *Science* 299:389–92.

Longline catch rates: Oral presentation by Randall Arauz regarding Costa Rica's Dorado long-liners. Circle hooks in Latin America: Largacha, E., M. Parrales, L. Rendón, V. Velásquez, M. Orozco, and M. Hall. 2005. *Working with the Ecuadorian Fishing Community to Reduce the Mortality of Sea Turtles in Longlines: The First Year, March 2004–March 2005.* Western Pacific Regional Fishery Management Council.

THE OTHER GRAND CANYON

Larvaceans: Robison, B. H., et al. 2005. "Giant Larvacean Houses: Rapid Carbon Transport to the Deep Sea Floor." *Science* 308:1609–11. **Coral growth directly proportional to carbonate:** Langdon, C. 2003. "Effect of Elevated CO_2 on the Community Metabolism of an Experimental Coral Reef." *Global Biogeochemical Cycles* 17:1–14. **Carbon dioxide and ocean acidification:** Raven, J., et al. 2005. *Ocean Acidification Due to Increasing Atmospheric Carbon Dioxide.* Royal Society. Policy document 12/05. ISBN 0-85403-617-2. www.royalsoc.ac.uk. **And intensified storms:** Emanuel, K. 2005. "Increasing Destructiveness of Tropical Cyclones over the Past Thirty Years." *Nature* 436:686–88. **Also:** Webster, P. J., et al. 2005. "Changes in Tropical Cyclone Number, Duration, and Intensity in a Warming Environment." *Science* 309:1844–46. **And:** www.ucar.edu/news/releases/2005/hurricanestudy.shtml. **Commentary:** Stipp, D. 2005. "Katrina's Aftermath: The High Cost of Climate Change." *Fortune.* September 2, 2005. **Also:** Buncombe, A. 2005. "Hurricane Katrina: Global Warming May Be to Blame." *Independent* (London). August 31.

JAMURSBA *BELIMBINGS*

Wallace's Line: Diamond, J. 1997. "Mr. Wallace's Line." *Discover,* August, pp. 76–83.

Turtle economics and conservation tourism: Troëng, S., and C. Drews. 2004. "Money Talks: Economic Aspects of Marine Turtle Use and Conservation." WWF-International, Gland, Switzerland, www.panda.org. **For Sabah Island Green Turtle recovery see also:** Chan, E., and H. Liew. 1996. "Decline of the Leatherback Population in Terengganu, Malaysia, 1956–1995." *Chelonian Conservation and Biology* 2:196–203.

Leatherback status in Papua: Betz, W., and M. Welch. 1992. "Once Thriving Colony of Leatherback Sea Turtles Declining at Irian Jaya, Indonesia." *Marine Turtle Newsletter* 56:8–9. **Also:** Hitipeuw, C., P. Dutton, et al. Submitted. "Population Status and Inter-nesting Movement of Leatherback Turtles, *Dermochelys coriacea,* Nesting on the Northwest Coast of Papua, Indonesia." *Chelonian Conservation and Biology.*

St. Croix: Dutton, D. L., et al. 2005. "Increase of a Caribbean Leatherback Turtle *Dermochelys coriacea* Nesting Population Linked to Long-Term Nest Protection." *Biological Conservation* 126:186–94.

Recovery in the face of egging versus long-lining: Kaplan, I. C. 2005. "A Risk Assessment for Pacific Leatherback Turtles (*Dermochelys coriacea*)." *Canadian Journal of Fisheries and Aquatic Science* 62:1710–19.

Drive them to extinction: Spotila, J. R., et al. 1996. "Worldwide Population Decline of *Dermochelys coriacea:* Are Leatherback Turtles Going Extinct?" *Chelonian Conservation and Biology* 2:209–22.

"Fast, thorough, and long-lasting": Seminoff, J. A. (assessor), et al. 2004. "IUCN Red List Status Assessment, Green Turtle (*Chelonia mydas*)." IUCN Marine Turtle Specialist Group.

Taiwan reducing its long-liners: http://english.coa.gov.tw/content.php?catid=9923.

Leatherback recovery in South Africa: Hughes, G. R. 1996. "Nesting of the Leatherback Turtle (*Dermochelys coriacea*) in Tongaland, KwaZulu-Natal, South Africa, 1963–1995." *Chelonian Conservation and Biology* 2:153–58.

CHANT FOR THE ENCHANTED

Seri life, particularly attributing formation of Isla Tiburón to a Leatherback: Burkhalter, D. 1999. *Among Turtle Hunters and Basket Makers.* Tucson: Treasure Chest Books.

Various aspects of Seri culture and the Leatherback ceremony: Nabhan, G. P. 2003. *Singing the Turtles to Sea.* Berkeley: Univ. of California Press.

Significance of zigzag lines: Felger, R. S., and M. B. Moser. 1985. *People of the Desert and Sea.* Tucson: Univ. of Arizona Press.

INDEX

Entries in *italics* refer to maps.

ABOUT THE AUTHOR

CARL SAFINA is the winner of a MacArthur Fellowship, a Pew Fellowship, and the Lannan Literary Award. He is the founding president of Blue Ocean Institute, as well as being a World Wildlife Fund Senior Fellow and an adjunct professor at Stony Brook University. *The New York Times Book Review* called his *Song for the Blue Ocean* "a landmark book." It was selected as a *New York Times* Notable Book of the Year, a *Los Angeles Times* Best Nonfiction Selection, and a *Library Journal* Best Science Book. His *Eye of the Albatross* won a National Academies Communication Award and the John Burroughs Medal.